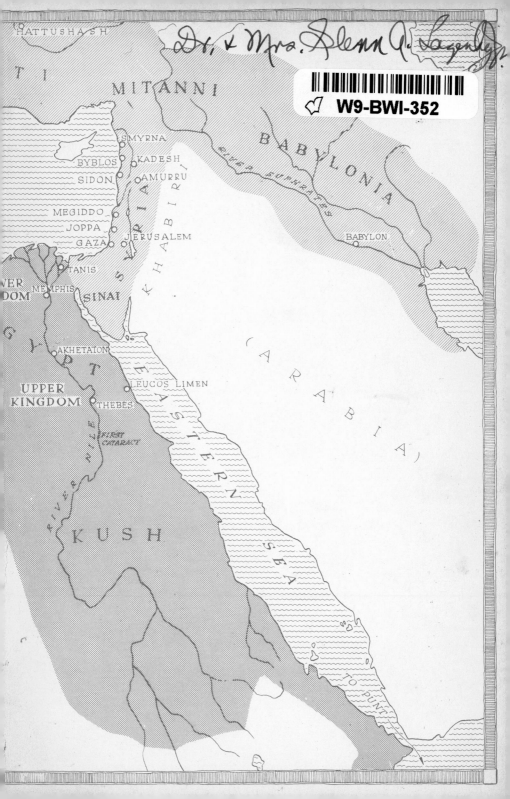

The Egyptian

The Egyptian

A NOVEL

BY MIKA WALTARI

TRANSLATED BY

NAOMI WALFORD

G. P. PUTNAM'S SONS

NEW YORK

Contents

BOOK I

The Reed Boat

I

I, SINUHE, the son of Senmut and of his wife Kipa, write this. I do not write it to the glory of the gods in the land of Kem, for I am weary of gods, nor to the glory of the Pharaohs, for I am weary of their deeds. I write neither from fear nor from any hope of the future but for myself alone. During my life I have seen, known, and lost too much to be the prey of vain dread; and, as for the hope of immortality, I am as weary of that as I am of gods and kings. For my own sake only I write this; and herein I differ from all other writers, past and to come.

I begin this book in the third year of my exile on the shores of the Eastern Sea, whence ships put out for the land of Punt, near the desert, near those hills from which stone was quarried to build the statues of former kings. I write it because wine is bitter to my tongue, because I have lost my pleasure in women, and because neither gardens nor fish pools delight me any more. I have driven away the singers, and the sound of pipes and strings is torment to my ear. Therefore, I write this, I, Sinuhe, who make no use of my wealth, my golden cups, my ebony, ivory, and myrrh.

They have not been taken from me. Slaves still fear my rod; guards bow their heads and stretch out their hands at knee level before me. But bounds have been set to my walking, and no ships can put in through the surf of these shores; never again shall I smell the smell of black earth on a night in spring.

My name was once inscribed in Pharaoh's golden book, and I dwelt at his right hand. My words outweighed those of the mighty in the land of Kem; nobles sent me gifts, and chains of gold were hung about my neck. I possessed all that a man can desire, but like a man I desired more—therefore, I am what I am. I was driven from Thebes in the sixth year of the reign of Pharaoh Horemheb, to be beaten to death like a cur if I returned—to be crushed like a frog between the stones if I took one step beyond the area prescribed for my dwelling

3

place. This is by command of the King, of Pharaoh who was once my friend.

But before I begin my book I will let my heart cry out in lamentation, for so an exile's heart must cry when it is black with sorrow.

He who has once drunk of Nile water will forever yearn to be by the Nile again; his thirst cannot be quenched by the waters of any other land.

I would exchange my cup for an earthenware mug if my feet might once more tread the soft dust in the land of Kem. I would give my linen clothes for the skins of a slave if once more I might hear the reeds of the river rustling in the spring wind.

Clear were the waters of my youth; sweet was my folly. Bitter is the wine of age, and not the choicest honeycomb can equal the coarse bread of my poverty. Turn, O you years—roll again, you vanished years—sail, Ammon, from west to east across the heavens and bring again my youth! Not one word of it will I alter, not my least action will I amend. O brittle pen, smooth papyrus, give me back my folly and my youth!

2

Senmut, whom I called my father, was physician to the poor of Thebes, and Kipa was his wife. They had no children, and they were old when I came to them. In their simplicity they said I was a gift from the gods, little guessing what evil the gift would bring them. Kipa named me Sinuhe after someone in a story, for she loved stories, and it seemed to her that I had come fleeing from danger like my namesake of the legend, who by chance overheard a frightful secret in Pharaoh's tent and fled, to live for many adventurous years in foreign lands.

This was but a childish notion of hers; she hoped that I, too, would always run from danger and avoid misfortune. But the priests of Ammon hold that a name is an omen, and it may be that mine brought me peril and adventure and sent me into foreign lands. It made me a sharer in dreadful secrets—secrets of kings and their wives—secrets that may be the bearers of death. And at the last my name made me a fugitive and an exile.

Yet I should be as childish as poor Kipa to fancy that a name can influence one's destiny; would it not have been the same if I had been called Kepru or Kafran or Moses? So I believe—yet Sinuhe was indeed exiled whereas Heb, the son of the Falcon, was crowned as Horemheb

4

with the red and white crown, to be king over the Upper and Lower Kingdoms. As to the significance of names, therefore, each must judge for himself; each in his own faith will find solace against the evils and reverses of this life.

I was born in the reign of the great King Amenhotep III and in the same year as that one who desired to live by truth and whose name may no longer be named because it is accursed—though at the time nothing of this was known. There was great rejoicing at the palace when he was born, and the King brought many sacrifices to the great temple of Ammon that he had built; the people also were glad, not knowing what was to come. The royal consort Taia had until then hoped vainly for a son, though she had been consort for twenty-two years and her name was written beside that of the King in the temples and upon the statues. Therefore, he whose name may no longer be named was proclaimed heir with elaborate ceremonial as soon as the priests had performed the circumcision.

He was not born until the spring in the sowing season, whereas I had come the previous autumn when the floods stood at their highest. The day of my birth is unknown, for I came drifting down the Nile in a little reed boat daubed with pitch, and my mother Kipa found me among the reeds on the shore close by her own doorstep. The swallows had just returned and were twittering above me, but I lay so still that she believed me dead. She brought me to her house and warmed me by the charcoal fire and blew into my mouth until I whimpered.

My father Senmut came back from visiting his patients, carrying two ducks and a bushel of flour. When he heard me crying, he thought Kipa had adopted a kitten and was about to rebuke her, but my mother said, "It is not a cat—I have a son! Rejoice, Senmut my husband, for a son has been born to us!"

My father called her an idiot and was angry until she showed me to him, and then he was moved by my helplessness. So they adopted me as their own child and even put it about among the neighbors that Kipa had borne me. This was foolish, and I do not know how many believed her. But Kipa kept the reed boat that brought me and hung it up in the roof above my bed. My father took his best copper bowl to the temple and had me registered in the book of births as his own son born of Kipa, but the circumcision he did himself, for he was a doctor and feared the priests' knives because they left infected wounds. He did not let the priests touch me. Also he may have wanted to save money, for a poor people's doctor is not a wealthy man.

I cannot, of course, recall these things, but my parents have told me of them so often and in such unvarying phrases that I must believe them and have no reason to suppose they lied. Throughout my childhood I never doubted that they were my parents, and no sadness darkened those years. They did not tell me the truth until my boy's locks were shorn and I became a youth. They told me then because they feared and honored the gods, and my father did not want me to live a lie my whole life through.

But who I was, whence I came, and who my parents were I never learned, though—for reasons I shall speak of later—I believe I know.

One thing is certain: I was not the only one to be carried down the river in a pitched-reed boat. Thebes with its palaces and its temples was a big city, and the mud hovels of the poor clustered thickly about the statelier buildings. In the time of the great Pharaohs Egypt had brought many nations under its sway, and with power and wealth came altered customs. Foreigners came to Thebes: merchants and craftsmen built temples there to their own gods. Great was the splendor and wealth of the temples and the palaces, great also the poverty outside the walls. Many poor people put their children out; many a rich wife, whose husband was away on his travels, abandoned the proof of her adultery to the river. Perhaps I was the son of a seaman's wife who had deceived her husband with some Syrian merchant. Perhaps—as I had not been circumcised—I was some foreigner's child. When my hair was cut and my mother had put it away in a little wooden box with my first sandals, I looked long at the reed boat she showed me. The struts were yellowed and broken and sooty with smoke from the brazier. It was tied with fowler's knots, but that was all it could tell me of my parentage. It was then that my heart felt its first wound.

3

With the approach of age the soul flies like a bird back to the days of childhood. Now those days shine bright and clear in my memory until it seems as if everything then must have been better, lovelier than in the world of today. In this rich and poor do not differ, for there is surely none so destitute but his childhood shows some glint of happiness when he remembers it in age.

My father Senmut lived upstream from the temple walls, in a squalid, noisy quarter. Near his house lay the big stone wharves where the Nile boats discharged their cargoes, and in the narrow alley ways were the seamen's and merchants' taverns and the brothels to which the wealthy also came, borne on chairs from the inner city. Our neighbors were tax collectors, barge masters, noncommissioned officers, and a few priests of the fifth grade. Like my father, they belonged to the more respected part of the population, rising above it as a wall rises above the surface of the water.

Our house, therefore, was spacious in comparison with the mud huts of the very poor that huddled sadly along the narrow alleys. We had even a garden a few paces long with a sycamore in it that my father had planted. The garden was fenced from the street by acacia bushes, and for a pool we had a stone trough that contained water only at floodtime. There were four rooms to the house, and in one of them my mother prepared our food, which we ate on a veranda opening out of my father's surgery. Twice a week a woman came to help my mother clean the house—for Kipa was very cleanly— and once a week a washerwoman fetched our linen to her wash place on the river bank.

In this rowdy quarter, where there were many foreigners—a quarter whose degradation was revealed to me only as I grew out of child-hood—my father and his neighbors upheld tradition and all venerable customs. At a time when among even the aristocrats of the city these customs lapsed, he and his class continued rigidly to represent the Egypt of the past in their reverence for the gods, their purity of heart, and selflessness. It seemed as if they desired to dissociate themselves by their behavior from those with whom they were obliged to live and work.

But why speak now of what I only later understood? Why not rather remember the gnarled trunk of the sycamore, and the soughing of the leaves when I sought shelter at its foot from the scorching sun, and my favorite toy, the wooden crocodile that snapped its jaws and showed its red gullet when I pulled it along the paved street on a string? The neighbors' children would gather to stare at it in wonder. I won many a honey sweetmeat, many a shiny stone and snippet of copper wire by letting others drag it along and play with it. Only chil-dren of high rank had such toys as a rule, but my father was given it by the palace carpenter, whom he had cured of a boil that prevented him from sitting down.

In the morning my mother would take me with her to the vege-table market. She never had many purchases to make, yet she could spend a water measure's time choosing a bunch of onions and the whole of every morning for a week if it were a matter of choosing new shoes. By the way she talked one might have judged her to be rich and concerned merely with having the best; if she did not buy all that took her fancy—why, then it was because she wished to bring me up in thrifty ways. She would declare, "It is not the man with silver and gold who is rich, but the man who is content with little." So she would assure me, while her poor old eyes dwelt longingly upon the brightly colored woolen stuffs from Sidon and Byblos, as fine and light as down. Her brown, work-hardened hands caressed the ostrich feathers and the ornaments of ivory. It was all vanity, she told me—and herself. But the child's mind rebelled against these precepts; I longed to own a monkey that put its arm about its master's neck or a brilliant-feathered bird that shrieked Syrian and Egyptian words. And I should have had nothing against gold chains and gilded sandals. It was not until much later that I realized how dearly poor old Kipa longed to be rich.

Being but the wife of a poor physician, she stilled her yearnings with stories. Before we fell asleep at night she would tell me in a low voice all the tales she knew. She told of Sinuhe and of the shipwrecked man who returned from the Serpent King with countless riches, of gods and evil spirits, of sorcerers, and of the Pharaohs of old. My father often murmured at this and said she was filling my head with nonsense, but when it was evening and he had begun to snore, she would continue, as much for her own pleasure as for mine. I remember those stifling summer nights when the pallet scorched my bare body and sleep would not come; I hear her hushed, soothing voice; I am safe with her once more. . . . My own mother could hardly have been kinder or more tender than simple, superstitious Kipa, at whose hands blind and crippled storytellers were sure of a good meal.

The stories pleased me, but as a counterweight there was the lively street, that haunt of flies, the street that was filled with a thousand scents and smells. From the harbor the wind would bring the fresh tang of cedarwood and myrrh, or a breath of perfumed oil when a noble lady passing in her chair leaned out to curse the street boys. In the evenings, when Ammon's golden boat swung down to the western hills, there arose from all the nearby huts and verandas the smell of fried fish mingled with the aroma of newly baked bread. This smell of the poor quarter in Thebes I learned to love as a child, and I have never forgotten it.

It was during meals on the veranda that I received the first teachings from my father. He would enter the garden wearily from the

8

street or come from his surgery with the sharp odor of ointments and drugs clinging to his clothes. My mother poured water over his hands, and we sat on stools to eat while she served us. Sometimes while we were sitting there, a gang of sailors would reel along the street, yelling drunkenly, beating with sticks upon the walls of the houses, or stopping to relieve themselves by our acacias. My father, being a discreet man, said nothing until they had gone by; then he would tell me, "Only a Negro or a dirty Syrian does that in the street. An Egyptian goes between walls."

Or he would say, "Wine enjoyed in moderation is the gods' gift to us, and rejoices our hearts. One beaker hurts no one. Two loosen the tongue, but the man who drinks a jar of it wakes to find himself in the gutter, robbed and beaten."

Sometimes a breath of perfumed ointments would reach the veranda when a lovely woman went by on foot, robed transparently, with cheeks, lips, and eyebrows beautifully painted and in her liquid eyes a glint never seen in those of the virtuous. When I gazed spellbound upon such a one, my father would say gravely, "Beware of a woman who calls you 'pretty boy' and entices you, for her heart is a net and a snare, and her body burns worse than fire."

It was no wonder that after such teachings my childish soul began to fear the wine jar and beautiful women who were not like ordinary women, though both became endowed with the perilous charm of feared and forbidden things.

While I was yet a child, my father let me attend his consultations; he showed me his scalpels, forceps, and jars of medicine and explained their uses to me. When he examined his patients, I had to stand beside him and hand him bowls of water, dressings, oil and wine. My mother could not endure to see wounds and sores and never understood my interest in disease. A child does not appreciate suffering until he has experienced it. To me, the lancing of a boil was a thrilling operation, and I would proudly tell the other boys all I had seen to win their respect. Whenever a new patient arrived, I would follow my father's examination and questions with close attention until at last he said, "This disease can be cured," or "I will undertake your treatment." There were also those whom he did not feel competent to treat. Then he would write a few lines on a strip of papyrus and send them to the House of Life, in the temple. When such a patient had left him, he would usually sigh, shake his head, and say, "Poor creature!"

Not all my father's patients were needy. Patrons of nearby pleasure

9

houses were sent to him now and again to be bandaged after some brawl, and their clothes were of finest linen. Masters of Syrian ships came sometimes when they had boils or toothache. I was not surprised, therefore, when the wife of a spice dealer came for examination one day wearing jewelry and a collar sparkling with precious stones. She sighed and moaned and lamented over her many afflictions while my father listened attentively. I was greatly disappointed when at last he took up a strip of paper to write upon, for I had hoped he would be able to cure her and so acquire many fine presents. I sighed, shook my head, and whispered to myself, "Poor creature!"

The sick woman gave a frightened start and looked uneasily at my father. He wrote a line in ancient characters copied from a worn papyrus scroll, then poured oil and wine into a mixing bowl and soaked the paper in it until the ink had been dissolved by the wine. Then he poured the liquid into an earthenware jar and gave it to the spice dealer's wife as a medicine, telling her to take some of it whenever head or stomach began to pain her. When the woman had gone, I looked at my father, who seemed embarrassed. He coughed once or twice and said, "Many diseases can be cured with ink that has been used for a powerful invocation."

He said no more aloud, but muttered to himself after a time, "At least it can do the patient no harm."

When I was seven years old, I was given a boy's loincloth and my mother took me to the temple to attend a sacrifice. Ammon's temple in Thebes was at that time the mightiest in all Egypt. An avenue bordered with ram's-headed sphinxes carved in stone led to it, right through the city from the temple and pool of the moon goddess. The temple area was surrounded by massive brick walls and with its many buildings formed a city within the city. From the tops of the towering pylons floated colored pennants, and gigantic statues of kings guarded the copper gates on each side of the enclosure.

We went through the gates, and the sellers of Books of the Dead pulled at my mother's clothes and made their offers shrilly or in a whisper. Mother took me to look at the carpenters' shops with their display of wooden images of slaves and servants, which, after consecration by the priests, would serve their owners in the next world so that these need never lift a finger to help themselves.

My mother paid the fee demanded of spectators, and I saw white-robed, deft-handed priests slay and quarter a bull between whose horns a braid of papyrus bore a seal, testifying that the beast was without blemish or a single black hair. The priests were fat and holy, and their

10

shaven heads gleamed with oil. There were a hundred or so people who had come to attend the sacrifice, but the priests paid little heed to them and chatted freely to one another of their own affairs throughout the ceremony. I gazed at the warlike pictures on the temple walls and marveled at the gigantic columns, failing altogether to understand my mother's emotion when with tear-filled eyes she led me home. There she took off my baby shoes and gave me new sandals that were uncomfortable and chafed my feet until I grew used to them.

After the meal my father, with a grave look upon his face, laid his big, clever hand on my head and stroked with shy tenderness the soft locks at my temple.

"Now you are seven years old, Sinuhe, and must decide what you want to be."

"A warrior!" I said at once, and was puzzled by the disappointed look on his good face. For the best games the street boys played were war games, and I had watched soldiers wrestle and perfect themselves in the use of arms in front of the barracks and had seen plumed war chariots race forth on thundering wheels to maneuvers outside the city. There could be nothing nobler or grander than a warrior's career. Moreover, a soldier need not be able to write, and this was what weighed most with me, for older boys told terrible tales of how difficult the art of writing was and of how mercilessly the teachers pulled the pupils' hair if they chanced to smash a clay tablet or break a reed pen between their unskilled fingers.

It is likely that my father was never a notably gifted man, or he would surely have become something more than a poor man's doctor. But he was conscientious in his work and never harmed his patients and in the course of years had become wise through experience. He knew already how touchy and self-willed I was and made no comment on my resolve.

Presently, however, he asked my mother for a bowl, and going to his workroom, he filled the vessel with cheap wine from a jar.

"Come, Sinuhe," he said, and he led me out of the house and down to the river bank. By the quay we stopped to look at a barge from which stunted porters were unloading wares sewn up in matting. The sun was setting among the western hills beyond the City of the Dead, but these serfs toiled on, panting and dripping with sweat. The overseer stung them with his whip while the clerk sat placidly beneath his awning, checking off each bale on his list.

"Would you like to be one of those?" asked my father.

I thought this a stupid question and gaped at him without answering. No one wanted to be like the porters.

"They labor from early morning till late at night," said Senmut. "Their skins have coarsened like a crocodile's; their fists are gross as crocodile's feet. Only when darkness falls can they crawl to their miserable huts, and their food is a scrap of bread, an onion, and a mouthful of thin, bitter beer. That is the porter's life, the ploughman's life, the life of all who labor with their hands. Do you think they are to be envied?"

I shook my head, still looking at him in wonder. It was a soldier I desired to be, not a porter, a scratcher of the soil, a waterer of the fields, or a dung-caked shepherd.

"Father," I said as we went on, "soldiers have a fine time. They live in barracks and eat good food; in the evening they drink wine in the pleasure houses, and women smile at them. The leaders among them wear golden chains about their necks although they cannot write. When they return from battle, they bring with them booty and slaves who toil and follow trades to serve them. Why shouldn't I strive to become a warrior, too?"

My father made no answer but hastened his step. Near the big rubbish dump where flies buzzed in a cloud about us he bent down and peered into a low mud hovel.

"Inteb, my friend, are you there?"

Out crawled a verminous old man leaning on a stick. His right arm had been lopped off below the shoulder, and his loincloth was stiff with dirt. His face was dried and wizened with age, and he had no teeth.

"Is—is *that* Inteb?" I gasped, looking at the old man in horror. Inteb was a hero who had fought in the Syrian campaigns under Thothmes III, the greatest of the Pharaohs, and stories were still told of his prowess and of the rewards that Pharaoh had given him.

The old man raised his hand in a soldier's salute, and my father handed him the bowl of wine. Then they sat down on the ground for there was not even a bench outside the hut, and Inteb raised the wine to his lips with a trembling hand, careful not to waste a drop.

"My son Sinuhe means to be a warrior," my father smiled. "I brought him to you, Inteb, because you are the last survivor of the heroes of the great wars and can tell him of the proud life and splendid feats of soldiers."

"In the name of Set and Baal and all other devils!" cackled the other, turning his nearsighted gaze upon me. "Is the boy mad?"

12

His toothless mouth, dim eyes, dangling arm stump, and wrinkled, grimy breast were so terrifying that I crept behind my father and gripped his arm.

"Boy, boy," tittered Inteb, "if I had a mouthful of wine for every curse I have uttered upon my life and upon fate—miserable fate that made a soldier of me—I could fill the lake that Pharaoh has had made for his old woman. True, I have never seen it because I cannot afford to be ferried across the river, but I doubt not I could fill it—ay, and that there would be enough over to fuddle an army."

He drank again, sparingly.

"But," said I, my chin quivering, "the soldier's profession is the most honorable of all."

"Honor! Renown!" said Inteb, hero of the armies of Thothmes. "Droppings—ordure where flies are bred—no more! Many a lie have I told in my time to get wine out of the goggling blockheads who listened to me, but your father is an upright man whom I will not deceive. Therefore, son, I tell you that of all professions the warrior's is the most wretched and most degraded."

The wine was smoothing out the wrinkles in his face and kindling a glow in his wild old eyes. He rose and gripped his neck with his one hand.

"Look, boy! This scraggy neck was once hung with golden chains—five loops of them. Pharaoh himself hung them there. Who can reckon the lopped-off hands I have heaped before his tent? Who was the first to scale the walls of Kadesh? Who burst through the enemy ranks like a trumpeting elephant? It was I—I, Inteb the hero! And who thanks me for it now? My gold went the way of all earthly things, and the slaves I took in battle ran away or perished miserably. My right hand I left behind in the land of Mitanni, and I should long ago have been begging at street corners were it not for the charitable people who give me dried fish and beer now and then for telling their children the truth about war. I am Inteb, the great hero—look at me! I left my youth in the desert, robbed of it by starvation, privation, and hardship. There the flesh melted from my limbs, my skin toughened, and my heart hardened to stone. Worst of all, the parched desert dried my tongue, and I became the prey of unquenchable thirst, like every other soldier who returns alive from foreign wars. And life has been like the valley of death since I lost my arm. I need not so much as mention the pain of the wound and the agony when the army surgeons scalded the stump in boiling oil after the amputation—that is something your father can appreciate. Blessed be your name,

13

Senmut! You are a just man, a good man—but the wine is finished."

The old fellow fell silent, panted a little, and sitting down again upon the ground, he turned the earthenware bowl sadly upside down. His eyes were glowing embers, and he was once more an old, unhappy man.

"But a warrior need not know how to write," came my faltering whisper.

"H'm," said the old man and looked sideways at my father, who quickly took a copper bangle from his arm and handed it to him. Inteb called loudly, and at once a grimy boy ran up, took the ring and the bowl, and started for the tavern after more wine.

"Not the best!" shouted Inteb to him. "Get the sour—they'll give you more of it." He looked at me again reflectively. "A warrior need not write, only fight. If he could write, he would be an officer with command over the most valiant, whom he would send before him into battle. Anyone who can write is fit for command, but a man who cannot scribble pothooks will never have even so many as a hundred under him. What joy can he take in gold chains and honors when it is the fellow with the reed pen in his hand who gives the orders? Thus it is, and thus it will be—and so, my lad, if you would command men and lead them, learn to write. Then those with the gold chains will bow down before you, and slaves will carry you in a chair to the field of battle."

The dirty boy came back with a jar of wine and had the bowl full as well. The old man's face shone with joy.

"Your father Senmut is a good man. He can write, and he tended me in my palmy days when wine was plentiful and I used to see crocodiles and hippopotamuses where none were. A good man, though he *is* only a doctor and cannot handle a bow. He has my thanks."

I stared nervously at the wine jar to which Inteb plainly meant to turn his full attention and began to tug at my father's wide, drug-stained sleeve, fearful lest so much wine might result in our waking, bruised and beaten, in some gutter. Senmut looked at the jar also, sighed a little, and led me away. Inteb lifted up his shrill old voice in a Syrian song while the naked, sun-blackened boy laughed.

So I buried my martial dreams and no longer resisted when my father and mother took me next day to school.

4

My father could not afford to send me to any of the big temple schools where the sons—and sometimes daughters—of rich men, nobles and eminent priests were taught. My teacher was the old priest Oneh who lived not far away and held classes on his tumble-down veranda. His pupils were the children of artisans, merchants, dock foremen, and noncommissioned officers whose ambition sought to open a scribe's career for their sons. Oneh had in his time been steward to the Celestial Mūt in the temple and was therefore well fitted to give elementary writing lessons to children who later on would be keeping tally of merchandise, measures of grain, head of cattle, or provisions for the army. There were hundreds of such little schools in the great city of Thebes. Instruction was cheap, the pupils merely having to maintain the teacher. The charcoal seller's son replenished his brazier in winter, the weaver's son kept him in clothes, the corn chandler's boy saw that he never ran short of flour, and my father treated his many aches and pains and gave him herbal anodynes to take in his wine.

His dependence upon us made Oneh a gentle teacher. A boy who fell asleep over his tablets never had his ears boxed; he had but to filch some titbit for the old man next morning. Sometimes the corn merchant's son would bring a jug of beer. On such days we were all attention, for old Oneh would be inspired to tell us strange stories of the other world: of the Celestial Mūt, of the Creator, of Ptah and his companion gods. We would giggle, believing that we had distracted him from our difficult tasks and wearisome writing characters for the rest of the day; it was only later that I perceived old Oneh to be a wiser teacher than we took him for. There was a purpose in his recital of the legends to which his pious, childlike spirit gave life: they taught us the traditions of ancient Egypt. In them no evil deed went unpunished. Relentlessly each human heart was weighed before the high throne of Osiris. That mortal whose evil deeds were disclosed upon the scales of the Jackal-Headed One was thrown to the Devourer who was crocodile and hippopotamus combined, but more terrifying than either.

He told also of the surly Backward-Gazer, that dread ferryman without whose help no one could attain the fields of the blessed. When he rowed, he faced aft, never forward like the earthly boatmen of the Nile. Oneh would make us repeat by heart the phrases with which this being might be bribed and propitiated. He taught us to copy them out and then write them down from memory, correcting our faults with the gentle warning that the smallest error would wipe out all chance of a happy life in the hereafter. Were we to hand the Backward-Gazer a letter containing even a trivial mistake, we should be forced to wander like shadows for all eternity by the banks of those somber waters or, worse still, be engulfed in the hideous abysses of the realms of death.

I attended Oneh's school for some years. My best friend there was Thothmes, who was a year or so older than myself and who had been brought up from infancy to wrestle and to handle horses. His father was leader of a squadron of chariots and wielded a whip of office braided with copper wire: he had hopes that his son might become a high-ranking officer and therefore wished him to learn to write. But there was nothing prophetic about the illustrious name of Thothmes, despite his father's ambitions, for as soon as the boy began his schooling, he ceased to care for javelin throwing and charioteering. He learned his characters easily, and while the other boys struggled grimly with them, he drew pictures on his tablets: pictures of chariots, rearing horses, and wrestling soldiers. He brought clay to school, and while the ale jug told stories through Oneh's mouth, he modeled a comic little image of the Devourer snapping with clumsy jaws at a little bald old man whose humped back and pot belly could belong to none other than Oneh. But Oneh was not angry. No one could be angry with Thothmes. He had the broad face and short, thick legs of a peasant, but his eyes held a joyful glint that was infectious, and the birds and beasts he formed from clay with his clever hands delighted us all. I had sought his friendship first because he was soldierly, but the friendship persisted after he had ceased to show a trace of warlike ambition.

A miracle happened during my school days and happened so suddenly that I still remember that hour as one of revelation. It was a fair, cool day in spring when the air was full of bird song and storks were repairing their old nests on the roofs of the mud huts. The waters had gone down, and fresh green shoots were springing from the earth. In all the gardens seeds were being sown and plants bedded out. It was a day for adventure, and we could not sit still on Oneh's rickety old veranda, where the mud bricks crumbled under one's hand. I was scratching at those everlasting symbols—letters for cutting in stone and beside them the abbreviated signs used for writing on paper— when suddenly some forgotten word of Oneh's, some queer flash within myself, spoke and brought these characters to life. The pictures became a word, the word a syllable, the syllable a letter. When I set

16

picture to picture, new words leaped forth—living words, quite distinct from the symbols. Any yokel can understand one picture, but two together have meaning only for the literate. I believe that everyone who has studied writing and learned to read knows what I am trying to say. The experience was to me more exciting, more fascinating than snatching a pomegranate from a fruit seller's basket—sweeter than a dried date, delicious as water to the thirsty.

From that time I needed no urging but soaked up Oneh's learning as dry earth soaks up the flood waters of the Nile, and I quickly learned to write. In a little while I began to read what others had written, and by the third year I could already spell my way through tattered scrolls and read aloud instructive fables for the others to write down.

About this time I noticed that I did not look like the rest. My face was narrower, my skin lighter, and my limbs more slender than those of the other lads and of the people among whom I dwelt. But for the difference in dress, hardly anyone could have distinguished me from the boys who were carried in chairs or walked the streets attended by slaves. I was sneered at for this; the corn merchant's son would try to put his arm round my neck and called me a girl until I had to jab him with my stylus. He revolted me for he had an evil smell, but I liked to be with Thothmes, who never touched me. One day Thothmes said shyly, "I will model your likeness if you will sit for me."

I took him home, and there under the sycamore he made a likeness of me in clay and scratched the characters of my name upon it with a stylus. My mother Kipa, coming out with cakes for us, was badly frightened when she saw the image and called it witchcraft. But my father said that Thothmes might become artist to the royal household if he could only join the temple school, and jokingly I bowed down before Thothmes and stretched forth my hand at knee level as one does in the presence of distinguished persons. His eyes shone; then he sighed that it could never be, for his father thought it was time he came back to barracks and joined the school for charioteers. He could already write as well as was required of any future officer. My father left us then, and we heard Kipa muttering to herself in the kitchen; but Thothmes and I ate the cakes, which were greasy and good, and we were well content.

I was still happy then.

5

The day came when my father put on his newly washed best robe and set about his neck a broad collar embroidered by Kipa. He went to the great temple of Ammon, though privately he had no love for priests. But nothing ever happened in Thebes or indeed in the whole of Egypt at this time without their help and intervention. They administered justice so that a bold man against whom judgment had been given by Pharaoh's own court could appeal to them for redress. In their hands lay all instruction for the higher administrative posts. They foretold the height of the flood waters and the size of the harvest and from this assessed the taxes for the whole country.

I do not think it can have been easy for my father to humble himself before them. All his life he had been a poor man's physician in the poor man's quarter—a stranger to the temple and the House of Life—and now like other penniless fathers he had to wait in line outside the administrative department until it should please some holiness or other to receive him. I can see these poor fathers now, squatting in the temple courtyard in their best robes, dreaming ambitious dreams for their sons, for whom they coveted a better existence than their own. Many of them had come a long way on river boats, carrying their food with them. They spent their substance on bribes to doorkeeper and clerk for the privilege of a word with a gold-embroidered, perfumed, and anointed priest, who wrinkled his nose at the smell of them and gave them harsh words. And yet—Ammon stands in continual need of new servants. The greater his wealth and power, the greater the numbers of scribes he wears out in his service. However, there is not a father who does not regard it as a divine favor for his son to be received into the temple—ay, though in bringing the boy he brings a gift more precious than gold.

My father was fortunate in his visit, for noon had scarcely passed when his old fellow student Ptahor came by. In the course of time Ptahor had become skull opener to Pharaoh's household. My father ventured to address him, and he promised to honor our house in person and inspect me.

The day being fixed, my father saved up for a goose and the best wine. Kipa baked—and nagged. A luscious odor of goose fat floated out into the street till blind men and beggars gathered there to sing and play for their share of the feast. Kipa, hissing with rage, charged out with a bit of bread dipped in the fat for each of them and sent them packing. Thothmes and I swept the street from our door far into the city. My father had asked Thothmes to be at hand when the guest came, in the hope that he also might be favored with the great man's attention. Boys though we were, when my father lit the censer and set it to perfume the entrance way, we felt as awestruck as if we had been in a temple. I guarded the can of scented water and kept the flies off the dazzling white linen cloth Kipa had set aside for her own burial, but which was now brought forth as a towel for Ptahor.

We had long to wait. The sun set, and the air grew cooler. The incense in the porch all burned away, and the goose sizzled sorrowfully in the roasting pit. I grew hungry, and Kipa's face lengthened and stiffened. My father said nothing but would not light the lamps when darkness fell. We all sat down on stools in the porch and avoided one another's eyes, and it was then I learned what bitter grief and disappointment the rich and mighty in their thoughtlessness can bring upon the poor.

But at last there came the glow of a torch along the street. My father jumped up and hastened to the kitchen for an ember to light both the lamps. I raised the water pitcher in trembling hands while Thothmes breathed heavily beside me.

Ptahor, the opener of royal skulls, arrived unpretentiously in a chair borne by two Negro slaves and preceded by a fat torchbearer who was evidently drunk. With puffings and cheerful cries of greeting Ptahor stepped from the chair to hail my father, who bowed and stretched forth his hands at knee level. The guest laid his hands on Senmut's shoulders, either to show him that ceremony was needless or to steady himself. Thus supported he kicked at the torchbearer and told him to sleep it off under the sycamore. The Negroes, without waiting for orders, dumped the chair in the acacia bushes and squatted on the ground.

Still leaning on my father's shoulder, Ptahor stepped into the porch, where I poured water over his hands despite his protests. When I handed him the linen cloth, he said that as I had rinsed his hands I might now dry them. When I had done this, he thanked me and said I was a handsome boy. My father led him to the seat of honor— a chair with a back, borrowed from the spice merchant—and he sat down, his inquisitive little eyes peering about him in the light of the suet lamps. For a time there was silence. Then, clearing his throat apologetically, he asked for something to drink as the long journey had made him dry. My father, delighted, poured out wine for him.

Ptahor sniffed at it and tasted it suspiciously, then emptied the cup with evident enjoyment and gave a contented sigh.

He was a bowlegged, shaven-headed little man with a breast and belly that sagged beneath the thin robe. His collar, set with precious stones, was now soiled like the rest of his dress, and he smelled of oil, wine, and sweat.

Kipa served him with spice cakes, small fish fried in oil, fruit, and roast goose. He ate politely though it was clear that he had just come from a good meal, and he tasted and praised every dish to Kipa's great delight. At his desire I took beer and food to the Negroes, but they returned the courtesy by shouting insults and asking whether old swagbelly was ready to go. The servant snored beneath the sycamore, and I had no wish to wake him.

The evening grew extremely confused, as my father, too, drank more than I had ever seen him do, so that at last Kipa, sitting in the kitchen, was overcome with woe and sat rocking back and forth with her head in her hands. When the pitcher was empty, they drank father's medicinal wine. When that was gone, they started upon ordinary table beer; for Ptahor assured us that he was not particular.

They talked of their student days in the House of Life, swaying and embracing each other as they sat. Ptahor related his experiences as royal skull surgeon, affirming that it was the last branch in which any physician should specialize, being more suited to the House of Death than the House of Life. But there was little work attached to it, and he had always been lazy, as Senmut the Tranquil would certainly remember. The human head—except for the teeth, ears, and throat, which required their own specialists—was in his view the simplest thing to study, and so he had chosen it.

"But," said he, "if I had had any decency I should have remained what I was: an honest physician bringing life to his patients. As it is, my lot is to deal out death when kinsfolk grow weary of the old or the incurable. I should be like you, friend Senmut—poorer perhaps, but leading a more honest, a more wholesome life."

"Never believe him, boys!" said my father—for Thothmes was sitting with us now and held a small wine cup in his hand. "I am proud to call Pharaoh's skull borer my friend; in his own line he is the most highly skilled in all Egypt. Do I not remember the prodigious trepanning operations by which he saved the lives of mighty and humble alike and astonished the world? He releases evil spirits that drive men to madness and takes their round eggs from men's brains.

Grateful patients bestow gold and silver upon him, chains and drinking cups."

"But grateful kinsfolk have done more," put in Ptahor thickly. "For if by chance I heal one in ten, one in fifteen—no, let us say one in a hundred—so much more certain is the death of the others. Have you heard of a single Pharaoh who lived three days after his skull had been opened? No, the mad and incurable are put under my flint knife —and the richer and more illustrious, the quicker they come. My hand releases men from pain, divides inheritances—land, cattle, and gold— my hand raises Pharaohs to the throne. Therefore they fear me, and none dares speak against me, for I know too much. But what increases knowledge increases sorrow, and I am a most unhappy man!"

Ptahor wept a little and blew his nose on Kipa's shroud.

"You are poor but honest, Senmut," he sobbed. "Therefore, I love you, for I am rich and rotten—rotten—a lump of ox dung upon the road."

He took off his jeweled collar and hung it about my father's neck, and then they began to sing songs whose words I could not understand though Thothmes listened with interest and told me that riper songs were not to be heard even in barracks. Kipa began to weep loudly in the kitchen. One of the Negroes came over from the acacia bushes, lifted Ptahor in his arms and would have carried him to his chair, for it was long after bedtime. But Ptahor struggled and uttered pitiful cries, called upon the watchmen to help him and vowed that the Negro meant murder. As my father was of no help, Thothmes and I drove the Negro off with sticks until he flew into a rage and went, swearing violently and taking comrade and chair with him.

Ptahor now emptied the beer jug over himself, asked for oil to rub on his face, and tried to bathe in the pool. Thothmes whispered to me that we ought to get the old men into bed, and so it came about that my father and the royal skull surgeon fell asleep on Kipa's bed with arms about each other's necks, slobbering oaths of eternal friendship to the last.

Kipa wept and tore her hair and sprinkled herself with ash from the roasting pit. I was tormented by the thought of what the neighbors would say, for the roaring and racket had sounded far and wide into the still night. Thothmes was placid, however, for he had seen wilder doings in barracks and in his father's house when the charioteers talked of the old days and of the punitive expeditions into Syria and the land of Kush. He contrived to quiet Kipa, and after we had cleared away the traces of the feast as best we could, we, too, went

21

to bed. The servant snored on beneath the sycamore, and Thothmes lay down beside me in my bed, put his arm about my neck, and talked about girls for he also had drunk wine. But I found this wearisome, being a year or two younger than he, and soon feel asleep.

Early in the morning I was awakened by bumping and sounds of movement in the bedroom, and on entering I saw my father still sound asleep in his clothes with Ptahor's collar about his neck. Ptahor was sitting on the floor holding his head in his hands and asking in a woeful voice where he was.

I greeted him respectfully and told him that he was still in the harbor quarter, at the house of Senmut the physician. This quieted him, and he asked for beer in the name of Ammon. I pointed out to him that he had emptied the beer jug over himself, as his robe testified. He then rose, drew himself up with a dignified frown, and went out. I poured water over his hands, and he bowed his bald head with a groan, bidding me pour water over that, too. Thothmes, who had also awakened, brought him a can of sour milk and a salt fish. When he had eaten, he grew more cheerful. He went out to the sycamore where the servant lay sleeping and began to beat him with his stick till the fellow woke and stood up, his garment stained from the grass and his face earthy.

"Miserable swine!" cried Ptahor and smote him again. "Is it thus you mind your lord's affairs and bear the torch before him? Where is my chair? Where is my clean robe? And my medicinal berries? Out of my sight, contemptible thief and swine!"

"I am a thief and my lord's swine," said the servant meekly. "What are my lord's commands?"

Ptahor gave him his orders, and he went off to look for the chair. Ptahor settled himself comfortably under the sycamore, leaned against the trunk, and recited a poem concerning morning, lotus flowers, and a queen bathing in the river, and then related to us many things that boys love to hear. Kipa meanwhile awoke, lit the fire, and went in to my father. We could hear her voice right out in the garden, and when my father emerged later in a clean robe, he looked sorrowful indeed.

"You have a handsome son," said Ptahor. "He carries himself like a prince, and his eyes are gentle as a gazelle's." Young as I was, I understood that he spoke thus to make us forget his behavior of the night before. After a while he went on, "Has your son talent? Are the eyes of his soul as open as those of his body?"

Then Thothmes and I fetched our writing tablets. The royal skull

surgeon, gazing abstractedly into the topmost branches of the sycamore, dictated a little poem, which I still remember. It ran thus:

> *Rejoice, young man, in thy youth,*
> *For the throat of age is filled with ashes*
> *And the body embalmed smiles not*
> *In the darkness of the grave.*

I did my best, first writing it down in ordinary script and then in
pictures. Lastly I wrote the words "age," "ashes," "body," and "grave"
in all the ways in which they can be written, both in syllables and letters. I showed him my tablet. He found not one mistake, and I knew
that my father was proud of me.

"And the other boy?" said Ptahor, holding out his hand. Thothmes
had been sitting apart, drawing pictures on his tablet, and he hesitated
before handing it over, though there was mirth in his eyes. When we
bent forward to look, we saw that he had drawn Ptahor fastening his
collar about father's neck, then Ptahor pouring beer over himself,
while in the third picture he and my father were singing with their
arms round each other's shoulders—such a funny picture that you
could see what manner of song it was that they were singing. I wanted
to laugh but dared not for fear that Ptahor might be angry. For
Thothmes had not flattered him; he had made him just as short and
bald and bandy and swagbellied as he really was.

For a long time Ptahor said nothing but looked keenly from the
pictures to Thothmes and back again. Thothmes grew a little scared
and balanced nervously on tiptoe. At last Ptahor asked, "What do
you want for your picture, boy? I will buy it."

Thothmes, crimson in the face, replied, "My tablet is not for sale.
I would give it—to a friend."

Ptahor laughed.

"Good. Let us then be friends, and the tablet is mine."

He looked at it attentively once more, laughed, and smashed it to
pieces against a stone. We all started, and Thothmes begged forgiveness if he had offended.

"Am I wroth with water when it reflects my image?" returned
Ptahor mildly. "And the eye and the hand of the draftsman are more
than water—for I know now how I looked yesterday, and I do not
desire that others shall see it. I smashed the tablet but acknowledge
you as an artist."

Thothmes jumped for glee.

Ptahor turned to my father and, pointing to me, solemnly pro-

23

nounced the ancient oath of the physician: "I will undertake his treatment."

Pointing then to Thothmes he said, "I will do what I can." And, having thus come into doctors' talk again, they both laughed contentedly. My father, laying his hand upon my head, asked, "Sinuhe, my son, will you be a physician like me?"

Tears came into my eyes, and my throat tightened till I could not speak, but I nodded in answer. I looked about me, and the garden was dear to me; the sycamore, the stone-set pool—all were dear to me.

"Sinuhe, my son," he went on. "Will you be a physician more skilled than I, better than I—lord of life and death and one to whom all, be they high or low, may entrust their lives?"

"Neither like him nor like me!" broke in Ptahor. He straightened himself, and a shrewd glint came into his eye. "A true physician, for that is the mightiest of all. Before him Pharaoh himself stands naked, and the richest is to him one with the beggar."

"I would like to be a real physician," I said shyly, for I was still a boy and knew nothing of life nor that age ever seeks to lay its own dreams, its own disappointments, on the shoulders of youth.

But to Thothmes Ptahor showed a gold ring that was about his wrist and said, "Read!"

Thothmes spelled out the characters there inscribed and then read aloud uncertainly, "'A full cup rejoiceth my heart.'" He could not repress a smile.

"There is nothing to laugh at, you rascal!" said Ptahor gravely. "This has nothing to do with wine. If you are to be an artist you must demand that your cup be full. In the true artist Ptah reveals himself—the creator, the builder. The artist is more than a reflecting pool. Art indeed may often be nothing but flattering water or a lying mirror, yet the artist is more. So let your cup never be less than full, son, and do not rest content with what men tell you. Trust rather to your own clear eyes."

He promised that I should soon be summoned as a pupil to the House of Life and that he would try to help Thothmes enter the art school in Ptah's temple, if such a thing were possible.

"But, boys," he added, "listen carefully to what I say and then forget it at once—or forget at least that it was the royal skull surgeon who said it. You will now fall into the hands of priests; you, Sinuhe, will become one yourself in course of time. Your father and I were both initiated into the lowest grade, and no one may follow the physician's calling without being so initiated. When you come among them, be

24

wary as jackals and cunning as serpents, that you be not blinded and misled. But outwardly be as harmless as doves, for not until the goal is attained may a man appear as he is. Remember!"

We conversed further until Ptahor's servant appeared with a hired chair and fresh clothes for his master. The slaves had pawned Ptahor's own chair at a neighboring brothel and were still sleeping there. Ptahor gave his servant authority to redeem both chair and slaves, took leave of us, assuring my father of his friendship, and returned to the fashionable quarter of the city.

But next day he sent a present to Kipa—a sacred scarab carved from a precious stone, to be placed next her heart beneath the shroud at her burial. He could have given my mother no greater joy, and she forgave him everything and ceased lecturing my father Senmut upon the curse of wine.

BOOK

The House o

I

IN THEBES in those days all higher education was in the hands of the priests of Ammon, and it was not possible to study for an important post without a certificate from them. As everyone knows, the Houses of Life and of Death had stood for untold ages within the temple walls, and also the theological schools for priests in the higher grades. That the faculties of mathematics and astronomy should be subordinate to the priesthood can be understood, but when both juridical and mercantile training were taken over, misgivings arose in the minds of the more alert among the educated classes that the priests were meddling with matters that concerned Pharaoh and the taxation department alone. Initiation was not, indeed, indispensable to membership in the merchants' and lawyers' guilds, but as Ammon controlled at least a fifth of the land of Egypt, and therefore also of its commerce, those who wished to become merchants on a large scale or enter the administration found it wise to qualify for the lowest grade of priesthood and submit themselves as the faithful servants of Ammon.

Before I might set foot in the House of Life I had to pass the examination for admission to the lowest grade of priesthood in the theological faculty. This took me more than two years, for at the same time I had to accompany my father on his visits to the sick and from his experience gain knowledge that would profit me in my future career. I lived at home as before but had to attend one lecture or another every day.

Candidates for the lowest grade were divided into groups according to the profession they were to follow afterward. We, that is to say those who were to be disciples in the House of Life, formed a group on our own, but I found no close friend among my companions. I had taken Ptahor's wise warning to heart and kept myself aloof, meekly obeying every order and feigning stupidity when the others jested or blasphemed as boys will. Among us were the sons of medical specialists whose advice and treatment were requited in gold. And there were with us also the sons of country doctors, often older than the rest of us, full-grown, gawky, sunburned fellows who strove to hide their shyness and addressed themselves laboriously to their tasks. There were lads from the lower classes who wanted to rise above their fathers' trade and social level and had a natural thirst for knowledge, but they received the severest treatment of any, for the priests were by nature mistrustful of all who were not content with the old ways.

My caution stood me in good stead, for I soon noticed that the priests had their spies and agents among us. A careless word, a spoken doubt, or a joke among friends soon came to the knowledge of the priests, and the culprit was summoned for examination and punishment. Some were flogged, and some even expelled from the House of Life, which was thenceforth closed to them forever, both in Thebes and in the rest of Egypt.

My ability to read and write gave me a marked advantage over many of my fellows, including some of the older ones. I considered myself ripe to enter the House of Life, but my initiation was delayed. I lacked courage to ask the reason since that would have been regarded as insubordination to Ammon. I frittered away my time in copying out Texts of the Dead, which were sold in the forecourts, and grew rebellious and depressed, for already many of the less talented among my fellows had begun their studies in the House of Life. But under my father's direction I was to gain a better grounding than they, and I have since reflected that Ammon's priests were wise. They saw through me, noted my defiance and my unbelief, and therefore put me to this test.

At last I was told that my turn had come to hold vigil in the temple. I lived in the inner rooms for a week, during which time I was forbidden to leave the precincts. I had to fast and purify myself, and my father hastened to cut my hair and invite the neighbors to a feast in celebration of my maturity. For from this time, being now ripe for initiation—simple and meaningless though the ceremony in fact was—I would be regarded as fully grown, superior to my neighbors and to all other boys of my age.

Kipa had done her best, but to me her honey bread was tasteless, and the mirth and coarse jests of the neighbors were no diversion. In the evening after the guests had gone Senmut and Kipa caught my sadness, too. Senmut began to tell me the truth about my birth, Kipa prompting when his memory failed, while I gazed at the reed boat above my bed. Its blackened, broken struts made my heart ache. In all the world I had no real father and mother but was alone beneath the stars in a great city. I was, perhaps, but a miserable foreigner in the land of Kem or my origin a shameful secret. . . .

There was pain in my heart when I went to the temple wearing the initiation robe that Kipa, with such care and love, had made for me.

2

There were twenty-five of us young men and boys who were preparing to be received into the temple. When we had bathed in the temple pool, our heads were shaved and we put on coarse clothes. The priest appointed as our director was not so pettily meticulous as some. Tradition entitled him to subject us to every kind of humiliating ceremony, but there were some among us of high rank and others who had already taken their law examination—full-grown men who were entering Ammon's service to make their future more secure. These had brought plentiful provisions with them and made the priests presents of wine; some even ran off at night to the pleasure houses, for initiation held no meaning for them. I served with an aching heart and with many bitter thoughts in my mind, contenting myself with a piece of bread and a cup of water—the traditional diet for novices— and waiting in mingled hope and foreboding for what was to come.

For I was so young that I had an unspeakable longing to believe. It was said that Ammon himself appeared at the initiation and spoke individually to each candidate; it would have been ineffable comfort to find release from myself in the awareness of some ultimate and universal purpose. But before the physician even Pharaoh stands naked; already as a child I had seen sickness and death at my father's side, and my eye had been trained to greater keenness than others of my age possessed. To a doctor nothing must be too sacred, and he bows to nothing but death; that my father taught me. Therefore, I doubted, and all that I had seen in the temple during those three years had only deepened my unbelief.

Yet I hoped that behind the veil in the dimness of the holy of holies I should find the Unknown, that Ammon would appear to me and bring peace to my heart.

I was musing upon this as I wandered along the colonnades to which laymen had access. I surveyed the colorful sacred pictures and the inscriptions that told of the stupendous gifts the Pharaohs had brought back to Ammon from the wars, as the god's share of the spoils. And there I met a lovely woman whose robe was of linen so transparent

31

that her breasts and loins might be seen through it. She was straight and slender, her lips, cheeks, and eyebrows were colored, and she looked at me in unabashed curiosity.

"What is your name, you handsome boy?" she asked, her eyes lingering upon the gray shoulder cloth that showed me to be a candidate for initiation.

"Sinuhe," I answered in confusion, not daring to meet her gaze; but she was so beautiful that I hoped she would ask me to be her guide about the temple. Such requests were often made to the novices.

"Sinuhe," she repeated thoughtfully, surveying me. "Then you must be easily frightened and flee when a secret is confided to you."

This was an allusion to the Sinuhe of the story, and it annoyed me; there had been enough of that teasing at school. I drew myself up and looked her in the eye, and her glance was so strange and clear and searching that I felt my face beginning to burn and a flame seemed to be running over my body.

"Why should I fear?" I retorted. "A physician-to-be dreads no secrets."

"Ah," she smiled, "the chick has begun to cheep before it has cracked the shell. But tell me, have you among your comrades a young man named Metufer? He is the son of Pharaoh's master builder."

It was Metufer who had filled the priest with wine and given him a gold bracelet as initiation present. I felt a pang as I told her that I knew him and offered to fetch him. Then it struck me that she might be his sister or some other kinswoman; this cheered me and I smiled at her boldly.

"How am I to fetch him, though, when I do not know your name and cannot tell him who has sent me?"

"He knows," returned the woman, tapping the pavement impatiently with her jeweled sandal. I looked at the little feet, unsoiled by dust, and at the beautiful toenails lacquered bright red. "He knows who it is. Perhaps he owes me something. Perhaps my husband is on a journey, and I am waiting for Metufer to come and console me in my grief."

My heart sank once more at the thought that she was married, but I said briskly, "Very well, fair unknown! I will fetch him. I will say that a woman younger and fairer than the moon goddess calls for him. He will know then who it is, for whoever has seen you once can never forget you."

Scared at my own presumption I turned to go, but she caught hold of me.

32

"Why such haste? Wait! You and I may have something more to say to one another."

She surveyed me again until my heart melted in my breast and my stomach seemed to have slipped down to my knees. She stretched forth a hand heavy with rings and bracelets, touched my head and said kindly, "Is not that handsome head cold, being so newly shaven?" Then softly, "Were you speaking the truth? Do you think I am beautiful? Look more closely."

I looked at her, and her robe was of royal linen, and in my eyes she was fair—fairer than all the women I had seen—and in truth she did nothing to hide her beauty. I looked at her and forgot the wound in my heart, forgot Ammon and the House of Life. Her nearness burned my body like fire.

"You do not answer," she said sadly, "and need not. In those splendid eyes of yours I must appear a hag. Go then and fetch the young candidate Metufer, and be rid of me."

I could neither leave her nor speak, though I knew she was teasing. It was dark between the huge temple pillars. Dim light from some distant stone tracery gleamed in her eyes, and there was no one to see us.

"Perhaps you need not fetch him." She was smiling now. "Perhaps I should be content if you delight me and take your pleasure with me, for I know of no other to give me joy."

Then I remembered what Kipa had told me of women who entice handsome boys; I remembered it so suddenly that I started back a pace.

"Did I not guess that Sinuhe would be afraid?"

She approached me again, but I raised my hand in dismay to hold her off, saying, "I know now what manner of woman you are. Your husband is away, and your heart is a snare, and your body burns worse than fire."

But though I spoke this way, I could not flee from her.

She was taken aback but smiled again and came close against me.

"Do you believe that?" she said gently. "But it is not true! My body does not burn at all like fire; indeed, it is said to be desirable. Feel for yourself!"

She took my limp hand and carried it to her belly. I felt her beauty through the thin stuff so that I began to quake, and my cheeks burned.

"You still do not believe me," she said with feigned disappointment. "My dress is in the way, but stay—I will draw it aside." She pulled

33

away her robe and held my hand to her bare breast. It was soft and cool beneath my hand.

"Come, Sinuhe," she said very softly. "Come with me, and we will drink wine and take our pleasure together."

"I may not leave the precincts of the temple," I said in a fright and was ashamed of my cowardice and desired her and feared her as I would have feared death. "I must keep myself undefiled until I have received my consecration, or I shall be driven from the temple and never again be admitted to the House of Life. Have pity on me!"

I said this knowing that if she asked me once again I must follow her. But she was a woman of the world and knew my distress. She looked about her thoughtfully. We were still alone, but people were moving to and fro nearby, and a guide was loudly reciting the marvels of the temple to some visitors and begging copper from them before showing them new wonders.

"You are a very shy young man, Sinuhe!" she said. "The rich and great must offer gold before I call them to me. But you would remain undefiled."

"You would like me to call Metufer," I said desperately. I knew that Metufer would never hesitate to slip out of the temple when night fell, although it was his turn to watch. He could do such things, for his father was Pharaoh's master builder—but I could have slain him for it.

"Perhaps I no longer wish you to call Metufer," she said, looking mischievously into my eyes. "Perhaps I should like us to part friends, Sinuhe. Therefore I will tell you my name, which is Nefernefernefer, because I am thought beautiful and because no one who has pronounced my name can resist saying it once more, and again. It is a custom also for parting friends to give one another keepsakes. Therefore I want a gift from you."

I was once more aware of my poverty, for I had nothing to give her: not the most trifling little ornament, not the smallest copper ring— nor if I had could I have offered such things to her. I was so bitterly ashamed that I bent my head, unable to speak.

"Then give me a present to revive my heart," she said, and she raised my chin with her finger and brought her face quite close. When I understood what she wanted, I touched her soft lips with mine. She sighed a little.

"Thank you. That was a beautiful gift, Sinuhe. I shall not forget it. But you must be a stranger from a far country since you have not yet learned how to kiss. How else is it possible that the girls of

34

Thebes have not taught you, though your hair is shorn for manhood?"

She drew from her thumb a ring of gold and silver in which was set a large stone without any inscription and put it on my hand.

"I give you a present also, Sinuhe, so that you may not forget me. When you have been initiated and have entered the House of Life, you can have your seal engraved upon this stone, like men of wealth and position. But remember that it is green because my name is Nefernefernefer, and because it has been said that my eyes are as green as Nile water in the heat of summer."

"I cannot take your ring, Nefer," and I repeated it "nefernefer" and the repetition gave me untold joy, "but I shall not forget you."

"Silly boy! Keep the ring because I wish it. Keep it for a whim of mine, and for the interest it will pay me some day."

She shook a slim finger before my face, and her eyes laughed as she said, "And remember to beware of women whose bodies burn worse than fire!"

She turned to go, forbidding me to follow her. Through the temple door I saw her step into a carved and ornamented chair that was awaiting her in the courtyard. A runner went before and shouted to clear a way, the people standing aside whispering and looking after her. When she had gone, I was seized with a deadly emptiness as if I had dived headfirst into a dark abyss.

Metufer noticed the ring on my finger some days later; he gripped my hand suspiciously and stared at it.

"By all the forty just baboons of Osiris! Nefernefernefer, eh? I would never have believed it." He looked at me with something like respect although the priest had set me to scrub the floors and carry out the most menial tasks because I had not had the wit to give him a present.

Then I conceived such a hatred of Metufer and his words as only a youth can feel. However much I longed to ask him about Nefer I would not stoop to it. I hid my secret in my heart, for a lie is more lovely than the truth and a dream purer than earthly contact. I contemplated the green stone upon my finger, remembering her eyes and her cool bosom, and seemed still to sense her perfumed ointments on my fingers. I held her, and her soft lips still touched mine—in consolation, for by then Ammon had revealed himself to me and my faith was gone.

When I thought of her, I whispered with burning cheeks, "My sister." And the word was a caress in my ears, for from untold ages its meaning has been and will ever be, "My beloved."

35

3

But I shall tell how Ammon revealed himself to me.

On the fourth night it was my turn to watch over the peace of Ammon. There were seven of us boys: Mata, Mose, Bek, Sinufer, Nefru, Ahmose, and I. Mose and Bek were also candidates for the House of Life, and so I knew them but not the others.

I was weak with fasting and suspense. We were in a solemn mood and walked unsmilingly after the priest—may his name perish in oblivion—as he led us to the enclosed part of the temple. Ammon's ship had sailed beyond the hills in the west, the watchmen had blown their silver horns, and the temple gates were shut. But the priest who guided us had eaten a good meal of meat from the sacrifices and fruits and sweet cakes; oil dripped down his face, and his cheeks were rosy with wine. Laughing to himself, he raised the veil and let us look into the holy of holies. In his alcove, which was carved out of one huge block of stone, stood Ammon. The jewels in his headdress and collar sparkled green, red, and blue like living eyes in the light of the sacred lamps. In the morning under the direction of the priest we were to anoint him and clothe him afresh, for each morning he required a new robe. I had seen him before at the Spring Festival when he was carried out to the forecourt in his golden boat and all the people prostrated themselves before him, and when the river was at its height, I had seen him sail upon the sacred lake in his ship of cedarwood. But then as a lowly novice I had but glimpsed him at a distance. His red robe had never made so fierce an impact as now, by lamplight, in the inviolate silence of the sanctuary. Red was worn by gods and Pharaohs alone, and as I gazed at his lifted face, I felt as if the very slabs of stone lay upon my breast to stifle me.

"Watch and pray before the evil," said the priest, clinging to the border of the curtain, for he was unsteady on his legs. "Perchance he will call you. It is his custom to reveal himself to the postulants, addressing them by name and speaking, if they be found worthy."

Hurriedly he made the holy signs, mumbled the divine name of Ammon, and pulled the veil back into place without troubling even to bow and stretch forth his hands at knee level.

He went, leaving us alone in the darkness of the inner antechamber, whose stone floor struck cold to our bare feet. But when he had gone, Mose brought forth a lamp from beneath his shoulder cloth while Ahmose walked coolly into the sanctuary and fetched some of the sacred flame with which to kindle it.

"We should be fools to sit in darkness," said Mose, and we felt safer, though I think we were none of us without fear. Ahmose brought out bread and meat; Mata and Nefru started throwing dice on the flagstones, calling the score so loudly as to wake the echoes in the hall. But when Ahmose had eaten, he rolled himself in his shoulder cloth and, after swearing a little at the hardness of the stones, settled down to sleep; a little later Sinufer and Nefru lay down beside him for warmth.

But I was young and I watched, though I knew that the priest had been given a jar of wine by Metufer, whom he had invited with one or two other distinguished candidates to his room, and therefore would not be coming to take us by surprise. I watched, though I knew from the tales others had told me that it was the custom for would-be initiates to spend their vigil in eating, gaming, and sleeping.

My night was long. While the others slept, I was filled with devotion and aspiration, and I reflected that I had kept myself pure and fasted and obeyed all the old commandments so that Ammon might reveal himself to me. I repeated his holy names and listened to every rustle with senses alert—but the temple was void and cold. With the approach of morning the veil of the sanctuary stirred in the draft, but nothing further happened. As daylight began to creep into the hall, I blew out the lamp with a heavy heart and woke my companions.

Soldiers blew their horns, on the walls the guard was changed, and from the forecourts came a murmur like the rushing of distant waters. We knew that day and its work had begun. At last the priest entered in a great hurry and with him, to my surprise, Metufer. A strong reek of wine came from them; they were walking arm in arm, the priest swinging the keys of the sacred shrines in his hand. Prompted by Metufer, he gabbled off the holy formulas before greeting us.

"Postulants Mata, Mose, Bek, Sinufer, Nefru, Ahmose, and Sinuhe! Have you watched and prayed as you were commanded, that you might be acceptable to the Most High?"

"We have watched and prayed," we answered with one voice.

"Has Ammon revealed himself to you according to his word?"

The priest belched, and his eyes traveled over us unsteadily. We glanced sideways at each other and hesitated. At last Mose faltered, "He has revealed himself." One after the other my companions repeated, "He has revealed himself." Last of all Ahmose firmly and reverently declared, "Most certainly did he reveal himself." He stared the priest straight in the eye, but I said nothing. I felt as if a hand were squeezing my heart, for to me my companion's words were blasphemy.

Metufer said impudently, "I also have watched and prayed to be worthy of initiation, for this next night I have other things to do than to tarry here. And to me also Ammon appeared, as the priest can testify. His form was that of a huge wine jar, and he spoke to me of many sacred matters that it is not fitting I should repeat to you; but his words were as refreshing to me as wine so that I thirsted to hear more and yet more until the dawn."

Then Mose plucked up courage and said, "To me he appeared in the shape of his son Horus, perching upon my shoulder like a hawk and saying, 'Blessed be thou, Mose, and thy family and all thy deeds, that thou may'st come to dwell in a house with two gates and have command over many servants.'"

Now the others also hastened to relate what Ammon had said to them; they talked eagerly, several at a time, while the priest listened and nodded and laughed. I do not know whether they spoke of their dreams or whether they were lying. I only know that I stood apart and said nothing.

At last the priest turned to me, knitted his shaven eyebrows, and said sternly, "And you, Sinuhe! Are you not worthy? Did not Ammon appear to you in any shape at all? Have you not seen him even in the likeness of a little mouse? For he manifests himself under many forms."

My entry into the House of Life was at stake, so I summoned courage and answered, "At dawn I saw the holy veil of the sanctuary stirring a little, but I have seen nothing else, and Ammon did not speak to me."

Then everyone burst out laughing; Metufer laughed and slapped his knees and said to the priest, "He's simple." Then tugging his wine-soaked sleeve, he whispered something to him, his eyes still upon me.

The priest looked at me again sternly and said, "If you have not heard the voice of Ammon you cannot be initiated. Yet, for all that, we may find a remedy, for I believe you to be a steadfast youth, full of honest purpose."

When he had said this, he vanished into the holy of holies, and Metufer came forward to me. When he saw my woeful face, he smiled in a friendly way and said, "Have no fear!"

A moment later we all jumped, for through the darkness of the hall came the braying of a supernatural voice that was unlike the voice of any man. It seemed to come from everywhere at once: from the roof, the walls, and between the pillars—and we looked about us to discover whence it came.

"Sinuhe, Sinuhe, thou sluggard, where art thou? Come swiftly and bow down before me, for I have but little time and cannot tarry all day for thee."

Metufer drew aside the veil of the sanctuary and, pushing me in, gripped the back of my neck and bent me to the floor and into the attitude in which salutation is made to gods and Pharaohs. But I raised my head at once and saw that the holy of holies was full of light.

A voice came from Ammon's mouth, saying,

"Sinuhe, Sinuhe, thou swine and baboon! Wast thou then drunk and sleeping when I called thee? Verily thou should'st be cast into a pool of slime and eat mud all thy days; nevertheless, for thy youth's sake I will have mercy, despite thy foolishness, thy uncleanness, and thy sloth. For I have compassion on those who believe in me, but all others shall be cast into the abyss of the Kingdom of Death."

Many more things were spoken by the voice, with howls, revilings, and curses, but I no longer remember it all nor desire to remember, such was my humiliation and bitterness of spirit. For as I listened, I could detect through the superhuman reverberations the voice of the priest, and this discovery so shocked and horrified me that I could no longer give ear to it. After the voice had ceased, I remained lying before the statue of Ammon until the priest came in and kicked me aside. My companions made haste to bear incense, ointments, cosmetics, and red cloths.

Each of us had a task allotted to him, and remembering mine, I went out to the forecourt to fetch a vessel of holy water and the consecrated towels for washing the god's face, hands, and feet. On my return I saw the priest spit in Ammon's face and rub it with his dirty sleeve. Then Mose and Nefru painted his lips and cheeks and eyebrows. Metufer anointed him and laughingly rubbed holy oil into the priest's face and his own. Lastly the statue was undressed to be washed and wiped as if it had befouled itself, and then a red pleated skirt and an apron were fastened round it, a cloth hung across its shoulders, and its arms thrust into sleeves.

When all this had been done, the priest collected the cast-off garments and took charge of the washing water and the towels. All this was to be divided up and sold in the forecourt to wealthy travelers, the water being dispensed as a remedy for skin diseases. Then we were free to go out into the sunshine of the court, where I vomited.

39

My brain and heart were as empty as my belly, for I no longer believed in the gods. But when the week had passed, my head was anointed with oil, and having sworn the priestly oath, I was given a certificate. On this document was the great seal of the temple of Ammon and my name, and it entitled me to enter the House of Life.

So we entered it, Mose, Bek, and I. Its gate was opened to us, and my name was inscribed in the Book of Life as my father Senmut's name had been inscribed before me and his father's name before him. But I was happy no longer.

4

In the House of Life, which was part of the great temple of Ammon, the teaching was supervised nominally by the royal physicians, each in his own branch. We saw them but seldom, however, for their practices were large, they received costly presents from the wealthy, and they lived in spacious houses outside the city. But, when any patient came to the House of Life whose sickness puzzled the ordinary doctors, or if these would not venture to undertake the cure, a royal physician would come to treat him and to demonstrate his proficiency before those who were specializing in his branch. Thus even the poorest sufferer might have the benefit of a royal physician's care, to the glory of Ammon.

The training period was a long one even for those with talent. We had to take a course on drugs and potions, learn the names and properties of herbs and the seasons and hours at which they must be gathered, and also dry them and make extracts from them; for a physician must be able to prepare his own remedies at need. Many of us grumbled at this, not seeing the use of it, since by merely writing a prescription one could obtain from the House of Life all the known remedies correctly mixed and measured. Later, however, this knowledge was to stand me in good stead, as I shall show.

We had to learn the names of the different parts of the body, also the functions and purpose of every human organ. We learned to handle scalpel and forceps, but above all we had to accustom our hands to recognize disease both through the natural orifices of the body and through the skin; from the eyes also we had to detect the nature of a disorder. We must be able to deliver a woman in childbirth when the midwife's help was of no avail. We must stimulate and alleviate pain as occasion required and learn to distinguish between trifling complaints and severe ones, between ailments of mental and physical

40

origin. We had to know truth from falsehood in the patients' talk and what questions to ask in order to gain a clear picture of the complaint.

The long period of probation was followed by the day when—after ceremonial purification—I was clothed in a white gown and started work in the reception hall, where I learned to draw teeth from the jaws of strong men, to bandage wounds, lance boils, and set broken limbs. None of this was new to me; thanks to my father's teaching I made good progress and was promoted to the charge and instruction of my companions. Sometimes I received gifts such as are given to doctors, and I had my name engraved on the green stone that Nefer-nefernefer had given me so that I could set my seal below my prescriptions.

I was put to ever more exacting tasks. I went on duty in the rooms where the incurably sick lay and attended renowned physicians at their treatments and at the operations, in which for every one that was cured ten died. I learned that death holds no terrors for a doctor and for the sick comes often as a merciful friend so that their faces after release are apt to be more serene than at any time during their life of drudgery.

Yet I was blind and deaf until the day of awakening came as it had come in my childhood, when pictures, words, and letters sprang to life. Once more my eyes were opened, and I woke as from a dream; my spirit welled up in its joy because I asked myself "why?" The dread key to all true knowledge is "why?" It is mightier than the reed of Thoth, more potent than inscriptions in stone.

It happened thus: A wife came to me who had had no children and who believed herself to be barren, for she was already forty years of age. But her monthly flow had ceased, and she was uneasy; she came to the House of Life because she feared that an evil spirit had taken possession of her and poisoned her body. As was prescribed in such cases, I planted grains of corn in some earth, watering half of them with Nile water and the rest with the woman's urine. I then exposed the soil to the warmth of the sun and bade the woman return in two days. When she came again, the seeds had sprouted, those which had been watered with Nile water being small and the other shoots green and strong.

What had been written of old was true, and I said to the astonished woman, "Rejoice, for holy Ammon in his grace has blessed your womb, and you shall bring forth a child like other favored women."

The poor soul wept for joy and gave me a silver bangle from her wrist weighing two deben,* for she had long ago given up hope. And as soon as she could believe me, she asked, "Is it a son?" thinking me omniscient. I plucked up courage, looked her in the eye, and said, "It is a son." For the chances were even and at that time my gambling luck was good. The woman rejoiced still more and gave me a bracelet from her other wrist, of two deben weight.

But when she had gone, I asked myself how it was possible for a grain of corn to know what no doctor could discover and know it before the eye could detect the signs of pregnancy? Summoning up my resolution, I asked my teacher. He merely looked at me as if I were half-witted and said, "It is so written." But this was no answer.

I took courage again and asked the royal obstetrician in the maternity house. He said, "Ammon is chief of all the gods. His eye sees the womb that receives the seed; if he permits germination, why should he not also allow corn to grow when moistened with water from the pregnant woman's body?"

He, too, stared at me as if I were half-witted, but his was no answer.

Then my eyes were opened, and I saw that the doctors in the House of Life knew the writings and the traditions but no more. If I asked why a festering wound must be burned while an ordinary one is merely dressed and bandaged and why boils are healed with mildew and cobwebs, they said only, "So it has always been." In the same way a surgeon might perform the hundred and eighty-two operations and incisions prescribed, and perform them according to his experience and skill, well or badly, quickly or slowly, more or less painfully; but more he cannot do because only these are described and illustrated in the books, and nothing else has ever been done.

There were some cases in which the sufferer grew thin and pale, though the doctor could find in him no disease or injury; he could be revived and cured by a diet of raw liver from the sacrificial beasts, bought at a high price, but one must on no account ask why. There were some who had pains in their bellies and whose hands and feet burned. They were given purges and narcotics; some recovered, others perished, but no doctor could say beforehand who would live and whose belly would swell so that he died. No one knew why this was; no one might seek to know.

I soon noticed that I was asking too many questions, for people began to look at me askance, and those who had come after me were set in authority over me. Then I took off my white robe, cleaned myself,

* A deben weighs approximately 3¼ ounces.

42

and left the House of Life, taking with me two silver rings that together weighed four deben.

5

When I left the temple—a thing I had not done for years—I saw that while I had been working and studying Thebes had changed. I noted it as I walked along the Avenue of Rams and through the markets. There was restlessness everywhere; people's dress had become more elaborate and costly so that one could no longer distinguish men from women by their wigs and pleated skirts. From wine shops and pleasure houses came shrill Syrian music; foreign speech was heard in the streets, where Syrians and wealthy Negroes rubbed shoulders with Egyptians unabashed. The wealth and power of Egypt were immeasurable; for centuries past no enemy had entered its cities, and men who had never known war had reached middle age. But I cannot tell whether the people were any happier on this account, for their eyes were restless, their movements hurried, and they seemed always to be waiting impatiently for some new thing and could not be content with the day that was passing.

I walked alone along the streets of Thebes with a heavy and rebellious heart. On coming home, I found that my father Senmut had aged; his back was bent, and he could no longer distinguish written characters. My mother Kipa was old also; she panted as she moved and talked of nothing but her grave. For with his savings my father had bought a tomb in the City of the Dead on the west bank of the river. I had seen it: it was a handsome tomb built of mud bricks with the usual inscriptions and pictures on the walls, and all about it were hundreds and thousands of similar graves that the priests of Ammon sold to honest, thrifty folk at a high price—a price they paid to obtain immortality. I had written out a death book to be laid in their tomb so that they should not go astray on the long journey: a fine, fairly written book, though not adorned with colored pictures like those sold in the book court of Ammon's temple.

My mother gave me food, and my father asked about my studies, but beyond this we found nothing to say to each other; the house was strange to me, as were the street and the people in the street. My heart grew heavier still until I remembered the temple of Ptah and Thothmes who had been my friend and was to become an artist. I thought: I have four deben of silver in my pocket. I will seek out my friend

Thothmes, that we may rejoice together and make merry with wine, for I shall find no answer to my questions.

So I took leave of my parents, saying that I must return to the House of Life, and shortly before sunset I found the temple of Ptah. Having learned from the porter where the art school lay, I entered and inquired for the student Thothmes; only then did I hear that he had been expelled long ago. The students spat upon the ground before me when they spoke his name, because the teacher was present; when he turned his back, they counseled me to go to a tavern called the Syrian Jar.

I found this place; it lay between the poor quarter and the rich and had an inscription over the door praising the wine from Ammon's vineyard and also that from the harbor. Inside there were artists squatting on the floor drawing pictures while an old man sat in sad contemplation of the empty wine bowl before him.

"Sinuhe, by all the potters' wheels!" cried someone, rising to greet me with his hands lifted in wonder. I recognized Thothmes, though his shoulder cloth was dirty and tattered and his eyes were bloodshot and there was a big bump on his forehead. He had grown older and thinner, and there were lines at the corners of his mouth, but his eyes still held that cheerful, impudent, irresistible glint, and he bent forward till our cheeks touched. I knew then that we were still friends.

"My heart is heavy," I said to him. "All is vanity, and I have sought you out so that we may rejoice our hearts with wine—for no one answers when I ask why."

Thothmes lifted his apron to show that he lacked the means to buy wine.

"I carry four deben of silver on my wrists," said I with pride. Thothmes then pointed at my head, which was still shaven because I wanted men to know that I was a priest of the first grade: it was all I had to be proud of. But now I was vexed that I had not let my hair grow and said impatiently, "I am a physician, not a priest. I think I read over the door that wine from the harbor can be had here; let us see if it is good."

Thothmes ordered mixed wine, and a slave came to pour water over our hands and set roasted lotus seeds on a low table before us. The landlord himself brought the brightly colored goblets. Thothmes raised his, spilled a drop on the ground, and said, "For the divine Potter! May the plague consume the art school and its teachers!" And he recited the names of those he hated most.

I also raised my goblet and let a drop fall on the ground.

44

"In the name of Ammon! May his boat leak to all eternity, may the bellies of his priests rupture, and may the pestilence destroy the ignorant teachers in the House of Life!" But I said this in a low voice and looked about me lest a stranger should overhear my words.

"Have no fear," said Thothmes. "So many of Ammon's ears have been boxed in this tavern that they have had enough of listening—and all of us here are lost already. I could not find even bread and beer if I had not hit upon the idea of making picture books for rich men's children."

He showed me the scroll he had been working on when I came. I could not help laughing, for there he had drawn a fortress defended by a quaking, terrified cat against the onslaught of mice, also a hippopotamus singing in a treetop while a dove climbed painfully up the tree by means of a ladder.

There was a smile in Thothmes' brown eyes, but it faded as he unrolled the papyrus further and disclosed the picture of a bald little priest leading a big Pharaoh on a rope to the temple, like a beast of sacrifice. Next he showed me a little Pharaoh bowing before a massive statue of Ammon. He nodded at my questioning look.

"You see? Grown people laugh at the pictures, too, because they're so crazy. It is ridiculous for a mouse to attack a cat or a priest to lead a Pharaoh—but those who know begin to reflect upon a number of things. Therefore, I shall not lack for bread and beer—until the priests have me clubbed to death in the street. Such things have happened."

"Let us drink," I said, and drink we did, but my heart was not gladdened. Presently I put my question to him. "Is it wrong to ask why?"

"Of course it is wrong, for a man who presumes to ask 'why' has no home nor resting place in the land of Kem. All must be as it has been—and you know it. I trembled with joy when I entered the art school—I was like a thirsty man who has found a spring, a hungry man clutching at bread. And I learned many fine things. . . . Oh, yes. I learned how to hold a pen and handle a chisel, how to model in wax what will be hewn from stone, how stone is polished, how colored stones are fitted together, and how to paint on alabaster. But when I longed to get to work and make such things as I had dreamed of, I was set to treading clay for others to handle. For high above everything stands the convention. Art has its convention no less than writing, and he who breaks with it is damned.

"From the beginning of time it has been laid down how one should represent a standing figure and how a sitting one, how a horse lifts his hooves, how an ox draws a sled. From the beginning the technique has been fixed; whoever departs from it is unfit for the temple, and stone and chisel are denied him. O Sinuhe, my friend, I, too, have asked why—and only too often. That is why I sit here with bumps on my head."

We drank and grew merry, and my heart lightened as if a boil in it had been lanced, for I was no longer alone.

"Sinuhe, my friend, we have been born into strange times. Everything is melting—changing its shape—like clay on a potter's wheel. Dress is changing, words, customs are changing, and people no longer believe in the gods—though they may fear them. Sinuhe, my friend, perhaps we were born to see the sunset of the world, for the world is already old, and twelve hundred years have passed since the building of the pyramids. When I think of this, I want to bury my head in my hands and cry like a child."

But he did not weep, for we were drinking mixed wine in brightly colored goblets, and each time the landlord of the Syrian Jar refilled them he bowed and stretched forth his hands at knee level. From time to time a slave came to pour water over our hands. My heart grew light as a swallow on the threshold of winter; I could have declaimed verse and taken the whole world into my arms.

"Let us go to a pleasure house," said Thothmes laughing. "Let us hear music and watch girls dancing and gladden our hearts—let us not ask 'why' any more or demand that our cup be full."

We walked along the streets. The sun had set, and I met for the first time that Thebes where it is never night. In this flaring, noisy quarter torches flamed before the pleasure houses, and lamps burned on columns at the street corners. Slaves ran here and there with carrying chairs, and the shouts of runners mingled with the music from the houses and the roarings of the drunk.

Never in my life had I set foot in a pleasure house, and I was a little scared. The one to which Thothmes led me was called the Cat and Grapes. It was a pretty little house, full of soft, golden lamplight. There were soft mats to sit on, and young—and in my eyes lovely— girls beat time to the music of flutes and strings. When the music stopped, they sat with us and begged me to buy them wine, as their throats were as dry as chaff. Then two naked dancers performed a complicated dance requiring great skill, and I followed it with interest. As a doctor I was accustomed to the sight of naked girls and yet had never seen breasts swaying or little bellies and bottoms moving so seductively as these.

46

But the music saddened me again, and I began to long for I knew not what. A beautiful girl took my hand and pressed her side to mine and said my eyes were those of a wise man. But her eyes were not as green as the Nile in the heat of summer, and her dress, though it left her bosom bare, was not of royal linen. So I drank wine and neither looked into her eyes nor felt any wish to call her "my sister," or take pleasure with her. And the last I remember of that place is a vicious kick from a Negro and a lump I got on my head when I fell down the steps. So it came about just as my mother Kipa had foretold: I lay in the street without a copper piece in my pocket until Thothmes drew my arm over his strong shoulder and led me to the jetty, where I could drink my fill of Nile water and bathe my face and my hands and my feet.

That morning I entered the House of Life with swollen eyes and a smarting lump on my head, a dirty shoulder cloth, and without the smallest wish to ask, "Why?" I was to be on duty among the deaf and those with ear diseases, so I washed myself quickly and put on the white robe. On the way I met my chief, who began to upbraid me in phrases I had read in the books and knew by heart.

"What is to become of you if you run along the walls by night and drink without keeping tally of your cups? What is to become of you if you idle away your time in pleasure houses, smiting wine jars with your stick to the alarm of honest citizens? What is to become of you if you shed blood and run from the watchmen?"

But when he had done his duty, he smiled to himself with relief, took me to his room, and gave me a potion to cleanse my stomach. My spirits rose as I realized that wine and pleasure houses were winked at in the House of Life provided one stopped asking why.

6

So, I, too, was smitten with Thebes fever and began to love the night more than the day, the flickering of torches more than sunlight, Syrian music more than the moans of the sick, and the whispering of pretty girls more than crabbed old writings on yellow papers. But no one had anything to say against this as I fulfilled my tasks in the House of Life, satisfied my examiners, and kept a steady hand. It was all part of the initiate's life; few students could afford to set up house on their own and marry during their training, and my teacher gave me to understand that I would do well to sow my wild oats, give rein to my body, and be of a merry heart. But I meddled with no woman though I thought I knew that their bodies did not really burn worse than fire.

The times were full of unrest, and great Pharaoh was ill. I saw his shriveled old man's face when he was carried to the temple at the autumn festival adorned with gold and precious stones, motionless as a statue with his head bowed beneath the weight of the double crown. The physicians could not longer help him; rumor had it that his days were numbered and that his heir would soon succeed him—and the heir was but a stripling like myself.

There were services and sacrifices in the temple of Ammon, and Ammon could not help his divine son though Pharaoh Amenhotep III had built for him the mightiest temple of all time. It was said that the King had grown wroth with the Egyptian gods and that he had sent swift messengers to his father-in-law, the king of Mitanni in Nahara, desiring that the miracle-working Ishtar of Niniveh be sent to heal him. But to the joy of the priests even foreign gods could not cure Pharaoh. When the river began to rise, the royal skull surgeon was summoned to the palace.

In all the time I had been in the House of Life I had not once seen Ptahor, for trepanning was rare and during my training period I had not been allowed to attend the specialists at their treatments and operations. Now the old man was carried in haste from his villa to the House of Life, and I was careful to be at hand when he entered the purifying room. He was as bald as ever, his face had grown wrinkled, and his cheeks hung lugubriously on either side of his discontented old mouth. He recognized me, smiled and said, "Ah, is it you, Sinuhe? Have you come so far, son of Senmut?"

He handed me a black wooden box in which he kept his instruments and bade me follow him. This was an unmerited honor that even a royal physician might have envied me, and I bore myself accordingly.

"I must test the steadiness of my hand," said Ptahor, "and open a skull or two here, to see how it goes."

His eyes were watery, and his hand trembled slightly. We went into a room in which lay incurables, paralytics, and those with head injuries. Ptahor examined a few and chose an old man for whom death would come as a release, also a strong slave who had lost his speech and the use of his limbs from a blow on the head in a street brawl. They were given narcotics to drink and were then taken to the operating theater and cleansed. Ptahor washed his own instruments and purified them in fire.

48

My task was to shave the heads of both patients with the keenest of razors. Then the heads were cleaned and washed once more, the scalps massaged with a numbing salve, and Ptahor was ready for his work. First he made an incision in the scalp of the old man and pushed the edges back regardless of the copious flow of blood. Then with swift movements he bored a hole in the bared skull with a large tubular bore and lifted out the circle of bone. The old man began to groan, and his face turned blue.

"I see nothing the matter with his head," said Ptahor. He replaced the bit of bone, stitched the edges of the scalp together, and bandaged the head; whereupon the old man gave up the ghost.

"My hands appear to tremble somewhat," remarked Ptahor. "Perhaps one of the young men would bring me a cup of wine."

The onlookers, besides the teachers in the House of Life, consisted of all the students who were to become head surgeons. When Ptahor had had his wine, he turned his attention to the slave, who had been bound and drugged, yet still sat savagely glowering at us. Ptahor asked that he might be bound yet more firmly and that his head might be gripped in a vice that not even a giant could have shifted. He then opened up the scalp and this time was careful to stanch the flow of blood. The veins at the edges of the incision were cauterized and the blood stopped by special medicaments. Ptahor let other doctors do this, to spare his own hands. In the House of Life there was as a rule a "blood stancher," a man of no education whose mere presence would stop a flow of blood in a short time, but Ptahor wished this to be a demonstration and desired also to save his strength for Pharaoh.

When Ptahor had cleansed the outside of the skull, he pointed out to us the place where the bone had been crushed in. By means of bore, saw, and forceps he removed a piece of skull as large as the palm of one's hand and then showed us how clotted blood had gathered among the white convolutions of the brain. With infinite care he removed the blood bit by bit and freed a bone splinter that had been forced into the brain substance. This operation took some time, so each pupil could follow his movements and impress the look of a brain upon his own memory. Next Ptahor closed the opening with a plate of silver that had been prepared meanwhile to correspond in shape to the piece of bone that had been removed and fixed it firmly in position with tiny clips. Then he stitched the edges of the wound together, bandaged it, and said, "Wake him." For the patient had long ago lost consciousness.

The slave was freed from his bonds, wine was poured down his throat, and he was given strong drugs to inhale. Presently he sat up

49

and let forth a stream of curses. It was a miracle no one who had not witnessed it could have believed, for the fellow had previously been dumb and unable to move his limbs. This time I had no need to ask why, for Ptahor explained that the bone splinter and the blood on the surface of the brain had been the cause of the symptoms.

"If he is not dead within three days, he is cured," said Ptahor. "In two weeks he will be able to thrash the man who stoned him. I do not think he will die."

With friendly courtesy he thanked all who had helped him, naming me among them, though I had but handed him his instruments as they were needed. I had not understood his purpose in this, but in giving me his ebony box to carry he had singled me out to be his assistant in Pharaoh's palace. I had now served him at two operations and was therefore experienced and more useful to him than even the royal physicians where the opening of a skull was concerned. I did not understand this and was amazed when he said, "We're now ripe to deal with the royal skull. Are you ready, Sinuhe?"

Wrapped in my simple doctor's mantle, I stepped up beside him in the carrying chair. The blood stancher sat on one of the poles, and Pharaoh's slaves ran with us to the landing stage, at so smooth a pace that the chair never swayed. Pharaoh's ship awaited us, manned by picked slaves who rowed swiftly: we seemed rather to fly over the water than float upon it. From Pharaoh's landing stage we were borne rapidly to the golden house. I did not wonder at our haste, for soldiers were already marching along the streets of Thebes, gates were being closed, and merchants were carrying their goods into the warehouses and closing doors and shutters. It was clear from this that Pharaoh was soon to die.

BOOK 3

Thebes Fever

I

A GREAT concourse of people from every walk of life had gathered by the walls of the golden house, and even the forbidden foreshore was thronged with boats—the wooden rowing boats of the rich and the pitched-reed boats of the poor. At the sight of us a whisper ran through the crowd like the rushing of distant waters, and the news that the royal skull surgeon was on his way sped from mouth to mouth. Then the people held up their hands in grief, while cries and lamentations followed us up to the palace; for everyone knew that no Pharaoh had ever lived until the third sunrise after his skull had been opened.

Through the gate of lilies we were taken to the royal apartments; court chamberlains were our servants and prostrated themselves before us, for we carried death in our hands. A temporary cleansing room had been prepared, but after exchanging a few words with Pharaoh's own physician, Ptahor raised his hands in sorrow and performed the cleansing ceremonial in but a perfunctory manner. The sacred fire was borne after us, and having passed through a series of splendid rooms, we entered the royal bedchamber.

Great Pharaoh lay beneath a golden canopy; the bedposts were protecting gods, and the bedstead was supported by lions. His swollen body was naked, stripped of all the symbols of sovereignty. He was unconscious, his aged head hung sideways, and he breathed stertoriously, saliva running from the corner of his mouth. So shadowy and ephemeral is mortal glory that he could not have been distinguished from any of the old men who lay dying in the reception hall of the House of Life. But on the walls of the room he was depicted as speeding in a chariot drawn by swift, plumed horses; his powerful arm drew back the bowstring, and lions, pierced by his arrows, fell dead about his feet.

We prostrated ourselves before him, knowing—as all who had seen death must know—that Ptahor's arts were useless here. But since throughout the ages the skull of Pharaoh has been opened as a last resort, if natural death has not already supervened, it must be opened now, and we set about our task. I lifted the lid of the ebony box and in the flame purified once more the scalpels, bores, and forceps. The court physician had already shaved and washed the head of the dying man, and Ptahor ordered the stancher of blood to sit upon the bed and take Pharaoh's head in his hands.

Then the royal consort Taia stepped to the bed and forbade him. Hitherto she had stood by the wall with her arms raised in the gesture of grief, motionless as an image. Behind her stood the young heir to the throne, Amenhotep, and his sister Baketamon, but I had not yet dared to raise my eyes to them. Now that a stir ran through the room I looked, and recognized them from the statues in the temples. The prince was of my own age but taller. Princess Baketamon had noble and very lovely features and large, oval eyes. But more majestic than either was the royal consort Taia, though she was short and plump. Her complexion was very dark and her cheekbones broad and prominent. It was said that by birth she was a woman of the people and had Negro blood in her veins; I do not know if this is so, for it is but hearsay. Even if it be true that her parents bore no honorable titles in the records, yet her eyes were intelligent, bold, and piercing, and her whole bearing radiated power. When she moved her hand and looked upon the stancher of blood, he seemed dust beneath her broad, brown feet. I understood her feelings, for the fellow was an ox driver of low birth and could neither read nor write. He stood with bent head and hanging arms, with his mouth open and a vacant expression on his face. Unskilled, untalented though he was, he yet had the power to stop the flow of blood by his mere presence. Therefore he had been called from his plow and his oxen to be paid his fee in the temple, and despite all cleansing ceremonial the smell of cattle dung clung about him. He himself could not account for his powers. He possessed them, as a jewel may be found in a clod of earth, and they were such as cannot be acquired through study or spiritual exercises.

"I do not permit him to touch the god," said the Queen. "I will hold the god's head if it be needful."

Ptahor protested that the task was an unpleasant and bloody one; nevertheless, she took her place on the edge of the bed and most carefully raised the head of her dying husband into her lap, heedless of the saliva that dripped onto her hands.

"He is mine," she said, "and no one else shall touch him. It is from my arms that he shall enter the realms of death."

"He shall step aboard the ship of his father the sun," said Ptahor, incising the scalp with his flint knife. "Of the sun was he born, to the

54

sun shall he return, and all people shall praise his name from ever-lasting to everlasting— In the name of Set and all devils, what is the blood stancher about?"

He had been talking to distract the Queen's thoughts from the oper-ation, as a skillful doctor will talk to a patient to whom he is causing pain, but the last phrase was hissed at the peasant, who was leaning against the door post with sleepy, half-shut eyes. Sluggish blood had begun to well from Pharaoh's head and run down into his consort's lap so that she flinched and her face turned a yellowish gray. The man roused himself from his thoughts—thoughts no doubt of his oxen and his irrigation ditches—remembered his duty, and approaching the bed, he looked at Pharaoh and raised his hands. The flow of blood ceased at once, and I washed and cleaned the head.

"Forgive me, my little lady," said Ptahor, taking the bore from my hand. "To the sun—ay, indeed, straight to his father in the golden ship, the blessing of Ammon be upon him."

While he was speaking, he spun the bore swiftly and deftly between his hands so that it grated its way into the bone. The prince opened his eyes, took a step forward, and his face quivered as he said, "Not Ammon but Ra-Herachte shall bless him, and he manifests himself in Aton."

"Ay, indeed, Aton," murmured Ptahor soothingly. "Aton, of course —a slip of the tongue." He took his flint knife again and the ebony-handled hammer, and with light taps began to remove the piece of bone. "For I remember that in his divine wisdom he raised up a temple to Aton. That was surely soon after the prince's birth, was it not, fair Taia? One moment."

He glanced uneasily at the prince, who was standing by the bed with clenched fists and twitching face.

"A mouthful of wine would steady my hand and do the prince no harm. At such a time as this one might well break the seal of a royal jar. There!"

I handed him the forceps, and he jerked out the piece of bone with a grating noise.

"A little light, Sinuhe!"

Ptahor heaved a sigh, for the worst was over, and so did I. The same feeling of relief seemed to be communicated to the unconscious Pharaoh, for his limbs stirred, his breathing grew slower, and he sank into a yet deeper coma. Ptahor contemplated Pharaoh's brain thought-fully in the bright light, where it lay exposed: it was grayish blue, and it quivered.

55

"Hm," he said musingly. "What is done is done. May his Aton do the rest for him, for this is a matter for gods, not men."

Lightly and carefully he fitted the piece of bone back into place, smearing size into the crack, drew together the edges of the wound, and bandaged it. The royal consort laid his head over a neck rest of rare wood and looked at Ptahor. Blood had dried upon her, but she did not heed it. Ptahor met her fearless gaze without making obeisance, and said in a low voice, "He will live until dawn, his god permitting."

Then he raised his hands in a gesture of sorrow, and so did I. But when he raised them to show sympathy, I dared not follow his example, for who was I to pity royalty? I purified the instruments in fire and put them back in the ebony box.

"Your reward shall be great," said the Queen, and she signed to us that we might go. A meal had been prepared for us in another room, and Ptahor looked with delight at the many wine jars that stood along the wall. Having closely examined the seal of one of these, he caused it to be opened, and a slave poured water over our hands.

When were were alone again, Ptahor explained to me that Ra-Herachte was the god of the Amenhoteps and that Aton was his manifestation: a god of great antiquity, older indeed than Ammon.

"It is said that the present heir to the throne is the divine son of this Aton," went on Ptahor. He took a draught of wine. "It was in the temple of Ra-Herachte that the royal consort saw her vision, after which she bore a son. She took with her a very ambitious priest whom she favored; his name was Eie, and he saw to it that his wife was engaged as wet nurse to the heir. His daughter Nefertiti drank milk from the same breasts as the prince and played with him in the palace like a sister, so you may fancy what will come of that."

Ptahor drank again, sighed, and went on. "Ah, for an old man there is nothing more delightful than drinking wine and gossiping about what does not concern him. If you but knew, Sinuhe, how many secrets lie buried behind this old forehead. Perhaps there are kingly secrets among them. Many wonder why it is that no son has ever been born alive in the women's wing of the palace, for that is against all medical law—and the man lying there with the opened skull was no milksop, either, in the days of his joy and strength. He found his consort on a hunting trip; they say Taia was the daughter of some fowler and dwelt among the reeds of the Nile, but that the king made her his equal because of her wisdom and venerated her parents, too, and filled their tomb with the costliest of gifts. Taia had nothing against his pleasures so long as the women of the harem bore no man children. In this she had wonderfully good fortune, such as one could hardly believe possible if it had not happened."

Ptahor looked sideways at me and glancing round said quickly, "But, Sinuhe, never believe any stories you may hear; they are only put about by ill-natured people—and everyone knows how gentle the queen is and how wise and what a gift she has for gathering useful men about her. Yes, yes . . ."

I led Ptahor out into the fresh air; night had fallen, and in the east the lights of Thebes outshone the red glow in the sky. I was flushed with wine and felt again the city's fever in my blood. Stars twinkled above my head, and the garden was filled with the scent of flowers.

"Ptahor," I said, "when the lights of Thebes shine to the night sky, then—then I thirst after love!"

"There is no love," said Ptahor emphatically. "A man is sad when he has no woman to lie with, and when he has lain with one, he is still sadder. So it has ever been and ever will be."

"Why?"

"Not even the gods know that. And never talk to me of love unless you want me to open your skull for you. I will do that for nothing and without requiring the smallest present from you and so save you much sorrow."

It now seemed best for me to take upon myself the duties of a slave; I lifted him in my arms and carried him to the room that had been put at our disposal. He was so little and old that I was not even breathless. When I had lain him down upon the bed, he fell asleep at once, after some little groping for a wine cup. I covered him with soft skins, as the night was cold, and went out again to the terrace of flowers—for I was young, and youth desires no sleep on the night of a king's death.

The murmuring voices of those who were passing the night by the palace walls reached the terrace like the distant sough of wind through rushes.

I awoke amid the scent of flowers as the lights of Thebes glowed a garish red against the eastern sky; I remembered a pair of eyes green as Nile waters in the heat of summer—and found I was no longer alone.

The light from the stars and from the thin sickle of the moon was so faint that I could not see whether a man or a woman was approaching, but someone drew near and peered into my face. I stirred, and the

57

newcomer, in a voice of authority that was yet shrill—almost childish —demanded, "Is it the Lonely One?"

I recognized the prince's voice and his lanky figure and prostrated myself before him not daring to speak. But he nudged me impatiently with his foot.

"Stand up, you fool. No one can see us, so you need not bow to me. Keep that for the god whose son I am—for there is but one, and all others are his manifestations. Did you know that?" Without waiting for an answer he added reflectively, "All others but Ammon, who is a false god."

I made a gesture of protest and said, "Oh!" to show I feared such talk.

"Let be!" he said. "I saw you standing by my father, handing knife and hammer to that crazy old Ptahor. So I called you the Lonely One. To Ptahor my mother gave the name of Old Monkey. You must bear these names if you have to die before leaving the palace. But *I* thought of yours."

I thought he must be mad to talk thus wildly, though Ptahor had said that we must die if Pharaoh did, and the stancher of blood believed it. My hair prickled on my scalp, for I did not wish to die.

The prince was panting; his hands twitched, and he mumbled to himself: "Restless . . . I would be—I would be in some other place. It is my god revealing himself. I know it—I fear it. Stay with me, Lonely One. He crushes my body with his strength, and my tongue is afflicted. . . ."

I trembled, thinking him delirious. But he said to me in a commanding voice, "Come!" and I followed him. He led me down from the terrace and past Pharaoh's lake, while from behind the walls came the murmuring voices of the mourners. I was in great dread, for Ptahor had stated that we might not leave the palace before the death of the king, but I could not gainsay the prince.

He held his body tense and walked with such rapid, jerky steps that I had hard work to keep up with him. He was wearing only a loin-cloth, and the moon shone on his fair skin, his slender legs, and feminine thighs. It shone on his prominent ears and the tormented, agitated face that seemed to tell of some vision he alone could see.

When we reached the shore, he said, "We will take a boat. I am going eastward to meet my father."

Without hesitating to choose his craft, he stepped into the nearest; I followed him, and we began to row across. No one sought to hinder us, though we had stolen the boat. The night was uneasily astir; other craft were out on the river, and the red glow of Thebes showed ever brighter in the sky ahead. When we reached the farther shore, he set the boat adrift and started to walk forward as if he had been this way many times before. Others were abroad also, and we went unchallenged by the watch. Thebes knew that the king would die that night.

The pace was wearing him out. Yet I wondered at the toughness of that young body, for though the night was cold, the sweat ran down my back as I followed him. The stars moved across the heavens, and the moon went down, and still he walked until we came up out of the valley into the desert, leaving Thebes behind us. The three hills in the east—the city's guardians—loomed before us black against the sky.

At last he sank down panting in the sand and said in a frightened voice, "Hold my hands, Sinuhe, for they tremble, and my heart thuds against my ribs. The hour draws near—it draws near for the world is desolate—you and I are alone. Where I go, you cannot follow—and I do not want to be alone."

I gripped his wrists and felt that his whole twitching frame was bathed in cold sweat. The world about us was indeed desolate; far off some jackal howled for a death; slowly the stars paled and space about us turned a wan gray. Suddenly he shook off my hands and rising lifted his face to the east, to the mountains.

"The god is coming!" he said softly, with awe in his distracted, blazing face. "The god is coming." Then again in a loud voice he shouted into the desert, "The god is coming!"

The air grew brighter, the hills before us flamed gold, and the sun rose—and with a shrill cry he sank swooning to the ground, his mouth moving, his limbs twitching convulsively and churning up the sand. But I was no longer afraid, for I had heard such cries in the forecourt of the House of Life and knew what to do. Lacking a peg to wedge between his teeth, I tore a strip from my loincloth, rolled it up, and stuffed it into his mouth. Then I began to massage his limbs. He would be sick and dazed when he awoke. I looked about me for help, but Thebes lay behind us, and not the meanest hovel was in sight.

At that instant a falcon flew past me with a screech, swooping out of the rays of the rising sun into an arc above us, then sank again, and made as if to alight upon the prince's forehead. Startled, I instinctively made the holy sign of Ammon; had the prince had Horus in his mind when he greeted his god, and was Horus here manifest? The boy moaned, and I bent to tend him. When I raised my head again, it seemed that the bird had taken human shape. Before me stood a young man, godlike, beautiful in the sun's rays. He carried a spear and wore the coarse shoulder cloth of a poor man. Though I did not believe in the gods, for safety's sake I prostrated myself before him.

"What's this?" he asked in the dialect of the Lower Kingdom. "Is the lad sick?"

Feeling very foolish, I rose to my knees and greeted him in the ordinary way.

"If you are a robber," I said, "you'll get little from us, but I have here a sick boy, and the gods may bless you for your help."

He screeched like a hawk, and the bird fell from the air to alight upon his shoulder.

"I am Horemheb, son of the falcon," he said proudly. "My parents are but cheese makers, but it was foretold at my birth that I should win command over many. The falcon flew before me, and I followed, having found no shelter for the night in the city. Thebes is shy of spears after dark. But I mean to enter Pharaoh's service as a warrior. They say he is sick, therefore he may need strong arms to protect his sovereignty."

The prince moaned, passed his hands gropingly over his face, and contorted his limbs. I removed the rag from his mouth, wishing I had water with which to revive him. Horemheb surveyed him and asked coolly, "Is he dying?"

"He is not," I replied impatiently. "He has the holy sickness."

Horemheb gripped his spear as he looked at me.

"You need not despise me though I come barefoot and am poor. I can write passably and read what is written, and I shall have command over many. Which god has taken possession of him?"

The people believe that a god speaks through those suffering from the holy sickness, hence his question.

"He has his own god," I answered, "and I think he is a little queer in the head."

"He is cold." Horemheb drew off his cloak and spread it over the prince. "Morning in Thebes is chilly, but my own blood suffices to keep me warm. My god is Horus. This is surely a rich man's son, for his skin is white and delicate, and he has never worked with his hands. And who are you?"

"A physician and initiate of the first grade of priesthood in Ammon's temple in Thebes."

The heir to the throne sat up, moaned, and looked dazedly about him. His teeth chattered as he spoke.

"I have seen! The instant was as a cycle of time—I was ageless—he

60

stretched forth a thousand hands above my head in benediction, and in every hand the symbol of eternal life. Must I not then believe?"

At the sight of Horemheb his eyes cleared, and he was beautiful in his radiant wonder.

"Is it you whom Aton, the one god, has sent?"

"The falcon flew before me, and I followed; that is why I am here. I know no more than that."

The prince looked with a frown at the other's weapon.

"You carry a spear," he said in rebuke.

Horemheb held it forth.

"The shaft is of choice wood," he said. "Its copper head longs to drink the blood of Pharaoh's enemies. My spear is thirsty, and its name is Throat Slitter."

"Not blood!" cried the prince. "Blood is an abomination to Aton. There is nothing more terrible than flowing blood."

"Blood purifies the people and makes them strong; it makes the gods fat and contented. As long as there is war, so long must blood flow."

"There will never be war again," declared the heir to the throne. Horemheb laughed.

"The lad's daft! War there has always been and always will be, for the nations must test each other's worth if they are to survive."

"All peoples are his children—all languages—all complexions—the black land and the red." The prince was gazing straight into the sun. "I shall raise temples to him in every land, and to the princes of those lands I shall send the symbol of life—for I have seen him! Of him was I born and to him I shall return."

"He is mad," said Horemheb to me, shaking his head in compassion. "I can see he needs a doctor."

The prince raised his hand in greeting to the sun, and his face was once more filled with a passionate beauty as if he were looking into another world. We let him finish his prayer and then began to lead him toward the city. He made no resistance. The fit had left him weak; he staggered and moaned as he went; so at last we carried him between us, and the falcon flew ahead.

When we came to the edge of cultivation, we saw a royal carrying chair awaiting us. The slaves had lain down upon the ground, and out of the chair stepped a fat priest whose head was shaven and whose dark face was grave and beautiful. I stretched forth my hands at knee level before him, for I took him to be Eie, of whom Ptahor had spoken. But he did not heed me. He threw himself prostrate before the prince

61

and hailed him as king, so I knew that Amenhotep III was dead. The slaves then hastened to tend the new Pharaoh. His limbs were washed, massaged, and anointed, he was robed in royal linen, and upon his head was set the royal headdress.

Meanwhile Eie spoke to me. "Did he meet his god, Sinuhe?"

"He met his god, and I watched over him that no evil might befall. How do you know my name?"

He smiled. "It is for me to know all that goes on within the palace walls. I know your name and that you are a physician and that I might therefore entrust him to your care. You are also one of Ammon's priests and have sworn him your oath."

There was a hint of menace in his tone as he said this. Throwing out my hands, I exclaimed, "What signifies an oath to Ammon?"

"You are right and have nothing to repent of. And this spearman?"

He pointed to Horemheb, who was standing apart, testing the spear point on his hand, with the falcon perched upon his shoulder.

"It were better perhaps that he should die," he added, "for Pharaoh's secrets are shared by few."

"He covered Pharaoh with his cloak when it was cold and is ready to wield his spear against Pharaoh's enemies. I believe he will be more useful to you alive than dead, priest Eie."

Eie threw a gold ring from his arm toward him, saying carelessly, "You may call upon me some time at the golden house, spearman."

But Horemheb let the gold ring fall in the sand at his feet and looked defiantly at Eie.

"I take my orders from Pharaoh, and if I am not mistaken, Pharaoh is he who bears the royal headdress. The falcon led me to him, and that is sign enough."

Eie remained unruffled.

"Gold is costly and is always of use," he remarked. He picked up the gold ring and put it back upon his arm. "Make your obeisance to Pharaoh, but you must lay aside your spear in his presence."

The prince stepped forward. His face was pale and drawn but lighted still by a secret ecstasy that warmed my heart.

"Follow me," he said, "follow me, all of you, upon the new way, for the truth has been revealed to me."

We walked with him to the chair, though Horemheb mumbled to himself, "Truth lies in my spear." The porters set off at a trot to where the boat awaited us alongside the landing stage. We returned as we had come, unobserved, though the people stood packed outside the palace walls.

62

We were allowed to enter the prince's room, and he showed us big Cretan jars upon which were painted fish and other creatures. Word came that the Queen Mother was on her way to make her obeisance to him, so he gave us leave to go, promising to remember us both. When we had left him, Horemheb said to me in perplexity, "I am at a loss. I have nowhere to go."

"Stay here with an easy mind," I counseled him. "He promised to remember you, and it is as well to be at hand when he does. The gods are capricious and quickly forget."

"Stay here and buzz around with these flies?" he demanded, pointing to the courtiers who were swarming at the prince's door. "No, I have good reason to be uneasy," he went on somberly. "What is to become of an Egypt whose ruler is afraid of blood and believes that all nations and languages and colors are of equal merit? I was born a warrior, and my warrior sense tells me that such notions bode ill for such a man as I."

We parted, and I bade him ask for me at the House of Life if ever he needed a friend.

Ptahor was waiting for me in our room, red eyed and irritable.

"You were absent when Pharaoh drew his last breath at dawn," he growled. "You were absent, and I slept; and neither of us was there to see Pharaoh's soul fly from his nostrils straight into the sun, like a bird."

I told him what had happened that night, and he raised his hands in great astonishment.

"Ammon keep us! Then the new Pharaoh is mad."

"I think not," said I doubtfully. "I think he has knowledge of a new god. When his head has cleared, we may see wonders in the land of Kem."

"Ammon forbid! Pour me out some wine, for my throat is as dry as roadside dust."

Shortly after this we were conveyed under guard to a pavilion in the House of Justice, where the Keeper of the Seal read the law to us from a leather scroll and told us that we must die since Pharaoh did not recover after his skull had been opened. I looked at Ptahor, but he only smiled when the executioner stepped forward with his sword.

"Let the stancher of blood go first," he said. "He is in a greater hurry than we are, for his mother is already preparing pease pottage for him in the Western Land."

The stancher of blood took a warm farewell of us, made the holy sign of Ammon, and knelt meekly on the floor before the leather

63

scrolls. The executioner swung his sword in a great arc above the head of the condemned man, till it sang in the air, but stopped short as the edge just touched the back of his neck. But the blood stancher fell to the floor, and we thought he had swooned from terror, for there was not the smallest scratch upon him. When my turn came, I knelt without fear; the executioner laughed and touched my neck with his blade without troubling to frighten me more. Ptahor considered he was too short to be required to kneel, and the executioner swung his sword over his neck, too. So we died, the law was accomplished, and we were given new names engraved in heavy gold rings. In Ptahor's ring was written "He Who Is Like a Baboon" and in mine "He Who Is Alone." Then Ptahor's present was weighed out to him in gold and mine also, and we were clad in new robes. For the first time I wore a pleated robe of royal linen and a collar heavy with silver and precious stones. When the servants tried to lift the blood stancher and revive him, they found him stone dead. I saw this with my own eyes and can vouch for its truth. But why he died I do not know, unless from the mere expectation. Simple though he may be, a man who can arrest the flow of blood is not like other men.

Henceforth, being officially dead, I could not sign my name as Sinuhe without adding He Who Is Alone, and at court I could be known by no other name.

3

When I went back to the House of Life in my new clothes and with the gold ring on my arm, my teachers bowed before me. Yet I was still a pupil and had to write a detailed account of Pharaoh's operation and death, attesting it with my name. I spent much time over this and ended with a description of the soul of Pharaoh flying from his nostrils in the shape of a bird and passing straight into the sun. Later I had the satisfaction of hearing my report read to the people on each of the seventy days during which Pharaoh's body was being prepared for immortality. During the whole of this period of mourning all pleasure houses, wine shops, and taverns in Thebes were closed so that to buy wine or hear music one had to enter by the back door.

But when these seventy days had passed, I learned that I was now a qualified physician and might start to practice in whatever quarter of the city I chose. If on the other hand I preferred to pursue my studies in one or other of the special branches—among the dentists or ear doctors, for instance, or the obstetricians, layers-on-of-hands, surgeons, or in any other of the fourteen different subjects in which instruction was given at the House of Life—I need only choose my branch. This was a special mark of favor, testifying how amply Ammon rewarded his servants.

I was young, and the learning in the House of Life no longer absorbed me. I had been seized with the fever of Thebes; I desired wealth and fame; I desired to profit by the period of my fame among the people. With the gold I had received I purchased a small house on the outskirts of the fashionable quarter, furnished it according to my means, and bought a slave—a scraggy fellow with one eye, but good enough for me. His name was Kaptah. He assured me that his one eye was my good fortune, for now he could tell my would-be patients in the waiting room that he had been stone blind when I had bought him and that I had given him back partial sight. I had pictures painted on the walls of the waiting room. In one of these Imhotep the Wise, the god of doctors, was shown giving me instruction. I was painted small before him, as the custom is, but below the picture was an inscription that ran thus:

Wisest and most skillful of thy disciples
is Sinuhe, Son of Senmut, He Who Is Alone.

Another picture showed me making sacrifice to Ammon, that I might be seen to do him honor and win the confidence of my patients. But in a third, great Pharaoh looked down upon me from the heavens in the shape of a bird, while his servants weighed out gold for me and clothed me in new robes.

I commissioned Thothmes to do these paintings for me although he was not an authorized artist and his name did not appear in the book in the temple of Ptah. But he was my friend, and because of his work those who looked upon the pictures for the first time raised their hands in astonishment, saying, "In truth he inspires faith, this Sinuhe, son of Senmut, He Who Is Alone, and will surely cure all his patients by his skill."

When all was ready, I sat down to await the sick. I sat for a long time, but none came. In the evening I went to a wine shop, having still a little gold and silver left from Pharaoh's gifts. I was young and fancied myself a clever doctor; I had no misgivings about the future and together with Thothmes made good cheer over my wine. In loud voices we discussed the affairs of the Two Kingdoms, for everywhere —in the market, before the merchants' houses, in the taverns and pleasure houses—such matters were vigorously debated by all at this time.

It had come to pass as the old Keeper of the Seal had foretold. When the body of great Pharaoh had been made proof against death and attended to its resting place in the Valley of the Kings, where the doors of the tomb had been sealed with the royal seal, the Queen Mother ascended the throne bearing in her hands the scourge and the crook. Upon her chin was the beard of sovereignty and the lion's tail was about her waist. The heir was not yet crowned Pharaoh, and it was said that he desired to purify himself and perform his devotions to the gods before he assumed power. But when the Queen Mother dismissed the old Keeper of the Seal and raised Eie, the unknown priest, to honor at her right hand so that he surpassed in rank all the illustrious men of Egypt—then the temple of Ammon hummed like a beehive, there were ill omens, and misfortune attended the royal sacrifices. The priests interpreted many strange dreams that men had had. Winds veered from their usual quarter against all the laws of nature, and there was rain for two days running in the land of Egypt. Merchandise standing at the wharves suffered damage, and grain rotted. Certain pools on the outskirts of Thebes were turned to blood, and many went to see them. But the people were not yet afraid, for such things had happened in every age when the priests were angered. Though there was unrest and much empty talk, the mercenaries at the barracks—Egyptians, Syrians, Negroes, and Shardanas—were given lavish presents by the Queen Mother, and good order was maintained. The might of Egypt was undisputed; in Syria it was upheld by the garrisons, and the princes of Byblos, Smyrna, Sidon, and Gaza—who in their childhood had dwelt at Pharaoh's feet and grown up in the golden house—mourned his death as if he had been their father, and wrote letters to the Queen in which they declared themselves dust beneath her feet.

The King of the land of Mitanni, in Naharani, sent his daughter as a bride to the new Pharaoh as his father had done before him and as had been agreed with the celestial Pharaoh before his death. Tadu-khipa, for such was her name, arrived in Thebes with servants and slaves and asses laden with merchandise of great value. She was a child just six years old, and the prince took her to wife, for the kingdom of Mitanni was a wall between the wealth of Syria and the lands of the north, and guarded the caravan routes all the way from the land of the twin rivers to the sea. Rejoicing ceased among the priests of Se-khmet, the celestial daughter of Ammon, and the hinges of her temple gates were rusted fast.

It was of this we spoke, Thothmes and I; we rejoiced our hearts with wine as we listened to Syrian music and watched the dancing girls. The fever of the city was in my blood; yet each morning my one-eyed servant came to my bedside deferentially and brought me bread and a salt fish and filled my beaker with ale. Then I would wash myself and sit down to await my patients, to listen to their woes and to heal them.

4

It was floodtime. The waters had risen as high as to the temple walls, and when they sank again, the land sprouted forth in tender green, birds built their nests, and lotus flowers blossomed in the pools amid the perfume of acacias. One day Horemheb came to my house and greeted me. He was dressed in royal linen with a gold chain about his neck. In his hand he carried a whip denoting that he was an officer in Pharaoh's household. But now he held no spear.

"I come for counsel, Sinuhe the Lonely," said he.

"What can you mean? You are as strong as a bull and as bold as a lion. There is nothing a doctor can do for you."

"I ask you as a friend not as a physician," he said sitting down. Kaptah poured water over his hands, and I offered him cakes my mother Kipa had sent me and wine from the harbor, for my heart rejoiced at the sight of him.

"You have been promoted then. You are now an officer of the household and no doubt the light of all women's eyes."

His face darkened. "And what filth it all is! The palace is full of flies that blow on me. The Theban streets are hard and hurt my feet, and my sandals chafe them sore."

He kicked off the sandals and rubbed his toes. "I am an officer in the bodyguard, yes—but some of the officers are ten-year-olds whose side locks are still unshorn, and because of their high birth they laugh at me and mock me. Their arms have not strength to draw the bowstring, and their swords are gold and silver toys; they might cut meat with them but never strike down an enemy. The soldiers drink and lie with the household slave girls and are without discipline. In the military school they read outdated treatises—they have never seen war or known hunger and thirst or fear of the enemy."

He rattled the chain about his neck impatiently and went on. "What are chains and honors when they are won not in battle but in prostrations before Pharaoh? The Queen Mother has tied a beard to her chin and girded herself with the tail of a lion, but how can a warrior look up to a woman as his chief? In the days of the great Pharaohs the warrior was a man not altogether despised, but now the Thebans look upon his profession as the most contemptible of all and shut their doors to him. I waste my time. The days of my youth and strength trickle away while I study the arts of war under those who would turn and fly at the mere sound of a Negro war cry. By my falcon! Soldiers are made upon the field of battle and nowhere else, and they are tried in the clash of arms. I will stay here no longer!"

He smote the table with his whip, overturning the wine cups, and my servant fled with a yelp of fear.

"Horemheb, my friend—you are ill after all. Your eyes are fevered, and you are bathed in sweat."

"Am I not a man?" He smote his chest. "I can lift a brawny slave in either hand and crack their heads together. I can bear heavy burdens as a soldier should, I can run long distances without becoming breathless, and I fear neither hunger and thirst nor the desert sun. But all this is shameful in their eyes, and the women in the golden house admire only such men as do not need to shave; they like them with slender wrists and hairless chests and hips like girls'. They admire the ones who carry sunshades and paint their mouths red and twitter like the birds in the trees. I am despised for being strong and for having sunburned skin and hands, that show that I can work."

He fell silent, staring before him. At length he emptied his goblet. "You are alone, Sinuhe—and so am I, for I guess what is to come. I know that I was born to a high command and that one day both kingdoms will have need of me. But I can no longer bear to be alone, Sinuhe. There are sparks of fire in my heart; my throat feels tight; I cannot sleep. I must get away from Thebes—the filth stifles me, and the flies soil me."

Looking at me then, he said in a low voice, "Sinuhe, you are a doctor. Give me a remedy that will conquer love."

"That is easy. I can give you berries that when dissolved in wine will make you strong and hot as the baboon so that women sigh in your arms and roll their eyes. That is easily done."

"Nay, you misunderstand me, Sinuhe. There is nothing wrong with my strength. I want a remedy for folly. I want a remedy to quieten my heart—and turn it into stone."

"There is no such remedy. A smile—a glance from green eyes—and the physician's arts are powerless. This I know. But the wise say that one evil spirit can be driven out by another. Whether this is true I know not—but I fancy the second might be worse than the first."

"What do you mean?" he demanded irritably. "I am weary of twisted phrases."

"Find another woman to drive the first from your heart. That is all I meant. Thebes is full of lovely, seductive women who paint their faces and wear the thinnest of linen. You may find one among them to smile upon you, being young and strong with slender limbs and a gold chain about your neck. But I do not understand what keeps you from the one you desire. Even though she be married, there is no wall too high for love to surmount. When a woman desires a man, her cunning can remove all barriers. Stories from both kingdoms prove that. The love of women is said to be as constant as the wind, blowing always and merely changing its direction. Women's virtue, they say, is like wax and melts in the heat. So it has been and ever will be."

"She is not married," snapped Horemheb. "You are beside the mark with your prattle of constancy and virtue. She does not even see me though I dwell under her eyes nor take my hand if I stretch it forth to help her into her chair."

"She is then a lady of some distinction?"

"Vain to speak of her. She is lovelier than the moon and the stars and more remote. Truly I could more easily grasp the moon in my arms. Therefore, I must forget—therefore, I must leave Thebes or die."

"You have surely not fallen victim to the charms of the Queen Mother," I exclaimed jestingly, for I wanted to make him laugh. "She is too old and fat to please a young man."

"And she has her priest," returned Horemheb with contempt. "I believe they were adulterers while the king yet lived."

I stopped him with my raised hand and said, "You have drunk from many poisoned wells since you came to Thebes."

"The one I desire paints her lips and cheeks yellow red, and her oval eyes are dark, and no one has yet touched those limbs veiled by the royal linen. Her name is Baketamon, and in her veins flows the blood of the Pharaohs. Now you know all my madness, Sinuhe. But if you tell anyone or remind me of it with so much as a word, I will seek you out and slay you wherever you may be—I will put your head between your legs and throw your body on the wall."

I was greatly alarmed at what he said, for that a man of low birth should raise his eyes to Pharaoh's daughter to desire her was a dire thing indeed. I answered, "No mortal may approach her. If she is to marry anyone, it will be her brother, the heir, who will raise her up to be his equal as royal consort. And thus it will be, for I read it in her eyes at the deathbed of the King when she looked at no one but her

69

brother. I feared her as a woman whose limbs will bring no warmth to any man, and emptiness and death dwell in her glance. Depart, Horemheb, my friend; Thebes is no place for you."

He retorted impatiently, "All this I know better than you, and your chatter is as the buzz of flies in my ear. Let us rather return to what you said of the evil spirits, for my heart is full; and, when I have drunk wine, I long for some woman to smile at me, whoever it be. But her robe must be of royal linen; she must wear a wig and paint her lips and cheeks yellow red, and to awaken my desire her eyes must be curved like the rainbow."

I smiled. "You say wisely. Let us therefore debate the matter like friends."

"Listen! Among my fellow officers is one Kefta from Crete, whom I once had occasion to kick. He now respects me, and he invited me to go with him today to a reception at a house near the temple of some cat-headed god. I have forgotten the name of the god, having felt no inclination to go."

"You mean Bast. I know the temple, and the place is in all likelihood well suited to your purpose, for light women pray much to the cat-headed one and make sacrifice to win wealthy lovers."

"But I do not go without you, Sinuhe. I am of low birth, ignorant of behavior in Thebes and especially among the women of Thebes. You are a man of the world and were born here, and you must come with me."

I was flushed with wine, and his confidence in me was flattering; I would not confess that my knowledge of women was as slight as his. I sent Kaptah for a carrying chair and bargained with the porters while Horemheb drank more wine to give himself courage. The men carried us to the temple of Bast. When they saw that torches and lamps burned before the doors of the house we were to visit, they began to complain loudly of their payment until Horemheb slashed at them with his whip and they fell into injured silence.

I led the way in, and no one seemed surprised at our coming. Cheerful servants poured water over our hands, and the aroma of hot dishes, of ointments and flowers, was wafted out as far as the veranda. Slaves adorned us with garlands, and we stepped boldly into the great hall.

When we had entered, I had no eyes for any but the woman who came toward us. She was clad in royal linen so that her limbs gleamed through it like the limbs of a goddess. On her head she wore a heavy blue wig, and she had much red jewelry; her eyebrows were blackened, and beneath her eyes was painted a green shadow. But greener

70

than all green were the eyes themselves, like the Nile in the heat of summer, so that my heart was drowned in them. For this was Nefernefernefer, whom I had once met in the colonnade of Ammon's great temple. She did not recognize me but smiled at Horemheb, who raised his officer's whip in greeting. Kefta, the young Cretan, was there also; he ran up to Horemheb and embraced him, calling him his friend.

No one heeded me, and I had leisure to gaze at the sister of my heart. She was older than I remembered, and her eyes no longer smiled but were hard as green stones. They did not smile though her mouth smiled, and they rested first upon the gold chain about Horemheb's neck. But my knees were weak as I beheld her.

There was much shouting and laughter; overturned wine jars and crushed flowers lay about the floor, and the Syrian musicians handled their instruments to such purpose that no conversation could be heard. It was evident that there had been a great deal of drinking, for one woman vomited. A servant handed her a bowl too late so that her dress was befouled and everyone laughed.

Kefta the Cretan embraced me, also, smearing salve all over my face as he did so and calling me his friend. But Nefernefernefer looked at me and said, "Sinuhe! I once knew a Sinuhe; he also was to be a physician."

"I am that Sinuhe," I said, looking her in the eye and trembling.

"No, you are not he." She made a gesture of denial. "The Sinuhe I knew was a young boy with eyes as clear as a gazelle's—but you are a man with the ways of a man. There are two furrows between your eyebrows, and your face is not smooth like his."

I showed her the ring with the green stone that I wore on my finger, but she shook her head, pretending to be puzzled, and said, "I must be entertaining a robber in my house, who has killed that Sinuhe and stolen the ring I once gave him in token of our friendship. His name also you have stolen, and the Sinuhe who pleased me no longer lives."

She raised her hands in the gesture of grief, and in my bitterness I took the ring from my finger and handed it to her, saying, "Take back your ring then, and I will go and vex you no longer."

But she said, "Do not go!" and again, laying her hand lightly on my arm as she had done once before, she said softly, "Do not go!"

And I did not go though I knew that her body would burn me worse than fire and that never again could I be happy without her. Servants poured out wine for us, and wine was never more delectable in my mouth than then.

The woman who had been ill rinsed her mouth and drank more wine. Then she drew off her soiled gown and threw it down; she also removed her wig so that she was quite naked. She pressed her breasts together with her hands, telling the servants to pour wine between them, and she let any drink there who cared to. She reeled down the room laughing loudly—young, beautiful, reckless—and, pausing before Horemheb, she offered him the wine between her breasts. He bent his head and drank. When he raised it again, his face was dark, and he looked the woman in the eyes, seized her bare head in his hands, and kissed her. Everyone laughed, and the woman laughed with them. Then becoming shy all at once, she demanded a fresh gown. Servants clad her, and she put on her wig again. She sat close to Horemheb and drank no more. The Syrian musicians played on; I felt the fever of Thebes in my blood and knew that I was born to live in the sunset of the world—that nothing mattered any more as long as I might sit beside the sister of my heart and gaze on the greenness of her eyes and the redness of her lips.

Thus it was through Horemheb that I came to meet Nefernefernefer my beloved once again; but it would have been better for me if I had never met her.

5

"Is this your house?" I asked her as she sat beside me, surveying me with her hard green eyes.

"This is my house, and these are my guests. I have guests every evening, for I do not care to be alone."

"And Metufer?" I asked, for I wished to know all, despite the pain it might cause me. She frowned a little.

"Did you not know that Metufer is dead? He died because he misused money Pharaoh had given his father for the building of a temple. Metufer died, and his father is no longer the royal master builder. Did you not know that?"

"If that is true," I said smiling, "I can almost believe that Ammon punished him, for he mocked the name of Ammon." I told her how Metufer and the priest had spat in the face of Ammon's statue to wash it and how they had rubbed themselves with Ammon's sacred ointment.

She smiled, but her eyes had a hard, distant look in them. Suddenly she said, "Why did you not come to me then, Sinuhe? If you had sought me, you would have found me. You did ill in not coming and in visiting other women with my ring on your finger."

"I was but a boy and I feared you—but in my dreams you were my sister, Nefernefernefer, and—laugh at me if you will—I have never yet lain with any woman. I have been waiting to see you again."

She laughed and made a gesture of disbelief.

"You are certainly lying. In your eyes I must seem an ugly old woman, and it diverts you to mock me and lie to me." Her eyes were gay now as in other days, and she looked so much younger that my heart swelled and ached as I looked at her.

"It is true that I have never touched any woman," I said, "but it may not be true that I have waited for you. Let me be honest. Very many women have come before me, young and old, pretty and plain, wise and simple; but I have looked upon all alike with the eye of a physician; and not one of them has stirred my heart; though why this should be I cannot tell."

"Perhaps when you were a little boy you fell from the top of a wagon load and landed astride the shaft, so that ever since then you have been melancholy and happier alone"; and, as she laughed, she touched me lightly as no woman had ever touched me. Reply was needless, for she knew herself that what she said was untrue. She quickly withdrew her hand, whispering: "Let us drink wine together. I may yet take my pleasure with you, Sinuhe."

We drank wine while the slaves carried some of the guests out to their chairs, and Horemheb put his arm about the woman beside him, calling her his sister. He took the gold chain from his neck and would have hung it about hers.

But she resisted and said angrily, "I am a decent woman and no harlot!" Rising, she moved away in an offended manner, but in the doorway beckoned secretly and Horemheb followed her. I saw nothing more of either of them that evening.

Those who yet remained went on drinking. They staggered about the floor tripping over stools and rattling sistra they had filched from the musicians. They embraced, calling each other brother and friend—and then fell out with blows and cries of gelding and eunuch.

I was drunk, not with wine but with the nearness of Nefernefernefer and with the touch of her hand, until at last she made a sign and the servants began to put out the lights, carry away tables and stools, and gather up the trampled garlands. Then I said to her, "I must go."

But each word stung my heart like salt in a wound, for I dreaded losing her, and every moment not spent in her company seemed to me wasted.

"Where will you go?" she asked in feigned surprise.

"I go to keep watch tonight in the street before your house. I go to make sacrifice in every temple in Thebes, in thanksgiving to the gods that I have met you again. I go to pluck blossoms from the trees to strew in your path when you leave your house and to buy myrrh with which to anoint your door posts."

She smiled and said, "It would be better if you did not go, for flowers and myrrh I have already. And if you go fired so with wine, you will run astray among strange women. That I will not allow."

Her words filled me with joy. I would have seized her, but she resisted me, saying, "Stop! My servants can see us. Though I live alone, I am no contemptible woman."

She led me out into her garden, which lay in moonlight and was filled with the scent of myrtle and acacia. The lotus flowers in the pool had closed their chalices for the night, and I saw that the edge of the pool was inlaid with colored stones. Servants poured water over our hands and brought us roast goose and fruits steeped in honey, and Nefernefernefer said, "Eat and enjoy yourself here with me, Sinuhe."

But my throat was roughened by desire, and I could not swallow. She gave me a mocking look and ate greedily. Each time she glanced at me the moonlight was mirrored in her eyes. I would have drawn her into my arms, but she pushed me away, saying, "Do you not know why Bast, the goddess of love, is portrayed as a cat?"

"I care neither for cats nor gods," said I, reaching out to her, my eyes blurred with desire. She pushed my hands aside.

"Quite soon you may touch me. You may lay your hands on my breast and my stomach if it will quiet you, but first you shall listen to me and learn why a woman is like a cat and why passion, too, is like a cat. Its paws are soft, but they hide claws that rip and tear and stab mercilessly into your heart. Ay, indeed, a woman is like a cat, for a cat also takes pleasure in tormenting its prey and torturing it without ever tiring of the game. Not until the creature is maimed will she devour it and then set forth to seek another victim. I tell you this because I would be honest with you; I have never wished you ill. No, I have never wished you ill," she repeated absently, taking my hand and moving it to her breast while the other she placed in her lap. I trembled, and the tears sprang from my eyes. Then she pushed me away again.

74

"You may leave me now, never to return, and then I shan't hurt you. But if you don't go now, you can't blame me for anything that may happen."

She gave me time to go, but I did not. Sighing a little then as if weary of the game, she said, "So let it be. You must have what you came for, but be gentle, for I am tired, and I fear I may fall asleep on your arm."

She took me to her room and to her couch of ivory and ebony. There, slipping off her robe, she opened her embrace to me.

It was as if my whole self were being burned away to ashes by her body.

Soon she yawned and told me, "I am very sleepy—and I must believe that you have never lain with a woman before, for you go about it very clumsily and give me no pleasure. But when a youth takes his first woman, he gives her a priceless treasure. I will ask no other present of you. But go now and let me sleep, for you have had what you came for."

And when I sought to embrace her again, she defended herself and sent me away. I went home with a body molten and seething, knowing that never should I be able to forget her.

6

On the following day I told my servant Kaptah to send away all my patients and bid them seek other doctors. I sent for a barber, washed and anointed myself with sweet-smelling oils, dressed, and ordered a chair, telling the porters to run. I desired to hasten to the house of Nefernefernefer without soiling my clothes or feet with dust. Kaptah looked after me with concern and shook his head, for I had never before left my workroom in the middle of the day, and he feared that if I neglected my patients the fees would dwindle. But I had one thought only, and my body burned as with fire—a glorious fire.

A servant admitted me and led me to Nefernefernefer's room. She was adorning herself before the mirror and looked at me with hard, indifferent eyes.

"What do you want, Sinuhe? You weary me."

"You know very well what I want," I said, trying to gather her into my arms and remembering her ardor of the night before. But she pushed me roughly away.

"Is this malice or stupidity? To come now! A merchant has arrived from Sidon with a jewel that was once a queen's—a forehead ornament from a tomb. This evening someone is to give it to me; I have long yearned for a gem such as no one else possesses. Therefore I shall make myself beautiful and let them anoint my body."

She undressed without embarrassment and stretched herself upon the bed for a slave girl to rub salve into her limbs. My heart rose into my throat, and my hands sweated at the sight of her beauty.

"Why tarry, Sinuhe?" she asked when the slave had gone, leaving her lying there unconcernedly upon her bed. "Why have you not gone? I must dress."

Giddiness seized me, and I rushed at her, but she warded me off so adroitly that I could not take her and stood there finally shedding tears of thwarted desire.

I said at last, "If I could buy you that jewel I would, as you well know—but no one else shall touch you—I will die first."

"Ah?" she said, her eyes half shut. "You forbid anyone else to touch me? And if I give up this day to you, Sinuhe—if I eat and drink and play with you today—since no one knows what tomorrow will bring—what will you give me?"

She stretched out on the bed so that her flat belly was hollowed. There was not a hair on her, either on her head or on her body.

"I have indeed nothing to give you," and I looked about me as I said it—at the floor of lapis lazuli inlaid with turquoises and at the many golden cups that were in the room. "Truly I have nothing to give you."

My knees gave beneath me, and I was turning away when she stopped me.

"I am sorry for you, Sinuhe," she said softly, stretching her lithe body once more. "You have already given me what you had that was worth giving—although its value appears to me much overrated. But you have a house and clothes and all the instruments that a physician needs. You are not altogether poor, I think."

Trembling from head to foot, I said, "All that is yours, Nefernefernefer, if you wish. It is worth little, but the house is fitted up for a doctor's use. A student in the House of Life might give a good price for it if his parents had the means."

"Do you think so?"

She turned her naked back to me, and as she contemplated herself in the glass, she drew her slender fingers along the black lines of her brows.

"As you will. Find a scribe, then, to record this so that all you possess may be transferred to me in my name. For though I live alone, I am not a woman to be despised, and I must make provision for the future when perhaps you will cast me off, Sinuhe."

I stared at her naked back; my tongue grew thick in my mouth, and my heart began to beat so violently that I turned hastily and went. I found a law scribe who quickly made out the necessary papers and dispatched them to the royal archives for safekeeping. When I returned, Nefernefernefer had clothed herself in royal linen and wore a wig as red as gold; neck, wrists, and ankles were adorned with the most splendid jewelry. At the entrance a handsome chair awaited her.

Handing her the scribe's receipt I said, "All that I possess is now yours, Nefernefernefer, even to the clothes I have on. Let us now eat and drink and take our pleasure together this day, for no one knows what tomorrow may bring."

She took the paper carelessly, put it in an ebony casket and said, "I am sorry, Sinuhe, but I find that my monthly trouble is upon me so you cannot come to me as I had wished. You had better go now until I have made the appointed purification, for my head is heavy, and my body pains me. Come another day, and you shall have your desire."

I stared at her with death in my breast and could not speak. She stamped with impatience.

"Away with you. I am in a hurry."

When I sought to touch her, she said, "Do not smudge the paint on my face."

I went home and set my belongings in order, that all might be ready for the new owner. My one-eyed slave followed every step I took, shaking his head, till his presence maddened me. I burst out, "Do not hang at my heels; I am no longer your master. Another owns you now. Serve him obediently when he comes, and do not steal so much from him as you did from me, for it may be his stick is harder than mine."

Then he cast himself to the ground, raising his hands above his head in the depth of his grief and weeping bitterly.

"Do not send me away, lord, for my old heart has grown into your ways and will break if you banish me. I have always been faithful to you, young and simple though you are. What I have stolen from you I have stolen with due regard to your advantage. I have run about the streets on my old legs in the noonday heat, crying your name and merits, though the servants of other physicians have beaten me and cast dung upon me."

77

My heart was as if filled with salt, and I had a bitter taste in my mouth as I looked at him.

But I was touched, and gripping him by the shoulders I said, "Get up, Kaptah! Of what use is all this outcry? It is not from displeasure that I dismiss you, for I have been content with your service, though you have often shown your temper in a shameless manner by slamming doors and clattering the dishes when something has vexed you. And your pilfering has not angered me, for it is a slave's right. I have been forced to hand you over against my will, for I had nothing else to give; my house has gone, too, and all that I possess, so that not so much as the clothes upon my back are my own. You lament in vain."

Kaptah tore his hair and groaned, "This is an evil day!"

He mused heavily for a time, and then went on, "You are a great doctor, Sinuhe, despite your youth, and the world lies before you. It will be best, therefore, if I make haste to gather up those things that are of most value, and when darkness comes, we can fly. We can make our way to the Red Lands, where no one knows you, or to the islands in the sea where the wine is sparkling and the women joyous. In the land of Mitanni, also, and in Babylon, where the rivers flow in the wrong direction, the arts of Egyptian physicians are highly regarded so that you may grow rich and I may become the servant of a respected master. Hasten, therefore, lord, that we may pack up your belongings before dark," and he tugged at my sleeve.

"Kaptah, Kaptah! Spare me this witless chatter. My heart is grieved to death, and my body is no longer my own. I am bound with fetters that are stronger than copper chains though you do not see them. I cannot fly, for to be absent from Thebes is to be in a glowing furnace."

My servant sat on the floor, for his feet were afflicted with painful swellings that I treated from time to time when I had leisure.

He said, "It is clear that Ammon has abandoned us—which I cannot wonder at since you so seldom go to make sacrifice to him. Nevertheless, I have faithfully sacrificed one fifth of what I have stolen from you in thankfulness for having been given a young and simple master. Now he has abandoned me also. Well, well . . . We must change gods and hasten to make sacrifice to some other who will perhaps divert the evil from us and make all well again."

"No more of this nonsense. You forget we have nothing to sacrifice since all is now another's."

"A man or a woman?"

78

"A woman," I answered—for what need was there to conceal it? When he heard this, he burst out in fresh lamentation. "Oh, that I had never been born into this world! Oh, that my mother had strangled me in my navel cord at birth! For there is no bitterer fate for a slave than to serve a heartless woman—and heartless must she be who has done this to you."

"She is in no way heartless," I answered him—for so foolish is man that I needs must talk of Nefernefernefer even to my slave, having no one else in whom to confide. "Naked upon her couch she is more beautiful than the moon. Her limbs gleam with costly oils, and her eyes are green as the Nile in the heat of summer. Happy are you and enviable, Kaptah, if you are permitted to live near her and breathe the same air."

Kaptah made yet louder outcry.

"She will sell me for a porter or a quarryman—my lungs will be choked, and blood will spurt from under my nails, and I shall perish in the mud like a mangled donkey."

In my heart I knew that this might be the truth, for in the house of Nefernefernefer there would scarcely be bread and houseroom for such as he. Tears fell from my eyes, also, though I didn't know whether I wept for him or for myself. When Kaptah saw this, he fell silent at once and stared at me aghast, but I bowed my head in my hands and cared not that my slave should see me weep. Touching my head with his broad hand, he said ruefully, "This is all my doing—I should have kept better watch over my master. But I did not dream he was so white and pure—like a cloth before its first washing. For that alone would explain it. I marveled, indeed, that my master never sent me out for a girl when he came back at night from the wine shop, and the women I sent you for your pleasure went peevishly away, calling me rat and carrion crow. And there were young and comely ones among them. But my trouble was wasted, and like a blockhead I rejoiced, thinking you would never bring a wife into your house to cuff me on the head and throw scalding water over my feet whenever she had quarreled with you. Fool, blockhead that I was! It is the first firebrand that burns down the hut."

He also said much more, and the sound of his voice was as the buzzing of flies in my ears. At length he ceased and prepared food for me and poured water over my hands. But I could not eat, for my body was on fire; and, when evening came, one thought alone filled my mind.

BOOK 4

Nefernefernefer

I

EARLY in the morning I went to Nefernefernefer's house, but she was still sleeping. When I roused her servants, they swore and threw slops over me, so I sat in the doorway like a beggar until I heard movement and talk in the house and then tried once more to enter.

Nefernefernefer lay upon her bed. Her face looked small and white, and her green eyes were dark from wine drinking.

"You bore me," she said. "What is it you want?"

"To eat and drink and take pleasure with you," I replied heavily, "for so you promised."

"That was yesterday. Today is a new day."

A slave girl drew off Nefer's rumpled dress and oiled and rubbed her limbs. Nefer regarded herself in the mirror, painted her face, put on her wig, and taking up the new ornament of pearls and precious stones set in antique gold, she placed it on her forehead.

"It is beautiful," she said, "and worth the price, though I am as weary as if I had been wrestling all night."

"So you lied to me yesterday, and there was nothing to hinder us," I said, though in my heart I had known it.

"I was mistaken—but my time should have come, and I fear you have got me with child, Sinuhe, for I was limp in your arms, and you were violent." But she smiled mockingly.

"So your jewel comes from a royal tomb in Syria—wasn't that what you told me yesterday?"

"Ah," she said softly. "It was found beneath the pillow of a Syrian merchant—but do not let that vex you. He was a paunchy man, as fat as a pig, and he smelled of onions. I have what I sought and do not mean to see him again."

She took off wig and ornament and dropped them carelessly on the floor beside the bed. Her bare skull was smooth and comely as she stretched herself out again and pillowed her head on her clasped hands.

"I am weary, Sinuhe, and you abuse my weariness by thus devouring me with your eyes when I have not strength to prevent you. You should remember that though I live alone I am not a woman to be despised."

"You know very well that I have no more to give you, for you already possess all that was mine."

I bowed my head down to the edge of the bed and caught the perfume of her ointments and of her body. She put out her hand to touch my hair, then withdrew it quickly, laughing and shaking her head.

"What deceivers men are! You lie to me, too, Sinuhe. I cannot help my fondness for you—I am weak."

But when I would have taken her in my arms, she pushed me away and sat up, saying in a voice of bitter resentment, "Weak, lonely though I may be, I will have no dealings with cheats and swindlers. You never told me that your father Senmut has a house in the poor quarter near the harbor. The house is worth little, but the ground it stands on lies near the quays, and his furniture might fetch something at the market. I might eat and drink and take pleasure with you today if you were to give me this property of yours—for no one knows what tomorrow may bring, and I must guard my reputation."

"My father's property is not mine," I said aghast. "You must not ask of me what is not mine to give, Nefernefernefer."

She tilted her head sideways, watching me with her green eyes.

"Your father's property is your lawful inheritance, Sinuhe, as well you know. And further, you never told me that he is blind and that he has entrusted you with the stewardship of his possessions so that you can dispose of them as if they were your own."

This was true, for when my father's sight had grown dim, he had given me his seal and asked me to look after his property as he could no longer see to sign his name. Kipa and he had often said that the house would fetch a good price and enable them to buy a little homestead outside the city and to live there until the time came for them to take possession of their tomb and start on the journey to immortality.

I could not speak, so overwhelmed was I with horror at the thought of deceiving the mother and father who trusted me. But Nefernefernefer half closed her eyes and murmured, "Take my head between your hands—touch my breast with your lips—for there is something about you that makes me weak, Sinuhe, so that I forget my own advantage where you are concerned. All day I will take my pleasure with you if you will make over your father's property to me, however little it may be worth."

84

I took her head between my hands, and it was smooth and small, filling me with fever unspeakable.

"So be it," I said, and my voice grated on my own ears.

But when I would have approached her, she said, "You shall enter into the realm that is already yours—but first seek out a law scribe to prepare the appointed documents, for I do not trust men's promises, and I must guard my reputation."

I left her to send for a scribe, and each step away from her was torment. I urged him to hasten, and when all was done, I pressed my father's seal on the paper and signed it with his name. But when I returned, the servants told me that Nefernefernefer was sleeping, and I had to wait until late evening for her to wake. At last she received me, took the scribe's receipt, and slipped it carelessly into the black casket.

"You are obstinate, Sinuhe, but I am a woman of honor and always keep my promises. Take what you have come for."

She lay upon the bed and opened her embrace, but took no pleasure in me. She turned her head aside to look at herself in the mirror, yawning behind her hands, so that the delight I sought was turned to ashes.

When I arose from her couch, she said, "You have had what you wanted, Sinuhe; now go, for you are very wearisome. Another day you may return, but you have no doubt had all you want."

I was like the shell of a blown egg as I staggered home. I desired to be at peace in a dark room, to bury my head in my hands and give vent to my misery in weeping. But on the veranda sat a stranger wearing a braided wig and a Syrian robe of many colors. He greeted me haughtily and said he had come to consult me as a physician.

"I do not receive patients any more," I told him, "for the house is no longer mine."

"I have evil swellings on my feet," he said, and he mixed Syrian words with his speech. "Your intelligent slave Kaptah recommended your skill in treating such swellings. Relieve me from my torment and you shall not regret it."

So stubborn was he that at length I led him into my room and called to Kaptah for hot water to wash my hands. There was no reply, but not until I examined the feet of the Syrian, did I recognize Kaptah's own gnarled and spavined joints. My slave plucked off his wig and burst into roars of laughter.

"What mummery is this?" I exclaimed, and I thrashed him till his laughter turned to howls. When I had thrown the stick aside, he said,

"Since I am no longer your slave but the slave of another, I may safely tell you that I think of making my escape and therefore wished to discover whether you would know me in this dress."

I reminded him of the punishments that threaten runaway slaves and told him that he was certain to be recaptured sooner or later, for what had he to live on? But he replied, "Last night, having drunk much beer, I had a dream. You, lord, lay in a burning furnace, but I came to you with stern words and lifting you by the scruff of the neck plunged you into flowing water that carried you away. I have since been to the market to ask an interpreter of dreams what this means. He said that my master is in danger and has a long journey before him and that I for my boldness should come by many blows. This dream is true, for one need but see your face, lord, to know that you stand in great peril. The blows I have had already—therefore the end of the dream also must be true. For this reason I have disguised myself, for I am resolved to go with you upon your journey."

"Your loyalty moves me, Kaptah," I said and strove to sound mocking. "It may well be that a long journey lies before me, but if so it is to the House of Death, where you will scarcely follow me."

"Tomorrow is hidden," was Kaptah's pert retort. "You are young and green as an unlicked calf, and I dare not let you set forth alone upon the troubled journey to the House of Death and the Western Land. Like enough I shall come with you to help you with my experience, for my heart is bound to you despite your foolishness. Though doubtless I have begotten many children in my time, yet I have never seen any of them and so have a whim to think of you as my son. By this I mean no offense; I seek merely to express my affection for you."

This was carrying insolence too far, but I had not heart enough to thrash him, and he was no longer my slave. I shut myself into my room and covered my head and slept like the dead until morning, for there is no narcotic like shame and remorse if they be deep enough. Yet when at last I awoke, the first things I remembered were the eyes of Nefernefernefer and her body, and I seemed to hold her smooth head in my hands and feel her bosom against mine. I washed, dressed, and anointed my face to go to her.

2

Nefernefernefer received me in her garden beside the lotus pool. Her eyes were clear and gay and greener than the waters of the Nile.

When she saw me she cried, "O Sinuhe! So you have come back—then I am perhaps not yet so old and ugly. What do you want?"

I looked at her as a starveling looks at bread until she tilted her head in displeasure.

"Sinuhe, Sinuhe—again? I live alone, indeed, but I am no contemptible woman, and I must guard my reputation."

"Yesterday I made over to you all my father's property; and he is now a poor man, though formerly a respected physician. Being blind, he must beg bread in his old age while my mother must wash the linen of others."

"Yesterday was yesterday, and today is today." Her eyes narrowed. "But I am not extortionate. You may sit beside me and hold my hand. I am happy today and would at least share my heart's gladness with you, if no other pleasure."

She laughed mischievously and stroked her belly with a light hand. "You do not ask why my heart is glad today, but I will tell you. You must know that a distinguished man from the Lower Kingdom has arrived in the city, and he brings with him a golden bowl of nearly a hundred deben weight, upon which are engraved many beautiful and diverting pictures. He is old, certainly, and so thin that his old shanks will chafe me, yet I believe that in the morning that bowl will adorn my house."

She feigned a deep sigh when I made no answer and sat with her dreamy gaze on the lotuses and the other flowers in that garden. Then slowly slipping off her robe, she stepped down into the pool. Her head rose from the water beside a lotus flower, and she was more fair than all the lotuses. Floating before me with her hands behind her head, she said, "You are silent today, Sinuhe! Surely it is not I who have unwittingly wounded you? I would gladly make amends if I could."

I answered in spite of myself, "You know well enough what it is I want, Nefernefernefer."

"Your face is flushed, and I can see the blood pulsing at your temples. Would it not be well to lay aside your robe and step down into the pool here with me to cool yourself this hot day? None can see us here, so do not hesitate."

I stripped and stepped down into the pool, and my side touched hers. But when I would have held her, she evaded me, laughing and splashing water into my face.

"I understand what you want, Sinuhe, though I am too bashful to look at you. But first you must give me a present, for you know that I am not a woman to be despised."

I shouted in my wrath, "Are you mad? You know you have robbed me of everything! I am ashamed and dare never again look my parents in the face. But I am still a physician, and my name is written in the Book of Life. Perhaps I may yet earn enough to give you a present worthy of you. Have pity on me now, for even in the water I burn as in fire and bite my hand till the blood flows when I look at you."

She stretched herself out on the water, her breasts rising above the surface like two rosy flowers. She looked at me from under her green-painted eyelids and said, "Can we think of nothing for you to give me? For I weaken, Sinuhe; it is troubling to me to see you naked in my pool. You are clumsy and without experience, yet I think that one day I could teach you much that you do not yet know—tricks to sharpen a man's pleasure and a woman's also. Consider this, Sinuhe!"

When I snatched at her, she stepped swiftly up out of the pool and standing behind a tree shook the water from her arms.

"I am but a weak woman, and men are deceivers—you, too, Sinuhe! My heart is heavy at the thought of it and the tears very near my eyes—for it is clear that you are tired of me. Were this not so, you would never have kept from me that your parents have furnished a fine tomb for themselves in the City of the Dead and have paid to the temple the sum needful for the embalming of their bodies against death and for the things necessary to their journey to the Western Land."

When I heard this, I tore at my breast with my hands till the blood came.

"Shall I rob my parents of immortality and let their bodies dissolve into nothingness like the bodies of beggars and slaves and those who are cast into the river for their crimes? You cannot demand such a thing of me!"

The tears were rolling down my cheeks. Though I groaned in anguish, I went up to her, and she pressed her nakedness against me, saying, "Give me your parents' tomb and I will whisper 'my brother' in your ear and be to you a fire of delight and teach you a thousand things unknown to you to bring you joy!"

I had no mastery of myself but wept.

"Be it so, and may your name be accursed to all eternity—but withstand you I cannot, so powerful is the spell by which you hold me."

"Speak not of sorcery, for that offends me. As you are tedious and out of humor, I will send a servant for the scribe while we eat and

88

drink to gladden our hearts, that we may enjoy one another when the papers are in order." And with a joyous laugh she ran into the house.

I dressed and followed her; servants poured water over my hands and bowed, stretching forth their hands at knee level. But behind my back they sniggered and mocked me though I pretended that their sneering was no more than the buzzing of flies in my ear. When Nefernefernefer came down, they fell silent; we ate and drank together, and there were five sorts of meat and twelve sorts of pastry, and we drank mixed wine, which goes quickly to the head. The law scribe came and wrote out the necessary papers. I made over to Nefernefernefer my parents' tomb in the City of the Dead, with its furnishings, also their deposit in the temple, defrauding them of immortality and of their hope of journeying to the Western Land. I pressed my father's seal upon the paper and signed it with his name, and the scribe undertook to dispatch the documents to the royal archives that same day and so make them legally valid. He handed the receipt to Nefernefernefer; she put it into the black casket and paid him for his trouble.

When he had gone, I said, "From this hour I am accursed and dishonored before gods and men—it is a high price to pay. Prove to me now that it is not too high."

But she smiled.

"Drink wine, my brother, that your heart may be gladdened."

When I would have seized her, she evaded me and filled my wine cup from the jar. Presently she glanced at the sun and said, "See, the day is spent, and it will soon be evening. What do you stay for?"

"Well you know!"

"And well you know which well is deepest and which pit is bottomless, Sinuhe. I must hasten to dress and paint my face, for a golden goblet awaits me, which tomorrow will adorn my house."

When I would have gathered her into my arms, she slipped from me with a shrill laugh and called out for the servants, who instantly obeyed her summons.

"How came this insufferable mendicant into my house? Throw him out instantly and let him never come within my doors again! If he resists, beat him."

The servants threw me out, numb as I was with wine and fury, and came again to beat me with sticks when I battered at the barred outer door. And when people began to gather about the spot because of my roaring, the servants declared, "This drunkard insulted our mistress, who lives in her own house and is not a woman to be despised."

They beat me until I was senseless and left me to lie in the street, where men spat upon me and dogs made water upon my clothes.

When I came to myself, I was without the will to rise and lay there motionless until the morning. The darkness hid me, and I felt that I should never dare to show my face again. The prince had named me He Who Is Alone and I was assuredly the loneliest mortal in the world that night. But when dawn came, when people began to move about the streets, and merchants displayed their merchandise before their booths, and the oxcarts rumbled by, I rose and left the city and hid myself among the reeds for three days and three nights without food or drink. Heart and body were one hideous wound. If any had spoken to me then, I should have screamed aloud, and I feared for my reason.

3

On the third day I bathed my hands and feet and washed the dried blood from my clothes. Turning my face toward the city, I went to my own house. But the house was no longer mine, and at the door was the signboard of another doctor. I called Kaptah, and he came running, sobbing for joy, and threw his arms about my knees.

"Master—for in my heart you are still my master, no matter who may give me orders. A young man has come here who fancies himself a great physician. He has been trying on your clothes and laughing in his delight. His mother has already been out into the kitchen to throw hot water over my feet and call me rat and dung fly. But your patients miss you—they say his hand is not as light as yours and that he does not understand their maladies as you do."

He babbled on, but his one red-rimmed eye was fixed upon me with a look of horror until I said at last, "Tell me all, Kaptah. My heart is already a stone within my breast and incapable of further pain."

Then, raising his arms to express the deepest woe, he declared, "I would have given my one remaining eye to spare you this grief—but evil is the day, and it is well that you came. Your parents are dead."

"My father Senmut and my mother Kipa," said I, raising my hands as custom demands, and my heart stirred in my breast.

"This day the servants of the law broke down their door, having yesterday given notice of eviction, but found them lying upon the bed no longer breathing. Today, therefore, you must bring them to the House of the Dead, for tomorrow their house is to be pulled down, by order of the new owner."

"Did my parents know why this happened?" I asked and could not look my slave in the face.

"Your father Senmut came to seek you; your mother led him, for he could not see. They were old and frail, and they trembled as they walked. But I did not know where you were. Your father said that it was better that way, and he told how the servants of the law had thrown him out of his house and set seals upon his chests and all his property so that he and his wife owned no more than the rags they had upon them. When he asked the reason for it all, the bailiffs laughed and said that his son Sinuhe had sold house and property and the tomb of his parents for gold to give to a bad woman. After long hesitation your father begged a copper piece of me, that he might dictate a letter to you through some scribe.

"But a new man had come to the house, and just then the mother of this man came for me and beat me with a stick because I was wasting my time in company with a beggar. Perhaps you will believe me when I tell you that I would have given your father the piece of copper, for though I have not yet been able to steal anything from my new lord, still I have copper and silver left of that I stole from you and my previous masters. But when I went back to the street, your parents had already gone. The mother of my new master forbade me to run after them and shut me into the roasting pit for the night so that I might not run away."

"My father left no message?"

"He left no message, lord."

Though my heart was a stone in my breast, my thoughts were serene as birds in cool air. Having reflected for a while, I said to Kaptah, "Give me all the copper and silver you have—give it to me quickly—and it may be that Ammon or some other god will reward you if I cannot. I must carry my parents to the House of Death, and I no longer have any means of paying for the embalming of their bodies."

Kaptah began to weep and lament, but at last he went to a corner of the garden, looking this way and that as a dog does that has buried a bone. Lifting up a stone, he drew forth a rag in which he had knotted his silver and copper, less than two deben, though it was the savings of a lifetime. He gave me all of it, though with many tears; blessed be he, therefore, to all eternity.

I hastened to my father's house, where I found the doors smashed and seals placed upon all that was within. Neighbors were standing in the garden; they raised their hands and shrank from me in horror, uttering no word. In the inner room Senmut and Kipa lay on their bed, their faces as rosy as when they were alive, and on the floor stood a still smoldering brazier in whose fumes they had perished, having tightly closed the shutters and the doors. I swathed their bodies in the shroud, heedless of the seals on it, and sought out a donkey driver, who agreed to carry away the bodies.

With his help I lifted them on to the ass's back and brought them to the House of Death. But at the House of Death they would not take them, for I had not sufficient silver to pay for even the cheapest form of embalming.

Then said I to the corpse washers, "I am Sinuhe, the son of Senmut, and my name is inscribed in the Book of Life, though a hard destiny has deprived me of silver enough to pay for my parents' burial. Therefore, I beseech you in the name of Ammon and of all the gods of Egypt; embalm the bodies of my parents, and I will serve you to the best of my skill for as long as it takes to complete their preservation."

They swore at my stubbornness and cursed me, but at last the pox-eaten foreman accepted Kaptah's money, hitched a hook under my father's chin and slung him into the great bath. He did the same to my mother, throwing her into the same bath. There were thirty of these baths. Every day one of them was filled and one emptied so that the bodies of the poor lay for thirty days steeped in salt and lye to preserve them against death. Nothing more than this was done for them though I did not know it at the time.

I had to return to my father's house with the shroud, which bore upon it the seal of the law. The foreman washer mocked me, saying, "Come back before tomorrow, or we will drag out the bodies of your parents and throw them to the dogs."

By this I saw that he fancied me a liar and no doctor.

I returned stony hearted to my father's house, though the crumbling mud bricks of its walls cried out to me, as did the sycamore in the garden and the pool of my childhood. Therefore, I turned swiftly away when I had put the covering back in its place, but in the doorway I met a scribe who plied his trade at a street corner by the spice dealer's. He said, "Sinuhe, son of Senmut the Just—is it you?"

"It is I."

"Do not run from me, for I have a message to you from your father. He did not find you at your house."

I sank to the ground and covered my head with my hands while the scribe brought out a paper from which he read aloud:

"I Senmut, whose name is inscribed in the Book of Life, and his wife Kipa send this greeting to our son Sinuhe, who in Pharaoh's house was given the name He Who Is Alone. The gods sent you to us; throughout your life you have brought us only joy, and great has been our pride in you. We are grieved for your sake because you have met with reverses, and we have not been able to help you as we should have wished. And we believe that in all you did you were justified and could not help yourself. Do not grieve for us though you must sell our tomb, for assuredly you would not have done this without good reason. But the servants of the law are in haste, and we have no leisure to await our death. Death is as welcome to us now as sleep to the weary—as home to the fugitive. Our life has been long and its joys many, but the greatest joy of all we had of you, Sinuhe— you who came to us from the river when we were already old and solitary.

"Therefore, we bless you. Do not grieve because we have no tomb, for all existence is but vanity, and it is perhaps best that we should vanish into nothingness, without seeking to encounter further perils and hardships on that difficult journey to the Western Land. Remember always that our death was easy and that we blessed you before we went. May all the gods of Egypt protect you from danger, may your heart be shielded from sorrow, and may you find as much joy in your children as we have found in you. Such is the desire of your father Senmut and your mother Kipa."

The stone of my heart was melted and flowed out in tears upon the dust. The scribe said, "Here is the letter. It does not bear your father's seal, nor could he see to write his name, but you will surely believe me when I tell you that I wrote it down word for word at his dictation; moreover, your mother's tears have blurred the characters here and there."

He showed me the paper, but my eyes were blinded by tears and saw nothing. Rolling it up he put it into my hand, and continued, "Your father Senmut was a just man and your mother Kipa a good woman—if rough-tongued at times, as is the way of women. So I wrote this for your father though he had not the smallest present to give me, and I will give the paper to you though it is good paper and could be cleaned and used again."

I reflected for a little and then said, "Nor have I any present for you, most excellent man. Take my shoulder cloth, for it is of good stuff though now dirty and creased. May all the gods of Egypt bless you, and may your body be preserved forever, for even you do not know the merit of the deed you have done."

He took the shoulder cloth and went, waving it above his head and laughing for joy. But I went to the House of Death clad only in a loincloth, like a slave or an ox driver, to serve the corpse washers for thirty days and nights.

4

As a physician I fancied I had seen all there was to see of death and suffering and had hardened myself to foul smells and the handling of boils and festering wounds. On beginning my service in the House of Death, I found I was a child and knew nothing. The poor, indeed, gave us but little trouble. They lay peacefully in their baths in the sharp smell of salt and lye, and I soon learned to handle the hook with which they were moved. But the bodies of those of the better class required more elaborate treatment, and to rinse out the entrails and put them in jars called for a hardened mind. Still more hardened must it be to witness Ammon's plundering of the dead, exceeding that of the living. The price of embalming varied according to means, and the embalmers lied to the kindred of the dead, charging for many costly oils, salves, and preservatives that they vowed they used, though all was but one and the same sesame oil. Only the bodies of the illustrious were prepared with the full measure of skill. The others were filled with a corrosive oil that consumed the viscera, the cavity being then stuffed with reeds steeped in resin. For the poor not even this was done; after their removal from the basin on the thirtieth day they were allowed to dry and were then handed over to their relatives.

The House of Death was supervised by the priests. Nevertheless, the body washers and embalmers stole all that they could lay their hands on and looked upon this as their right. Only those accursed of the gods or criminals fleeing from authority took service as corpse washers, and they could be recognized far off by the smell of salt and lye and cadavers inseparable from their trade so that people avoided them and would not admit them to wine shop or pleasure house.

Since I had volunteered to work among them, the corpse washers supposed me to be like one of themselves, and they hid none of their actions from me. Had I not already witnessed worse things, I should have fled appalled at the way in which they defiled the bodies of even the most distinguished, mutilating them in order to sell to sorceresses the organs these had need of. If there is a Western Land—which for my parents' sake I hope there may be—I believe many of the dead will marvel at their own dismembered condition when they start upon their journey, despite the sums paid to the temple for their burial.

But the greatest rejoicing in the House of Death occurred when the body of a young woman was brought in, no matter whether she were beautiful or plain. She was not immediately thrown into the bath, but for one night was kept as the corpse washers' bedfellow; they squabbled and cast lots as to who should have her first. For these men were so abhorred that not the wretchedest prostitute would submit to them, though they offered her gold. Not even Negresses would have them but held them in great dread.

When once a man had entered the House of Death and taken service there as a corpse washer, he left the place but seldom because of the abhorrence in which his caste was held, and he lived out his life among the carcasses. For the first few days they all seemed to me to be under the curse of the gods, and their talk as they mocked and defiled the bodies outraged my ears. Later I found that among even these there were skilled craftsmen who held their trade in high honor, regarding it as the most important of all, and among the best of whom it was hereditary. Each of them specialized in some branch, as did the physicians in the House of Life, so that one dealt with the head, another the belly, a third the heart, a fourth the lungs, until each part of the body had been treated for its eternal preservation.

Among them was an elderly man named Ramose, whose task was the most difficult of all: he had to detach the brain and draw it out through the nose with pincers, and then swill out the skull with purifying oils. He noted the deftness of my hands with astonishment and began to instruct me so that by the time I had completed half my service in the House of Death he made me his assistant, and life for me became more bearable. I helped him in his work, which was the cleanest and most highly regarded of any in that place, and so great was his influence that others no longer dared frighten me or throw guts and offal upon me. I do not know how it was he had this power, for he never raised his voice.

When I observed the thieving and saw how little was done to preserve the bodies of the poor though the fee was large, I resolved to help my parents by myself and steal for them eternal life. For to my mind, my sin against them was already so hideous that it could be made no blacker by a theft. The one hope and joy of their old age had been that of their own eternal preservation, and in my desire to fulfill this hope I embalmed them, with Ramose's assistance, and bound them in strips of linen, remaining for this purpose forty days and nights in the House of Death. My stay was thus prolonged in order to steal enough for the proper treatment of the bodies. But I had no tomb for them—not so much as a wooden coffin—and could do no more than sew them up together in an oxhide.

When I was ready to leave the House of Death, I became irresolute and my heart thudded in my breast. Ramose, who had noted my skill, invited me to remain as his assistant. I could then have earned and stolen much and lived out my life in the burrows of the House of Death without the knowledge of any of my friends and free from the vexations and sufferings of a normal life. Yet I would not—and who can tell why?

Having washed and purified myself most thoroughly, I stepped out of the House of Death, while the corpse washers shouted curses after me and jeered. They meant no ill by this; it was their way of talking to one another, and the only way they knew. They helped me to carry out the oxhide. Although I had washed, the passers-by gave me a wide berth, holding their noses and making insulting gestures, so steeped was I in the stench of the House of Death. No one would ferry me across the river. I waited until nightfall when, heedless of the watchman, I stole a reed boat and rowed my parents' bodies over to the City of the Dead.

5

The City of the Dead was strictly guarded by night and day, and I could not find one unwatched tomb in which to hide my parents so that they might live forever and enjoy the offerings that were brought for the rich and illustrious dead. So I bore them out into the desert, where the sun burned my back and drew the strength from my limbs till I cried out in the belief that I was dying. But I carried my burden up into the hills along dangerous tracks that only grave robbers dared to use and into the forbidden valley where the Pharaohs lie entombed.

Jackals howled in the night, venomous snakes of the desert hissed at me, and scorpions crawled over the hot rocks. I felt no fear, for my heart was hardened against all danger. Young though I was, I would have greeted death gladly if death had had a mind for me.

My return to sunlight and the world of men had made me feel again the bitterness of my shame, and life had nothing to offer me.

I had not learned then that death avoids a man who desires it, to snatch at him whose heart holds fast to life. Serpents darted from my path, scorpions did me no harm, and the heat of the desert sun did not stifle me. The watchmen of the forbidden valley were blind and deaf and never heard the rattle of stones as I climbed down. If they had seen me, they would have killed me instantly·and left my body to the jackals. So the forbidden valley opened out before me, deathly still and to me more majestic in its desolation than all the enthroned Pharaohs in their lifetime had ever been.

I walked about that valley all night, seeking the tomb of some great Pharaoh. Having come so far I felt that only the best was good enough for my parents. I sought and found a tomb whose Pharaoh had not long stepped aboard Ammon's boat, that the offerings might be fresh and the death ceremonies in his temple on the shore faultlessly performed.

When the moon went down, I dug a hole in the sand beside the doorway, and there I buried them. Far away in the desert jackals were howling. It seemed to me that Anubis was abroad, watching over my father and mother and bearing them company upon their last journey. And I knew that their hearts would not be found wanting in the great scales before Osiris, though they lacked the death books of the priests and the lies learned by rote to which the wealthy pinned their faith. Sweet was the relief in my soul as I scooped the sand over them, for they would live from everlasting to everlasting beside the great Pharaoh and humbly enjoy the good offerings set before him. In the Western Land they would journey in Pharaoh's boat, eat Pharaoh's bread, and drink his wine.

As I was heaping the sand over them, my hand struck against something hard, and I found that I was holding a sacred scarab carved in red stone, with tiny jewels for eyes, and engraved all over with holy signs. I trembled and my tears fell upon the sand, for it seemed to me that I had been given a sign from my parents telling me that they were contented and at peace. This I chose to believe, though I knew that the scarab must have fallen from among the furnishings of Pharaoh's tomb.

The moon had set, and the sky was growing pale. I bowed down in the sand; I raised my hands and said farewell to my father Senmut and my mother Kipa. May their bodies endure forever, and may their lives

97

in the Western Land be full of all delight. For their sake alone I could hope that such a land exists though I no longer believe it.

I regained the banks of the Nile that same day, drank of its waters, and lay down to sleep among the reeds. My feet were cut and torn, my hands bleeding. The desert had blinded me, and my body was scorched and blistered, but I lived, and slumber vanquished pain, for I was very weary.

6

In the morning I awoke to the quacking of ducks among the reeds; Ammon sailed in his golden boat across the sky, and from the far shore there came to my ears the murmur of the city. River craft glided under red sails; washerwomen clapped their boards together, laughing and calling out to each other as they worked. The morning was young and fresh, but my heart was empty and life like ashes in my hands.

I had made what atonement I could, and now there seemed no further purpose or goal to my existence. I wore a ragged loincloth, like a slave; my back was burned and scabby; and I possessed not so much as the smallest copper coin with which to buy food. I knew that if I moved I should soon run into the guards, who would challenge me. I should be unable to answer them, for I believed that the name Sinuhe was accursed and dishonored for all time.

I was brooding upon this when I became aware of some live creature near me, though at the first sight I did not imagine him to be human but rather some specter from an evil dream. There was a hole where the nose should have been, his ears had been cut off, and he was horribly emaciated. When I looked at him more closely, I saw that his hands were large and bony and his body tough and scarred as from burdens or the chafing of ropes.

When he saw that I had observed him, he spoke. "What is that you hold so tightly in your hand?"

I unclenched it and showed him Pharaoh's sacred scarab, which I had found in the sand of the forbidden valley, and he said, "Give it to me that it may bring me luck, for I stand in sore need of it, poor wretch that I am."

I answered, "I, too, am poor and own nothing but this scarab. I shall keep it as a talisman to bring me good fortune."

"Though I am poor and wretched, you shall have a piece of silver for it, though that is too much to give for a bit of colored stone. But I feel compassion for your poverty. Here is the piece of silver."

And indeed he dug a silver piece from his belt. Nevertheless, I became the more firmly resolved to keep the scarab and obsessed with the idea that it would prosper me, and so I told him.

He rejoined wrathfully, "You forget I might have slain you where you lay, for I was watching you for a long time as you slept, wondering what you held so tightly in your hand. I waited till you awoke, but I repent now of not having killed you, since you are so ungrateful."

"I see by your ears and nose that you are a criminal escaped from the quarries. You were welcome to kill me as I slept—it would have been a kindly action, for I am alone and have nowhere to go. But take heed and fly from here, for if the guards see you, they will flog you and hang you head downward from the walls or at the very least take you back whence you came."

"What sort of stranger are you not to know that I need not fear the guards, being a free man and no slave? I could enter the city if I wished, but I do not care to walk the streets, for my face terrifies the children."

"How can he be free who has been condemned to a lifetime of labor in the quarries, for so much I see by your nose and ears?" I sneered, thinking he boasted.

He answered, "Do you then not know that the prince, when he was crowned with the crown of the Upper and Lower Kingdoms, decreed that all bonds should be loosed and all slaves freed from mines and quarries so that those who work there now are free men and are paid for their toil?"

He laughed to himself and went on, "Many a stout fellow now dwells among the reeds and lives on the offerings from rich men's tables in the City of the Dead—for the watchmen fear us, and we fear no one, not even the dead. No man does who has been in the mines; there is no worse fate than to be sent there as a slave, as you well know. Many of us do not fear even the gods, though I believe that prudence is a virtue, and I am a pious man—if I *have* lived for ten years in a mine."

I heard now for the first time that the heir had come to the throne as Amenhotep IV and liberated all slaves and prisoners so that the mines and quarries in the east by the coast were deserted, also those of Sinai. For there was none in Egypt so mad as to work in the mines of his own free will. The royal consort was the Princess of Mitanni, who still played with dolls, and Pharaoh served a new god.

"His god is assuredly a very remarkable one," said the ex-slave, "for he causes Pharaoh to act like a madman. Robbers and murderers now wander freely through the Two Kingdoms, the mines are deserted, and the wealth of Egypt sees no increase. I, indeed, am innocent of evil-doing, being the victim of injustice, but such things have always happened and always will. It is crazy to cut the fetters from hundreds and thousands of criminals in order that one innocent man may be freed. But that is Pharaoh's affair not mine. Let him do my thinking for me."

He had been examining me as he spoke, feeling my arms and the scabs upon my back. He was not afraid of the smell that still hung about me from the House of Death, and it was clear he pitied me because of my youth, for he said, "Your skin is burned; I have oil. Will you let me rub you?"

He rubbed oil into my legs and arms, but swore as he did it.

"By Ammon, I know not why I do this, for of what use are you to me? No one oiled me when I was beaten and wounded and reviled the gods because of the injustice done to me."

I knew well enough that all slaves and convicts protest their innocence, but he was good to me, and I wished to be as much to him. Moreover, I was so lonely I dreaded that he might go and leave me to my desolation. So I said, "Tell me of the injustice that was done you, that I may grieve with you."

"Know then," he began, "that I was once a free man with land to till, a hut, a wife, oxen, and beer in my jar. But I had also a neighbor, an influential man named Anukis—may his body rot! No eye could measure his land; his cattle were as countless as grains of desert sand, and their bellowing was as the ocean's roar—yet he coveted also my little plot of ground. He caused me all manner of vexation, and after every floodtime, when the ground was measured afresh, the boundary stone was moved nearer to my hut, and I lost land. There was nothing I could do; the surveyors listened to him and not to me, because he gave them handsome presents."

The noseless one sighed and rubbed more oil into my back.

"Nevertheless, I might still be living in my hut had the gods not cursed me with a beautiful daughter. I had five sons and three daughters, for the poor breed rapidly. When they were full grown they were a help and a joy to me though one of the boys was stolen by a Syrian merchant when he was small. But my youngest daughter was very fair, and in my madness I was proud of her and did not make her do heavy work, or carry water, or tan her skin by toiling in the fields. It would have been wiser to cut off her hair and rub her face with soot, for my neighbor Anukis saw her and desired her and would have let me keep my field if I had given him my daughter. But this I would not agree to, for I hoped that with her beauty she would get a decent man for a husband—one who would care for me in my old age and show me kindness.

"At last his servants set upon me. I had nothing but my staff, but with that I smote one of them over the head so that he died. Then they cut off my nose and ears and sent me to the mines. My wife and children were sold as slaves, but the youngest one Anukis kept for himself, and when he had enjoyed her, he gave her to his servants. Therefore, I think it was unjust to send me to the mines. When after ten years the King freed me, I hastened home, but my cabin was torn down, alien cattle grazed in my meadows, and my daughter would have nothing to do with me but threw hot water over my feet in the cowmen's shack. I heard that Anukis was dead and that his tomb lies in the City of the Dead near Thebes and has a long inscription on the door. So I came to Thebes to rejoice my heart with what is written there. But I cannot read and no one has read it out to me though I found my way to the tomb by inquiry."

"If you wish it I will read the inscription for you," I said.

"May your body be preserved forever if you will do me this service, for I would know what is written of Anukis before I die."

We went together to the City of the Dead, unchallenged by the guards, and wandered between the rows of tombs until we reached a large one before which meat had been set forth and many sorts of cakes, fruit, and flowers. A sealed wine jar stood there also. The noseless one ate of the offerings, giving some to me, and then bade me read what was written upon the door. And this is what I read to him:

"I Anukis sowed seed and planted fruit trees, and my crops were plentiful because I feared the gods and sacrificed to them one fifth of all my harvest. The Nile greeted me with favor, and no one upon my land went hungry at any time during my life, nor did my neighbors lack food, for I brought water to their fields and fed them with my grain in lean years. I dried the tears of the fatherless and robbed not the widows but forgave them their debts, and my name is blessed from end to end of the land. To him whose ox died, I Anukis gave a new and healthy one. I was scrupulous in removing no landmarks nor in hindering the water from flowing over my neighbor's field. I walked in justice and piety all my days. These things did I Anukis do, that the gods might be gracious to me and lighten my journey to the Western Land."

The noseless one listened reverently, and when I had finished, he shed bitter tears, saying, "I am a poor man and I believe all that is written. Thus I see that Anukis was a pious man, revered in death. Future generations will read the inscription on the door of his tomb and do him honor. But I am miserable and an evildoer and have neither nose nor ears so that my shame is seen of all, and when I die, my body will be cast into the river, and I shall cease to be. Is not everything in this world great vanity?"

He broke the seal of the wine jar and drank. A watchman came up and menaced him with his stick, but my companion said, "Anukis was good to me in his day, and I would honor his memory by eating and drinking at his tomb. But if you lay hands upon me or upon my friend here beside me—a learned man—know that there are many sturdy fellows among the reeds, and some of us have knives and will come upon you by night and slit your throat."

He glared at the guard and was horrible to see. The man looked this way and that and went away. We ate and drank by the tomb of Anukis, and the roof above the offerings gave a cool shade.

He said, "I see now that it would have been better to give up my daughter willingly to Anukis. Perhaps he would have let me keep my hut and given me presents as well, for my daughter was beautiful and a virgin though now she is a worn-out pallet for his servants. I see that the rights of the rich and powerful are the only rights in this world and that the word of the poor man does not reach the ear of Pharaoh."

Raising the jar to his lips he laughed aloud and said, "Your health, most righteous Anukis, and may your body be preserved forever! I have no wish to follow you to the Western Land, where you and your like live merrily, unvexed by the gods. Yet it appears to me but right that you should continue in your loving kindness on earth and share with me the golden goblets and the jewels in your tomb, so this next night I shall visit you when the moon is veiled in cloud."

"What are you saying, Noseless?" I exclaimed in consternation and unthinkingly made the holy sign of Ammon. "You would not become a grave robber, for that is the vilest of all crimes in the eyes of gods and men!"

But Noseless, fired with wine, retorted, "You talk great nonsense in your learned way. Anukis is in my debt, and I, being less merciful than he, will enforce my demands. If you try to stop me, I will break your neck. If you are wise, you will help me since four eyes see better than two, and together we could bear away more from the tomb than I could manage alone. That is if there is no moon."

"I do not wish to be hung head downward from a wall and flogged," said I in a fright. But on reflection I knew that my shame could hardly be deeper though my friends should see me hanging thus, and death of itself held no terrors for me.

That night soldiers rowed across the river from the city to guard the tombs, but the new Pharaoh had not given them the presents that were customary after a coronation. So they murmured among themselves, and when they had drunk wine—for there was much wine among the offerings—they began to break open the tombs and despoil them. No one hindered Noseless and me when we violated the tomb of Anukis, overturned his chest, and took away as many golden cups and valuables as we could carry. At dawn a throng of Syrian merchants had gathered on the river bank to buy up the plunder and take it down the river in their ships. We sold our booty to them, receiving nearly two hundred deben in gold and silver, which we divided between us according to the weight stamped upon the metal. The price we got was but a fraction of the true value of the goods, and the gold was alloyed, but Noseless rejoiced greatly.

"I shall be a rich man, for in truth this trade is more profitable than staggering under burdens at the harbor or carrying water from irrigation ditches to the fields."

But I said, "The pitcher goes once too often to the well." So we parted, and I returned in a merchant's boat to the other shore and Thebes. I bought new clothes and ate and drank at a wine shop, for the smell of the House of Death was leaving me. But all day long there came from the City of the Dead across the river the notes of horns and the clash of arms. Chariots thundered along the paths between the tombs, and Pharaoh's bodyguard pursued the plundering soldiers and miners with spears till their death cries could be heard in Thebes. That evening the wall was lined with bodies hanging by the heels, and order was restored.

7

I slept one night at an inn, and then went to what had been my house and called for Kaptah. He came limping forth, his cheeks swollen with blows. When he saw me, he wept for joy and threw himself at my feet.

"Lord, you have come back though I believed you dead! I thought that if you were alive you would surely return for more silver and copper, for when once a man gives, he must go on giving. But you did not come though I have stolen from my new master as much as ever I did in my life, as you may see by my cheek and by my knee which he kicked yesterday. His mother, the old crocodile—may she rot!—threatens to sell me and I am in great fear. Let us leave this evil house, lord, and fly together."

I hestitated and he misunderstood me.

"I have indeed stolen so much that I can take care of you for a time, and when it is all gone, I can work for you if you will only take me away."

"I came but to pay my debt to you, Kaptah," I told him, and I counted gold and silver into his hand, many times the sum he had given me. "But if you like, I will buy your freedom from your master so that you may go where you will."

"And if you free me, where shall I go since all my life I have been a slave? Without you I am a blind kitten, a lamb forsaken by the ewe. Nor should you waste good gold upon my freedom—why pay for what is already yours?" He blinked his one eye in sly reflection. "A big ship is now fitting out for Smyrna, and we might perhaps venture to sail in her if we first make lavish sacrifice to the gods. It is only a pity that I have not found a powerful enough god since I gave up Ammon, who made such mischief for me."

Remembering the scarab I had found I gave it to Kaptah, saying, "Here is a god who is very powerful, though small. Guard him well, for I believe he will bring us luck; already I have gold in my purse. Clothe yourself as a Syrian, then, and escape if you must, but do not blame me if you are caught as a runaway slave. May the little god help you; we will so save our money to pay our passage to Smyrna. I can no longer look anyone in the face in Thebes or in the whole land of Egypt, so I will go never to return."

"Make no vows, for who knows what tomorrow may bring? A man who has once drunk of Nile waters cannot quench his thirst elsewhere. I know not what evil you have done—you drop your eyes when you speak of it—but you are young and will one day forget. A man's action is as a stone cast into a pool: it makes a splash and rings spread outward, but after a while the waters are still again, and there is no trace of the stone. Human memory is like that water. When sufficient time has passed, everyone will have forgotten you and your deed and you may return—and I hope that by then you will be rich and powerful enough to protect me also."

"I go and shall not return," I said resolutely. Just then Kaptah's mistress called him in a shrill voice. I went to wait for him at the street corner, and after a time he joined me there with a basket. In the basket was a bundle, and he jingled some coppers in his hand.

"The mother of all crocodiles has sent me marketing," he said delightedly. "As usual she gave me too little money, but it will all help, for I believe Smyrna lies a long way from here."

His dress and wig were in the basket. We went down to the shore and he changed his clothes among the reeds. I bought him a handsome staff such as is used by servants and running footmen in the houses of the great. Next we went to the quay where the Syrian ships were berthed and found a big, three-masted vessel, on which a rope the thickness of a man's body ran from stem to stern and from whose masthead fluttered the signal for sailing. The captain was a Syrian, and he was glad to hear that I was a physician, for he respected Egyptian medicine, and many of his crew were sick. The scarab was bringing us luck indeed, for he entered us on the ship's register and would take no money for our passage, which he said we should earn. From that moment Kaptah venerated the scarab as a god, anointing it daily and wrapping it in fine cloth.

We cast off, the slaves began to bend to their oars, and in eighteen days we reached the borders of the Two Kingdoms. In another eighteen days we reached the Delta, and in two more the sea lay before us, and there was no further shore in sight. When the ship began to roll, Kaptah's face turned gray, and he clung to the great rope. Presently he moaned to me that his stomach was rising to his ears and he was dying. The wind freshened, the ship rolled more steeply, and the captain headed her out to sea until we were beyond sight of land. Then I, too, grew uneasy, for I could not understand how he would ever find it again. I no longer laughed at Kaptah because I felt giddy myself and had unpleasant sensations. Presently Kaptah vomited and sank down upon the deck; his face was green, and he uttered never another word. I became alarmed, and when I saw that many other passengers were vomiting and moaning that they would perish and that they were strangely altered in the face, I hastened to the captain and told him that it was clear that the gods had put a curse on his vessel, as a terrible sickness had broken out on board despite my skill. I begged him to put back to land while he could still find any, or as a doctor I could not answer for the consequences. But the captain reassured me, saying we had a fair wind, which would bring us smartly along on our course, and that I should not mock the gods by calling this a storm. He swore by his beard that every passenger would be as spry as a young goat the moment he set foot on dry land and that I need not fear for my dignity as a physician. Yet, when I observed the misery of these travelers, I found it hard to believe him.

Why I myself did not fall so gravely ill I cannot say unless it was that immediately after my birth I had been put to rock on the Nile in a reed boat.

I sought to tend Kaptah and the others, but when I would have touched the passengers, they cursed me. When I offered Kaptah some strengthening food, he turned away his face and snapped his jaws noisily like a hippopotamus, to empty his belly though there was no more in it. But Kaptah had never before turned from food, and I began to think he really would die. I was greatly cast down for I had begun to grow used to his nonsense.

Night fell, and at last I slept, fearful though I was of the rolling of the ship, the terrifying smack of the sails, and the thunder of the seas against the hull. Days passed, but none of the passengers died; some indeed recovered enough to eat and walk about the deck. Only Kaptah lay still and touched no food yet showed some sign of life in that he began once more to pray to the scarab, from which I concluded that he had regained hope of reaching land alive. On the seventh day a coast line appeared, and the captain told me that we had sailed past Joppa and Tyre and would be able to make Smyrna direct, thanks to the favorable winds. How he knew all this I cannot even now make out. On the following day we sighted Smyrna, and the captain made lavish sacrifice in his cabin to the sea gods and others. The sails were lowered, the oarsmen manned their oars, and rowed us into the port of Smyrna.

When we had entered smooth water, Kaptah stood up and swore by his scarab that never again would he set foot aboard a ship.

BOOK 5

The Khabiri

I

I SPEAK now of Syria and of the different cities to which I came, and to this end I should explain first of all that the Red Lands differ from the Black Lands in every particular. There is, for example, no river there like ours; instead, water pours from the sky and wets the ground. Every valley has its hill, and beyond every hill lies another valley. In each of these dwells a distinct people governed by a prince who pays tribute to Pharaoh—or did at the time of which I write. The dress of the people is colorful and expertly woven of wool and it covers them from head to foot, partly, I think, because it is cooler in their country than in Egypt and partly because they think it shameful to expose their bodies except when they relieve themselves in the open— which to an Egyptian is abomination. They wear their hair long and allow their beards to grow and eat always within doors. Their gods, of which each city has its own, demand human sacrifice. From all this it may readily be seen that everything in the Red Land differs from the ways of Egypt.

It is also clear that to those distinguished Egyptians who held resident posts in the Syrian cities, supervising taxation or commanding the garrisons, their task appeared more of a punishment than an honor. They yearned for the banks of the Nile—all but a few, that is, who had succumbed to the alien ways. These had altered the style of their garments and their thoughts and made sacrifice to strange gods. Moreover, the constant intrigues among the inhabitants, the cheating and roguery of the taxpayers, and the squabbles between rival princes embittered the lives of the Egyptian officials.

I lived in Smyrna for two years during which I learned the Babylonian language, both spoken and written; for I was told that a man with this knowledge could make himself understood among educated people throughout the known world. The written characters, as is well known, are imprinted on clay with a sharp stylus, and all correspondence between kings is so conducted. Why this is so I cannot tell unless it be that paper will burn but a clay tablet endures forever as a testimony to the speed with which rulers forget their pacts and treaties.

Syria differs from Egypt also in that the physician must seek out his patients, who, instead of coming to him, trust to their gods to send him to them. Moreover, they give their presents before and not after they have been cured. This profits the doctor, for patients tend to be forgetful once they are well again.

It was my intention to follow my calling here quite unpretentiously, but Kaptah was of another mind. He wished me to lay out all I had in fine clothes and to hire criers who would make known my fame in every public place. These were to announce also that I did not visit patients but that they must come to me, and Kaptah forbade me to receive any who did not bring at least one gold piece with them as a present. I told him this was folly in a city where no one knew me and where the customs differed from those of the Black Land, but Kaptah stood his ground. I could do nothing with him, for when once he got an idea into his head, he was as stubborn as a donkey.

He persuaded me also to visit those doctors who were held in highest repute and to say to them:

"I am Sinuhe, an Egyptian physician to whom the new Pharaoh gave the name of He Who Is Alone, and I am a man of renown in my own country. I restore the dead to life and bring back sight to the blind if my god wills it—for I have a small but powerful god whom I carry with me in my traveling chest. Knowledge differs from one place to another, however, nor are diseases everywhere the same. For this reason I have come to your city to study maladies and to cure them and to profit by your learning and wisdom.

"I do not mean in any way to encroach upon your practice, for who am I to compete with you? I propose, therefore, that you send to me such patients as are under your god's displeasure so that you cannot cure them, and especially those requiring treatment with the knife—for the knife you do not use—that I may see whether my god will bring them healing. And should such a patient be cured I will give you half of what he gives me, for I have not come here for gold but for knowledge. Should I fail to cure him, I will take nothing from him at all but send him back to you with his gift."

The physicians whom I met in the streets and market places visiting their patients and to whom I spoke swung their cloaks and fingered their beards and said:

"You are young, but truly your god has blessed you with wisdom, for your words are agreeable to our ears. What you say of gold and of presents is wise as is also your allusion to the knife. For we never use knives to heal the sick, a man who comes under the knife being more certain of death than he who does not. One thing only we desire of you, and that is that you will effect no cures by sorcery, for our own witchcraft is very powerful, and in that branch there is too much competition both in Smyrna and in the other cities along the coast."

This was true, for there were many illiterate men haunting the streets who undertook to heal the sick by means of magic and lived fatly in the homes of the credulous until their patients either recovered or died.

In this way sick people with whom others had failed came to me, and I treated them, but those I could not cure I sent back to the physicians of Smyrna. From Ammon's temple I brought sacred fire to my house that I might carry out the prescribed purification and so venture to use the knife and to perform operations at which the physicians fingered their beards and marveled greatly. I was fortunate enough to give a blind man back his sight, although both physicians and sorcerers had smeared clay mixed with spittle upon his eyelids to no effect. I treated him with the needle, as the Egyptian manner is, thereby greatly enhancing my reputation. However, after some time the man lost his sight again, for the needle cure is but temporary.

The merchants and wealthy men of Smyrna led an idle and luxurious life; they were fatter than the Egyptians and suffered from breathlessness and stomach troubles. I used the knife on them till they bled like pigs. When my medical stores were exhausted, I found good use for my knowledge in the matter of gathering herbs upon the right days and under favorable aspects of moon and stars, for in this the men of Smyrna had little science, and I dared not trust to their remedies. To the obese I gave relief from their abdominal pains and saved them from suffocation by means of medicines I sold to them at prices graded according to their means. I quarreled with none but gave presents to the doctors and city authorities, while Kaptah spread a good report of me and gave food to beggars and storytellers that they might cry my praises in street and market and preserve my name from oblivion.

I earned a quantity of gold. All that I didn't spend or give away I invested with the merchants of Smyrna, who sent ships to Egypt, to the islands in the sea, and to the land of Hatti, so that I had a share in many vessels—a hundredth or a five-hundredth, according to my means at the time. Some ships were never seen again, but most of them returned, and my stakes in them—now doubled or tripled—were entered in the trading books. This was the custom in Smyrna, though unknown in Egypt. Even the poor speculated in this way and either increased their funds or became still more impoverished; ten or twenty of them would pool their copper pieces to buy a thousandth share in a vessel or her cargo. Thus I never had to keep gold in my house as a lure for robbers. Neither was I obliged to carry it with me when I traveled to other cities, such as Byblos and Sidon, in the course of my work, for then the merchant gave me a clay tablet to be presented at the business houses of those cities, by which I could obtain money from them whenever I required it.

Thus all went well with me. I prospered, and Kaptah grew fat in his expensive new clothes and anointed himself with fine oils. Indeed he became insolent, and I was compelled to thrash him. But why everything favored me so I cannot say.

2

Nevertheless, I continued in loneliness, and life gave me no delight. I even wearied of wine, for it never cheered me but turned my face as black as soot so that when I had drunk I desired only to die. Therefore, I sought ever to increase my knowledge that no moment of the day should find me idle—for in idleness I fretted over myself and my deeds—and at night I slept like the dead.

I acquainted myself with the gods of Smyrna to learn whether they might hold some hidden truth for me. Like all else, these gods differ from those of Egypt. Their great god was Baal, a cruel god who exacted human blood in return for his favor and whose priests were made eunuchs. He also required children. Moreover, the sea was greedy for sacrifice so that merchants and those in authority must be forever seeking new victims. No crippled slave was ever to be seen, and the poor were threatened with savage punishment for the least offense. Thus a poor man who stole a fish to feed his family was dismembered as a sacrifice on the altar of Baal.

Their female divinity was Astarte, also called Ishtar, like the Ishtar of Nineveh. She had many breasts and was robed every day afresh in jewels and thin garments, being served by women who for some reason were known as the virgins of the temple, though that they were not. On the contrary, they were there to be enjoyed—a mission regarded with favor by the goddess—and the more exquisite the enjoyment, the more gold and silver was offered to the temple by the client.

But the merchants of Smyrna guarded their own women with great strictness, shutting them up at home and clothing them from head to foot in thick garments lest they tempt the stranger. The men, however, visited the temple for the sake of variety and to win divine approval. Thus in Smyrna there were no pleasure houses like those of Egypt. If the temple girls were not to a man's liking, he had to take a wife or buy himself a slave girl. Slave girls were for sale every day, for ships were continually coming into port with women and children on board of every size and color, both plump and thin, to suit all tastes. But the crippled and unfit were purchased cheaply for sacrifice to Baal on behalf of the city council, who would then laugh and slap their chests and commend themselves for their cunning in thus deceiving their god.

I, too, made sacrifice to Baal since he was the god of the city and it was prudent to seek his favor. Being an Egyptian, I bought no human sacrifices for him; I gave him gold. Sometimes I visited Astarte's temple, which opened in the evenings, to listen to music and watch the temple women—whom I will not call maidens—dancing voluptuous dances to the glory of their goddess. Since it was the custom I lay with them, and I marveled at the practices they taught me of which I had known nothing. But I was not cheered and did all from curiosity. When they had taught me what they had to impart, I wearied of them and no longer visited their temple. To my mind there were no accomplishments so monotonous as theirs.

But Kaptah shook his head in concern for me, for my face was aging, the furrows between my brows were deepening, and my heart was sealed. His wish was that I should have a slave girl to beguile my leisure moments. Since he kept house and handled my money, he bought a girl for me who was to his own taste. He washed, dressed, and anointed her, and presented her to me one evening when, tired after the day's work, I desired only to go to bed in peace.

This girl was from the islands in the sea; she was plump, her skin white, her teeth faultless, and her eyes were round and gentle like the eyes of a heifer. She gazed at me in veneration and showed fear of the strange city to which she had been brought. Kaptah extolled her charms with the greatest earnestness, and to please him I took her. Yet, though I did my best to escape from my loneliness, my heart was not gladdened, and I could not bring myself to call her my sister.

In showing her kindness I erred, for it made her arrogant, and she disturbed me in my interviews with patients. She ate a great deal and grew fat and was forever demanding jewels and new clothes. Also she dogged my footsteps in a continual desire to take pleasure with me.

It was to no purpose that I made journeys inland and to the cities along the coast. On my return she was the first to greet me, with tears and persecution. I beat her, but in vain; then she grew hotter than before, and life in my house became intolerable.

But the scarab brought me good fortune, for one day King Aziru, the ruler of the inland province of Amurru, came to me. I doctored his teeth, making him one tooth of ivory to replace one that had been knocked out in battle and coating other damaged ones with gold. While he remained in the city, conferring with the authorities on administrative business, he visited me every day. He met my slave girl, whom I called Keftiu after the islands in the sea, being unable to pronounce her heathenish name, and he found delight in her. This Aziru was white skinned and as strong as a bull. His beard was blue black and glossy, and his eyes held a bold gleam so that Keftiu began to look upon him with desire—for women are ever captivated by what is new. He admired her plumpness above all, and her garments, which she wore in the Greek manner, greatly inflamed him. Though they covered her throat, they left her breast bare, and he was accustomed to seeing women veiled from head to foot.

At length he was unable to restrain his desire, and sighing deeply, he said to me, "Truly you are my friend, Sinuhe the Egyptian, and you have mended my teeth and caused my mouth to glisten with gold whenever I open it, which will greatly enhance my dignity in the land of Amurru. For this I will make you such gifts as shall cause you to raise your hands in wonder. Nevertheless, I am forced to pain you against my will.

"Ever since I laid eyes upon the woman in your house, she has pleased me, and I can no longer withstand my desire for her; it tears at me like a wildcat and not all your arts can heal that sickness. I have never seen her like and can well fancy your fondness for her when she warms your bed at night.

"Yet I desire her of you, that I may make her my wife among my other wives and release her from slavery. I tell you this openly, for you are a just man, and I will pay you whatever you ask. But I tell you openly also that if you will not give her up of your free will, I will come and take her by force and carry her off to my country, where you could never find her even if you dared to seek."

At these words of his I raised my hands in delight, but Kaptah who had overheard tore his hair and lamented, "Evil is the day, and better were it that my master had never been born than that you should now take from him the only woman in whom he has found pleasure. Nor

114

can her loss be made good, for to my lord she is dearer than all the gold in the world—all the jewels, all the incense—and she is fairer than the full moon, and her belly is round and white as a heap of wheat—though you have not yet seen it—and her breasts are like melons, which your own eyes can tell you."

Thus he babbled on, for since coming to Smyrna, he had learned the ways of merchants and hoped for a good price though both he and I desired nothing so much as to be rid of the girl. When Keftiu heard him, she wept also, saying that she would never forsake me—but as she wept she peeped admiringly between her fingers at the prince and his curly beard.

I raised my hands, and having quieted them, I assumed a grave expression.

"Aziru, King of Amurru and my friend! Truly this woman is dear to my heart, and I call her my sister, but your friendship is dearer to me than anything else. In token of this friendship I will give her to you without payment, and I beg you to accept of her and do with her all that the wildcat within you desires—for if I do not deceive myself, her heart is inclined toward you, and she will be content, for in her body also lurk many wildcats."

Aziru cried aloud for joy.

"Ah, Sinuhe, Egyptian though you be—and all evil comes out of Egypt—from this day you are my brother and my friend; throughout the land of Amurru your name shall be blessed; as my guest you shall sit at my right hand above all others, though they be kings. This I swear!"

He laughed so that his teeth flashed. Then as he looked at Keftiu, who had ceased weeping, his face changed. With glowing eyes he gazed at her, seized her by the arms so that the melons swayed, and swung her into his carrying chair without noticing her weight. So he departed, and neither I nor anyone else in Smyrna saw him for a while, for he shut himself up in his lodgings for three days and three nights. Kaptah and I rejoiced at having rid ourselves of the baggage, though he rebuked me for demanding nothing in exchange when Aziru would have given me whatever I asked.

But I replied, "By giving him this girl, I have secured his friendship. No one knows what tomorrow may bring. Though the land of Amurru is small and insignificant—being no more than grazing land for asses and sheep—yet a king's friendship is the friendship of a king, and its worth may prove more than gold."

Kaptah shook his head, but he smeared the scarab with myrrh and placed fresh dung before it in thanksgiving for being quit of Keftiu.

Before Aziru returned to his own country he called on me, and bowing to the ground he said, "I offer you nothing, Sinuhe, for you have given me that which cannot be requited with gifts. The girl is even more entrancing than I could have believed; her eyes are like bottomless wells, and I do not weary of her though she has pressed out my seed as oil is pressed from olives. To be frank with you, my country is not a wealthy one, and I can acquire gold in no other way than by taxing the merchants who travel through it or by making war on my neighbors—and then the Egyptians are over me like horseflies and often I lose more than I gain. So I cannot make you such gifts as your action merits. But I promise that whenever you come to me and whatever you ask of me I will give it you if it be in my power to do so—as long as you do not ask me either for this woman or for horses, for I have few of them and need them for my chariots. And if any man offend you, send word to me and my men shall slay him, wherever he may be. No one shall come to hear of it, and your name will not be mentioned in the affair. So great is my friendship for you."

Then he embraced me in the Syrian manner. I saw that he honored and admired me, for he took the gold chain from his neck and hung it about mine though his deep sigh as he did so told me how great was this sacrifice. Therefore, I took from my own neck a gold chain I had been given by the richest shipowner in Smyrna for saving his wife's life during a difficult labor, and I hung it about his neck. He lost nothing by the exchange, and this greatly pleased him. And so we parted.

3

Now that I was free of the woman my heart was as light as a bird. My eyes longed to see new things, and I was filled with restlessness and a desire to be out of Smyrna. Spring had come again. The earth was fresh and green; leaves budded on the trees; there was a cooing of doves and frogs croaked in the pools. In the harbor ships were being fitted out for long voyages. With the spring also came word that the Khabiri had swarmed in from the desert and were ravaging the Syrian borders from the south to the north, burning villages and besieging cities. But Pharaoh's armies came too, through the desert of Sinai from Tanis, and were giving battle to the Khabiri. They captured the chiefs and drove the enemy back into the desert. It happened every spring and had always happened. This time, however, the citizens of Smyrna were uneasy, for the city of Katna, garrisoned by Egyptian troops, had been plundered, the king slain, and all the Egyptians put to the sword without mercy shown to women or children and without any prisoners being taken and held for ransom. Such a thing had not been known within living memory, for the Khabiri were wont to avoid the fortified towns.

War had broken out in Syria, and I had never seen war. I set forth to join Pharaoh's forces and see whether it held some hidden truth for me and also to study the wounds inflicted by war clubs and other weapons. But above all I went because the commander of the troops was Horemheb, and in my loneliness I longed to see again the face of a friend and hear his voice. Having taken ship along the coast, I made my way inland with the supply column, among the ox-drawn sleds of grain and the donkeys laden with jars of oil and wine and sacks of onions. We came to a small city set on a hill and girdled by a wall; the name of it was Jerusalem. A small Egyptian garrison was stationed here, and here also Horemheb had set up his headquarters. But the rumors that had reached Smyrna greatly exaggerated the size of his force, which comprised but one squadron of chariots and a couple of thousand archers and spearmen, while the Khabiri hordes were said to be as the sands of the desert.

Horemheb received me in a dirty mud hut, with the words, "I knew a Sinuhe once. He, too, was a doctor and my friend."

He surveyed me, puzzled by the Syrian cloak I had taken to wearing. Like him I had aged, and my face had altered, but he knew me again and laughed, raising his gold-braided whip of office in salute.

"By Ammon, it is Sinuhe! I thought you were dead." He drove out his staff officers and the scribes with their maps and papers and ordered in wine. "Marvelous are the ways of Ammon that we should meet again here in the Red Land, in this filthy, miserable town."

At his words my heart stirred in my breast, and I knew that I had missed him. I told him as much as I thought fit of my life and adventures, and he said, "Come with us and share the honors of war! I mean to give these lousy Khabiri such a scalding that they will never forget me and will curse the day they were born. I was a green enough lad when we first met; you were a man of the world and gave me good counsel. I have learned—I have learned—and I carry a golden whip in my hand, as you see. But I won it by degrading service in Pharaoh's bodyguard, rounding up the robbers and convicts whom in his madness he had freed from the mines. Trouble enough they gave us before they were all destroyed.

117

"When I heard that the Khabiri were attacking, I asked Pharaoh to give me troops to repel them. No other senior officer cared to compete with me for command, for wealth and honors shower down more profusely in Pharaoh's neighborhood than they do in the desert—moreover, the Khabiri have sharp spears and their war cries are most horrible, as I have good reason to know. But at last I was able to gain experience and exercise my troops in real battle. However, Pharaoh's one concern is that I should build a temple here in Jerusalem to his new god and drive out the Khabiri without bloodshed!"

Horemheb burst out laughing and slapped his leg with his whip, and I laughed with him. Then he fell silent, and after another pull at the wine he went on:

"To be frank, Sinuhe, I have changed somewhat since we last met, as a man must who lives in Pharaoh's presence, whether he will or no. He disturbs me, for he thinks deeply—and talks—about his god, who differs from all other gods. I used often to feel as if a swarm of ants were loose in my brain. I could not sleep at night without wine and a woman to clear my head, so strange is this divinity of his. The god is without form though he is everywhere at once; his image is a circle and has hands, with which he blesses all that he has made; and slave and lord are equal in his sight. Tell me, Sinuhe, is this not the raving of a sick man? I can only think that he was bitten by a rabid ape when he was small—for who but a madman could fancy the Khabiri may be routed without bloodshed?"

He drank again.

"Horus is my god, and I have nothing against Ammon, either. But I can see that Ammon has grown too powerful, and the new god has set himself up in opposition to strengthen Pharaoh's sovereignty. That is what the Queen Mother herself said to me, and it was echoed by Eie, the priest who now carries the crook upon the King's right hand. With the help of Aton they intend to overthrow Ammon or at least to limit his power, for it is not fitting that Ammon's priests should rule Egypt over the head of Pharaoh. That is sound statesmanship, and as a warrior I can well understand that a new god is indispensable. If Pharaoh were content merely to raise temples to him and fee priests into his service, I should have nothing to complain of. But Pharaoh thinks and talks too much about him. Whatever the occasion, sooner or later he brings the conversation round to him, by which he makes those about him crazier than himself. He says that he lives by truth—but truth is like a sharp knife in the hands of a child; a knife should be carried in its sheath and used only when need occurs. So it is with truth, and for no one is truth more dangerous than for the ruler."

He took another draught of wine.

"I thank my falcon that I was able to leave Thebes, for the city is seething like a nest of serpents because of it, and I do not wish to involve myself in squabbles between gods. The priests of Ammon are already spreading pretty stories about Pharaoh's origins and fomenting sedition against the new god. His marriage also has caused indignation, for the Princess of Mitanni, who used to play with dolls, died suddenly, and Pharaoh has raised up Nefertiti, the daughter of the priest, to be his consort. Certainly this Nefertiti is beautiful and dresses well, but she is very willful and her father's daughter in everything."

"How did the Princess of Mitanni die?" I asked, for I had seen the scared, wide-eyed child gazing out at Thebes as she was carried, decked out and adorned like an image, along the Avenue of Rams to the temple.

"The physicians say she could not stand the climate," he laughed. "And that is a barefaced lie, for it is common knowledge that no country has so healthy a climate as Egypt. But you yourself know that the death rate among the royal children is high—higher than in the poor quarter though it seems hard to believe. It is wisest to name no names, but I would halt my chariot before Eie the priest's house if I dared."

After this we lay down in the tent to sleep.

In the morning I was roused by the sound of horns and saw the soldiers falling in by companies, while sergeants ran up and down the ranks yelling at them, buffeting them, and striking them with their whips. When all were paraded, Horemheb stepped out from the dirty hut with his golden whip in his hand, and a servant held an umbrella over his head and kept the flies off him with a fly whisk while he addressed the soldiers:

"Soldiers of Egypt! This day I lead you into battle, for my scouts report that the Khabiri are encamped beyond the hills. What their numbers are I cannot say, for these scouts took to their heels in a fright and never stayed to count them. I hope there will be enough to put an end to all of you so that I am spared the sight of your miserable faces and can go back to Egypt to raise an army of real men who love glory and the spoils of war."

He glared savagely at the troops, and the glare struck home: not one among them dared move an eyelash.

"I shall lead you into battle, and you are to know—every one of you —that I go in the forefront and shall not stay to see which if any of you follow. For I am the son of Horus; the falcon flies before me; and I mean to vanquish the Khabiri if I have to do it alone. Nevertheless, I tell you now that this evening my whip will drip blood, for with my own hands I will flog any who do not follow me. And I tell you that my whip bites deeper than the spears of Khabiri, which are of poor copper and brittle. There is nothing terrible about the Khabiri save their voice, which is indeed appalling. If any of you quail at the sound of shrieks, stop your ears with clay. Do not go into battle whining like old women—at least feign manhood: you wear loincloths, not skirts. If you defeat the Khabiri, you may share out their cattle among you and their other possessions, for they have collected much booty in the cities they have sacked. You may also divide their women among you; I think you will enjoy a tumble with them tonight, for the Khabiri women are comely and fiery, and they love bold warriors."

Horemheb paused and surveyed his men, who with one accord raised a great shout, struck their shields with their spears, and brandished their bows. He smiled and with a flick of his whip went on:

"I see that you burn for your thrashing, but first we are to consecrate a temple to Pharaoh's new god Aton. He is by nature an unwarlike god, and I do not think you will take much delight in him. Therefore, the main force may set out upon their march while the reserves stay behind to consecrate the temple and assure themselves of Pharaoh's favor toward us."

Once more the troops acclaimed him, then began to stream from the city in disorder, each company following its own standard, borne upon a pole. These emblems were lions' tails and hawks and crocodile heads, which went before them into battle. The light chariots drove on ahead to clear the road. But those officers who held the highest command remained behind with the reserves and followed Horemheb to the temple, which stood on a rise at the outskirts of the city. The temple was small and built of timber. It had been hastily knocked together and daubed with mud. It was unlike other temples, being open in the middle, where the altar stood. No god was to be seen so that the puzzled soldiers looked about to find him.

Horemheb told them, "The god is round and is like the sun's disk, so look into the sky if your eyes can endure the brightness. He holds out his hands over you in benediction, though my mind misgives me that today after your march his fingers upon your backs will feel like red-hot needles."

The soldiers murmured that Pharaoh's god was too distant. They desired one before whom they might prostrate themselves and whom they might touch with their hands if they dared. But they fell silent as the priest stepped forward, a slim youth with unshaven head, who bore a white cloth over his shoulder. His eyes were clear and eager, and upon the altar he offered up spring flowers and oil and wine, which made the soldiers laugh aloud. He also sang a hymn to Aton that was said to have been composed by Pharaoh. It was very long and monotonous, and the men listened to it with open mouths and very little comprehension.

> *"Most beautiful art thou upon the horizon,*
> *Living Aton, source of all things living!*
> *When thou arisest in the eastern sky*
> *All lands are filled with thy glory.*
> *Fair art thou, great art thou, radiant above the world.*
> *Thy beams embrace all lands and them hast thou created,*
> *And they are bound together with the rays of thy love.*
> *Far art thou, yet thy rays touch the ground;*
> *Exalted art thou; yet the soles of thy feet move upon the dust."*

The priest sang of darkness, of lions that slink from their lairs by night, and of serpents, and many of those who listened were afraid. He sang of the day's brightness and declared that when the birds spread their wings in the morning it was in adoration of Aton. He declared also that this new god quickened the babe in the womb and gave fertility to the seed of man. Listening to him, one might fancy that there was not one tiny thing in the world with which Aton did not concern himself, nor could even a chick crack its shell and cheep without Aton's help. The priest ended:

> *"Thou alone dwellest in my heart*
> *And no man knoweth thee but the King thy son.*
> *Thou sharest thy thought with him,*
> *Thou anointest him with thy power.*
> *The world lieth between thy hands as thou didst create it;*
> *By thy light do men live*
> *And if thou veil from them thy countenance they perish.*
> *Thou art life and men live through thee.*
> *All eyes are turned toward thy glory*
> *Until the hour of thy setting,*
> *All labor ceaseth*
> *When thou declinest in the West.*
> *Since thy creation of the world*

Thou has prepared it for the coming of thy son:
For him who was born of thee,
The King who liveth by the truth,
Lord of both Kingdoms, the Son of Ra,
Who liveth by the truth.
For the Lord of the Crowns didst thou create the world
And for his great consort, his beloved,
Queen of the Two Kingdoms, Nefertiti,
Who shall live and bloom from everlasting to everlasting!"

The soldiers listened and wiggled their toes in the sand. When at last the song came to an end, they shouted in relief and to the honor of Pharaoh, for all that they grasped of the hymn was the intention to praise Pharaoh and hail him as the son of the god, which was right and fitting: so it had ever been and ever would be. Horemheb gave the priest leave to go, and the young man, delighted by the acclamation of the troops, went away to write an account of the event to Pharaoh.

4

The men marched away, followed by ox sleds and pack asses. Horemheb dashed ahead in his chariot, while the senior officers proceeded in their chairs, complaining of the heat. I was content to sit on the back of a donkey like my friend the quartermaster, and I took with me my medical chest of which I expected to make good use.

The column marched until evening with only a brief rest during which the men were allowed to eat and drink. An ever increasing number grew footsore and dropped out by the roadside, unable to rise despite the kicks and whippings of the sergeants. The men swore and sang by turns. With the lengthening of the shadows came the whine of arrows from the rocks bordering the road and now and then a cry from the ranks, where a man clutched his shoulder, in which an arrow was sticking, or fell headlong upon the road. Horemheb did not stay to pick off the snipers but pressed onward until the troops were moving at a jog trot. The light chariots cleared the way ahead, and soon we saw lying along the roadside the bodies of Khabiri in ragged cloaks, their mouths and eyes crawling with flies. Some of our men fell out to turn these bodies over in search of plunder, but there was nothing left to take.

The quartermaster sweated on his donkey and bade me take his last greeting to his wife and children, for he felt that this was to be his last day. He told me where in Thebes his wife was to be found and begged me to see to it that no one looted his corpse—provided we were not all dead by evening, he added, with a gloomy shake of the head.

At last there opened out before us the wide plain on which the Khabiri were encamped. Horemheb gave order for the sounding of horns and disposed his troops for attack, spearmen in the center and bowmen on either flank. The chariots, save for a few of the heavier ones, he dispatched to play a certain part elsewhere, and they raced off at such speed that the dust whirled up and hid them. From the valleys beyond the hills rose the smoke from burning villages. The Khabiri on the plain seemed numberless, and their howls and yells filled the air as they advanced upon us, shields and spear points glinting menace in the sunlight.

Horemheb shouted with a loud voice, "Stiffen your knees, you toads, for the fighters among them are few, and what you see are cattle and women and children—all to be yours before nightfall. In their cooking pots hot food awaits you. Away with you now, that we may eat, for already I am as famished as a crocodile!"

But the Khabiri host rolled nearer, far outnumbering ours. Their spears looked sharp in the sunlight, and battle held no charms for me. The ranks of our spearmen wavered, and they looked this way and that as I did. The sergeants slashed with their whips and swore—and doubtless the men were too weary to turn and fly, for they stiffened their ranks, and the bowmen twanged nervously at their bowstrings, awaiting the signal.

When the Khabiri had drawn near, they uttered their war cry, a howl so horrible that the blood left my head and my legs gave beneath me. At that instant they charged, letting fly with their arrows as they ran. The sound of the arrows was bzzzt, bzzzt, like the buzzing of flies. I know of no more maddening noise than the singing of arrows past the ear. Yet I was heartened to see how little damage they did, for they either flew over our heads or were warded off by the shields.

Now Horemheb shouted, "Follow me, you scum!" His charioteers gave the horses their heads and away they went after him; the bowmen let fly their arrows as one man, while the spearmen charged after the chariots. A cry burst from all throats—a yell more terrifying than the howl of the Khabiri—for each man was shrieking for himself to drown his terror. I heard myself bellowing also at the full pitch of my lungs and found therein great relief.

The chariots thundered in among the attacking Khabiri, and away in the forefront, above the swirling dust and thrusting spears, glittered the plumed helmet of Horemheb. In the rear of the chariots charged the spearmen led by their battle standards—their lions' tails and hawks—while the bowmen scattered about the plain discharging volleys into the harassed enemy. From this moment all was one hideous, clashing, thundering, shrieking, howling confusion. Arrows whistled past my ears; my donkey shied and bolted into the thick of the struggle, and I yelled and kicked in my extremity but could not hold him. The Khabiri fought resolutely and without fear, and those of them who were trampled underfoot by the horses still lunged with their spears at those who charged over them, and many an Egyptian was slain as he stooped to lop off the hand of his victim in token of triumph. The reek of blood outdid the reek of sweating soldiers, and ravens circled down from the sky in ever growing flocks.

Suddenly the Khabiri uttered a shriek of rage and set off in full retreat, for they saw that those chariots which had been sent round the plain had entered their camp; their women were being attacked and the cattle driven off. This sight they could not endure but ran to the rescue, a move that was their undoing. The chariots rounded upon them and scattered them, and the remainder were dealt with by the spearmen and archers. When the sun had set, the plain was full of handless corpses, the camp was in flames, and from every quarter came the bellowing of frantic cattle.

In the delirium of victory our men prolonged the massacre, plunging their spears into all they saw, slaying men who had already laid down their arms, braining children with their clubs, and madly shooting arrows into the stampeding livestock until Horemheb ordered the horns to be sounded; whereupon officers and subordinates came to their senses and rounded up the rabble with their whips. But my mad donkey still galloped about the battlefield, bumping and jolting me upon his back like a sack of flour till I hardly knew whether I was alive or dead. The soldiers laughed at me and mocked me until at last one of them smote the donkey on the muzzle with the butt of his spear, bringing the beast to a halt so that I could climb down. Thenceforward I was known among them as the Son of the Wild Ass.

The prisoners were driven together into enclosures, the weapons stacked, and herdsmen sent forth to round up the cattle. So numerous were the Khabiri that many of them had made good their escape, but

Horemheb surmised that they would run all night and be in no great haste to return. In the light of the blazing tents and loads of forage the sacred chest was brought forth and placed before Horemheb. He opened it and lifted out Sekhmet, the Lion-headed, whose carven breast swelled proudly in the firelight. The soldiers, in high jubilation, sprinkled her with drops of the blood that was flowing from their wounds and cast down before her the severed hands in token of conquest. These formed a great heap, and some men brought to it as many as four and five. Horemheb conferred chains and bracelets upon them and honored the most valiant with promotion. He was dusty and bloodstained, and his golden whip was dripping, but his eyes smiled upon his warriors as he hailed them as his own jolly ruffians and bruisers.

There was much work for me, as the spears and clubs of the Khabiri inflicted horrible wounds. I labored in the light of the burning tents, and the cries of the wounded mingled with those of the women as they were dragged away by the soldiers, who cast lots for them. I washed and stitched together gaping wounds, thrust entrails back into gashed bellies, and replaced torn flaps of scalp. To those whose death was certain I gave beer and narcotics that they might pass away in peace during the night.

I attended also some of the Khabiri whose injuries had prevented flight, stitching and dressing their wounds. For what reason I did this I hardly know unless it was that I though Horemheb would get a better price for them when he sold them as slaves if I healed them first. But many of them cared nothing for my help and rather tore open their wounds afresh when they heard the crying of their children and the lamentations of their ravished women. They curled up their legs, drew their garments over their heads, and bled to death.

I watched them and felt less proud of the victory than before. They were but poor starving desert folk, tempted by the cattle and grain of the valleys to make these desperate raids into Syria. They were gaunt and suffered often from eye diseases. Though they were valiant and terrifying in war and left behind them a trail of burning villages, yet I could not but feel compassion when I saw them draw their ragged garments over their heads to die.

On the following day I met Horemheb and begged him to set up a guarded camp where the soldiers who had been most gravely wounded could recover since if they were taken straight to Jerusalem they would be sure to perish on the way.

Horemheb thanked me for my help, and said, "I never credited you

125

with such valor as you displayed yesterday, riding into the thick of battle on your mad donkey. You cannot have known that in war the physician's task does not begin until the battle is over. I have heard the men call you the Son of the Wild Ass, and if you wish it, I will take you into battle in my own chariot. Good fortune must surely attend you since you are still alive, though you carried neither spear nor club."

"Your men praise your name and swear to follow wherever you lead them," I said, to flatter him. "But how is it that you are not even wounded after charging alone into the thick of the spears? Are you protected by some powerful magic, or how comes it that you feel no fear?"

"I know that I am destined to perform great deeds, though how I know this I cannot tell you. A warrior either has good fortune on his side or he has not, and I have had it since the falcon led me to Pharaoh. It is true that my falcon did not love the palace and flew away never to return. But as we were marching across the desert of Sinai, enduring great hunger and greater thirst—for I suffered with my men to learn what they were feeling and so have command over them—I saw in some valley a burning bush. It was of living fire shaped like some big bush or tree, and it was not consumed but burned night and day. The earth round about it had a smell that went to my head and inspired me with courage. I saw it as I was driving ahead of my troops to hunt the wild beasts of the desert, and it was seen by no other save my charioteer, who can bear witness to the apparition. But from that moment I have known that no spear or arrow or war club can touch me before my appointed time."

I believed his account and was filled with awe, for he had no reason to invent such a tale for my amusement. Indeed, I hardly think he could have done so, being a man who believed only in what he could touch with his hands.

On the third day Horemheb divided his troops, sending some back to Jerusalem with the plunder—for not many traders came to the battlefield itself after our slaves, cooking pots, and grain—and another party he sent to herd the grazing cattle. I had set up a camp for the wounded, which was guarded by a special platoon, but the greater number of the sick men died. Horemheb himself set off with his chariots in pursuit of the Khabiri, for by questioning the prisoners he had learned that the fugitives had contrived to rescue and carry away their god.

He took me with him against my will, and I stood behind him

126

in the chariot, clutching him round the waist and wishing I had never been born. He drove like a maniac, and I thought every instant we should overturn and I should be flung out headfirst among the stones. But he only scoffed and told me he would give me a taste of war since I had come to find out what it had to say to me.

He gave me a taste of it: I saw the chariots sweep like a storm over the Khabiri—the happily singing, palm-waving Khabiri—as they drove their stolen cattle to their hiding place in the wilderness. His horses trampled down women and children and the aged; he was wreathed in the smoke of burning tents; and in blood and tears the Khabiri learned that it was better to live in poverty in the desert and starve to death in their dens than to raid wealthy, fertile Syria, that they might smear their sun-dried skins with oil and stuff themselves with stolen grain. Thus I tasted war—which was war no longer but persecution and murder—till Horemheb himself had had enough and turning, ordered the setting up of the boundary stones that the Khabiri had thrown down.

He had caught up with the Khabiri god, however, and swooped upon it like a hawk, scattering the bearers who dropped it and fled. The image was later chopped up into firewood and burned before Sekhmet. The warriors smote their chests saying, "See how we burn the god of the Khabiri!" The name of this god was Jehou or Jahveh; it was the only one the raiders possessed, and they had to return bereft to the wilderness. They were thus poorer, for all their erstwhile palm waving and songs of joy, than when they had set out.

5

Horemheb returned to Jerusalem, which was thronged with refugees from the border country, and he sold back to them their grain and cooking pots. At this they tore their clothes and cried, "These robbers are worse than the Khabiri!" But they suffered no hardship, for they were able to borrow money from their temples, from the merchants, and from the tax gatherers, who had streamed into Jerusalem from all over Syria. Thus Horemheb converted the spoils into gold and silver, which he distributed among his soldiers. I understood now why most of the wounded had died despite my care. There remained so much more booty for their comrades, who had also stolen the clothes and weapons and treasure of the sick and given them neither water nor food so that they perished. What wonder that unskilled surgeons were ever eager to follow the troops into battle or that, despite their incompetence, they returned so wealthy!

Jerusalem was full of noise and clamor and the din of Syrian instruments. The soldiers squandered the gold and silver on beer and girls till the traders, having thus regained their money, went away. Horemheb levied a tax upon the merchants both when they came and when they left and was thus a rich man though he had abstained from his share of the spoils.

He felt no elation, and when I went to take leave of him before setting forth for Smyrna, he said, "This campaign was over before it began, and in his letter to me Pharaoh upbraids me for shedding blood against his commands. I must go back to Egypt with my rats, to disband them and deliver their standards into the keeping of the temple. But what will be the outcome I know not, for these are the only trained troops in Egypt, and the rest are fit for nothing but dirtying walls and pinching women's rumps in the market place. By Ammon, it is easy enough in Pharaoh's golden palace to write songs in honor of one's god and to believe that all nations may be governed by love! Could he but hear the screams of mutilated men and the wailing of women in the burning villages when the enemy crosses the borders, he might think otherwise."

"Egypt has no enemies; she is too rich and too powerful," I said. "Also your fame has gone out over Syria, and the Khabiri will not remove the landmarks a second time. Why then should you not disband the troops, for in truth they rage in their cups like wild beasts, their sleeping dens stink, and they are verminous."

"You know not what you say," he retorted, staring before him and scratching at his armpits—for even the commander's hut was full of lice. "Egypt is self-sufficient and is therein mistaken. The world is large and in the hidden places seed is being sown from which fire and destruction will be harvested. I have heard, for example, that the King of the Amorites is diligently amassing horses and chariots, whereas it would be more becoming in him to pay his tribute to Pharaoh with greater punctuality. At his banquets his high officials talk only of how the Amorites once ruled the whole world—which is in a sense true, as the last of the Hyksos dwell in the land of Amurru."

"That Aziru is my friend and a vain man, for I gilded his teeth. And I think he has other things on his mind, for I have heard that he has taken a wife who draws the strength from his loins."

"You know many things," remarked Horemheb, looking at me attentively. "You are a free man, an independent man; you travel

128

from city to city hearing much that is hidden from others. If I were in your place and free, I should journey into every country seeking knowledge. I should go to the land of Mitanni, and also Babylon, and learn what manner of war chariots the Hittites now use and how they exercise their troops. I should visit the islands in the sea to note how big the ships there are, of which there is so much talk. But my name is known throughout all Syria, and perhaps I should not hear so very much. But you, Sinuhe, are clad in Syrian clothes and speak a language known to the educated of all nations. You are also a physician, and no one would imagine that you understand anything outside your profession. Moreover, your talk is simple and to my ears often childish, and you have a wide-eyed look. Yet I know that your heart is locked and what you carry within you is known to none. Isn't this true?"

"Perhaps. But what is it you want of me?"

"What would you say if I were to furnish you with a good supply of gold and send you to the lands I spoke of to practice your craft and spread the fame of both Egyptian medicine and your own healing powers? The rich and influential—even kings, perhaps—would summon you, and you would look into their hearts. While you followed your calling, you would let your eyes be mine and your ears mine so that when you returned to Egypt you might render me account of all you have seen and heard."

"I do not intend ever to return—and besides there is danger in what you propose. I have no desire to hang head downward from the wall of a foreign city."

"No one knows what tomorrow may bring. I think you will come back to Egypt, for he who has once drunk of Nile waters cannot quench his thirst elsewhere. Even the swallows and the cranes return each winter. Gold is but dust to me, and I would rather exchange it for knowledge. As for hanging, your talk is like the buzz of flies in my ear. I don't ask you to do ill or to break the laws of any place. Don't all great cities lure the traveler to visit their temples—do they not prepare all manner of banquets and diversions to attract him and his gold? You are welcome everywhere if you bring gold.

"Your arts also are welcome in lands where they slay the aged with an ax and expose the sick in the desert to die, as you know is done. Kings are proud and love to parade their soldiers to impress the stranger. You do no evil in noting how the men march and in what manner they are armed, in counting chariots and bearing in mind whether they are large and heavy or small and light and whether they carry two or three men—for I have heard that some employ a shield bearer as well as a charioteer. It is also important to note whether the troops are well fed and gleaming with oil or gaunt and verminous, with diseased eyes, like my own rats. There is a rumor that the Hittites have discovered some new metal and that weapons made of this can chip the edges of the finest copper ax. Whether this is true I don't know; it is possible that they have discovered some new way of hardening copper. However it may be, I should like to know more. But above all I would learn the hearts of the rulers and of the counselors. Look at me!"

I looked at him, and he appeared to grow before my eyes. He was godlike, and his look was a burning coal so that my heart quailed and I bowed before him.

He said, "Do you believe now that I am a man of authority?"

"My heart tells me that you can command me, but I do not know why this should be," I faltered, and my tongue was thick in my mouth. "Doubtless it is true that you are destined to hold command over many, as you said. I go, therefore, and my eyes shall be your eyes and my ears your ears. I don't know whether you will gain by what I see and hear, for in the matters you would learn of I am a dunce. Yet I will do it as well as I may and not for gold but because you are my friend and because plainly the gods have so willed it—if indeed there be any gods."

He said, "I don't think you will repent of being my friend. I will give you gold for your journey, nevertheless, for if I know anything of men, you will have need of it. You do not ask why this knowledge is more precious to me than gold, but this I can tell you: The great Pharaohs sent clever men to foreign courts, but the envoys of this Pharaoh are muttonheads who know no more than how to pleat their robes and wear their honors and in what order they must stand on the right or left hand of Pharaoh. So pay no heed to them if you should meet with any, but let their talk be as the buzz of flies in your ear."

When we parted, he laid aside his dignity, stroked my cheek, and touched my shoulders with his face, saying, "My heart is heavy because of your going, Sinuhe, for if you are alone, why, so am I. No man knows the secrets of my heart."

I believe that as he said this his thoughts were with the Princess Baketamon whose beauty had bewitched him.

He gave me much gold, more than I could have imagined—I believe he gave me all the gold he had won in the Syrian campaign—and he furnished me with an escort as far as the coast so that I could travel without fear of robbers. As soon as I arrived there, I placed the gold with a large trading company, exchanging it for clay tablets, which were safer to carry, being useless to thieves, after which I boarded a ship for Smyrna.

BOOK 6

The Day of the False King

I

BEFORE starting on a new book I must give glory to the days gone by when I journeyed unmolested through many lands acquiring wisdom, for such a time will hardly come again. I traveled through a world that for forty years had known no war. Kings everywhere protected caravan routes and the traders who used them, while their ships and Pharaoh's swept the seas of pirates. Frontiers were open; merchants and travelers who brought gold were welcome in every city, and there was neither bitterness nor dissension between men; they bowed to one another, stretching forth their hands at knee level, and learned one another's ways. Many of the educated spoke several languages and wrote two kinds of script.

Fields were watered and bore abundant crops, and in the Red Lands the river of the heavens did duty for our Nile and refreshed the earth. In those days cattle roved in safety over the grazing grounds, and the herdsmen carried no spears but played on pipes and sang merry songs. Vineyards prospered, and fruit trees bowed beneath their burdens; priests were fat and shiny with oil; and the smoke from countless sacrifices rose from the forecourts of temples in every country. The gods throve also and were gracious and grew fat upon burnt offerings. The rich became richer, the mighty yet mightier, and the poor poorer, as the gods have decreed, so that all were content and there was no murmuring. Such is the vision I have of this bygone time—a time never to return—when in my young manhood my limbs were unwearied by long journeys, when my eyes were eager for new things, and when my heart, thirsting for knowledge, drank its fill.

And now having praised the past when even the sun shone more brightly and the winds were gentler than in these evil days, I will tell of my journeys and of all I saw and heard. But first I must speak of my return to Smyrna.

When I came home, Kaptah ran to meet me, shouting and weeping for joy, and threw himself at my feet.

"Blessed be the day that brings my lord home!" he cried. "You have returned though I believed you dead in battle—I believed positively that you had been slit open with a spear because you were heedless of my warnings and went forth to see what war is like. Truly our scarab is a powerful god and has protected you, and blessed is the day. My heart is full of gladness at the sight of you, and the gladness flows from my eyes in tears—for I cannot restrain them though I fancied myself your heir and expected to take possession of all the gold you placed with the Smyrna merchants. Yet I do not grieve over this lost wealth, for without you I am like a kid that has lost its dam, and my days are dark. Nor have I stolen more from you than formerly but have guarded your house and property and all your interests so that you return richer than you went."

He washed my feet and poured water over my hands and tended me in every way with uninterrupted outcry till I ordered him to be silent.

"Make speedy preparation, for we are to set forth upon a journey that may take many years and that will be full of hardships; we go to the land of Mitanni and to Babylon and to the islands in the sea."

Then Kaptah cried, "Now truly I wish that I had never been born into this world and also that I had never grown fat and prosperous, for the more fortunate a man is the harder is it for him to renounce his ease. Were you to set forth for a month or two, as you have done before, I should say nothing but remain peacefully here in Smyrna. But if your journey is to last for years, you may never return and I never see you again. Therefore, I must come with you, taking our sacred scarab. Against such hazards you will need all possible good fortune, and without the scarab you would tumble into crevasses on your way and be transfixed by the spears of robbers. But it would be better to remain at our house in Smyrna."

For Kaptah had grown more impudent with every passing year and already spoke of our house and our scarab and when paying for something said our gold.

But I wearied of this, and of his lamentation, and said, "My heart tells me that one fine day you will hang by the heels from the wall for your insolence. Resolve, therefore, whether you will come with me or stay here—and above all cease this continual caterwauling when I would make ready for a long journey."

At this Kaptah fell silent and became resigned to his fate, and we made ready to depart. Since he had sworn never again to set foot aboard a ship, we joined a caravan that was on its way to northern Syria, for I desired to see the cedars of Lebanon, whence came the timber for the palaces and for the sacred boat of Ammon. Of the journey there was little to say; it was uneventful and no robbers attacked us. The inns were good, and we ate and drank well; at one or two of the stopping places sick people came to us, whom I tended. I journeyed in a chair, for I had had enough of donkeys. Though the dry wind parched my face so that I must be forever rubbing in oil and though the dust choked me and the sand fleas tormented me, yet these seemed but petty trials, and my eyes rejoiced at all they saw.

I saw forests of cedar and trees that were so huge that no Egyptian would believe me if I were to describe them. The fragrance of these woods was most marvelous, and the streams were clear, and it seemed to me that no one who lived in so beautiful a country could be altogether unhappy. But that was before I saw the slaves who felled and stripped the timber to send it down the hillside to the seashore. The misery of these slaves was terrible to witness; their arms and legs were covered with festering sores torn by the bark and by their tools, and on their backs the weals cut by the scourge were alive with flies.

At last we came to the city of Kadesh, where there was a fortress and a large Egyptian garrison. But the walls of the fortress were unguarded, the defenses had crumbled, and both officers and men lived in the city with their families, remembering that they were warriors only on the days when grain and onions and beer were distributed from Pharaoh's stores. We lingered in the city long enough for the riding sores on Kaptah's backside to heal. I cured many sick people, for the Egyptian physicians in this place were incompetent, and their names must long have been erased from the Book of Life—if indeed they had ever been inscribed there.

In this city I had a seal cut for me in a rare stone, as befitted my dignity; for seals also differ from those in Egypt, being worn not in a ring but hung about the neck in the form of cylinders that, when rolled over the tablet, leave their impression in the clay. The poor and illiterate merely press their thumbs upon it—if they ever have occasion to make their mark.

We continued our journey and crossed the border into Naharani, none hindering, where we came to a river flowing upward instead of down as the Nile does. We were told that we were in the land of Mitanni, and we paid the travelers' tax into the royal revenues. But because we were Egyptians, the people greeted us with respect, coming up to us in the street and saying:

"We bid you welcome; our hearts rejoice at the sight of Egyptians, for it is long since we beheld them. Our hearts also are uneasy, for your Pharaoh has sent us no soldiers, no arms, and no gold; and the rumor runs that he has offered to our king some new god of whom we know nothing, though we have already Ishtar of Nineveh and a number of others who have hitherto protected us."

They invited me to their houses and gave me food and drink, and they also served Kaptah because he was an Egyptian, though only my servant, so that he said to me, "This is a good land. Let us remain here, lord, and practice medicine, for it appears that these people are ignorant and credulous and would be easy to deceive."

The King of Mitanni and his court had gone up into the mountains for the hot season. I had no desire to follow them there, being impatient to see the wonders of Babylon, of which I had heard so much. But I did as Horemheb had commanded me and spoke with the great ones and with the humble; all told the same tale; all were uneasy. The land of Mitanni had formerly been powerful, but now it seemed a land floating in the air, walled in by Babylon in the east, by savage tribes in the north, and in the west by the Hittites, the name of whose country was Hatti. The more I heard of the Hittites, who were greatly feared, the firmer became my resolve to journey to the land of Hatti also, but first I desired to visit Babylon.

The inhabitants of the land of Mitanni were small of stature, their women were beautiful, and their children like dolls. It may be that they had been a mighty people in their time, for they said that they had once ruled over the peoples of the north and the south, the east and the west—but that is what every nation says. Ever since the time of the great Pharaohs this country had been dependent upon Egypt, and for two generations the daughters of its king had dwelt as wives in Pharaoh's golden house. By listening to the talk and the complaint of the Mitannians, I came to understand that their country had been designed as a shield for Syria and Egypt against the might of Babylon and of the savage peoples, to receive in its body the spears aimed at Pharaoh's sovereignty. For this reason, and this reason alone, the Pharaohs propped up the king's tottering throne and sent him gold, arms, and mercenaries. But the people did not understand this, and they were exceedingly proud of their country and its power.

I saw that it was a weary and declining nation with the shadow of death on its temples. The people were unaware of this, and they paid more attention to their food, preparing it in many remarkable ways; they also squandered their time in trying on new clothes—their pointed shoes and tall hats—and they were particular in the choosing of jewelry. Their limbs were slender like those of the Egyptians, and the women's complexions were so transparent that one might see the blood flowing blue in their veins. They spoke and behaved with delicacy and were taught in their childhood to walk gracefully, men as well as women. To live here was pleasant; even in the pleasure houses there was no brawling: all was silence and discretion so that I felt clumsy when I frequented them and drank my wine there. Yet my heart was heavy, for I had seen war and knew that if all that was said of the land of Hatti was true, then Mitanni was doomed.

Their medicine also was of a high standard, and their physicians skillful men who knew their trade and also a great deal that I did not know. I obtained from them a potion for expelling worms that was far less troublesome and unpleasant than any I had met with before. They could also cure blindness with the needle, and in this also I became more proficient. But they knew nothing of skull opening and said that only the gods could cure head injuries—and that even then the patients were never the same again so that it was better for them to die.

Nevertheless, the people were curious; they came to see me and brought their sick, being attracted by anything strange. Just as they loved to wear foreign clothes and jewelry and eat exotic dishes and drink imported wine, so they desired to be treated by an alien physician. Women came also and smiled upon me and told me of their maladies and complained that their men were lazy and tired and without virility. I understood well enough what they were after but was careful not to give way to them, for I did not wish to offend against the laws of a foreign land. Instead I gave them drugs to mix with their husbands' wine. I had obtained such drugs as would set even a dead man rutting from the doctors in Smyrna, the Syrians being the cleverest in the world in this matter and their medicines more powerful than those of Egypt. But whether the women gave these drugs to their husbands or to quite other men I do not know, though I fancy they preferred strangers, for they were free in their ways. Few of them had children, which again was a sign to me that the shadow of death hung over their land.

I must mention that these people no longer knew the boundaries of their own kingdom since the boundary stones were constantly being moved. The Hittites bore them away in their chariots and set them up where they pleased. If the Mitannians protested, the Hittites laughed and challenged them to put them back again if that was their desire. But that was not their desire, for if what was told of the Hittites was true, there had never on this earth been seen so cruel, so

139

formidable a people. Legend had it that their keenest pleasure was to hear the cries of the mutilated and to watch blood flow from open wounds. They cut off the hands of the Mitannian border folk who complained that the Hittite cattle trampled their fields and devoured their crops and then mocked them and told them to lift the boundary stones back into their places. They would cut off these peasants' feet also and tell them to run and complain to their king or slit their scalps and pull the skin down over their eyes so they could not see whither the landmarks had been carried. I cannot recount all the evil that the Hittites had done, all their cruelties and hideous practices. It was said that they were worse than locusts, for after locusts the earth brings forth again, but where the chariots of the Hittites had passed, no grass ever grew.

I did not wish to tarry any longer in the land of Mitanni, for I felt that I had learned all I desired to know, but my doctor's pride was hurt by the doubts of the Mitannian faculty, who did not believe what I had told them of skull opening. Now there came to my inn a distinguished man who complained that he had the roar of the sea continually in his ears, that he was given to swooning, and that he suffered from such excruciating pains in his head that if no one could cure him he desired to die. The physicians of Mitanni would not treat him.

I said to this man, "It is possible that if you let me open your skull you will be cured but more possible that you will die. From this operation only one in a hundred recovers."

He answered, "I should be mad not to agree to this, for then at least I have one chance in a hundred of survival. I do not trust to your curing me, but in dying by your hand there is no transgression in the sight of the gods as there would be in putting an end to my own life. If on the other hand you do cure me, I will gladly give you half of all I possess—and that is no mean sum—nor will you repent if I die, for then also my gifts will be liberal."

I examined him with great thoroughness, feeling every part of his head with my hand, but my touch gave him no pain, and no place on his head was more tender than any other.

Then Kaptah said, "Tap him on the head with a hammer; you have nothing to lose."

I tapped him with the hammer at different points, and he made no sign until suddenly he cried out and fell to the ground senseless. I concluded from this that I had found the spot where it would be best to open his skull.

Summoning the skeptical physicians, I said, "You may believe or you may not believe, but I mean to open the skull of this man to heal him though his death is the more probable result."

The doctors sneered, "This indeed should be worth seeing!"

I borrowed fire from the temple of Ammon, then purified myself and my distinguished patient and all that was in the room. When the noon light was brightest, I began my work. Slitting up the scalp, I stanched the copious bleeding with red-hot irons, though I was uneasy at the agony this caused him. But he told me that the pain was nothing to that he suffered every day. I had given him plentiful draughts of wine in which narcotics were dissolved so that his eyes protruded like those of a dead fish and he was cheerfully disposed. Next I opened the bone as carefully as I could with the instruments I had at my disposal, and he never even fainted but drew a deep breath and told me it already eased him when I removed the piece of bone. Now my heart rejoiced, for just where I had opened his head either the devil or the spirit of disease had laid its egg, as Ptahor had taught me. It was red and hideous and the size of a swallow's egg. With the utmost care I removed it, burning away all that held it to the brain, and showed it to the doctors, who laughed no longer. I closed the skull with a silver plate and stitched the scalp over it, and the patient never lost consciousness at any time. When I had finished, he rose and walked about and thanked me with all his heart, for he no longer heard the terrible roar in his ears, and the pains also had ceased.

This achievement brought me fame in the land of Mitanni, and my fame went before me into Babylon. Although my patient began to drink wine and enjoy himself, his body grew hot and he raved. On the third day he left his bed in his delirium, fell from the wall, and broke his neck. But all declared the fault was not mine and praised my science greatly.

Kaptah and I then hired a boat with oarsmen and journeyed down the river to Babylon.

2

The land under the sway of Babylon is called by many names; it is known as Chaldea and also the land of the Kassites after the people who live there. But I will call it Babylon, for everyone knows what land that is. It is a fertile country whose fields are threaded with irrigation ditches, and it is flat as far as the eye can see, differing from

141

Egypt in this as in everything else. Thus, for example, while Egyptian women grind their corn in a kneeling position and turning a round stone, the women of Babylon sit and grind two stones together, which is of course more toilsome.

There are so few trees that to fell one is regarded as an offense against gods and men and is punishable by law. But whoever plants a tree thereby wins the favor of the gods. The inhabitants of Babylon are fatter and oilier than other people and like all fat folk are given to laughter. They eat heavy, floury food, and I saw a bird there they call a hen, which could not fly but lived among the people and laid an egg as large as a crocodile's egg for them every day, though no one hearing this would believe it. I was offered some of these eggs to eat, for the Babylonians regard them as a great delicacy, but I never ventured to try them and contented myself with dishes familiar to me or of which I knew the ingredients.

The people of the country told me that Babylon was the greatest and most ancient of all the cities in the world, though I did not believe them, knowing that Thebes is both the greatest and the oldest. There is no city in the world like Thebes, though I will admit that Babylon astonished me with its size and wealth. Its very walls were as high as hills and formidable to see, and the tower they had built to their gods soared to the sky. The town houses were four and five stories high so that people lived their lives above and below each other, and nowhere—not even in Thebes—have I seen such magnificent shops and such a wealth of merchandise as in the trading houses of the temple.

Their god was Marduk, and to the honor of Ishtar a gateway had been built that was loftier than the pylons of Ammon's temple. It was covered with many-colored glazed tiles fitted together into pictures that dazzled the eyes in sunlight. From this gateway a broad road ran to Marduk's tower, up which a spiral way led to the summit— a way so smooth and wide that a number of chariots might have been driven up it abreast. At the top of this tower dwelt the astrologers, who knew all the heavenly bodies, calculated their paths, and proclaimed auspicious and inauspicious days so that all might regulate their lives thereby. It was said also that they could foretell a man's destiny, though for this they had to know the day and hour of his birth. Being ignorant of my own, I could not put their science to the test.

I had as much gold as I cared to draw from the temple counting house, and I took up my dwelling near the Gate of Ishtar at a large inn many stories high, on the roof of which were gardens of fruit trees and myrtle bushes and where streams flowed and fish leaped in the pools. This inn was frequented by eminent people visiting Babylon from their country estates—if they had no town house of their own—and also by foreign envoys. The rooms were carpeted with thick mats and the couches soft with the skins of wild animals, while on the walls were frivolous pictures very gaily and colorfully pieced together with glazed tiles. This inn was called Ishtar's House of Joy and belonged, like all else of note in the city, to the Tower of the God.

Nowhere else in the world are so many different sorts of people to be seen or languages to be heard as in Babylon. The citizens say that all roads lead thither and that it is the center of the world. Its people are first and foremost merchants; nothing is more highly regarded than commerce, so that even their gods trade among themselves. For this reason they have no love for war, and they maintain mercenaries and build walls merely to safeguard their business. Their desire is for roads in every country to be kept open to all, chiefly because they know themselves to be the greatest merchants of any and that trade is of more advantage to them than war. Yet they are proud of the soldiers who guard their ramparts and temples and who march every day to the Gate of Ishtar, their helmets and breastplates gleaming with gold and silver. The hilts of their swords also and their spearheads are adorned with gold and silver in token of their wealth. They inquire eagerly of the stranger whether he has ever before seen such troops and such chariots.

The King of Babylon was a smooth-faced boy who had to hang a false beard to his chin when he mounted the throne. He loved playthings and strange tales. My fame had sped before me from Mitanni, so that when I put up at Ishtar's House of Joy and had spoken with the priests and doctors of the tower, I received word that the King commanded my attendance.

Kaptah as usual was anxious, and said to me, "Do not go, but rather let us fly together, for of kings no good thing can come."

But I said, "You fool, do you not remember that we have the scarab with us?"

"The scarab is the scarab," he rejoined, "and I have not forgotten, but safety is better than hazard, and we must not try the scarab too high. If you are resolved to go, I cannot hinder you, and I will come, too, so that at least we may die together. But we must stand upon our dignity and request that a royal chair be sent to fetch us—and we will not go today, for by the custom of the country it is an evil day.

The merchants have closed their shops, and the people rest in their houses and do no work. If they did, it would miscarry, this being the seventh day of the week."

I pondered this and knew that he was right. Though to Egyptians all days are alike, save those proclaimed unpropitious according to the stars, yet in this country the seventh day might be unlucky for an Egyptian, also, and it was better to be prudent.

I said, therefore, to the King's servant, "You must take me for a simple foreigner indeed if you fancy I would appear before the King on such a day as this. Tomorrow I will come if your King will send a chair for me. I have no wish to come before him with dung between my toes."

The servant replied, "For these words of yours, Egyptian scum, I fear you will come before the King with a spear prodding your behind."

But he went and was certainly impressed, for the next day the King's chair came to Ishtar's House of Joy to fetch me. But the chair was a common one, such as is sent to bring tradesmen and other common people to the palace to show jewelry and feathers and apes.

Kaptah shouted loudly to the porters and to the runner, "In the name of Set and all devils! May Marduk scourge you with scorpions! Be off! As if it were seemly for my lord to travel in such a rickety old coop as that!"

The porters looked blank, and the runner threatened Kaptah with his staff. Onlookers began to gather at the inn door and laugh, saying, "In truth we long to see your lord for whom the King's chair is inadequate."

But Kaptah hired the great chair belonging to the inn, which required forty slaves to carry it; in this the ambassadors from powerful kingdoms went about their business, and in this also foreign gods were carried when they visited the city. And the bystanders laughed no longer when I came down from my room in a robe on which were embroidered in silver and gold the symbols of my calling. My collar glittered in the sunshine with gold and precious stones, while about my neck were hung chains of gold. The inn slaves followed with chests of cedarwood and ebony inlaid with ivory in which lay my medicines and my instruments. Indeed, there was no more laughing; rather they bowed before me, saying one to another, "Truly this man must be as the lesser gods in wisdom. Let us follow him to the palace."

At the palace gates the guards dispersed the throng with their spears and raised their shields as a barrier, a very wall of gold and

144

silver. Winged lions lined the way along which I was carried to the inner courts. Here an old man came to meet me whose chin was shaven after the fashion of scholars and in whose ears gleamed golden rings. His cheeks hung in discontented folds, and there was anger in his eyes as he addressed me.

"My liver is incensed because of the needless uproar you have caused by your arrival. The lord of the four quarters of the world is already asking what manner of man this is who comes when it suits him rather than when it suits the King—and who, when he does come, brings tumult with him."

I said to him, "Old man! Your speech is as the buzz of flies in my ear. Nevertheless, I ask who you may be to address me thus?"

"I am physician in chief to the lord of the four quarters of the world—and what swindler are you who come to entice gold and silver from the King? Know that if of his bounty he reward you with minted gold or silver, you must give half of it to me."

"I see that you would do better to talk to my servant, whose business it is to clear blackmailers and parasites from my path. Yet I shall be your friend since you are an old man and know no better. I shall give you these gold rings from my arm to show you that gold and silver are but as dust beneath my feet and that it is not for them that I have come but for wisdom."

I gave him the bracelets, and he was astonished and knew not what to say. He even allowed Kaptah to accompany me and brought us into the presence of the King.

King Burnaburiash sat on soft cushions in an airy room with the walls glowing with brightly colored tiles, a spoiled, sulky boy with his hand to his cheek. Beside him lay a lion that growled softly as we appeared. The old man prostrated himself to wipe the floor with his mouth before the King, and Kaptah did the same. When he heard the growl, however, he bounced up on hands and feet like a frog with a yelp of fear, which made the King burst out laughing and tumble backward on his cushions, squirming with mirth. Kaptah squatted on the floor, his hands raised defensively, while the lion also sat up and yawned at great length, then clashed its fangs together as the temple coffers close on a widow's mite.

The King laughed till the tears ran from his eyes. Then he remembered his pain and moaned and put his hand to a cheek so swollen that one eye was half closed. He scowled at the old man, who hastened to say, "Here is that stubborn Egyptian who would not come when

145

you summoned him. Say but the word, and the guards shall slit his liver."

But the King kicked at him, saying, "This is no time to talk nonsense but for him to heal me at once. The pain is terrible, and I fear that I may die since I have not slept for many nights nor eaten anything but broth."

Then the old man lamented, striking his head against the floor, "O lord of the four quarters of the world! We have done all we might to heal you; we have offered jaws and teeth in the temple to drive out the evil spirit that is lodged in your jaw. More we have not been able to do because you would not let us touch your sacred person. Nor do I think this unclean Egyptian can do better than we."

But I said, "I am Sinuhe the Egyptian, He Who Is Alone, Son of the Wild Ass, and I do not need to examine you to see that a tooth has caused your cheek to swell because you did not have it cleansed or drawn out in time as your physicians must surely have counseled you to do. Such pains are for children and the timid and not for the lord of the four quarters of the world, before whom the very lions tremble and bow their heads as I see with my own eyes. Nevertheless, I know your pain is great, and I will help you."

The King, still with his hand to his face, made answer, "You speak boldly. Were I well, I should have your impudent tongue cut out and your liver slit—but there is no time for that now. Cure me quickly, and your reward shall be great. But if you hurt me, I will have you slain without delay."

"Be it so. I have with me a small but remarkably powerful god, thanks to whom I did not come yesterday—for if I had, it would have been to no purpose. I can see that today the evil has ripened sufficiently for me to treat it, and this I shall do if you wish. But not even a king can the gods preserve from pain, though I declare to you that your relief when it is over will be so great that the pain will be forgotten and that I will make it as slight as any man in the world can make it."

The King hesitated for a while, scowling, with his hand to his cheek. He was a handsome boy when well, though spoiled, and I knew that I liked him. Feeling my eyes upon him, at last he said irritably, "What you have to do, do quickly."

The old man groaned and struck his head against the floor, but I paid him no heed. I ordered wine to be warmed, and with this I mixed a narcotic. He drank and after a time brightened a little, say-

146

ing, "The pain is leaving me, and you need not plague me with your knives and forceps."

But my will was stronger. Tucking his head firmly into my armpit, I made him open his mouth, then lanced the boil on his jaw with a knife purified in the fire Kaptah had brought with him. The fire was not, indeed, the holy fire of Ammon; Kaptah had carelessly allowed this to go out on the journey down the river. The new flame Kaptah had kindled with a fire drill in my room at the inn, believing in his simplicity that the scarab was potent as Ammon.

The King uttered loud cries when he felt the knife, and the lion with blazing eyes rose up and roared, lashing its tail to and fro; but soon the boy was busily spitting. His relief was sweet, and I helped him by pressing lightly on his cheek. He spat, and wept for joy, and spat again, exclaiming, "Sinuhe the Egyptian, you are a blessed man although you hurt me." And he spat on unceasingly.

But the old man said, "I could have done that as well as he, and better, if only you had permitted me to touch your sacred jaw. And your dentist would have done it best of all."

He was astonished when I said, "This old man says truly, for he could have done it as well as I, and the dentist would have done it best. But their wills were not as strong as mine, and so they could not free you from your pain. For a physician must venture to cause pain even to a king when it is unavoidable, without fearing for himself. These feared, but I do not fear, for all is one to me, and your men are welcome to slit my liver when I have cured you."

The King spat and pressed his cheek, and the cheek was no longer painful.

"I never heard a man speak as you speak, Sinuhe. Truly you have brought me great relief; wherefore, I pardon you your insolence—and I forgive your servant also though he saw me with my head under your arm and heard me cry out. I forgive him because he made me laugh with his capering." To Kaptah he added, "Do it again!"

But Kaptah said wrathfully, "It is inconsistent with my dignity."

Burnaburiash said smiling, "We shall see."

He called the lion, and the lion rose and stretched till its joints cracked, its intelligent eyes upon its master. The King pointed to Kaptah, and the lion strolled lazily toward him waving his tail, while Kaptah drew back and back and gazed on the beast as if bewitched. Suddenly the lion opened its jaws and gave a muffled roar; Kaptah whipped about and, seizing the door hangings, scuttled up them and perched upon the lintel. He squeaked with terror as the animal

147

dabbed up at him with its paw. The King laughed more than ever.

"Never did I see such clowning," he said.

The lion sat licking its chops while Kaptah clung to the lintel in great distress. But now the King ordered food and drink, declaring that he was hungry. The old man wept for joy that the King was cured, and many different foods were brought in on silver dishes, wine also in golden cups.

The King said, "Eat with me, Sinuhe! Ill though it befits my dignity, I will forget it today and not think of how you held my head under your arm and poked your fingers into my mouth."

So I ate and drank with him, and I told him, "Your pain is soothed, but may return at any time if the tooth that is the cause of it be not removed. Therefore, let the dentist draw it as soon as the swelling in your cheek has gone down, when it may be done without endangering your health."

His face darkened.

"You talk much and tediously, you crazy foreigner." Then after some reflection he added, "But it may be true, for the pain returns every autumn and spring when my feet are wet—and so badly that I wish I were dead. If it must be done then you shall do it, for I will not set eyes on that dentist again because of the needless pain he has caused me."

I answered him gravely, "Your dentist shall draw the tooth and not I, for in such matters he is the cleverest man in the country—cleverer also than myself—and I would not bring his anger upon my head. But if you wish it, I will stand beside you and hold your hands and encourage you while he does it, and I will soothe the pain with all the arts I have learned in many lands among many people. And this shall be done two weeks from today—for it is best to fix the time lest you repent of it. By then your jaw will be sufficiently healed, and meanwhile you shall rinse your mouth morning and evening with a remedy I shall give you, though it may sting and has an evil taste."

He grew angry. "And if I will not do this?"

"You must give me your sacred word that all shall be done as I have said—for indeed the lord of the four quarters of the world cannot go back upon that. And if you let it be done, I will divert you with my arts and turn water into blood before your eyes—I will even teach you to do this and amaze your subjects. But you must promise never to reveal the secret to anyone else, for it is sacred to the priests of Ammon, and I should not know it myself were I not a priest of the first grade, nor dare to teach it to you were you not a king."

As I finished speaking, Kaptah cried out pitifully from the door frame, "Take away this devil's beast or I shall climb down and slay it, for my hands are numb and my backside sore with sitting in this uncomfortable place which in no way befits my dignity."

Burnaburiash laughed more than ever at this threat. Then feigning gravity he said, "It would indeed be a woeful thing if you killed my lion, for I have brought it up from a cub, and it is my friend. I will call it away, therefore, that you may not commit this evil deed in my palace."

He called the lion to him, and when Kaptah had climbed down the hangings, he stood rubbing his cramped legs and glaring at the lion so that the King laughed again and slapped his knees.

"A more comical man I never saw in my life. Sell him to me, and I will make you rich."

But I did not wish to sell Kaptah. The King did not insist, and we parted friends. He had begun to nod by now, and his eyelids were drooping, for he had had no sleep for many nights.

The old physician followed me out, and I said to him, "Let us take counsel together about what is to happen in two weeks' time, for that will be an evil day, and we should be wise to make sacrifice to all suitable gods."

This greatly pleased him, for he was a pious man, and we agreed to meet in the temple to make sacrifice and to confer with the doctors about the King's tooth. Before we left the palace, he caused refreshment to be offered to the porters who had brought me; they ate and drank in the forecourt and praised me volubly. They sang aloud as they carried me back to the inn, crowds followed us, and from that day my name was famous in Babylon. But Kaptah rode his white donkey in a great rage and would not speak to me, for he had been wounded in his dignity.

3

Two weeks later I met the King's physicians in Marduk's tower, where we sacrificed a sheep together and the priests examined its liver; in Babylon the priests consult the livers of sacrificial beasts, interpreting therefrom much that is hidden from others. They told us that the King would be exceedingly wroth but that no man would lose his life because of it or suffer lasting hurt, though we must beware of claws and spears. Next we bade the astronomers consult the Book of the Heavens to learn whether the day was auspicious for this undertaking. They told us that the day was not unfavorable although we might have chosen a better. Next the priests at our request poured oil into water and in this sought to read the future. Having surveyed the oil, they said they saw nothing remarkable—or at least nothing of ill omen. As we left the temple, a vulture flew over us carrying in its claws a human head it had snatched from the wall. This the priests interpreted as a favorable sign—though to me it appeared very far from that.

Warned by the auguries, we dismissed the King's guard and shut the lion out, for when the King became angered, he might have set it upon us, to rend us, as the physicians declared had been known to happen. But King Burnaburiash came stoutly in, having fortified his liver with wine—as they say in Babylon—though when he saw the dentist's chair that had been conveyed to the palace he turned extremely pale and said that he had important affairs of state to see to, which he had forgotten while drinking.

He made as if to go, but while the other physicians lay face downward upon the floor, wiping it with their mouths, I seized the King's hand and encouraged him, saying that all would speedily be over if he would only have courage. I ordered the doctors to cleanse themselves, and I purified the dentist's instruments in the fire of the scarab, then rubbed numbing salves into the boy's gum till he commanded me to stop, saying that his cheek was like wood and he could no longer move his tongue. Then we set him in the chair, binding his head to it and putting wedges in his mouth so that he could not close it. I held his hands and cheered him, the dentist audibly invoked all the gods of Babylon to aid him and, putting the forceps into the boy's mouth, whipped out the tooth more deftly than I have ever seen it done. Despite the gags the King yelled in a terrible manner, and the lion began roaring outside the door, hurling itself against it till it creaked and scratching at it with its claws.

It was a terrifying moment, for when we had unbound the boy's head and taken the wedges from his jaws, he spat blood into a dish, shrieking and yelling, with the tears pouring down his face. He roared that his bodyguard should put us all to death; he called his lion and kicked over the holy fire and beat his physician with a stick till I took it from him and bade him rinse his mouth. This he did while the physicians lay at his feet quaking in every limb, and the dentist thought that his last hour was come. But the King quieted down and drank some wine, though with a wry mouth, and asked me to divert him as I had promised.

150

We went into the great banqueting hall, for the room in which the tooth had been drawn was no longer pleasing to the King. Indeed, he intended to close it forever and call it the Accursed Room. I poured water into a vessel and let the King and the other doctors taste it and satisfy themselves that it was, indeed, ordinary water. Next I poured the water slowly into another vessel, and as it ran into this, it was transmuted into blood so that the King and his physicians cried aloud in dismay.

After this the King rewarded his physicians richly and made the dentist a wealthy man, and he sent them all away. But he bade me stay, and I taught him how to change water into blood, giving him some of the substance that must be mixed with the water to bring the miracle about. It is a simple matter as everyone familiar with it knows, but every great art is simple, and the King marveled greatly and was full of my praises. He was not content until he had summoned to the garden all the distinguished men of the court and also people from the walls. In the sight of all he transmuted the water of the pool into blood so that both mighty and humble cried out in fear, prostrating themselves before him, to his very great satisfaction.

He had forgotten his tooth, and he said to me, "Sinuhe the Egyptian, you have cured me of a great evil and delighted my liver in many ways, therefore, you may ask of me what you will. Name the gift you desire, and I will give it you, whatever it may be, for I would rejoice your liver also."

I replied, "King Burnaburiash, lord of the four quarters of the world! As your physician I have held your head under my arm and grasped your hands when you uttered wrathful cries. It is not fitting that I, a stranger, should preserve such a memory of the King of Babylon when I return to my own country to tell of what I have seen here. Impress me, therefore, with a glimpse of your might! Hang a beard upon your chin, gird a tail about you, and command your warriors to parade before your face that I may behold your majesty and power— that I may prostrate myself humbly before you and kiss the dust. I ask no more than this."

My request pleased him, for he answered, "Truly no one has ever spoken as you do, Sinuhe. I will grant your request though for me it is most wearisome, for I must sit throughout a whole day on a golden throne till my eyes are tired and I am overcome with yawning. Nevertheless, it shall be as you wish."

He sent word to all parts of the country summoning his forces and fixed a day for the parade.

This parade took place at the Gate of Ishtar. The King sat upon a golden throne with the lion at his feet and with his chief dignitaries about him fully armed; he appeared to float in a cloud of gold and silver and purple. Below him along the broad road ran the warriors—spearmen and archers sixty abreast and chariots six abreast—and their passing took the whole day. The chariot wheels were thunderous, and the thud of running feet and the clatter of accouterments was like a tempest, making the eyes swim and the knees tremble.

I said to Kaptah, "It will not suffice for us to report that the Babylonian warriors are as the sands of the sea in number; we must count them."

He protested, "Lord, this cannot be done, for there are not so many numbers in the world."

Yet I reckoned as well as I might. The foot soldiers were sixty times sixty times sixty men, while of chariots there were sixty—for sixty is a sacred number in Babylon, as are also five and seven and twelve.

I noted, also, that the shields and weapons of the King's bodyguard blazed with gold and silver, their faces gleamed with oil, they were so fat that running made them breathless, and they panted past the King like a herd of oxen. But they were few in number; the troops from outlying districts were sunburned and dirty and smelled of urine. Many of them lacked spears, for the King's summons had taken them by surprise. Their eyes were sore from flies, and I reflected that soldiers in every country are alike. Moreover, their chariots were old and squeaky, one or two of them lost a wheel as they drove by, and the scythes fixed to them were green with verdigris.

That evening the King summoned me to his presence and said smilingly, "Did you see my might, Sinuhe?"

I prostrated myself at his feet, kissed the ground, and answered, "Truly there is no mightier monarch than yourself, and it is not for nothing that men call you lord of the four quarters of the world. My eyes are weary, my head whirls, and my limbs tremble with fear, for the number of your warriors is as the sands of the sea."

He smiled in delight.

"You have had your desire, Sinuhe. Let us now drink wine and rejoice our livers after this tedious day, for I have much to ask you."

I drank with the King, and he asked me many questions such as children and the young who have seen nothing of the world will ask.

My answers pleased him, and at last he said, "The wine has revived me and cheered my liver, and I go now to my women. But come you with me, for that as a physician you may do. I have a superabundance of wives and shall not be offended if you choose one for yourself tonight, provided you do not get her with child, for that would cause difficulties. I am also curious to see how an Egyptian lies with a woman, for every nation has its own customs. If I were to tell you the ways of those wives who come from distant lands, you would not believe me and would be greatly astonished."

He would not heed my refusal but led me to the women's house on walls of which he showed me pictures his artists had made of colored tiles. They depicted men and women taking pleasure with one another in many different ways. He showed me, also, some of his wives, who were clad in rich garments and adorned with precious stones. Among them were women and young girls from all known lands, and also some from the savage nations, whom merchants had brought. They varied in color and figure and chattered like monkeys in many different tongues; they danced before the King with bared bellies and diverted him in various ways, competing for his favor. He urged me continually to choose one of them for myself until at last I told him that I had promised my god to abstain from women whenever I was about to treat a patient. I was to perform an operation on one of the court officials on the following day, so I insisted that since I might not approach a woman it would be better for me to retire, lest I bring my calling into disrepute. The King accepted this and allowed me to go, but the women were sorely displeased and showed it by various gestures and sounds. They had never yet seen there a man in the prime of his manhood, but only eunuchs and the King, who was young and slender and still without a beard.

Before I went, the King said, laughing to himself, "The rivers have overflowed their banks, and the spring has come, and the priests have therefore chosen the thirteenth day from today for the spring festival and the Day of the False King. I have prepared a surprise for you on that day that I believe will greatly divert you, and I expect to enjoy it myself, also. I will not say what it is to be, for that would spoil my pleasure."

I went away full of misgivings, fearing that what amused King Burnaburiash would not amuse me at all, and in this Kaptah for once was of my opinion.

During my continued stay in Babylon I acquired much occult learning that was useful to a physician; the priestly art of prophecy especially was of interest to me. I learned also under the priests' direction to read the auguries in the livers of sheep, which revealed many hidden things, and spent much time studying the patterns formed by oil upon the surface of water.

Before I speak of the spring festival in Babylon and of the Day of the False King, I would mention a curious incident concerning my birth.

When the priests consulted a sheep's liver on my account and contemplated floating oil, they said, "There is some fearful secret connected with your birth that we cannot resolve and from which it appears that you are not merely an Egyptian as you believe but a stranger in the world."

I told them then that I had not been born like other men but had come drifting down the river in a reed boat and that my mother had found me among the reeds. Then the priests looked at one another and bowing low before me, said, "This we guessed."

They went on to tell me of their great King Sargon, who had gathered the four corners of the world under his sway and whose empire had stretched from the northern sea to the southern sea and who had ruled also over the islands in the sea. They told me that as a newborn child he had been carried down the river in a pitched-reed boat and that nothing was known of his birth until his mighty deeds showed that he was born of the gods.

At this my heart was filled with dread, and I tried to laugh the matter off.

"Surely you do not fancy that I, a doctor, am born of the gods?"

They did not laugh but said gravely, "That we do not know, but prudence is a virtue—therefore, we bow before you."

They bowed low before me once more until I had had enough and said, "Let us make an end of this foolery and return to our business."

They began once more to interpret the mazes of the liver but stole awestruck glances at me and whispered among themselves.

From this day the thought of my origin weighed upon my spirit, and my heart sank because I was a stranger in all four quarters of the world. I had a strong desire to question the astrologers, but as I did not know the precise hour of my birth, it was useless to ask since they could not have enlightened me. Nevertheless, at the priests' request they sought out the tablets relating to the year and the day of my coming down the river, for the priests also were curious. But all the astrologers could say was that if I had been born at such and such a time of day I must have been of royal blood and destined to rule over a nation of many people. This knowledge was no comfort to me, for, when I thought of the past, I remembered only the crime I had committed and

154

the shame I had brought upon myself in Thebes. It might be that the stars had cursed me from the very day of my birth and sent me in the reed boat to drive Senmut and Kipa to an untimely death and to rob them of the contentment of their old age—to rob them even of their tomb. And at this I shuddered, for if once the stars opposed me, I could not avoid my destiny but should continue to bring ruin and suffering upon those who held me dear. The future oppressed me, and I feared it, and I perceived that everything that had happened to me was designed to make me turn my heart from my fellows and live alone, for only solitude could save me from bringing destruction upon others.

4

It remains for me to tell of the Day of the False King.

When the young corn had begun to sprout and the fierce chill of the nights had given way to warmth, the priests went forth out of the city to bring their god from his tomb and to cry that he had risen again. Upon this the city of Babylon was transformed into a fair ground, where there was dancing and where gaily dressed crowds poured along the streets. The mob plundered the shops, making more commotion and uproar than the soldiers had after the great inspection. Women and girls went to the temple of Ishtar to collect silver for their wedding portions, and whoever chose might enjoy them without shame. The last day of the festival was the Day of the False King.

I was by now familiar with many customs in Babylon, yet I was astonished to see the King's bodyguard before dawn on that day crowding drunkenly into Ishtar's House of Joy, breaking open the doors and striking everyone they met with the butts of their spears as they shouted at the tops of their voices:

"Where is our king hiding? Bring him forth speedily, for the sun is about to rise, and the king must dispense justice to his people!"

The din was beyond description. Lamps were lighted, and the inn servants ran about the passages in a fright, while Kaptah, believing that riots had broken out in the city, hid beneath my bed. But I went to meet the soldiers, naked under my woolen robe, having just risen from sleep, and asked them, "What is it you want? Beware how you behave to me, for I am Sinuhe the Egyptian, the Son of the Wild Ass, whose name you have certainly heard."

At this they shouted, "If you are Sinuhe, then you are he whom we seek!"

They tore off my cloak so that I stood naked; whereupon they pointed me out to each other in wonder, having never before seen a circumcised man. Then they debated together, saying, "Can we let this man go free? He is a danger to our women, who love whatever is new and strange."

But when they had had enough of mockery, they released me, saying, "Waste no more of our time but deliver to us your servant, for we must bring him to the palace with all speed, today being the Day of the False King. It is the King's will that we hasten to the palace with the man."

When Kaptah heard this, he was so terrified that he began to tremble and shake the whole bed so that they found him and, dragging him forth with jubilation, made deep obeisance before him.

They said to one another, "This is a day of great rejoicing, for at last we have found our king who had hidden himself and disappeared from our sight. Our eyes are gladdened by him, and we hope he will reward our fidelity with many gifts."

The trembling Kaptah stared at them with eyes as big as snaffle rings, and at the sight of his amazement and terror they laughed more than ever and said, "This is indeed the king of the four quarters of the world, and we know his face!"

They bowed low before him, and those who stood at his back kicked him in the seat to hurry him.

Kaptah said to me, "Truly this city—truly this whole world is full of destruction, of maniacs and malignants against whom not even the scarab seems able to protect me. I cannot tell whether I stand on my head or my heels—it may be that I am sound asleep there upon the bed and in the grip of an evil dream. Anyway, I must go with them, for they are sturdy men. But save your own life, lord, if you may. Take down my body from the wall when they have hung me up by the heels, and embalm it for safety's sake. Do not let them throw me into the river."

The soldiers howled with delight when they heard him.

"By Marduk, we could have found no better king than this; it is a marvel that his tongue is not in knots with his talking."

Dawn was now breaking, and they smote Kaptah on the back with their spear shafts to hurry him and led him away. I dressed myself rapidly and followed them to the palace, where I found all the fore-courts and outer rooms full of noisy crowds. I was now sure that riots had broken out and that the gutter would run blood as soon as reinforcements arrived from the provinces.

156

But when I followed the soldiers into the great throne room, I saw Burnaburiash seated on his lion-footed golden throne beneath the canopy of sovereignty, robed in kingly raiment and with the symbols of power in his hands. Round about him stood the chief priests of Marduk, the counselors and the foremost men in the kingdom. But the soldiers never heeded them; they thrust Kaptah forward, making way with their spears until they reached the throne, where they paused.

There was suddenly silence; no one spoke until Kaptah suddenly said, "Take away that devil's creature, or I shall weary of this game and go away."

At this moment sunlight broke through the tracery of the east window, and everyone began to shout, "He is right! Take away this creature, for we have had enough of being governed by a beardless boy. This man is wise, therefore we make him king that he may rule over us."

I could not believe my eyes when I saw them set upon the King, jostling and laughing with rude utterance, to snatch the symbols from his hands and the robe from his back so that he was soon as naked as I when the soldiers surprised me. They pinched his arms and felt his thigh muscles and jeered at him.

"It is plain to see that he is newly weaned and his mouth still wet with his mother's milk. It is high time that the women in the women's house had some enjoyment, and we think that this old rogue, Kaptah the Egyptian, can ride in that saddle!"

Burnaburiash uttered no word of protest but laughed with them, while his lion in great uneasiness and perplexity slunk away with its tail between its legs, scared by the mob.

And then for all I knew I might have been standing on my head, for from the King they rushed to Kaptah, clothed him in the royal robe and forced him to take the symbols of majesty into his hands. They pushed him onto the throne and prostrated themselves before him, wiping the floor with their lips. First among them crawled Burnaburiash, stark naked, shouting, "This is as it should be! He shall be our king, and a better one we could not have chosen."

Then they all sprang up and proclaimed Kaptah king, and they stamped and squirmed and held their sides in mirth.

Kaptah stared at them goggle eyed, his hair on end beneath the royal diadem, which they had set awry on his head.

At length he said, "If I am indeed king, it is worth a drink. Make haste, therefore, to bring in wine, you slaves, if any is to be found here, or my stick shall dance on your backs, and I shall have you hung from the walls. Bring a great quantity of wine, for these gentlemen and friends who have made me king shall drink with me, while I myself mean to bathe up to my neck in wine."

His words evoked great rejoicing, and the shouting throng dragged him to a vast hall where many luscious dishes were set forth and much wine. Each one took what he fancied, and Burnaburiash donned a servant's apron and dashed about like a clown, stumbling over people's feet and spilling wine and sauce over their clothes so that many swore and flung gnawed bones at him. In all the outer courtyards food and drink were offered to the mob; oxen and sheep were quartered there; and the populace could scoop beer and wine from the pools and stuff themselves with a porridge prepared with cream and sweet dates. As the sun rose higher, an indescribable tumult prevailed.

As soon as opportunity offered, I approached Kaptah and said to him privately, "Kaptah, follow me; let us fly unobserved, for no good can come of this."

But Kaptah had drunk wine, and his belly was swollen with good food. He replied, "Your words are as the buzz of flies in my ear. Never did I hear such witless talk. Am I to go now when all these good people have made me king and bow before me?"

He wiped the grease from his mouth and, shaking a gnawed donkey bone at me, shouted, "Take away this scum of an Egyptian before I lose my temper and let my stick dance on his back!"

It might have gone ill with me, but at that moment a horn was sounded, and a man announced that it was now time for the king to go down and dispense justice to his people; whereupon I was forgotten.

Kaptah was somewhat taken aback when they began to lead him toward the House of Justice and said that he was content to leave the business to the appointed judges—sound men whom he trusted. But the people countered this with heat and indignation, and shouted, "We will witness the king's wisdom to prove to ourselves that he is the right king and knows the laws."

So Kaptah was lifted to the throne of justice; before him were laid scourge and fetters, the symbols of justice; then the people were called on to step forward and lay their cases before the king.

When Kaptah had pronounced judgment on some of these, he grew weary of the business; he stretched himself and said, "Today I have eaten and drunk and—as I think—toiled and racked my brain enough. As king I am lord also of the women's house, where so far as I know some four hundred wives await me. I must therefore inspect these

158

possessions of mine, for wine and majesty have strangely fired me, and I feel as strong as a lion."

When the people heard this, they raised a tremendous shout, which seemed as if it would never end. They followed him back to the palace, where in the courtyard before the door of the women's house they took up their stand. But Burnaburiash was no longer laughing; he rubbed his hands nervously and scratched his leg with the other foot.

When he saw me, he came up and said rapidly, "Sinuhe, you are my friend, and as a physician you may enter the house of the King's women. Follow him and see that he does nothing he may be sorry for later. I shall have him flayed alive and set his head to dry upon the wall if he touches my women; if he behaves well, I promise him an easy death."

I said to him, "Burnaburiash, I am indeed your friend and wish you well, but tell me what all this means, for my liver is heavy to see you in the place of a servant and mocked by all."

He answered me impatiently, "Today is the Day of the False King as everyone knows; hasten now to follow him, lest evil befall."

I made no move to obey, though he seized me by the arm, but said only, "I do not know the customs of your country; you must explain to me what all this signifies."

"Each year on the Day of the False King the stupidest, craziest man in Babylon is chosen king to rule from dawn to sunset in full majesty and power, and the King himself waits upon him. And never have I seen a more comical king than Kaptah, whom I chose for that reason. He does not know what is to happen to him, and that is drollest of all."

"What then is to happen?"

"At sunset he will be slain as suddenly as he was crowned. I can kill him cruelly if I choose, but mostly I give them a gentle poison in their wine, and they fall asleep without knowing they are to die. Hasten now and see to it that your servant commits no folly of which he may repent before sundown."

But there was no need to fetch Kaptah, who now came tumbling from the house in a great rage, with blood streaming from his nose and with his hand over his one eye. He said amid howls and yells, "See what they have done to me! They offered me old hags and Negresses, but when I would have tasted a tender kid, it turned into a tiger and gave me a black eye and hit me on the nose with a slipper!"

Burnaburiash was so helpless with laughter that he had to steady himself by catching on to my arms, and Kaptah continued with his lamentation.

"I dare not open the door to that house, for the young woman in there is raging like a wild beast, and I know not what is to be done —unless you, Sinuhe, go in and open her skull and so release the evil spirit that is in her. In truth she must be possessed; how else would she dare lay hands on the King and smite me on the nose with her slipper so that blood flows from me as from a stuck ox?"

Burnaburiash nudged me and said, "Go in, Sinuhe, and see what has happened. You know the place now, and today I may not enter it. Then come and tell me. I think I know which girl it is, for one was brought here yesterday from the islands in the sea from whom I expect much enjoyment though she should first be drugged with poppy juice."

He pestered me until I went into the women's house, where all was turmoil. The eunuchs did not hinder me, knowing that I was a physician. Old women who in honor of the day had clad themselves in all their splendor and painted their wrinkled faces came clustering about me, demanding with one voice, "What became of him, our beloved, our heart's flower, our little he-goat for whom we have waited since morning?"

A big Negress, whose breasts hung down on her belly like black cooking pots, had undressed so as to be the first to receive Kaptah, and she cried, "Give me my beloved that I may press him to my bosom! Give me my elephant that he may wind his trunk about me!"

But the harassed eunuchs said, "Do not heed these women. Their task is but to entertain the false king, and they have drunk their livers full of wine while waiting for him. But truly we need a physician, as the girl who was brought here yesterday is mad. She is stronger than we are and kicks us very severely, and we do not know what will come of this, for she has a knife and is as savage as a wild beast."

They took me to the women's court the colored tiles of which glowed in the sunshine. In the middle of this was a round pool in which stood carved water monsters spouting water from their jaws. The frenzied woman had climbed up on these; her clothes had been torn by the eunuchs as they tried to catch her, and she was drenched from having swum across the pool, and from the many jets of water that spurted about her. With one hand she clung to the mouth of a spouting porpoise and in the other she held a flashing knife. What with the rushing of the water and the screams of the eunuchs I could not hear a word she said. Despite her torn dress and wet hair she was certainly a beautiful girl. She confused me, and I said wrathfully to the eunuchs, "Go away and let me speak with her and calm her; shut off the water that I may hear what she says, for I see she is shouting."

160

When the rushing of the water was stilled, I heard that she was not shouting but singing. I could not understand the words of the song, for they were in a language I did not know. Her head was thrown back, her eyes sparkled green as a cat's, and her cheeks were flushed with excitement.

I called to her in a passion, "Cease that screeching, wildcat—throw away the knife and come here that we may talk together and that I may heal you, for you are certainly mad."

She broke off her song and answered me in imperfect Babylonian —it was even worse than mine, "Jump into the pool, baboon, and swim hither for me to let blood from your liver, for I am exceedingly angry!"

"I mean you no harm!"

"Many a man has said that to me and lied. I may not approach a man even should I so desire, for I have been dedicated to my god to dance before him. That is why I carry this knife, and I will give it my own blood to drink rather than that a man should touch me. Least of all shall that one-eyed devil come fumbling at me, for he looked more like a blown-up bag than a man."

"Dance your fill, you maniac, but put away that knife; for you might hurt yourself, and that would be a pity since the eunuchs tell me they paid a quantity of gold for you in the slave market on behalf of the King."

"I am no slave; I was stolen away in secret as you would see if you had eyes in your head. But can't you speak some respectable language that these people can't follow? The eunuchs are lurking among the pillars with ears pricked to hear what we are saying."

"I am an Egyptian," I answered in my own tongue, "and my name is Sinuhe, He Who Is Alone, Son of the Wild Ass. By profession I am a physician, so you need not fear me."

She jumped into the water then and swam over to me, knife in hand. Throwing herself down before me she said, "I know that Egyptian men are weak and will not take a woman by force; therefore, I trust you and beg you to forgive me for keeping my knife since it seems likely that this very day I shall have to open my veins lest my god be defiled through me. But if you fear the gods and wish me well, then save me and take me away from this land, though I may not reward you as you would then deserve, for it is forbidden."

"I have no mind whatever to help you escape," I snapped at her. "That would be an injury to the King, who is my friend and who has paid a mountain of gold for you. Moreover, I can tell you that the blown-up bag who was here is but the false king who reigns for today only, and tomorrow the real king will visit you. He is still a beardless boy and agreeable in his person, and he expects to find much delight with you when he has once tamed you. I do not think the power of your god can reach you here, and you would lose nothing by submission to the inevitable. It will be best, therefore, for you to make an end of this folly and to clothe and adorn yourself for him. You look far from comely with your wet hair and with the red from your lips smeared all over your face."

These observations had their effect, for she felt her hair and wetting her finger tip rubbed her eyebrows and lips with it. Then she smiled at me—she had a small and lovely face—and said softly, "My name is Minea, and you may call me that when you take me away and we fly together from this evil land."

I raised my hands in exasperation and turning walked quickly away, but her face so tormented me that I retraced my step and said, "Minea, I will speak for you to the King; more I cannot do. Meanwhile dress and compose yourself. If you wish it, I will give you a sedative drug so that you no longer care what is done with you."

"Try that if you dare! Nevertheless, since you take my part, I will give you this knife, which has protected me hitherto—for I know that once I have done this you will protect and not betray me and that you will take me out of this land."

She smiled at me under her dripping hair until I left her, carrying her knife and suffering deep mortification. For I perceived that she was more cunning than I in that by giving me her knife she bound her destiny with mine and I could not evade her.

Burnaburiash met me on my way from the women's house and was most curious to know what had happened.

"Your eunuchs have done a poor stroke of business," I told him, "for Minea, the girl they bought for you, is raving and will not come near a man because her god has forbidden it. It will be best, therefore, if you leave her in peace until she changes her mind."

But Burnaburiash only laughed happily.

"Truly I anticipate much delight with her, for I know that kind of girl; with them the stick is the best argument. I am still young, and my beard has not grown, and I am often weary in the arms of women; I find greater pleasure in looking on and listening to their cries when the eunuchs lash them with thin wands. Therefore, this stubborn girl pleases me well since she gives me occasion to have her whipped by the eunuchs, and I swear that this very night she shall be beaten until

162

her skin swells up and prevents her lying on her back, whereby my pleasure shall be greater than before."

He rubbed his hands as he left me and tittered like a girl. As I stood and watched him go, I knew that he was no longer my friend, nor did I wish him well. And Minea's knife still lay in my hand.

5

After this I could not join in the general merrymaking, although the palace and its forecourts swarmed with people who drank wine and beer and wildly applauded Kaptah's clowning—for he had already forgotten the awkwardness in the women's house. His black eye had been treated with slabs of fresh raw meat so that it was no longer painful though richly colored. But what was amiss with me I do not know.

I reflected that I still had much to learn in Babylon since my studies relating to the livers of sheep were not yet completed, and I still could not pour oil into water as proficiently as the priests. Moreover, Burnaburiash was much in my debt both for my professional skill and for my friendship, and I knew that by remaining his friend I should receive lavish presents at my departure. Yet the more I pondered over this, the more persistently was I haunted by Minea's face. I thought also of Kaptah, who was to die that evening for a stupid whim of the King's, altogether without my consent, although he was my servant.

The upshot of it was that I hardened my heart against the King, who, by offending me thus, convinced me of my right to offend against him—though my heart told me that the mere thought was a breach of all the laws of friendship. But I was a solitary foreigner, unbound by local custom. That afternoon, therefore, I went down to the river bank and hired a ten-oared boat, and I told the oarsmen:

"Today is the Day of the False King, and I know that you are drunk with joy and beer and will not willingly go rowing. But I will give you double the customary reward, for my wealthy uncle has died, and I must take his body to lay it among his forefathers—and do it swiftly before his children or my brother begin to dispute the inheritance and leave me penniless. Therefore, I will pay you lavishly, if you row with speed despite the length of the journey—for my forefathers are gathered at our old home on the borders of Mitanni."

The boatmen grumbled, but I bought them two jars of beer and told them they might drink till sundown as long as they held themselves in readiness to start as soon as it was dark. At this they made violent protest.

"In no circumstances will we set forth after dark, for the night is full of many devils both large and small, also evil spirits that utter ghastly cries and will perhaps capsize our boat or slay us."

But I answered, "I go to make offering in the temple that no harm may come to us in the course of our journey, and the jingling of all the silver I will give you when we arrive will drown the howls of devils."

I went to the tower and sacrificed a sheep in the forecourt; not many people were about, for most of the citizens had assembled at the palace to celebrate the feast of the False King. I contemplated the liver of the sheep, but my thoughts were in such a turmoil that it told me little enough. I noticed merely that it was darker than usual and had an evil smell so that I was filled with misgivings. I collected the blood of the sheep in a leather bag, which I carried under my arm to the palace. When I stepped into the women's house, a swallow flew past my head, which warmed my heart and made my body valiant, for it was a bird from my homeland, and I took it as a good omen.

In the women's house I said to the eunuchs, "Leave me alone with this mad woman that I may drive the devil out of her."

They obeyed and took me to a small room where I explained to Minea what she was to do, and I gave her the knife and the bag of blood. She promised to follow my directions and I left her, shutting the door after me and telling the eunuchs that no one must disturb her, as I had given her a medicine to drive the devil out of her—a devil who might take possession of the first one who opened the door without my permission. They needed no further admonition.

By now the setting sun was filling the palace rooms with ruddy light. Kaptah was eating and drinking again while Burnaburiash waited upon him, laughing and tittering like a girl. All over the floor drink-sodden men were slumbering in pools of wine. I said to Burnaburiash, "I wish to convince myself that Kaptah will have a painless death, for he is my servant, and I owe it to him to be so assured."

"Hurry, then," he said, "for the old man is already mixing the poison with the wine and your servant must die at sunset as custom demands."

I found the old man, the King's physician. When I told him that the King had sent me, he believed me and said, "Mix the poison yourself, for my hands are shaky with wine drinking, and my eyes are so blurred that I can see nothing, so heartily have I laughed today at your servant's frolics."

164

I threw away his mixture and poured poppy juice into the wine, though not enough to cause death. Then, carrying the goblet to Kaptah, I said, "Kaptah, it may be that we shall never meet again, for your dignities have gone to your head and by tomorrow you will not deign to know me. Drink, therefore, from the cup I now offer you, so that upon my return to Egypt I shall be able to say that the lord of the four quarters of the world was my friend. When you have drunk, you will know that I mean you nothing but good, whatever may befall. Remember also our scarab!"

Kaptah said, "The talk of this Egyptian would be like the buzz of flies in my ears if my ears were not already so full of the buzz of wine that I cannot hear what he says. But the cup I have never spurned as all here know and as I have striven to prove today to all my subjects, with whom I am greatly pleased. Therefore, I will drain the cup you offer me though I know that I shall feel wild asses kicking in my head tomorrow."

He emptied the goblet, and at that moment the sun went down. Torches were brought in and lamps lighted. All rose and stood in silence so that quietness reigned throughout the palace. Kaptah put off the Babylonian diadem, saying, "This accursed crown weighs down my head, and I am weary of it. Also my legs are numb and my eyelids like lead. I had better go to bed."

So saying he dragged a heavy tablecloth over himself and lay down to sleep upon the floor. With the cloth, jars and wine cups came tumbling down on him so that he bathed in wine to his neck, even as he had promised to do in the morning. The King's servants undressed him and put the wine-drenched robe on Burnaburiash, set the royal diadem on his head and the symbols of majesty in his hands, and led him to take his place upon the throne.

"This has been a tiring day," he said. "Yet in the course of it I have not failed to note one and another of you who have shown me insufficient respect during the revels, no doubt in the hope that I should choke myself and never regain my throne. Drive those sleepers out with whips, chase the rabble from the courtyards, and put this fool into the jar of eternity if he is dead, for I am weary of him."

Kaptah was rolled on to his back, and the physician, having examined him with shaking hands and dim eyes, declared, "He is as dead as a dung beetle."

Servants bore in a great earthenware urn such as Babylonians use for the entombing of their dead, and into this Kaptah was put, the top being then sealed with clay. The King gave orders that the jar was to be carried down to the vaults beneath the palace and placed among those of previous false kings.

At this point I intervened, saying, "This man is an Egyptian and circumcised like myself. Therefore, I must embalm his body after the Egyptian custom, and for his journey to the Western Land I must furnish him with all necessary things so that he may eat and drink and take his pleasure after death without the necessity of toil. This may take thirty days or it may take seventy days, according to the rank the dead man has held during his lifetime. With Kaptah I think it will take but thirty days, as he was my servant. After that time I will bring him back to his place among his predecessors, the other false kings, in the vaults beneath your house."

Burnaburiash listened curiously and said, "So be it. Do with him as you will since it is the custom of your land; I shall not quarrel over customs, for I also pray to gods I do not know to propitiate them for sins I may unknowingly have committed. Prudence is a virtue."

I bade the servants carry Kaptah out in his jar and put him in a carrying chair that stood waiting by the palace wall. Before leaving I said to the King, "For thirty days you will not see me, for during the period of embalming I cannot show myself among men, lest I transmit to them the devils that swarm about the corpse."

On reaching the carrying chair I pierced a hole in the clay that sealed the jar, to give Kaptah air to breathe, and then returned secretly to the palace and the women's house. The eunuchs rejoiced to see me, for they feared that at any moment the King might come.

But when I had opened the door of the room in which I had left Minea, I returned at once, tearing my hair and lamenting. "Come and see what has happened, for there she lies dead in her blood with the bloodstained knife beside her, and her hair also is bloody!"

The eunuchs came and were aghast—for eunuchs have a great horror of blood—and they dared not touch her but began weeping and crying out in terror of the King's wrath.

I said to them, "We are involved in the same misfortune, you and I. Quickly bring a mat in which I may roll the body; then wash the blood from the floor, that none may know what has occurred. For the King anticipated much pleasure from this girl, and his wrath will be terrible if he learns that you and I in our blundering have let her die as her god required. Make speed, therefore, to put another girl in her place—one from a foreign land for choice, who does not speak your tongue. Dress her and adorn her for the King, and if she resists, beat her with sticks before his eyes, for this is especially pleasing to the King, and he will reward you richly."

The eunuchs perceived the wisdom of my words, and after bargaining with them for a while, I gave them half the silver they declared to be the price of a new girl. They brought me a mat in which I rolled Minea, and they helped me to carry her across the dark courtyards to the chair already occupied by Kaptah in his jar.

When we reached the river bank, I bade the porters lift the jar down into the boat, but the mat I carried myself and hid below the deck. Then I said to the porters, "Slaves and sons of dogs! This night you have heard and seen nothing, should anyone ask you. To remind you of this I give each one of you a silver piece."

Prancing with delight they shouted, "Truly we have served an illustrious lord, but our ears are deaf, and our eyes are blind, and we have seen and heard nothing this night."

I let them go, well knowing that they would get drunk without delay, as has been the way of porters in all ages, and that in their cups they would babble of all they had seen. As there were eight of them and they were burly men, I could not kill them and throw them into the river as I might have wished.

As soon as they were gone, I woke the boatmen. In the light of the rising moon, they unshipped their oars and pulled away from the city, yawning and cursing their fate, for their heads were dizzy with all the beer they had drunk.

Thus I took flight from Babylon, though for what reason I did all this I cannot say; doubtless it was written in the stars before the day of my birth, and was inevitable.

BOOK 7

Minea

I

WE SUCCEEDED in getting clear of the city unchallenged by the watch, for there was free access to the river at night, and I crept beneath the deck to lay my weary head to rest. But still there was no peace, for Minea had unrolled herself from the mat and was washing herself clean of blood, scooping up the river water in her hands while the moonlight sparkled in the drops that fell between her fingers.

She looked at me unsmilingly and said in reproach, "By your advice I have made myself filthy, and I smell of blood and shall surely never again be clean, and it's all your fault. What's more, when you carried me, you squeezed me much harder than was necessary so that I could not breathe."

Her talk annoyed me, and I was very tired, so I snapped at her, "Hold your tongue, accursed woman! When I think of all you have made me do, I feel like throwing you into the river, where you could wash to your heart's content. Had it not been for you, I should now be sitting on the right hand of the King of Babylon, and the priests of the tower would impart to me all their wisdom, concealing nothing, and I should be the wisest physician in the world. For your sake I have forfeited the presents I might have earned by the practice of my calling. My gold is dwindling, and I dare not present the tablets that entitle me to draw money in the temple counting houses. All this is on your account, and I curse the day I saw you; every year on this day I shall wear sackcloth and ashes."

She trailed her hand in the moonlit river, the water cleaving before it like molten silver, as she said in a low voice and with her face averted, "If this is so, let me jump into the river as you desire. Then you will be rid of me."

She rose and would have leaped in, but I seized and held her, saying, "Have done with this folly! If you jump in, all my contriving will have been in vain. In the name of all the gods let me sleep in peace, Minea, and do not bother me with these whims, for I am very tired."

With this I crawled under the mat and drew it closely about me, for the night was chilly although spring had come and storks were crying among the reeds. She crept in beside me, murmuring, "If I can do nothing else, I can at least keep you warm."

I was too weary for further argument but fell asleep and slept soundly in her warmth, for she was young and her body like a little stove beside me.

When I awoke, we had come far upstream, and the boatmen were grumbling. "Our shoulders are like wood, and our backs ache. Do you seek our death? Is your house afire that we must race to quench it?"

I hardened my heart and said, "Whoever slackens will feel my stick; you will take your first rest at noon. Then you may eat and drink, and to each of you I shall give a mouthful of date wine to revive you, and you will feel as airy as birds. But if there is any murmuring, I shall invoke all the devils against you; for you must know that I am a priest and a magician."

I said this to frighten them, but the sun was shining brightly and they did not believe me. They said only, "He is alone and we are ten!" and the nearest of them tried to smite me with his oar.

At that moment a thunderous noise came from the bow: it was Kaptah beating on the inside of the jar, cursing and yelling. The rowers turned gray in the face and one after another leaped overboard into the river and swam away out of sight. The boat swung across the stream, but I dropped the anchor stone. Minea came up from the cabin combing her hair, and at that instant all my fear left me, for she was fair, and the sun was shining, and the storks were crying among the reeds. I ran forward to the funeral urn and said loudly as I broke the clay seal, "Stand up, you man within there!"

Kaptah stuck his tousled head out of the jar, and I have never seen a more bewildered man. He moaned, "What is this foolery? Where am I? Where is my royal diadem, and where are the symbols of my majesty? I am naked and chilled—also my head is full of wasps, and my limbs are like lead as if I had been bitten by a venomous serpent. Beware how you make sport of me, Sinuhe, for it is dangerous to jest with kings!"

I wanted to punish him for his arrogance of the day before, so I looked blank and said, "I don't know what you are saying, Kaptah; you must still be in a fog of wine. You will remember that when we left Babylon you drank too much and became so violent in the boat and talked so wildly that the boatmen had to shut you up in that jar lest you should do them some harm. You were babbling of kings and judges and much else."

Kaptah shut his eyes and strove to recollect himself, and at last he replied, "Lord, never again will I drink wine, for wine and dreams have led me into a terrible adventure—an adventure so altogether ghastly that I cannot relate it to you. But this I can say: It seemed to me that by the grace of the scarab I was a king, dispensing justice from my throne, also that I entered the women's house and took exceedingly great pleasure there with a beautiful girl. Many other things happened, also, but I don't dare think of them now."

Just then he saw Minea. Ducking hastily down into the jar again, he said in a pitiful voice, "Lord, I am not yet quite recovered—or else I am still dreaming—for there in the stern of the boat I seem to see the girl whom I met in the women's house."

He touched his black eye and swollen nose and mourned aloud. Minea went up to the jar, pulled out his head by the hair and said, "Look at me! Am I the woman with whom you took pleasure last night?"

Kaptah gazed at her in terror, shut his one eye, and moaned, "All ye gods of Egypt have mercy on me and pardon me for having worshiped strange gods and made sacrifice to them—but you are she! Forgive me, for it was but a dream."

I helped him out of the jar and gave him a bitter stomach-cleansing potion, then tying a rope about his waist I dipped him in the river despite his protests, and held him floating in the water to clear his head of the poppy juice and wine. But when I had hauled him aboard again, I relented, saying, "May this be a lesson to you for your rebelliousness toward me, your master. Everything that happened to you is true and had it not been for my help you would now be lying lifeless in a jar among all the other false kings."

I then told him all that had taken place, and I had to tell it many times before he grasped it all and believed me. Finally I told him, "Our lives are in danger, and what has passed no longer seems funny, for as surely as we sit here in this boat, we shall hang head downward from the wall if the King finds us—and he may do even worse. Good planning is now essential, and you must hit on some way for us to escape with our lives into the land of Mitanni."

Kaptah scratched his head and mused. At length he said, "If I have understood you rightly, all that has happened is true and no wineborn delusion. This being so, I will praise this day as a good day, for

I can now drink wine without misgivings for my head's sake though I thought that never again in my life should I dare to taste it."

He crept into the cabin, broke the seal of a wine jar, and took a deep draught, for which he praised all the gods of Egypt and of Babylon by name, and he also praised many other gods whose names he did not know. For each divinity he named he bowed forward over the wine jar till at last he sank down on the mat in slumber, snoring like a hippopotamus.

I was so enraged at his behavior that I would have rolled him into the water and drowned him, but Minea said, "Kaptah is right: to each day its own vexations. Therefore, why shouldn't we drink wine and be happy in the place the river has brought us to? For it is a beautiful place, and we are hidden by the reeds. Storks are crying among them, and I see others flying with outstretched necks to build their nests; the waters gleam green and gold in the sunlight, and my heart is as arrowy as a bird now that I am freed from slavery."

I considered her words and they were wise.

"Since both of you are mad, why shouldn't I also be mad? Truly it is all one to me whether my hide hangs drying on the wall tomorrow or ten years from now, for all this was written in the stars before our birth, as the priests of the tower have taught me. The sun shines in glory, and in the fields along the river bank the corn is showing green. Therefore, I shall bathe in the river and try to catch fish in my hands as I did when a child, for this day is as good as any other."

And so we bathed in the river and dried our clothes in the sun, and we ate and drank wine. Minea made sacrifice to her god and danced his dance for me in the boat so that my breast tightened as I watched her, and I breathed with difficulty.

I finally said to her, "Only once in my life have I called a woman 'my sister,' but her embrace was a fire and her body a parching desert that brought me no refreshment. Therefore, I beseech you, Minea, set me free from the spell in which your limbs have bound me. Do not look at me with eyes that are like moonlight on the river, or else I shall call you 'my sister,' and you will lead me into destruction and death as the other woman did."

Minea looked at me curiously.

"You must have known strange women, Sinuhe—but perhaps those of your country are different. Don't be uneasy on my account. It is far from my purpose to seduce you as you seem to fear. My god has forbidden me to approach a man, on pain of death."

She took my head between her hands and laid it against her knees, and stroking my cheeks and hair, she said, "This is a stupid head to make you speak so ill of women, for though there be women who poison all wells, certainly there are others who are like a fountain in the desert—like dew on a parched meadow. But, though you have a thick and uncomprehending head and your hair is black and stiff, I like to hold it in my hands. There is that about you—in your eyes and your hands—that I find lovely and alluring. Therefore, I am sad that I cannot give you what you wish—sad not only for your sake but for mine if such an immodest confession can please you."

The water rippled against the boat, green and gold, and I held her strong, beautiful hands in mine. I held them like a drowning man and looked into her eyes that were like moonlight on the river and yet as warm as a caress.

"Minea, my sister!" I said. "I am weary of all the gods whom men have raised up for themselves—for fear, as I believe. Renounce your god, therefore, for his demand is cruel and useless—and today more cruel than ever. I will bring you to a country beyond the reach of his power though we have to journey to the edge of the world and eat grass and dried fish among savage tribes and sleep on reeds till our life's end. For somewhere there must be a bound set to the power of your god."

She held tightly to my hands and turned away her head.

"My god has set his boundary within my heart so that wherever I go I am within his reach—and if I give myself to any man I must die. Today as I behold you, my god seems to me cruel and foolish to demand this, but I can do nothing against him. Tomorrow all may be different—you will tire of me and forget me, for that is the way of men."

"No man knows what tomorrow will bring," I said impatiently, for all my being blazed toward her like a bundle of reeds that has been scorched year in, year out by the sun until kindled by a spark. "Your talk is but empty evasion to torment me—as all women love to do—and you enjoy my torment."

She withdrew her hands with a reproachful look.

"I am no ignorant woman, for besides my own language I speak that of Babylon and yours also and can write my name in three sorts of letters both on clay and paper. Moreover, I have been in many great cities, and I have danced before many different people, who have marveled at my art, until I was stolen away by merchants when our ship foundered. Ever since childhood I have grown up in the stables of the god and have been initiated into his secret ritual so that no power or witchcraft can separate me from him. If you also had danced before bulls and in the dance swung yourself between sharp horns and tickled a bellowing muzzle in play with your foot, you would understand. But I believe you have never seen youths and girls dancing before bulls."

"I have never even heard of it. But if I am to spare your virginity for the benefit of bulls, then it is a matter beyond all understanding, though I have heard that in Syria the priests who perform the secret ritual of the earth mother sacrifice maidens to he-goats, and these maidens are chosen from among the people."

She smote me hard on both cheeks, and her eyes burned as the eyes of a wildcat burn in the dark as she cried in a fury, "I find there is no difference between a man and a he-goat, for your thoughts turn on bodily things only so that a goat would answer your lusts as well as a woman. Sink then beneath the ground and leave me in peace; plague me no more with your lovesickness, for you know as much about it as a pig knows of silver."

Her speech was harsh and her blows severe. I left her and went aft. To pass the time I opened my medicine chests and began to clean my instruments and weigh out drugs. She sat in the bows, drumming her heels on the bottom of the boat in her exasperation; presently she threw off her clothes in a passion, rubbed her body with oil and began so wild and violent a dance that the boat rocked. I could not resist a sideways glance, for her performance was masterly beyond belief. She could bend backward without effort till she rested on her hands, arching her body like a bow, then raise her feet straight up into the air. All the muscles of her body quivered under the gleaming skin, she grew breathless, and her hair billowed about her head, for the dance demanded a degree of skill such as I have never seen equaled though I have watched dancing girls in the pleasure houses of many lands.

As I watched her, my anger melted away, and I brooded no longer upon what I had lost through stealing this capricious, ungrateful girl. I remembered also that she had been ready to stab herself to death in defense of her maidenhood and knew that I had behaved ill in demanding of her what she could not give. When she had danced so long that the sweat ran down her body and every muscle quivered with exhaustion, she covered herself, head and all, with a garment, and I heard her weeping. Then I forgot my drugs and instruments. Hastening to her, I touched her shoulder gently and asked, "Are you ill?"

176

She made no answer, but pushed my hand away and wept the more. I sat down beside her, and my heart was full of grief.

"Minea, my sister, do not weep—do not weep at least because of me, for truly I never mean to touch you—never, never—even if you were to ask me. I would save you all pain and sorrow and would have you stay always as you are."

She raised her head and wiped away her tears in a gesture of annoyance.

"I fear neither pain nor sorrow, you fool. And I do not weep because of you but because of my fate, which has separated me from my god and made me as weak as a rag so that a glance from a blockhead makes my knees give beneath me."

I held her hands, and she did not withdraw them but turned to me at length, to say, "Sinuhe, in your eyes I must appear ungrateful and vixenish, but I can't help it, for I don't know what has come over me. I would gladly tell you of my god so that you might understand me better but to speak of him to the uninitiated is forbidden. I can tell you only that he is the god of the sea and lives in a dark house, and no one who has entered that house has ever returned but dwells with him eternally. But there are some who say that he resembles a bull although he lives in the sea. We who are dedicated to his service are trained to dance before bulls. It is said also that he is like a man despite his bull's head, but I believe this is no more than a tale.

"I know only that every year twelve are chosen by lot from among those dedicated to enter his house one at a time when the moon is full, and there is no greater joy for those so dedicated than to enter this house. The lot has already fallen to me, but before my turn came, our ship foundered, as I have told you. The merchants stole me away and sold me in the slave market of Babylon. All my youth I have dreamed of the wonderful mansions of the god and of his couch and of immortality. Although we who are consecrated have permission to return to this world after a month is past, no one yet has ever done so—so I think the world has nothing to offer those who have once beheld the god."

A cloud seemed to veil the sun as she spoke; the scene took on a wan and deathly hue in my eyes, and I was seized with trembling, for I knew that Minea was not for me. Her story was like the stories told by the priests of every land—and she believed it, which barred her from me forever. I did not want to vex or sadden her.

Warming her hands between mine, I said only, "I understand that you desire to return to your god, so I will bring you over the sea to

177

Crete—for I know now that that is where you come from. I guessed it when you spoke of bulls, but what you said of the god in the dark house makes me sure of it. It is what merchants and seamen in Smyrna have told me though I never believed them until now. They would have it that the priests slew all who tried to return from the god's house, lest any should learn from them what he is like. That was only the talk of sailors and the common people; you being in-itiated will know better."

"I must go back—you know it!" she pleaded. "Nowhere else on earth should I find peace. I rejoice at every day to be spent with you, Sinuhe, and not because you delivered me from evil but because no one has ever treated me as you have. I have not the same yearning for the god's house as before but go to it with sorrow in my heart. If it be granted me, I will return to you after the allotted time—still, I don't think that will be, for no one has ever come back. Our time is short, and nobody knows what tomorrow may bring as you say, so let us enjoy every day as it comes, Sinuhe, and waste no thought on what is to come. That is best."

Another man might have taken her by force, carried her to his own land, and lived there with her all his days. I knew that she was speaking the truth and that she would never have a happy day if she betrayed her god; rather the time would come when she would curse me and flee from me. Such is the power of the gods when men believe in them, though over those who do not believe they can have none.

Doubtless these things were written in the stars before my birth and were unsusceptible of change. So we ate and drank in our boat, hidden by the reeds, and the future was remote from us. Minea bent her head and swept her hair across my face, smiling. When she had drunk wine, she touched my mouth with her wine-scented lips and the pain she caused my heart was sweet—sweeter perhaps than if I had taken her, though I did not think it then.

2

At dusk Kaptah awoke and crept out from under the mat, rub-bing his eyes and yawning.

"By the scarab—and not altogether forgetting Ammon—my head is no longer like an anvil. I could feel in harmony with the world once more if only I had something to eat, for my stomach feels as if it were full of ravening lions."

Without asking leave he joined us in our meal and crunched birds baked in clay, spitting the bones overboard. At the sight of him I was reminded of our plight.

"You drunken bat! You should have cheered us with good counsel and helped us out of this, for we shall soon all three be hanging by the heels in a row. Instead, you drank yourself sodden and snored face downward like a pig in the mire. Say quickly what is to be done, for the King's soldiers must already be in pursuit to slay us."

Kaptah scratched his head.

"This boat is indeed too large for three of us to row upstream. To speak truth I have no love for oars; they raise blisters on my hands. We should therefore go ashore and steal two donkeys on which to load our bundles. Let us dress in shabby garments so as not to attract attention, and we must bargain and haggle at the inns. You must not let it be known that you are a physician but feign to be of some other trade. We shall be a company of mummers traveling from village to village, entertaining the rustics in the evening on the threshing floors. No one chases jugglers, and thieves think them not worth the trouble of robbing. You can tell the yokels' fortunes in oil, as you have learned to do; I can tell them funny stories without end; and the girl can dance for her bread. It would never do to steal the boat from the poor boatmen, who are no doubt lurking somewhere in the reeds, waiting only for darkness to murder us. We should be wise to set off at once."

Evening was upon us, and there was no time to be lost. Kaptah was certainly right in supposing that the boatmen would conquer their fears and return to fetch their boat, and they were ten strong men. We smeared ourselves with their oil and soiled our clothes and faces with mud, then divided the remains of my gold and silver between us, hiding it in our girdles and other garments. My medicine chest, which I was unwilling to leave, we rolled up in the mat and laid on Kaptah's back, despite his protests. Then, letting the boat drift in among the reeds, we waded ashore. In the boat we left food and a couple of wine jars, Kaptah believing that the men would stay to get drunk, after which they would not trouble to pursue us. If they tried to accuse us before the judges when they were sober, they would give conflicting evidence, and their story would be so confused that the judges would drive them away with sticks—or so I hoped.

Thus we began our wandering and came in time to a caravan route that we followed all night, though Kaptah cursed the day he was born because of the weight of the bundle that sat askew on his shoulders. In the morning we reached a village whose inhabitants greeted us warmly and with respect because we had dared to travel by night regardless of devils. They gave us porridge made with milk and sold us two donkeys; they held festival when we left them, for they were simple folk who had not seen minted gold for many months but paid their taxes in grain and cattle and dwelled in mud huts among their beasts.

Day after day we trudged the roads of Babylonia. We met merchants; we stepped out of the way of rich men's chairs and bowed as they passed. The sun burned our skins, and our clothes became tattered, and we grew accustomed to staging our performances on threshing floors of beaten earth. I poured oil into water and foretold lucky days and abundant harvests, men children, and profitable marriages—for I pitied their poverty and was loath to prophesy anything but good. They believed me and rejoiced greatly. If I had told them the truth, I should have spoken of unrelenting tax gatherers, hard blows, corrupt judges, fevers at floodtime, locusts and flies, scorching drought and bad water in summer, heavy toil and, after toil, death—for that was their life. Kaptah told them stories of sorcerers and princesses and of foreign lands where people carried their heads under their arms and turned into wolves once a year. They believed his stories and venerated him and fed him well. Minea danced for them every day to keep in practice for her god, and they marveled at her art, saying, "Never have we seen the like of this!"

The journey was profitable to me, for it taught me that, if the rich and powerful are everywhere alike and think in the same way, so also are the poor the same the world over. Their thoughts are the same though their customs differ and their gods bear different names. My heart melted toward them for their great simplicity, and I could not refrain from healing the sick when I saw them, from lancing boils and cleansing eyes that I knew would otherwise soon be sightless— and all this I did of my own will, asking nothing in return.

But why I so exposed myself to the peril of discovery I cannot say. Perhaps my heart was softened by Minea, whom I saw every day and whose youth warmed my side at night when we lay on those earthen floors that smelled of straw and pungent manure. Perhaps I did it for her sake, to propitiate the gods by meritorious actions; but it may also be that I desired to test my skill, lest my hands lose their steadiness and my eyes their keenness in the detection of disease. For the longer I live the more clearly do I see that what a man does he does for many reasons—reasons of which he himself may be unaware; therefore, his actions are as dust beneath my feet, since I cannot know his motives or his purposes.

We encountered much hardship. My hands grew callused, the soles of my feet thickened, and the dust blinded my eyes. Nevertheless, when I recall this journey of ours along the dusty Babylonian roads, it seems beautiful, and I cannot forget it. Nay, I would give much of what I have known and possessed in this world if I might make that journey once more, with youth, keen eyes, and unwearying body restored to me and Minea beside me, her eyes gleaming like moonlight on the river. Death shadowed us all the way—a death that would have been no easy one if we had been discovered and had fallen into the hands of the King. But in those distant days I never thought of death nor feared it, though life was more precious to me than ever before, walking thus beside Minea and watching her dance on the sprinkled threshing floors. In her company I forgot the crime and shame of my youth, and every morning when I awoke to the bleating of kids and the lowing of cattle my heart was as light as a bird; I would step out to see the sun rise and sail like a golden ship into the gentle blue of the sky.

At last we reached the ravaged border country, but herdsmen, believing us to be poor, showed us the way so that we entered the land of Mitanni and came as far as Naharani without paying tribute or encountering the guards of either King. Only when we came to the great city, where people did not know each other, did we venture into the bazaars, where we bought new clothes and washed and dressed ourselves according to our station, after which we put up at the best inn. Since my gold was fast running out, I lingered a while in that city to practice my calling, finding many patients and healing many sick, for the people of Mitanni were as curious as ever and loved all that was strange. Minea also attracted attention by her beauty, and many offered to buy her of me. Kaptah rested after his labors and grew fat and met many women who granted him their favors for the sake of his stories. When he had drunk in the pleasure houses, he would tell of his day as King of Babylon, and everyone laughed and slapped his knees and cried, "Never have we met such a liar! His tongue is as long and fluent as the river."

So the time passed until Minea began to gaze at me with misgiving, and at night she lay awake weeping. Then I said to her, "I know that you yearn for your own country and your god, and we have a long journey before us. Yet I must first visit the land of Hatti, where the Hittites live, for reasons I cannot tell you. I believe that from their country one may sail for Crete—though of this I am not sure—and if you prefer it I will take you straight to the Syrian coast, whence vessels bound for Crete sail every week. But I have heard that a caravan is soon to start from here to take the yearly gifts from the King of Mitanni to the King of the Hittites, and with this we may travel in safety and see and hear many new things. However, the decision shall not be mine but yours."

In my heart I knew that I deceived her, for my desire to visit the land of Hatti was simply my desire to keep her with me longer before relinquishing her to her god.

But she replied, "Who am I to meddle with your plans? I go with you willingly wherever it may be since you have promised to take me back to my country. Where you go, I go, and should death overtake us, I will mourn not for my sake but for yours."

I therefore resolved to join the caravan as a physician and so travel under the protection of the King of Mitanni to the land of Hatti, which is also called Cheta. When Kaptah heard this, he broke out in imprecations and invoked the gods to his aid.

"Hardly are we out of the jaws of one death before my lord yearns to plunge down the gullet of another. Everyone knows that the Hittites are wild beasts and worse. By the scarab! Cursed be the day I was born into this world to suffer the whims of my lunatic master!"

I had to call him to order with a stick, after which I said, "Be it as you wish! I will send you in company with some merchants direct to Smyrna, and pay for your journey. Look after my house there until I return, for I am sick to death of your eternal lamentations."

But Kaptah blazed up again, saying, "And where would be the sense in that? How can I allow my lord to journey alone to the land of Hatti? I might as well loose a newborn kid among hounds, and my heart would never cease to upbraid me for the crime. I ask but one question: Is the land of Hatti reached by sea?"

I told him that so far as I knew there was no sea between the lands of Hatti and Mitanni.

"Blessed be my scarab," Kaptah replied, "for if it had been necessary to go by sea I could not have accompanied you since I have sworn to the gods never to set foot on a sea-going ship."

He then began to gather our things together and make ready for our departure, and I left all to his care, for in these matters he was handier than myself.

3

The journey with the Mitannian envoy was uneventful, and there is little to say about it, for the Hittites escorted us the whole way in their chariots and saw to it that we had food and drink at every stopping place. The Hittites are hardy, caring for neither cold nor heat, for they live among barren hills and are trained to hardship and privation from their childhood. They are fearless and dogged in battle; they scorn the weaker nations and subdue them, while they honor the valorous and seek their friendship.

Their nation is divided into many clans and villages ruled by princes whose power over them is absolute, but who are in turn subject to the great king who dwells in his city of Hattushash, among the mountains. He is their high priest, their commander-in-chief, and their supreme judge. In him is united all the authority by which men are ruled, divine as well as temporal, and I know of no king in whom is vested equal power, absolute though all royal authority is held to be. In other countries, Egypt included, the priests and judges have more control over the king's actions than is generally supposed.

In speaking of the great cities of the world men will mention Thebes and Babylon and sometimes Nineveh, which I have not seen. But I have never heard them speak of Hattushash, which is the great city of the Hittites and the seat of authority, set in the mountains like an eagle's eyrie at the heart of the hunting grounds. Yet this city may well be compared with others; and when I remember that its gigantic buildings are of hewn stone and its walls impregnable and more massive than any I have seen, I must acknowledge this city to be one of the greatest. It remains a secret from the world because the King has closed it to foreigners. Only accredited envoys are admitted to have audience of the King and deliver to him their gifts, and even these men are closely watched during the time they remain in Hattushash. Therefore, the citizens do not willingly talk to strangers even if they know their language. Should one make inquiry of them, they reply, "I do not understand" or "I do not know," and look about them uneasily lest someone should see them in converse with a stranger. They are not churlish by nature, however, but friendly, and they love to see foreign clothes, if these are handsome, and follow the wearers about the streets.

They do not hire soldiers, as do civilized peoples, but are themselves warriors, the men being divided into classes corresponding to their military rank. Thus the most distinguished are those who can afford to keep a chariot, and their status is determined not by their origins but by their proficiency in arms. All men of fighting age gather yearly for military exercises under the direction of their commanders. Hattushash is not a city of commerce like the other great cities but is full of forges and workshops from which come a steady clang of hammers, for in these workshops are forged arrowheads and spear heads and the wheels and frames of chariots.

At the time of my arrival in the land of Hatti the great King Shubbiluliuma had reigned for twenty-eight years. His name was so dreaded that people bowed and held up their hands when they heard it, crying aloud his praises, for he had brought order to the land of Hatti and subjugated many peoples. He lived in a stone palace in the middle of the city, and many stories were told of his birth and his heroic deeds, as they are told of all great rulers. I never saw him though; not even the envoys from Mitanni saw him. They had to leave their gifts on the floor of the reception hall, amid the jeers of the soldiers.

At first there seemed little for a physician to do in Hattushash, for as I understood it, the Hittites were ashamed of illness and concealed it as long as they could. Puny and deformed children were killed at birth, and ailing slaves were also put to death. For this reason their doctors had little skill and were ignorant, illiterate men, though they treated wounds and contusions well enough and had effective remedies also for the ailments peculiar to mountain districts, remedies that rapidly diminished the heat of the body and of which I was glad to learn. But if any man found himself afflicted with a disease that threatened to be fatal, he chose death rather than a cure, lest he should be maimed or feeble for the rest of his life. For the Hittites had no fear of death as civilized people have, but they held debility in great dread.

Yet in the main all great cities are alike, and the eminent and wealthy of every country are alike. When my fame spread among the people, a number of them came to my inn seeking cures; their maladies were known to me and I could treat them. But they preferred to come to me disguised, secretly and under cover of darkness, that their dignity might not be diminished. For this reason also they gave me munificent presents, and in the end I acquired much gold and silver in Hattushash, though at first I had feared to leave it as a beggar.

The Hittites were strict in their behavior, and men of the better class could not appear drunk in the streets without loss of dignity, but as in all other great cities, they did drink a great quantity of wine and also pernicious mixed wines. I treated the cramps resulting from this and stilled their trembling hands when they were to appear before the King. I let Minea dance for their entertainment; they admired her greatly and gave her rich presents without desiring more of her—for the Hittites were generous when anything pleased them. Having won their good will in this way I ventured to ask them about many things I could not openly have inquired into. I learned most from the King's Keeper of the Archives, who spoke and wrote many languages, dealt with the King's foreign correspondence, and was not bound by custom. I let him believe that I had been banished from Egypt never to return, and that I had no other object in traveling abroad than to acquire wealth and learning. He trusted me and was willing to answer my questions in return for good wine and Minea's dancing.

"Why is Hattushash closed to foreigners?" I asked him. "And why must caravans and merchants keep to certain roads, although your country is rich and your city vies with any other in marvels? Would it not be better for others to learn of your might and sing your praises among themselves as your land well merits?"

He tasted his wine and said, as his eyes strayed greedily to Minea's slender limbs, "Shubbiluliuma, our great king, said when he ascended the throne, 'Give me thirty years and I will make the land of Hatti the most powerful realm the world has ever seen.' Those thirty years will soon have expired, and I think that before long the world will hear more about the land of Hatti than it cares to know."

"But in Babylon I saw sixty times sixty times sixty men march past their king, and the sound of their feet was as the roar of the sea. Here perhaps I have seen as many as ten times ten men at once, and I cannot understand what you do with all the chariots that are being built in the city workshops. Of what use are chariots in mountain country? They are intended for fighting in the plains."

He laughed.

"For a physician you are very inquisitive, Sinuhe the Egyptian! Perhaps we earn our little crust of bread by selling chariots to the kings of the flat countries." He narrowed his eyes knowingly.

"That I do not believe!" I said boldly. "As readily would a wolf lend his fangs to a hare."

He roared with laughter, smiting his knees till the wine slopped out of his cup.

"I must tell the King that! Perhaps even during your lifetime you may see a great coursing of hares, for the justice of the Hittites is different from the justice of the plains. In your land I believe the rich rule the poor; in ours the strong rule the weak. The world will learn a new lesson before your hair is gray, Sinuhe."

"The new Pharaoh in Egypt also has a new god," I said with feigned simplicity.

"That I know, for I read all the King's letters. This god is a great lover of peace and declares that there is no dispute between nations that cannot be settled peaceably. We have nothing against this god; on the contrary we like him very well—so long as he rules in Egypt and in the plains. Your Pharaoh has sent our great king an Egyptian cross that he calls the symbol of life, and he will certainly have peace for some years to come provided he sends us plenty of gold, that we may store up still more copper and iron and grain, build new workshops, and fashion more and heavier chariots than before. For all of these much gold is needed, and our king has gathered together here in Hattushash the cleverest armorers of many different countries and rewards them lavishly. But why he does this I believe no doctor's wisdom can divine!"

"The future you foretell may please crows and jackals, but it does not cheer me, and I find in it no cause for laughter. In Mitanni stories are told of your crimes in the border country—stories so frightful that I will not repeat them, for they are unbecoming a cultured people.'

"What is culture?" he asked, refilling his wine cup. "We also can read and write and amass numbered clay tablets in our archives. Our aim is to instill fear among the enemy peoples so that when the time comes they will submit to us without a struggle and so save themselves needless injury and loss. For we do not love destruction for its own sake; we prefer to annex countries and cities in as undamaged a state as possible. A timid foe is a foe half vanquished."

"Is everyone then your enemy? Have you no friends at all?"

"Our friends are all those who make submission to us and pay us tribute," he explained. "We let them live in their own way and do not interfere much with their customs and their gods so long as we are the rulers. Our friends are also all those who are not our neighbors— at least until such time as they become our neighbors, for then we tend to discover offensive traits in them that disturb harmony and force us into war against them. So it has been hitherto, and so I fear it will be henceforth, from what I know of our great king."

"Have your gods nothing to say about this? In other countries it is often they who determine what is right and what wrong."

"Right and wrong? Right is what we desire, and wrong is what our neighbors desire. That is a very simple principle that facilitates

186

both life and statesmanship and that in my opinion differs little from the teaching of the gods in the plains. As I understand it, these gods hold that to be right which the wealthy desire and that wrong which the poor desire."

"The more I learn about the gods the sadder I become," I said dejectedly.

That evening I told Minea, "I have learned enough about the land of Hatti and have found what I came to seek. I am ready to leave, for there is a smell of corpses here, and it stifles me. Death broods over me like an oppressive shade while I remain, and I don't doubt the King would have me impaled on a stake if he knew what I have discovered. Let us flee from this corruption; it makes me feel that I would rather have been born a crow than a man."

With the help of some of my more eminent patients I succeeded in getting a permit to travel by a prescribed route to the coast and there to board a ship. My patients bewailed my departure and urged me to stay, assuring me that if I continued to practice among them I should be wealthy in a few years. However, no one sought to prevent my going, and I laughed and joked with them and told them the stories they enjoyed so that we parted friends and they gave me many presents in farewell. We left the fearful ramparts of Hattushash, behind which lurked the world of the future, and rode on our donkeys past the blinded slaves who turned the thundering millstones, past the corpses of sorcerers impaled on either side of the road. I made all possible speed, and in twenty days we arrived at the port.

4

We tarried there for a while—though it was a noisy town, full of vice and crime—for when we saw a ship bound for Crete, Minea would say, "That one is too small and will sink, and I have no wish to be shipwrecked a second time." And when we saw a larger one, she would say, "That is a Syrian ship, and I will not sail in her." And of a third she would object, "The master of the vessel has evil eyes, and I fear he will sell us as slaves in a foreign land."

So we stayed on in the seaport, and I for one did not regret this. I had plenty to do there, cleansing and stitching up gashes and opening crushed skulls. The harbor master himself eventually came to me, for he was suffering from a pox. I knew the disease from my Smyrna days and was able to cure it with a remedy used by the physicians there.

When I had cured him he said, "What shall I give you, Sinuhe, for your great skill?"

I replied, "I do not want your gold. Give me the knife in your girdle, and the obligation will be mine; I shall also have a lasting gift by which to remember you."

But he objected, saying, "The knife is a common one; no wolves run along its edge, nor is there silver inlay in the handle."

But he said this because the knife was of Hittite metal, of which it was forbidden to give or sell any to strangers. I had been unable to buy such a weapon, not liking to insist for fear of arousing suspicion. In Mitanni such knives were to be seen only among the most distinguished persons, and their price was ten times their weight in gold—and even then their possessors would not sell them because there were but few of them in the known world. But for a Hittite such a knife had no great value since he was forbidden to sell it to a foreigner.

The harbor master knew that I was soon to leave the country, and reflecting that he could find better use for his gold than to give it away to a doctor, he did in the end present me with the knife. It was so sharp that it shaved hair more easily than the finest flint blade and could make nicks in copper without damaging its own edge. I was delighted with it and resolved to silver-wash the blade and fit to it a handle of gold as did the Mitannians when they had acquired such a knife. The harbor master bore no grudge but was my friend because I had wrought him a lasting cure.

In this town there was a field in which wild bulls were kept as was often the case at seaports, and the youth of the place were wont to display their litheness and valor in encounters with these beasts, hurling darts into their shoulders and leaping over them. Minea was overjoyed to see them and desired to test her skill. In this way I first saw her dance among wild bulls; it was like nothing I had ever seen before, and my heart froze as I watched. For a wild bull is the most terrible of all savage beasts—worse even than an elephant, which is gentle when not irritated—and its horns are long and sharp as brad awls; with one stroke it will slit a man's body or toss him high in the air and trample him underfoot.

But Minea danced before them wearing only a flimsy garment, and she stepped lightly aside when they lowered their heads and charged at her with dreadful bellowings. Her face was flushed, and with growing excitement she threw off her silver hair net so that her hair floated in the wind. Her dance was so rapid that the eye could not follow all her movements as she leaped up between the horns of an attacking beast, held fast to them and then, thrusting with her feet against its forehead, threw herself upward in a somersault, to land on its back. I gazed spellbound at her performance; I believe her awareness of this urged her on to do things I could never have believed a human being could accomplish. So I looked on with my body streaming with sweat, and I could not sit still, although those who sat behind me on the benches swore at me and tugged at my shoulder cloth.

On her return from the field she was loudly applauded. Garlands were set upon her head and about her neck, and the other young people presented her with a bowl on which bulls were painted in red and black. All exclaimed, "We have seen nothing like it!" and the sea captains who had been to Crete said, as they blew wine fumes through their nostrils, "Even in Crete there is hardly such another to be seen."

But she came to me and leaned against me, and her thin dress was wet with sweat. She leaned against me, and every muscle in her strong, slender body was quivering with weariness and pride. I said to her, "I have never seen anyone like you." My heart was weighed down with grief, for now that I had seen her dance before the bulls, I knew that they had come between us like some evil sorcery.

Soon after this a ship from Crete put into the harbor; she was neither too small nor too large, and the captain's eyes were not evil. He spoke Minea's own language; and she said to me, "This ship will take me safely home to my god, so now you will leave me gladly, because I have caused you much vexation and loss."

"You know very well, Minea, that I am coming to Crete with you."

She looked at me with eyes like the sea in moonlight; she had colored her lips, and her eyebrows were thin black lines.

"I do not know why you would come with me, Sinuhe, since the ship will take me straight home in safety, and no further evil can befall me."

"You know as well as I do, Minea."

She laid her long, strong fingers in mine and sighed.

"We have gone through much together, Sinuhe, and I have seen so many people that my mother country has grown dim in my memory like some fair dream, and I do not yearn after my god as I did formerly. Therefore, I have put off this voyage with empty excuses as you well know—but when I danced once more before the bulls, I knew that I must die if you were to possess me."

"Yes, yes, I know. We have been all through this before; it is a tedious, pointless, and oft-repeated tale. I do not mean to ravish you, for the matter is not worth the plaguing of your god. Any slave girl can give me what you refuse—there is no difference, as Kaptah says."

Then her eyes glistened green as a wild cat's eyes in the dark; she drove her nails into my hand and hissed, "Make haste then and find your slave girl, for the sight of you revolts me. Run away now to the grimy girls in the harbor whom you so desire, but know that thereafter I shall not recognize you and will perhaps even shed your blood with your own knife. What I can forgo you also can forgo."

I smiled at her.

"No god has forbidden me this thing!"

"I forbid it—and dare you to come to me afterward!"

"Be easy, Minea, for really I am weary of the matter. There is nothing more monotonous than taking pleasure with a woman, and having tried it, I feel no desire to repeat the experience."

But she flared up again and said, "Your talk wounds the woman in me, and I fancy you would not find—everyone—so monotonous."

I found I could say nothing to please her, though I did my best. That night she did not lie beside me as usual but took her mat into another room and covered her head to sleep.

I called to her, "Minea! Why don't you warm me? You are younger than I am; the nights are cold, and I shiver."

"That is not true, for my body burns as if I were in a fever, and I cannot breathe in this stifling heat. I would rather sleep alone—but if you are cold, have a brazier brought to your room, or take a cat to lie beside you, and trouble me no more."

I went and felt her, and her body was hot and shivery under the blanket. I said, "You are ill, perhaps. Let me tend you."

She kicked and pushed me away, saying angrily, "Be off now! I do not doubt that my god will heal this sickness."

But after a little while she said, "Give me something, Sinuhe, or my heart will break."

I gave her a soothing medicine, and at last she slept; but I watched until the harbor dogs began barking in the wan light of dawn.

Then came the day of departure, and I said to Kaptah, "Pack up our belongings, for we are going aboard a ship bound for Keftiu's island, which is also Minea's."

"I guessed this, but I did not rend my clothes, for then I should have had to mend them—and it is not worth strewing ashes in my hair for such a false dealer as you! Didn't you swear when we left Mitanni that we need not put to sea? Nevertheless, I have resigned myself and will say nothing; I will not even weep lest I lose the sight

190

of my one remaining eye—so bitterly have I already wept on your account in the countries to which your folly has led us. I merely say at once, to avoid subsequent mistakes, that this is my last voyage— my stomach tells me so. But I shall not trouble even to reproach you, for the bare sight of you and the physician's smell of you are revolting to me. I have put our things together and am ready to depart, for without the scarab you cannot venture forth in a ship, and without the scarab I cannot hope to travel the land route to Smyrna and preserve my life. Therefore, I go with the scarab and either die on board or drown in the sea with you."

I marveled at Kaptah's reasonable attitude—until I learned that he had inquired among the seafarers in the harbor concerning remedies for seasickness and had bought magic talismans from them. Before we sailed, he tied these objects about his neck, drew his girdle tight, and drank an intoxicating herbal mixture so that when he stepped aboard his eye was staring like that of a boiled fish. He begged in a thick voice for fat pork, which the sailors had assured him was the best preventive of seasickness. He lay down on his bunk and fell asleep with a pig's shoulder blade in one hand and the scarab gripped in the other. The harbor master took our clay tablet and bade us farewell; then the oarsmen unshipped their oars and rowed us out of the bay.

Thus began the voyage to Crete. The captain made sacrifice in his cabin to the sea god and others, then gave the command to hoist sail; the vessel heeled over and began to cleave the water while my stomach rose to my throat—for ahead there was no shore line. Ahead was but the endless, rolling sea.

BOOK 8

The Dark House

BEFORE us rolled the boundless waters, but I feared nothing for Minea was with me, Minea who breathed the sea air and was herself again, with moonlight in her eyes. She stood in the bows by the figure-head, leaning forward and drinking in the air as if with her own strength she would draw us more speedily along our course. The sky over us was blue, and the sun shone; the wind was not too boisterous but fresh and steady and blowing from the right quarter—or so the captain said. Having become accustomed to the motion of the vessel, I suffered no sickness, though fear of the unknown assailed my heart when on the second day out the last of the white-winged, circling sea birds forsook the ship. Instead, the dolphin team of the sea god attended us, their smooth backs flashing as they tumbled in the water. Minea shouted aloud and hailed them in her own tongue, for they brought her greetings from her god.

Nor were we alone on the waters; we sighted a Cretan warship whose hull was hung with copper shields and who dipped her pennant when she saw that ours was not a pirate vessel. Kaptah rose from his bunk when he found himself able to stand and talked to the sailors, boasting of his journeys in many lands. He told of his voyage from Egypt to Smyrna, of a storm that ripped the sail from the mast, and of how he and the captain were the only ones aboard who could eat, while the rest lay about the deck groaning and puking into the wind. He told also of most fearful sea monsters that haunted the Nile delta and would engulf any fishing boat which ventured too far out to sea. The sailors gave him as good again and described certain pillars at the farthest ends of the ocean, which supported the heavens, and of fish-tailed maidens who lay in wait for seafarers and put spells on them to seduce them. They told tales of sea monsters that made the hair rise on Kaptah's head and sent him running to me with a gray face, to cling to my shoulder cloth.

Minea grew daily more radiant. Her hair floated in the wind, her eyes were like moonlight on the waters, and she was so slender and beautiful to see that my heart melted within me as I beheld her and remembered how soon she would be gone. To return to Smyrna or to Egypt without her seemed an empty thing. Life was like ashes in my mouth at the thought of the time when she would not put her hands in mine or press against my side and when I should behold her no longer.

The captain and his men held her in deep veneration when they heard that she danced before bulls and that the lot had fallen to her to enter the god's house at the full moon, although she had hitherto been prevented by shipwreck. When I tried to ask them about their god, they made no answer; some said, "We do not know" and others, "We do not understand your tongue, stranger." I knew only that the Cretan god ruled the sea and that the islands in the sea sent their young men and their maidens to dance before his horned beasts.

The day came when Crete rose like a blue cloud from the ocean and the seamen uttered cries of joy, while the captain made sacrifice to the god of the sea who had sent us fair weather and a following wind. The mountains of Crete and its steep, olive-clad shores rose before my eyes, and I saw a strange land of which I knew nothing, though I was to leave my heart buried there. But Minea saw in it her homeland and wept with joy at the bare hills and the tender green of the earth within the sea's embrace. Then the sail was lowered; the oarsmen unshipped their oars and rowed the ship alongside the quay, past other craft from every land—both warships and merchantmen—which lay at anchor in the roads. There must have been a thousand vessels, and Kaptah surveying them said he could not have believed there were so many in the world. Here were neither towers nor walls nor any fortifications, and the city adjoined the port; so assured was Crete's sovereignty of the seas—so powerful its god.

2

I shall now speak of Crete and of what I have seen there, but of what I think of the country and its god I shall say nothing; I shall seal my heart and let my eyes report. Nowhere in the world, then, have I beheld anything so strange and fair as Crete, though I have journeyed in all known lands. As glistening spume is blown ashore, as bubbles glow in all five colors of the rainbow, as mussel shells are bright with mother of pearl, so was Crete lucent to my eyes. Nowhere are human pleasures so immediate, so capricious, as here. No one acts but by the impulse of the moment, and the minds of the people veer from hour to hour. For this reason it is difficult to extract promises from them or make agreements. They are fair of speech and of great charm, because they delight in the music of words; death is not acknowledged among them, nor do I believe they have named it. It is concealed, and when a man dies, he is removed in secret that others be not oppressed. I believe they burn the bodies of their dead, though of this I cannot be sure, for throughout my stay I saw not one dead person nor any graves save those of former kings. These had been built of huge stones in some bygone age, and today people go far out of their way to avoid them as if by turning their thoughts away from death they might escape it.

Their art also is strange and wayward. Every painter paints as the fancy takes him, heedless of rules, and he paints only such things as in his own eyes are beautiful. Vases and bowls blaze with rich color; round their sides swim all the strange creatures of the sea. Flowers grow upon them, butterflies hover over them, so that a man accustomed to an art regulated by convention is disturbed when he sees the work and thinks himself in a dream.

Buildings are not imposing like the temples and palaces of other countries, convenience and luxury being the aim rather than outward symmetry. Cretans love air and cleanliness; their lattice windows admit the breeze, and their houses contain many bathrooms where both hot and cold water runs from silver pipes into silver baths at the mere turn of a tap. In the privies, running water sluices out the pans with a rushing sound, and nowhere else have I seen such a refinement of luxury. Nor is it only the rich and eminent who live in this fashion, but all save those about the harbor, where foreigners and dock laborers have their dwellings.

The women spend endless time in washing themselves, in plucking hairs from their bodies, and in tending, beautifying, and painting their faces, so they can never be ready at any stated time but arrive at receptions when it suits their convenience. Strangest of all are their clothes. They wear dresses woven of gold or silver, which cover all their bodies save for the arms and bosom—for they are proud of their lovely breasts. But the wide, pleated skirts are adorned with a thousand embroideries or with the paintings of artists. Also they have dresses put together of numberless pieces of beaten gold in the form of cuttlefish, butterflies, and palm leaves, and their skin gleams through between them. They dress their hair high and with complexity, devoting whole days to the task, and they wear small, light hats that they fasten to the hair with gold pins, so as to seem poised like butterflies. Their bodies are lithe and slim and their loins as narrow as a boy's so that they have difficulty in bearing children and avoid this as far as they can, thinking it no shame to be childless or to have but one or two.

The men wear ornamented boots to the knee, but their loincloths are simple, and they gird themselves tightly, being vain of their slender waists and broad shoulders. They have small, handsome heads and delicate limbs, and like the women they allow no hair upon their bodies. Only a few of them speak foreign tongues, for they prefer their own country to others, which do not offer the same ease and gaiety. Although they derive their wealth from seafaring and commerce, I met those who refused to visit the harbor because of its evil smells and who could not perform the simplest calculation but in all things relied upon their stewards. Able foreigners may, therefore, speedily acquire wealth if they are content to live in the harbor quarter.

They have instruments that play without a musician, and they claim to be able to put music into writing so that one may learn to play without ever having heard the piece performed. The musicians of Babylon also declared that they could do this, and I will not contradict them or the Cretans since I know nothing of music and the instruments of many different lands have perplexed my ear. Nevertheless, I can well understand the saying current in other parts of the world: "He lies like a Cretan."

No temples are to be seen there, and they pay little heed to the gods but content themselves with serving their bulls. This they do, however, with great enthusiasm so that a day seldom passes without a visit to the field. I do not think this is to be attributed so much to their piety as to the excitement and pleasure afforded by the dancing.

Nor can I say that they display much veneration for their king, for he is their equal save that he lives in a palace many times larger than those of his subjects. They are as much in his company as in anyone's; they jest with him and tell stories, come to his receptions at whatever hour they please and leave when they are bored or in response to some fresh whim. They drink wine in moderation, for cheerfulness' sake, and they are very free in their ways. They are never drunk, however, for they consider this barbarous, nor have I seen anyone vomit from excess of drinking at their banquets as often happens in Egypt and elsewhere. Nevertheless, desire for one another is readily kindled, and they enjoy each other's wives or husbands how or when the fancy takes them. The youths who dance before the bulls stand highest in the women's favor. Many distinguished men learn this art though not initiates; they do it for pleasure and at times attain a proficiency equal to that of the dedicated youths to whom women are forbidden, as men are forbidden to the girls. This last I cannot understand, for from their way of life one would not expect them to attach much importance to the matter.

Upon our arrival in the harbor we put up at the foreigners' inn, which was the most luxurious of any I have seen though not large. Ishtar's House of Joy in Babylon, with all its dusty magnificence and its loutish servants, seemed in comparison a very barbarous place. At this inn we washed and dressed, and Minea put up her hair and bought new clothes that she might show herself to her friends.

I was astonished to behold her—she wore on her head at tiny hat like a lamp and on her feet high-heeled shoes that were awkward to walk in. I would not vex her by any remark but gave her earrings and a necklace of different-colored stones, which the merchant told me was fashionable that day, though for the morrow he could not answer. I surveyed also with astonishment her bared breasts with nipples painted red, which swelled forth from the silver sheath about her body; she avoided my eyes, saying defiantly that her breasts were nothing to be ashamed of but would stand comparison with those of any woman in Crete. After closer inspection I did not deny this, for she may well have been right.

Next we were conveyed to the town itself. With its gardens and airy houses it was like another world after the crowds, noise, fish smells, and chaffering of the port. Minea took me to an elderly man of some distinction who was her special patron and friend; it had been his custom to stake money on her in the field of bulls, and Minea looked on his house as her own. He was studying the list of bulls when we came and noting the bets he would make on the following day.

When he saw Minea, he forgot his papers in his joy, embraced her without reserve, and cried, "Where have you been hiding? I have not seen you for so long a time that I fancied you must already have entered the house of the god. Yet I have chosen no one to take your place, and your room stands empty—that is if my servants have remembered to keep it so and my wife has not had it pulled down to make room for a pool; she has just now a fancy for breeding different kinds of fish and can think of nothing else."

"Helea—breeding fish?" exclaimed Minea in astonishment.

Somewhat embarrassed the old man replied, "It is Helea no longer. I have a new wife, and she has with her just now an uninitiated youth to whom she is showing her fish; I do not think she would want to be disturbed. But present your friend to me that he may be my friend also and this house his."

"My friend is Sinuhe the Egyptian, He Who Is Alone, and by profession he is a doctor," said Minea.

"I wonder how long he will remain alone here," the old man jested. "But surely you are not ill, Minea, that you come in company with a physician? That would distress me, for I am hoping you will dance before the bulls tomorrow and turn my luck. My steward down at the port has been complaining that my income no longer covers my expenses—or perhaps it is the contrary? I do not well remember, for I can make nothing of his complicated accounts, which he constantly thrusts before me in the most tedious manner."

"I am not ill, but this friend has rescued me from many perils, and we have journeyed far to return to my homeland. I was shipwrecked on my way to dance before bulls in Syria."

"Indeed?" said the old man uneasily. "I hope that despite your friendship you have kept your virginity, or you will be excluded from the competitions—and there are also other vexations as you are well aware. I am indeed distressed, for I note that your breasts have developed in a suspicious manner and your eyes have a moist shine in them. Minea, Minea! You have not cast yourself away?"

"No!" said Minea in wrath. "And when I deny it you may trust to my word and need not examine me as they did in the Babylonian slave market. You seem scarcely to understand that it is thanks to my friend here that I have returned safely after many perils. I thought my friends would rejoice to see me, but you think only of your bulls and your wagers!" She began to weep with rage, and her tears left streaks of eye black on her cheeks.

The old man was greatly disturbed and cast down, and he said, "I doubt not that you are overwrought from your travels, for in foreign countries you may not even have been able to take your daily bath. Nor do I think that the bulls of Babylon can be compared with ours —and that reminds me that I should long ago have been at Minos', though the matter escaped my mind. I had better go at once. If my wife should come, tell her I am with Minos and that I did not wish to disturb her and the young aspirant. Or I might go to bed since no one at Minos' will observe whether I am there or not. On the other hand if I went I could look in at the stables on the way and learn how that new bull is shaping—the one with the patch on its flank. Perhaps after all I had better go. A truly exceptional beast!"

Absently he took his leave of us, but Minea said to him, "We shall also go to Minos' that I may present Sinuhe to my friends."

So we went to the palace of Minos, on foot because the old man could not make up his mind whether or not it was worth while to take a chair for so short a distance. Not until we reached the palace did I discover that Minos was the king and that their kings were always called Minos to distinguish them from other people. But which Minos of his line he might be was unknown, for no one had the patience to reckon and record them.

There were countless rooms in this palace; on the walls of the reception hall were depicted billowing seaweeds and cuttlefish and jellyfish swimming in transparent waters. The great room was filled with people, each more rarely and extravagantly dressed than the last, and they moved about conversing in lively tones with one another, laughing loudly and drinking chilled drinks—wine and fruit juice—from small cups, while the women compared dresses. Minea presented me to many of her friends, who all displayed the same absent-minded courtesy; King Minos said a few friendly words to me in my own language, thanking me for having saved Minea for their god and brought her home. She should now enter the god's house at the first opportunity, he said, although her turn according to the lot she had drawn was now past.

Minea went about the palace as if it were her own, leading me from room to room, crying out in pleasure at the sight of some object familiar to her, and greeting the servants, who returned her salutation as if she had never been away. I learned that any eminent Cretan could visit his country estates or set forth on a journey whenever the fancy took him, and though he forgot to mention it to his friends, no one would wonder at his absence. On his return he would join the rest again as if he had never been away. This habit must have softened the fact of death for them, for when anyone disappeared, no one inquired for him and he was forgotten. His absence from an appointment or a meeting or a reception caused no remark since he might have taken it into his head to do something else instead.

At length Minea took me to a room that was perched on a rock above the rest of the building. Its wide windows commanded a view over smiling fields and plowland, olive groves and plantations beyond the city. She told me that this was her room; all her possessions were there as if she had left it but yesterday, though the clothes and jewelry were now out of date and could no longer be worn. Only now did I learn that she was a kinswoman of Minos, though I should have guessed this from her name. Gold and silver and costly presents were meaningless to her since she had been accustomed from childhood to have whatever she desired. From childhood also she had been dedicated to the god and had been brought up in the house of the gods, where she lived when she was not staying at the palace, or with her old patron, or with friends. They are as casual in their dwelling places as in every other particular.

Next Minea took me to the house of the bulls, which was a city in itself, with stalls and arenas, meadows and paddocks, school buildings and priests' houses. We went from stall to stall, breathing the rank smell of these beasts. Minea wearied not of calling them by pet names and enticing them, though they tried to gore her between the posts of the partitions, bellowing and pawing the sand with their sharp hoofs.

She met there boys and girls whom she knew, although these dancers were in general not friendly, being jealous of their skill and unwilling to impart their tricks to one another. But the priests who trained both bulls and dancers received us warmly, and when they heard that I was a physician, they asked me many questions concerning the digestion of bulls and their diet and the gloss of their coats, although they must have known more of these matters than I. Minea stood high in their favor and was at once allotted a beast and a place in the program for the following day; she was eager to display to me her proficiency with the very best beasts.

Finally Minea took me to a little building where the high priest of the Cretan god lived alone. Just as Minos was always named Minos, so was the chief priest always Minotauros, and for some reason he was the most venerated and dreaded man in Crete. His name was not willingly mentioned and he was referred to as "the man in the little bull house." Even Minea feared to visit him though she would not confess this to me; I saw it from her eyes, whose every shade I had learned to know.

When we had been announced, he received us in a dim room. At first I fancied that we beheld the god himself and believed all the tales I had been told, for I saw a man with the golden head of a bull. When we had bowed before him, he removed this head and revealed his own face; nevertheless despite his courteous smile I did not like him, for there was in his expressionless face something of sternness and cruelty. I could not define what it was, for he was a handsome man, very dark and born to command. Minea had no need to tell him anything; he already knew of her shipwreck and her travels. He asked no unnecessary questions but thanked me for my good will to Minea and through her to Crete and its god. He told me that rich presents awaited me at my inn with which he fancied I should be well content.

"I am indifferent to presents," I said. "Knowledge is of more value to me than gold, and to increase it I have journeyed in many countries so that I am now familiar with the gods of Babylon and of the Hittites. I hope to acquaint myself with the god of Crete, of whom I have heard much that is marvelous, and who loves virgins and pure boys in contrast to the gods of Syria, whose temples are pleasure houses and who are served by castrated priests."

"We have a great number of gods whom the people worship," he replied. "In the harbor there are temples to the glory of foreign gods, where you may make sacrifice to Ammon or the Baal of the port if you so desire. But I would not mislead you, and acknowledge that the might of Crete depends upon that god who has been worshiped in secret from as far back in time as our knowledge goes. The initiates alone may know him, and that only when they meet him face to face. No one has returned to tell us of his shape."

"The gods of the Hittites are the heavens and the rain that falls from the heavens and fructifies the earth. The god of Crete I understand to be the god of the sea since the wealth and power of Crete derive from the sea."

"Perhaps you are right, Sinuhe," he said with a strange smile. "Know, however, that we Cretans worship a living god, differing herein from the people of the mainland who worship dead gods and images of wood. Our god is no image although bulls are accounted as his symbols, and as long as our god lives, so long endures the Cretan sovereignty of the seas. Thus it has been foretold, and we are assured of it though we also put great trust in our warships, with which no other seafaring nation can compete."

"I have heard that your god dwells in the mazes of a dark mansion," I persisted. "I would gladly see this labyrinth, of which I have heard much. But I do not understand why the initiates never return from it, though they have permission to do so when they have been there for the space of one moon."

"The highest honor, the profoundest bliss, that can fall to the lot of an initiate is to enter the mansion of the god," said Minotauros, repeating words I had heard countless times before. "Therefore the islands in the sea vie with one another in sending their fairest maidens and the flower of their young men to dance before the bulls so that they may take part in the drawing of lots. I do not know whether you have heard stories of the sea god's mansions; life there is altogether different

203

from that which we know so that no one who has entered it desires to return to the torment and sorrow of the world. How say you, Minea? Do you fear to enter?"

Minea made no reply and I said, "I have seen the bodies of seamen washed up on the beach at Smyrna; their faces and bellies were swollen, and no joy was reflected in their features. That is all I know of the mansions of the sea god, but I do not doubt your word, and I wish all good to Minea."

Minotauros said coldly, "You shall see the labyrinth for the night of the full moon is near, and upon that night Minea will enter the house of the god."

"And if she refuse?" I demanded fiercely, for his words angered me and froze my heart with despair.

"Such a thing has never happened. Be easy, Sinuhe the Egyptian. When Minea has danced before the bulls she will enter the god's house of her own free will."

He donned the golden bull's head once more as a signal that we might retire, and his face was hidden from us. Minea took my hand and led me away; she was no longer happy.

3

Kaptah was at the inn when I returned and had drunk copiously in the wine shops of the harbor. He said to me, "Lord, for servants this land is the Western Land; no one beats them or remembers how much gold was in his purse or what jewels he had. If a master be wroth with his servant and order him to leave his house, the servant has but to hide himself and return the following day when his master has forgotten the whole matter."

This he said in his customary manner as if he were drunk, but then he shut the door, and having assured himself that no one was listening, he went on, "Lord, strange things are coming to pass in this country. The seamen in the wine shops say that the god of Crete has died and that the priests in great fear are seeking a new god. This is dangerous talk for which sailors have already been hurled from the clifftop to be devoured by cuttlefish, for it has been foretold that the might of Crete will crumble when the god dies."

A wild hope blazed up in my heart. I said to Kaptah, "On the night of the full moon Minea is to enter the house of that god. If he is indeed dead—and it may be so, for the people come to know all things at last though no one tell them—then Minea will perhaps come back to us from the god's house, whence no one has hitherto returned."

On the following day I secured a good place in the great amphitheater whose stone benches rose up like steps one behind the other so that everyone could see the bulls without difficulty. I greatly admired this cunning device, never having seen another like it; in Egypt, at processions and displays, high platforms are erected that all may behold the god and the priests and those who dance.

The bulls were let into the ring one by one, and each dancer in turn carried out a routine that was complex and exacting. It included many different feats, which must all be faultlessly performed in a prescribed order. Most difficult of all was the leap between the horns and from there the back somersault into the air, which must end with the dancer standing on the bull's back. Not even the most proficient could execute the whole without some fault, for much depended on the behavior of the beast, how it stood, charged, or lowered its head. The wealthy and eminent of Crete made wagers among themselves at every event, each backing his favorite. When I had seen a few of these, I could not understand their eagerness, for the bulls all looked alike to me, and I could not distinguish one event from the next.

Minea also danced, and I feared for her life until her marvelous agility and skill so bewitched me that I forgot her danger and rejoiced with the rest. Here the girls danced naked, and the boys also, for so treacherous was the sport that the smallest garment would have hindered their movements and imperiled their lives. To my thinking Minea was the loveliest of all as she danced there, her skin gleaming with oil, although I must admit that among the rest were some exceedingly beautiful girls who won great applause. But I could spare no glance for any but Minea. Compared with the others she was out of practice by reason of her long absence, and she won not a single garland. Her old patron, who had wagered on her success, was full of bitterness and resentment until he forgot the silver he had lost and went to the stables to make fresh bets, which as Minea's patron he had a right to do.

When I met Minea in the bulls' house after the performance, she looked about her and said to me coldly, "Sinuhe, I shall see you no more, for my friends have invited me to a feast; also I must prepare for my god since the moon is full the night after tomorrow. Therefore, it is likely that we shall not meet again before I enter the house of the god, unless you would care to accompany me thither with the rest of my friends."

"So be it," I said. "I have much to see in Crete; the customs and also the clothes of the women divert me greatly. As I sat watching your performance, several of your women friends invited me to their houses, and I found delight in gazing on their faces and their breasts—even though these women were a little fatter and more frivolous than you."

She seized me by the arms in a fury; her eyes blazed and her breath came quickly as she said, "I forbid you to make merry among my friends when I am absent! For my sake you should wait until I have gone, Sinuhe. And though doubtless in your eyes I am too thin—which never occurred to me before—yet do this out of friendship for me since I ask it of you."

"It was a jest. I have no wish to trouble your peace since you have doubtless much to do before you enter the house of the god. I will return therefore to my inn and heal the sick, for in the harbor are many who need my help."

I left her, and for a long while afterward the smell of the horned beasts was in my nostrils. Never shall I forget the smell of the Cretan stables, and to this day, when I see a herd and catch the scent of it, I am seized with sickness and cannot eat, and my heart aches in my breast. Nevertheless, I went from her to my patients at the inn; I treated them and soothed their suffering until darkness fell and lamps were lit in the pleasure houses of the harbor. Through the walls came the sound of music and laughter—for even slaves had caught the carefree manners of their masters, each living as if he would never die and as if pain, grief, and loss had no existence.

It was dark; I sat in my room, where Kaptah had already spread my sleeping mat, in darkness, for I would have no lamp lit. The moon rose large and bright but not yet quite full, and I hated the moon because it was to sever me from the only one in the world who was my sister. I also hated myself for being weak and timid and uncertain of my own desires. Then the door opened, and Minea came cautiously in. She was no longer dressed in the Cretan manner but wore the same simple dress in which she had danced for the mighty and the humble of many lands, and her hair was bound with a golden ribbon.

"Minea!" I cried in amazement. "Why have you come? I thought you were preparing for your god."

She said, "Speak softly, for I do not want others to hear us."

She sat close against me and staring at the moon she went on quaintly, "I do not like my sleeping place in the house of bulls, and I am not as happy among my friends as formerly. But why I should come to visit you at this inn in the harbor, which is so unseemly a thing to do, I cannot tell you. Should you wish to sleep, however, I shall not disturb you—I will go.

"I could not sleep and I felt a craving for the old smell of drugs and herbs; I wanted to pinch Kaptah's ear once more and pull his hair for the nonsense he talks. Travels and strange peoples have distracted me so that I no longer feel at home among the bulls nor elated at the applause on the field, and I do not even long for the god's house as before. The talk of those about me is like the babbling of silly children, their mirth is like sea froth on the beach, and their pleasures are no pleasures to me. My heart is a void, and my head also is empty; there is no single thought that I can call my own. Everything is pain, and I have never in my life known such distress. I beg you, therefore, to hold my hand again as you used to do. I fear no evil—not even death —as long as you hold my hands, Sinuhe, though I know only too well that you would prefer to look on plumper and more beautiful women than I am and hold their hands."

I said to her, "Minea, my sister! My childhood and youth were like a clear, deep-running brook. My manhood was a great river, which spread and spread, covering much soil, but its waters were turgid, and they settled into foul, stagnant pools. But when you came to me, Minea, you gathered up all these waters; they poured joyously down a deep channel so that all within me was cleansed. The world smiled at me, and evil was easily brushed aside. For your sake I sought goodness; I healed the sick without regard to gifts, and the dark gods had no power over me. Thus it was when you came. Now that you go, the light goes also, and my heart is like a lonely crow in the desert. I bear good will to no one any more. I hate men, and I hate the gods and will not hear them spoken of.

"So it is with me, Minea, and therefore I tell you: In the world are many countries but only one river. Let me carry you with me to the Black Land by the shores of that river, where wild duck cry in the reeds and every day the sun rows across the heavens in his golden boat. Come with me, Minea; we will break a jar together and be man and wife, never more to part from one another. Life will be easy for us, and when we die, our bodies will be preserved so that we may meet in the Western Land and live there together forever."

But she crushed my hands in hers; she touched my eyelids, my mouth, and my throat with her finger tips and said, "Sinuhe, if I would, I could not follow you, for there is not a single ship that would carry us from Crete, and no captain would dare to conceal us on board. I am guarded already for my god's sake, and I will not allow you to be slain for mine. I cannot go with you. Since I have danced before the bulls, their will is stronger than my will though I cannot explain this to you because you have not felt it. Therefore on the night of the full moon I must enter the god's house, and no power on earth can prevent me. Why it is I do not know—and it may be that no one knows but Minotauros."

My heart was like an empty tomb in my breast as I said, "No one knows what tomorrow will bring, and I cannot believe that you will return from that house. In the golden mansions of the sea god you may drink eternal life from his fountain, forgetting all earthly things—forgetting even me—though I believe none of this. It is a fairy tale, and nothing that I have yet seen in any country inclines me to believe fairy tales. Know, therefore, that if you have not returned within the allotted time I will enter the god's house myself and fetch you. I will fetch you even if you do not wish to return. This is my purpose, Minea, were it to be my last act upon earth."

But she laid her hand on my mouth in terror and glancing about her exclaimed, "Hush! You must never utter such things—or even think them. The god's house is dark, and no stranger can find his way in it. For a noninitiate there lurks a frightful death. Nor would you be able to make your way in, for it is guarded by gates of copper. I am glad of that, knowing that in your madness you might really do as you say and hurl yourself to destruction. Believe me, I will come back of my own free will, for my god cannot be so malignant as to hinder me from coming back to you if I so desire. He is a most fair and lovely god, who guards the might of Crete and bears good will toward everyone, so that the olive trees flourish and grain ripens in the fields and ships sail from port to port. He directs the winds in our favor and guides the vessels when they are beset by fog, and no evil befalls those under his protection. Why then should he feel ill will toward me?"

From childhood she had grown up beneath the shadow; her eyes were blinded, and I could not open them though I had cured the blind with needles and given them back their sight. In impotent fury I caught her in my arms and kissed her and caressed her limbs, and her limbs were as smooth as glass, and she was to me a very fountain in the desert.

She did not resist me but pressed her face against my neck and trembled, and her tears were hot on my neck as she said, "Sinuhe, my friend, if you doubt my return, I shall deny you nothing. Do with me as you will if it can give you joy, even though I must die because of it

208

—for in your arms I do not fear death; nothing matters but that my god takes me from you."

I asked her, "And would it give you joy?"

Her reply was hesitant.

"I do not know. I know only that my body is restless and comfortless away from you. I know only that a mist rises before my eyes, and my knees are weak when you touch me. I used to hate myself for this and feared your touch. At that time all was straightforward, nothing quenched my joy, and I gloried only in my skill and litheness and my maidenhood. Now I know that your touch is sweet to me though it might bring me pain—yet I do not know. Perhaps afterward I should be sad. But if you were happy—then your gladness is mine, and I desire no other."

Loosening my embrace, I stroked her hair and her eyes and her throat and said, "For me it is enough that you came here tonight as you were when we walked the roads of Babylon together. Give me the golden ribbon from your hair; I ask no more of you than that."

She looked at me doubtfully, and smoothing her hands over her loins, she said, "I am perhaps too thin, and you fancy my body would give you no pleasure. Doubtless you would prefer a gayer woman than myself. But I would be gay—I would do all you wish so as not to disappoint you, and I would give you as much pleasure as I could."

I smiled at her, stroked her smooth shoulders, and said, "Minea, no woman is more beautiful to me than you are, and no one could give me greater joy, but I would not take you for my pleasure while you were in distress for the sake of your god. I know of something we can do that would give happiness to us both. After the custom of my country we will take a jar and break it between us. When we have done this, we are man and wife though I do not possess you and though there are no priests to witness it or write our names in the temple book. Let Kaptah bring us a jar, therefore, that we may perform this rite."

Her eyes widened and shone in the moonlight, and she clapped her hands and smiled joyfully. And so I went to seek Kaptah—but found him sitting on the ground outside my door, rubbing his tear-stained face with the back of his hand. When he saw me, he wept aloud.

"What is it, Kaptah?" I asked. "Why do you weep?"

He answered unabashed, "Lord, I have a tender heart, and I could not restrain my tears when I heard all that you and that slender-hipped girl were saying. Never in my life have I heard anything so moving."

I kicked him angrily and said, "Do you mean you have been listening at the door and have heard all we said?"

Innocently he replied, "That is what I mean, for other listeners were trespassing at your door who had no business with you but who came to spy on the girl. Therefore, I drove them away with threats and sat by the door to guard your peace, thinking that you would not welcome a disturbance in the middle of an important conversation. As I sat here, I could not but hear what was said, and it was so beautiful—though childish—that I was obliged to weep."

When he had so spoken, I could not be angry with him for his simplicity and said only, "If you have been listening, you will know what we need. Hasten to fetch me a jar."

"What manner of jar shall it be, lord," he said evasively. "Do you desire an earthenware jar or a stone one, painted or plain, tall or short, wide or narrow?"

I struck him with my stick, though lightly, for my heart was full of good will and told him, "You know well enough what I mean and that for my purpose any jar will do. Let us have no more dodging, but bring me quickly the first jar you can lay hands upon."

He said, "I am already speedily on my way and spoke those words to give you time to consider what you are about. To break a jar with a woman is an important step in a man's life, which should not be taken hastily or without due reflection. But of course I shall fetch the jar since you wish it and shall not hinder the matter."

Kaptah brought us an old oil jar that smelt of fish, and we smashed it together, Minea and I. Kaptah was witness to the marriage, and he laid Minea's foot upon his neck and said, "From this moment you are my mistress and will order me about as my lord does—or even more —but I hope that you will not throw scalding water over my feet when you are angry. Further, I hope that you affect soft, heelless slippers; I do not like heels on slippers for they leave bruises and bumps on my head. I mean to serve you as faithfully as I serve my master since for some strange reason my heart has become strongly attached to you, although you are thin and your breasts are small and I do not understand what my lord fancies he sees in you. Also I intend to steal as conscientiously from you as from him, regarding your advantage rather than my own."

In saying this he became so moved that he wept again and uttered loud lamentation. Minea stroked his back and his fat cheeks and consoled him until he grew more composed, whereupon I made him sweep up the fragments of the jar and sent him from the room.

That night we lay as we had been wont to lie, Minea and I. She slept in my arms, her breath upon my neck and the caress of her hair at my cheek. But I did not possess her, for what was no joy to her was none to me. I fancy that my joy was sweeter and more profound than if she had been mine, though of this I cannot be sure, never having made the comparison. One thing I know: I felt charity toward all men, and there was not one evil thought left in my heart; every man was my brother, every woman my mother, and every girl my sister both in the Black Land and in the Red Lands under the same moonlit sky.

4

On the following day Minea danced once more before the bulls, and my heart quaked for her, though she came to no harm. But a young man among her companions slipped from the forehead of his beast and fell to the ground, where the bull slit open his body and trampled him beneath its hoofs so that the spectators round the arena rose up and shrieked with horror and delight. When the bull had been driven off and the dancer's body borne out to the stables, the women ran to look at him. They touched his bleeding limbs, their breath came quickly, and they exclaimed, "What a sight to see!" But the men said, "It is long since we beheld such excellent contests as those of today." They settled their wagers with one another without regret, weighing out gold and silver, and they drank wine together and made merry in their houses so that the lights shone brightly until very late. Wives went astray from their husbands into strange beds, but no one frowned at this for it was their custom.

I lay alone on my mat, for that night Minea could not come. Early in the morning I hired a chair in the harbor and set forth to follow her to the god's house. She was borne thither in a golden carriage drawn by plumed horses, and her friends attended her in chairs or on foot with much noise and laughter, throwing flowers over her and halting by the wayside to drink wine.

The way was long but all were well provisioned, and they broke off branches and fanned each other and stampeded the peasants' sheep and indulged in many other tricks. The house of the god lay in a desert place at the foot of a mountain near the seashore, and when the party drew near to this, they lowered their voices and spoke in whispers, and the laughter ceased.

This house is difficult to describe, for it was like a low hill upon which grew grass and flowers, and it ran directly into the mountain. The entrance was barred by lofty gates of copper, and before it was a small temple where dedication took place and where the watchmen were quartered. It was dusk when the procession arrived here. Minea's friends stepped from their chairs, threw themselves down on the grass and began eating and drinking and playing tricks on one another, having forgotten their recent solemnity—for Cretans have short memories. As darkness fell they lit torches and chased each other through the thickets until the cries of women and men's laughter rang out in the darkness, but Minea sat alone in the temple where none might approach her.

I watched her as she sat. She was arrayed in gold like a divine image, and on her head she wore a great gilded headdress; she tried to smile at me, but the smile was joyless. When the moon rose, they took from her the jewelry and gold, dressed her in a simple robe, and bound her hair in a silver net. Then the guards drew back the bars of the copper gates, which opened with a deep, rumbling noise; ten men were needed to move each gate. Beyond, all was yawning darkness. There was a profound silence. Minotauros girded himself with a golden girdle, hung a sword at his side, and put on the golden bull's head so that he ceased to resemble a man. A kindled torch was set in Minea's hand; Minotauros led her into the dark house, where they disappeared, and the torchlight died away. Then the thunderous copper gates were shut again and secured with the huge bars that required many strong men to draw them, and I saw Minea no more.

I was seized with such an agony of despair that my heart felt like an open wound from which my life's blood was ebbing away. I fell on my knees and bowed my head to the earth. In that hour I knew that never again should I see Minea, although she had promised to return and live her life with me. I knew that she would not come back. Why I should have been persuaded of this just at this moment I cannot say since hitherto I had wavered, and believed, and feared, and hoped, and sought to convince myself that the god of Crete was different from all other gods and would release Minea for the sake of the love that bound her to me. Now I hoped no longer but lay with my face to the ground, while Kaptah sat beside me wagging his head in his hands and lamenting.

The flower of Cretan youth ran past me with torches in their hands; they danced intricate dances and sang songs whose words I could not understand. Once the gates of copper had been closed, they were seized with such frenzy that they leaped and danced and ran till they were weary, and their voices rang in my ears like the squawk of crows from a city wall.

212

After a while Kaptah ceased lamenting and said, "If my eyes do not deceive me—and I have not yet drunk enough to see double—Hornhead has come out of the mountain. I do not know how, for no one has opened the copper gates."

He spoke truly. Minotauros had returned, and the golden bull's head gleamed with terrifying luster in the moonlight where with the others he danced the ceremonial dance. On seeing him, I could not control myself but sprang up and sped to him, seized him by the sleeves and asked, "Where is Minea?"

He struck away my hands and wagged his mask, but when I would not give way, he removed it and said wrathfully, "It is forbidden to disturb the sacred ritual, but being a stranger, you doubtless are ignorant of this, and I will pardon you provided you do not raise your hand to me again."

"Where is Minea?" I asked him again.

"I left Minea in the darkness of the god's house as is ordained and returned to dance the ceremonial dance in honor of the god. What more do you want of Minea since you have been rewarded already for bringing her back?"

"How could you return when she did not?" I demanded, pressing forward to him, but he thrust me aside, and the dancers came between us. Kaptah seized my arm and dragged me away. It was well he did, or who knows what might have happened?

He said to me, "You are foolish to attract so much attention; it would be better to dance with the rest and laugh and sing as they do, or else it may go ill with you. I know now that Minotauros came out through a little door beside the copper gates. I went to look at it and saw a watchman lock it and take away the key. But now drink wine, lord, and compose yourself. Your face is distorted like that of one possessed, and you roll your eyes like an owl."

He gave me wine to drink, and I slumbered there on the grass in the moonlight, while the glare of torches flickered before my eyes. He had deceitfully mixed poppy juice with the wine. So he was avenged for what I had done to him in Babylon to save his life, but he put me into no jar. He spread a blanket over me and prevented the dancers from trampling me underfoot. In his turn he may have saved my life, for in despair I might have run my blade into Minotauros and slain him. He sat beside me all night through until the wine jar was empty, then fell asleep and blew wine fumes into my ear.

I awoke late the next day. So powerful had been the drug that at first I wondered where I was. When I remembered, I was calm and clear headed and thanks to the dose I raved no longer. Many of those who took part in the procession had returned to the city, but some still slept among the bushes, men and women together, their bodies shamelessly uncovered, for they had drunk and danced till morning. When they awoke, they donned fresh clothes, and the women put up their hair again, discontented because they could not bathe; the streams were too cold for such as were accustomed to hot water from silver taps.

But they rinsed their mouths and rubbed ointment into their faces, painted lips and eyebrows, and said yawningly to one another, "Who stays to await Minea, and who goes back to the city?"

Most of them were now weary of the revelry and returned to the city in the course of the day. Only the youngest and most insatiable remained to divert themselves further, on the pretext of awaiting Minea's return, the true reason being an encounter during the night with one or other in whom they had found pleasure. The wives took this opportunity of sending their husbands back to the city to be rid of them. Now I understood why there was not a single pleasure house in the city but only in the harbor. Having beheld their play during this night and the day following, I reflected that girls who made it their profession would have been hard put to rival the women of Crete.

Before Minotauros left I said to him, "Have I leave to await Minea's return in company with her friends, foreigner though I am?"

He surveyed me malevolently and answered, "There is nothing to prevent you. But I fancy that there is just now a ship lying in the harbor that will take you back to Egypt—for you wait in vain. No one who has been dedicated to the god has ever returned."

But I persisted coaxingly, with the air of a simpleton: "It is true that I was somewhat taken with Minea, though it was tedious to be denied her for the sake of her god. But to speak truly I do not expect her to return; like the others I give that as my reason for remaining here, for there are many enchanting girls—and wives also—who like to look into my eyes and lay their breasts seductively between my hands, and that is a thing I have never before experienced. Minea was in fact a damnably jealous and quarrelsome girl who interfered with my pleasures though she could offer me none herself. Furthermore, I must ask your forgiveness if I was so drunk last night as unwittingly to offend you. I cannot quite call to mind the matter, being still a little fuddled."

I thickened my speech in saying this and blinked and moaned about my headache until he smiled, taking me for an idiot, and replied, "If that is how the matter stands I shall not hinder your enjoyment, for in Crete we are not narrow in our views. Stay, therefore, and await Minea as long as you wish, but take care to get no one with child, for that—as you are a foreigner—would be unsuitable. Let not this counsel wound you; I offer it as one man to another that you may understand our customs."

I assured him that I would be careful and babbled of my alleged experiences with the temple maidens of Syria and Babylon until he thought me a bigger fool than before and very tedious. He patted me on the shoulder and turned away to start upon the journey to the city. Nevertheless, I believe he adjured the watchman to keep an eye on me, and I believe also that he bade the Cretans to entertain me, for soon after he had gone a flock of women came to me. They hung garlands about my neck and looked into my eyes and leaned upon me until their naked breasts pressed against my arm. They took me with them in among the laurel bushes to eat and drink. Thus it was I saw their wantonness, and they were not shy of me. I drank heavily and feigned intoxication so that they had no joy of me but grew weary and smote me, calling me swine and barbarian.

Kaptah came and dragged me away by the arms, insulting me loudly because of my drunkenness, and he offered to take my place with them for their enjoyment. They tittered at the sight of him, and the youths mocked him, pointing at his great belly and his bald head. But he was a foreigner, and women everywhere are attracted by what is foreign. When they had done laughing, they let him join their company, giving him wine and stuffing his mouth with fruit, leaning against him and calling him their he-goat and being outraged at the smell of him—until his smell also began to seem alluring.

So that day passed until I was sickened by their gaiety and wantonness and could fancy no more tedious life than theirs, for lawless caprice is in the end more wearisome than a life of purpose. They whiled away the night as before, and my anguished dreams were broken by the cries of women, pretending to flee from pursuing youths who snatched at their clothes to pull them off. But in the morning they were weary and cloyed and longed to bathe, and the greater number returned that day to the city. Only the youngest and most indefatigable lingered by the copper gates.

On the third day these also went, and I let them take my chair, which had awaited me. Those who had come on foot were unfit to walk and staggered as they went from immoderate lechery and want

215

of sleep; moreover it suited my purpose that none should wait for me. Every day I had given the guards wine, and when I brought them a jar at dusk, they were not surprised but received it joyfully. They had few pleasures in their loneliness, which lasted a month at a time, from the coming of one initiate to that of the next. If they marveled at all it was that I remained behind to await Minea, but as I was a foreigner they supposed me simple and drank my wine.

When I saw that the resident priest was of their opinion, I said to Kaptah, "The gods have now decreed that we must part. Minea has not returned, nor do I think she will unless I fetch her. But no one who has entered that dark house has ever come out again, and it is not to be expected that I shall do so. I have therefore written for you a clay tablet and attested it with my Syrian seal so that you may return to Syria and draw my money from the merchants' houses. You may sell my house if you wish. When you have done this, you are free to come and go. If you fear that in Egypt you may be seized as a runaway slave, then stay in Smyrna and live in my house on my money. As matters now stand, you have not even to arrange for the embalming of my body. If I do not find Minea, I don't care whether or not my body is preserved. Go therefore, and may the good luck of the scarab go with you—for you may keep the scarab since you have more faith in it than I. I do not think I shall need it on the journey I am now to take."

Kaptah was silent for a long time and he did not look at me. At length he said, "Lord, I bear you no grudge if at times you have beaten me with needless severity, for you did it with good intent. But more often you have listened to my counsel and have talked to me as a friend rather than as to a servant, so that at times I have been concerned for your dignity until your stick once more established the divinely ordained division between us. The situation now is that I have set Minea's little foot upon my head and am thus responsible to her as her servant. Nor can I allow you to enter that dark house alone, so that even if I cannot attend you thither as your servant—since you have ordered me to leave you, and I must obey your orders even if they are foolish—yet as a friend I shall come with you. For I cannot leave you alone and certainly not without the scarab—although like you I believe that even the scarab can hardly help us in this matter."

He spoke so gravely and thoughtfully that I scarcely knew him, nor did he whine as was his custom. But to my mind it was mad for two of us to seek death where one would suffice. I told him this, and again ordered him to leave me.

But he was obstinate and said, "If you will not let me come with you, then I will follow after you. But I would rather come with you, for so greatly do I fear that dark house that my body turns to water at the thought of it. For that reason I hope you will allow me to bring a jar of wine so that I may take a mouthful now and then upon the way to give me courage, lest I shriek out in my terror and disturb you."

I finished off the discussion, saying, "Cease this chattering and bring the wine if you wish, but let us start now for I believe the guards are asleep and overcome by the drink I mixed for them."

The guards were sleeping soundly, and the priest also, so I was able to remove the key without difficulty from the place in the priest's house where I had observed it. We also took with us a dish of embers and some torches, though we did not light them then, for the moon was bright and the little door was easy to unlock. We stepped into the house of the god and shut the door behind us. In the darkness I heard Kaptah's teeth rattle against the rim of the wine jar.

5

When Kaptah had fortified his valor with wine, he said in a faint voice, "Lord, let us light a torch. Its glow will not be seen from outside, and this obscurity is worse than the darkness of death: that is unavoidable, but we have entered this of our own free will."

I blew on the charcoal and, lighting a torch, perceived that we were in a large vault, the entrance of which was closed by the copper gates. From this vault issued ten passages leading in different directions and separated from one another by massive walls of brick. I was prepared for this as I had heard that the god of Crete dwelt in a labyrinth, and the Babylonian priests had taught me that labyrinths were constructed on the same plan as the viscera of sacrificial beasts. For this reason I believed that I might find my way, so often had I beheld the entrails of bulls at the sacrifice, and I assumed that the Cretan labyrinth was built on this plan.

Therefore, I pointed to the passage that lay farthest to one side and said, "We will go in there."

But Kaptah said, "We are in no great hurry, and nothing was ever lost by caution. Let us beware of going astray, and above all let us ensure that we find our way back—if we are ever to come back, which I gravely doubt."

Upon this he took a ball of thread from his pouch and fastened the end of it to a bone pin, which he drove between the bricks. The device was so cunning in its simplicity that I should never have hit on it myself, though I did not say this lest I lose dignity in his eyes but merely told him sharply to hasten. So I entered the mazes of the dark house with the image of bovine entrails impressed on my memory, while Kaptah following unrolled the thread.

We wandered endlessly about in the darkness, while new passages continually opened out before us. At times we came up against a wall and had to turn and go some other way. At last Kaptah stood still and sniffed the air. Then his teeth chattered, and the torch wavered in his grasp as he said, "Lord, do you smell the bulls?"

I, too, was by now aware of a repulsive stench like the stench of bulls, though even more vile, and it seemed to issue from the very walls as if the whole labyrinth had been a gigantic cattle shed. I ordered Kaptah to continue without breathing in, and when he had taken a deep draught from the wine jar, we hurried forward until my foot slid on some slippery object. On bending down, I found it to be the rotting skull of a woman, to which hair still adhered. Then I knew that I should not see Minea alive again, but a lunatic urge to make sure drove me forward. I cuffed Kaptah and forbade him to whimper, and we went on, unrolling the thread as we advanced. But soon we encountered another wall and had to turn about.

All at once Kaptah stopped short, pointing to the ground; his scanty hair rose on his head, and his face was contorted and gray. I followed his gaze and observed some dried cattle dung on the ground —but the heap was as high as a man so that if a bull had left it the creature must have been big beyond belief.

Kaptah had the same thought, for he said, "This cannot be from a bull, for such a bull could not enter these passages. I believe it is the droppings of a monstrous serpent!"

So saying he took another deep draught from the jar, his teeth chattering against the rim, and I reflected that the maze seemed made for the movements of such a serpent and was seized with the impulse to turn back. But then I remembered Minea, and impelled by wild despair, I pressed forward, dragging Kaptah with me and gripping my knife in a moist hand, though I knew that no knife could help me.

As we continued, the stench of the passages grew ever more appalling, resembling the miasma from some enormous grave, and it was difficult for us to breathe. Yet I rejoiced, knowing that we were near our goal. We rushed onward until a faint light was perceptible in the passages. We were now into the mountain itself; the walls were no longer bricked but hewn from soft rock. Now the way led downward, and we stumbled over human bones and heaps of dung until at last a great cavern opened before us. We stood on a rocky ledge overhanging an expanse of water and were enveloped in most foul and poisonous air.

Light entered this cavern from the sea, a dreadful greenish light that enabled us to see without torches, and somewhere in the distance we could hear waves thundering against the rocks. On the surface of the water before us floated what appeared to be a row of immense leather sacks, until the eye perceived them to be one huge, dead animal—an animal more huge and more terrifying than can be imagined, which emitted the stench of corruption. Its head had sunk into the water; it was that of a colossal bull. The body resembled the body of a serpent, which, made light by decomposition, rocked its hideous curves on the water. I knew that I beheld the god of Crete—knew also that it had been dead for months. Where then was Minea?

As I thought of her, I thought also of all those who had preceded her. I thought of the youths to whom women were forbidden and of the girls who must preserve their maidenhood in order to enter into the bliss and glory of the god. I thought of their skulls and bones lying in the passages of the dark house. I thought of the monster pursuing them through the maze and blocking the way with its monstrous bulk so that neither their leaps nor any other stratagem could help them.

This leviathan had lived on human flesh—one meal in the month— a meal furnished by the rulers of Crete in the form of the fairest girls and most perfect youths, because these rulers fancied that by so doing they could maintain the sovereignty of the seas. From out of the dread depths of the ocean the creature must once, long ago, have been driven into the cavern by some tempest. A barrier had been thrown across the entrance to prevent its return and the labyrinth built for it to run in. It had then been fed with sacrifices until it died, and there could be no other such monster in the whole world. Where then was Minea?

Mad with despair I shouted Minea's name and awoke the echoes in the cavern until Kaptah pointed to the rock on which we stood; it was stained with dried blood. Following the track of this down into the water, my eyes beheld Minea's body, or what was left of it. It stirred slowly along the bottom, dragged by sea crabs that were tearing at it ravenously. Her face was gone and I recognized her only by the silver net over her hair. I did not have to look for the sword gash in her breast, for I knew that Minotauros had followed her here, thrust his blade through her from behind, and thrown her into the water, that none might learn that the god of Crete was dead. This he must have done to many a boy and girl before Minea.

When I had seen and comprehended it all, a terrible cry burst from my throat. I sank down in a swoon and would certainly have fallen from the ledge to join Minea had not Kaptah dragged me to safety, as he afterward told me. Of what then befell I know nothing save by Kaptah's account, so mercifully profound was the swoon following upon anxiety, torment, and despair.

Kaptah told me that he mourned long beside my body, believing me to be dead, and he wept also for Minea until his good sense returned to him. Having felt me and found that I was alive, he reflected that he could save me at least though he could do nothing for her. He had seen the bodies of other youths and girls whom Minotauros had slain; the crabs had torn all the flesh from these bones so that they lay smooth and white upon the sandy bed of the sea.

Then he began to be stifled by the smell. When he found that he could not carry both me and the wine jar, he resolutely drank the rest of the wine and threw the empty jar into the water. So greatly fortified was he by this that he succeeded in half dragging, half carrying me back to the copper gates by means of the thread we had unrolled on our way in. After a moment's reflection he thought it best to roll it up again as he went so as to leave no trace of our visit. It seems that in the light of his torch he noted secret signs on the walls, no doubt set there by Minotauros to help him find his way. Kaptah told me he had thrown the wine jar into the water to give Minotauros something to think about when next he carried out his bloody work.

Day was dawning as he brought me out. He locked the door behind him and put the key back in the priest's house—for the priest and the guards were still sleeping, drugged with the wine I had mixed for them. Next he took me to a hiding place in a thicket on the bank of a stream. There he bathed my face and rubbed my hands until I came to my senses. I do not remember anything of this either. It seems I was much distracted and unable to speak, and he therefore gave me a sedative drug. I did not return to clear consciousness until much later when we were approaching the city, he leading and supporting me. Thereafter I remember everything.

I recall no suffering, nor did my thoughts turn often to Minea. She was now a remote shade in my soul, as if I had known her in some other life. Instead I reflected that the god of Crete was dead and that

220

the might of Crete would now decline according to the prophecy. I was in no way cast down by this although the Cretans had shown me kindness, and their mirth sparkled like sea spray on the shore. When I came near the city, I was glad to think that those airy, delicate buildings would one day be in flames and that the lecherous cries of women would turn to mortal shrieks, that Minotauros' mask of gold would be beaten flat and divided among the rest of the spoils, and that nothing would remain of the splendid majesty of Crete. The very island would sink again into the sea from which, with other marvels of the deep, it had once arisen.

I thought also of Minotauros, and without ill will, for Minea's death had been easy, and she had not had to flee from the monster with every trick her art had taught her; she died before she knew what had befallen her. I reflected that Minotauros was alone in the knowledge that the god was dead and that Crete must fall and I guessed that his secret could be no easy one to bear. I was not sure his task had ever been easy, even in the days when the monster still lived and he sent the flower of his country's youth into that dark house, month after month, year after year, knowing what happened to them there.

No, I felt no rancor. I sang and laughed like a madman as I walked, leaning upon Kaptah. He easily convinced those of Minea's friends whom we met that I was still drunk after having awaited her return. They found it natural, seeing that I was a foreigner and too ignorant to know how barbarous it must appear to them to be publicly drunk in the middle of the day. At last he was able to hire a chair, and he took me back to the inn where, having drunk a great quantity of wine, I sank into a long and profound slumber.

When I awoke, my head was cool and clear, and the past remote. I thought again of Minotauros. Should I set forth and slay him? But I knew that it would serve no useful purpose. By telling the truth, I could save the lives of all those who were still to draw lots, or who had already drawn them, for the privilege of entering the house of the god. But I knew that truth is an unsheathed knife in the hands of a child and readily turns against its holder.

As a foreigner, therefore, I felt that the god of Crete was no concern of mine—and Minea was gone. Crabs and crayfish would gnaw at her delicate bones, and she would rest forever on the sandy floors of the sea. I told myself that all had been written in the stars long before the day of my birth, and this brought me consolation. I spoke of it to Kaptah, but he said that I was ill and must rest, and he forbade anyone to see me.

I was greatly vexed with Kaptah at this time, for he persisted in stuffing me with food although I felt no hunger at all and desired only wine. I suffered from a continual and unquenchable thirst and was calmest when I had drunk enough to distort my vision. At such times I became aware that things might not be quite as they seem. For the drinker sees everything double when he has drunk enough. To him this is true vision even while he knows in his heart that it is false. And what is this but the very essence of truth? When with patience and self-mastery I sought to expound this to Kaptah, he would not listen but bade me lie down, close my eyes, and compose myself.

I can now appreciate the severity of my disorder, though I have forgotten my thoughts since the wine tended to confuse me and darken my understanding. Yet I think the good wine saved my reason and helped me through the worst when I had lost Minea forever and with her my faith in the gods and in humanity.

Something in me evaporated in the fumes of the wine. I had felt something like it before when in my boyhood I saw the priest of Ammon spit on the face of the god in the sanctuary and rub it with his sleeve. The river of life was choked and its waters spreading—spreading into a wide lake whose surface was fair, a mirror to the starry heavens. Thrust a staff into it, and the water was clouded and the bottom but slime and corruption.

One morning I awoke in the inn to see Kaptah sitting in a corner of the room weeping silently and rocking his head between his hands. I bowed my head over the wine jar and having drunk said roughly, "What do you weep for, dog?"

It was the first time for many days that I had troubled to speak to him, so weary was I of his foolish solicitude. He raised his head and answered, "A ship is now lying in the harbor ready to sail for Syria, the last, it is said, that will leave before the winter gales set in. That is all I weep for."

I said to him, "Run away to your ship, then, before I beat you again. At least I shall be spared the sight of your unendurable face and the sound of your everlasting lamentations and complaints."

Having said this, I was ashamed and pushed away the wine jar. A bitter consolation lay in the thought that there was at least one creature dependent on me, though it was but a runaway slave.

Kaptah said, "Truly, lord, I, also, am weary of your sottishness. The dead are dead and don't return. Let's go away from here while we may. Your gold and silver—all that you amassed in the course of your journeys—you have thrown out of the window. With your shaking hands I do not believe that you could effect a single cure; you cannot so much as hold a wine jar. At first I thought it well for you to drink for the sake of your peace of mind; I urged you to do it, continually breaking the seals of new jars—and I drank also myself. Moreover, I boasted to others: See what a master I have! He drinks like a hippopotamus—he drowns both gold and silver in his wine, recklessly, and makes exceedingly merry. Now I boast no longer and am ashamed on my master's account, for there are limits to everything, and to my mind you exceed them.

"I will never condemn a man who drinks himself into a passion and brawls in the street and gets his head broken. That is a sensible custom, which relieves the mind in many kinds of grief, and I have often done the same. The resulting disorders should be treated prudently with beer and salt fish, after which a man resumes his labor, as the gods have ordained and decency requires. But you drink as if each day were your last, and I fear you wish to soak yourself into your grave. If this is your aim, you would do better to drown in a bath of wine, for this is a speedier method, pleasanter also, and no dishonor."

I considered his words. I surveyed my hands, which had been those of a healer but which now shook as if they had a will of their own and I were no longer their master. I thought of the knowledge I had accumulated in many lands and saw that excess was foolishness. It was as foolish to eat and drink immoderately as to give way to extremes of joy and sorrow.

Therefore, I said to Kaptah, "Let it be as you say, but know that the matter was already evident, and it is not your words that persuade me. They are as the tedious buzzing of flies in my ear. I shall leave drinking for a time and do not purpose to open another jar. I have brought order among my thoughts and intend to return to Smyrna."

Kaptah skipped joyfully across the room and went out to arrange for our departure, and on that same day we went aboard. The rowers dipped their oars, and we glided from the harbor, past the scores and hundreds of vessels lying at anchor and past the copper-shielded Cretan warships. Once outside the harbor the men shipped their oars; the captain made sacrifice in his cabin to the sea god and others and gave orders for the hoisting of the sail. The vessel heeled over and sped on her way. Astern of us the island of Crete melted like a blue cloud— a shadow—a dream—and we were alone on the rolling expanse of the ocean.

BOOK 9

The Crocodile's Tail

I

SO I ripened to manhood, and when I returned to Smyrna, I was no longer young. I had been absent from that city for three years, during which I had acquired knowledge, both good and evil, of many countries. The ocean winds blew the wine fumes from my head, cleared my eyes, and restored strength to my limbs. I ate and drank and behaved like other people, save that I spoke less than they and was even more solitary than before. Solitude is some men's destiny—a destiny of mature years—but I had been lonely from childhood, a stranger in the world since the reed boat had carried me to the Theban shore. I had no need to adapt myself to loneliness as many must, since from the beginning it was home to me and a refuge in the dark.

But as I stood by the ship's figurehead amid the green, rolling waters and the wind blew folly from my mind, I saw far off two green eyes like moonlight on the sea; I heard Minea's spontaneous laughter and watched her dance on a threshing floor beside the roads of Babylon, in her flimsy dress young and slight as a tender reed. And her image was not grievous to me but rather a sweet torment such as a man feels on waking from a dream that is lovelier than life. When I thought of her, I rejoiced at having known her and would not have renounced one hour of her company, knowing that without her there would have been less of myself. The ship's figurehead was of cold, painted wood, but the face was a woman's. As I stood beside it with my face to the wind, I felt my manhood strong within me and was aware that there would yet be many women in my life since for a solitary man it is comfortless to lie every night alone. Yet I fancied that to me all these women would be but painted wooden figures and that, when in the darkness I took them to me, I should seek in them only Minea—only the glint of moonlight, the warmth of a slender body, the fragrance of cypress, which would remind me of Minea. Thus, by the figurehead of the ship, I bade her farewell.

My house in Smyrna was still standing though the shutters had been broken open by thieves. They had carried away all that was worth taking of such possessions as I had not entrusted to the safekeeping of the merchants. Since I had been away so long, my neighbors had begun to use the space before my house as rubbish dump and privy, the stench of which was very foul. Rats scuttled over the floor as I entered my rooms and tore the cobwebs from the lintels.

My neighbors were not pleased to see me. They averted their eyes and said to one another, "He is an Egyptian and all evil comes from Egypt." Therefore I went first to an inn, bidding Kaptah set my house in order so that I could once more live there, and then visited the merchants' houses where I had placed my funds. After my three years' traveling I had returned a poor man, for besides my own earnings I had lost what Horemheb had given me, mostly to the priests of Babylon on Minea's account.

The wealthy shipowners were astonished to see me. Their noses grew even longer than before and they tugged thoughtfully at their beards, for my long absence had encouraged them to think that my wealth was now theirs. Nevertheless, they rendered me strict account, and although certain ships had foundered and I had lost my share in them, yet others had proved exceedingly profitable. When all had been assessed, it appeared that I was now wealthier than I had been at my departure and I need have no concern for my livelihood in Smyrna.

Nevertheless, the owners invited me into their rooms, offered me wine and honey bread, and pulling long faces, they said to me, "Sinuhe the physician! You are our friend, but although we are glad to trade with Egypt, we do not like to see Egyptians making their way in among us. The people murmur and are sorely vexed by the tribute they must pay to Pharaoh. Egyptians have lately been stoned in the streets, dead pigs have been cast into their temples, and our people will not show themselves publicly in their company. You, Sinuhe, are our friend, and we respect you highly for your skill in healing, which we still remember. For this reason we would make all clear to you, that you may act accordingly and with prudence."

Their words bewildered me since before my departure people had vied with one another for the favor of the Egyptians and invited them to their houses. Just as Syrian customs had been adopted in Thebes, so here in Smyrna men followed the fashion of the Egyptians. Yet Kaptah bore out their words when in high indignation he called at the inn.

"An evil spirit has certainly crept into these people, for they conduct themselves like mad dogs, feigning ignorance of the Egyptian tongue. They threw me out of the tavern where I went to refresh my parched

228

throat when they saw I was Egyptian. They shouted evil words after me and the children showered me with dung. Then I went to another tavern, for my throat was as dry as chaff and I craved the strong Syrian beer. But here I never uttered a sound—a hard thing for me, as you know. However, I was prudent and dipped my reed into my beer with the others in silence, and I listened to what they were saying. They said that Smyrna was once a free city, paying tribute to none, and that they no longer wished their children to be born the bondsmen of Pharaoh. Other Syrian cities were once free also, and therefore all Egyptians should be clubbed and driven forth—this was the duty of every man who loves freedom and is weary of being Pharaoh's serf. Such was their nonsense, although it is well known that Egypt's protection is for Syria's benefit rather than its own. If left to themselves, the cities of Syria would be like wildcats in a sack, rending and tearing at each other, to the great detriment of farming and commerce. These people boasted of their power and spoke of some alliance between all their cities. As an Egyptian I became so sickened with their talk that when the landlord turned his back I went away without paying and snapped my drinking-reed."

I did not have to walk far in the city before observing the truth of Kaptah's words. No one molested me, for I had learned to wear Syrian clothes, but those who had known me before now turned away when we met, while other Egyptians in the city went guarded. Even so, men mocked them and pelted them with rotten fruit and fish. I felt no concern, however. Doubtless the people of Smyrna were incensed over the new taxes, and tumult such as this was apt to subside quickly since Syria had as much profit from Egypt as Egypt from Syria. I did not fancy that the cities of the coast could long maintain themselves without Egyptian grain.

I had my house set in order, received patients, and treated them as before. As before they came, for pain and disease do not inquire after a man's race but only after his skill.

Yet they would argue with me, saying, "Tell us, you Egyptian, is it not unjust that Egypt should extort tribute from us, exploit us, and batten on our poverty like a blood-sucking leech? How unjust also that we may not repair our walls and towers if we so desire and are willing to bear the cost of it ourselves! Our own councilors are competent to govern us well and fairly without Egyptian interference in the coronation of our rulers or the administration of our justice. By Baal, if it were not for the Egyptians, we should flourish and prosper. They are upon us like locusts, and your Pharaoh is now forcing a new god upon us so that we lose the favor of our own."

I did not desire to bandy words with them, but I said this, "Against whom would you build your walls and towers if not Egypt? It is doubtless true that your city was free within its own walls in the days of your great-grandfathers, but you shed blood and impoverished yourselves in countless wars with neighbors whom you still hate, while your princes were licensed despots under whom neither rich nor poor knew security. Now you are protected from your enemies by the shields and spears of Egypt, and Egypt's laws secure the rights of rich and poor alike."

But this incensed them; their eyes reddened and their nostrils quivered as they retorted, "Egypt's laws are filth to us and its gods an abomination. What if our princes were despots, and unjust—which we do not believe! They were our own princes, and our hearts tell us that injustice in a free land is better than justice in a land enslaved."

I said, "I see among you no signs of slavery; rather you grow fat and boast of wealth gained at the expense of Egyptian stupidity. If you were free, you would plunder one another's ships and cut down one another's fruit trees. On your journeys inland your lives would no longer be secure."

But they would not listen. They flung down their gifts and left, saying, "You are an Egyptian in your heart though you wear Syrian clothes. Every Egyptian is an oppressor and an evildoer, and the only good Egyptian is a dead one."

In consequence of these things I was now ill at ease in Smyrna. I began to gather in all that was mine in preparation for departure. I must go to Egypt, according to my promise, to meet Horemheb and tell him of all I had seen. But I made no great haste, for my spirit quailed at the thought of drinking Nile water once again, and so the time slipped by.

One evening I was returning in the dark from Ishtar's temple, which I visited upon occasion—as a thirsty man will drink without regard to the source of his refreshment. Some men came along the wall toward me, saying to one another, "Is not this man an Egyptian? Shall we suffer a circumcised man to lie with our virgins and defile our temple?"

I said, "Your virgins, for whom I could suggest a more fitting term, care neither for race nor person. They weigh their pleasure by the gold the man has in his purse. I do not quarrel with them for this since it is my custom to take pleasure with them, and I intend to continue when it so pleases me."

230

At this they drew their cloaks before their faces, threw themselves on me, and bore me to the ground, then beat my head against the wall until I thought I was about to die. But as they set about robbing me and were dragging the clothes off me before throwing me into the harbor, one of them saw my face and said, "Is it not Sinuhe, the Egyptian doctor and King Aziru's friend?"

I acknowledged this and swore that I would slay them and throw their carcasses to the dogs. My head ached exceedingly, and I was much too angry to be frightened. They released me, restored my clothes, and fled, holding their cloaks before their faces. I could not think why they did so, for with me in their power they had no reason to heed my threat.

<h1 style="text-align:center">2</h1>

A few days later a messenger rode up to my door on a horse, which was a rare sight, for an Egyptian never travels on horseback and a Syrian very seldom. It is chiefly the desert raiders who journey in this fashion, the horse being a tall, unruly creature that kicks and bites when a man tries to mount it, and throws him off, and behaves quite differently from the donkey, which is amenable to all uses. This man rode up to my door on a lathery, gasping beast, from whose mouth blood was trickling. The man's garments told me that he came from the hills of the sheep country, and in his face I read intense agitation.

He rushed up to me and barely gave himself time to utter a greeting before crying out to me in his excitement, "Order out your carry chair, Sinuhe, and follow me speedily. I come from the land of Amurru, whose king, Aziru, has sent me to fetch you. His son is sick, and no one knows what ails the boy. The King rages like a lion in the wilderness and breaks the bones of everyone who comes near. Therefore take your medicine chest and follow me in haste, or I will cut your head from your shoulders and kick it along the street."

"My head alone would be of little use to the King. Yet I pardon you your impetuousness and will follow you—not on account of your threats but because King Aziru is my friend and I would help him."

I ordered Kaptah to fetch a chair, and I followed the messenger, rejoicing in my heart. I was so lonely that I looked forward to meeting even Aziru, whose teeth I had once coated with gold. But I was no longer so happy when we came to the mouth of a pass, for then I and my medicine chest were hoisted into a chariot and drawn by wild horses. We careered over stones and rocks until I feared that every one of my limbs would be broken, and I cried out shrilly in my terror. My companion on his weary horse was left far in the rear, and I hoped that he might break his neck.

On the other side of the range I was hauled from the chariot into another drawn by fresh horses. I hardly knew whether I was on my head or my heels, and I could only scream at the drivers, "You filth! You carrion! You dung beetles!" and thump them on the back with my fists when we came to the smoother stretches, and I dared loosen my hold upon the edge of the cart. They did not heed me but shook the reins and cracked the whip so that we leaped over the stones and I thought the wheels would fly off.

Our journey to Amurru was thus not a lengthy one, and before sunset we came to a city that was encircled by newly built, lofty walls. These were patrolled by soldiers bearing shields, but the gates stood open to us. We drove through the city amid the braying of donkeys and the yelling of women and children, while baskets of fruit flew through the air and countless pitchers were crushed beneath the wheels, for the drivers paid no heed to any in their path.

When I was lifted from the vehicle, I could no longer walk but reeled like a drunken man. The drivers rushed me by the arms into the house, followed by slaves with my medicine chest. We had come no farther than the outer wall, which was hung with shields and breastplates and tasseled spears, when Aziru collided with us, trumpeting like a wounded elephant. He had rent his clothes and cast ashes on his hair, and he had scratched his face with his nails until it bled.

Aziru then embraced me warmly and wept and said, "Heal my son, Sinuhe—heal him, and all that is mine shall be yours."

I said to him, "Let me first see your son that I may find out if I can heal him."

He led me quickly to a large room heated by a brazier although it was summer. The air within was stifling. In the middle of the floor stood a cradle in which lay a baby less than a year old, swathed in woolen garments. He was screaming so hard that he was blue black in the face and sweat stood in beads upon his forehead. Although he was still so small, he had thick black hair like his father. I could not see that much ailed him. If he had been dying, he could not have roared so lustily. Lying on the floor beside the cradle was Keftiu, the woman I had once given to Aziru. She was fatter and whiter than ever, and her mountainous flesh shook as she struck her forehead on the floor in her grief and mourned and shrieked. From the corners of the room came the outcry of slaves and nurses whose faces were swollen and bruised from the blows that Aziru had dealt them because they could not heal his son.

"Be of good courage, Aziru," I said. "Your son is not dying, but I must cleanse myself before I examine him. And take away the accursed brazier before we all choke!"

Keftiu raised her head quickly from the floor and said in a fright, "The child will catch cold!" Her eyes lingered on me. Then she smiled and sat up, tidied her hair and her dress, and said, "Sinuhe, is it you?"

But Aziru wrung his hands and groaned, "The boy can take no food but spews up all he eats, and his body is hot. For three days now he has taken scarcely anything—only wept so that my heart breaks to hear it."

I bade him drive out the nurses and the slave women, and he obeyed me meekly, altogether forgetting his majesty. When I had cleansed myself, I undid the baby's woolen clothes and took them off, then opened the shutters so that the room was freshened by the cool evening air. The child at once grew quieter. His crying ceased and he began to kick his fat legs. I felt his body and his belly until all at once I thought of something and put my finger in his mouth. I had guessed rightly: the first tooth was showing like a pearl in his jaw.

Then I exclaimed wrathfully, "Aziru, Aziru! Was it for this your wild horses dragged hither the cleverest physician in Smyrna? Nothing ails your child—he is merely as impatient and irritable as his father. It may be he has had a little fever, but that has now abated. If he vomited, it was because he had the good sense to save his own life, for he has been overstuffed with rich milk. It is time that Keftiu weaned him and accustomed him to proper food, or he will soon bite off his mother's nipples. You must know that your son wept in petulance at the cutting of his first tooth—and if you do not believe me, see for yourself."

I opened the baby's mouth and showed Aziru the tooth. He broke out in wild jubilation, clapped his hands, and danced about the room till the floor shook beneath him. I showed Keftiu the tooth also, and she vowed she had never seen so fair a tooth in the mouth of any child. When she would have swathed the baby in the woolen things again, I forbade her and wrapped him in a cool linen cloth lest he be chilled by the evening air.

Aziru continued to dance and stamp and sing in his raucous voice and was not at all abashed at having dragged me from so great a distance. He insisted upon displaying his son's tooth to the members of his court and to his officers. Even the guards from the walls were called in to behold it. They pressed about the cradle amid a clanking of spears and shields and admired the child and tried to poke their dirty thumbs into his mouth to see the tooth, until I drove them all from the room, bidding Aziru take thought for his dignity and control himself.

Aziru looked foolish and said, "Truly I may have forgotten myself and made a needless pother. Many nights I have lain awake by his cradle with a sick heart. But you must understand that he is my son and my first-born, my prince, my jewel, the apple of my eye, my little lion who one day will wear the crown of Amurru and rule over many. For truly I mean to make this land a great one, worth the inheriting, so that he will come to praise his father's name. Sinuhe, Sinuhe, you don't know how grateful I am to you for lifting this stone from my heart. You must acknowledge that you have never seen so fine a man child, not in all your travels. Look at his hair—at the swarthy lion's mane—and tell me whether you have ever before seen such hair on a child of that age! You saw yourself that his tooth is like a pearl, faultless and gleaming—and look at his limbs!"

I grew so weary of his prattle that I bade him and his child take themselves to the nethermost pit. I told him my limbs were crippled from that hideous drive so that even now I hardly knew whether I stood on my head or my heels. But he appeased me, and putting his arm about my shoulders, he offered me many kinds of food on silver dishes, roast mutton and rice cooked in fat, also wine from a golden goblet. I was refreshed and forgave him.

I remained as his guest for some days. He gave me lavish presents and much gold and silver; his wealth had greatly increased since last we met. In what manner his poor country had grown rich he would not tell me but laughed in his beard and said that the wife I had given him had brought him good fortune. Keftiu was cordial also and showed me marked respect—no doubt recalling the stick with which I had so often tested the toughness of her skin. She followed me about, swaying and jingling in all her opulence, looking at me fondly and caressing me with her smile. So burning a love did Aziru bear toward her that he seldom visited his other wives, and from courtesy only. They were the daughters of tribal chieftains whose alliance he had thus prudently secured.

I had traveled so widely and seen so many countries that he felt impelled to boast of his might. He told me much that later he may have regretted mentioning. Thus I learned that the men who had attacked me in Smyrna and would have cast me into the harbor were agitators

234

whom he had sent forth, and it was they who reported to him that I was once more in Smyrna.

He deplored what had happened but added, "Truly there shall be many broken skulls among the Egyptians, and many an Egyptian soldier shall be cast into the harbor before Smyrna and Byblos and Sidon and Gaza have learned that Egyptians are not invulnerable—that their blood flows and life leaves them when their hides are pierced. The merchants of Syria are overcautious, the princes timid, and the people as sluggish as oxen. It is for the alert to lead them and show them where their advantage lies."

I asked him, "Why must this be, Aziru, and why do you bear so great a hatred toward Egyptians?"

He stroked his curly beard with a sly smile and said, "Who says I hate them, Sinuhe? I do not hate you. I grew up in Pharaoh's golden house, like my father before me and all other Egyptian princes. I learned there that in the eyes of the educated all peoples are much of a muchness. No nation is either braver or more chickenhearted, crueler or more compassionate, wickeder or more virtuous than another. Among all races there are heroes and cowards, straight men and crooked—and this is true also of Syria and Egypt. Rulers therefore hate no one and acknowledge no difference between nations—but hatred is a great force in the ruler's hand! It is more potent than many weapons, for without hatred no arm is strong enough to wield a weapon. Therefore I am doing what I can to kindle hatred between Syria and Egypt, and I shall blow on the flame until it blazes up into a fire to consume Egyptian sovereignty in Syria. All the cities, all the races of Syria shall learn that Egyptians are more despicable and cowardly and cruel, more corrupt, greedy, and thankless than Syrians. They shall learn to spit when they hear them mentioned and regard them as usurpers, oppressors, bloodsuckers, torturers, and defilers of children until their hatred can move mountains."

"But none of this is true, as you said yourself."

Throwing out his hands with a shrug he said, "What is truth, Sinuhe? When their blood has soaked up enough of the truth I offer them, they will swear by all their gods that it is the only truth and will believe no one who affirms the contrary. They will be persuaded that they are stronger, braver, and more righteous than any other people in the world. They will fancy that they love freedom more than they fear death and starvation and hardship, and they will be ready to pay any price to gain it. I shall teach them this. Many already believe it, and each believer will convert others until the new truth has run like wild fire throughout Syria. It is also a truth that Egypt once entered Syria with fire and blood and therefore with fire and blood must be driven out."

"Which freedom is it you speak about to them?" I asked, fearing his talk on Egypt's account.

He raised his hands once more and smiled gently.

"Freedom is a word with many meanings; some mean one thing by it and some another, but this is of no importance so long as the freedom is never attained. Many are needed to achieve freedom. When it has been won, it is safest not to share it but to keep it for oneself. I believe that the land of Amurru will one day be called the cradle of freedom. A nation that believes all it is told is like a herd of cattle that can be driven through a gate by means of a stick, or like a flock of sheep that follows the bellwether without reflecting where it is bound. And perhaps it is I who drive the herd and lead the flock."

"You must indeed have the brain of a sheep to talk thus dangerously. When Pharaoh hears of it, he will send his chariots and his spears against you. He will break down your walls and hang you and your son head downward from the bows of his warship when he returns to Thebes."

Aziru only smiled.

"I do not think that I am in any danger from Pharaoh, for I have received the symbol of life from his hands and have raised a temple to his god. He believes in me more than in anyone else in Syria—more than in his own envoys or in the officers of the garrison who worship Ammon. I will now show you something very diverting."

He led me to the walls and showed me a dried-up, naked body hanging by the heels; it was crawling with flies.

"Look closely," he said, "and you will see that this man is circumcised: he is indeed an Egyptian. He was one of Pharaoh's tax gatherers who made so bold as to come prying here to find out why I was a year or two in arrears with my tribute-money. My soldiers had good sport with him before they hung him on the wall for his impudence. By this I have ensured that Egyptians do not willingly travel through the land of Amurru, even in large bands, and the merchants prefer to pay their taxes to me rather than to them. You will grasp the significance of this when I tell you that Megiddo is under my dominion, obeying me and not the Egyptian garrison, who cower in the fortress and dare not venture into the streets of the city."

"The blood of this poor man will be on your head," I said appalled. "Your punishment will be terrible when the deed is known, for one may trifle with anything in Egypt rather than with its tax gatherers."

I sought to explain to him that he had a mistaken notion of the wealth and majesty of Egypt and warned him against being puffed up. Even a leather sack swells when filled with air yet when pricked collapses. But Aziru merely laughed and flashed his golden teeth, then ordered in more roast mutton on heavy silver dishes so as to display his wealth.

His study was filled with clay tablets, for messengers brought him intelligence from all the cities in Syria. He received tablets also from the King of the Hittites and from Babylon, of which he could not refrain from boasting, though he would not let me see their contents. He was most curious to hear from me about the land of the Hittites, but I perceived that he knew as much of it as I did. Hittite envoys visited him and spoke with his warriors and chieftains.

When I understood this, I said, "The lion and the jackal may make alliance to hunt the same prey—but did you ever see the choicest morsels fall to the jackal's share?"

He only laughed. "Great is my thirst for knowledge, and like you I seek to learn new things, though affairs of state prevent me from traveling as you do, who are without responsibility and as free as the birds of the air. What harm, then, if the Hittite officers advise my chieftains in the arts of war? They have new weapons and experience that we lack. This can only be of service to Pharaoh, for should war ever come —why, Syria has long been Pharaoh's shield and often a bloody one. This is something we shall remember when we come to cast our accounts together."

When he spoke of war I thought of Horemheb and said, "I have enjoyed your hospitality too long and must now return to Smyrna if you will place a chair at my disposal. Never again will I step into one of your terrifying chariots. I would rather be clubbed at once. Smyrna has become a wilderness for me, and doubtless I have sucked the blood of poor, indigent Syria too long. I intend to take ship for Egypt. We may not meet for a long time—perhaps never—for the memory of Nile water is sweet in my mouth. Who knows but that I shall remain to drink of it since I have seen enough of the world's evil and have also learned something of it from you."

Aziru replied, "No one knows what tomorrow may bring. Rolling stones gather no moss, and the restlessness glowing in your eyes will not allow you to stay long in any one place."

We parted friends; he gave me a chair and many presents, and his

237

warriors escorted me back to Smyrna lest any should offer me violence because I was an Egyptian.

At the gateway into Smyrna a swallow darted like an arrow past my head; my mind was troubled and the street scorched my feet. When I had reached my house I said to Kaptah, "Gather up our belongings and sell this house. We are bound for Egypt."

3

It is needless to describe our voyage, which is to me now as a shade or an unquiet dream. When at last I stepped aboard the vessel that would bring me on my way to Thebes, the city of my childhood, such intense and boundless longing filled my soul that I could neither stand nor sit nor lie, but paced to and fro over the crowded deck, among the rolled-up mats and bales of merchandise. The smell of Syria lingered in my nostrils, and each passing day increased my eagerness to see, in place of the rock-bound coast, a certain low-lying land green with beds of reeds. When the vessel lay to for days on end at the quays of the cities along the coast, I had not serenity enough to explore these places or to gather information; the braying of donkeys on the shore mingled with the cries of the fish sellers and the murmur of foreign tongues into a roar that to my ears was indistinguishable from that of the sea.

Spring had come again to the Syrian valleys. Seen from offshore the hills were red as wine, and in the evenings the foaming surf of the beaches gleamed a pearly green. The priests of Baal made shrill commotion in the narrow alleys. They gashed their faces with flint knives until the blood flowed, while women with burning eyes and disheveled hair followed the priests, pushing wooden barrows. But all this I had seen many times before; their alien ways and brutish frenzy revolted me when before my eyes there floated a faint vision of my homeland. I had thought that my heart was hardened, that I had by now adapted myself to all customs and all faiths, that I understood the folk of all complexions and despised none, and that my one purpose was to gather knowledge. However, the consciousness that I was on my way home to the Black Land swept like a reviving flame through my heart.

I laid aside my foreign thoughts like foreign garments and was Egyptian once more. I longed for the smell of fried fish at dusk in the alleyways of Thebes when the women light their cooking fires before the mud huts. I longed for the savor of Egyptian wine and for the waters of the Nile with their scent of fertile mud. I longed for the whisper of the papyrus reeds in the evening breeze, for the chalice of the lotus flower unfolding on the shore, for the picture writing in the temples, for the colorful pillars with their eternal images, and for the smell of incense between those pillars. So foolish was my heart.

I was coming home although I had no home and was a stranger upon the earth. I was coming home and memory stung me no more. Time and knowledge had silted like sand over that bitterness. I felt neither sorrow nor shame; only a restless yearning gnawed at my heart.

Astern of us dropped the Syrian land: prosperous, fertile, seething with hatred and unrest. Our vessel, urged forward by the oars, glided past the red beaches of Sinai, and the desert winds blew hot and dry over our faces although it was spring. Then there came a morning when the sea was yellow, and beyond it the land lay like a narrow green ribbon. The seamen lowered a jar and brought up in it water that was not salt; it was Nile water and tasted of the mud of Egypt. No wine ever tasted so delectable to me as this muddy water, hauled up so far from land.

Kaptah said, "Water is always water, even in the Nile. Have patience, lord, until we find an honest tavern where the beer is clear and foaming, so that a man need not suck it through a straw to avoid the husks of grain. Then and then only shall I know that I am home."

His godless talk jarred on me, and I said, "Once a slave always a slave, even when he is robed in fine wool. Have patience, Kaptah, until I find a flexible cane—such a one as can be cut only in the reed swamps of the Nile—and then, indeed, you shall know that you are home."

He was not offended, but his eyes filled with tears, his chin quivered, and he bowed before me, stretching forth his hands at knee level.

"Truly, lord, you have the gift of hitting upon the right word at the right moment, for I had already forgotten how sweet is the caress of a slender cane on the legs and backside. Ah, my lord Sinuhe, it is an experience that I wish that you also might share. Better than water or beer, better than incense, better than wild duck among the reeds— more eloquently than these does it speak of life in Egypt, where each fills his proper place and nothing changes. Do not wonder if in my emotion I weep, for only now do I feel that I am coming home after seeing much that is alien and perplexing and contemptible. O blessed cane that sets each in his proper place and resolves all problems, there is none like you!"

He wept a little and then went to anoint his scarab, but I noted that he no longer used as fine oil as before. Land was near, and he fancied no doubt that once in Egypt his own natural guile would suffice him.

239

When we berthed in the great harbor of the Lower Kingdom I realized for the first time how weary I was of brightly colored, voluminous clothes, curly beards, and thick bodies. The narrow hips of the porters, their loincloths, their shaven chins, their speech which was that of the Lower Kingdom, the smell of their sweat, of the river mud, of the reeds and the harbor—all was different from Syria; all was familiar.

The Syrian clothes I wore began to irk and stifle me. When I had finished my business with the harbor clerks and had written my name on many papers, I went at once to buy new clothes. After so much wool, fine linen was sweet to the skin. But Kaptah resolved to continue as a Syrian, for he feared lest his name might still figure on the list of runaway slaves, though he had obtained a clay tablet from the authorities in Smyrna, certifying that he had been born a slave in Syria, where I had lawfully bought him.

Next we embarked with our baggage on a river boat to continue our voyage up the Nile. Days went by and carried us further into the life of Egypt. On either side of the river lay the drying fields where slow oxen drew the wooden plows and laborers walked the furrows with bowed heads, sowing their grain. Swallows skimmed with anxious twitterings above the leisurely flowing water and the mud into which they would soon vanish during the heat of the year. Curving palms lined the banks, and in the shade of tall sycamores clustered the low huts of the village. The boat touched at the landing stages of towns great and small, and there was not a harbor tavern to which Kaptah did not run, to moisten his throat with Egyptian beer, to boast and tell fantastic tales of his travels and my skill, while his audience of dock laborers listened and laughed and jested and invoked the gods.

So I saw again the peaks of the three hills against the eastern sky, the eternal guardians of Thebes. Buildings now stood closer together; poor villages gave place to rich suburbs until the city walls rose up like hills. I saw the roof of the great temple and its pillars, the countless buildings about it, and the sacred lake. Westward the City of the Dead stretched away to the hills. The death temple of the Pharaohs glowed white against the yellow slopes, and the rows of pillars in the temple of the great queen still bore up a sea of flowering trees. Beyond the hills lay the forbidden valley with its snakes and scorpions where, in the sand at the entrance to the tomb of the great Pharaoh, the dried bodies of my parents Senmut and Kipa lay in eternal rest. Further south along the shore rose the golden, airy house of Pharaoh, hazy among its walls and gardens. I wondered whether my friend Horemheb dwelt there.

The boat came alongside a familiar stone quay. Nothing was changed, and not many streets away was the place where I had spent my childhood, little dreaming that one day I was to lay waste my parents' life. The sands of time, which had drifted over these bitter memories, stirred a little. I longed to hide myself and cover my face and felt no joy, though the noise of a great city was in my ears once more, and though the haste and restless movements of the people brought to my own senses the feverish pulse of Thebes. I had made no plans for my return, having resolved to let all depend upon my meeting with Horemheb and upon his position at court. But when my feet touched the stones of the quay a plan sprang ready formed into my head, a plan that promised neither fame nor wealth—no lavish gifts in return for all the knowledge I had amassed, as had formerly been my dream—but obscurity and a simple life among poor patients. Yet my mind was filled with a strange serenity when I saw my future revealed. This resolve, this hidden fruit of experience, had ripened within me unseen. When I heard the roar of Thebes about me and my feet touched the burning stones of the wharf, I was a child again, watching with solemn, curious eyes the work of my father Senmut among the sick.

I drove away the porters who noisily importuned me, squabbling among themselves the while, and I said to Kaptah, "Leave our baggage in the boat and hasten to buy me a house—no matter which—a house near the harbor in the poor quarter, near the place where my father's house stood before they pulled it down. Do this in haste that I may take up my dwelling there today and tomorrow begin to ply my trade."

Kaptah's jaw dropped, and his face was a blank mask. He had fancied that we should first put up at the best inn and be waited on by slaves. Yet for once he uttered no word of protest, but having gazed into my face, he shut his mouth and went his way with a drooping head.

That evening I moved into a house in the poor quarter that had belonged to a copperfounder. My baggage was conveyed thither, and there I spread my mat on the earthen floor. Cooking fires were glowing before the huts of the poor, and the smell of fried fish floated over all that dirty, wretched, sickly quarter. Then the lamps were lit above the doors of the pleasure houses, and Syrian music began to jangle from the taverns, blending with the roars of tipsy seamen, and the sky over Thebes glowed red from the countless lights in the center of the city.

241

I had traveled many outlandish roads to their end, gathering wisdom and fleeing eternally from myself, and I had come home.

4

On the following morning I said to Kaptah, "Find me a doctor's sign to set above my door, a simple one, without ornament or paint. And should any ask for me, say nothing of my fame or ability, but only that the physician Sinuhe receives patients—poor as well as rich—and requires only such gifts as their means allow."

"Poor folk?" repeated Kaptah in heartfelt dismay. "Lord, you are not ill? You have not drunk marsh water or been stung by a scorpion?"

"Do as I command if you wish to stay with me. If this simple house is not to your mind and if the reek of poverty offends your delicate Syrian nose, then you are free to come and go as you choose. I fancy you have stolen enough from me to be able to buy your own house and to take a wife if you so desire. I shall not prevent you."

"A wife?" exclaimed Kaptah in still greater dismay. "Truly, lord, you are sick and feverish in the head. Why should I take a wife, who would oppress me and smell my breath when I returned from the city and who, when I awoke in the morning with an aching head, would be standing beside me with a stick in her hand and a mouth full of evil words? Why take a wife when the commonest slave girl will do my business? I have already debated this matter with you. But you are my lord; your way is my way and your punishment mine, although I had thought to reach peace and quiet at last after all the terrible hardships you have brought on me. If rushes are good enough for you to sleep on, then they suffice me also. The wretchedness about us has this advantage, that there are taverns and pleasure houses within reach. The tavern called the Crocodile's Tail, of which I have spoken, lies not far away.

"I hope you will excuse me if I take myself there today and get drunk. All this has shaken me severely, and I need to recover. This I could not have believed! Only a madman hides a jewel in a dung heap, yet in the same manner you bury your skill and your science."

"Kaptah," I said. "Everyone is born naked into the world, and in disease there is no difference between poor and rich, Egyptians and Syrians."

"That may be, but in the gifts they bring their doctor, there is a great difference," said Kaptah sententiously. "Yours is a beautiful thought,

242

and I should have nothing against it, were some other man to put it into effect, now that at last after all our miseries we are able to swing on the golden bough. This notion of yours better suits one born in slavery; I myself had such thoughts when I was younger, until the stick drove sense into me."

"That you may know my full purpose," I went on, "I will tell you that should I ever come on an abandoned child I shall adopt it and bring it up as mine."

"And for what reason?" demanded Kaptah bewildered. "There is a home for foundlings in the temple. Some of them are brought up to be low-grade priests, while others, being made eunuchs, lead a more brilliant life in the women's houses of Pharaoh and the nobles than their mothers could ever have dreamt of. If you desire a son—which is understandable—nothing is easier to achieve. Should you not wish to buy a slave, you can always seduce some poor girl who would be happy and thankful to you for caring for her child and so freeing her from shame. But children are troublesome and the joy of them is certainly exaggerated—although I cannot say much about this since I have never seen any of mine, of whom there must be a number growing up here and there about the world. You would be wiser to buy a young slave girl this very day. She would also be of help to me, for my limbs are stiff, and my hands shake as a result of all our hardships, especially in the mornings. To look after your house and prepare your food is too much for me to do when I have also to supervise your investments."

"I had not thought of that, Kaptah. Yet I shall not buy a slave. You may hire a servant if you wish, for it is no more than you deserve. If you remain in my house, you are free to come and go as you please because of your fidelity, and I believe that with the help of your thirst you can obtain much valuable information for me. Therefore, do as I have said and ask me no more questions, for my resolve has been formed by something within me that is stronger than myself and that may not be gainsaid."

Upon this I went out to ask after my friends. At the Syrian Jar I asked for Thothmes, but a new landlord was there who could tell me nothing of a certain poor painter who lived by drawing cats in picture-books for rich men's children. I then went to the barracks to inquire for Horemheb, but the place was empty. In the courtyard were no wrestlers, no spearmen lunging at sacks stuffed with rushes, nor were the great cauldrons steaming in the cooking sheds as formerly. All was deserted.

A taciturn sergeant of the Shardanas stared at me, wriggling his toes

243

in the sand. His face was bony and unoiled, but he bowed when I asked for Horemheb, Pharaoh's commander who some years ago had waged war against the Khabiri in Syria. He was still commander, the man told me in broken Egyptian, but had been absent for some months in the land of Kush, where he was to disband the garrisons and release the troops from service. No one knew when he would return. I gave the man a silver piece because he seemed so dejected, and at this he forgot his dignity as a Shardana, smiled, and in his delighted astonishment swore by the name of some unknown god. When I would have left he detained me, pointing with a listless hand to the courtyard.

"Horemheb is a great officer who understands soldiers, and is without fear himself," he said. "Horemheb is a lion, Pharaoh a hornless goat. The barracks are empty, no pay, no food. My comrades beg about country. What will come, I don't know. Ammon bless you for the silver; you are a good man. I haven't drunk for months, and my belly is full of dread. I left my own country for many promises. Egyptian recruiting officers went from tent to tent and promised much silver, much women, much drink. Now? No silver, no drink, no women!"

He spat to show his disgust and ground the spittle into the dust with his callused foot. He was a very sorrowful Shardana, and I was concerned for him, gathering from what he said that Pharaoh had dismissed his soldiers and disbanded the troops that had been levied abroad in the days of his father. My thoughts turned to old Ptahor, and in order to find out where he might be, I summoned up my courage and went to the House of Life in the temple of Ammon to seek his name among the records. But the keeper of the records told me that the royal skull surgeon had lain in the City of the Dead for a year and more. So I found not one single friend in Thebes.

Being already in the temple, I went to the great hall of pillars, into the holy twilight of Ammon. The fragrance of incense hung about the colored stone columns with their manifold sacred inscriptions, and far above swallows darted in and out through the stone tracery of the windows. But the temple was almost empty and the forecourt also, and in the countless booths and workshops there was less chaffering and bustle than in former days. Shaven, oily-headed priests in white cloaks regarded me diffidently, and the people in the forecourt conversed in low voices, with many sideways glances as if they feared eavesdroppers. The busy hum of this courtyard, so familiar to me in my student days, when it was like the soughing of wind through reeds, was muffled now to silence. I bore no love for Ammon but despite myself was seized

244

with melancholy, as a man must be who thinks of his youth, whether that youth were good or evil.

When I stepped out between the pylons and the gigantic statues of the Pharaohs, I observed that a new temple had grown up beside the old, of massive proportions and utterly strange in its design. There were no enclosing walls, and when I entered, I found that the colonnade surrounded an open court, on the altar of which offerings of grain, flowers, and fruit had been placed. A great carven relief showed Aton showering his rays on Pharaoh, who made sacrifice, each ray ending in a hand of benediction that held the cross of life. The heads of the white-robed priests were not shaven; most of these men were but youths. Their faces glowed in ecstasy as they sang that holy song whose words I remembered having heard once before, in far-off Jerusalem. But more impressive than priests or images were the forty huge pillars from each of which the new Pharaoh, carved in proportionate size, gazed at the observer with his arms tightly crossed over his breast, holding in his hands the crook and the scourge of majesty.

That these sculptured pillars were representations of Pharaoh I could plainly see, for I recognized that haunting, passionate face, that broad-hipped form with its slender arms and legs. I was seized with awe-struck admiration for an artist skilled enough and bold enough to carve these statues, for the free art that my friend Thothmes had once longed for was apparent here, in sinister perversion. All deformities in Pharaoh's body had been unnaturally emphasized—the swollen thighs, the slender ankles, and the thin, fanatical neck—as if they possessed some occult significance. Most terrifying of all was Pharaoh's face—that queerly long face with the slanting eyebrows and prominent cheekbones, with the secret, ironical smile of the dreamer and blasphemer hovering about the thick lips. In Ammon's temple the stone Pharaohs sat on either side of the pylons, majestic, godlike giants. Here, this swollen, gangling creature in human shape stared down from forty pillars on to the altars of Aton, a man who saw further than other men. The whole of his stone-imprisoned form was instinct and tense with fanaticism.

I trembled to the depths of my being when I beheld these pillars, because for the first time I was seeing the fourth Amenhotep as he may have seen himself. I had met him once when he was a frail, puny youth, racked by the holy sickness. Surveying him with the eye of a physician—albeit a callow one—I had taken his words for the ravings of delirium. Now I saw him as the sculptor had seen him, with mingled love and hatred—a sculptor unrivaled in Egypt for courage.

245

For if any forerunner of his had dared to create such a likeness of Pharaoh, he would have been mutilated and hung head downward from the wall for treason.

There were but few people in this temple. Some of them, to judge by the royal linen, heavy collars, and jewels they wore, were nobles and members of the royal household. The common folk listened to the chanting of the priests with dull, stupid faces, for the words were new and differed widely from the ancient invocations that had been handed down for two thousand years—ever since the building of the pyramids. The ears of the faithful were accustomed to these old prayers since childhood. The people could understand them with their hearts though they might not often reflect upon their meaning.

Yet when the hymn was over, an old man, who from his dress seemed to be a countryman, stepped reverently forward to speak with the priests and to buy an appropriate talisman, or protecting eye, or strip of paper inscribed with some magic text if these were to be had at a moderate price. The priests told him that such objects were not sold in their temple since Aton required neither magic, gifts, nor sacrifices but came freely to everyone who believed in him. The old man, outraged, went his way muttering of lies and foolery, and I saw him enter the old familiar gateway of Ammon.

An elderly fisherwoman next approached the priests, and looking at them with benevolent respect, she asked, "Does no one offer rams or oxen to Aton, so that you poor, skinny lads can get a little meat now and then? If your god is as strong and powerful as he is said to be—stronger even than Ammon though this I cannot quite believe—his priests should be fat and gleam with good living. I am but a simple woman and know no better, but from my heart I could wish you much meat and fat."

The priests laughed and whispered among themselves like mischievous boys. The eldest of them regained his gravity and said to the woman, "Aton desires no blood sacrifices, and it is not fitting that in his temple you should speak of Ammon, for Ammon is a false god whose throne is soon to fall and whose temple will crumble in ruins."

The woman stepped back hastily, spitting on the ground and making the holy sign of Ammon, and she cried, "It was you who said that and not I. May the curse fall on you."

She hurried away, and with her went others, who glanced over their shoulders at the priests in dismay. But these laughed loudly and called after the people with one voice, "Go then, ye of little faith—but

246

Ammon is a false god! Ammon is an idol, and his dominion shall fall like grass beneath the sickle."

Then one of those who retreated took a stone and threw it, and it struck one of the priests in the face so that blood flowed. He covered his face with his hands, lamenting bitterly, while the other priests began to call for the guards. But the aggressor had already taken to his heels and mingled with the throng before the pylons of Ammon's temple.

All this gave me much to think about. Going up to the priests, I said to them, "I am indeed an Egyptian, but I have long dwelt in Syria and do not know this new god whom you call Aton. Will you not in charity enlighten my ignorance and explain to me who he is, what he requires, and how he is to be worshiped?"

They hesitated and studied my face, suspecting mockery, but at length they answered, "Aton is the one god. He has created the land and the river, mankind and the beasts, and all that is upon earth. He is eternal and was worshiped as Ra in his earlier manifestations, but in our own time he has revealed himself as Aton to his son Pharaoh, who lives by truth. He is the only god, and all others are idols. He spurns no one who turns to him. Rich and poor are equal in his sight, and every morning we greet him in the disk of the sun. He blesses the earth with his rays; he shines upon good and evil alike and offers to everyone the cross of life. If you receive it, you are his servant, for his being is love. He is deathless and eternal and everywhere present; nothing can come to pass without his will. By the power of Aton Pharaoh can look into the hearts of all men and see even their most secret thoughts."

But I protested, "Then he is not human, for it lies in the power of no man to see into the heart of another."

They conferred with one another, and replied, "Though Pharaoh himself may desire to be no more than human, yet we do not doubt that in essence he is divine, and this is shown by his visions during which he can live many lives in a short space of time. But this can be known only by those whom he loves, for which reason the artist has portrayed him on these pillars as both man and woman since Aton is the living force that quickens the seed of man and brings forth the child from the womb."

Then I raised my hands in mock despair, and clutching my head exclaimed, "I am but a simple man, as simple as that woman just now, and I cannot altogether grasp this wisdom of yours. Moreover it appears

247

obscure even to yourselves since you must take counsel with one another before you can reply to me."

They rejoined eagerly, "Aton is perfect even as the disk of the sun is perfect, and all that is and lives and breathes in him is perfect. Human thought is imperfect and like a mist, and therefore we cannot perfectly enlighten you since we ourselves do not know all but must learn his will day by day. To Pharaoh alone is his will wholly revealed —to Pharaoh his son, who lives by truth."

The words struck home, for they showed me that these priests were steadfast in their hearts even though they dressed in fine linen and oiled their hair and delighted in the admiration of women and made fun of the simple. The element in me that had come to maturity, independently of my will or learning, responded to these words. For the first time I reflected that human thought might indeed be imperfect and that beyond it there might exist such things as the eye could not see, nor the ear hear, nor the hand grasp. Could it be that Pharaoh and his priests had found this ultimate truth and named it Aton?

5

It was dusk when I returned to my house. Above my door hung a simple signboard, and in the courtyard squatted a few grimy folk patiently awaiting me. Kaptah, looking discontented, was sitting in the porch fanning the flies away from his face and legs with a palm leaf. The flies had come with the patients, but to console him he had a newly broached jar of ale.

I bade him first send in to me a mother who held an emaciated baby in her arms. The remedy for her was a few copper pieces with which to buy herself proper food so that she might suckle her child. Next I tended a slave who had crushed some fingers in a mill, setting the bones and joints in place and administering a soothing draught that he might forget his pain. Then came an old scribe with a growth as big as a child's head upon his neck, so that he was pop eyed and held his head awry and found difficulty in breathing. I gave him an extract of seaweed that I had learned of in Smyrna, although I did not think it could do much for him now. He brought out two copper pieces from a clean rag and offered them to me with pleading eyes, ashamed of his poverty. I did not take them, telling him that I should call upon his services when next I needed any writing done. He departed rejoicing because he had saved his money.

248

A girl from a nearby pleasure house also begged my help, for her eyes were so scabby that they handicapped her in her profession. I cleansed her eyes and mixed her a lotion with which to bathe them and rid them of the evil. Shyly she stood naked before me to offer me the only gift she had. Being unwilling to wound her by a rebuff, I told her that I must abstain from women on account of an important treatment I was about to give. She this believed and admired me for my self-discipline. Moreover, so that her willingness might not be altogether in vain, I removed a few disfiguring warts from her flank and belly, having first rubbed in a numbing salve to render the operation almost painless, and she went her way rejoicing.

Thus my first day's work brought me less than enough to buy salt for my bread, and Kaptah sneered as he served me with a fat goose prepared in the Theban manner, a dish unmatched in any other part of the world. He had brought it from a superior wine shop in the city and kept it hot in the roasting pit. He poured into a colored glass goblet the best wine from Ammon's vineyard, mocking me meanwhile for my profitable day's work. But I was light of heart and happier because of the work than if I had treated a wealthy merchant and been rewarded with a gold chain. And I should add that the mill slave returned in a few days to show me his fingers, which were healing well, and to give me a whole crock of meal he had stolen for me, whereby my first day's work did not go wholly unrewarded.

But Kaptah said, "I believe that from today your fame will spread throughout the quarter, and by dawn your courtyard will be full of patients. I seem to hear the beggars babbling to one another, 'Hasten to the copperfounder's house at the corner, for a physician has come there who heals the sick without payment, painlessly and with great skill, who gives copper to penniless mothers and performs beautifying operations on poor girls from the pleasure houses, requiring no gifts. Hasten thither! The firstcomer gets most, for the man will soon be obliged to sell his house and go elsewhere.'

"But the blockheads are wrong. By good fortune you are the possessor of gold, which I shall cunningly set to work for you. Never in your life need you suffer want but may eat goose every day if you wish and drink the best wine and still prosper, provided you are content to remain in this modest house. But since you never conduct yourself as others do, I shall not be surprised to wake one morning with ashes in my hair because you have sold the house and me with it—such is the fatal restlessness of your heart. Truly, it would not astonish me; therefore, lord, it would be as well to record on paper

249

that I am free to come and go as I please, and to dispatch this paper to the royal archives. The spoken word is forgotten and vanishes, but paper endures forever if it bear your seal in clay and if you offer suitable gifts to the King's scribes. I have a special reason for this request of mine, but I shall not at this time trouble your head and waste your time with it."

It was a mild evening in spring; the fires of dung crackled before the mud huts, and from the harbor the wind bore the scent of cedarwood and of the perfumed waters of Syria. The fragrance of the acacias blended sweetly with the reek of fried fish. I had eaten goose prepared in the Theban manner and drunk wine, and I was full of contentment.

I bade Kaptah pour wine for himself also in an earthenware cup, and I said, "You are free, Kaptah, and have long been so as you know, for notwithstanding your impudence you have been my friend rather than my slave since the day when you lent me silver and copper, believing that you would never see it again. Be free, Kaptah, and be happy! Tomorrow the King's scribe shall make out the legal papers upon which I will affix both my Egyptian and my Syrian seals. But tell me now in what manner you have invested my fortune so that it works for me though I earn nothing. Did you take the gold to the temple coffers as I bade you?"

"No, lord!" answered Kaptah, looking me straight in the face with his one eye. "I did not do your bidding as it was foolish, and I have never obeyed your foolish orders but have acted according to my own good sense. I can safely tell you this now that I am free and you have drunk wine in moderation and will not be wroth. Moreover, knowing your hasty and impulsive nature, which age has not yet mellowed, I have taken the precaution of hiding your stick. I tell you this so that you may not attempt to find it when I have begun to relate what I have done. Only simpletons send their gold to the temple for safekeeping, for the temple pays them nothing for it but rather exacts gifts for hiding it in cellars and setting a guard on it. It is stupid for this reason also: The taxation department then knows the amount of your gold, with the result that it dwindles rapidly away where it lies until there is none left. The only reasonable purpose in amassing gold is to put it out to work so that one may sit with folded hands and chew lotus seeds roasted in salt to induce a pleasurable thirst. I have run about the city all day on my stiff legs to inquire as to the best manner of placing your funds, while you took your walks abroad.

Thanks to my thirst I learned a great deal, among other things that Ammon is selling land."

"Therein you lie!" I exclaimed, for the mere notion was absurd. "Ammon never sells—he buys. Ammon has always bought and now owns one fourth of all the land in the country. And what he has once held he will never relinquish."

"Of course, of course," said Kaptah soothingly, pouring more wine into my glass beaker and—with less ostentation—into his own earthenware one. "Every sensible man knows that land is the only property that endures and maintains its value, provided one remains on good terms with the surveyors and has the wit to reward them after each floodtime. Nevertheless it is true that Ammon is selling land hastily and in secret to any of the faithful who have money. I also was greatly dismayed to hear of this and inquired into it more closely. Ammon is indeed selling land, and cheaply. You know that he owns the most fertile tracts, and if matters stood as they did formerly, nothing would be more tempting than such a purchase, for profit is sure and speedy. Ammon has sold very extensive areas of land and amassed in his vaults all the ready gold in Egypt, so that the price of real estate has dropped to a marked degree. But all these matters are secret, and I should have heard nothing of them had not my most serviceable thirst brought me among the very men who know."

"Do not tell me you have bought land, Kaptah?" I cried in dismay, but he reassured me.

"I am not so foolish, lord, for you should know that I was not born with dung between the toes, slave though I am, but in a stone-paved street among tall houses. I know nothing of land. Ammon's offer is so strangely tempting that a jackal must be lurking in it somewhere, and this is borne out by wealthy men's suspicions of the temple safes. I believe that the whole affair is the result of Pharaoh's new god. But I, seeking only your advantage, have bought for you a number of profitable buildings in the city: shops and dwelling houses, for these pay a substantial yearly rent. The purchases await only your seal and signature to be complete. Believe me, I have bought them cheap, and should the sellers make me presents afterward, that is none of your affair but a matter between myself and them arising out of their stupidity. In these dealings I steal nothing whatever from you. But I would not protest if you were to offer me a present or so since I have arranged the business so favorably."

I reflected a little and replied, "No, Kaptah, I shall make you no presents because you plainly intend to divert to yourself a portion of

251

the rents and also to make your own arrangements with the builders when they estimate their yearly repairs."

Kaptah, unabashed, assented readily to my words. "That is exactly how I saw the matter, for as your wealth is my wealth, so your advantage must be mine. Yet I will admit that when I heard of Ammon's transactions I began to take an intense interest in agriculture. I went to the corn exchange and there wandered from tavern to tavern listening and learning. With your gold and by your permission, lord, I mean to purchase stocks of grain—of next summer's harvest—that is the most profitable way and the prices are still very reasonable. I propose to keep it in store and carefully secured, for something tells me that the price of corn will rise as time goes on. Now that Ammon is selling and every fool becomes a farmer, the harvest cannot continue to be so abundant as formerly. Therefore I have bought storehouses for the grain, dry and soundly built; when we no longer have need of them we can lease them to corn merchants on advantageous terms."

To my mind Kaptah was giving himself unnecessary trouble and vexation, but the plans amused him and I had nothing against the investments so long as I had not to concern myself with their management. And I told him so.

Studiously concealing his satisfaction, he went on with an air of irritation, "There was a further most profitable enterprise that I desired to engage in on your behalf. One of the largest slave-trading houses is for sale, and I think I may say that I know all that is to be known about slaves, having been one my whole life; I should certainly make you rich in a very short time. I know how to conceal faults and failings in a slave and can use a stick to the best advantage—something you cannot do, lord, if you will allow me to mention it now that your stick is hidden. Yet I am oppressed by misgivings that this excellent opportunity will be wasted and that you will not agree to the scheme. Am I right?"

"You are quite right, Kaptah. The slave trade is something we will not embark upon, for it is a dirty and degrading business—though why this should be so I do not know since everyone buys slaves, uses slaves, and needs slaves. So it has ever been and ever will be, yet something tells me I could not be a slave trader, nor would I have you one."

Kaptah sighed with relief and said, "I read your heart aright, lord, and so we escaped that evil—for, thinking the matter over, I suspect that I might have paid undue attention to the women when assessing their value and so squandered my forces. I can no longer afford to

252

do this since I am growing old; my limbs are stiffening and my hands shake very grievously, especially in the mornings when I wake and before I have had time to grasp the beer jar. Having thus examined my heart, let me hasten to assure you that all the houses I have bought for you are respectable, yielding modest but certain profit. Not one pleasure house did I buy, nor slums whose moldering hovels bring in better returns than the snug houses of the well-to-do. But I have one favor to ask you."

All at once Kaptah became diffident and regarded me searchingly with his one eye to assess the gentleness of my mood. I myself poured wine into his cup and encouraged him to speak out, for I had never seen Kaptah uncertain of himself and it aroused my curiosity.

At length he said, "My request is impudent and presumptuous, but since by your own pronouncement I am free, I make bold to utter it, in the hope that you will not be angry. I desire you to come with me to the wine shop in the harbor called the Crocodile's Tail, of which I have often spoken to you, so that we may enjoy a measure of wine together and that you may see what manner of place it is that I dreamed of when I sucked muddy beer through a reed in Syria and Babylon."

I burst out laughing and was not offended, for the wine had put me in a good humor. There was melancholy in the spring twilight, and I was very lonely. Unbecoming and singular though it might be for a master to go with his servant to a miserable harbor tavern and to taste a drink that because of its potency was called crocodile's tail— yet I remembered that Kaptah had once of his own free will accompanied me through a certain dark doorway, well knowing that no one had ever come out of it alive. I laid my hand on his shoulder and said, "My heart tells me that a crocodile's tail is the very thing to finish off the day. Let us go."

Kaptah leaped for joy as slaves will, forgetting the stiffness of his bones. He ran and fetched my stick from its hiding place and wrapped my shoulder cloth about me. We then set off to the harbor and to the Crocodile's Tail, while over the water the wind brought the scent of cedarwood and the green-growing earth.

6

The Crocodile's Tail lay in the middle of the harbor quarter, crowded in among big warehouses in a dim alley. Its mud-brick walls were immensely thick so that in summer it was cool and in winter conserved its warmth. Above the door, besides a beer jar and a wine jar, there hung a huge dried crocodile with shiny glass eyes, its gaping jaws full of many rows of teeth. Kaptah drew me inside eagerly, called the landlord, and made his way to some cushioned seats. He was well known in the place and quite at home; the other customers, having glanced suspiciously at me, resumed their conversations. I saw to my astonishment that the floor was of wood and that the walls also were paneled. On these walls hung trophies from many long voyages: Negro spears and plumes, mussels from the islands in the sea, and painted Cretan bowls.

Kaptah followed my gaze with pride and said, "You will certainly be marveling that the walls are of wood as in rich men's houses. Know that all the planks are from old ships which have been broken up, and although I do not willingly think of sea voyages, I must mention that this yellow, sea-worn plank has sailed to the land of Punt and this brown one has scraped along the quays of the islands in the sea. But if you approve, let us enjoy a 'tail,' which the landlord himself has mixed for us."

A beautiful goblet was placed in my hand, molded in the form of a mussel shell, of the kind that must be held on the palm of the hand. I did not look at it, having eyes only for the woman who brought it to me. She was perhaps no longer as young as most serving girls, nor did she walk about half naked to catch the eye and the senses of the customers. She was decently dressed, with a silver ring in one ear and silver bangles about her slender wrists. She met my gaze fearlessly and did not drop her eyes as is the way of most women. Her eyebrows were plucked fine, and in her eyes could be seen both a smile and a sorrow. They were warm, brown, living eyes, and it did one's heart good to look into them. I took the cup she offered on the flat of my hand, and Kaptah did the same.

Still looking into her eyes I said in spite of myself, "What is your name, loveliness?"

Her voice was low as she answered, "My name is Merit, and it is not seemly to call me loveliness as shy boys do when they first seek to caress the loins of a serving girl. I hope that you will remember this if ever you honor our house again, Sinuhe the physician, You Who Are Alone."

Mortified I answered, "I have not the least desire to caress your loins, fair Merit. But how did you know my name?"

She smiled, and the smile was beautiful on her brown face as she

254

said mockingly, "Your fame has gone before you, Son of the Wild Ass, and seeing you I know that fame has not lied but spoken truly in every particular."

In the depths of her eyes there lay, like a mirage, some remote grief; it sought my heart through her smile and I could not be angry with her.

"If by fame you mean Kaptah here—this former slave of mine whom today I have made a free man—you know very well that his word is not to be trusted. From birth his tongue has been incapable of distinguishing truth from falsehood but loves both equally well—unless indeed it has a bias toward falsehood. I have been unable to cure this either by doctoring or beating."

She said, "Falsehood may be sweeter than truth when one is much alone and past the spring of life. I like to believe your words when you say 'fair Merit,' and I believe all that your face tells me. But will you not taste of the crocodile's tail I have brought you? I am curious to know whether it may be compared with any of the drinks in the strange lands you have visited."

Still with my eyes on her I raised the bowl and drank. Then I looked at her no longer. The blood rose to my head, I began to choke, and my throat seemed on fire.

When at last I found my breath again I gasped, "I will take back what I said of Kaptah, for in this matter at least he did not lie. Your drink is stronger than any I have tasted and more fiery than the earth oil the Babylonians burn in their lamps. I do not doubt that it would fell even a strong man like a blow from a crocodile's tail."

My body was afire, and in my mouth lingered the tang of spices. My heart took wings like a swallow and I said, "By Set and all the devils, I cannot think how this drink has been mixed, nor do I know whether it has bewitched me, Merit, or your eyes. Magic flows in my limbs and my heart is young once more—do not be surprised if I put my hand on your loins, for it is this bowl that will be to blame and not I."

Demurely she drew back and raised her hands in mockery. She was slender and long-limbed and she smiled as she said, "It does not become you to swear. This is a decent tavern, and I am not yet so very old nor so very far from being a virgin—though you may not believe this. As to this drink, it is all the dowry my father has provided, for which reason this slave of yours has diligently courted me, hoping to obtain the secret with me, and for nothing. But he is one eyed and old and fat, and I do not fancy that a mature woman could take much

255

pleasure in him. And so instead he has had to buy the tavern, and he hopes also to buy the formula, though truly much gold will have to be weighed out before we can agree on that."

Kaptah was pulling desperate faces to silence her.

I tasted the drink again and as its fire coursed through my body I remarked, "In truth I believe that Kaptah would be willing to break a jar with you for the sake of this drink although he knows that after the wedding you would soon begin to throw hot water over his feet. Even without it I can well understand his feelings when I look into your eyes—though you must remember that just now the crocodile's tail speaks in me, and tomorrow I may not answer for my words. Is it true, then, that Kaptah owns this wine shop?"

"Begone, you insolent baggage!" cried Kaptah, adding a string of gods' names he had learned in Syria. Then turning to me, he went on in a pleading tone, "Lord, the matter came out too suddenly. I intended to prepare you for this gradually and beg your approval, being still your servant. But it is true that I have bought this house of the landlord, and I also intend to worm the secret of the drink from his daughter. It has made this place famous up and down the river wherever cheerful men assemble, and I have remembered it daily when I have been far away. As you know, I have robbed you all these years as well and cleverly as I am able, and I have been at some pains to invest my own silver and gold, for I must think of my old age.

"Even in my youth the innkeeper's trade was to me the most enviable and alluring," he went on, for the crocodile's tail was making him sentimental. "In those days, it is true, I fancied he could drink as much beer as he liked for nothing. Now I know that he must be moderate in this and must never be drunk, and this will be very wholesome; too much beer sometimes affects me strangely so that I seem to see hippopotamuses and other hideous objects. An innkeeper is forever meeting people who may be useful to him and hears all that is going on, and this greatly tempts me since from my youth up I have ever been exceedingly inquisitive. My tongue will be of great service to me, and I believe that with my stories I shall so entertain my guests that they will unwittingly empty cup after cup and marvel when the hour of reckoning arrives. After ripe reflection, it seems as if the gods intended me for an innkeeper, though by some error I was born a slave. Yet even this is now an advantage, for truly there is no trick or lie by which a customer may seek to slip away without paying that I do not know or have not tried myself in my time."

Kaptah emptied his bowl, rested his head on his hands smiling.

"Furthermore," he went on, "the business is the safest and soundest of all, for whatever may come to pass, thirst remains. Though Pharaoh's power be shaken or the gods fall from their thrones, yet taverns and wine shops will never lose their patronage. Man drinks wine in his gladness and in his grief. When he prospers he drinks, and in wine he drowns his failures. The place is mine already, and for the present the landlord manages it with the help of this witch Merit, and we are to share the profits until I settle here to rest in my old age. We have made an agreement to this effect and have sworn to it by all the gods of Egypt. I do not fancy he will cheat me more than is reasonable, for he is a pious man and goes to the temple at all the festivals to make sacrifice—although I believe he does this partly because several of the priests come here. But I do not doubt his piety; it is no more than fitting, and a wise man will always combine his commercial and spiritual affairs, nor—nor—indeed I forget where I was and what I meant to say, for this is a day of great rejoicing for me, and I rejoice most of all that you have taken no offense but still regard me as your servant although I am the landlord of a tavern— a business not everyone considers respectable. . . ."

After this speech Kaptah began to drool and weep laying his head in my lap and throwing his arms about my knees in maudlin emotion.

Taking him by the shoulders I jerked him into his seat again and said, "Truly I do not think you could have found a more suitable occupation or better security for your old age, yet there is one point which I do not understand. If the landlord knows that his tavern is so profitable and he possesses the secret of the crocodile's tail, why did he agree to sell it to you instead of keeping it for himself?"

Kaptah regarded me reproachfully with tears in his one eye, and said, "Have I not said a thousand times that you have a singular gift for poisoning all my joy with your common sense, which is more bitter than wormwood. Say, as he does, that we have been friends from our youth up and love each other as brothers, and we desire to share our happiness and good fortune! I see from your look that this does not suffice for you, and I confess that in this deal also a jackal lies concealed. Rumors are abroad that there will be widespread disturbances when Ammon and Pharaoh's god strive with one another for power. As you know the taverns suffer first at such times; their shutters are smashed and their landlords whipped and cast into the river, jars are overturned and the furniture knocked to pieces, and in the worst cases, when the place has been drunk dry, it is set on fire. This is the more certain to happen if the owner is on the wrong side, and this

257

man is a man of Ammon and everyone knows it. He can scarcely change his skin at this time of day. He has had doubts of Ammon since hearing that Ammon has begun to sell land, and I have of course done my best to fan these doubts. You forget, lord, that we have the scarab. I am persuaded that it can spare a little protection for the Crocodile's Tail although it is of course busy with your various interests."

I pondered for some time, and said at length, "At any rate, Kaptah, I must acknowledge that you have achieved a great deal in one day."

He waved aside my praise, saying, "You forget, lord, that we disembarked yesterday. But truly I have not let grass grow under my feet. Incredible as it may seem to you, even my tongue is weary, since one single crocodile's tail can cause it to stumble."

We then rose to depart, bidding the landlord farewell, and Merit came with us to the door, the silver bangles jingling on her wrists and ankles. In the darkness of the doorway I laid my hand on her loins and felt her nearness.

She removed my hand firmly and pushed it from her, saying, "Your touch might please me, but I will not consent to it while the crocodile's tail speaks through your hands."

Abashed I raised my hands and regarded them, and they reminded me most vividly of the feet of a crocodile. We took the shortest way home, spread out our mats, and slept very deeply that night.

7

Thus began my life in the poor quarter of Thebes. As Kaptah had foretold, I had many patients, and lost more money than I earned. I required many costly medicines, and it was not worth my while to heal the starving if they could not buy enough meal and fat to regain their strength. The gifts I received were of small value though they gave me joy, and even greater joy was it to learn that the poor had begun to bless my name. Every evening the sky over Thebes glowed red with the lights of the inner city. I was weary after my day's work, and even at night my thoughts were with the sufferings of my patients. I thought also of Aton, Pharaoh's god.

Kaptah engaged an old woman to keep house for us, a woman who did not disturb me and who was weary of life and of men as her face showed. She cooked well and was quiet and never stood in the porch to insult the poor because of their smell or to drive them away from me with harsh words. I soon grew accustomed to her, and she was never in my way. She was a shadow, and I ceased to notice her. Her name was Muti.

So month followed month. The unrest in Thebes increased, and nothing was heard of Horemheb's return. The sun scorched the gardens yellow and the hottest part of the summer was at hand. At times I craved a change and went with Kaptah to the Crocodile's Tail to joke with Merit and look into her eyes, though she remained remote from me and made my heart sore. I listened to the talk of the other customers and soon observed that it was not everyone who was given a seat and a goblet in this house. The customers were picked and chosen, and although some of them might live by grave robbing or blackmail, they forgot their trade when at the tavern and comported themselves in a decent manner. I believed Kaptah when he told me that in this house only such people met as had a use for one another. No one had a use for me, and here also I was a stranger, although I was tolerated and men were not shy of me, because I was Kaptah's friend.

I heard a great deal here; I heard Pharaoh cursed as well as praised, but his new god was for the most part mocked. But one evening an incense dealer came to the tavern with torn garments and ashes in his hair.

He came to soothe his sorrows with a crocodile's tail and shouted, "May this false Pharaoh be cursed to all eternity—this bastard, this usurper, who acts according to his own whims, to the detriment of my sacred calling. Hitherto I have made my best profits on materials I obtain from the land of Punt, and the voyages on the Eastern Sea are not at all hazardous. Every summer ships have been fitted out for the trade routes, and during the following year at least two out of every ten ships have returned with no more than a water measure's delay. Thus I have always been able to make accurate assessment of my holdings and profits. But now! Was there ever greater madness? At the last refit Pharaoh himself came down to the harbor to inspect the fleet. He saw the seamen lamenting aboard the ships and their wives and children weeping on the shore, slashing their faces with sharp stones as is only seemly on such an occasion, for it is well known how many sail and how few return. It has been so ever since the days of the great queen. Nevertheless, believe it or not, this cranky boy, this damned Pharaoh forbade the vessels to sail and has decreed that no more ships are to be fitted out for Punt. Ammon save us! Every honest merchant knows what that means. It means ruin for countless

259

men, poverty and starvation for the wives and children of seamen. Consider the fortunes invested in ships and warehouses, in glass beads and earthenware jars! Think of the Egyptian agents who must now languish forever in the straw huts of the land of Punt, abandoned by the gods!"

Not until the incense dealer had been given the third crocodile's tail on the flat of his hand did he grow quieter. Then he made haste to beg forgiveness if in his grief and indignation he had uttered disparagement of Pharaoh.

"Yet," he went on, "I believe Queen Taia, who is a wise and discerning woman, should govern her son better. I believed Eie the priest also to be a sensible man, but they all seek to overthrow Ammon and allow Pharaoh to give free rein to his madness. Poor Ammon! A man commonly comes to his senses once he has broken a jar with a woman and married, but this Nefertiti, this royal consort, thinks only of her clothes and of her indecent fashions. Believe it or not, the women of the court now paint themselves green round the eyes with malachite and go with their robes open from the navel downward in the sight of men."

Kaptah was curious and said, "I have never seen such fashions in any other land, though I have encountered many curiosities, especially in the matter of women's dress. Do you mean to tell me that women now walk abroad with their private parts uncovered, the Queen also?"

The incense dealer was offended and replied, "I am a man of decorum, with a wife and children. I did not lower my eyes below the navel, nor would I counsel you to do anything so unbecoming."

Merit now interposed wrathfully, "It is your own mouth that is shameless and not these new summer fashions, which are wonderfully cool and do full justice to a woman's beauty, provided she has a fair and well-formed belly and a navel that has not been disfigured by an unskilled midwife. You might safely have allowed your eyes to travel lower, for beneath the open robe there is a narrow loincloth of finest linen that cannot offend the eye of decorum."

The incense dealer would have liked to reply to this, but the third crocodile's tail was stronger than his tongue. Therefore he laid his head in his hands and wept bitterly over the dress of the court women and over the fate of the Egyptians abandoned in the land of Punt.

When Kaptah and I were leaving, I said to Merit at the door, "You know that I am alone, and your eyes have told me that you also are alone. I have pondered over the words you once said to me and believe that at times a lie can be sweeter than truth for a solitary person whose first springtime is past. I should like you to wear such a new summer dress as you were speaking of, for you are shapely and your legs are long, and I do not think you will need to be ashamed of your belly when I walk with you along the Avenue of Rams."

This time she did not put aside my hand but pressed it gently and said, "Perhaps I will do as you suggest."

Yet her promise gave me no pleasure when I stepped out into the hot evening air; rather I was filled with melancholy. From far out upon the river came the lonely notes of a double-reed pipe.

On the following day Horemheb returned to Thebes and with him an armed force. But to tell of this and of all else that happened, I must begin on a new book. Yet I should first mention that in the course of my practice I twice had occasion to open skulls; one patient was a powerful man and the other a poor woman who believed herself to be the great Queen Hatshepsut. Both recovered and were cured, though I believe the old woman was happier in thinking herself queen than when her reason was restored.

BOOK 10

The City of the Heavens

I

THE summer was it its hottest when Horemheb returned from the land of Kush. The swallows had long vanished into the river mud; the pools about the city stagnated while locusts and flea beetles attacked the crops. But in Thebes the gardens of the wealthy were green and cool and luxuriant, and on either side of the Avenue of Rams flowers bloomed in all the colors of the rainbow. Only the poor lacked water, and their food alone was polluted by the dust that fell everywhere like a net, filming the leaves of the acacias and sycamores in their quarter of the city. Southward, on the farther shore, Pharaoh's golden house with its walls and gardens rose through the heat haze with the blue, misty glow of a dream. Although the hottest season was now upon us, Pharaoh had not left for his summer palaces in the Lower Kingdom but remained in Thebes. From this everyone knew that something was about to happen. As the heavens darken before a sandstorm, so the hearts of the people were overshadowed with dread.

No one was surprised to see warriors marching into Thebes at dawn on all the southern roads. With dusty shields, gleaming copper spearheads, and strung bows the black troops marched along the streets and stared about them in wonder, the whites of their eyes flashing in their sweaty faces. They followed their barbarous standards into the empty barracks, where cooking fires soon began to blaze and stones were heated to put in the great earthenware cauldrons. Meanwhile, ships of the fleet were berthing alongside the quays, and the chariots and plumed horses of the officers were put ashore from the transports. There were no Egyptians to be seen among these troops, who were for the most part Nubians from the south and Shardanas from the desert in the northwest. They occupied the city; watch fires were kindled at the street corners, and the river was closed. Gradually in the course of the day labor ceased in workshop and mill, in office and warehouse. The merchants carried in their goods from the street and barred their shutters, and the keepers of taverns and pleasure houses hurried to hire sturdy fellows with cudgels to protect their premises. The people

265

arrayed themselves in white and began to stream from all quarters of the city toward the great temple of Ammon, until its courts were crammed and many were gathered outside the walls.

Meanwhile the word flew round that during the night the temple of Aton had been defiled and desecrated. The rotting carcass of a dog had been thrown on the altar, and the watchman had been found with his throat slit from ear to ear. When the people heard this they shot sidelong glances of fear, but many could not refrain from secret jubilation.

"Cleanse your instruments, lord," said Kaptah gravely. "I believe that before nightfall there will be much work for you to do. If I do not mistake, you will be opening skulls also."

Yet nothing noteworthy took place before the evening; a few drunken Nubians plundered shops and raped a couple of women. The guards seized them, and they were flogged in the sight of the people, which brought little consolation either to the merchants or to the women. Hearing that Horemheb was aboard the commander's ship, I went to the harbor, though with little hope of speech with him. The guard heard me with indifference and went to announce my arrival, then to my surprise returned to summon me to the captain's cabin. Thus for the first time I boarded a warship and looked about me with great curiosity, yet only the armament and the more numerous crew distinguished it from other vessels, since merchantmen also had gilded bows and colored sails.

So once more I encountered Horemheb. He seemed to me even taller and of greater dignity than before; his shoulders were broad, and the muscles of his arms powerful. But there were lines in his face, and his eyes were bloodshot and weary. I bowed low before him and stretched forth my hands at knee level.

He exclaimed with a bitter laugh, "See, it is Sinuhe, the Son of the Wild Ass! In truth you come at an auspicious hour!"

He did not embrace me because of his dignity, but turned to a fat, pop-eyed little officer who stood beside him panting in the heat. Horemheb handed him his golden whip of office saying, "Here it is, then —take charge!" Removing his gold-embroidered collar, he set it about potbelly's neck and added, "Assume command, and may the blood of the people flow over your filthy hands." Then he turned abruptly to me.

"Sinuhe, my friend, I am free to go with you wherever you will, and I hope you have a mat in your house where I can stretch my bones, for by Set and all devils I am mortally weary of arguing with maniacs."

He then laid his hands on the shoulders of the little officer, who was a head shorter than himself, and said, "Look well upon him, friend Sinuhe, and impress what you see upon your memory, for here is a man in whose hands lies the destiny of Thebes this day. Pharaoh put him in my place when I told Pharoah he was mad. And having seen him you may readily surmise that Pharoah will soon have need of me again!"

He laughed and smote his knees, but there was no mirth in his laughter; it frightened me. The little officer looked at him meekly, his eyes popping with the heat and the sweat running down his face and neck and between his fat breasts.

"Be not angry with me, Horemheb," he said in a high voice. "You know that I have not coveted your whip of office; I prefer my cats and the peace of my garden to the din of war. But who am I to set myself against the commands of Pharaoh? And he declares that there will be no war, but that the false god shall fall without bloodshed."

"He declares the thing he hopes for," answered Horemheb. "His heart runs ahead of his reason as a bird outstrips a snail, so that his words have no weight. You should think for yourself and shed blood moderately, with due consideration, even though it may be the blood of Egyptians. By my falcon, I will flog you with my own hand if you have left your good sense in the cages with your pedigreed cats, for in the time of the late Pharaoh you were an eminent warrior, I hear, which is doubtless why Pharaoh has entrusted you with this tedious task."

He thumped the new commander on the back so that the little fellow gulped and gasped, and the words he had meant to say stuck fast in his throat. Horemheb sprang up on deck in two strides, and the soldiers straightened themselves and greeted him with raised spears.

He waved his hand at them, crying, "Farewell, scum! Obey this little pedigreed pussy, who now bears the whip of command. Obey him as if he were a child, and see to it that he does not tumble off his chariot or hurt himself with his own knife."

The soldiers laughed and shouted his praise, but he grew wroth and shook his fist at them, saying, "I shall not bid you farewell! We shall meet again in a little while, for I can see your purpose in your eyes. I say to you: Behave yourselves and remember my words, or I shall have the hide of your backs in ribbons when I come again."

He asked where I lived and told the officer of the watch, but he forbade him to send his baggage to my house, believing it to be safer aboard the warship. Then as in the old days he laid his arm about my neck and sighed, "Truly, Sinuhe, if anyone has earned an honest carouse tonight, it is I."

I told him of the Crocodile's Tail, and he appeared so much interested that I ventured to beg for a special guard to be posted at Kaptah's tavern. He gave the necessary orders to the officer of the watch, who promised to pick out some reliable older men for the purpose. In this way I was able to do Kaptah a service that cost me nothing.

I was by then aware that the Crocodile's Tail contained a number of small private rooms where grave robbers and receivers of stolen goods were wont to settle their accounts and where at times distinguished ladies kept appointments with muscular porters from the harbor. I took Horemheb to such a room. Merit brought him a crocodile's tail in a shell; he swallowed it at one draught, coughed somewhat and said, "O—oh!" He asked for another, and when Merit had gone to fetch it, he remarked that she was a beautiful woman and asked what there was between us. I assured him that there was nothing; nevertheless I was glad that Merit had not yet acquired her new open-fronted dress. But Horemheb made no advances; he offered her respectful thanks, and taking the cup upon the flat of his hand, he tasted it warily.

With a deep sigh he said, "Sinuhe, tomorrow blood will flow through the streets of Thebes, and I can do nothing to prevent it. Pharaoh is my friend, and I love him despite his madness; I once covered him with my shoulder cloth, and it was then that my falcon bound our destinies together. Perhaps I love him because of his madness, but I will not be involved in this struggle for I have my own future to think of and would not have the people hate me. O Sinuhe my friend! Much water has flowed down the Nile since the day of our last meeting in that stinking Syria. I have just come from the land of Kush, where by Pharaoh's command I have disbanded the garrisons and brought the Negro troops back to Thebes, so that in the south the country is undefended. If this goes on, it can be but a question of time before disturbances break out in Syria. Revolt may bring Pharaoh to his senses—but meanwhile the country is impoverished. Ever since his coronation the mines have been worked by very few and without profit. Disciplining the lazy with sticks is no longer permitted; instead, they are put on short rations. Truly my heart trembles for Pharaoh's sake, and Egypt's, and for the sake of his god—though of gods, being

268

a warrior, I know nothing. I say only that many—a very great many—will perish on account of that god. It is madness, for surely the gods exist to keep the people quiet and not to sow unrest among them."

After a pause he went on, "Tomorrow Ammon is to be deposed and I for one shall not regret him, for he has grown too powerful to share Egypt with Pharaoh. It is statesmanlike of Pharaoh to overthrow him, for then he can confiscate his vast possessions, which may yet prove our salvation. The priests of other gods have been overshadowed by Ammon and are envious—but neither do they love Aton, and it is the priests who rule the people's hearts. For this reason disaster must follow."

"But," said I, "Ammon is a hateful god, and his priests have kept the people in darkness for too long and stifled every living thought, until no one dares say a word without Ammon's leave. Whereas Aton offers light and a life of freedom—a life without fear—and that is a great thing, a very great thing, my friend Horemheb."

"I do not know what you mean by fear," he said. "The people must be controlled by fear. If the gods govern them, the throne needs no weapons to support it. Were Ammon content to be Pharaoh's servant, he would fully deserve his place, for no nation can be ruled without fear. That is why Aton, with his gentleness and his cross of love, is an exceedingly dangerous god."

"He is a greater god than you believe," I said quietly, hardly knowing why I said it. "Perhaps he is in you, without your knowledge—and in me. If the people understood him, he could save them all from fear and darkness. But it is more likely that many must die on his account, as you say, for those things that are eternal can only be imposed upon the general run of men by force."

Horemheb regarded me impatiently as one looks at a babbling infant. Then, inspired by the crocodile's tail, he regained his good humor and said, "At least we are agreed that it is time to oust Ammon, and if it is to be done, it should be done suddenly, by night and in secret, and all over the country at the same time. The priests of the highest grades should be executed at once and the others sent to the mines and quarries. But Pharaoh in his foolishness desires to do all openly with the knowledge of the people and in the light of his god—for the sun's disk is his god, no new doctrine, by the way. The thing is lunacy and will cost much blood. I would not agree to its execution since I had not been told of his plans beforehand. By Set and all devils, if I had known of the matter, I should have planned it well and overthrown Ammon so swiftly that he himself could hardly have grasped what had happened. But now every street boy in Thebes knows of the plan; the priests are rousing the people in the temple courtyards, men are breaking branches in their gardens to serve as weapons, and women go to the temple with washing clubs hidden beneath their clothes. By my falcon, I could weep at Pharaoh's madness."

He bowed his head in his hands and shed tears over the trials that were to beset Thebes. Merit brought him the third crocodile's tail and gazed so admiringly upon his broad back and swelling muscles that I sharply bade her be gone and leave us alone. I tried to tell Horemheb of what I had seen in Babylon, in the land of Hatti and in Crete, until I saw that the crocodile had already clouted him on the head with its tail and he was slumbering heavily with his head in his hands. He lay that night in my arms, and I held vigil over his sleeping, hearing all night the reveling of soldiers in the tavern. Kaptah and the landlord felt bound to entertain them, that they might the more readily protect the house when disturbances began. But I did not enjoy myself, for I reflected that in every house in Thebes knives were being whetted, stakes sharpened, and pestles bound with copper. I think there were few in the city who slept that night—certainly Pharaoh was not among them—but Horemheb, a warrior born, slept soundly.

2

All night long the crowds watched before the temple. The poor lay on the cool lawns of the flower gardens while the priests made continual and lavish sacrifice to Ammon and dispensed sacrificial meat, bread, and wine to the people. They called on Ammon in a loud voice and promised eternal life to all who believed in him and gave their lives for his sake.

The priests might have prevented bloodshed if they had so wished. They had but to submit, and Pharaoh would have left them in peace and not persecuted them since his god abominated persecution and hatred. But power and wealth had gone to their heads so that not even death deterred them. They knew that neither the people nor Ammon's few guards could oppose an armed force trained and toughened in war, but that such an army would sweep all aside as rising waters sweep aside dry straw. They desired bloodshed between Ammon and Aton so as to make a murderer and criminal of Pharaoh, who would then be allowing dirty Negroes to shed the pure blood of Egypt. They desired sacrifice to be made to Ammon that he might endure to all eternity, even were his image to be overthrown and his temple closed.

After this long night the disk of Aton rose at last above the three eastern hills, and cool darkness gave place to the scorching heat of the day. In every street and public place horns were blown, and heralds read aloud a proclamation in which Pharaoh affirmed that Ammon was a false god and had now been deposed, that he was accursed to all eternity, that his name should be erased from all inscriptions and monuments and also from the tombs. All the temples of Ammon, both in the Upper and Lower Kingdoms; all his land, cattle, slaves, buildings, gold, silver, and copper were forfeit to Pharaoh and his god. Pharaoh promised to transform the temples into open walks and the gardens into public parks and the sacred lakes into public lakes where the poor might bathe and draw water freely. He promised to divide the land of Ammon among those who owned no land, that they might cultivate it in Aton's name.

The people listened to this proclamation in silence, as custom required. Then everywhere—in the streets and squares and before the temples—there arose a thunderous roar of "Ammon! Ammon!" So tremendous was the shout that the very stones and walls seemed to give it utterance. And now the black troops faltered. Their faces turned gray beneath the red and white paint, their eyes rolled white in their heads, and as they looked about them they saw that despite their numbers they were but a few in this mighty city they were seeing for the first time. Because of the great noise there were not many who heard that Pharaoh, to dissociate his name from that of Ammon, that day assumed the name of Akhnaton, the favored of Aton.

The shout woke even Horemheb, who stretched himself and murmured smilingly, with his eyes still shut, "It is you, Baket, the beloved of Ammon, my princess? Did you call me?"

But when I nudged him in the side, he opened his eyes, and the smile fell from his face like an old garment. He felt his head and said, "By Set and all devils, yours was a potent drink, Sinuhe. I was dreaming, I think."

I said to him, "The people are calling on Ammon."

Then he remembered everything and was in haste to go. We went through the wine shop, where we stumbled over the bare legs of girls and soldiers. Horemheb snatched a loaf from the shelf and emptied a jug of beer, and together we hastened to the temple through streets deserted as never before. On the way he washed at a fountain, plunging his head into the water with much puffing and blowing, for the crocodile's tail still pounded in his head.

271

The plump little cat, whose name was Pepitamon, was disposing his troops and chariots before the temple. When he received word that all was ready and that every man understood his orders, he rose up in his gilded chair and cried out in a shrill voice, "Soldiers of Egypt! Bold men of Kush! Valiant Shardanas! Go now and overturn the image of Ammon the accursed, according to Pharaoh's command, and great shall be your reward!"

Having said this, he felt that he had done all that was required of him, and he sat himself down again contentedly on the soft cushions of his chair and let his slaves fan him, for it was already exceedingly hot.

But before the temple stood a countless throng of white-clad people, men and women, old folk and children, and they did not yield before the advancing troops and chariots. With a great shout they cast themselves down so that the horses trampled on them and the wheels rolled over their bodies. The officers saw that they could not advance without bloodshed and called on their men to retire until they had received further orders, for Pharaoh had forbidden the shedding of blood. But blood already was flowing over the stones of the square, where the injured groaned and shrieked, and there was great excitement among the people when they saw the soldiers draw back. They believed the victory was theirs.

Meanwhile, Pepitamon remembered that in his proclamation Pharaoh had changed his name to Akhnaton and suddenly resolved to change his also, to find favor with Pharaoh. When the officers came to take counsel with him, sweating and perplexed, he affected not to hear them, but opened his eyes wide and said, "I know of no Pepitamon. My name is Pepitaton; Pepi the blessed of Aton."

The officers, each of whom carried a gold-braided whip and commanded a thousand men, were exceedingly irritated, and the commander of the chariots exclaimed, "To the bottomless pit with Aton! What is this foolery? Give us your orders!"

Then Pepitaton mocked them, saying, "Are you warriors or women? Disperse the people but shed no blood, for that Pharaoh has expressly forbidden."

When the officers heard this they looked at one another and spat on the ground. Then, since there was nothing more they could do, they returned to our men.

While these high councils were in progress, the people pressed forward on the retreating Negroes, wrenching up stones from the street and hurling them, swinging their pestles and broken boughs and shouting. The crowd was very great, and men exhorted one another with yells. Many Negroes felled by stones lay on the ground in their own blood. The horses went wild with the outcry of the people and reared and shied so that the charioteers had much ado to hold them. When the commander of the chariots returned to his troop, he found that the best and most costly animal of all had had an eye knocked out and was lame in one leg, having been struck by a stone.

This made the man so savage that he began to howl with rage and cried, "My arrow of gold, my roebuck, my sunbeam! They have put out your eye and broken your leg—but in truth you are dearer to my heart than all these people and the gods put together. Therefore I will be revenged—but let us not shed blood, for that Pharaoh has expressly forbidden!"

At the head of his chariots he tore into the mob, and every charioteer snatched up the noisiest of the rebels into his chariot, while the horses trampled the aged and the children and the shouts were turned to groaning. But those whom the soldiers caught up they strangled in the reins so that no blood flowed; then they wheeled and drove back with the corpses trailing behind them to strike terror into the hearts of the people. The Nubians unstrung their bows, charged in, and strangled their victims with the bowstrings. They also strangled children, and defended themselves against stones and blows with their shields. But every painted Negro who became separated from his fellows was trampled underfoot by the rabble and torn to pieces. They succeeded in dragging down the driver from one chariot, and they smashed his head against the paving stones amid howls of frenzy.

The royal commander-in-chief Pepitaton grew uneasy as time passed, and the water clock beside him gurgled away, and the roar of the people met his ear like the rushing of a torrent. He summoned his officers and rebuked them for the delay, and he said, "My Sudanese cat Mimo is to kitten today; I am anxious about her because I am not there to help her. In the name of Aton go in and overturn that accursed statue that we may all go home, or by Set and all devils I will snatch the chains from your necks and break your whips; I swear it!"

When the officers heard this, they knew that they were betrayed, whatever the outcome, and they resolved at least to save their honor as soldiers. They re-formed their men and charged, hurling the people aside like chaff before a flood; the spears of the Negroes were reddened, blood flowed over the square, and a hundred times a hundred men, women, and children perished that morning in the name of Aton. For when the priests saw that the soldiers were attacking in earnest, they closed the pylon gates, and the people fled this way and that like stampeded sheep. Negroes drunk with blood pursued them and slew them with arrows, while the charioteers stormed though the streets transfixing every fugitive with their spears. But in their flight the people forced their way into the temple of Aton, overturned the altars, and slew such priests as they caught, and the pursuing chariots thundered in after them. Thus the stone pavement of Aton's temple was soon running with blood and strewn with the dying.

But the walls of Ammon's temple blocked the way for Pepitaton's black troops, who were not accustomed to storming such defenses, nor did their battering rams avail to force the copper gates. The soldiers could do no more than encircle the temple, and from the walls the priests yelled imprecations upon them, and the temple guards let fly at them with their arrows and hurled their spears, so that many a painted Negro fell, and to no purpose. From the open place before the temple rose the thick reek of blood, and flies from all over the city gathered there in the billowing dust. Pepitaton came in his golden chair and turned gray in the face at the hideous stench; he bade slaves burn incense about him, and he wept and rent his clothes at the sight of the countless dead.

Yet his heart was full of uneasiness on account of Mimo the Sudanese cat, so he said to his officers, "I fear that Pharaoh's wrath will be most terrible, for you have not overturned the image of Ammon, but instead the blood flows in streams along the gutters. I must hasten to Pharaoh to report on what has passed, and I shall try to speak on your behalf. At the same time I shall be able to call at my house, to see my cat, and change my clothes, for the smell here is fearful and soaks into the very skin. We cannot storm the temple walls today. Pharaoh himself must decide what is to be done now."

Nothing further occurred that day. The officers withdrew their men from the walls and from among the dead, and they caused the supply wagons to be driven up that the Nubians might eat.

During the nights that followed, fires raged in the city, houses were rifled, painted Negroes drank wine from golden cups, and Shardanas lay in soft, canopied beds. All the dregs of the city slunk forth: thieves, tomb robbers, and footpads who had no fear of the gods, not even of Ammon. Piously they blessed the name of Aton and entered his temple, which had been hastily cleansed, receiving the cross of life at the hands of such priests as survived. They hung this about their necks as a protecting talisman which would enable them to steal, murder, and pillage at their ease under cover of night. Many years were to pass

274

before Thebes reverted to what it had once been, for during these days power and wealth drained away from it like blood from a plethoric body.

3

Horemheb stayed at my house, sleepless and haggard. His eyes grew more somber every day, and he had no stomach for the food Muti repeatedly set before him. Muti, like many other women, was greatly taken with Horemheb and had more respect for him than for myself, who, learning or no learning, was nothing but a flabby-muscled man.

Horemheb said, "What do I care for either Ammon or Aton? But they have let my men run wild so that many backs must come under my lash and heads must fall before I can bring them to their senses. And this is a great pity, for they are good fighting men when disciplined."

Kaptah grew richer every day, and his face shone with grease. He now spent his nights at the Crocodile's Tail, for the officers and sergeants of the Shardanas paid for their drams with gold, and in the back rooms of the tavern lay ever growing heaps of stolen treasure, jewels and coffers and mats, which the customers gave in exchange for wine without asking about the price. No one attacked the house, and thieves walked wide of it, for it was guarded by Horemheb's men.

By the third day my stock of medicines was exhausted, and it was impossible to buy more, even for gold. My arts were vain in the face of the disease that spread through the poor quarter from the corpses and foul water. I was tired, and my heart was like a wound in my breast, and my eyes were bloodshot from lack of sleep. I was sickened with everything—with the poor, with wounds, with Aton—and I went to the Crocodile's Tail where I drank mixed wine until I fell alseep.

In the morning Merit roused me; I was lying on her mat with her beside me. Deeply ashamed I said to her, "Life is like a cold night, but truly it is sweet when two lonely mortals keep one another warm, though their hands and eyes tell lies for the sake of their friendship."

She yawned sleepily.

"How do you know that my hands and eyes are lying? I am weary of smiting soldiers over the fingers and kicking their shins; here by your side, Sinuhe, is the only safe place in the city—a place where no one will lay a hand on me. Why this should be I cannot tell, and I am

275

a little offended, for I am said to be beautiful nor is there anything amiss with my belly, though you have not deigned to look at it."

I drank the beer she offered me, to clear my aching head, and found nothing to say. She looked into my eyes with a smile, though in the depths of her brown ones sorrow lay still, like the dark waters at the bottom of a well.

She said, "Sinuhe, I would help you if I could, and I know that in this city there is a woman who owes you an immeasurable debt. In these days roofs are floors, and doors open outward, and payment for many old debts is demanded in the streets. Perhaps it would do you good also to go adunning and so lose the belief that every woman is a wilderness."

I said that I had never believed this of her, but I went and her words remained with me, for I was but human. My heart was swollen with the sight of carnage, and I had tasted the frenzy of hatred so that I was afraid for myself. I remembered the temple of the cat and the house beside it though time had drifted like sand over these memories. But during the days of terror the dead rose from their graves and I remembered my father Senmut in his tenderness and my good mother Kipa; there was a taste of blood in my mouth as I thought of them. At this time no one in Thebes was too rich or too eminent to be in danger when he walked abroad, and I need only have hired a few soldiers to carry out my purpose. But as yet I did not know what my purpose was.

On the fifth day there was an uneasiness even among the officers under Pepitaton's command, for the soldiers ceased to obey the notes of the horn and insulted their leaders in the streets, snatching the golden whips from them and snapping them across their knees. The officers went to Pepitaton who was growing weary of a warrior's life and missed his cats, and they persuaded him to seek audience of Pharaoh, tell him the truth, and relinquish his collar of office. And so on the fifth day Pharaoh's messengers came to my house to summon Horemheb before Pharaoh. Horemheb rose like a lion from his couch, washed and dressed, and went back with the men, growling to himself at the thought of all he would say to Pharaoh. Now even Pharaoh's authority was tottering, and no one knew what tomorrow might bring.

When he stood before him, he said, "Akhnaton, there is not a moment to be lost, and I have no time to remind you of all I counseled you to do. If you desire all to be as it was, give me your authority for three days, and on the third day I will restore it to you. You need never know of what has passed."

276

Pharaoh said to him, "Will you overthrow Ammon?"

Horemheb answered, "Truly you are a man possessed! Yet after what has happened Ammon must fall if Pharaoh's majesty is to survive. Therefore, I will overthrow him—but do not ask how it will be done."

Pharaoh said, "You shall not harm his priests, for they know not what they do."

Horemheb answered him and said, "In truth your skull should be opened, for it is plain that nothing else will cure you. Nevertheless I will obey your command for the sake of that hour when I covered your weakness with my shoulder cloth."

Then Pharaoh wept and handed him his whip and his crook for three days. How this matter came about I know only from what Horemheb told me, and after the manner of warriors he was given to fanciful embellishment. Be that as it may, he returned to the city in Pharaoh's gilded carriage and drove through street after street calling the soldiers by name. He took the trustiest among them with him and caused horns to be sounded, mustering the men under their standards: their falcons and lions' tails. The search went on all night. Yells and howls were heard from the men's sleeping quarters, and canes by the score were worn to shreds in the hands of the castigators, whose arms grew weary and who groaned that never before had they known such toil. Horemheb sent his best men on patrol through the streets to grab every man who did not obey the horns and lead him to be flogged; many whose hands and garments were bloody had their heads cut off in the sight of their fellows. When morning dawned, the riffraff of Thebes had scuttled back to their holes like rats, for everyone caught thieving or house breaking was speared on the spot.

Horemheb also summoned together all the builders in the city and bade them tear down the houses of the wealthy and break up ships for their timber, and he set laborers to building battering rams and siege towers, so that the noise of hammering filled the night. But above all other noises rose the yells of Nubians and Shardanas under the lash, an agreeable sound to the citizens of Thebes.

Horemheb wasted no time in vain negotiation with the priests, but as soon as it grew light he gave his officers their orders. Siege towers were placed at five points about the temple walls while at the same time battering rams began to thunder against the gates. No one was wounded, for the soldiers made roofs of their shields. The priests and temple guards could make no stand against so determined and well concerted an attack. They dispersed their forces and ran hither and thither in panic about the walls, while from the courts below came the cries of terrified people who were sheltering there. When the chief priests saw that the gates were giving way and that Negroes were gaining the walls, they caused horns to be sounded for a truce that the lives of the people might be saved. They were of the opinion that Ammon had had sacrifice enough and they desired to spare the remainder of the faithful for service in the future. The gates were therefore opened and the soldiers allowed the packed masses to escape as Horemheb had commanded. The people fled, calling upon Ammon, and were content to hasten home, for the uproar had abated and they were weary indeed of standing so long in the courtyards beneath the burning sun.

Thus Horemheb took possession of the forecourts, stores, stables, and workshops of the temple without severe casualties. The Houses of Life and Death also were brought under his control, and he sent physicians from the House of Life into the city to heal the sick, but he did not meddle with the House of Death, for those who dwell there are apart and in sanctuary whatever may befall in the outside world. The priests and guards made a last stand in the great temple to protect the holy of holies; the priests laid spells on the guards and drugged them that they might fight to the death without feeling pain.

The battle in the great temple went on until nightfall, but by then the bewitched guards had all been slain with such priests as had made armed resistance, and there remained only the priests of the highest grade who had gathered about their god in the sanctuary. Horemheb gave order for the fighting to cease and at once sent men to gather up the dead and throw them into the river.

Then, approaching the priests of Ammon, he said, "I wage no war against Ammon, for I serve Horus, my falcon. Nevertheless I must obey the command of Pharaoh and depose your god. Would it not be more agreeable for both yourselves and me if no image were found in the holy of holies for the soldiers to desecrate? For I do not wish to commit sacrilege, though because of my oath I must serve Pharaoh. Reflect upon my words; to that end I will allow you a water measure's time. Thereafter you may depart in peace, and none shall raise his hand against you since I do not seek your lives."

These words were agreeable to the priests, who had braced themselves to die for the sake of Ammon. They remained in the sanctuary until a measure of water had run from the water clock. Then Horemheb with his own hand tore down the veil of the sanctuary and let the priests depart. When they had gone, the sanctuary was empty and no image of Ammon was to be seen. The priests had made haste to demolish it, and they bore away the pieces under their cloaks, that later they might proclaim a miracle and affirm that Ammon still lived. Horemheb caused seals to be set on all stores, and he sealed the cellars where the gold and silver was hidden with his own hand. That evening, by the light of torches, stone masons set to work to efface the name of Ammon from every statue and inscription. During the night Horemheb had the square cleared of bodies and fragments of bodies and sent men to quench the fires that still raged in some parts of the city.

When the wealthier and more aristocratic Thebans learned that Ammon had been deposed and that peace and good order had been restored, they arrayed themselves in their finest clothes, lit lamps before their houses, and went out into the streets to celebrate Aton's victory. Members of the court, who had taken refuge in Pharaoh's golden house, were now ferried back across the river to the city. Soon the sky over Thebes glowed red from the festival torches and lamps, and people strewed flowers in the streets and shouted and laughed and embraced one another. Horemheb could not prevent them plying the Shardanas with wine nor hinder noble ladies from embracing Nubians who carried impaled upon the points of spears the shaven heads of the priests they had slain. Thebes rejoiced that night in the name of Aton. In the name of Aton all was permitted and there was no difference between Egyptian and Negro. In testimony of this the court ladies admitted Nubians to their houses, shook out their new summer dresses, and enjoyed the virility of the black men and the sour, blood smell of their bodies. And when a wounded temple guard crawled out into the open from the shadow of the wall, calling on Ammon in his delirium, they smashed his head against the stones of the street, and the ladies danced in jubilation round the body.

These things I saw with my own eyes, and having seen them, clutched my head in my hands, indifferent now to all that happened. I reflected that no god can cure man of his madness. I ran to the Crocodile's Tail, and with Merit's words blazing up in my heart, I called the soldiers who were on guard there. They obeyed me, having seen me in company with Horemheb, and I led them through that night of delirium, past revelers dancing in the streets, to the house of Nefernefernefer. There also torches and lamps were burning and from the house, which had suffered no pillage, the noise of drunken revelry rang out into the street. When I had come thus far, my knees began to quake, and my stomach sank.

I said to the soldiers, "These are the orders of Horemheb, my friend and the King's commander-in-chief. Go into the house where you will find a woman who carries her head haughtily and whose eyes are like green stones. Bring her here to me, and should she resist, smite her over the head with the butt of a spear but do her no other harm."

The soldiers strode in cheerfully. Soon the startled guests came reeling out, and servants called for the guards. My men soon returned with fruit and honey bread and jars of wine in their hands, and with them they carried Nefernefernefer. She had struggled, and they had struck her with a spear so that her smooth head was bloody and her wig had slipped off. I laid my hand on her breast, and her skin was smooth as warm glass, but to me it was as if I had laid my hand on a snakeskin. I felt her heart beating and knew that she was unharmed, yet I wrapped her in a dark cloth as corpses are wrapped and lifted her into a chair. The watch did not interfere when they saw that I had soldiers with me. These attended me to the gateway of the House of Death, while I sat in the swaying chair with Nefernefernefer's senseless body in my arms. She was beautiful still but more repulsive to me than a serpent. So we went on through the riotous night to the House of Death, where I gave the soldiers gold and dismissed them, and I also sent away the chair.

With Nefernefernefer in my arms I entered the House and I said to the corpse washers who met me, "I bring you the body of a woman whom I found in the street; I do not know her name or her family, but I fancy the jewels she is wearing will reward you for your trouble if you will preserve her body forever."

The men swore at me, saying, "Madman, do you think we have not had enough carrion to deal with in these days? And who will reward us for our trouble?"

But when they had unwound the black cloth, they found that the body was yet warm, and when they took off the dress and the jewels, they saw that she was fair—fairer than any woman who had yet been brought to the House of Death. They said no more to me but laid their hands on her breast and felt her heart beating. They swiftly covered her once more in the black cloth, winking and grimacing at one another with delighted laughter.

Then they said to me, "Go your way, stranger, and blessed be this act of yours. We shall do our best to preserve her body forever, and should it depend on us alone, we will keep her with us seventy times seventy days, that her body may be preserved indeed."

Thus did I exact payment from Nefernefernefer for the debt in

280

which she stood to me on my parents' account. I wondered how she would feel when she awoke in the recesses of the House of Death, robbed of her wealth and in the power of corpse washers and embalmers. If I knew anything of them, they would never let her return to the light of day. This was my revenge, for it was through her that I ever came to know the House of Death. But my revenge was childish, as I was later to discover.

At the Crocodile's Tail I saw Merit and said to her, "I have enforced my demands, and in a more terrible manner than anyone has ever done. But my revenge gives me no relief, my heart is yet emptier than before, and despite the warmth of the night my limbs are cold."

I drank wine, and it was as dust in my mouth. I said, "May my body perish if ever I lay my hand upon a woman again, for the more I think of woman the more do I fear her; her body is a wilderness and her heart a mortal snare."

She stroked my hands, and her brown eyes looked into mine as she said, "Sinuhe, you have never known a woman who wished you well."

And I answered, "May all the gods of Egypt save me from a woman who wishes me well. Pharaoh also wishes only well, and the river is full of bobbing corpses because of his well wishing."

I drank wine, and I wept, saying, "Merit, your cheeks are smooth as glass and your hands are warm. Let me touch your cheeks with my lips this night and put my cold hands into your warm ones so that I may sleep without dreaming, and I will give you whatever you desire."

She smiled sadly and said, "The crocodile's tail speaks through your mouth, but I am accustomed to that and I take no offense. Know therefore, Sinuhe, that I require nothing of you and never in my life have required anything of a man; from none have I taken a gift of any value. What I give I give from my heart, and to you also I give what you ask, for I am as lonely as you."

She took the wine cup from my trembling hand, and having spread her mat for me, she lay down beside me, warming my hands in hers. I brushed her smooth cheeks with my lips and breathed in the fragrance of cedar from her skin, and I took pleasure with her. She was to me as my father and my mother—she was as a brazier on a winter's night and a beacon on the shore that guides the seaman home through a night of tempest. When I fell asleep, she was to me Minea—Minea whom I had lost forever—and I lay against her as if on the floor of the sea with Minea. I saw no evil dreams but slept soundly, while she whispered in my ear such words as mothers whisper whose children fear the dark. From that night she was my friend, for in her arms I could believe once more that there was something greater than myself beyond my understanding, for which it was worth while to live.

Next morning I said to her, "Merit, I have broken a jar with a woman who is now dead, and I still have the silver ribbon with which I bound her long hair. Yet for the sake of our friendship, Merit, I am ready to break the jar with you if you wish it."

Yawning she held the back of her hand across her mouth and said, "You must drink no more crocodiles' tails, Sinuhe, since they make you talk so foolishly next day. Remember that I grew up in a tavern and am no longer an innocent girl who might take you at your word —and be sorely disappointed!"

"When I look into your eyes, Merit, I can believe that there are good women in the world," I said, and I brushed her smooth cheeks with my mouth. "That was why I said it, that you might know how much you are to me."

She smiled.

"You note that I forbade you to drink crocodiles' tails, for a woman first shows her fondness for a man by forbidding him something, to feel her own power. Let us not talk of jars, Sinuhe. You know that my mat is yours whenever you are thus lonely and sorrowful. But be not offended if you find that there are others lonely and sorrowful besides yourself, for as a human being I too am free to choose my company, and I hold you in no way bound. And so, in spite of all, I will give you a crocodile's tail with my own hand."

So strange is the mind of man and so little does he know his own heart that my soul at this moment was as free and light as a bird, and I recalled nothing of the evil which had come to pass during those days. I was content and tasted no more crocodiles' tails that day.

4

Next morning I came to fetch Merit to watch Pharaoh's festival procession. Despite her tavern upbringing she looked very lovely in the summer dress that was made in the new fashion, and I was not at all ashamed to stand beside her in places reserved for the favored of Pharaoh.

The Avenue of Rams was brilliant with banners and lined with the vast crowds who had come to see Pharaoh. Boys had climbed the trees in the gardens on either side, and Pepitaton had ordered countless baskets of flowers to be set out along the road so that, according to custom, the spectators could strew them in Pharaoh's path. My mood was hopeful for I seemed to glimpse freedom and light for the land of Egypt. I had received a golden bowl from Pharaoh's house and had been nominated skull surgeon to his household. Beside me stood a mature and lovely woman who was my friend, and around us in the reserved places we saw only happy, smiling people. Yet profound silence reigned; the squawking of crows could be heard from the temple roof—for crows and vultures had taken up their abode in Thebes and were so gorged that they could not rise and fly back to their hills.

It was a mistake for Pharaoh to allow painted Negroes to walk behind his chair. The mere sight of them aroused the fury of the people. There were few who had not suffered some injury during the preceding days. Many had lost their homes by fire, the tears of wives had not yet dried, men's wounds still smarted beneath the bandages, and their bruised and broken mouths could not smile. But Pharaoh Akhnaton appeared, swaying high in his chair above the heads of the people and visible to them all. Upon his head he wore the double crown of the Two Kingdoms—lily and papyrus. His arms were crossed on his breast, and his hands were hard clenched about the crook and whip of royalty. He sat motionless as an image, as the Pharaohs of all ages have sat in the sight of the people, and there was a dread silence as he came, as if the sight of him had struck men dumb. The soldiers guarding the route raised their spears with a shout of greeting, and the more eminent of the onlookers also began to shout and throw flowers in front of the royal chair. But against the menacing hush of the crowd, their cries sounded thin and pitiful, like the buzz of a solitary midge on a winter's night, so that they soon fell silent and looked at one another in amazement.

Now, against all tradition, Pharaoh moved. He raised the crook and whip in ecstatic greeting. The crowd surged back and suddenly from its manifold throat broke a cry as terrible as the thunder of bursting seas among the rocks.

"Ammon! Ammon! Give us back Ammon, the king of all gods!"

As the mob billowed and swayed and the cry rolled out ever louder, the crows and vultures winged upward from the temple roof and flapped their black pinions above the chair of Pharaoh. And the people cried, "Away with you, false Pharaoh! Begone!"

The shout alarmed the bearers so that the chair halted in its course. When they again moved forward, goaded by the nervous officers of the guard, the people poured in an irresistible flood across the Avenue of Rams, swept away the chain of soldiers, and threw themselves pell-mell before the chair to block its advance.

It was no longer possible to follow exactly what was happening. The soldiers began to belabor the people with their cudgels to clear the way, but soon they had recourse to spears and daggers in their own defense. Sticks and stones sang through the air, blood flowed across the street, and above the roar rose the screams of the dying. But not one stone was cast at Pharaoh, for he was born of the sun like all other Pharaohs before him. His person was sacred, and no one in the crowd would have dared even in his dreams to lift a hand against him, though in their hearts all hated him. I do not believe that even the priests would have done so unheard of a thing. Pharaoh looked on unmolested. Then he arose, forgetting his dignity, and called out to halt the soldiers, but no one heard his cry in all the din.

The mob stoned the guards, and the guards defended themselves and slew many of the people, who cried out unceasingly, "Ammon! Ammon! Give us back Ammon!" and also, "Away with you, false Pharaoh! Begone! Thebes will have none of you!" Stones were cast on those of high rank, and the people surged threateningly about the reserved enclosures, so that women threw away their flowers, dropped their phials of perfume, and fled.

At Horemheb's command the horns were sounded. From courts and sidestreets came the chariots that he had disposed there out of sight lest the people be provoked. Many were crushed beneath the hoofs and wheels, but Horemheb had ordered the removal of the scythes from the sides of the chariots to prevent unnecessary bloodshed. They drove slowly and in a prearranged order, encircling Pharaoh's chair and also protecting the royal family and others in the procession, and so escorting them away. But the crowds would not disperse until the royal barges were seen rowing back across the river. Then they broke out in jubilation, and their rejoicing was yet more terrible than their anger. The ruffians among the crowd besieged the houses of the rich until the soldiers restored order and the people dispersed to their homes. Evening drew on and the crows circled down to tear at the bodies that remained lying in the Avenue of Rams.

Thus Pharaoh Akhnaton was confronted for the first time by his raging people and saw blood flowing on his god's account. He never forgot this sight. Hatred dropped poison into his love, and his fanaticism grew until at last he decreed that everyone who spoke the name

284

of Ammon aloud or held his name concealed on images or vessels should be sent to the mines.

I speak of these events before coming to the time in which they took place, to make plain their cause. That same evening I was summoned hastily to the golden house, for Pharaoh had had an attack of his sickness. His physicians feared for his life and sought to share the burden of responsibility, for he had spoken of me. He lay long like one dead; his limbs grew cold, and his pulse was no longer to be detected. After a period of delirium during which he bit his tongue and lips until the blood flowed, he came to himself. He then dismissed all the other physicians, for he could not endure the sight of them.

"Summon the boatmen," he said to me, "and hoist red sails on my ship. Let my friends come with me, for I am going upon a journey and will let my vision lead me until I find a land belonging neither to gods nor to men. This land I will dedicate to Aton and build there a city that shall be the city of Aton. I will never again return to Thebes."

He said also, "The conduct of the Thebans is more hateful to me than all that has gone before—more loathsome, more contemptible than anything my forebears ever saw, even among foreigners. Therefore I spurn Thebes and leave it to its own darkness."

So intense was his agitation that he demanded to be carried to his ship while yet ailing, nor could I as his physician prevent him.

Horemheb said, "It is better so. The people of Thebes will have their way, and Akhnaton will have his; both will be satisfied, and there will be peace in the land once more."

I attended Pharaoh on his voyage down the river. He was too impatient to wait even for the royal family but set sail first. Horemheb ordered an escort of warships to accompany the vessel that he might come to no harm.

So beneath her red sails Pharaoh's ship glided down the river, and Thebes fell behind. Walls, temple roofs, and the gilded tips of the obelisks sank below the horizon, and lastly the three peaks, the eternal guardians of Thebes, vanished also. But the memory of Thebes remained with us for many days, for the river was full of fat crocodiles whose tails splashed up the foul waters, and a hundred times a hundred swollen corpses drifted with the current. There was no shoal or clump of reeds without its body, held fast by clothes or hair, and all because of Pharaoh Akhnaton's god. But he knew nothing of this, for he lay in his cabin on soft mats, where servants anointed him with

285

perfumed oils and burned incense about him, that he might not smell the smell of his god.

When we had been sailing for ten days, the river was pure again, and Pharaoh stepped into the bows to look about him. The earth was summer yellow; farmers were gathering in their harvest, and in the evenings the cattle were driven down to the water's edge to drink, and herdsmen blew on their double pipes. When the people saw Pharaoh's ship, they arrayed themselves in white and ran down to the shore, where they shouted their greetings and waved their branches of palm. The sight of these contented people was better than any medicine to Pharaoh. Now and then he would give orders for the ship to put in to the bank, and he would go ashore to talk to the people, to touch them, and to bless the women and children with his hands. The sheep also came shyly up, to nuzzle and nibble at the hem of his robe, and he laughed for joy.

In the darkness of night he stood in the bows gazing at the burning stars, and he said to me, "I will divide all the land of the false god among those who are content with little and have labored with their hands, that they may be happy and bless the name of Aton. I will divide all the land among them, for my heart rejoices at the sight of plump children and laughing women and men who labor in the name of Aton without fear or hatred of any."

He said also, "The heart of man is dark; I should not have believed this had I not seen it for myself. For so lucent is my own clarity that I do not comprehend the darkness, and when light pours into my heart, I forget all the hearts that are twisted and shadowy. There must be many who do not comprehend Aton, though they see him and feel his love, for they have lived their lives in darkness, and their eyes do not know the light when they see it. They call it evil and say that it hurts their eyes. Therefore I leave them alone and do not trouble them, but I will not dwell among them. I gather about me those who are dearest to me and will remain among them, never to leave them, that I may not suffer those evil pains in my head through seeing things that oppress my spirit and are hideous in the sight of Aton."

Screwing up his eyes at the stars, he went on, "Night is abomination to me. I do not love the darkness; I fear it. I do not love the stars, for when they shine, jackals slink from their dens, lions leave their lairs and roar with blood lust. Thebes is night to me, and so I spurn it—in truth I spurn all that is old and crooked and put my faith in the young and in children. The spring of the world is born of them. Those who from childhood dedicate themselves to the teaching of Aton are purified, and so the whole world shall be purified. Schools shall be transformed, the old teachers driven forth, and new texts written for children to copy. Moreover I will make writing simpler than it now is, for we need no pictures to understand it; I shall cause a script to be adopted that even the humblest may quickly learn. There shall no longer be a gulf between scribes and people; the people shall learn to write so that in every village—even the smallest—there shall be one to read what I shall write to them. For I shall write to them often, of many things that they should know."

Pharaoh's talk disturbed me. I knew this new script that was easy to learn and to read; it was not sacred writing, nor was it as beautiful or as rich in content as the old, and every self-respecting scribe despised it.

Therefore I said, "Popular script is ugly and barbarous, and it is not sacred writing. What will become of Egypt if everyone is made literate? Such a thing has never been. No one will then be content to labor with his hands; the soil will lie untilled, and people will take no pleasure in their ability to write when they are starving."

I should not have said this, for he cried out in high indignation, "So near to me then is the darkness! It stands beside me in you, Sinuhe. You cast doubts and obstacles in my path—but truth burns like fire within me. My eyes pierce all barriers as if they were barriers of pure water, and I behold the world that will come after me. In that world is neither hatred nor fear; men share their toil with one another and there are neither rich nor poor among them—all are equal—all can read what I write to them. No man says to another 'dirty Syrian' or 'miserable Negro'. All are brothers, and war is banished from the world. And seeing this, I feel my strength increase; so great is my joy that my heart is near to bursting."

Once more I was persuaded of his madness. I led him to his sleeping mat and gave him soothing medicine. Yet his words were a torment, and my heart felt the sting of them, for there was something in me that had matured to receive his message.

I said to my heart, His mind is greatly disordered because of his sickness, nevertheless the disorder is both beneficient and infectious. I could wish that his visions might come true although my reason tells me that such a world could exist nowhere but in the Western Land. Still my heart cries out that his truth is higher than all other truths that have been spoken and that no greater truth will ever be spoken after him, notwithstanding that bloodshed and ruin break from his

287

footprints. If he lives long enough, he will overthrow his own great kingdom.

And as I gazed at the stars through the darkness I reflected, I Sinuhe am a stranger in the world and do not even know who brought me into it. Of my own will I became the poor man's physician in Thebes, and gold means little to me, though I prefer a fat goose to dry bread and wine to water. None of that is so important that I could not abstain from it. Having no more than my life to lose, why should I not be a prop for his weakness—stand at his side and encourage him, without misgivings? For he is Pharaoh! The power is his and there is no more wealthy or more fertile land in the whole world than Egypt, and who knows but Egypt may survive the trial? If such a thing could be, then indeed the world would be renewed: men would be brothers and there would be neither rich nor poor. Never before has a man been offered such an opportunity to bring his truth into being, for this man is born Pharaoh, and the chance will never come again. Here is the one moment in all ages of the world when his truth may be made reality.

Such were my waking dreams aboard the rocking ship, while the night wind bore to my nostrils the fragrance of ripe grain and of the threshing floors. But the wind chilled me and the dream melted and I said to myself ruefully, If only Kaptah were here to hear his words! For although a physician is a clever man and can heal many maladies, yet the world's sickness and misery is so great that not all the doctors in the world could cure it even if they were competent—and there are ills before which physicians are powerless. Thus Akhnaton may be a physician for the human heart, but he cannot be everywhere. There are hearts so hardened and blackened that not even his truth can avail them anything. Kaptah would say, Even were the time to come when there would be neither poor nor rich, yet there will always be wise and stupid, sly and simple, for so there have ever been and ever will be. The strong man sets his foot on the neck of the weakling; the cunning man runs off with the simpleton's purse and sets the dunce to work for him. Man is a crooked dealer and even his virtue is imperfect. Only he who lies down never to rise again is wholly good. Already you may see the fruits of that goodness, and those who have most reason to bless it are the crocodiles of the river and the gorged crows on the temple roof.

Pharaoh Akhnaton spoke with me, and I spoke with my weak and vacillating heart. On the fifteenth day we reached land that belonged neither to a god nor to any eminent man. From the shore its hills

288

shaded from golden yellow into blue. The soil lay uncultivated, and only a few herdsmen guarded their flocks there and lived in reed huts along the bank. Here Pharaoh went ashore and dedicated the land to Aton in order to found on it a new city; this future city he named Akhetaton, the City of the Heavens.

Ship after ship followed, and he gathered together his master builders and architects and showed them where the main streets were to run, where his golden palace and the temple of Aton were to stand. As his followers joined him he pointed out to each the site of his house. The builders drove away the herdsmen and their sheep, tore down their reed huts, and built quays along the shore. For these builders Pharaoh allotted space for their own town outside the city where, before starting the work commanded of them, they were allowed to build mud houses for themselves. Five streets ran north and south, five east and west; the houses that lined them were all of identical height and each contained two similar rooms. The roasting pit was in the same place in every house, as was every mat and pitcher. Pharaoh bore good will to all his workmen and wished them to share the same benefits, that they might dwell happily in their own place outside Pharaoh's city and bless the name of Aton.

Then came winter and the season of flood. Pharaoh did not return to Thebes as was his custom but remained aboard his ship which was now the seat of government. As stone was laid upon stone and column after column was erected, he rejoiced greatly. Often he would break into malicious laughter when he beheld the beautiful, delicate timber houses rising along the streets, for the thought of Thebes corroded his mind like poison. On this city of Akhetaton he spent all the money he had won from Ammon, and he divided Ammon's land among the very poor.

I had much work to do, for although Pharaoh himself improved in health and spirits as he beheld his city blossom from the soil on its colored pillars, yet sickness raged among the workmen before the ground had been drained; also there were many building accidents because of the haste imposed upon the men.

As soon as the river had fallen, Horemheb landed at Akhetaton in company with members of the court, though he did not intend to stay longer than was needful to persuade Pharaoh to change his mind about disbanding the army. Pharaoh had commanded him to release the Nubians and Shardanas from his service and send them home, but Horemheb had delayed fulfillment of the order on all manner of pretexts, having reason to fear that revolt would soon break out in Syria and being minded to lead the troops into that country.

But Pharaoh Akhnaton was unshakable in his resolve and Horemheb but wasted his time in Akhetaton. Every day their conversations were the same.

Horemheb said, "There is serious unrest in Syria and the Egyptian colonies there are feeble. King Aziru is fomenting hatred toward Egypt. I have no doubt that when the time is ripe he will start open revolt."

Pharaoh Akhnaton said, "Have you seen the floors in my palace on which artists are just now creating reed swamps and swimming ducks in the Cretan manner? As to a revolt in Syria, I think it unlikely, for I have sent to all its princes the cross of life. King Aziru in particular is my friend, having received the cross of life from me and raised a temple to Aton in the land of Amurru. No doubt you have already seen the colonnaded hall of Aton beside my palace here. It is worth seeing, although the pillars are of brick only, to save time—moreover the thought of slaves toiling in the quarries is repugnant to me. But to return to Aziru—you have no grounds to doubt his loyalty; I have received from him countless clay tablets in which he seeks eagerly to learn new things of Aton. If you wish, my scribes can show you these tablets as soon as our archives are in order."

Horemheb answered, "I spit on his clay tablets—they are as foul and as false as himself. But if it is your firm resolve to disband the army, let me at least reinforce the frontier troops, for already the tribes of the south are driving their herds within our boundary stones, to the grazing grounds in the land of Kush and in Syria. They are burning the villages of our black allies, which is no hard task since they are built of straw."

Akhnaton said, "I believe it is not ill will that drives them but poverty. Our allies must share their grazing with the southern tribes, and I will also send them the cross of life. Nor do I believe they fire the villages through set purpose. As you say, these are easily kindled, and one should not condemn whole tribes for the sake of a few villages. But if you will, then by all means strengthen the frontier guards in the land of Kush and in Syria since you are answerable for the safety of the realm—but see to it that they are guards only and not a standing army."

Horemheb said, "Akhnaton, my mad friend, you must let me reform the garrison troops all over the country, for the disbanded men are robbing right and left in their poverty and stealing the tribute hides of the peasants, whom they beat with sticks."

Pharaoh Akhnaton said, as one pointing a moral, "See what came of your refusal to listen to me! Had you spoken more of Aton to these men, they would not now be acting thus, but their hearts are darkened, the scars of your whip lash burn their backs, and they know not what they do. And by the by, have you noticed that both my daughters can now walk? Meritaton takes care of the younger one, and they have an enchanting little gazelle for a playfellow. Well there is nothing to prevent your hiring the disbanded men as guards up and down the country, provided they remain guards and are not embodied into a standing army for war. And to my mind it would be well to break up all the chariots, for suspicion breeds suspicion, and we have to convince our neighbors that whatever happens Egypt will never have recourse to war."

"Would it not be simpler to sell the chariots to Aziru or the Hittites? They pay well for chariots and horses," sneered Horemheb. "I can see that it would not pay you to keep a regular army when you bury all the wealth of Egypt in a swamp or make bricks of it."

They disputed thus day after day until by sheer tenacity Horemheb gained the position of commander-in-chief of the frontier troops and of all the garrisons. It was Pharaoh who decided how they should be armed, namely with wooden spears. Their numbers were left for Horemheb to determine. Horemheb then summoned all district commanders to Memphis because it lay in the middle of the country and on the borders of the Two Kingdoms. He was on the point of embarking for that city when a river courier arrived, with a stack of letters and clay tablets from Syria, full of alarming news. His hopes were rekindled. These communications showed beyond dispute that King Aziru, having learned of the disturbances in Thebes, considered the moment favorable for the annexation of certain cities beyond his borders. Megiddo, the key to Syria, was also in revolt, and Aziru's forces were besieging the fortress to which the Egyptian garrison had retired and from which they were now appealing to Pharaoh for speedy help.

But Pharaoh Akhnaton said, "I fancy King Aziru has good reason for his actions. He is a fiery man, and it may be that my envoys have offended him. I will not judge him until he has opportunity to defend himself. But one thing I can do, and it was wrong of me not to think of it before. Now that a city of Aton is rising in the Black Land I must build another in the Red Land—in Syria—and in Kush. Megiddo

291

is a junction for the caravan routes and therefore the most suitable place, but I suspect that just now it is too disturbed to permit building.

"But you have spoken to me of Jerusalem, where you built a temple to Aton during your campaign against the Khabiri—a campaign for which I can never forgive myself. It is not so central as Megiddo, being farther south; nevertheless I shall take immediate steps for the building of a city of Aton in Jerusalem so that in future that shall be the center of Syria, though now it is only a tumbledown village."

When Horemheb heard this, he broke his whip, threw it at Pharaoh's feet, and went aboard his ship. And so he sailed to Memphis to reorganize the garrison troops throughout the country. Yet his stay in Akhetaton had had this advantage: I had been able to tell him quietly and at leisure all that I had seen and heard in Babylon, Mitanni, the land of Hatti, and in Crete. He listened in silence, nodding now and again as if what I told him were not altogether news, and he fingered the knife I had been given by the harbormaster. All that I recounted to him of roads, bridges, and rivers he caused to be set down in writing, also any names I mentioned. Finally I told him to consult Kaptah in the matter, for Kaptah was as childish as himself in his memory for all manner of useless things.

He departed from Akhetaton in anger, and Pharaoh rejoiced to see him go. The conversations with Horemheb had greatly plagued him so that even the sight of the man gave him a headache.

To me he said musingly, "It may be the will of Aton that we lose Syria, and if so, who am I to oppose it since it must be for the good of Egypt? For the wealth of Syria has eaten at Egypt's heart. All superfluity, all softness, vices, and evil practices have come from there. Were we to lose Syria, Egypt would return to simpler ways—to ways of truth—and that is the best thing that can befall it. The new life must start here and spread among all nations."

My heart rose up against his talk and I said, "The commander of the Smyrna garrison has a son named Rameses—a lively boy with big brown eyes who loves to play with pretty stones. I treated him once for chickenpox. And in Megiddo there dwells an Egyptian woman who, having heard of my skill, once visited me in Smyrna. Her belly was swollen; I opened it with my knife and she lived. Her skin was soft as wool, and she walked beautifully like all Egyptian women, even though her belly was swollen and here eyes were bright with fever."

"I do not understand why you tell me of these things," said Akhnaton, and he began to make a sketch of a temple he beheld in his mind's eye. He constantly vexed his architects and master builders with drawings and explanations though they understood their business better than he.

"I mean that I can see that little Rameses with his mouth cut and bruised and the locks at his temple clotted with blood. I see the woman from Megiddo lying naked and bleeding in the courtyard of the fortress while men from Amurru violate her. Yet I acknowledge that my thoughts are trivial compared with yours and that a ruler cannot remember every Rameses and every soft-skinned woman among his subjects."

Pharaoh clenched his fists, and his eyes darkened as he cried, "Sinuhe, can you not understand that if I must choose death rather than life, then I will choose the death of a hundred Egyptians rather than that of a thousand Syrians? Were I to give battle in Syria so as to liberate every Egyptian there, then many—both Syrians and Egyptians —would lose their lives in the war. Were I to meet evil with evil, only evil could result. But if I meet evil with good, the resulting evil is less. I will not choose death rather than life, and so I stop my ears to your talk. Speak to me no more of Syria if you love me and if my life is dear to you. When I think of that, my heart feels all the suffering those who die for my will's sake must undergo—and a man cannot long endure the sufferings of many. Give me peace for the sake of Aton and of my truth."

He bowed his head, and his eyes were swollen and bloodshot in his grief, and his thick lips trembled. I left him in peace, but in my own ears I heard the thunder of battering rams against the Megiddo walls and the cries of outraged women in the woolen tents of the Amorites. I hardened my heart against these sounds for I loved him, for all his madness, and perhaps I loved him the more because of it, for his madness was more beautiful than the wisdom of other men.

5

The founding of the new city brought division into the royal family. for the Queen Mother refused to follow her son into the desert. Thebes was her city, and the golden house of Pharaoh, glowing hazy blue and russet among its walls and gardens by the river, had been built by Pharaoh Amenhotep for his beloved. Taia, the Queen Mother, had begun life as a poor fowler girl in the reed swamps of the Lower Kingdom. She would not leave Thebes, and Princess Baketamon stayed

293

with her. Eie the priest, bearer of the crook on the right hand of the King, ruled and sat in judgment there on the King's throne with the leather scrolls before him. Life in Thebes went on as before; only the false Pharaoh was absent—and unregretted.

Queen Nefertiti returned to Thebes for the birth of her next child, for she dared not be brought to bed without the help of the physicians and the Negro sorcerers of Thebes. Here she bore her third daughter, whose name was Ankhsenaton and who would in time be queen. To ease the birth, the sorcerers narrowed and lengthened the child's head as they had done with the other princesses. When the girl grew up, all the court ladies, and others who wished to be in the fashion and to imitate the styles of the court, took to wearing false backs to their heads. But the princesses themselves kept their heads close shaven to show off the fine shape of their skulls. Artists also admired it, and they carved and drew and painted numerous portraits of them without suspecting that this distinctive feature was but a result of the magicians' arts.

When Nefertiti had born her child she returned to Akhetaton and took up her residence in the palace, which in the meantime had been set in habitable order. She left the other women behind in Thebes, being vexed at having given birth to three daughters and unwilling to let Pharaoh waste his virility on the couches of others. Akhnaton was content to have it so, for he was weary of fulfilling his duty in the women's house and wanted no one but Nefertiti, as all who beheld her beauty could well understand. Not even her third confinement had dimmed her loveliness. She seemed younger and more radiant than before, but whether this change in her was due to the city of Akhetaton or to the black men's witchcraft I cannot say.

Thus Akhetaton rose from the wilderness in a single year; palm trees waved proudly along its splendid streets, pomegranates ripened and reddened in the gardens, and in the fish pools floated the rosy flowers of the lotus. The whole city was a blossoming garden, for the houses were of wood, airy and fragile as pavilions, and their columns of palm and reed were light and brightly colored. The gardens entered the very houses, for the paintings on the walls were of palms and sycamores swayed by the breezes of eternal spring. On the floors were beds of reeds and multicolored swimming fish, and ducks with brilliant wings rose in flight. In this city nothing was lacking to rejoice the heart of man. Tame gazelles wandered in the gardens, while in the streets the lightest of carriages were drawn by fiery horses adorned with ostrich plumes. The kitchens were fragrant with keen spices brought from every part of the world.

Thus the City of the Heavens was completed, and when autumn returned and swallows emerged from the mud to dart in restless flocks above the rising waters, Pharaoh Akhnaton consecrated the city and the land to Aton. He consecrated the boundary stones north, south, east, and west, and on each of these stones was the representation of Aton shedding the benediction of his rays on Pharaoh and the house of Pharaoh. Inscriptions on the stones recorded Pharaoh's vows never again to set foot beyond these boundaries. For this ceremony the workmen laid stone-paved roads to the four quarters of the land so that Pharaoh might drive to the borders in his golden carriage attended by his family in their carriages and chairs and by the members of his court, who strewed flowers as they went, while flutes and stringed instruments sounded in praise of Aton.

Not even in death did Pharaoh intend to leave the city of Aton. When the building of it was finished, he sent his workmen to the eastern hills within the consecrated land, to hew out eternal resting places. They found work enough to last their whole lives through and were never able to return to their birthplace. They did not greatly desire to do so but accustomed themselves to dwelling in their own town and in Pharaoh's shadow, for grain was measured to them abundantly, their oil jars were never empty, and their wives bore them healthy children.

When Pharaoh had decided to build tombs for himself and his nobles and to present one to each of his distinguished followers who would live in the City of the Heavens with him and who believed in Aton, he built also a House of Death outside the city so that the bodies of those who died in Akhetaton should be preserved forever. To this end he summoned from Thebes those embalmers and washers who held the foremost place in their craft. They came down the river in a black ship, and their smell was borne before them on the wind so that the people hid in their houses with bowed heads, reciting prayers to Aton. Many also prayed to the old gods and made the holy sign of Ammon, for when they smelled the body washers' smell Aton seemed far away and their thoughts turned to their earlier dieties.

The embalmers stepped ashore from the vessel with all their materials, blinking with eyes that were accustomed to the dark and swearing bitterly at the light, which hurt them. They entered swiftly into the new House of Death, taking their smell with them so that the place became a home for them, which they never left again. Among

295

them was old Ramose, the expert of the pincers, whose task was to extract the brain. I met him in the House of Death, for the priests of Aton held the House of Death in horror, and Pharaoh had placed it under my charge. When he had gazed at me for some time he knew me again, and marveled. I made myself known to him to gain his confidence, for uncertainty gnawed like a worm at my heart and I desired to know how my revenge had prospered at the House of Death in Thebes.

When we had spoken a little of his work, I asked, "Ramose my friend, did you ever have under your hands a beautiful woman who was brought to the House of Death during the Terror and whose name I believe was Nefernefernefer?"

He regarded me, bent backed and blinking like a tortoise, and said, "In truth, Sinuhe, you are the first distinguished man who has ever called a corpse washer his friend. My heart is greatly moved, and the information you require is doubtless of great import since you so address me. Surely it was not you who brought her one dark night, swathed in the black robe of death? For if you were that man you are the friend of no corpse washer, and if they come to hear of it, they will stab you with poisoned knives and so inflict upon you a most hideous death."

His words caused me to tremble, and I said, "Whoever may have brought her, she deserved her fate. Yet from your words I suspect that she was not dead but came to life under the hands of the washers."

Ramose answered, "Most certainly that frightful woman was restored to life, though how you know of this I prefer not to guess. She awoke, for such women never die—and if they die, they should be burned so that they can never return. When we came to know her we gave her the name of Setnefer: the devil's beauty."

A dreadful suspicion seized me and I asked, "Why do you speak of her as of something that has been? Is she not still in the House of Death? The washers vowed that they would keep her there for seventy times seventy days."

Ramose rattled his knives and pincers angrily, and I believe he would have struck me if I had not brought him a jar of the best wine in Pharaoh's cellar. He merely felt its dusty seal with his thumb and said, "We bore you no ill will, Sinuhe; you were to me as my own son, and I would have kept you all your life in the House of Death and taught you my art. We embalmed the bodies of your parents as only those of the eminent are embalmed and did not spare the finest oils and balsams. Why then did you wish us so ill as to bring that terrible

296

woman to us alive? Know that before her coming we led a simple, hard-working life, rejoicing our hearts with beer and greatly enriching ourselves by thefts of jewelry from the dead, without regard to sex or standing, and also by selling to sorcerers such organs as they require for their spells. But after the coming of that woman the House of Death became like some abyss of the underworld. The men knifed one another and fought together like mad dogs. She stole all our wealth from us—all the gold and silver we had amassed in the course of years and hidden in the House of Death—nor did she scorn copper. Even our clothes she took from us, for having robbed the young men of all they possessed she set them on to steal from the old ones such as I, whose lust could no longer be kindled. No more than thirty times thirty days had passed before she had stripped us naked of possessions. Then she left, taking all her wealth with her, and we could not prevent her, for if one placed himself in her path he was opposed by another—for the sake of a smile or a touch of her fingers. Thus she took from us our property and our peace. She had by then no less than three hundred *deben* of gold, to say nothing of silver, copper, linen bands, and salves that for years we had stolen from the dead, as the custom is. She vowed to return to us in a year to see how much we had been able to save by then. There is more theft in the House of Life than there has ever been before; moreover the washers have learned to pilfer from each other and not only from the bodies, so that our peace has altogether departed. By this you may understand why we gave her the name of Setnefer, for she is exceedingly fair though her beauty is of Set."

It was now I learned how childish my revenge had been since Nefernefernefer returned unharmed from the House of Death richer than before and, as I believe, suffered no ill effects from her stay save the smell, which soaked into her body and for some time prevented her from plying her trade. My revenge had eaten at my own heart and left her unharmed. When I knew this, I knew also that revenge brings no satisfaction. Its sweetness is brief and it turns against the avenger, to eat at his heart like fire.

BOOK II

Merit

I

EVERYONE has seen water running from a water clock. So also does human life trickle away, though it is measured not by water but by events. This is a profound truth, to be grasped only in old age when a man's time runs away to nothing, in monotony. A single day in an eventful period leaves its mark upon him and can seem longer than a year or so of monotonous labor that leaves his heart unchanged. I learned this truth in the city of Akhetaton, where my time flowed smoothly by like the current of the Nile and my life was a brief dream—a lovely, fading song. The ten years I spent in the shadow of Pharaoh Akhnaton in the golden palace of the new city were shorter than any one of the years of my youth: those years of travel and of change.

At Akhetaton I added nothing either to my wisdom or to my science; rather I drew on what I had gathered in so many countries, as a bee survives the winter on the honey it has stored up in the comb. Yet, as running water alters the shape of a stone, so time may have changed my heart; though of this I remained unaware. I was less lonely than before. I may have grown quieter, less puffed up over myself and my talents, though I can claim no credit for this; it was because Kaptah no longer lived with me, but was far away in Thebes, where he managed my property and the Crocodile's Tail.

The city of Akhetaton shut itself away within the dreams and visions of Pharaoh and was unconcerned with the outside world. All that happened beyond Aton's boundary stones was as remote and unreal as moonlight upon water. The only reality was what took place within the city of Akhetaton. Yet in looking back upon it now one sees that the opposite may have been true: Akhetaton and its doings were but shadow and illusion, while reality lay in the hunger, suffering, and death beyond its borders. For all that was unpleasing to Akhnaton was hidden from him, and when any matter arose in which a decision from him was necessary, it was presented to him as it were, veiled and sweetened, and with gentleness, lest the sickness in his head return.

During this time Eie the priest ruled in Thebes as bearer of the crook on the King's right hand. Pharaoh had left behind him all such administrative duties as were tedious or unpleasant, placing full trust in Eie, who was his father-in-law—and a man of great ambitions. Eie was the true ruler of the Two Kingdoms, since all that touched on the life of the common people, whether farmers or townsmen, lay in his hands. Once Ammon had been overthrown, no power was left to rival that of Pharaoh—which was Eie's—and Eie hoped that the disturbances would soon subside. Nothing could have been more to his mind than the city of Akhetaton, which kept Pharaoh far away from Thebes. He did what he could to collect funds for the building of it and for its adornment and was continually sending lavish gifts to render Akhetaton still more acceptable to Pharaoh. Peace might have come again and all have been as before—save for Ammon only—but for the fact that Pharaoh was a stumbling block to Eie.

Eie's government was shared by Horemheb in Memphis, who was answerable for security and good order throughout the country. His ultimately was the power behind the rods of the tax gatherers and behind the hammers that hewed away the name of Ammon from all images and inscriptions and penetrated the very tombs for this purpose. Pharaoh Akhnaton permitted the tomb of his own father to be opened so that the name of Ammon might be effaced from its inscription. Nor did Eie oppose him so long as he remained content with such innocent pastimes. He preferred the thoughts of Pharaoh to be engaged in religious matters which did not affect the everyday life of the people.

For some time after the days of terror in Thebes, Egypt lay calm as a summer lake. Eie delegated the collection of revenues to his chief officers, which saved him much trouble. These leased taxation rights to the tax gatherers of cities and villages and substantially enriched themselves. If the poor bewailed their lot and bestrewed their heads with ashes when the tax gatherers visited them, it was no more than they had done in every age.

In Akhetaton the birth of a fourth daughter was a greater misfortune than the fall of Smyrna. Queen Nefertiti began to suspect that she was the victim of witchcraft and went to Thebes to seek help from her mother's Negro sorcerers. It was indeed strange for a woman to give birth to four girls and not a single boy. Nevertheless it was her fate to give Pharaoh Akhnaton six daughters in all and no son—and her fate was bound with his.

As time went on, the tidings from Syria grew ever more alarming. Whenever a courier ship berthed, I went to the King's archives to study the latest tablets with their renewed appeals for help. As I read them, I seemed to hear the singing of arrows past my ears and smell the smoke of burning houses. Through the respectful phrases I could hear the shrieks of the dying and of mutilated children. The men of Amurru were brutal, and they had been schooled in the arts of war by Hittite officers. Not one single garrison in Syria was able to withstand them. I read messages from the King of Byblos and the Prince of Jerusalem. They pleaded their age and their fidelity; they invoked the memory of the late Pharaoh and their friendship for Akhetaton in their appeals for help, until Pharaoh was weary of their supplications and sent their letters to the archives unread.

When Jerusalem had fallen, the last of the faithful cities capitulated, Joppa also, and formed alliances with King Aziru. Then Horemheb journeyed from Memphis to have audience of Pharaoh and to demand from him an army with which to organize resistance in Syria. Hitherto he had but carried on a secret war with letters and money, in order to save at least one outpost in that country.

He said to Pharaoh Akhnaton, "Let me hire at least one hundred times one hundred spearmen and archers, and a hundred chariots, and I will win back Syria for you. Now that even Joppa has yielded, Egyptian power in Syria is lost."

Pharaoh Akhnaton was greatly cast down when he heard that Jerusalem had been destroyed, for he had already taken steps to make it a city of Aton, to pacify Syria. He said, "This old man in Jerusalem —I cannot just now recall his name—was a friend of my father's. When I was a boy, I saw him in the golden house at Thebes, and he had a long beard. By way of compensation I will pension him out of Egyptian funds although the revenues have notably diminished since trade with Syria ceased."

"He is hardly in a condition to enjoy a pension," returned Horemheb dryly. "An exquisite bowl ornamented with gold has been fashioned of his skull, at Aziru's command and sent by him as a gift to King Shubbiluliuma in Hattushash—unless my spies are very much in error."

Pharaoh's countenance went gray, and his eyes were bloodshot, but mastering his agony, he said quietly, "I find it hard to believe such a thing of King Aziru, whom I considered my friend and who so

303

willingly received the cross of life at my hands. But perhaps I have been mistaken in him and his heart is blacker than I supposed. But, Horemheb, you desire of me an impossibility in asking for spears and chariots, for already the people are complaining at the taxes and the harvest has been less abundant than I hoped."

"For the sake of your Aton, at least give me an authority for ten chariots and ten times ten spearmen, that I may take them to Syria and save what may be saved."

But Pharaoh Akhnaton said, "I cannot wage war for Aton's sake, for bloodshed is abomination to him. I would rather relinquish Syria. Let Syria be free and form its own federal state, and let us trade with it as before—for Syria cannot do without Egyptian grain."

"Do you suppose that they will be content with that, Akhnaton?" exclaimed Horemheb thunderstruck. "Every Egyptian slain, every breached wall, every city captured increases their self-esteem and urges them to ever more outrageous demands. After Syria will come the copper mines of Sinai, without which we can no longer forge spears and arrowheads."

"I have already said that wooden spears suffice for the guards," retorted Pharaoh irritably. "Why do you torment me with ceaseless talk of spears and arrowheads so that the words go round and round in my head when I try to compose a hymn to Aton?"

"After Sinai comes the turn of the Lower Kingdom," went on Horemheb bitterly. "As you said yourself, Syria cannot do without Egyptian grain, although I hear they are now obtaining it from Babylon. But if you do not fear Syria, then fear at least the Hittites, to whose lust for power there are no bounds."

Pharaoh Akhnaton laughed in a pitying manner as any sensible Egyptian would have laughed to hear such talk, and he said, "For as long as we can remember not one single enemy has set foot within our borders, and none would dare. Egypt is the wealthiest and mightiest of all kingdoms upon earth. I have sent the cross of life to King Shubbiluliuma also, and—at his own request—gold, so that he can erect a life-size figure of me in his temple. He will not disturb the peace of Egypt since he may have gold of me whenever he asks it."

The veins in Horemheb's forehead swelled, but having by now learned to master his feelings he said no more. I told him that as a physician I could no longer allow him to weary Pharaoh, whereupon he turned and followed me out.

When we reached my house, he slapped himself sharply on the thigh with his golden whip, saying, "By Set and all devils! A dung cake on the road is of more use than his cross of life. Yet certainly of all things this is the maddest: when he looks me in the eye, lays his hand on my shoulder, and calls me his friend, I believe in his truth, although I know but too well that he is wrong and I am right! That strange force in him is ever replenished in this city, which is as gaudy as a harlot and smells like one. If one might bring before him every human being in the world, for him to speak to each of them, touch them with his gentle fingers, and pour his strength into them, I believe that he might change the world—but it is not possible. Faugh! If I stayed long in this place, I should begin to grow breasts like the courtiers—and end by giving suck!"

2

When Horemheb had returned to Memphis, his words remained with me, haunting me, and I blamed myself for being a bad friend to him and a bad counselor to Pharaoh. Yet my couch was soft beneath its canopy, my cooks served me little birds dressed with honey, there was no lack of antelope roasts, and the water ran quickly from my clock.

The second of Pharaoh's daughters, Meketaton, was seized by a wasting sickness; her little cheeks glowed with fever and her collarbones began to show through the skin. I sought to strengthen her with tonics, giving her a solution of gold to drink, and I bewailed my fate that no sooner had Pharaoh's attacks ceased than his daughter must fall ill so that I had no peace by night or day. Pharaoh also grew uneasy, for he loved his daughters dearly. The two eldest, Meritaton and Meketaton, accompanied him to his balcony on audience days and threw down golden chains and other tokens to those whom Pharaoh desired to honor.

As is the way of men, Pharaoh grew fonder of this ailing daughter than of the other three. He gave her balls of ivory and silver, and a little dog that followed her everywhere and slept at the foot of her bed. He grew thin and lost sleep because of his anxiety, rising several times each night to listen to the child's breathing; every cough of hers tore at his heart.

In the same way also this little girl meant more to me than my property in Thebes, or Kaptah, or the year of famine, or all the people then starving and dying in Syria on Aton's account. I lavished on her my utmost care and skill, neglecting my other distinguished patients, who were suffering from gluttony and boredom and above all from headaches since this was Pharaoh's complaint. By humoring their headaches I had acquired much gold, but I was weary of gold and groveling.

I was often so curt with my patients that they said, "His dignity as physician to the household has gone to his head! Because he fancies that Pharaoh listens to him, he ignores what others have to say."

Yet when I thought of Thebes and Kaptah and the Crocodile's Tail, I was filled with melancholy, and my heart was hungry with a hunger I could not assuage. I was growing bald beneath my wig and there were days when, forgetting my duties, I dreamed daydreams and walked the Babylonian roads again with my nostrils full of the smell of dried grain on earthen threshing floors. I noticed that I had put on weight and that my sleep was heavy and that I needed a carrying chair because even a short walk left me breathless, although formerly the longest distances could never so affect me.

But when autumn came again and the river rose and the swallows emerged from the slime of the river bed to dart restlessly in the air above, the health of Pharaoh's daughter mended. She smiled and no longer felt the pains in her chest. My heart followed the swallows in their flight, and with Pharaoh's leave I boarded a ship for Thebes. He bade me greet on his behalf all the river-side settlers among whom he had divided the land of the false god, and he sent greetings also to the schools he had founded and hoped to hear good tidings of them on my return.

I touched at many villages and summoned the elders to talk with me. The journey was more comfortable than I had hoped, for Pharaoh's pennant fluttered at the masthead, my bed was soft, and there were no flies on the river. My cook followed me in the kitchen boat, and gifts were brought to him from all the villages so that I had no lack of fresh food. But when the settlers visited me, I saw that they were mere skeletons, their wives stared about them with terrified eyes, afraid of every sound, and the children were sickly and bowlegged. These people showed me their corn bins, which were less than half full, and the grain in them was speckled red as if it had been exposed to a shower of blood.

They said to me, "At first we thought that our failures were the result of ignorance since we had never tilled the soil before. We know now that the land Pharaoh divided among us is accursed, and he who cultivates it is accursed also. At night, unseen feet trample down our crops; unseen hands break the fruit trees we have planted. Our cattle

306

perish without cause, our irrigation ditches are stopped up, and we find carrion in our wells so that even drinking water is lacking. Many have abandoned their land and returned to the towns poorer than they were before, reviling the name of Pharaoh and his god. But we have persevered, trusting to the magic cross and the letters Pharaoh has sent us. We hang these out on stakes in our fields as a protection against locusts. But Ammon's magic is more powerful than the magic of Pharaoh. Our faith is failing us, and we mean to leave this noisome land before we all die as the wives and children of many have already done."

I also visited their schools, and when the teachers saw the cross of Aton on my clothes, they hid their canes and made the sign of Aton, while the children sat cross legged on the threshing floors staring at me so fixedly that they neglected to wipe their noses.

The teachers said, "We know that there is no greater madness than the notion that every child should learn to read and write, but what would we not do for Pharaoh, whom we love and who is our father and our mother and whom we venerate as the son of his god? But we are learned men and it ill befits our dignity to sit on threshing floors, to wipe the noses of grimy children and draw ugly signs in the sand— for we have no tablets or reed pens—moreover these new characters can never reproduce all the wisdom and knowledge that, with great trouble and cost, we have acquired. Our salaries are irregularly paid, and the parents reward us very meagerly; their beer is weak and sour, and the oil in our jars is rancid. Yet we persist, to demonstrate to Pharaoh that it is impossible to teach all children to read and write, for only the best pupils whose heads are soft and receptive can learn."

I tested their proficiency, with which I was far from satisfied. Still less pleased was I by their swollen faces and unsteady gaze, for these teachers were broken-down scribes to whom no one would give employment. They had accepted the cross of Aton for the sake of their livelihood.

The settlers and elders of the villages swore bitterly in the name of Aton and said, "Lord Sinuhe, speak for us to Pharaoh, and beg him at least to lift from us the burden of these schools, or we cannot long survive. Our boys come home black and blue from the beatings, and with torn locks, and these terrible teachers are insatiable as crocodiles. They eat us out of house and home, they extort our last coppers from us and the hides of our cattle to buy themselves wine. When we are out in the fields, they enter our houses and take pleasure with our wives, saying that this is the will of Aton in whose sight there is no difference between man and man or between woman and woman. Truly we desired no change in our lives, for if indeed we were poor in the cities, yet we were happy also. Here we see nothing but muddy ditches and lowing cattle. They were right who warned us, saying, 'Beware of change: among the poor it must always be for the worse. Whatever changes are made in the world, be assured that with them the grain measure of the poor must dwindle and the oil sink in their jars.' "

My heart told me that they were right in what they said, and I would not dispute it but continued on my journey. I was filled with sadness on Pharaoh's account and I marveled that all he touched he blighted so that the diligent grew lazy because of his gifts and only the worthless clustered about Aton like flies on a carcass. Then my heart was seized with a terrible suspicion: What if Pharaoh and the noble idlers about his court—even I myself during the past few years— were no more than parasites, vermin, fleas in a dog's coat? The flea may fancy that the dog exists solely for the benefit of fleas and for their nourishment. Pharaoh and his god might be such fleas, giving much vexation and doing no good whatever since dogs are all the better for being free of vermin.

Thus my heart awoke after its long sleep, and it spurned the city of Akhetaton. I looked about me with fresh eyes, and nothing that I saw was good. But in this my eyes may have been distorted by the magic of Ammon, who in hidden ways governed the whole of Egypt, the City of the Heavens being the only place in the land over which he had no control. Where truth lay I cannot say, for although there are those who think always in the same manner and draw in their heads like tortoises at the hint of any new thing, yet my thoughts have ever been modified by what I have seen and heard. Many things have therefore influenced my thinking even when I have not understood them well.

I saw once more the three hills on the horizon, the eternal guardians of Thebes. The roof of the temple and its walls rose before my eyes, but the tips of the obelisks no longer blazed in the sunshine, for their gilding had never been renewed. Yet the sight of them was refreshment to my heart, and I poured wine into the waters of the Nile as seamen do who return after a long voyage—though their libation is of beer since they prefer to keep their wine, if any, for themselves. I saw again the great stone wharves of Thebes and caught the harbor smell: the smell of rotting grain and foul water, of spices and herbs and pitch.

When in the poor quarter I beheld the house that had been the copperfounder's, it appeared to me exceedingly cramped and narrow, and the alley before it filthy, full of flies and stench. Nor did the sycamore in the court delight me although I had planted it myself and it had grown tall in my absence, so spoiled was I by the wealth and abundance of Akhetaton. I was sorrowful and ashamed because I could not rejoice over my home.

Kaptah was not there, but only my cook Muti, who exclaimed bitterly, "Blessed be the day that brings my lord home, but the rooms are not cleaned and the linen is in the wash and your arrival causes me much trouble and vexation, although I expect but little happiness from life in general. Yet I am not at all astonished at your sudden coming, for that is the way of men from whom nothing good is to be expected."

I pacified her, telling her that I would sleep on board that night. Having asked for Kaptah I left her and was carried to the Crocodile's Tail. Merit met me at the door and did not recognize me because of my fine clothes and my chair.

She said, "Have you reserved your place here for this evening? For if not I cannot allow you to enter."

She had grown somewhat plumper, and her cheekbones were less sharp, but her eyes were the same save for a few lines about them.

My heart was warmed and laying my hand on her loins I said, "I can understand that you have forgotten me, for many must be the lonely, sorrowful men you have warmed on your mat—nevertheless I fancied I might find a seat in your house and a cup of chilled wine, even if I do not presume to think of that same mat."

She cried out in astonishment, "Sinuhe, is it you? Blessed be the day that brings my lord home!"

She laid her strong, lovely hands on my shoulders and, scanning my face narrowly, went on, "Sinuhe, what have you been doing? If your solitude was once that of a lion, it is now that of a lapdog, and you are on a leash." She took off my wig, stroked my bald head kindly, and went on. "Sit then, Sinuhe, and I will bring you chilled wine, for you are sweating and out of breath from your wearisome journey."

I said anxiously, "On no account bring me a crocodile's tail, for my stomach is no longer equal to that—to say nothing of my head."

Stroking my knee, she mocked me, saying, "Am I already so old and fat and ugly that when you meet me for the first time for years you think only of your stomach? And you were never wont to fear

309

headaches in my company—indeed, so eager were you for those crocodiles' tails that I had to restrain you."

I was abashed at her words, for she spoke the truth, and truth has
often this effect.

So I answered her, "Oh, Merit my friend—I am already old, and
finished."

But she retorted, "So you fancy, but your eyes when you look at me
are far from old, and I am glad of this."

"Merit, for the sake of our friendship, make haste to bring me a
crocodile's tail lest I become outrageous in my manner toward you,
which would ill become my dignity as skull surgeon to the household,
especially in a harbor tavern."

She brought me the drink in a shell and set it on my palm. The
drink burned my throat, which was accustomed to mellow wines, yet
the burning was sweet to me for my other hand rested upon her
flank.

"Merit," I said, "you once told me that a lie may be sweeter than the
truth to one who is alone and whose first spring is over. And so I
tell you that my heart still flowers and is young at the sight of you;
long are the years that have severed us, and not one day of them has
passed but I have whispered your name to the wind; I have sent my
greeting to you with the swallows as they flew upstream, and every
morning I have awakened with your name on my lips."

She looked at me, and in my sight she was slender still, and beautiful. In the depths of her eyes was a glint of smiles and sorrow, as in the
waters of a deep well. She stroked my cheek with her hand and said,
"You speak beautifully, Sinuhe—why should I not also confess that
my heart has yearned for you and my hands have sought yours when
at night I have lain alone upon my mat? Whenever by reason of the
crocodile's tail some man has talked nonsense to me, I remembered
you with sadness. But in Pharaoh's golden house there must be many
fair women, and no doubt as a physician you have used your leisure
hours conscientiously on their behalf."

It is true that I had taken pleasure with some of the court ladies
who in their boredom came to ask my professional advice. Their skin
was smooth as fruit and soft as down, and in winter especially it was
warmer to lie two in a bed than singly. But it was trivial and I have
not troubled to record it in my book. I replied, "Merit, if I have not
always slept alone, it is true that you are the only woman who is my
friend."

The crocodile's tail worked within me. My body was growing as young as my heart, and a sweet fire ran through my veins as I said, "Doubtless many men have shared your mat during this time, but you would do well to warn them of me as long as I remain in Thebes, for when roused I am a violent man! When I fought against the Khabiri, the soldiers of Horemheb named me the Son of the Wild Ass."

She raised her hands in mock terror and said, "That is what I have so greatly dreaded, for Kaptah has told me of many wild skirmishes and brawls into which you were led by your fiery nature and from which you were rescued only through his fidelity and resolution."

When I heard Kaptah's name and guessed at all the shameless lies he must have told her of myself and my life in foreign lands, my heart melted within me, and tears streamed from my eyes as I cried, "Where is Kaptah, my former slave and servant, that I may embrace him? For my heart has missed him sorely, unbecoming though it be in me to speak thus of a slave."

Merit strove to silence me.

"Truly I see that you are unaccustomed to crocodiles' tails and my father is looking wrathfully in our direction because of your noise. You will not see Kaptah before evening, for his time is taken up with important business at the corn exchange and in the taverns. You will be astounded when you meet him, for he hardly remembers that he was once a slave and carried your sandals on a stick across your shoulders. I will take you out for a breath of cool air before he comes. You will doubtless wish to see how Thebes has changed since you were here, and in this way we can be alone."

She went to change her dress and anoint her face and adorn herself with gold and silver. Only by her hands and feet could she have been distinguished from a lady of the aristocracy, though perhaps few ladies had so clear and steady a glance as hers or so proud a mouth. I bade the slaves carry us along the Avenue of Rams, and we sat close together in the chair so that I breathed the scent of her ointments, which was the scent of Thebes, more pungent and intoxicating than all the rare cosmetics of Akhetaton. I held her hand in mine, and there was not one evil thought left in my heart. After a long journey I had come home.

We approached the temple, where black birds circled and squawked above the emptiness, for they had never returned to their hills but settled within the precincts. This was accursed ground and repugnant to the people. We stepped from the chair and wandered through the deserted forecourts; the only folk we saw were those about the Houses of Life and of Death. To move these institutions would have been too costly and troublesome a business. Merit told me that people avoided the House of Life also, for which reason most of the physicians had moved into the city itself to carry on their profession. We walked in the temple garden, but grass overgrew the paths, and its trees had been felled and stolen. The only people we encountered in the gardens which Pharaoh had turned into a public park and playground were one or two dirty, skulking vagabonds who gave us sidelong looks.

Merit said, "You chill my heart in bringing me to this evil place. Doubtless, the cross of Aton will protect us though I would prefer you to remove it from your collar since because of it you might be stoned. Hatred is still rife in Thebes."

She spoke truly. When we had come back to the open place before the temple, the people spat on the ground when they saw my cross. I was astonished to observe one of the priests of Ammon walking boldly among the crowd with his head shaven, despite Pharaoh's order, and arrayed in white. His face gleamed, his robe was of the finest linen, and he seemed to have suffered no hardship. The people made way for him with veneration. Prudence bade me keep one hand on my breast to hide the cross of Aton, for I was loath to be the cause of needless uproar.

We paused by the wall where a storyteller sat on his mat with an empty bowl before him. His audience stood in a ring, and the poorest among them sat on the ground, having no need to consider their clothes. The story he was telling I had never heard before, for he spoke of a false Pharaoh who had lived many, many years ago and whose mother was a black witch. By the will of Set, this witch won the love of the good Pharaoh and gave birth to the false one, who sought the ruin of the Egyptian people and would have bound them in slavery to Nubians and savages. He overthrew the statues of Ra so that Ra cursed the land, which became barren. The people were drowned by mighty floods, locusts devoured the standing crops, and pools were transformed into foul-smelling blood. But the days of the false Pharaoh were numbered, for the power of Ra was greater than that of Set. The false Pharaoh died a miserable death, as did also the witch his mother, and Ra struck down all those who had denied him, and he divided their houses and goods and land among those who had remained steadfast to him throughout these trials and believed in his return.

This tale was very long and very exciting, and the people shuffled their feet and raised their hands in impatience to hear what the conclusion might be. My mouth also hung open as I listened. When the story was ended and the false Pharaoh received his punishment and was hurled into the bottomless pit—when his name had been cursed and Ra had rewarded his faithful—then the listeners leaped and cried out in their delight and threw coppers into the storyteller's bowl.

I was greatly puzzled and said to Merit, "This is a new tale, which I have never heard before, although I fancied I had learnt them all as a child since my mother Kipa was passionately fond of them and favored the storytellers highly—to such a degree that my father Senmut would sometimes menace them with his stick when she fed them in our kitchen. Yes, this is a new story. Were it not impossible, I should say that it concerns Pharaoh Akhnaton and the false god whose name we dare not speak aloud. This tale should be forbidden!"

Merit smiled.

"Who can forbid a story? This one is told in both Kingdoms, at every gateway and beneath every wall in the smallest villages, and the people love it. When the guards threaten the storytellers, these maintain that the tale is an ancient one—and they can prove it, for the priests have found it in writings that are centuries old. Therefore the guards cannot prevent it although I have heard that Horemheb, who is a stern man and cares nothing for proofs and writings, has had a few storytellers hung from the walls and has thrown their bodies to the crocodiles."

Merit held my hand and smiled as she continued, "Many prophecies are spoken of in Thebes. Whenever two men meet, they tell one another of the prophecies they have heard, and of ill omens. As you know the grain stocks are dwindling, the poor people starve, and taxes lie heavily upon rich and poor. Worse things are foretold, and I tremble when I think of all the evil with which these prophecies threaten us."

I withdrew my hand from hers, and my heart also. The crocodile's tail had long cleared from my head, which now ached. My spirits drooped, and her dull stubbornness did nothing to cheer me. So we returned sulkily to the tavern, and I knew that what Pharaoh Akhnaton had said was true: "Aton shall separate the child from its mother and the man from the sister of his heart until his kingdom is established upon earth." But I had no wish to be separated from Merit because of Aton, and so I remained in an exceedingly ill humor until the evening I saw Kaptah.

No one could long remain sullen at the sight of Kaptah rolling in through the tavern door, huge and ponderous as a farrowing sow—so fat that he had to turn sideways to get in. His face was as round as the full moon and gleaming with sweat and expensive oils; he wore a fine blue wig and had hidden his empty eye socket with a disk of gold. He had ceased to wear Syrian dress but was clothed in the Egyptian fashion, in the finest garments the tailors of Thebes could produce, and his wrists and thick ankles jingled with heavy gold rings.

When he saw me he cried out with his arms raised in surprise, then bowed low before me and stretched forth his hands, a posture his belly made difficult of achievement.

"Blessed be the day that brings my lord home!"

His feelings overcame him, and he wept, throwing himself on his knees to embrace my legs and making such clamor that I recognized my old Kaptah despite the royal linen and the gold bangles, the costly oil and the blue wig. I raised him by the arms and embraced him, and I seemed to be hugging a fat ox that smelled of new bread, so powerfully did the odor of the corn exchange hang about him.

He smelled my shoulders politely also, dried his tears, and laughed, "This is for me a day of such great joy that I will offer every customer now sitting in my house one crocodile's tail free! Should they desire a second they must pay for it themselves."

He led me into the inner part of the house and gave me soft mats to recline on. He allowed Merit to sit beside me while servants and slaves brought me the best the house could offer. His wines were comparable to those of Pharaoh, and his roast goose was a Theban goose, which has no parallel in the whole of Egypt, for it is fed with rotten fish, which imparts to the meat the finest, most delicate flavor.

When we had eaten and drunk he said, "Sinuhe, my lord and master, I trust that you have carefully examined all reports and accounts prepared for you by the scribes at my bidding and dispatched to your house in Akhetaton during these past years. Perhaps you will permit me to charge this dinner to our expense account, also the crocodiles' tails that in my great joy I have presented to the customers. This will be all your advantage, for I have the greatest trouble in deceiving Pharaoh's taxation department on your behalf."

I said to him, "This is all mumbo-jumbo to me; I understand not a word of it. Do what seems best, for you know I place full trust in you. I have read your records and accounts yet must confess that I understood but little of them, since they contain an inordinate quantity of figures and my head ached long before I came to the end of the sums."

Kaptah laughed delightedly, and the laugh rumbled from his belly as from under soft cushions. Merit also laughed, for she had drunk wine with me and was now leaning back with her hands behind her head so that I might observe how beautiful still was the curve of her breasts beneath her dress.

Kaptah said, "Oh, Sinuhe, my lord and master, I rejoice to see that you have kept your childish disposition and understand no more of everyday things than does a swine of pearls—though it is far from my intention to liken you to a pig. Rather I render thanks and praise to all the gods of Egypt on your behalf since they might well have given you as a servant some thief or good-for-nothing who would have beggared you, while I have made you rich."

I pointed out that he had no need to thank the gods for this but rather my good judgment since I had bought him myself in the slave market—and cheaply, because he had lost one eye in a tavern brawl.

At the recollection of these things I was moved and said, "Truly I shall never forget my first sight of you, bound by the ankle to the slave stake and shouting shameless words to the women who passed by or begging beer from the men. Yet I was wise to buy you although I was doubtful of this at the time."

Kaptah's face darkened and twisted itself into many folds as he replied, "I do not care to be reminded of such old and tedious matters, which are unbecoming to my dignity." He went on to praise the scarab very highly, saying, "You were wise to leave the scarab with me to watch over your affairs, for it has made you rich—richer than you could ever have dreamed—despite the tax gatherers who swarm over me like flies. I have had to hire two Syrian bookkeepers to keep special books for their benefit, for no one—not Set himself—could make head or tail of Syrian bookkeeping. And talking of Set, my thoughts turn to our old friend Horemheb to whom I have lent money in your name as you know. I will not speak of him now but of your wealth, little though you may grasp of such matters. Thanks to me you are richer than many Egyptian nobles. Wealth means possession not of gold but of houses and stores and ships and quays, cattle and land and orchards and slaves. You own all these although you may be unaware of it since I have been compelled to enter many items in the names of servants and scribes to evade taxation. Pharaoh's taxes bear hardly upon the well-to-do who must pay more than the

315

poor, so while a poor man hands over one fifth of his grain, a rich man is compelled to give a third or even half. This is iniquity—the most godless iniquity of all that Pharaoh has perpetrated. This and the loss of Syria have beggared the country. What is strangest of all, as national wealth decreases, the poor become poorer than before and the rich become richer. Not even Pharaoh can alter this."

Having drunk once more Kaptah began to boast of his dealings in grain.

"Our scarab, lord, is strange in that on the first day of our return from our travels it brought me to the wine shop patronized by corn merchants. I began at once to purchase grain on your behalf and already in the first year was able to make a profit since Am— I mean certain large pieces of land lay fallow and unsown as you know. Grain is a remarkable commodity in that it may be bought and sold before it is ever sown, and also because its price rises from year to year as by witchcraft so that the buyer cannot help making a profit. For this reason I do not intend to sell but shall continue to buy it and store it in my granaries until the price by measure is paid in gold, as is bound to happen if this state of things continues."

Kaptah, having examined my face, poured out more wine for all three of us and went on gravely, "However, no man stakes all he has on a single throw, and so I have spread your profits evenly among many ventures so as to play as it were with several dice on your behalf, my dear lord. I have stolen no more from you than formerly— not half what I have earned for you by my sagacity; hardly even a third, although I know of no one from whom it would be more rewarding to steal, my dear and blessed lord Sinuhe."

Merit leaned back on her mat, smiling, and laughed aloud at my bewildered expression as I sought to grasp all that Kaptah was saying. He continued his explanations.

"You must understand, lord, that when I speak of profits I mean net profits, all that is left after taxation. I have also had to subtract certain presents for the taxation officers because of my Syrian bookkeeping and great quantities of wine with which it was needful to ply them to make them squint when they examined my figures. That alone was no small item, for they are astute men with unusual powers of resistance; they grow fat in their profession. From time to time I have distributed grain to the poor that they might bless my name. When times are unsettled, it is well to live in harmony with the poor. This distribution of grain is an excellent stroke of business since Pharaoh in his madness allows a rebate on all corn so distributed.

316

When I give a measure of grain to a poor man, I cause him to testify with his thumbprint that he has received five measures, for the poor cannot read—and if they could they would be so thankful for one measure that they would bless my name and press their fingers at the foot of any document I put before them."

When Kaptah had delivered himself of all this he folded his arms in a challenging manner, puffed out his chest, and awaited my praise. But his words had set my mind to work and I thought hard for some time. At length I asked, "Then we have large stocks of grain?"

Kaptah nodded vigorously, still awaiting my commendation, but I went on, "If such is the case you must hasten to the settlers who are cultivating the accursed land and distribute the grain among them for seed, for they have none. What corn they have is speckled as if blood had rained on it. The river has fallen, and the time of plowing and sowing has come; you must go in haste."

Kaptah regarded me compassionately with a shake of the head, and said, "My dear lord, you should not vex your valuable head with matters you do not understand, but let me do your thinking for you. The matter stands thus: We dealers first profited from the settlers by lending grain to them, for they were compelled by poverty to pay back two measures for every one borrowed. If they were unable to pay, we made them slaughter their cattle and took the hides in payment for debt. When grain increased in price, this arrangement became un-profitable, and it is now to our advantage to let as much land as possible remain unsown this spring so that the price of grain may rise still higher. Let us therefore not be such maniacs as to lend the settlers corn for sowing, for that would be to damage our own interests, and I should make enemies of all the corn merchants."

But in this I was resolute, and I said sharply, "Do as I order, Kaptah, for the grain is mine, and I am not thinking now of profits but of men whose ribs show through their skins like the ribs of miners—of women whose breasts hang like empty bags—of children walking bowlegged on the river bank, their eyes crawling with flies. It is my will that you should divide this grain among them for sowing and that you should help them by every means to get it sown. I desire you to do this for Aton's sake and for the sake of Pharaoh Akhnaton, whom I love. Do not give it to them free, for I have seen how gifts breed laziness and ill will and sloth and greed. Were they not given land and cattle for nothing? And still they failed. Use your stick on them, Kaptah, if it be needful. See to it that the corn is sown and reaped. When you come to claim your own again, I will permit you to rake nothing off for yourself: you will take from them one measure for every one lent."

When Kaptah heard this he tore his clothes and lamented.

"Measure for measure, lord? Madness, for where am I to steal if not from your profits? In other respects also your talk is foolish and godless. Besides the corn merchants I shall have the priests of Ammon against me—and I may safely speak his name aloud now that we are sitting in a closed room with none to hear or inform against me. I call his name aloud, lord, for he lives still, and his power is more formidable than ever before. He curses our houses and our ships and our warehouses and shops—this tavern he curses also so that it may be wise to transfer it to Merit's name if she agrees—and I am indeed thankful so much of your property is entered under other names so that the priests cannot learn of it and call down maledictions on it."

Kaptah babbled on to gain time in the hope that I should repent of my purpose. When he saw that I was resolved, he swore bitterly and said, "Have you been bitten by a mad dog, lord? Or stung by a scorpion? I thought at first that this was some feeble jest of yours. The plan will make us poor; nevertheless perhaps the scarab can help us. Moreover—to be quite frank—I do not like to look on thin people myself but turn my eyes the other way. I wish that you would do the same, for what a man doesn't see he need never know. I have soothed my conscience by the distribution of grain among the poor since this was profitable. What I most dislike about your plan is that you require me to venture on uncomfortable journeys and tramp about in the mud, where doubtless I shall stumble and fall into some irrigation ditch—and then you will have my life upon your conscience, lord, for I am a tired old man, and my limbs are stiff. I should miss my soft couch and Muti's soups and steaks; also walking makes me breathless."

But I was pitiless.

"You are a bigger liar than ever, Kaptah, for you have grown younger during these years instead of older. Your hands do not tremble as they did, nor was your eye red when you first came in, but only now since you have drunk too much wine. As a physician I prescribe this uncomfortable journey for you because of the love I bear you. You are altogether too fat, which is a strain on your heart and constricts your breathing. I hope that you will thin down in the course of this expedition and become a respectable human being once more so that I need not blush for my servant's obesity. Don't you remember how we rejoiced as we walked the dusty Babylonian roads

318

—with what rapture you rode your donkey among the mountains of Lebanon, and with what even greater rapture you descended from the beast in Kadesh? Truly, if I were younger—that is, had I not so many important missions to fulfill here on Pharaoh's behalf—I would come with you myself, for many will bless your name because of this journey."

We wrangled no more, and Kaptah resigned himself to the project. Late into the night we sat drinking. Merit also drank, and she bared her brown skin that I might brush it with my lips. Kaptah recited his memories of the roads and threshing floors of Babylonia. If he had accomplished as much as he claimed, then my love for Minea must have rendered me blind and deaf at the time. For I did not forget Minea although I lay that night on Merit's mat and took pleasure with her so that my heart was warmed and my loneliness melted away. Nevertheless, I did not call her my sister, but lay with her because she was my friend, and she did for me the friendliest thing that a woman may do for a man. I was willing to break the jar with her, but she would not, saying that she was tavern bred and I too wealthy and eminent a man for her. But I think it was that she desired her freedom and my continued friendship.

4

On the following day I had to visit the golden house for an audience of the Queen Mother, whom all Thebes now called the black witch. I think that despite her ability and wisdom she had earned the name. She was a merciless old plotter. The great power she wielded had shriveled every good quality.

When I had returned to the ship, changed into royal linen, and assumed the symbols of my dignity, my cook Muti came from the copperfounder's house in a great rage and said to me, "Blessed be the day that brought you home, lord, but is it in any way fitting that you should go rioting among the pleasure houses all night without even coming home for breakfast, although I have taken very great pains to prepare the food you like? Moreover, I stayed up all night to bake and roast and have thrashed the idle slaves to speed them with the cleaning of the house, until my right arm aches with weariness. I am now an old woman and have lost my faith in men, nor have you done anything to raise my opinion of them. Come home now, and eat the breakfast I have prepared for you—and bring the harlot with you if you cannot bear to be parted from her even for a day."

Such were her words although she held Merit in high honor and admired her. It was her way of talking, to which I had grown accustomed. Her acrimony was melodious to me, making me feel that I had come home. Having sent word to Merit at the Crocodile's Tail, I went with her willingly.

She walked with dragging feet beside my chair and kept up a constant muttering: "I hoped that you had settled down and learned to behave decently during your long sojourn among royalty, but it is plain that you have done nothing of the kind and are as unruly as before. Yet I seemed to read peace and composure in your face yesterday. I was also glad to note that your cheeks were somewhat plumper, for when a man grows fat he grows tranquil. It will certainly not be my fault if you lose weight here in Thebes, but the fault of your own graceless courses. All men are alike and all evil in the world springs from the little tool they hide beneath their loincloths because they are ashamed of it—as well they may be."

So incessant was her nagging that I was reminded of my mother Kipa. I should certainly have been moved to tears had I not quickly snapped at her, "Shut your mouth, woman, for your chatter disturbs my thoughts and is like the buzz of flies in my ear."

She fell silent at once, delighted at having teased me into shouting at her and so making her feel that the master had indeed come home.

She had prepared the house very handsomely for my reception. Bunches of flowers were tied to the pillars of the entrance, the garden was swept, and the carcass of a cat that had lain before my door now lay before that of the neighbor. She had hired children to stand in the street and shout "Blessed the day that brings our lord home!" She had done this because she was indignant that I had no children of my own; she would have liked me to have some if they could have been obtained without a wife. I gave the children copper, and Muti distributed honey cakes among them, and they went away rejoicing.

Then Merit came, very beautifully arrayed and with flowers in her hair, and her hair gleamed with perfumed oil so that Muti sniffed and wiped her nose as she poured water over our hands. The food she had prepared for us was sweet to my palate, for it was Theban food. In Akhetaton I had forgotten that nowhere in the world is there to be found such food as in Thebes.

I thanked Muti and praised her skill, which delighted her although she tried to scowl and snort, and Merit complimented her also.

320

Whether this meal in the copperfounder's house was in any way memorable or noteworthy I do not know. I mention it for my own sake because it was then I felt happy, and I said, "Stay your course, water clock, for this hour is a good hour. Let it never pass."

While we were eating, people had gathered in my courtyard: people from the poor quarter, who had arrayed themselves in their best clothes and come to greet me and to bewail their aches and pains.

They said, "We have sorely missed you, Sinuhe. While you dwelled among us we did not value you at your true worth. Only when you had gone did we perceive how much good you did us, and how much we lost in losing you."

They brought me presents, very modest ones, for these people were poorer than ever because of Pharaoh Akhnaton's god. Among them was the old scribe who held his head askew because of the growth in his neck; I was astonished to find him still alive. There also was the slave whose fingers I had healed; he held them up proudly and moved them before my eyes. A mother showed me her son who had grown up handsome and sturdy; he had a black eye, and there were scars on his legs, and he told me he could thrash any boy of his size in the neighborhood.

And there was the girl whose eyes I had healed and who ill repaid me by sending to me all the other girls from the pleasure house, that I might remove disfiguring birthmarks and warts from their skin. She had prospered, having earned enough to buy a public bath near the market, where she also sold perfumes and supplied the merchants with the addresses of young and free-hearted girls.

All brought gifts, saying, "Do not scorn our presents, Sinuhe, royal physician though you be and a dweller in Pharaoh's golden house, for our hearts rejoice to see you, so long as you do not speak to us of Aton."

I did not so speak but received them one by one, according to their ailments. I listened to their woes, prescribed for them, and gave them treatment. Merit put off her beautiful dress in order to help me. She bathed their sores, purified my knife in fire, and mixed narcotic drinks for those who were to have a tooth extracted. Whenever I looked at her I was glad—and I looked at her often as we worked, for she was fair and shapely. Her bearing was graceful and she was not ashamed to put aside her dress to work, as poor women do, nor did any of my patients wonder at it, being too much concerned with their own troubles.

The day wore on while I received patients and talked to them as in former times, rejoicing in my knowledge when I could effect their cure. Often I drew full breath and said, "Stay your course, water clock; water, cease your flow, for not many of my hours will be so fair." I forgot the visit that I must pay to the Queen Mother, who had been informed of my arrival. I think I forgot because I had no wish to remember, being happy.

By the time the shadows lengthened, the last of my patients had left the court. Merit poured water over my hands and helped me to cleanse myself. With gladness I did the same for her, and we dressed.

When I would have stroked her cheek and brushed her mouth with mine, she pushed me away, saying, "Make haste to visit your witch, Sinuhe, and lose no time, that you may return before nightfall. My sleeping mat awaits you with impatience. Yes, I feel that the mat in my room awaits you very eagerly—though why this should be I do not know. Your limbs are soft, Sinuhe, and your flesh flabby, nor are your caresses in any way remarkable. Nevertheless, to me you are different from all other men, and I can well understand the feelings of my mat."

She hung the symbols of my dignity about my neck and set the doctor's wig on my head, stroking my cheeks as she did so so that despite my dread of the Queen Mother's anger I had no wish to leave Merit and go to the golden house. But I urged my bearers and my oarsmen until we came alongside the palace walls. My boat touched at the landing stage just as the sun was setting behind the western hills, and the first stars appeared.

Before I speak of my conversation with the Queen Mother I must mention that only twice during these years had she visited her son in the city of Akhetaton. Each time she upbraided him for his madness, thereby troubling him sorely, for he loved his mother and was blind to her character—blind as sons often are until they marry and their eyes are opened by their wives. But Nefertiti had not opened Pharaoh Akhnaton's eyes, for the sake of her father. Queen Taia and Eie lived freely together at this time and no longer attempted to conceal their lust, and I do not know whether the royal house had ever before witnessed such open shame. Yet I cast no slur on Pharaoh Akhnaton's origins, for I believe them to have been divine. If he had had none of the late Pharaoh's blood in his veins, he would have had no royal blood at all. Then he would have been a false Pharaoh as the priests averred, and everything that happened would have been yet more iniquitous and meaningless and mad. I prefer to believe what my heart and my reason tell me.

The Queen Mother received me in a private room where many little

322

birds with clipped wings hopped and twittered in their cages. She had never forgotten the trade of her youth but still loved to catch birds in the palace garden, by liming the branches of trees and by means of nets. When I entered, she was braiding a mat of colored rushes. She addressed me sharply and rebuked me for my delay.

Then she asked, "Is my son at all recovered from his madness, or is it time to open his skull? He makes far too much ado about this Aton of his and stirs up the people, which is no longer needful, since the false god is overthrown and there is no one to compete with Pharaoh for power."

I told her of his condition, of the little princesses and their games, of their gazelles and dogs, and of how they went rowing on the sacred lake of Akhetaton. She was mollified and, bidding me sit at her feet, offered me beer. She did this not from miserliness but because she preferred beer to wine.

As she drank, she spoke to me frankly and gave me her full confidence, which was but natural since I was a physician. Women tell their physicians much they would never think of confiding to others. In this respect Queen Taia was no different from other women.

Her tongue being loosened by the beer, she spoke thus, "Sinuhe, you to whom my son by some foolish whim gave the name of The Lonely —though you do not appear to me to be so—you are a tranquil man and no doubt in your heart a good man. Though how it profits a man to be good I do not know; only stupid people are good, being incapable of anything else, as I have myself observed. Be that as it may, your presence calms me strangely. This Aton, whom in my foolishness I allowed to attain power, now makes me very uneasy. It was never my intention that the matter should be carried so far. I invented Aton in order to depose Ammon, so that my power and that of my son should be increased. To be precise it was Eie who thought of him, my husband as you know—unless you are too simple to know even this. However, he is my husband although it has not been possible for us to break the jar together. This miserable Eie, then, who has no more virility in him than a cow's teat, brought Aton from Heliopolis and stuffed the boy's head with him.

"I have no notion what my son fancies he sees in Aton. Even as a child he was given to daydreams, and I can only suppose that he is mad and that his skull should be opened—and what can ail him that his wife, Eie's beautiful daughter, bears him girl after girl, though all my dear sorcerers have done their best to help her?

"Why do people hate my sorcerers? They are treasures, black though they be, and though they wear pins of ivory through their noses and stretch their lips and lengthen their children's skulls. Yet I know the people detest them so that I must keep them hidden in the recesses of the golden house. I cannot do without them, for no one can tickle the soles of my feet as they do or prepare me potions that enable me to enjoy life still and take pleasure. But if you think I have pleasure in Eie any longer you are greatly mistaken, nor do I rightly understand why I cling to him so when it would be better to let him fall. Better for myself, that is. My dear Negroes are now my only joy."

The great queen mother giggled to herself as the old washerwomen in the harbor giggle together over their beer, and went on, "These Negroes of mine are doctors of great skill, Sinuhe, although through ignorance the people call them magicians. Even you might learn something from them. Since you are a physician and will not betray me, I will tell you that I take pleasure with them now and again, for they prescribe this for my health—moreover an old woman like me must have some distraction. I do not indulge in this in order to experience something new, as do the women of the court who in their depravity enjoy the Negroes in the manner of rakes who have tasted all things and are jaded, and affirm that rotten flesh is the most savory. It is not thus I love my Negroes, for my blood is young and red and needs no artificial stimulant. To me they are a secret that brings me nearer to the warm sources of life—nearer to the sun, the soil, and the beasts."

Her manner was now more somber. She drank no more beer but resumed the braiding of the bright rushes. Not daring to meet her eyes, I kept mine on her dark, nimble fingers.

As I remained silent, she went on, "Nothing is won by goodness; the only thing in the world that signifies is power. Those who are born with it do not perceive its worth, but only those who like myself were born with dung between the toes. Indeed, Sinuhe, I can estimate the value of power. I have done everything for its sake, to preserve it for my son and for my son's son, that my blood might endure on the golden throne of the Pharaohs. I have shrunk at nothing to achieve this. In the sight of the gods my deeds may be evil, but truth to tell I do not concern myself unduly about them since the Pharaohs stand above them. When all is said and done, neither good nor evil deeds exist: good is that which succeeds, and evil that which fails and is discovered. Nevertheless, my heart quakes at times, and my bowels are as water when I reflect on my actions. I am but a woman, and all women are superstitious. But I hope that in this matter my Negroes will be able to help me. It tears at my heart to see Nefertiti bearing one daughter after another. I feel each time as if I had thrown a stone behind me, only to find it lying in the path ahead like some attendant curse."

She muttered invocations between her thick lips and shifted her feet uneasily on the floor, but all the while her nimble fingers knotted the bright rushes into a mat. As I looked at them, my heart was chilled. For the knots she tied were those of a fowler, and were familiar to me. Yes, I knew them; they were peculiar to the Lower Kingdom. As a child I had seen them in a sooty reed boat that hung above my mother's bed.

When this had flashed upon me, my tongue was frozen and my limbs numb. On the night of my birth a mild west wind had been blowing, carrying the boat down the flood waters and bringing it to rest on the shore near my father's house. The thought that dawned on me as I watched the Queen Mother's fingers was so outrageous and terrible that I strove to put it from me, telling myself that anyone might use fowler's knots in making a reed boat. Yet fowlers plied their trade in the Lower Kingdom, and I had never seen such knots tied by anyone in Thebes. As a boy I had often examined the sooty boat with its broken strands and marveled at the knots that held it together, though at that time I was unaware of its link with my own destiny.

But the Queen Mother never noticed how I suddenly stiffened. She expected no answer but plunged into her own thoughts and memories. She said, "I may appear to you an infamous and repulsive woman, Sinuhe, now that I have spoken thus openly. Do not judge me too sternly because of my deeds, but seek to understand. It is not easy for a young fowler girl to enter Pharaoh's women's house, where everyone despises her for her dark skin and broad feet—where she is pricked by a thousand needles and has no refuge but a whim of Pharaoh and the beauty and youth of her body. Can you wonder if I did not look too closely into the ways and means to be used when I sought to bind Pharaoh's heart to me—when night after night I accustomed him to the strange practices of the blacks until he could no longer live without my caresses, and until through him I ruled Egypt? In this way I defeated all intrigues in the golden house, avoided all snares and tore aside the nets that were spread about my path, nor did I shrink from revenge when I had cause for it. I stilled all tongues with fear and ruled the golden house according to my will—and my will was that no other wife should bear a son to Pharaoh until I had done so. Therefore, no other wife did bear him a son, and the daughters that were born I married off at birth to eminent men, so strong was my will. Yet I dared not bear children at first lest I become ugly in his sight,

325

for in the beginning I kept my hold over him by my body alone and had not yet entangled his heart in a thousand other nets. Moreover he was aging, and the embraces by which I dominated him made him weak so that, when at last I judged the time ripe for breeding, I bore him, to my horror, a girl. This daughter is Baketaton, whom I have not yet married off; she is another arrow in my quiver. The wise keep many arrows in their quiver and never trust to one alone. Time passed, and I was in great agony of mind until at last I bore a son. I have taken less delight in him than I had hoped since he is mad, for which reason I fasten all my hopes on *his* son, though yet unborn. So great is my power that not one wife in Pharaoh's household bore him a son during all those years but only daughters. As a physician, Sinuhe, must you not acknowledge that this magic art of mine is remarkable?"

Trembling I looked into her eyes and said, "Your magic is of a simple and despicable order, great queen mother: your fingers braid it into the bright rushes for all to see."

She dropped the work as if it had burned her, and her beer-reddened eyes rolled in her head in dismay as she exclaimed, "Are you also a magician, Sinuhe, or is this matter known to all the people?"

I told her, "Everything is known to them at last. Although none may have witnessed your actions, yet the night has seen you—the night wind has whispered of your deed in many ears. Though you could silence the tongues of men, yet you could not stifle the night wind's utterance. Nevertheless, the magic carpet beneath your fingers is exceedingly handsome, and I should be grateful for it as a gift. I would set great value on it—certainly a higher value than anyone else to whom you might present it."

As I spoke, she grew calmer. She continued to work with fingers that trembled, and she drank more beer. When I had stopped she gave me a cunning look and said, "Perhaps I will give you this mat if I ever finish it, Sinuhe. It is a beautiful and precious mat since I have made it with my own hands—a royal mat. One gift deserves another. What will you offer me, Sinuhe?"

I laughed and answered indifferently, "As a gift in return, Queen Mother, I will give you my tongue although I would be glad if you would let it stay where it is. It will not profit my tongue to speak against you, therefore, it is yours."

She muttered to herself and shot me a sidelong glance, then said, "Why should I accept as a gift that which is already in my power? No one would stop me from taking your tongue. I might take your hands also so that you could not write what you were prevented from uttering. Furthermore I could take you to my cellars to greet my dear Negroes, whence you might never return since they like to use humans for their sacrifices."

But I said to her, "Clearly you have drunk too much beer, Queen Mother. Drink no more tonight lest you encounter hippopotamuses in your dreams. My tongue is yours and I hope to receive your mat when it is finished."

I rose to go, and she giggled as old women do when tipsy.

"You divert me greatly, Sinuhe—you divert me greatly!"

I left her and returned unmolested to the city, and Merit shared her mat with me. I was no longer quite happy. My thoughts ran on the soot-blackened reed boat that hung above my mother's bed, on the dark fingers that fashioned a mat with fowler's knots, and on the night winds that carried the fragile boats downstream from the walls of the golden house to the Theban shore. I was no longer quite happy, for what increases knowledge increases vexations, and this was a vexation I could well have dispensed with, being no longer young.

5

The official pretext for my journey to Thebes was a visit to the House of Life. It was years since I had entered it although my position as skull surgeon to Pharaoh entailed this obligation. Also I feared that I might have lost something of my skill since during the whole of my stay in Akhetaton I had not opened a single skull. So I went to the House of Life, where I discoursed and instructed those pupils who had chosen to specialize in this branch. As students were no longer required to qualify for the lowest grade of priesthood before entering the House of Life, I fancied that knowledge also would have been freed from the bonds of convention and would have advanced, because the pupils were no longer forbidden to ask "why."

But in this I was greatly disappointed. These boys were immature and lacking in any desire to ask "why." Their highest ambition was to obtain knowledge ready made from their teachers and have their names entered in the Book of Life so that they might start to practice and to earn money without delay.

There were now so few patients that weeks passed before I had opportunity to open the three skulls I had set myself as a test for my skill. These operations won me high regard; both physicians and students flattered me and praised the steadiness and dexterity of my hands.

However, I was oppressed by the suspicion that these hands were less skillful than they had once been. My eyes had dimmed so that I was unable to detect disease with my former ease and assurance and was obligated to ask numerous questions and perform lengthy examinations in order to arrive at my conclusions. For this reason I received patients daily at my house and treated them for nothing, with the sole purpose of regaining my former proficiency.

Of the three skulls I dealt with in the House of Life, one I opened from compassion because the sick man was incurable and suffered intolerable pain. Both the remaining cases were interesting and demanded the full exercise of my skill.

One was a man who a year or so before had fallen on his head from a rooftop, where he had been disporting himself with another man's wife. He had fallen while fleeing from the husband but regained consciousness later without apparent injury. After some time he fell ill of the holy sickness and suffered successive attacks, which invariably followed the drinking of wine. He saw no visions but merely shouted in a furious voice, kicked, and bit his tongue, and could not contain his water. So greatly did he dread these attacks that he begged to undergo the operation. I laid bare the whole surface of his brain, which in many parts was black with old blood. The cleansing process took a considerable time and could not have been fully performed without injury. The man suffered no further attacks, however, for he died on the third day after the operation, as is usual. Nevertheless this operation was acclaimed as highly successful; I was praised for my performance, and the students took careful note of all I did.

The other case was a simple one: the patient was a young boy whom the guards had found lying senseless in the street, having been robbed. His head was beaten in, and he was at the point of death. I chanced to be at the House of Life when he was brought in and saw that I had nothing to lose by operating as the physicians refused to attend him, being convinced that he must die. I opened the crushed skull as rapidly as possible, removed the splinters of bone from his brain, and covered the hole with a plate of purified sliver. He recovered and was still alive when I left Thebes two weeks later, although he found difficulty in moving his arms and could feel nothing when his hands and the soles of his feet were tickled with a feather. I believed that in time he would be completely cured. The case was remarkable in that its urgency had given me no time to shave his head before operating, and when I had stitched the scalp together again over the silver plate, the hair went on growing as before and entirely hid the scar.

328

Although I was treated with respect in the House of Life because of my position, the older physicians avoided me and withheld their confidence, for I was from Akhetaton, while they were governed by fear of the false god. I never spoke to them of Aton and discussed professional matters only with them. Day after day they sought to read my mind, and sniffed about me like dogs on a trail until I marveled at their behavior.

At length, after the third skull operation, a certain physician of exceptional wisdom and proficiency approached me and said, "Royal Sinuhe, you must have observed that the House of Life is emptier than in former days and that our knowledge is less sought after than it once was, although there are as many sick people as ever in Thebes, and more. You have traveled in many countries, Sinuhe, and seen many cures, yet I doubt if you have seen such healing as is performed secretly in Thebes today. This healing requires neither knife nor fire, neither medicine nor bandages. I have been instructed to tell you of it and to invite you to witness some examples. You must promise not to speak of what you see, and you must suffer your eyes to be blindfolded when you are conveyed to the sacred healing place, that you may remain in ignorance of where it lies."

His words repelled me, for I feared trouble with Pharaoh, and yet my curiosity was aroused. I said, "I have indeed heard that strange things are happening in Thebes. Men tell tales and women see visions, but of cures I have heard nothing. As a physician I am exceedingly skeptical of cures effected without knife or fire, medicine or bandages, and I prefer not to involve myself in deceptions lest my name be taken falsely, to testify to things that do not exist and cannot occur."

He protested eagerly.

"We believed you to be without prejudice, royal Sinuhe, since you are widely traveled and have learned much that is unknown in Egypt. Flowing blood can be stanched without the use of forceps or hot irons; why then may not cures be effected without knives or fire? Your name shall not be linked with the affair, of that we can assure you, but we have our reasons for desiring you in particular to see these things and to satisfy yourself that there is no deception. You are alone, Sinuhe, an impartial witness. That is what we want."

His words astonished me and whetted my curiosity. As a doctor I was ever eager to learn new things, and I agreed to come. When darkness had fallen, he called at my house with a carrying chair. I stepped into it, and he bound my eyes with a cloth so that I might not see the direction we were taking. On our arrival he led me through passages

329

and up and down many steps until I was weary and told him I had had enough of the foolery. He pacified me, removed the bandage from my eyes, and led me to a stone hall where many lamps were burning.

Three sick people lay on litters on the floor, and a priest came to meet me, shaven headed and gleaming with oil. He addressed me by name and invited me to examine the patients thoroughly and satisfy myself that there was no trickery. His voice was steady and gentle and his aspect wise. I did as he asked, assisted by the surgeon from the House of Life.

I saw that these people were unfeignedly ill and unable to rise from their litters. One was a young woman whose limbs were wasted and shriveled and lifeless; only her dark, frightened eyes moved in her emaciated face. The second was a boy whose whole body was covered with hideous eruption and many bloody scabs. The third was an old man whose legs were paralyzed so that he could not walk; the affliction was genuine; though I drove a pin into his leg, he felt no pain.

At length I said to the priest, "I have examined these patients with the utmost care. Were I their physician, I could do no more than send them to the House of Life. The woman and the old man could hardly be cured even there, although the boy's sufferings might be alleviated by daily sulphur baths."

The priest smiled and bade us both sit on seats that were at the end of the room, in semidarkness, and wait there patiently. Next he summoned slaves who lifted up the litters of the sick and set them on the altar, and then he kindled an intoxicating incense. From the passage came the sound of singing, and a group of priests entered, chanting the hymns of Ammon. Having taken up positions about the sick people, they began to pray, to leap, and to shout. They leaped and shouted until the sweat poured down their faces; they cast off their shoulder cloths, swung bells in their hands, and gashed their breasts with sharp stones.

I had seen similar rites in Syria, and I contemplated their ecstasy with the cold eye of a physician. Their shouts grew louder, and they beat on the stone walls with their fists. The wall opened, and the sacred image of Ammon loomed over them in the lamplight. At that instant the priests fell silent, and their silence followed the din with stunning force. The countenance of Ammon shone out at us from the dark recess, glowing with celestial light.

Suddenly the chief one among the priests stepped forward to the sick people, and calling each of them by name, he cried, "Arise and walk, for great Ammon has blessed you because of your faith in him!"

330

With my own eyes I saw the three sick people rise uncertainly from their beds, staring at the image of Ammon. Trembling all over they rose to their knees and then stood feeling their limbs incredulously until they broke out into weeping, praying, and blessing the name of Ammon. The stone walls closed; the priests departed, while slaves bore away the incense and lit many bright lamps, that we might examine the sick people a second time. Now the young woman could move and walk a few steps when he guided her. The old man could walk by himself, and the eruption had vanished from the skin of the young boy, which was now clean and smooth. All this had taken place within a few water measures' time. I could never have believed it had I not seen it with my own eyes.

The priest who had welcomed us came up with a triumphant smile and said, "What do you say now, royal Sinuhe?"

I looked him fearlessly in the eye and answered, "I perceive that the woman and the old man were under some spell that fettered their wills, and magic is cured by magic if the magician's will be stronger than that of those bewitched. But an eruption is an eruption and is not to be cured by spells but by months of treatment and medicinal baths. Therefore I must confess that I have seen nothing to compare with this."

His blazing eyes were on me as he demanded, "Do you then acknowledge, Sinuhe, that Ammon is still king of all gods?"

But I said, "I wish that you would not pronounce the name of the false god aloud, for Pharaoh has forbidden it, and I am the servant of Pharaoh."

I saw that he was incensed at my words, yet he was a priest of the highest grade, and his will conquered his heart.

Mastering his feelings, he said smiling, "My name is Hrihor; you may denounce me by it to the guards. But I do not fear the guards of false Pharaoh, or his whip or his mines. I heal all those who come to me in the name of Ammon. Let us not dispute these matters; let us rather converse like men of culture. Allow me to invite you to my cell for some wine; you must certainly be weary after sitting for many water measures' time on a hard seat."

He led me through stone passages to his cell. By the pressure of the air I knew that we were underground and guessed that these were the vaults of Ammon, of which many tales are told but which no layman is supposed to have seen. Hrihor dismissed the physician from the House of Life, and he and I alone entered his cell—a dwelling place that lacked no comfort to rejoice a man's heart. His bed was canopied, his coffers and chests were of ivory and black wood, his mats were soft, and the whole room was fragrant with rare spices. Courteously he poured perfumed water over my hands, bade me sit, and offered me honey cakes, fruit, and a venerable, full-bodied wine from Ammon's vineyard, spiced with myrrh.

We drank together, and he said, "Sinuhe, we know you; we have followed your steps, and we are aware that you bear great love toward the false Pharaoh, also that his false god is less alien to you than we could wish. Yet I assure you that in his god no more is comprehended than exists already in Ammon. Pharaoh's hatred and persecution have but purified Ammon and made him stronger than before. However, I will not allude to divine matters but will appeal to you as a man who has cured the sick without requiring gifts and as an Egyptian who loves the Black Lands more than the Red. Pharaoh Akhnaton is a curse to the poor and ruin to all Egypt, and he must be overthrown before the evil he has engendered becomes so great as to be irredeemable even by bloodshed."

I drank his wine and said, "I have had enough of gods; I care not for them. But Pharaoh Akhnaton's god is different from any that have ever been. He has no image, and all men are equal before him; all, whether poor men, slaves, or even foreigners, have value in his sight. I believe that one cycle is at an end and a new one beginning; at such times even the incredible can happen—things against all reason. Never in any age has such an opportunity occurred for renewing the world and making all men brothers."

Hrihor raised his hand in protest, smiling, and said, "I see that you dream daydreams, Sinuhe, although I believed you to be a man of sense. My aims are less ambitious. I desire only that all shall be as it was, that the poor may receive full measure and the laws be enforced. I desire only that every man be left to follow his trade in peace and in what faith he chooses. I desire distinction between slave and lord, servant and master; the continued supremacy and honor of Egypt, as a land where children may be born each into his own station and continue in it to his life's end and where no vain restlessness eats at men's hearts. All these things do I desire, and therefore Akhnaton must fall."

He touched my arm appealingly and leaning forward went on, "You, Sinuhe, are a man of moderation and peace, and wish ill to none. We live in a time when each of us must make his choice. He who is not with us is against us and must one day suffer for it. You are not so foolish as to believe that Pharaoh's rule can long endure? It is a matter of indifference to me which gods you serve; Ammon can survive without your faith. But it is in your power, Sinuhe, to remove the curse from Egypt. It is in your power to restore to Egypt its former majesty."

His words disturbed me. I drank more of the wine, and my mouth and nostrils were filled with the rich fragrance of myrrh. With a forced laugh I said, "You must have been bitten by a rabid dog or stung by a scorpion, for indeed I have little power of any kind—I cannot even heal the sick as well as you."

He rose.

"I will show you something."

Taking up a lamp, he led me out into the passage, where he opened a door that was secured with many locks. He held the lamp to illuminate a cell blazing with gold and silver and precious stones, and he said, "Have no fear: I shall not tempt you with gold. I am not so foolish. But it will do you no harm to see that Ammon is still richer than Pharaoh. I will now show you something else."

Opening another massive copper door, he threw light into a little cell where, on a stone shelf, lay a waxen image crowned with the double crown, its breast and temples transfixed with sharp bone pins. Involuntarily I raised my hands and recited the prayers that give protection from sorcery, such as I had learned before my initiation as priest of the first grade. Hrihor regarded me with a smile, and the lamp in his hand was steady.

"Do you believe now that Pharaoh's days are nearly numbered? We have bewitched this image in the name of Ammon and pierced its head and its heart with the sacred pins. Yet the workings of sorcery are slow, and much evil may yet come to pass. Moreover, his god is able to protect him somewhat from our magic. Now that you have seen this, I would speak with you further."

He secured the doors again with care and led me back to his room, where he refilled my cup with wine. The wine slopped over my chin, and the rim of the cup clattered against my teeth, for I knew that with my own eyes I had seen a sorcery more potent than all others and one that no one hitherto had been able to withstand.

Hrihor said, "From this you may see that Ammon's power extends even to Akhetaton. Do not ask me how we acquired hairs from his head and clippings from his nails to mix with the wax. I tell you only that we did not buy them for gold but were given them in the name of Ammon."

Regarding me narrowly and weighing his words with care, he went on, "Ammon's power increases daily as you saw when I healed the sick in his name. His curse on Egypt daily becomes more terrible; the

333

longer Pharaoh lives, so much more must the people suffer for his sake—and sorcery is slow. What would you say, Sinuhe, if I gave you a medicine to cure Pharaoh's headaches so that he need never again suffer pain?"

"Men are always subject to pain," I said. "Only the dead never feel it."

His burning eyes were on me, and his will chained me to my seat. I could not even raise my hand as he said, "That may be true, but this medicine leaves no trace. No one will blame you, and not even the embalmers will notice anything unusual in his entrails. You need know nothing of it at all; merely give Pharaoh a potion to relieve his headaches. When he has taken it, he will fall asleep, never again to suffer pain or sorrow."

He raised his hand to prevent my speaking and went on, "I do not bribe you with gold, but if you will do this thing, your name shall be blessed for all eternity and your body shall never be destroyed but shall endure forever. Invisible hands will protect you all the days of your life, and there is no human desire of yours that shall not be fulfilled. This I promise you, having authority so to do."

He raised his hands. His burning eyes held me, and I could not avoid his gaze! I could not move or rise or even raise my hands. He said, "If I say to you 'Arise,' you will do so. If I say 'Raise your hands,' you will raise them. But I cannot compel you to bow before Ammon against your will nor induce you to perform deeds to which your heart is opposed. This limits my power over you. I conjure you, Sinuhe, for the sake of Egypt give him this medicine, and cure his headaches forever."

His hands fell. I could move once more and raise the wine cup to my lips, and I trembled no longer. I breathed in the fragrance of myrrh and said to him, "Hrihor, I promise nothing, but give me the drug. Give me this merciful medicine, for perhaps it is better than poppy juice, and the time may come when Pharaoh himself desires to sleep without waking."

He gave me the potion in a vessel of colored glass and said, "The future of Egypt lies in your hands, Sinuhe. It is not fitting that any man's hand be raised against Pharaoh, but so bitter is the misery among the people that the day may come when they remember that even Pharaoh is mortal—that a knife will draw his blood. This must not be, for it would undermine the authority of the Pharaohs. The fate of Egypt lies in your hands, Sinuhe."

I secured the medicine within my girdle and said mockingly, "Upon

334

the day of my birth the fate of Egypt lay in certain swarthy fingers that knotted reeds together. There are things you do not know, Hrihor, though you fancy yourself omniscient. I have the drug, but remember I promise nothing."

He smiled, raised his hands in farewell, and said, according to custom, "Great shall be your reward."

He then accompanied me through the passages, concealing nothing. His eyes could penetrate men's hearts, and he knew that I should not betray him. I can affirm that the vaults of Ammon lie beneath the great temple, but I will not divulge in what manner they are entered since the secret is not mine.

6

A few days later the death of Taia, the Queen Mother, occurred. She died of the bite of an asp while overhauling fowling nets in the palace gardens. Her own physician was not at hand as is often the case with physicians when they are most needed, and I was summoned from Thebes. But when I arrived at the golden house, I could do no more than certify her death, for which I could not be blamed, for the bite of an asp is always fatal unless the wound can be incised before the pulse has beaten a hundred times, and the veins above it closed.

Custom required that I should remain in the golden house until the porters from the House of Death arrived to bear away the body. Thus it was I encountered the somber priest, Eie, beside the bier.

He touched the swollen cheeks of the Queen Mother and said, "It was time she died, for she was a repulsive old woman who intrigued against me. Her own acts condemned her, and I hope that now she is dead the unrest among the people will subside."

I do not think that Eie had murdered her, for he would scarcely have dared to do that: joint crimes and shared secrets form bonds more powerful than those of love.

News of the death spread through Thebes. The citizens arrayed themselves in their best clothes and gathered joyfully in the streets and squares. To gain their favor, Eie caused Queen Taia's Negro sorcerers to be driven with whips from the cellars of the golden house. There were four of them, also a witch woman as fat and ugly as a hippopotamus. The guards drove them out through the Papyrus Gate, where the mob fell on them and tore them to pieces. Not all their witchcraft availed to save them then. Eie had all the materials of their craft burned where they lay, their drugs and sacred tree stumps also, which I regretted, for I should have been glad to examine these things.

No one in the palace mourned the death of the Queen or the fate of her sorcerers. Only Princess Baketaton approached her mother's body, and as she laid her beautiful hands upon those dark ones, she said, "Your husband did ill, Mother, in letting the people tear your black sorcerers in pieces."

She also said to me, "These magicians were in no way wicked, and they did not willingly dwell here. They longed to return to their jungles and their straw huts. They should not have been punished for my mother's deeds."

Such was my meeting with Princess Baketaton. She spoke with me, and I was impressed by her proud bearing and her lovely head. She asked after Horemheb and spoke sneeringly of him.

"Horemheb is of low birth, and his speech is rough, but if he took a wife, he might breed a great race. Can you tell me, Sinuhe, why he has not done so?"

I said to her, "You are not the first to ask this, royal Baketaton, and for your beauty's sake I will tell you what I have never dared tell anyone. When as a boy Horemheb came to the palace, he chanced to see the moon. Since then he has been unable to look on any woman to break the jar with her. How is it with you, Baketaton? No tree can bloom eternally; it must also bear. As a physician I should rejoice to see your belly swell in fruitfulness."

She tossed her head proudly and said, "You know very well, Sinuhe, that my blood is too sacred to be mingled even with the purest blood of Egypt. Better it would have been for my brother to take me to wife, in accordance with tradition, and I should doubtless long ago have borne him a son. Were the power mine, I should have Horemheb's eyes put out, so degrading is it to think that he has dared to raise his eyes to the moon. Frankly, Sinuhe, the very thought of men repels me, for their touch is coarse and their hard limbs can bruise a fragile woman. I believe the pleasure they give us is greatly overrated."

But her eyes began to glitter with excitement, and she breathed hard as she spoke. Perceiving that such talk gave her intense pleasure, I said, "I have seen my friend Horemheb burst a strong copper ring on his arm, merely by bracing his muscles. His limbs are long and graceful, and his chest resounds like a drum when he strikes it with his fists in anger. The court ladies pursue him like cats, and he can do what he likes with anyone."

Princess Baketaton looked at me. Her painted mouth quivered, and her eyes blazed as she exclaimed wrathfully, "Sinuhe, your words are exceedingly repugnant to me, and I do not know why you plague me with this Horemheb. He was born with dung between the toes, and even his name revolts me. Why must you talk thus in the presence of the dead?"

I did not care to remind her who had first turned the conversation to Horemheb. I feigned repentance and said, "Oh, Baketaton, remain a flowering tree, for your body grows no older and you will blossom for many years to come. Had your mother no trusted lady-in-waiting who could mourn by her body until the House of Death sends to fetch it? I would weep myself, but I am a physician and my tears ran dry long ago in the continued presence of death. Life is a day of heat, and death perhaps a cool night. Life is a shallow bay, Baketaton, and death the clear, deep water."

She said, "Speak not of death, Sinuhe, for life is still sweet to me. It is shameful that there is no one to mourn beside my mother. I may not weep, for it is inconsistent with my dignity, but I will send for some court lady to weep with you, Sinuhe."

I jested with her.

"Divine Baketaton, your beauty has stirred me, and your speech has fed my fire with oil. Send me some old hag, that I be not tempted to seduce her, and so bring disgrace upon a house of mourning."

She shook her head in rebuke.

"Sinuhe, Sinuhe! Have you no shame at all? Even if you do not fear the gods—for this is reported of you—you should feel respect for death."

Being a woman, she was not offended at my words and went away to fetch a lady of the court to weep by the bier until the porters from the House of Death should arrive.

I had had reason for my godless talk and now waited impatiently for the arrival of a mourner. She came, and she was older and uglier than I had dared to hope. The widows of Taia's late husband still lived in the women's house, and also Pharaoh Akhnaton's wives, with the wet nurses and the ladies-in-waiting.

This old woman was named Mehunefer, and her face showed me that she loved men and wine. As her duty required, she began to weep and sob and tear her hair beside the dead queen.

I fetched wine, and after she had been mourning for some time, she consented to taste it. As a physician I assured her that it would sustain her in her great sorrow. Then I began to lay seige to her and to praise her former beauty. I spoke also of children and of Pharaoh Akhnaton's little daughters.

337

At last with feigned simplicity I asked, "Is it true that the Queen Mother was the only one of immortal Pharaoh's wives to bear him a son?"

Mehunefer shot a terrified glance at the dead woman and shook her head to silence me. I plied her once more with fair and flattering words, spoke of her hair and clothes and jewels, and also of her eyes and lips. At last she altogether forgot her weeping and gazed at me enchanted.

A woman will always accept such talk, however false she knows it to be. The older and uglier she is the more readily will she do so, because she desires to believe it. Thus we became good friends. When the porters from the House of Death came and carried away the body, she invited me to her room with much solicitude and drank more wine with me. Gradually her tongue loosened; she stroked my cheeks, called me a handsome boy, and recounted to me a quantity of palace gossip of the most shameless order, to inflame me.

She nuzzled at my shoulders and ears, but I held her from me and said, "The great Queen Taia was clever at tying reeds, was she not? Did she not fashion little boats of them and send them down the river by night?"

These words of mine severely startled her, and she demanded how I knew it. But the wine distorted her judgment, and being desirous of displaying her knowledge, she said, "I know more than you! I know that at least three newborn boys floated away downstream like the children of the very poor. Before the coming of Eie, the old witch feared the gods and was loath to soil her hands with blood. It was Eie who taught her how to administer poison, so that Princess Tadukhipa of Mitanni died while she was yet weeping and calling for her son and would have fled from the palace to seek him."

"O fair Mehunefer!" said I, stroking her heavy, painted cheeks. "You take advantage of my youth and inexperience and stuff me with tales that have no truth in them. The Princess of Mitanni bore no son. If she did, then when did the birth occur?"

"You are far from being young and inexperienced, Sinuhe the physician!" she sniggered. "On the contrary, your hands are sly and false, and falsest of all is your tongue, which spits brazen lies into my face. Yet such lies are sweet to an old woman's ears, and I cannot choose but tell you of the Princess of Mitanni, who might have become the royal consort. Know then, Sinuhe, that Princess Tadukhipa was but a little girl when she arrived at the women's house of Pharaoh Amenhotep. She played with dolls and grew up in the women's house, just like that other little princess who was married to Akhnaton and who also died. Pharaoh Amenhotep did not possess her but loved her as a child and played with her and gave her toys of gold.

"But Tadukhipa grew to womanhood, and at fourteen her limbs were delicate and slender, her skin was ashen fair like the skin of all Mitannian women, and there was a distant gaze in her dark eyes. Then Pharaoh fulfilled his duty to her as he fulfilled it joyfully with many women despite Taia's intrigues, for in such matters a man is difficult to restrain until the roots of his tree are dried up. Thus a seed began to sprout for Tadukhipa, and after a little while for Taia also, who rejoiced, for she had already given Pharaoh a daughter—namely, this haughty Baketaton."

She fortified her tongue with wine and continued garrulously, "It is well known that Taia's seed was native to Heliopolis, but it is as well not to speak of that. She endured great anguish during the period of Tadukhipa's pregnancy and did what she could to procure a miscarriage—as she did with many others in the women's house—with the help of her Negro sorcerers. Within the last few years she had sent two newborn boys down the river, but these were of less account, being the sons of minor wives who feared Taia greatly; she gave them many presents and reconciled them to finding girl babies beside them instead of boys. But the Princess of Mitanni was a more dangerous rival, for she was of royal blood and had powerful friends; she hoped to become the royal consort in place of Taia if only she might bear a son. Yet so great was Taia's influence and so fierce became her disposition as the seed ripened within her that no one dared oppose her. Moreover Eie, whom she had brought with her from Heliopolis, stood at her side.

"When the Princess' time was come, her friends were sent away and the Negro sorcerers surrounded her—to 'ease her pains' they said. When she begged to see her son, they showed a dead girl-baby. But she did not believe what Taia told her, and I, Mehunefer, know that the child she bore was a son, that he lived, and that during the same night he was set to drift down the river in a reed boat."

I laughed loudly and asked, "How should you, of all people, know that, fair Mehunefer?"

She flared up, and wine trickled down her chin from her cup.

"By all the gods! I gathered the reeds with my own hands since Taia was loath to wade into the water while with child."

Aghast at her words I sprang up, emptied my goblet on the floor, and rubbed the spilled wine into the mat with my foot to show my horror.

339

Mehunefer grasped my hands, and dragging me down again beside her, she said, "I never meant to tell you that, and I have done myself harm thereby. There is I know not what about you, Sinuhe, that so irresistibly works on me that my heart has no secrets from you. I confess: I cut the reeds, and Taia fashioned a boat of them, for she would not entrust the secret to servants, and she had bound me to her by witchcraft and by my own deeds. I waded out and cut the reeds, which she knotted together in the darkness, laughing to herself and uttering profanities in her delight at thus vanquishing the Princess of Mitanni.

"I soothed my heart by pretending that someone would surely find the child, although I knew this could never be. The babes who drift down the river either perish in the heat of the sun or are snapped up by crocodiles and birds of prey. But the Princess of Mitanni would not be silenced. The color of the dead baby's skin differed from that of her own; the shape of its head also was different. She would not believe that she had borne it. The women of Mitanni have skin as smooth as the skin of a fruit, with the color of smoke or pale ash, and their heads are small and beautiful. She began to weep and mourn, and she tore her hair and reviled Taia and the sorcerers until Taia bade them administer a narcotic and gave it out that Tadukhipa had lost her reason because her child was stillborn. After the manner of men, Pharaoh believed Taia rather than Tadukhipa. Thenceforth Tadukhipa began to pine away, and at last she died. Before she died, she attempted several times to fly from the golden house and seek her son, wherefore it was generally supposed that her reason had been darkened."

I looked at my hands, and they were pale compared with Mehunefer's monkey paws; the skin was the color of smoke. So intense was my agitation that I put my question in a strangled voice, "Fair Mehunefer, can you tell me when it was that all this came about?"

She stroked the nape of my neck with her swarthy fingers and said in wheedling tones, "Oh, handsome boy, why do you waste precious moments on these bygone things when you might make better use of your time? Since I can refuse you nothing, I will tell you that it happened when the great Pharaoh had reigned for twenty-two years, in the autumn when the waters stood at their highest. Should you wonder at my accuracy, know that Pharaoh Akhnaton was born in the same year, albeit in the following spring, in the sowing season. That is how I remember."

At her words I froze with horror and could make no defensive

340

movement, nor even felt her wine-wet mouth on my cheeks. She put her arm about me and pressed me to her, calling me her little bull and her dove. I held her at bay with my thoughts in a turmoil, and my whole being revolted against this terrible knowledge. If what she said was true, then the blood of the great Pharaoh ran in my veins. I was Pharaoh Akhnaton's half-brother and might have been Pharaoh before him had not the guile of Taia overcome my dead mother's love. I stared before me in sudden understanding of my loneliness: royal blood is ever alone among the people.

But Mehunefer's importunity brought me to myself. I was forced to exert myself to the utmost to withstand her caresses, which were repugnant to me. I urged her to more wine, that she might become too sodden to remember what she had told me. Then she became altogether abominable, and I was compelled to drug her wine with poppy juice to send her to sleep and so be quit of her.

When at last I left her room in the women's house, night had fallen, and the guards and servants of the palace pointed at me and tittered among themselves. I fancied this was because I staggered in my gait and my clothes were crumpled. At my house Merit was awaiting me, being uneasy at my long absence and wishing to learn particulars of the Queen's death. When she saw me, she clapped her hands to her mouth and Muti did the same, and they exchanged looks.

At length Muti said to Merit in a bitter voice, "Have I not told you a thousand times that men are all alike and not to be trusted?"

But I was worn out and desired to be alone with my thoughts, and I said to them angrily, "My day has been wearisome, and I cannot endure your nagging."

Then Merit's eyes grew hard and her face dark with anger. Holding a silver mirror before my face she said, "Look at yourself, Sinuhe! I have never forbidden you to take pleasure with strange women, but I could wish you might conceal the matter so as not to wound my heart. You cannot pretend, in your defense, that you were lonely and sorrowful when you left the house today."

I looked at my face and was greatly shocked, for it was smeared with Mehunefer's paint. Her mouth had left red patches on my cheeks and temples and on my neck. I appeared like a victim of the plague. Ashamed, I made speed to wipe my face while Merit mercilessly held the mirror.

When I had washed my face with oil, I said repentantly, "You have misunderstood the whole matter, Merit, my most dear. Let me explain."

341

She looked at me coldly.

"No explanations are needed, Sinuhe, and I do not wish you to soil your lips with lies for my sake. That face of yours was impossible to misunderstand."

I had much ado to soothe her. Muti burst into tears on her behalf. Covering her face, she retired to the kitchen, spitting her contempt for men in general. I had more difficulty in pacifying Merit than I had had in ridding myself of Mehunefer.

At last I cursed all women and said, "Merit, you know me better than anyone and should therefore be able to trust me. Believe that if I so wished I could explain the matter to your full satisfaction, but the secret may well belong to the golden house. For your own sake it is better that you should not learn it."

Her tongue was sharper than the sting of a wasp as she retorted, "I thought I knew you, Sinuhe, but it seems there are abysses in your heart that I never even suspected. You do well to protect the woman's honor, and far be it from me to pry into your secret. You are free to come and go as you will, and I thank all the gods that I had sense enough to preserve my freedom and refused to break the jar with you—that is, if you ever meant what you said. Ah, Sinuhe, how foolish I have been to believe your lying words, for you have been whispering those same words into beautiful ears all this evening—and I wish I were dead."

I would have stroked her soothingly, but she drew back.

"Keep your hands away from me, Sinuhe, for you must be weary after rolling on the soft mats of the palace. I have no doubt that they are softer than my mat and that you found there younger and more beautiful companions than myself."

So she went on, piercing my heart with small, smarting wounds until I thought I should go raving mad. Only then did she leave me, forbidding me even to accompany her to the Crocodile's Tail. I should have suffered more keenly still at her going if my thoughts had not been raging within me like tempestuous seas and if I had not longed to be alone with them. I let her go, and I fancy she was amazed that I did so without protest.

I lay awake all that night, and as the hours went by my thoughts became clear and detached with the melting away of the wine fumes, and my limbs shook with cold because I had no one to warm me. I listened to the gentle trickle of the water clock. The water did not cease its flow, and time went by unmeasured so that I felt remote even from myself.

342

I said to my heart, "I, Sinuhe, am what my own actions have made me. Nothing else is of any significance. I, Sinuhe, brought my foster parents to an untimely death for the sake of a cruel woman. I, Sinuhe, still keep the silver ribbon from the hair of Minea, my sister. I, Sinuhe, have seen a dead sea monster floating on the water and the head of my beloved moving as crabs tore at her flesh. Of what importance is my blood? All was written in the stars before ever I was born, and I was predestined to be a stranger in the world. The peace of Akhetaton was a golden falsehood and this most terrible knowledge is but salutary; it has roused my heart from its slumber and convinced me that always I must be alone."

When the sun rose in gold beyond the eastern hills, the shadows fled, and so strange is the heart of man that I laughed bitterly at the phantoms of my own brain. Every night abandoned children must have drifted with the current in boats tied with fowler's knots, nor was the ashen color of my skin any evidence since a physician passes his days under roofs and awnings and so remains pale of complexion. No, in the light of day I could find no conclusive proof of my origin.

I washed and dressed, and Muti served me with beer and salt fish. Her eyes were red with weeping, and she despised me because I was a man. I then took a chair to the House of Life, where I examined patients, passing afterward by the deserted temple and out between the pylons, followed by the squawk of fat crows.

A swallow sped past me toward the temple of Aton, and I followed. The temple was not empty now. Many were there, listening to the hymns of Aton and raising their hands in his praise, while the priests instructed the people in Pharaoh's truth. This in itself was of no great significance. Thebes was a large city, and curiosity might bring together a crowd in any part of it. I saw once more the carvings on the temple walls, and from the forty pillars Pharaoh Akhnaton gazed down on me with that face, which was so disturbing in its passion. I saw also the great Pharaoh Amenhotep sitting, old and frail, on his throne, his head bent beneath the weight of the double crown. Queen Taia sat beside him. Then I paused before a representation of Princess Tadukhipa of Mitanni making sacrifice to the gods of Egypt. The original inscription had been hewn away, and the new one declared that she was sacrificing to Aton although Aton was not worshiped in Thebes during her lifetime.

This image was carved in the old convention and showed her as a young and lovely woman, scarcely more than a girl. The little head beneath its royal headdress was beautiful, and her limbs delicate and slender. I gazed long upon the statue, while the swallow darted above my head with joyful twitterings, and I wept over the destiny of this lonely girl from a foreign land. For her sake I could have wished to be as beautiful as herself, but my limbs were heavy and soft and my head bald beneath the doctor's wig. Thought had plowed furrows in my forehead, and my face was puffy with high living in Akhetaton. I could not imagine myself as her son. Nevertheless, I was profoundly moved and wept for her loneliness in Pharaoh's golden house. And still the swallow darted joyfully about my head. I remembered the fine houses and the plaintive people of Mitanni; I remembered also the dusty roads and the threshing floors of Babylon and knew that youth had slipped past me forever and that my manhood had sunk into stagnation at Akhetaton.

Thus my day was spent, and when evening came, I went to the Crocodile's Tail to eat and to be reconciled with Merit. She received me coldly and treated me like a stranger when she served me. When I had eaten, she asked, "Did you meet your beloved?"

I retorted irritably that I had not gone out after women but had worked in the House of Life and visited Aton's temple. To make clear to her my sense of insult, I described minutely every step I had taken that day, but she regarded me throughout with a mocking smile.

"Never for a moment did I fancy that you had gone to visit women, for last night you were exhausted and are capable of nothing further, bald and fat as you are. I meant only that your beloved was here to ask for you, and I directed her steps to the House of Life."

I sprang up so violently as to overturn my seat, and cried, "What do you mean, idiot woman?"

"She came here to seek you, arrayed like a bride; she had adorned herself with glittering jewels and painted herself like a monkey, and the reek of her ointments wafted as far as the river. She left you a greeting and a letter also, in case she should not find you—and from my heart I wish you would tell her to keep away, for this is a respectable house and she had the air of a brothel keeper."

She handed me an unsealed letter, and I opened it with shaking hands. When I had read it, the blood surged into my head and my heart thudded in my breast. This is what Mehunefer wrote to me:

Greetings to Sinuhe the physician from his heart's sister Mehunefer, Keeper of the Needle Case in Pharaoh's golden house. My little bull, my dove, Sinuhe! I woke alone on my mat with an aching head and a still more aching heart, for my mat was deserted and you were gone.

344

Only the scent of your ointments clung to my hands. Oh, that I might be the cloth about your loins or the essence in your hair or the wine in your mouth, Sinuhe! I journey from house to house seeking you, and I will not cease this labor until I find you, for my body is full of ants at the thought of you, and your eyes are to me a delight. Hasten to me when you receive this—hasten on the wings of a bird, for my heart longs for you. If you do not come, I will fly to you more swiftly than any bird. Mehunefer, the sister of your heart, greets you.

I read this terrible effusion several times without daring to look at Merit. At last she snatched the letter from my hand, broke the stick on which it was rolled, tore up the paper, and stamped on it, saying furiously, "I could have understood you, Sinuhe, if she were young and fair, but she is old and wrinkled and ugly as a sack though she slaps paint on her face as upon a wall. I cannot imagine what you are thinking of, Sinuhe! Your behavior makes you a laughing stock all over Thebes, and I, too, am made ridiculous."

I rent my clothes and clawed at my breast and cried, "Merit, I have committed an appalling blunder, but I had my reasons and never dreamed that I should be visited with so terrible a retribution! Seek out my boatmen and bid them hoist sail. I must fly, or this abominable hag will come and lie with me by force, and I am powerless to keep her at a distance. She writes that she will fly to me more swiftly than a bird, and so I believe she may!"

Merit saw my fear and my anguish and seemed at last to understand, for she broke into helpless laughter. Finally she said, in a voice that still shook with mirth, "This will teach you to be more careful where women are concerned, Sinuhe, or so I hope. We women are fragile vessels, and I know myself what a magician you are, Sinuhe my beloved!"

Her mocking was merciless. With feigned humility she said, "Doubtless this fine lady is more delightful to you than I can be. At least she had had twice as many years in which to perfect herself in the arts of love, and I cannot presume to compete with her. I fear that for her sake you will cruelly cast me off."

So acute was my distress that I took Merit to my house and told her everything. I told her the secret of my birth and all that I had wheedled out of Mehunefer. I told her also why I wished to believe that my birth had nothing to do with the golden house or the Princess of Mitanni. As she listened, she fell silent and laughed no more but stared past me into the distance. The sorrow in her eyes darkened, and at last she laid her hand on my shoulder.

"Now I understand much that was a riddle to me. I understand why your solitude cried out to me, voiceless, and why my heart melted when you looked at me. I too have a secret, and of late I have been sorely tempted to impart it to you, but now I thank the gods that I have not done so. Secrets are heavy to bear and dangerous. It is better to keep them to oneself than to share them. Yet I am glad you have told me everything. As you say, you will be wise not to fret yourself with vain brooding over what may never have happened. Forget it as if it were a dream, and I also will forget."

I was curious to know her secret, but she would not speak of it, only touched my cheek with her lips, put her arm about my neck, and wept a little.

At length she said, "If you stay in Thebes you will have trouble with Mehunefer, who will persecute you daily with her passion until your life is made intolerable. I have seen such women and know how terrible they can be. The fault is partly yours in that you made her believe all manner of nonsense, and cleverly. It seems wisest for you to return to Akhetaton. First write to her and conjure her to leave you in peace, or she will pursue you and break the jar with you in your defenselessness. That is a fate I would not wish for you."

Her counsel was good, and I set Muti to gathering up my belongings and rolling them in mats. I then sent slaves to seek out my boatmen in the taverns and pleasure houses of the town. Meanwhile, I composed a letter to Mehunefer, but being unwilling to wound her, I wrote with great courtesy, thus:

Sinuhe, the royal skull surgeon, greets Mehunefer, Keeper of the Needle Case in the golden house at Thebes. My friend, I sorely repent of my excited mood if it has led you to a misunderstanding of my heart. I cannot meet you again, for such an encounter might lead me into sin, my heart being already engaged. For this reason I am going away, hoping that you will remember me merely as a friend. With my letter I send you a jar of drink called 'crocodile's tail,' which I hope may somewhat assuage any grief you may be feeling. I assure you that I am nothing to grieve for, being a tired old man in whom a woman such as you could find no delight. I rejoice that we have both been preserved from sin; that I shall not see you again is the sincere hope of your friend Sinuhe, Physician to the Household.

346

Merit shook her head at this letter, objecting that its tone was too gentle. In her opinion I should have expressed myself more curtly and told Mehunefer that she was an ugly old hag and that I was seeking escape from her persecution in flight. But I could not have written thus to any woman. After some argument Merit allowed me to roll up the letter and seal it although she continued to shake her head in foreboding. I sent a slave to the golden house with the letter and also the wine jar, to insure that on this evening at least Mehunefer would not pursue me. Believing myself rid of her, I heaved a sigh of relief.

When the letter was on its way and Muti was rolling my chests and coffers in mats for the journey, I looked at Merit and was filled with unspeakable sadness at the thought of losing her through my own stupidity. But for that I might well have remained in Thebes for some time to come.

Merit also seemed plunged in thought. Suddenly she asked, "Are you fond of children, Sinuhe?"

Her question bewildered me. Looking into my eyes she smiled a little sadly and said, "Have no fear! I do not intend to bear you any, but I have a friend with a four-year-old son, and she has often said how fine it would be for the boy to sail down the river and see the green meadows and the rolling plow land, and the water fowl and cattle, instead of the cats and dogs in the dusty streets of Thebes."

I was much disturbed.

"You cannot mean me to take a rampaging infant on board to deprive me of my peace and bring my heart into my mouth continually for fear he may tumble overboard or thrust his arm into the jaws of a crocodile?"

Merit smiled, but sorrow darkened her eyes as she replied, "I do not want to cause you any vexation, but the voyage would do the boy good. I myself carried him to be circumcised and have some obligations toward him. I intended to come with the boy, of course, to see that he did not fall into the water. In this way I should have had good and sufficient reason for accompanying you. But I shall do nothing against your will; let us forget the matter."

At this I shouted for joy and clapped my hands above my head.

"Truly this is a day of joy for me! In my dullness I never thought that you could come with me to Akhetaton, and you incur no injury to your reputation on my account if you bring a child with you as a pretext for your journey."

"Quite so, Sinuhe," she said, with the irritating smile affected by women in discussing matters that men do not understand. "My reputation will not be endangered if I bring a child. Oh, fools that men are! Nevertheless, I forgive you."

Our departure was sudden because of my dread of Mehunefer, and we sailed at dawn. Merit brought the child to the ship swathed in blankets and still sleeping. His mother did not come although I would gladly have seen a woman who dared to call her child Thoth, for parents seldom presume to give their children the names of gods. Thoth is the god of writing and of all sciences, human and divine, so that the temerity of this woman was the greater. The boy slept peacefully in Merit's arms, unburdened by his name, and never woke until the eternal guardians of Thebes sank below the horizon and the sun shone hot and golden on the river.

He was a brown, handsome, plump little boy; his hair was black and smooth as silk, and he had no fear of me but crept into my arms. I liked to hold him so, for he was quiet. He looked at me with his dark, thoughtful eyes as if he had long contemplated the riddles of existence. I grew very fond of him and made him little reed boats and let him play with my doctor's things and smell the different drugs. He loved the smell of them and poked his nose into all the jars.

He was no trouble to us aboard ship. He neither fell into the water nor stuck his arm into the jaws of any crocodile, nor did he break my reed pens. Our voyage was all sunshine and good fortune, for Merit was with me. Every night she lay on the mat beside me, and the little boy slept peacefully nearby. It was a happy journey, and until the day of my death I shall remember the soughing of the reeds in the wind and the evenings when cattle were driven down to the water's edge to drink. There were hours when my heart swelled with happiness as a ripe fruit bursts with the abundance of its juice.

I said to Merit, "Merit, my beloved, let us break the jar that we may be together forever, and perhaps one day you will bear me a son, like this little Thoth. You if anyone could give me just such a quiet, brown little fellow as he is. Truly I have never before desired children, but now my youth is past and my blood freed of its passion. When I look at little Thoth, I long to beget a child by you, Merit."

She laid her hand on my mouth and turned away her head, saying softly, "Sinuhe, talk not so foolishly, for you know I grew up in a tavern. Perhaps I am no longer able to bear children. You, who carry your destiny in your heart, may find it better to remain alone and be able to order your life and actions untrammeled by wife or child— this I read in your eyes when first we met. No, Sinuhe, do not talk thus to me. Your words make me weak, and I would not shed tears

348

when such happiness enfolds me. Others fashion their own destinies and bind themselves with a thousand bonds, but you bear your destiny in your heart, and it is a greater one than mine. I love this little boy and we have many hot, bright days before us on the river. Let us pretend that we have broken the jar together and are man and wife, and that Thoth is our own son. I shall teach him to call you father and me mother, for he is small and will soon forget, and it will do him no harm. We will steal a scrap of life from the gods for these few days. Let no grief or fear of the morrow dim our happiness."

So I dismissed all evil thoughts; I shut my eyes to the misery of Egypt and to the starving people in the villages along the banks, and I lived for each day as it came. Little Thoth put his arms about my neck, pressed his cheek to mine, and called me "Father." His tender body was a delight to my arms. Each night I felt Merit's hair against my neck; she held my hands in hers and breathed on my cheek. She was my friend, and I was no longer tormented by any evil dreams. The days slipped by: swiftly as breaths they passed and were gone. I will speak no more of them because their memory catches at my throat like chaff, and dew from my eyes blurs the script. Man ought not to be too happy, for nothing is more fleeting and elusive than happiness.

7

Thus I returned to Akhetaton, but now I was changed and saw the City of the Heavens with other eyes. With its fragile, brilliant sunlit houses beneath the deep blue of the sky the city appeared to me as a bubble or a fleeting mirage. Truth did not dwell here, but outside. Truth was starvation, suffering, misery, and crime.

Merit and Thoth returned to Thebes, taking with them my heart, so that I once more beheld things as they were, with cold eyes, and all that I saw was evil. Before many days had passed, truth came to Akhetaton, and Pharaoh was compelled to meet it face to face on the terrace of the golden house. From Memphis Horemheb sent a group of fugitives from Syria in all their wretchedness to speak with Pharaoh. He paid their passage, and I believe also that he bade them exaggerate their plight. They presented a hideous spectacle in the City of the Heavens. The nobles about the court sickened and shut themselves into their houses at the sight of them, and the guards closed the gates of the golden house. They cried aloud and threw stones at the walls until Pharaoh heard them and had them admitted to the inner court.

They said, "Hear from our bruised mouths the cry of your peoples! In the land of Kem power is but a shadow, and beneath the thunder of battering rams and the roar of flames flows the blood of those who trusted in you and set their hopes on you."

They raised their arm stumps to Pharaoh's golden balcony and cried, "Look at our hands, Pharaoh Akhnaton! Where are our hands?"

They pushed forward men whose eyes had been put out and went their way groping, and old men whose tongues had been torn out gaped emptily and howled. They cried to him, saying, "Do not ask us of our wives and daughters, for their fate is more terrible than death at the hands of Aziru's men and of the Hittites. They put out our eyes and cut off our hands because we trusted you, Pharaoh Akhnaton!"

Pharaoh hid his face in his hands, and he spoke to them of Aton. Then they laughed at him very terribly and reviled him, saying, "We know that you sent the cross of life to our enemies also. They hung it about the necks of their horses, and in Jerusalem they cut off the feet of the priests and bade them leap for joy to the honor of your god."

Then Pharaoh Akhnaton uttered a dreadful cry; the holy sickness seized him, and he fell senseless on the balcony. The guards would have driven away these homeless ones, but in their desperation they resisted. Their blood flowed between the stones of the inner court, and their bodies were cast into the river. Nefertiti and Meritaton, the ailing Meketaton and little Ankhsenaton saw it all from the balcony and were never to forget it. It was then that they beheld for the first time anguish and death, which are the fruits of war.

I had Pharaoh swathed in wet cloths, and when he came to himself, I gave him sedatives, for this attack had been so severe I feared for his life. He slept, but when he awoke his face was gray and his eyes were red with the pains in his head.

"Sinuhe, my friend, we must put an end to this. Horemheb tells me that you know Aziru. Go to him and buy peace. Buy peace for Egypt though it cost all the gold I have and impoverish the country."

I protested vigorously.

"Pharaoh Akhnaton, send your gold to Horemheb and he will swiftly buy peace with spears and chariots, and Egypt need suffer no disgrace."

He clutched his head.

"By Aton, Sinuhe! Can you not see that hate engenders hate, and vengeance sows vengeance, and blood breeds blood until we drown in blood? How are the victims served if their sufferings be avenged by the infliction of suffering on others? This talk of disgrace is but prejudice. I command you: Go to Aziru and buy me peace."

I was aghast.

"Pharaoh Akhnaton, they will put out my eyes and tear out my tongue before I can approach Aziru to speak with him, and his friendship will avail me nothing for he will assuredly have forgotten it by now. I am unaccustomed to the exertions of war, which I greatly fear. My limbs are stiff, my movements slower than they were, nor can I order my phrases as glibly as others who have been trained to lies since childhood and who serve you at the courts of foreign kings. Send another if you would purchase peace."

He insisted stubbornly, "Go as I command you. Pharaoh has spoken."

But I had seen the fugitives in the courtyard of the palace. I had seen their broken mouths, their empty eye sockets, and the stumps of their arms. I felt strongly disinclined for the journey and went home with the intention of taking to my bed and feigning sickness until Pharaoh should have forgotten this fancy of his.

On the way I met my servant, who said to me in some astonishment, "It is well that you have come, my lord Sinuhe, for a ship has just arrived from Thebes bringing a woman whose name in Mehunefer; she says she is your friend. She awaits you in your house, arrayed like a bride, and the house is fragrant with her ointments."

I turned swiftly about and ran to the golden house.

"Be it as you say, Pharaoh. I will go to Syria, and may my blood be upon your head. But if I am to go, let me depart at once. Let your scribes prepare the necessary tablets, certifying my rank and authority, for Aziru has great respect for tablets."

While the scribes were busy with these, I hastened to the workshop of my friend Thothmes. I had discovered he was a sculptor in Akhetaton. He was my friend and did not spurn me in my hour of need. He had just completed a statue of Horemheb to be set up in Hetnetsut, which was the warrior's birthplace. It was of brown sandstone and fashioned according to the new rules, very lifelike, although to my mind Thothmes had exaggerated the bulk of the arm muscles and the breadth of the chest so that Horemheb appeared more like a wrestler than the commander-in-chief of Pharaoh's forces. But it was the custom in this new art to exaggerate all things even to ugliness, that truth be not slighted. Thothmes wiped the image with a wet rag to show me how beautiful was the sheen on Horemheb's muscles and how well the color of the stone matched that of his skin.

He said to me, "I think I will travel with you as far as Hetnetsut

351

and take this figure with me, to insure that it is set up in the temple there in a position befitting Horemheb's rank and my own. Yes, I will come with you, Sinuhe, and let the river wind blow the wine fumes of Akhetaton from my head. My hands tremble with the weight of hammer and chisel, and fever frets at my heart."

The scribes brought me the clay tablets, with Pharaoh's blessing, and when Horemheb's statue had been carried aboard, we set sail down the river. My servant had orders to tell Mehunefer that I had gone to the war in Syria and there perished. I felt there was but little falsehood in this, for I feared that I should indeed die a hideous death on this journey. I had further bidden my servant convey Mehunefer aboard some vessel bound for Thebes, with all due honor and if need be by force. "For," said I, "should I, against all expectations, return and find Mehunefer in my house, I will have all my slaves and servants beaten, I will have their ears and noses cut off, and send them to the mines for the rest of their lives."

My servant looked me in the eye and, seeing that I was in earnest, was duly frightened and promised to obey my orders. So with a mind relieved, I sailed down the river with Thothmes. Being convinced that I was bound for certain death at the hands of Aziru's men and of the Hittites, we did not spare the wine. Thothmes declared that it was not the custom to be sparing of wine when going to war, and he could speak with authority having been born in barracks.

BOOK 12

The Water Clock
Measures Time

I

In my official capacity I was received with full honors by Horemheb at Memphis, but as soon as we were alone together, he began slapping his leg with his whip, and he asked impatiently, "What ill wind blows you hither as Pharaoh's envoy, and what new maggot has hatched out in his brain?"

I told him that my mission was to journey to Syria and buy peace at any price from Aziru. Horemheb swore bitterly at this.

"Did I not guess that he would ruin all the plans I have laid with such care and cost? Know that thanks to me Gaza is still in our hands, so that Egypt holds one bridgehead in Syria for military operations. Moreover, by means of gifts and threats I have induced the Cretan battle fleet to guard our sea communications with Gaza, this being partly in Crete's own interest since a strong and independent Syrian federation would threaten its naval supremacy. Know also that King Aziru has much ado to control his own allies, and many Syrian cities are at war with one another now that the Egyptians have been expelled. Those Syrians who have lost home and possessions have joined guerrilla forces, which are in control of the desert from Gaza to Tanis and are now in conflict with Aziru's troops. I have armed them with Egyptian weapons, and many valiant men from Egypt—former soldiers, robbers, and runaways from the mines—have joined them. Most important of all, the Hittites have at last invaded Mitanni with their full strength; they have wiped out the people and the Mitannian kingdom is no more. The Hittite forces are detained there by this victory; Babylon grows uneasy and is equipping troops to defend its boundaries, and the Hittites have now no time to give Aziru adequate support. If he is wise, Aziru will go in fear of them since their conquest of Mitanni, which was Syria's shield against them. The peace Pharaoh offers would be most welcome, for it would allow him time to consolidate his position and look about him. Give me half a year, or even less, and I will buy an honorable peace for Egypt; with singing arrows and thundering chariots I will force Aziru to fear the gods of Egypt."

But I objected, "You cannot make war, Horemheb, for Pharaoh has forbidden it and allows you no gold for such a purpose."

"I spit on his gold! I have borrowed right and left—borrowed myself into beggary to equip an army for Tanis. By my falcon, Sinuhe! You could not mean to ruin everything and journey to Syria as a peace maker?"

I told him that Pharaoh had already given me his commands and furnished me with all necessary tablets for the conclusion of peace. It was useful to know that Aziru himself desired it, for in that case he would be willing to concede it cheaply.

At this Horemheb flew into a rage; he kicked over his seat and shouted, "Now in truth if you buy peace from him, to Egypt's shame, I will have you flayed alive and thrown to the crocodiles when you return, friend though you may be; this I swear! Go then, speak to Aziru of Aton. Be simple, tell him that Pharaoh of his infinite goodness will have mercy on him! Aziru will never believe you, for he is a crafty man, but he will puzzle himself into a fit before he lets you go; he will bargain and haggle and stuff you to the teeth with lies. But on no account are you to yield Gaza. Tell him also that Pharaoh cannot answer for the guerrillas and their plundering—for these free forces will in no circumstances lay down their arms; they give not a rap for Pharaoh's tablets—I see to that! You need not tell Aziru this of course. Tell him that they are gentle, patient men whom sorrow has blinded but who will assuredly exchange their spears for shepherds' crooks as soon as peace has been signed. But do not yield Gaza, or I will flay you with my own hand: so much anguish have I suffered, so much gold have I scattered in the sand, so many of my best spies have I sacrificed in order to open the gates of Gaza to Egypt."

I remained in Memphis for several days, debating the terms of peace with Horemheb and disputing with him. I met envoys from Crete and Babylon, also distinguished fugitives from Mitanni. From their talk I formed a picture of all that had happened, and I was filled with ambition, aware for the first time of being an important factor in the great game, the stakes of which were the destinies of men and cities.

Horemheb was right: at this moment peace was a more valuable gift to Aziru than to Egypt, although events in the world at large bore promise of no more than an armistice. Having stabilized conditions in Syria, Aziru would turn once more against Egypt. The future now depended on whether the Hittites, having established

356

their sovereignty in Mitanni, would march on Babylon or Egypt through Syria. Reason suggested that they would aim at the weakest point, and Babylon was arming while Egypt lay defenseless. The land of Hatti was an uncomfortable ally for anyone; nevertheless, to Aziru it afforded support. In joining with Egypt against the Hittites he was threatened with certain defeat so long as Pharaoh Akhnaton reigned and Aziru had thus only sand at his back.

Horemheb told me that he would meet Aziru somewhere between Tanis and Gaza, where Aziru's chariots were engaging the guerrillas. He described conditions in Smyrna, numbering the houses that had been burned during the siege and giving the names of eminent persons who had been slain, so that I marveled at all he knew. Then he gave me an account of his spies who had visited the Syrian cities and followed Aziru's troops in the guise of sword swallowers, jugglers, fortunetellers, oil merchants, and slave traders.

Both Horemheb's officers and the fugitives told me such hideous tales of the men of Amurru and of the free Egyptian forces that my heart quailed and my knees turned to water as the hour of my departure approached.

Horemheb said, "You may choose whether to go by land or by sea."

"Perhaps it will be safer to go by land," I replied uncertainly. He nodded.

"From Tanis onward you shall have an escort of a few spears and chariots. Should they fall in with Aziru's troops, they will abandon you in the desert and make off with all speed. It is possible that Aziru's men, seeing you to be an Egyptian of high rank, will impale you on a stake in the Hittite manner, and urinate on your clay tablets. It is also possible that despite your escort you will fall into the hands of the guerrilla forces who will strip you and set you to turning their millstones until such time as I can ransom you for gold—but I do not think you would last so long, as their whips are fashioned of hippopotamus hide. Or they might as readily slit you open with their spears and leave you to the crows, which is by no means the worst way of ending one's days but on the whole a fairly easy death."

My heart quailed more than ever, and despite the summer heat my limbs were cold. I said, "I bitterly regret having left my scarab with Kaptah, for it might have done more to help me than Pharaoh's Aton, whose power seems not to extend to these godless places. For the sake of our friendship, Horemheb, should you hear that I am turning millstones as a prisoner in any place, be prompt to purchase my freedom, and do not spare the gold, for I am a rich man—richer than you think

—although I cannot now furnish you with a full statement of my property, of which even my own knowledge is incomplete."

He answered, "I know of your wealth and have borrowed a considerable quantity from you through Kaptah as I have from other rich men, being fair minded and unwilling to deprive you of the privilege of lending. For our friendship's sake I hope you will not dun me for the gold as this might strain the friendship or even break it. Go then, Sinuhe my friend, go to Tanis and there pick up an escort for your journey into the desert. May my falcon protect you, for I cannot; my authority does not extend so far. Should you be taken prisoner I will buy your freedom; should you die I will avenge you. May this knowledge comfort you when some spear is slitting your belly."

"Should you hear that I am dead, do not waste your vengeance on me," I said bitterly. "You will bring no comfort to my crow-pecked skull by bathing it in the blood of your victims. Do but greet the Princess Baketaton on my behalf, for she is a fair and desirable woman, although haughty, and at her mother's deathbed she asked after you."

Having loosed this poisoned arrow over my shoulder, I left him, somewhat comforted, and went to bid scribes to draw up my will and attest it with all necessary seals. This document, by which I bequeathed my whole estate to Kaptah, Merit, and Horemheb, I deposited in the archives of Memphis. I then took a ship for Tanis, where, in a sun-baked fortress at the edge of the desert, I met with Horemheb's frontier guards.

These men drank beer, cursed the day of their birth, hunted antelope in the desert, and drank more beer. Their mud huts were dirty and smelt of urine, and the women they had there were of the lowest sort. In a word, they lived the usual life of frontier troops and longed for the day when Horemheb would lead them into battle in Syria. Any fate, though it were death itself, was to be preferred to the unbearable monotony of their existence in those ovenlike quarters among the sand fleas. They were full of ardor; they vowed they would form the spearhead of the free forces and press forward to Jerusalem and even to Megiddo, sweeping before them the stinking Syrians as the rising Nile sweeps away dry reeds.

My escort equipped themselves for the journey. Waterskins were filled and horses brought in from the grazing ground, while smiths reinforced the wheels of the chariots. By Horemheb's command ten chariots were allotted me, each drawn by two horses and leading a spare. In them, besides the driver, were a foot soldier and a javelin

358

thrower. When the leader of the troop reported to me, I scanned him very narrowly, for I was entrusting my life to him. His loincloth was as ragged and dirty as those of his men, and the desert sun had burned him black; only his silver-braided whip distinguished him from the rest. I had the more confidence in him—more than if he had worn fine clothes and had an attendant to shield him from the sun.

When I spoke of a carrying chair, he forgot his respect and burst out laughing. I believed him when he said that our only safeguard was speed and that I must therefore go with him in his chariot, leaving chairs and other home comforts behind me. He promised that I should sit on a sack of forage if I wished, but assured me that I would do better to stand and learn to balance myself to the motion, or the desert would jolt the breath from my body and crack my bones against the sides of the chariot.

I drew myself up and told him that this would be by no means my first ride in a chariot. I had once driven from Smyrna to Amurru in the shortest possible time so that even Aziru's men marveled at my speed though at that time I had been younger than I now was. The officer, whose name was Juju, listened politely, after which he committed my life to all the gods of Egypt and I stepped up behind him into his chariot. There he broke out his standard and roared at the horses, and away we went along a caravan route into the desert. I bounced about on the forage sacks, clung to the sides with both hands, bumped my nose, and bewailed my condition. My groans were drowned in the din of the wheels, and the drivers behind me yelled madly for joy at driving out into the desert away from the scorching hell of the huts.

Thus we drove the whole day, and I spent the night on the sacks more dead than alive, bitterly cursing the day of my birth. Next morning I tried to stand in the chariot, holding to Juju's girdle, but after a while the wheel went over a stone and I flew out in a high arc, landing on my head in the sand, where prickly plants tore my face. But I was past caring for this. When night came Juju seemed uneasy about my condition. Although he was keeping the men short of water, he spared some to pour over my head. He held my hands and comforted me, saying that the journey had been fortunate so far and that if the free forces did not surprise us on the following day either, the fourth day should bring us up with some of Aziru's scouts.

At dawn I was roused by Juju rolling me roughly out of the chariot onto the sand. He threw out my tablets and chest after me, then turning his horses he commended me to the protection of the gods and tore

359

off at full gallop, followed by the rest of the chariots, and their wheels struck sparks from the stones.

When I had rubbed the sand from my eyes, I saw a group of Syrian chariots advancing toward me from the hills and fanning out in battle order. I rose and waved a palm branch above my head in token of peace, although the branch had shriveled and withered in the course of my journey. The chariots whirled by unheeding—except that an arrow sang past my ear and plunged into the sand behind me—and tore after Juju and his men. I saw, however, that these made good their escape.

Finding that pursuit was vain, Aziru's chariots returned to me, and the leaders stepped out. I announced my rank and showed them Pharaoh's tablets, but they took no heed of these. They robbed me, opened my traveling chest, took my gold, and then stripped the clothes off me and bound me by the wrists to the tail of a chariot. When they drove off, I had to run behind—run until I was near suffocating while the sand scraped the skin from my knees.

I should certainly have died on that journey had not Aziru's camp lain immediately beyond the range of hills. With half-blinded eyes I saw a great assembly of tents among which horses were grazing; a wall of chariots and ox sleds encircled the camp. After that I knew nothing more until I awoke to find slaves throwing water over me and rubbing oil into my limbs. An officer who could read had seen my clay tablets, and I was now treated with all respect and given back my clothes.

As soon as I could walk, I was taken to Aziru's tent, which smelt of tallow and wool and incense. Aziru advanced to meet me roaring like a lion; golden chains jingled about his neck, and his curly beard was in a silver net.

He came to me and embraced me, saying, "I am distressed that my men have treated you ill. You should have told them your name and explained that you were Pharaoh's envoy and my friend. You should also have waved a palm branch over your head as a token of peace, as good custom requires. My men tell me that you rushed at them brandishing your knife, so that in self-defense they were compelled to seize you."

My knees burned as with fire, and my wrists ached. Consumed with bitterness I replied, "Look at me and see if your men were in danger! They broke my palm branch and robbed me, and they trampled on Pharaoh's tablets. You should have them flogged to teach them respect for Pharaoh's envoy."

360

But Aziru threw open his garment in mockery and raised his hands. "You must certainly have had some evil dream, Sinuhe! Can I help it if you have hurt your knees on the stones in the course of your wearisome journey? I should not dream of flogging my best men for the sake of a miserable Egyptian, and the words of Pharaoh's envoy are as the buzz of flies in my ear."

"Aziru, king of many kings, order at least that man to be flogged who shamefully jabbed my behind in many places as I ran after the chariots. Have him flogged, and I shall be content. Know that I bring peace as a gift to you and to Syria!"

Aziru laughed aloud and smote his breast.

"What is it to me if that pitiful Pharaoh crawl before me in the dust, begging for peace? Yet your words are reasonable. Since you are my friend and the friend of my consort and my son, I will have that man flogged who speared you in the backside to hasten you, for that was at variance with good custom. As you know, I fight with clean weapons for lofty aims."

So I had the pleasure of seeing my worst tormentor flogged in the sight of the assembled troops before Aziru's tent. His comrades had no pity but mocked him and howled with laughter when he shrieked, for they were warriors and glad of any break in their life of tedium. Without doubt Aziru would have let them beat the man to death, but when I saw the blood flow and the flesh loosen from his ribs, I raised my hands and gave him back his life. I then had him carried to the tent Aziru had set aside for me—to the indignation of the officers who had been quartered there—and his comrades began to acclaim me with enthusiasm, fancying that I intended to follow up the whipping with many ingenious tortures. But I anointed his back with the same salves I had rubbed into my own knees and buttocks, and I bound up his wounds and let him drink his fill of beer. The man thought I was mad and lost all respect for me.

In the evening Aziru invited me to a meal of roast mutton and rice cooked in fat, which I ate in his tent with him and his officers, and with such Hittite officers as there were in the camp. The mantles and breastplates of these were adorned with designs of double-headed axes and winged suns. We drank wine together, and all treated me with kindness and good will, as a simpleton who came to offer peace just when they most needed it. They talked loudly of Syria's freedom and future power and of the yoke of the oppressor, which they had lifted from their shoulders. But when they had drunk sufficiently, they began to quarrel among themselves, and at last a man from Joppa drew his knife and stabbed a man from Amurru in the neck. No great harm was done, for the artery was not severed and I was able to treat the wound effectively, in acknowledgment of which he gave me many fine presents. For this act also I was held by all to be of feeble intellect.

2

When the meal was over, Aziru dismissed his officers and the Hittites, that they might pursue their quarrels in their own tents. He showed me his son, who accompanied him on his campaigns, although he was but seven years old, and had grown into a fine boy with cheeks like downy peaches and brilliant black eyes. His hair was as black and curly as his father's beard, and he had his mother's fair complexion.

Aziru said to me as he stroked the child's hair, "Have you ever seen a finer boy? I have won many crowns for him, and he shall be a great ruler. So far shall his sovereignty extend that I hardly dare think of it. Already with his own sword he has slit the belly of a slave who insulted him; he can read and write and has no fear of battle—for I have taken him into battle also though only when quelling rebellion in the villages where his young life was not in danger."

Keftiu remained in Amurru while Aziru was at the wars, and Aziru longed for her sorely and told me that he had tried in vain to still his longing with women prisoners and with the temple virgins who followed the army; whoever had once tasted Keftiu's love could never forget her. And she had bloomed yet more luxuriantly with the years, he told me, so that were I to see her now I should not believe my eyes. But he carried his son with him, not daring to leave him in Amurru because one day the boy would bear the united crowns of Syria.

During our conversation there came to our ears the sound of shrieks. Aziru became exceedingly angry and said, "The Hittite officers are torturing their women again. I can do nothing to stop them, for I depend on their prowess in the field; nevertheless, I am unwilling that they should teach my men these evil practices."

I knew the Hittites; I knew what one might expect of them. Grasping the opportunity, I said, "Aziru, king of kings, break with these Hittites in time, before they crush the crowns on your head—and your head likewise! There is no trusting them. Make peace with Pharaoh while the Hittites are yet bound by the campaign in Mitanni. Babylon is arming against them as you know and will send no more grain if you remain their friend. When winter comes, famine will prowl the

362

land like a ravening wolf unless you make peace with Pharaoh so that he may send corn to your cities as before."

He replied, "You talk foolishly, for the Hittites are good to their friends, but to their foes they are terrible. Yet I am not bound to them by any treaty—although they send me beautiful gifts and shining breastplates—and I am free to make a separate peace. I love peace better than war and fight only to gain a peace that will be honorable. I will be reconciled with Pharaoh if he will restore Gaza, which he took from me by treachery, and if he will disarm the robber hordes of the desert and make reparation with grain and oil and gold for all the devastation the Syrian cities have suffered during the conflict. Egypt alone is to blame for this war, as you know."

He stared at me impudently and smiled behind his hand, but I answered him with heat.

"Aziru, you bandit, you cattle thief, you butcher of the innocent! Don't you know that in every smithy throughout the Lower Kingdom spearheads are being forged, and the number of Horemheb's chariots is already greater than that of the fleas in your bed? And these fleas will bite you sorely once the harvest has ripened. This Horemheb, whose fame is known to you, spat on my feet when I spoke to him of peace. For the sake of his god, Pharaoh desires peace rather than the shedding of blood. I give you one last chance, Aziru. Egypt will keep Gaza, and you must scatter the desert hordes yourself, for Egypt is in no way answerable for their deeds. Your own cruelty has forced these Syrians to flee into the desert, there to take arms against you. Furthermore, you shall release all Egyptian prisoners and pay compensation for the losses Egyptian traders have sustained in Syrian cities and restore to them their property."

Aziru tore his clothes and his beard and cried aloud in his resentment, "Have you been bitten by a mad dog, Sinuhe, that you rave thus? Gaza must be ceded to Syria, the Egyptian traders shall answer for their own losses, and the prisoners shall be sold as slaves as custom requires. Nothing prevents Pharaoh from buying their freedom if he has gold enough for the purpose."

I said to him, "If you make peace you can build massive, lofty towers for your cities so that you need no longer fear the Hittites, and Egypt will support you. The merchants of those cities will grow rich when they can trade with Egypt free of tribute, and the Hittites, having no warships, cannot hinder your commerce. All the advantages will be on your side, Aziru, if you make peace. Pharaoh's terms are moderate, and I can make no concessions."

Day after day we debated, and many times Aziru tore his clothes, and poured ash on his hair, and called me a shameless robber, and wept over the fate of his son, who would certainly die in a ditch, beggared by Egypt. Once I even left his tent and called for chair and escort to Gaza. I had stepped up into the chair before Aziru called me back. Yet I think he delighted in this haggling, being a Syrian, and fancied he had got the better of me when I yielded certain points. He can never have suspected my mandate from Pharaoh to buy peace at any price, even to the ruination of Egypt.

Thus I maintained my self-assurance and through my negotiating won terms that were very advantageous to Pharaoh. Time was on my side, for conflict within Aziru's camp was intensifying. Every day more men departed for their own cities, and he could not prevent them, for his authority was as yet insufficiently established.

One night two assassins entered his tent and wounded him with their knives but not mortally. He slew one, while his small son awoke and thrust his little sword into the back of the other so that he also died. On the following day Aziru called me to his tent and in terrible words accused me so that I was exceedingly frightened. Afterward we came to a final settlement. In Pharaoh's name I made peace with him and with all the cities of Syria. Egypt was to retain Gaza, the routing of the free forces was to be left to Aziru, and Pharaoh reserved the right to buy the freedom of Egyptian prisoners and slaves. On these conditions we drew up a treaty of eternal friendship between Egypt and Syria. It was recorded on clay tablets and confirmed in the names of the thousand gods of Syria and the thousand gods of Egypt and also in the name of Aton. Aziru cursed in a hideous manner as he rolled his seal upon the clay, and I also tore my clothes and wept as I pressed my Egyptian seal on it. In our hearts we were well pleased. Aziru gave me many presents, and I promised to send many also, him and to his wife and son, by the first ship to sail from Egypt er terms of peace.

were in agreement when we parted; Aziru even embraced me lled me his friend. I lifted up his handsome boy, praised his touched his rosy cheeks with my lips. Yet both Aziru and I the treaty we had made in perpetuity was not worth the written on. He made peace because he was forced to, and e it was Pharaoh's wish. Our peace hung in the air, a prey since all depended on which way the Hittites would ni, on Babylon's fortitude, and on the Cretan warships maritime trade.

Aziru at any rate began to dismiss his forces, and he furnished me with an escort to Gaza, issuing at the same time an order to the troops there to raise the profitless siege of that city. Yet I came near to death before ever I reached Gaza. When we drew near to its gates and my escort waved palm branches and shouted that peace had been made, the Egyptian defenders began to let fly their arrows at us and cast their spears, and I thought my last hour had come. The unarmed soldier who held his shield before me received an arrow in this throat and fell bleeding while his comrades fled. Terror paralyzed my legs, and I crouched beneath the shield like a tortoise, weeping and crying out most pitifully. When because of the shield the Egyptians could not get at me with their arrows, they poured down boiling pitch from huge jars, and the pitch ran seething and hissing along the ground toward me. By good fortune I was protected by some large stones so that I received only slight burns on my hands and knees.

At this spectacle Aziru's men laughed until they fell down and then lay writhing on the ground with laughter. At last their commander ordered the horns to sound, and the Egyptians consented to let me into the city. They would open no gates but lowered a reed basket at the end of a rope, into which I must creep with my clay tablets and my palm branch, and so they hauled me up the wall.

I sharply rebuked the garrison commander for this, but he was a rough, obstinate man. He told me he had met with so much treachery among the Syrians that he did not intend to open the gates of the city without express orders from Horemheb. He would not believe that peace had been signed, although I showed him all my clay tablets and spoke to him in the name of Pharaoh; he was a simple, stubborn fellow. Yet but for his simplicity and stubbornness Egypt would assuredly have lost Gaza long before; therefore I have no right to reproach him too severely.

From Gaza I sailed back to Egypt. In case we should sight enemy ships I ordered Pharaoh's pennant run up at the masthead, with all the signals of peace. At this the seamen were filled with contempt for me and said that a vessel so prinked and painted looked more like a whore than a ship. When we reached the river, the people gathered along the banks waving palm branches and praising me because I was Pharaoh's envoy and the bringer of peace. Even the seamen began to respect me at last and forgot that I had been hauled up the walls of Gaza in a basket.

When I was once again in Memphis and Horemheb had read my clay tablets, he warmly commended my skill as a negotiator, to m' great astonishment since he was by no means given to applauding any deeds of mine. I could not understand it until I learned that the warships of Crete had been ordered home. Gaza would soon have fallen into Aziru's hands had war continued, for without sea communications the city was lost. Therefore Horemheb gave me high praise and made speed to send many ships to Gaza, laden with troops, arms, and provisions.

During my stay with King Aziru, King Burnaburiash of Babylon had sent an envoy to Memphis with his suite, bringing many gifts. I received him on board Pharaoh's ship, which was there awaiting me, and we journeyed up the river together. The voyage was pleasant, for he was a venerable old man of profound learning, with a white, silky beard that hung to his breast. We conversed together of stars and sheeps' livers and so lacked no topic for discussions, for one may talk all one's life through of stars and livers without ever exhausting the theme.

We discussed affairs of state also, and I noted that he was deeply disturbed by the growing power of the Hittites. The priests of Marduk foretold that their power was to be limited and would endure less than a hundred years; they would then be annihilated by a savage white race from the West. This was little comfort to me since I was born to live during the period of their supremacy. I wondered how any people could come from the West, where there was no land save the islands in the sea. Nevertheless since the stars had spoken it I was persuaded of its truth, having met with so many marvels in Babylon that I more readily believed the stars than my own knowledge.

He had with him some of the finest mountain wine. As we rejoiced our hearts with it, he told me that signs and omens in ever increasing numbers presaged the end of an era. He and I were both aware that we were living in the sunset of the world and that night was before ⸱. Many upheavals must occur, many people be swept from the face ⸱he earth as the Mitannians had already been swept, and old gods efore the new gods are born and a new cycle begun. He inquired agerly about Aton, and he wagged his head and stroked his eard when I spoke of him. He acknowledged that no other such ever revealed himself on earth and thought that this appear- might well signify the beginning of the end; so dangerous a his had never been spoken before.

asant journey, we came to Akhetaton, and I seemed to grown in wisdom since leaving it.

During my absence Pharaoh's headaches had returned, and anxiety gnawed at his heart because he was aware that everything he touched miscarried. His body glowed and burned in the fire of his visions and was wasting away. To hearten him, Eie the priest had decided to arrange a thirty-years festival for him that autumn, after the harvest when the waters had begun to rise. It mattered not at all that Pharaoh Akhnaton had reigned for very much less than thirty years since it had long been the custom for Pharaohs to celebrate that anniversary whenever they wished.

Great numbers of people had arrived at Akhetaton for the feast, and one morning when Akhnaton was walking beside the sacred lake, two assassins fell on him with knives. A young pupil of Thothmes was sitting on the bank making drawings of the ducks, for Thothmes made his pupils draw from life and not from patterns. This boy warded off the ruffians' knives with his stylus until the guards had rushed up and overpowered them, and Pharaoh suffered no more than a wound in the shoulder. But the boy died, and his blood flowed over Pharaoh's hands. Thus did death appear to Akhnaton. Amid the autumn glory of his garden he saw blood running over his hands. He watched death darken the eyes and slacken the jaw of the young boy, for Pharaoh's sake.

I was summoned in haste to bind up Akhnaton's wound, which was slight, and in this way I chanced to see the two assassins. One was shaven headed, and his face gleamed with sacred oil, and the ears of the other had been cut off for some shameful offense. As the guards bound them, they tore at their bonds, shouting hideous imprecations in the name of Ammon. They would not cease even when the guards struck them on the mouth until the blood flowed. Doubtless the priests had bewitched them so that they could feel no pain.

This was an alarming incident, for never yet had anyone dared to raise his hand openly against Pharaoh. Pharaohs may have died unnaturally before that time, but such deaths were not openly contrived. What was done was done secretly, by poison perhaps, or a thin cord, or by suffocation beneath a mat so as to leave no trace. Now and again also the skull of some Pharaoh had been opened against his will. But this was the first open assault, and it could not be hushed up.

The prisoners were questioned in the presence of Pharaoh but refused to speak. When they opened their mouths, it was to invoke Ammon's aid and curse Pharaoh although the guards smote them on the mouth with their spear shafts. And at the sound of that god's name even Pharaoh grew so enraged that he allowed the guards to go on striking until the men's faces were battered and bloody and the teeth flew from their mouths. The prisoners still called on Ammon to help them, and Pharaoh at length forbade further violence.

Then they cried out in their defiance, "Let them torture us, false Pharaoh! Let them crush our limbs, gash our flesh, burn our skins, for we feel no pain!"

So hardened were they that Pharaoh turned aside to wrestle with himself. Regaining control, he was bitterly ashamed because he had allowed the guards to strike the men in the face. He said, "Release them! They know not what they do."

When the guards had unbound the ropes of rushes, the captives swore worse than before. They foamed at the mouth and shouted in unison, "Kill us, accursed Pharaoh! In the name of Ammon give us death, false Pharaoh, that we may win eternal life!"

When they perceived that Pharaoh meant to free them unpunished, they wrenched themselves from the hands of the guards and dashed head first against the courtyard wall so that their skulls were fractured and they died soon afterward.

Everyone in the golden house knew that Pharaoh's life must henceforth be in danger. His adherents doubled the guard and would not let him long out of their sight, although in his sorrow he desired always to wander alone in his garden and by the shore. Those who believed in Aton roused themselves to more ardent devotion, while those who professed the faith for the sake of wealth and position began to fear for their places and increased their zeal in Pharaoh's service. Thus in both kingdoms fanaticism increased, and the people were stirred up as much on Aton's account as on Ammon's.

In Thebes, also, ceremonies and processions were arranged in celebration of the thirtieth anniversary. Baskets of gold dust were conveyed thither; ostrich feathers, panthers in cages, giraffes, little monkeys, and parrots with brilliant plumage were brought along the river, that the people might behold the wealth and majesty of Pharaoh and praise his name. But the people of Thebes surveyed the festival procession in silence. There was street fighting, and the cross of Aton was ripped from men's clothing. Two of Aton's priests were clubbed to death when they ventured forth among the crowds unguarded.

Worst of all, the foreign envoys were witnesses to these things, and learned also of the attack on Pharaoh's life. Aziru's ambassador had many agreeable tales to tell his master on his return to Syria. He took with him many costly presents from Pharaoh to Aziru, and I also sent presents to Aziru and his family by the hand of his envoy. I sent his son a whole little army carved in wood, with gaily painted spearmen and archers, horses and chariots; I had ordered half to be made like Hittites and half like Syrians, in the hope that he would let them fight each other when he played. These figures were fashioned by the highly skilled woodcarvers of Ammon, who had been out of work since the temples and the temple workshops closed. I paid more for them than I did for all my presents to Aziru.

Pharaoh Akhnaton suffered greatly at this time and wrestled with doubt; his faith was so much shaken that he would sometimes cry out bitterly because his visions had faded and Aton had foresaken him. At last, however, he turned the attempted assassination to account, deriving from it new strength and the conviction that his mission was yet loftier than before and his works of more vital importance since there was still so much darkness and fear in the land of Egypt. He tasted the bitter bread and salt water of hatred, and that bread could not satisfy his hunger nor that water quench his thirst. Yet he believed he acted in loving kindness when he redoubled the persecution of Ammon's priests and sent to the mines those who spoke the name of Ammon aloud. The greatest sufferers were of course the simplehearted and the poor, for the secret power of Ammon's priests was formidable, and Pharaoh's guards dared not interfere with them. Thus hatred bred hatred, and unrest continued to increase.

Having no son, Pharaoh sought to secure his throne by marrying his two elder daughters, Meritaton and Ankhsenaton, to the sons of trusted followers at his court. Meritaton broke the jar with a boy named Sekenre, who held the rank of Pharaoh's cup bearer and believed in Aton. He was an excitable boy of fifteen, much given to daydreaming, and was pleasing to Pharaoh Akhnaton. Pharaoh allowed him to assume the royal headdress and chose him for his successor since he no longer expected to have a son of his own.

But Ankhsenaton broke the jar with a ten-year-old boy named Tut, upon whom were conferred the dignities of Master of the Horse, and Overseer of the Royal Building Works and Quarries. He was a slender, sickly boy who played with dolls and liked sweetmeats and was obedient and docile. There was no evil in him, if no particular good, and he believed all he was told, echoing the words of the last speaker. These boys were of the noblest blood in Egypt, and by marrying his daughters to them, Pharaoh thought to secure to himself and Aton the alliance of their two illustrious families. The boys pleased him because they had no wills of their own; in his fanaticism he would tolerate no difference of opinion nor listen to his counselors.

Outwardly all went on as before, but the attempt on Pharaoh's life was an evil sign. Worse still, he stopped his ears to human voices and would listen only to those within him. Life became oppressive in Akhetaton; the streets were quieter, and the people laughed less than formerly and spoke in an undertone as if some secret fear were looming over the City of the Heavens. Often I would be roused from my thoughts while at work beside the murmuring water clock and looking out would be aware of a sudden, deadly hush over the city; not a sound would reach me save that of my clock as it measured out immeasurable time. At such moments the murmur of it seemed sinister, as if an allotted span were drawing to its close. Then carriages would roll again past my house, and I would see the colored plumes waving above the horses' heads. With the cheerful clatter of the wheels would mingle the voices of servants plucking fowls in the kitchen court. Then I would be reassured and fancy that I had had a bad dream.

Nevertheless there were cold, clear moments when I saw the city of Akhetaton as no more than the fair rind of a fruit that inwardly was eaten away by maggots. The grubs of time sucked the substance from its gay life so that joy faded and laugher died in Akhetaton. I began to yearn for Thebes and had no need to seek out pretexts for the journey; my heart abundantly supplied me with these. So it was with many who fancied themselves devoted to Pharaoh; they left Akhetaton, some to see their estates, others to marry off their kinfolk. Many returned to Akhetaton, but some did not, being now indifferent to Pharaoh's favor and relying more on the secret power of Ammon I arranged for Kaptah to send me a number of papers testifying that my presence in Thebes was necessary, that Pharaoh might not prevent my going.

4

Once I had stepped aboard and was on my way up the river, my soul seemed liberated from a spell. Spring had come again, the river had fallen, and the swallows were flashing above the swift yellow waters. The fertile mud had spread over the fields, and fruit trees were in blossom. I hastened, filled with the sweet unrest of spring, like a bridegroom hastening to his beloved. So much is man the slave of his heart that he will shut his eyes to what does not please him and believe all that he hopes. Freed from the spell and the prowling fear

370

of Akhetaton, my heart was jubilant as a bird released from its cage. It is hard to be bound by the will of another, as everyone in Akhetaton was bound by the fevered, fitful, and oppressive will of Pharaoh. To me, his physician, he was but a man, and this slavery was worse for me than for those to whom he was a god.

I rejoiced at seeing once more with my own eyes and hearing with my own ears, at speaking with my own tongue and living according to my will. Such freedom is in no way harmful; rather it made me humble and melted the bitterness from my heart. The greater my distance from Pharaoh the more clearly did I see him as he was and wish him well. The nearer I came to Thebes the more immediate and living were the memories in my heart, and the greater were Pharaoh Akhnaton and his god.

Therefore my hope and my belief were the same, and I rejoiced, feeling that I was a good man and better than many others. If I am to be honest with myself and live in truth, I must confess that I felt myself to be a better man than Pharaoh himself since I harmed no one willingly, forced my faith on none, and in the days of my youth had tended the poor without requiring gifts. As I pursued my way up the river, I saw everywhere the traces of Pharaoh Akhnaton's god. Though it was now the height of the sowing season half the fields of Egypt lay unplowed, unsown, and barren save for weeds and thistles, and the flood waters had filled the ditches with mud that no one cleared away.

Ammon was exerting his power over the hearts of men, driving the settlers from the land that had been his, and cursing Pharaoh's fields also, so that plowmen and laborers fled from them and hid themselves in the cities. A few of the settlers remained in their huts, scared and bitter.

I spoke with them and said, "Madmen! Why do you not plow and sow? You will die of hunger when the winter comes."

They looked at me with enmity because my clothes were of the finest linen and answered, "Why should we sow, when the bread that grows in our fields is accursed, killing those who eat it as the speckled grain has already killed our children?"

So remote lay the city of Akhetaton from the life of reality that it was only now I learned that the speckled grain caused the death of children. I had not heard of such a sickness before. It spread from child to child; their bellies swelled, and they died with pitiful moaning. Neither physicians nor sorcerers could help them. It seemed to me that this sickness could not originate from the grain but rather from the flood waters whence came all the infectious diseases of winter. It is true that this one killed only children, but when I surveyed the grown people who dared not sow their fields, preferring to submit to death by famine, I saw that the illness had killed at least their hearts. I did not blame Pharaoh Akhnaton for all I saw, but Ammon, who so poisoned the lives of these people in the fields that they chose death rather than life.

Impatience to look once more upon Thebes drove me onward. The sweat poured down the faces of my oarsmen. With reproach they showed me their hands, which were blistered and swollen because I urged them to such speed. I promised to heal the sores with silver, and I quenched their thirst with beer in my desire for goodness.

But as they pulled, their haunches braced askew, I heard them mutter one to another, "Why should we row this fat swine if all men are equal before his god? Let him try it himself, to learn how it feels, and then heal his hands with silver if he can!"

The stick at my side cried out to lay about me, but my heart was filled with goodness because I was on my way to Thebes. Having reflected on the men's words, I perceived their justice.

I went among the speakers and said, "Oarsmen, give me an oar!"

I stood and rowed among them until the hard wood of the oar rubbed blisters on the palms of my hands, and the blisters turned to sores. My back strained sideways until I thought my spine would crack, and I drew my breath with pain.

But I said to my heart, "Will you give up the labor you took on yourself, for your slaves to mock and scorn you? This and much more than this they endure every day. Experience their toil, their sweat, their swollen hands, that you may know what the boatmen's life is like. You, Sinuhe, once required your cup to be full!"

So I rowed until I was near swooning and the servants had to carry me to my bed.

The next day also I rowed with my flayed hands, and the oarsmen no longer laughed at me but begged me to cease, saying, "You are our lord, and we your slaves. Row no more, or floor becomes roof for us, and we shall seem to walk backward with our feet in the air. Row no more, for there must be order in all things; every man has his station as ordained by the gods, and yours is not the oarsman's stretcher."

But I rowed among them all the way to Thebes; my food was their bread and their porridge and my drink the bitter beer of slaves. Every day I could row for a longer time; every day my limbs grew wirier;

every day I took more delight in living and noted that I had ceased to be short winded.

My servants were uneasy on my account and said to one another, "Surely a scorpion has bitten our master, or he has gone mad like everyone else in Akhetaton, madness being an infectious disorder. Yet we do not fear him, for we have the horn of Ammon hidden beneath our clothes."

But I was not mad and had no intention of rowing beyond Thebes.

So we approached the city, and the scent of it reached us far out on the river—a scent surpassing all others for one who was born in that place. I bade my servants rub healing salves into my hands and wash me and dress me in my best clothes. The loincloth was too wide for me, for much of my belly had melted away in rowing, and it was necessary to tighten it about me with pins, which they very woefully did. I laughed at them and sent them to warn Muti of my arrival, not daring to present myself unannounced.

I divided silver among the rowers, and gold also, and I said to them, "By Aton! Go, eat and fill your bellies! Rejoice your hearts with good beer and take pleasure with the beautiful girls of Thebes, for Aton is the giver of joy and loves simple delights, and he loves the poor better than the rich, because their pleasures are artless."

At this the faces of the boatmen darkened; they fingered the silver and gold and said, "We would not offend you, but tell us whether this be accursed silver and accursed gold since you speak to us of Aton. For such we cannot accept; it burns our fingers and turns to dust as is well known."

They would not have said this to me had I not rowed with them and won their confidence. I reassured them.

"Go quickly and exchange it for beer if such are your misgivings. But have no fear; neither my gold nor my silver is accursed. You may see from the stamp on it that it is the old, pure metal, unalloyed by the copper of Akhetaton. You are foolish men, ignorant of what is good for you, if you fear Aton; in him there is no cause for dread."

They made answer, "We have no fear of Aton, for who fears an impotent god? You know well enough whom we fear, lord, although because of Pharaoh we may not speak his name aloud."

Exasperation burned within me, and I would dispute no longer. I dismissed them and they went, leaping and laughing and singing their boatmen's songs. I too would gladly have leaped and laughed and sung, but this would have been inconsistent with my dignity. I made my way directly to the Crocodile's Tail without even waiting

373

for a carrying chair. After long separation, I saw Merit and she was lovelier to me than before. Yet I must acknowledge that love, like all passions, colors vision. Merit was no longer very young, but in the full ripeness of her summer she was my friend and nearer to me in her way than anyone had ever been.

When she saw me, she bowed deeply and raised her hands, then came forward to touch my shoulders and my cheeks also, smiling and saying, "Sinuhe, Sinuhe! What has happened to make your eyes so clear, and what has become of your belly?"

"Merit, my most dear! My eyes are bright with longing and the fever of love, and my belly melted away in melancholy as I hastened to you, my sister."

Wiping her eyes she said, "Oh, Sinuhe! How far does a lie surpass the truth in sweetness when one is alone and one's spring has flowered in vain! When you come, spring is here once more, and I believe in all the old stories."

I shall say no more of this meeting, for I must speak also of Kaptah. His belly had certainly not melted away; he was more corpulent than ever, and more rings jingled about his neck and wrists and ankles, while the disk of gold that hid his empty eye socket was now set with precious stones. On seeing me, he wept and shouted for joy, and said, "Blessed be the day that brings my lord home!" He led me to a private room and bade me sit on a soft mat, while Merit served us with the best the Crocodile's Tail had to offer, and we rejoiced together.

Kaptah rendered account of my wealth and said, "My lord Sinuhe, you are the wisest of men—you are more crafty than the grain dealers, and few have ever got the better of them. Last spring you deceived them with your guile, even if the scarab had some share in this. You will remember that you bade me distribute all your corn among the settlers for seed, requiring of them measure for measure only, for which reason I called you mad. And by the gauge of common sense it was indeed the act of a madman. Know then that thanks to your cunning you are twice as wealthy as before. I can no longer carry the sum of your estate in my head, and I am exceedingly vexed by Pharaoh's tax gatherers, whose impudence and rapacity are now boundless. As soon as the merchants heard that the settlers were to have seed the price of grain fell immediately and fell still further when the news of peace came since everyone then sold to be free of their commitments, by which the merchants suffered great loss. But at that point I bought at a very low price grain that had not even been reaped. In the autumn I gathered in measure for measure as you had commanded, so that by

374

this means I regained also my former stocks. In all confidence I may tell you, lord, that the settlers' grain is as good as any other and harms no one. I believe that the priests and their followers have secretly splashed blood on the corn in the bins so that it is speckled and acquires an evil smell. With the coming of winter the price of grain rose again, because Eie in Pharaoh's name shipped some to Syria after peace was made, in order to crowd Babylonian grain from the Syrian markets. Therefore the price has never stood higher than at present. Our profits are enormous, and they will increase the longer we hold onto our stocks. Next autumn famine will creep into the land because the fields of the settlers are unplowed and unsown; the slaves flee from Pharaoh's fields, and the farmers are hiding their corn lest it be taken from them and sent to Syria. For all this I can do no more than sing your praises to the heavens, lord, for you are more crafty than I, although I believed you mad."

In great excitement he continued, "I praise these times, which make the rich man richer, whether he will or no. They are indeed very strange times, for now gold and silver flows from nowhere into my chests and coffers. By selling empty jars I have made as much profit as through grain. All over Egypt there are men who purchase empty jars of any kind, and when I heard this, I hired slaves by the hundred to buy up jars. People gave them their used ones for nothing, only to have the smelly vessels removed from their courtyards. If I say that this winter I have sold a thousand times a thousand jars I may exaggerate somewhat, but not much."

"What fool is buying empty jars?" I asked.

Kaptah gave me a sly wink with his one eye and said, "The buyers affirm that in the Lower Kingdom a new way has been discovered of preserving fish in salt and water. Having gone into the matter, I know that these jars are being sent to Syria. Shiploads of them have been discharged at Tanis—and at Gaza also—whence they are conveyed into Syria by caravan. What the Syrians do with them all is a mystery. No one can perceive how it pays them to buy used jars for the price of new ones."

Kaptah's tale of the jars was remarkable, but I did not puzzle my head over it, the grain question being one of more importance to me.

When I had listened to Kaptah's full account, I said to him, "Sell all you have if need be, and buy grain; buy all the stocks you can, no matter at what price. Do not buy any that has not yet been harvested, but only that which you see with your own eyes and can run through your fingers. Consider also whether you can buy back what has already been shipped to Syria, for although Pharaoh by the terms of the peace treaty must send it thither, yet Syria can always import grain from Babylon. Truly in the autumn famine will creep into the land of Kem; therefore let that man be cursed who sells grain from Pharaoh's stores to vie with the grain of Babylon."

At this Kaptah further commended my wisdom.

"You say well, lord. When these affairs have been brought to a happy conclusion, you will be the wealthiest man in Egypt. I believe I can still buy grain, though it be at usurer's prices. But the man you have cursed is that simple priest Eie, who sold grain to Syria at the beginning of peace while the price was still low. In his foolishness he sold enough to supply Syria for many years because Syria paid immediately and in gold, and he needed a great quantity of gold for Pharaoh's anniversary festival. The Syrians will not sell it back to us, for they are wily merchants, and I fancy they will wait until we have come to weigh a grain of corn in gold. Only then will they sell it back to us, and so suck all the gold of Egypt into their coffers."

But I soon forgot corn, and the famine that threatened Egypt, and the future that had lain hidden in darkness since sunset had cast its blood-red glow over Akhetaton. I looked into Merit's eyes, and my heart drank its fill of her beauty, and she was the wine in my mouth and the balsam in my hair. We parted from Kaptah, and she spread her mat for me to lie on. I did not hesitate now to call her my sister, although I had once supposed that I could never again call any woman so. She held my hands in the darkness of night, and her breath was on my neck, and my heart had no secrets from her, and I spoke to her without falsehood or deceit. Her heart preserved its secret from me, and I never guessed what it might be. By her side I did not feel like a stranger in the world, for her body was to me a home, and her mouth kissed away my loneliness—and yet this was but a fleeting illusion through which I must pass, that the measure of my experience be fulfilled.

At the Crocodile's Tail I again saw little Thoth, and the sight of him warmed my heart. He laid his arms about my neck and called me "Father," so that I could not but be touched by his good memory. Merit told me that his mother had died and that she had taken him to live with her since in carrying him to be circumcised she engaged, according to custom, to bring him up should his own parents be unable to do so. Thoth was quite at home in the Crocodile's Tail, where the customers made much of him and brought him presents and playthings, to please Merit. I was greatly charmed with him, and during my stay in Thebes I took him back to the copperfounder's house. Muti was delighted at this, and as I watched his play at the foot of the sycamore and heard him romping and arguing with the other children in the street, I remembered my own childhood and envied him. He liked it here so well that he spent his nights with me also, and for my own enjoyment I began to teach him although he was not yet of an age to go to school. I found him intelligent; he quickly learned the signs and characters of writing, and I determined to pay for him to be educated at the best school in Thebes, which children of high rank attended. This made Merit very happy. Muti never wearied of baking honey cakes for him and telling him stories. She now had had her way: there was a son in my house but no wife to worry her or throw hot water over her feet, as is the way of wives when they have quarreled with their husbands.

I might have been happy, but there were disturbances in Thebes at that time to which I could not close my eyes. Not a day passed without fighting in the streets, and the endless disputes over Ammon and Aton resulted in bloodshed and broken heads. Pharaoh's guards and magistrates found plenty to do, for every day men, women, and children were bound with ropes and taken to the wharf, to be sent to forced labor in Pharaoh's fields—and even to the mines—on Ammon's account. But their departure was not that of criminals, for people gathered on the quays to greet them and sprinkle them with flowers. The prisoners raised their bound hands and said, "We will soon return!" And others, "Indeed we will soon return to taste the blood of Aton!" Because of the people the guards dared not silence the prisoners and did not beat them until the ships had carried them from the shore.

Thus the people of Thebes were divided among themselves, son against father, wife against husband, for Aton's sake. Just as the followers of Aton wore the cross of life at their necks or on their garments, so the horn was the mark of Ammon's faithful, and they too wore it visibly. No one could prevent them since for ages past this horn had been accepted adornment on clothes or in jewelry.

To my surprise, the power of Aton had notably increased in Thebes during the past year, and at first I was at a loss to know why this was. Many settlers had fled back to the city, and having lost everything, they brought Aton with them in their bitterness, and they accused the priests who poisoned their grain and those who stopped up their irrigation ditches and let their cattle trample over the fields. Many who had learned the new script and attended Aton's schools were eager on his behalf, as youth will always be eager in opposing age. The

377

porters and slaves of the harbor spoke thus, "Our measure has dwindled to half of what it was, and we have no more to lose. In the sight of Aton there is neither lord nor slave, neither master nor servant, whereas Ammon exacts from us full payment."

The hottest champions of Aton were the thieves, tomb robbers, and traitors who had greatly enriched themselves by informing and now feared retribution. All those who in one way or another earned their bread by him and desired to keep in favor with Pharaoh held fast to Aton likewise. Thus the people were divided until honest, peaceful citizens were weary of it all and, losing their faith in any god, lamented bitterly, "Whether Ammon or Aton, it is all one to us. We desire only to live in peace and do our work, but we are torn this way and that until we don't know whether we are standing on our heads or our heels."

But he suffered most who sought to keep an open mind and allow every man his own faith. All with one accord fell on him and reviled him, accusing him of sloth and indifference, of stupidity and a hardened nature, of obstinacy and backsliding, until he was tormented into accepting cross or horn, whichever he fancied might cause him least vexation.

Many houses displayed one or other of the signs; wine shops, alehouses, and pleasure houses displayed them, so that horns drank in one place and crosses in another. The girls who plied their trade by the walls hung cross or horn about their necks as best pleased their clients. Every evening crosses and horns roved the streets in their drunkenness and smashed lamps, quenched torches, and rattled shutters and came to blows with one another. I could not say which faction was worse, being equally appalled by them both.

The Crocodile's Tail also had been compelled to display its sign, although Kaptah had not desired this, preferring to agree with everyone from whom he could milk silver. It was not left to his choice, for every night the cross of life was scrawled on the tavern walls, surrounded by indecent pictures. This was very natural, as the corn merchants nursed a bitter hatred for Kaptah, who had impoverished them by distributing corn to the settlers, and it was in vain that in the tax returns he had declared the tavern under Merit's name. It was alleged further that certain of Ammon's priests had met with violence in his house. Kaptah's regular customers belonged to the dubious rich of the harbor who shrank from no means of acquiring wealth and who had all declared for Aton since it was through him that they had prospered.

378

land like a ravening wolf unless you make peace with Pharaoh so that he may send corn to your cities as before."

He replied, "You talk foolishly, for the Hittites are good to their friends, but to their foes they are terrible. Yet I am not bound to them by any treaty—although they send me beautiful gifts and shining breastplates—and I am free to make a separate peace. I love peace better than war and fight only to gain a peace that will be honorable. I will be reconciled with Pharaoh if he will restore Gaza, which he took from me by treachery, and if he will disarm the robber hordes of the desert and make reparation with grain and oil and gold for all the devastation the Syrian cities have suffered during the conflict. Egypt alone is to blame for this war, as you know."

He stared at me impudently and smiled behind his hand, but I answered him with heat.

"Aziru, you bandit, you cattle thief, you butcher of the innocent! Don't you know that in every smithy throughout the Lower Kingdom spearheads are being forged, and the number of Horemheb's chariots is already greater than that of the fleas in your bed? And these fleas will bite you sorely once the harvest has ripened. This Horemheb, whose fame is known to you, spat on my feet when I spoke to him of peace. For the sake of his god, Pharaoh desires peace rather than the shedding of blood. I give you one last chance, Aziru. Egypt will keep Gaza, and you must scatter the desert hordes yourself, for Egypt is in no way answerable for their deeds. Your own cruelty has forced these Syrians to flee into the desert, there to take arms against you. Furthermore, you shall release all Egyptian prisoners and pay compensation for the losses Egyptian traders have sustained in Syrian cities and restore to them their property."

Aziru tore his clothes and his beard and cried aloud in his resentment, "Have you been bitten by a mad dog, Sinuhe, that you rave thus? Gaza must be ceded to Syria, the Egyptian traders shall answer for their own losses, and the prisoners shall be sold as slaves as custom requires. Nothing prevents Pharaoh from buying their freedom if he has gold enough for the purpose."

I said to him, "If you make peace you can build massive, lofty towers for your cities so that you need no longer fear the Hittites, and Egypt will support you. The merchants of those cities will grow rich when they can trade with Egypt free of tribute, and the Hittites, having no warships, cannot hinder your commerce. All the advantages will be on your side, Aziru, if you make peace. Pharaoh's terms are moderate, and I can make no concessions."

363

Day after day we debated, and many times Aziru tore his clothes, and poured ash on his hair, and called me a shameless robber, and wept over the fate of his son, who would certainly die in a ditch, beggared by Egypt. Once I even left his tent and called for chair and escort to Gaza. I had stepped up into the chair before Aziru called me back. Yet I think he delighted in this haggling, being a Syrian, and fancied he had got the better of me when I yielded certain points. He can never have suspected my mandate from Pharaoh to buy peace at any price, even to the ruination of Egypt.

Thus I maintained my self-assurance and through my negotiating won terms that were very advantageous to Pharaoh. Time was on my side, for conflict within Aziru's camp was intensifying. Every day more men departed for their own cities, and he could not prevent them, for his authority was as yet insufficiently established.

One night two assassins entered his tent and wounded him with their knives but not mortally. He slew one, while his small son awoke and thrust his little sword into the back of the other so that he also died. On the following day Aziru called me to his tent and in terrible words accused me so that I was exceedingly frightened. Afterward we came to a final settlement. In Pharaoh's name I made peace with him and with all the cities of Syria. Egypt was to retain Gaza, the routing of the free forces was to be left to Aziru, and Pharaoh reserved the right to buy the freedom of Egyptian prisoners and slaves. On these conditions we drew up a treaty of eternal friendship between Egypt and Syria. It was recorded on clay tablets and confirmed in the names of the thousand gods of Syria and the thousand gods of Egypt and also in the name of Aton. Aziru cursed in a hideous manner as he rolled his seal upon the clay, and I also tore my clothes and wept as I pressed my Egyptian seal on it. In our hearts we were well pleased. Aziru gave me many presents, and I promised to send many also, to him and to his wife and son, by the first ship to sail from Egypt under terms of peace.

We were in agreement when we parted; Aziru even embraced me and called me his friend. I lifted up his handsome boy, praised his valor and touched his rosy cheeks with my lips. Yet both Aziru and I knew that the treaty we had made in perpetuity was not worth the clay it was written on. He made peace because he was forced to, and Egypt because it was Pharaoh's wish. Our peace hung in the air, a prey to every wind, since all depended on which way the Hittites would turn from Mitanni, on Babylon's fortitude, and on the Cretan warships that protected the maritime trade.

364

Aziru at any rate began to dismiss his forces, and he furnished me with an escort to Gaza, issuing at the same time an order to the troops there to raise the profitless siege of that city. Yet I came near to death before ever I reached Gaza. When we drew near to its gates and my escort waved palm branches and shouted that peace had been made, the Egyptian defenders began to let fly their arrows at us and cast their spears, and I thought my last hour had come. The unarmed soldier who held his shield before me received an arrow in this throat and fell bleeding while his comrades fled. Terror paralyzed my legs, and I crouched beneath the shield like a tortoise, weeping and crying out most pitifully. When because of the shield the Egyptians could not get at me with their arrows, they poured down boiling pitch from huge jars, and the pitch ran seething and hissing along the ground toward me. By good fortune I was protected by some large stones so that I received only slight burns on my hands and knees.

At this spectacle Aziru's men laughed until they fell down and then lay writhing on the ground with laughter. At last their commander ordered the horns to sound, and the Egyptians consented to let me into the city. They would open no gates but lowered a reed basket at the end of a rope, into which I must creep with my clay tablets and my palm branch, and so they hauled me up the wall.

I sharply rebuked the garrison commander for this, but he was a rough, obstinate man. He told me he had met with so much treachery among the Syrians that he did not intend to open the gates of the city without express orders from Horemheb. He would not believe that peace had been signed, although I showed him all my clay tablets and spoke to him in the name of Pharaoh; he was a simple, stubborn fellow. Yet but for his simplicity and stubbornness Egypt would assuredly have lost Gaza long before; therefore I have no right to reproach him too severely.

From Gaza I sailed back to Egypt. In case we should sight enemy ships I ordered Pharaoh's pennant run up at the masthead, with all the signals of peace. At this the seamen were filled with contempt for me and said that a vessel so prinked and painted looked more like a whore than a ship. When we reached the river, the people gathered along the banks waving palm branches and praising me because I was Pharaoh's envoy and the bringer of peace. Even the seamen began to respect me at last and forgot that I had been hauled up the walls of Gaza in a basket.

When I was once again in Memphis and Horemheb had read my clay tablets, he warmly commended my skill as a negotiator, to my great astonishment since he was by no means given to applauding any deeds of mine. I could not understand it until I learned that the warships of Crete had been ordered home. Gaza would soon have fallen into Aziru's hands had war continued, for without sea communications the city was lost. Therefore Horemheb gave me high praise and made speed to send many ships to Gaza, laden with troops, arms, and provisions.

During my stay with King Aziru, King Burnaburiash of Babylon had sent an envoy to Memphis with his suite, bringing many gifts. I received him on board Pharaoh's ship, which was there awaiting me, and we journeyed up the river together. The voyage was pleasant, for he was a venerable old man of profound learning, with a white, silky beard that hung to his breast. We conversed together of stars and sheeps' livers and so lacked no topic for discussions, for one may talk all one's life through of stars and livers without ever exhausting the theme.

We discussed affairs of state also, and I noted that he was deeply disturbed by the growing power of the Hittites. The priests of Marduk foretold that their power was to be limited and would endure less than a hundred years; they would then be annihilated by a savage white race from the West. This was little comfort to me since I was born to live during the period of their supremacy. I wondered how any people could come from the West, where there was no land save the islands in the sea. Nevertheless since the stars had spoken it I was persuaded of its truth, having met with so many marvels in Babylon that I more readily believed the stars than my own knowledge.

He had with him some of the finest mountain wine. As we rejoiced our hearts with it, he told me that signs and omens in ever increasing numbers presaged the end of an era. He and I were both aware that we were living in the sunset of the world and that night was before us. Many upheavals must occur, many people be swept from the face of the earth as the Mitannians had already been swept, and old gods die before the new gods are born and a new cycle begun. He inquired very eagerly about Aton, and he wagged his head and stroked his white beard when I spoke of him. He acknowledged that no other such god had ever revealed himself on earth and thought that this appearance now might well signify the beginning of the end; so dangerous a teaching as his had never been spoken before.

After a pleasant journey, we came to Akhetaton, and I seemed to myself to have grown in wisdom since leaving it.

366

No one made bold to persecute me, because I was physician to the household, and the inhabitants of the poor quarter by the harbor knew me and my works. Therefore, no crosses or shameful pictures appeared on my walls, and no carcasses were flung into my courtyard. Even the drunken rioters avoided my house when they wandered the streets at night, shrieking the name of Ammon to annoy the watch. Respect for those who bore the sign of Pharaoh was in the people's very blood, despite all the priests could do to convince them that Akhnaton was a false Pharaoh.

But one hot day little Thoth came home from playing, beaten and bruised, with blood running from his nose and a tooth missing from his jaw. He came in sobbing although striving to be very brave, and Muti was aghast. She wept with rage as she washed his face, then seizing a washing club in her bony fist she cried, "Ammon or Aton, it is all one—but this the rush weaver's brats shall pay for!"

She was gone before I could stop her, and soon from the street came the howls of boys, cries for help, and the oaths of a grown man. Thoth and I peeped fearfully out through the door and saw Muti thrashing in the name of Aton all five sons of the rush weaver, his wife, and the man himself. Presently she returned, still panting with fury, and when I sought to upbraid her and explain that hatred bred hatred and vengeance begot vengeance, she came near to clubbing me also. In the course of the day her conscience began to trouble her, and having packed honey cakes and a jar of beer in a basket, she took them to the rush weaver and made peace with him and his wife and children. After this incident the man held Muti in veneration, and his boys became the friends of Thoth. They pilfered honey cakes from our kitchen and together fought as much with horns as with crosses whenever young partisans strayed into our street to make mischief.

5

There remains little to say of this sojourn in Thebes. A day came when Pharaoh Akhnaton summoned me because his headaches had become worse, and I could no longer postpone my departure. I bade farewell to Merit and little Thoth, for to my sorrow I could not take them with me on this journey since Pharaoh had commanded me to return with all possible speed.

I said to Merit, "Come after me, you and little Thoth! Dwell with me in my house at Akhetaton, and we will all be happy together."

379

Merit said, "Take a flower from its place in the desert, plant it in rich soil, and water it every day, and it will wither and die. So would it be with me in Akhetaton, and your friendship for me would wither and die likewise when you compared me with the women of the court. They would take care to stress every point in which I differ from them—for I know women, and men also, I believe. It would ill become your rank to keep a tavern-bred woman in your house who year after year has been fumbled after by sots."

I said to her, "Merit, my beloved, I will come to you as soon as I may, for I hunger and thirst every hour that I am absent from you. Many have left Akhetaton never to return, and perhaps I shall do the same."

But she answered, "You say more than your heart can answer for, Sinuhe. I know you. I know that it is not in your nature to forsake Pharaoh when others forsake him. In the good days you might have done it, but now you cannot. Such is your heart, Sinuhe, and perhaps it is for this reason that I am your friend."

Her words set my heart in a turmoil, and there was a prickling in my throat as of chaff when I reflected that I might lose her. Very earnestly I said to her, "Merit, Egypt is not the only country in the world. I am weary of battles between gods and of Pharaoh's madness. Let us fly to some place far away and live together, you and I and little Thoth, without fear of the morrow."

But Merit smiled and the sorrow in her eyes grew and darkened as she said, "Your talk is vain, and you know yourself that it is, yet even your lies please me because they show that you love me. But I do not think that you could live happily anywhere save in Egypt, nor I anywhere save in Thebes. No, Sinuhe, no man can escape his own heart. In course of time, when I had grown old and ugly and fat, you would sicken of me and hate me because of all you had missed on my account. I would rather give you up than see that happen."

"You are my home and my country, Merit. You are the bread in my hand and the wine in my mouth, and you know it well. You are the one being in the world in whose company I am not lonely, and for that I love you."

"Yes, indeed!" rejoined Merit a little bitterly. "I am but the cushion to soften your loneliness—when I am not your worn mat. But that is how it must be, and I desire nothing else. Therefore, I do not tell you the secret that eats at my heart and which perhaps you should know. I will keep it to myself although in my weakness I had meant to tell you. It is for your sake I conceal it, Sinuhe, for your sake only."

She would not confide her secret to me, for she was prouder than I and perhaps lonelier, although at that time I did not understand and thought only of myself. It is my belief that all men do so when they love, though this is no excuse for me. Men who believe they think of anything but themselves when they love are deluded, as they are in many other matters.

Once more, then, I departed from Thebes and went back to Akhetaton, and of that which followed there is nothing but evil to relate.

BOOK 13

Aton's Kingdom on Earth

I

UPON my return to Akhetaton I found Pharaoh exceedingly ill and in need of my help. His face was narrower, his cheekbones protruded, and his neck seemed even longer than before. It was incapable now of supporting the weight of the double crown, which pulled his head backward when he wore it on state occasions. His thighs had swollen, although his legs below the knees were mere sticks; his eyes also were puffy from constant headaches and were ringed with purple shadows. They did not look directly at anyone; his gaze wandered into other realms, and he often forgot the people with whom he spoke. The headaches were made worse by his custom of walking uncovered in the midday sun, to receive its rays of benediction upon his head. But the rays of Aton shed no blessing; they poisoned him so that he raved and saw evil visions. Perhaps his god was like himself, too liberal with his loving kindness, too overwhelming and profuse for his blessing to be other than a blight to all it touched.

In Pharaoh's lucid moments, when I applied wet cloths to his head and administered mild sedatives to soothe the pain, his dark, afflicted gaze would rest upon me in such unspeakable disillusion that my heart was moved for him in his weakness and I loved him; I would have sacrificed much to spare him this anguish.

He said to me, "Sinuhe, can it be that my visions are lies—the fruit of a sick brain? If so, then life is inconceivably hideous, and the world is ruled not by goodness but by a boundless evil. But this cannot be so, and my visions must be true. Do you hear, Sinuhe, the stiff-necked? My visions must be true although his sun no longer illuminates my heart, and my friends spit on my couch. I am not blind. I see into the hearts of men. I see into your heart also, Sinuhe—your weak and vacillating heart—and I know that you believe me mad. Yet I forgive you because of the light that once shone into that heart."

When pain assailed him he moaned and cried, "Men take pity on a sick animal, Sinuhe, and dispatch it with a club, and a spear brings release to the wounded lion—but to a man no one will show mercy!

385

My disillusion is more bitter to me than death because his light streams into my heart. Though my body die, yet shall my spirit live eternally. Of the sun am I born, Sinuhe; to the sun shall I return—and I long for that return because of the bitterness of my desolation."

With the coming of autumn he began to recover although it might have been better if I had let him go. But a physician may not allow his patient to die if his arts can avail to cure him—and this proves often the doctor's curse. Pharaoh's health improved and with this improvement came reserve; he would converse no further with me or with others. His eyes were hard now, and his solitude profound.

He had spoken no more than the truth when he said that his friends spat on his couch, for having borne him five daughters Queen Nefertiti wearied of him and came to loathe him and sought by every means to cause him pain. When for the sixth time the seed quickened within her, the child in her womb was Pharaoh's in name only. She lost all restraint and took pleasure with anyone, even with my friend Thothmes. Her beauty was regal still although her spring had flowered and passed, and in her eyes and her mocking smile lay something that men found irresistible. She conducted her intrigues among Pharaoh's adherents, to alienate them from him. So the circle of protecting love about him thinned and melted away.

Her will was strong, her understanding disturbingly acute. A woman who combines malice with intelligence and beauty is dangerous indeed—more dangerous still when she can add to this the power of a royal consort. For too many years Nefertiti had been content to smile and to rule by her beauty, to find delight in jewels, wine, verses, and adulation. Now, after the birth of the fifth daughter, something seemed to snap; she believed then that she would never bear a son and laid the blame for this upon Akhnaton. It must be remembered that in her veins ran the black blood of Eie the priest, the blood of injustice, treachery, and ambition.

Let it be said in her defense that never until now could an ill word have been spoken of her; no scandal about her was uttered abroad. She had been faithful; she had surrounded Pharaoh Akhnaton with the tenderness of a loving woman, defending his madness and believing in his visions. Many were amazed at her sudden transformation and saw in it a token of the curse that brooded like a stifling cloud over Akhetaton. So great was her fall that she was reputed to take pleasure with servants and Shardanas and hewers of tombs, though I will not believe this. When once people find something to talk of, they love to exaggerate and make more of it than the facts will warrant.

386

However this may be, Pharaoh shut himself away in his solitude. His food was the bread and gruel of the poor, and his drink was Nile water, for he desired to regain clarity by the purification of his body, in the belief that meat and wine had darkened his sight.

From the outside world no more joyful tidings came to Akhetaton. Aziru sent many tablets from Syria full of remonstrance and complaint. His men desired to return to their homes, he said, to tend their flocks and herds, to till their fields and enjoy their wives, for they were lovers of peace. But robber bands, armed with Egyptian weapons and led by Egyptian officers, made continual raids into Syria from the Sinai desert and were a permanent danger to the country, so that Aziru could not allow his men to return home. The commandant in Gaza was also behaving in an unbecoming manner and in contravention of the peace treaty, both in the spirit and the letter. He closed the gates of the city to peaceful traders and admitted only those whom he thought fit. Aziru made many other complaints and said that anyone save himself would long ago have lost all patience, but that he was long suffering because of his love of peace. Yet unless an end were put to these incidents, he would not answer for the outcome.

Babylon likewise was incensed at Egypt's competition for the Syrian grain markets; King Burnaburiash was far from content with the presents he had received from Pharaoh and put forward many demands.

The Babylonian ambassador in Akhetaton pulled his beard, shrugged his shoulders, and threw out his hands, saying, "My master is like a lion that rises uneasily in its lair and sniffs the wind, to learn what the wind will bring. He set his hopes on Egypt, but if Egypt is too poor to send him gold enough to hire strong men and build chariots, I do not know what will come of it. Though my master will ever prove a good friend to a powerful and wealthy Egypt, the friendship of a poor and impotent country is of no value to him, but rather a burden. I may say that my master was severely shocked and surprised when Egypt in its weakness yielded Syria. Everyone is his own nearest neighbor, and Babylon must consider Babylon."

A Hittite deputation, among which were many distinguished chiefs, now arrived at Akhetaton. These men declared that they had come to confirm the hereditary friendship between Egypt and the land of Hatti and at the same time to acquaint themselves both with the customs of Egypt, of which they had heard much that was good, and with the Egyptian army, from whose arms and discipline they believed they might learn a great deal. Their behavior was cordial and correct, and they brought munificent presents to the officers of the household. Among the gifts they offered to young Tut, Pharaoh's son-in-law, was a knife of blue metal, keener and stronger than all other knives. I was the only other in Akhetaton in possession of such a blade—one that had been given me by a Hittite harbor master, as I have related—and I counseled Tut to have his also set in gold and silver in the Syrian manner. Tut was so greatly delighted with this weapon that he said he would have it with him in his tomb. He was a delicate, sickly boy who thought of death more often than do most children of his age.

These Hittite chiefs were indeed agreeable and cultured men. Their large noses, resolute chins, and their eyes that were like those of wild creatures entranced the women of the court. From morning till night and from night till morning they were brilliantly entertained in the palaces of the great.

They said smiling, "We know that many dreadful things are told of our land by the invention of envious neighbors. We are therefore delighted to be able to appear before you in person so that you may see for yourselves that we are a cultured nation and that many of us can read and write. We are also peaceful and do not seek war; we seek only such knowledge as may be useful to us in our endeavors to educate and instruct our people. Do not believe the nonsense that is talked about us by the fugitives from Mitanni. They are bitter because in their fear they abandoned their country and all that was theirs. We can assure you that no evil would have befallen them if they had remained. But you must understand that the land of Hatti is cramped and we have many children, for the great Shubbililiuma takes great delight in children. Therefore we need space for our offspring and new grazing grounds for our cattle. And further, we could not endure to see the oppressions and wrongs that prevailed in the Land of Mitanni—indeed, the natives themselves appealed to us for help, and we marched into their country as liberators not conquerors. In Mitanni there is room enough for ourselves and our children and our cattle and we do not meditate further annexations, for we are a peace-loving people."

They raised their goblets with arms held straight and spoke in praise of Egypt, while the women gazed with desire at their sinewy necks and wild eyes.

And they said, "Egypt is a glorious land, and we love it. In our country also there may be something for Egyptians to learn—such Egyptians as are friendly toward us and desire to acquaint themselves with our customs."

388

They spoke many fair words to the eminent of Akhetaton, who dealt with them frankly, concealing nothing. But to my mind these strangers brought with them the smell of corpses. I remembered their bleak land and the sorcerers spitted on stakes by the roadside, and I did not mourn when they left Akhetaton.

The city had changed. Its inhabitants had been infected by some frenzy, and never before had people eaten and drunk and played so feverishly as at this time. But the gaiety was unwholesome, for they reveled only to forget the future. Often a deadly stillness would fall over Akhetaton so that laughter froze in men's throats and they looked at one another in fear, forgetting what they had been about to say. Artists also were gripped by this singular fever. They drew and painted and carved more diligently than ever as if they felt that time was slipping through their hands. They exaggerated truth to a fantastic degree; distortion grew beneath their chisels and pencils; they vied with one another to produce ever more strange and extravagant forms until they vowed they could represent a feature or a movement by a few lines and patches.

I said to my friend Thothmes, "Pharaoh Akhnaton raised you from the dust and made you his friend. Why do you carve his likeness as if you bitterly hated him? Why have you spat on his couch and outraged his friendship?"

Thothmes said, "Do not meddle with things you fail to understand, Sinuhe. Perhaps I hate him, but I hate myself more. The fire of creation burns within me, and my hands have never been so skillful as now. Perhaps it is when the artist is unsatisfied and hates himself that he best creates—better than when he is content and full of love. I create all from within myself, and in every piece of sculpture I hew myself in stone, to survive eternally. There is no one like me: I surpass all others and for me there are no rules to break. In my art I stand above rules and am more god than man. When I create form and color, I vie with Aton and outdo him, for all that Aton creates is perishable but what I create is eternal."

When he spoke thus, he had been drinking, and I forgave him his words, for torment burned in his face and from his eyes I saw that he was profoundly unhappy.

During this time the harvest was gathered in from the fields, the river rose and fell, and it was winter. With winter famine came to the land of Egypt, and no one could tell what new disaster the morrow might bring. News came that Aziru had opened the greater number of the Syrian cities to the Hittites and that the light chariots of these had driven across the Sinai desert, attacking Tanis and laying waste the surrounding country.

2

This news brought Eie in haste from Thebes and Horemheb from Memphis, to take counsel with Pharaoh Akhnaton and save what might be saved. In my capacity of physician I was present at this meeting, fearing lest Pharaoh become overexcited and fall ill because of the calamities of which he must hear. But Pharaoh was reserved and cold and remained master of himself throughout.

Eie the priest said to him, "The storehouses of Pharaoh are empty, and the land of Kush has not paid tribute this year although I had set my hopes upon those revenues. Great hunger prevails in the land, and the people are digging up the water plants from the mud and eating the roots; they also eat locusts and beetles and frogs. Many have perished and many more must do so. Even with the strictest distribution Pharaoh's grain is insufficient, while that of the merchants is too dear for the people to buy. The minds of all are possessed of great dread. Countrymen fly to the cities, and town dwellers fly to the land, and all say that this is the curse of Ammon and that it is Pharaoh's new god that has brought them this suffering. Therefore, Pharaoh Akhnaton, be reconciled with the priests and restore to Ammon his power, that the people may worship him and be pacified. Give him back his land that he may sow it, for the people dare not. Your land also lies unsown because the people believe it is accursed. Be reconciled with Ammon while there is yet time, or I wash my hands of the consequences."

But Horemheb said, "Burnaburiash has bought peace from the Hittites, and Aziru, yielding to their pressure, has become their ally. The numbers of their troops in Syria are as the sands of the sea and their chariots as the stars in the sky. They spell the doom of Egypt, for in their cunning the Hittites have carried water into the desert in jars. Having no fleet, they have carried thither infinite quantities of water so that when spring comes even a mighty army may cross the desert without succumbing to thirst. They bought in Egypt a large number of the jars, and the merchants who sold them have dug their own graves. The chariots of Aziru and of the Hittites have made reconnaissance raids into Tanis and into Egyptian territory and have thereby broken the peace. The damage they have done is indeed trivial, but I have set tales afoot of terrible devastation, and of the cruelty of the

Hittites, so that the people are ripe for battle. There is yet time, Pharaoh Akhnaton! Let the horns sound, let the banners fly—declare war! Gather together all those able to bear arms on the training grounds, call in all the copper in the country for spears and arrowheads, and your sovereignty shall be saved. I myself will save it by an incomparable war; I will defeat the Hittites and reconquer Syria for you. I can do all this if Egypt's resources be placed at the disposal of the army. Hunger makes warriors even of cowards. Ammon and Aton are all one to me; the people will forget Ammon once they are at war. Their unrest will find outlet against the enemy, and a victorious conflict will establish your power more firmly than before. I promise you a war of conquest, Pharaoh Akhnaton, for I am Horemheb, the Son of the Falcon. I was born to great deeds, and this is the hour for which I have been waiting all my life."

When Eie heard this he said hastily, "Do not believe Horemheb, Pharaoh Akhnaton, my dear son! Falsehood speaks with his tongue, and he is lusting for your power. Be reconciled with the priests of Ammon and declare war, but do not put Horemheb in command. Give it to some tested veteran who has studied in the old writings the arts of war as practiced in the times of the great Pharaohs, a man in whom you can place full trust."

Horemheb said, "Did we not now stand in Pharaoh's presence, Eie the priest, I would punch your dirty nose. You measure me by your own measure and betrayal speaks with your tongue, for you have in secret already negotiated with the priests of Ammon and come to terms with them behind Pharaoh's back. I will not fail the boy whose weakness I once shielded with my shoulder cloth by the hills of Thebes; my goal is the greatness of Egypt, and only I can save it."

Pharaoh asked, "Have you spoken?"

They answered with one voice, "We have spoken."

Then Pharaoh said, "I must watch and pray before I make my decision. Tomorrow summon all the people together—all those who love me, both high and low, lords and servants. Call also the quarrymen and stone masons from their town. I will speak through these to all my people and reveal to them my purpose."

They did as he commanded and bade the people assemble the next day, Eie in the belief that he would be reconciled with Ammon, Horemheb in the hope that he would declare war on Aziru and the Hittites. All that night Pharaoh watched and prayed and paced incessantly through his rooms, taking no food and speaking to none, so that as his physician I was concerned for him. On the following day he was

391

carried before the people. He sat on his throne, and his face was clear and radiant as he raised his hands and spoke.

"By reason of my weakness there is now famine in the land of Egypt; by reason of my weakness the enemy threatens our borders. The Hittites are now preparing to invade Egypt through Syria, and soon their feet will be treading the black soil. All this has come to pass because of my weakness—because I have not clearly heard the voice of my god or performed his will. Now my god has revealed himself to me. Aton has appeared to me, and his truth burns in my heart so that I am no longer either weak or doubting. I overthrew the false god, but in the infirmity of my purpose I allowed other gods to reign by the side of Aton, and the shadow of them has darkened Egypt. On this day all the old gods must fall, that the light of Aton may prevail as the only light throughout the land of Kem. On this day the old gods must vanish and Aton's kingdom on earth begin!"

When the crowds heard this, a ripple of horror ran through them, and many prostrated themselves before Pharaoh.

But Akhnaton raised his voice and continued with firmness, "Ye who love me, go now and overthrow the old gods in the land of Kem. Break down their altars; smash their images; pour away their holy water; pull down their temples; expunge their names from all inscriptions—enter the very tombs to do so—that Egypt may be saved. Officers, grasp clubs in your hands; sculptors, exchange your chisels for axes; workmen, take your sledge hammers and go forth into every province, every city and village, to overturn the old gods and efface their names. Thus will I liberate Egypt from the thralldom of evil."

Many fled from him aghast, but Pharaoh drew a deep breath, and his face glowed in exaltation as he cried, "May Aton's kingdom come on earth! From this day forward let there be neither slave nor lord, neither master nor servant; let all be equal and free in the sight of Aton! No one shall be bound to till the land of another or grind another's mill, but each man shall choose the work he will do and be free to come and go as he pleases. Pharaoh has spoken."

There was no further stir among the multitude. All stood dumb and motionless, and as they stared at Pharaoh, he grew in their sight, and the shining ecstasy in his countenance so dazzled them that they raised a shout of fervor and said to one another, "Such a thing was never before seen, yet truly his god speaks through him and we must obey."

The people dispersed in a ferment with bickering among themselves. Some came to blows in the streets, and the adherents of Pharaoh slew old men who spoke against him.

But when the people had dispersed, Eie said to Pharaoh, "Akhnaton, throw away your crown and break the crook, for the words you have spoken have already overturned your throne."

Pharaoh Akhnaton replied, "My words have brought immortality to my name, and I shall hold sway in the hearts of men from everlasting to everlasting."

Then Eie rubbed his hands together, spat on the ground before Pharaoh, and rubbed the spittle into the dust with his foot as he said, "If this is to be the way of it, I wash my hands and act as I think best. I am not answerable to a madman for my actions."

He would have gone, but Horemheb seized him by the arm and neck and held him easily although Eie was a powerful man.

Horemheb said, "He is your Pharaoh! You shall do his bidding, Eie, and not betray him. If you betray him, I will run you through the belly though I have to summon a regiment to do it. His madness certainly is deep and dangerous, yet I love him and will stand fast at his side because I have sworn him my oath. There is a spark of reason in his raving. If he had done no more than overthrow the old gods, civil war would have followed. In freeing the slaves from mill and field, he spoils the priests' game and gains the people to his side, even if the result be greater confusion than before. It is all one to me—but, Pharaoh Akhnaton, what shall we do with the Hittites?"

Akhnaton sat with his hands limp upon his knees and said nothing. Horemheb went on, "Give me gold and grain, arms and chariots, horses, and full authority to hire warriors and summon the guards to the Lower Land, and I think I can withstand the onslaught of the Hittites."

Then Pharaoh raised his bloodshot eyes to him, and the glow faded from his face as he said, "I forbid you to declare war, Horemheb. If the people desire to defend the Black Land, I cannot prevent it. Grain and gold—to say nothing of arms—I have none to give you, and if I had, you should not have it, for I will not meet evil with evil. You may make your dispositions for the defense of Tanis, but shed no blood and defend yourselves only if attacked."

"Be it as you say," said Horemheb. "Let lunacy prevail! I will die in Tanis at your command, for without grain and gold the most valiant army cannot long survive. But no doubts or half measures! I will defend myself according to my own good sense. Farewell!"

He went, and Eie also took his leave of Pharaoh, with whom I remained alone. He looked at me with eyes filled with unspeakable weariness and said, "Virtue has gone out of me with my words,

393

Sinuhe, yet even in my weakness I am happy. What do you mean to do?"

I looked at him in bewilderment, and smiling slightly he asked, "Do you love me, Sinuhe?"

When I confessed that I loved him, his madness notwithstanding, he said, "If you love me, you know what you have to do."

My mind rose up against his will, although inwardly I well knew what he required of me. At length I said in irritation, "I fancied you had need of me as a physician, but if not, then I will go. It is true I shall make but a poor hand at overturning the images of gods, and my arms are overweak for wielding a sledge hammer, but your will be done. The people will flay me alive and crush my head with stones and hang my body head downward from the walls, but how should that concern you? I will go then to Thebes, where there are many temples and where the people know me."

He made no answer and I left him in wrath.

On the following day Horemheb boarded his ship for Memphis, whence he was to proceed to Tanis. Before he went, I promised to lend him as much gold as I could lay my hands on in Thebes and to send him half the grain I possessed. The other half I thought to put to my own uses. Perhaps it was just this failing that determined my whole life: half I gave to Akhnaton and half to Horemheb. To no one did I give the whole.

3

Thothmes and I made the journey to Thebes, and while we were yet far from it, corpses came drifting downstream toward us. Swollen and rocking they came; the shaven heads of priests were to be seen among them, men of high and low degree, guards and slaves. The crocodiles had no need to swim upstream, for in cities and villages throughout the length of the river great numbers lost their lives and were cast into the Nile.

When we came to Thebes, many parts of the city were on fire. Even from the City of the Dead flames were leaping, for the people were robbing the tombs and burning the embalmed bodies of priests. Frenzied crosses hurled horns into the water and beat them down with stakes until they drowned, from which we deduced that the old gods had already been overthrown and that Aton had conquered.

We went straight to the Crocodile's Tail where we met Kaptah. He had put off his fine clothes, muddied his hair, and assumed the gray garment of the poor. He had also removed the gold plate from his eye and was now zealously serving drinks to ragged slaves and armed porters from the harbor.

"Rejoice, my brothers," he said, "for this is a day of great happiness! There are now neither lords nor slaves, neither high nor low, but all are free to come and go as they will. Today drink wine at my expense. I hope you will remember my tavern should fortune favor you and enable you to come by silver and gold in the temples of the false gods or in the houses of bad masters. I am a slave like yourselves and was born so, in proof of which behold my eye, which a cruel master blinded with his stylus when angry with me for having drunk a jar of his beer and refilled it with my own water. Such wrongs will never again be wrought. No one will ever again labor with his hands or feel the rod because he is a slave; all shall be joy and jubilation, leaping and pleasure continually."

Not until he had babbled thus far did he notice Thothmes and myself. Looking somewhat foolish, he led us to a private room.

He said, "You would be wise to dress in cheaper clothes and to soil your hands and faces, for slaves and porters roam the streets praising Aton. In Aton's name they beat everyone who seems to them too fat and who has never labored with his hands. They have forgiven me my paunch because I was once a slave and because I have distributed grain among them and let them drink for nothing. Tell me what ill fortune brings you to Thebes just now, for in these days it is a most unhealthy place for those of high rank."

We showed him our axes and sledge hammers and told him that we had come to overturn the images of false gods and to hew away their names from all inscriptions.

Kaptah nodded sagely and said, "Yours may be a clever plan and acceptable to the people so long as they do not learn who you are. Many changes are on the way, and the horns will be revenged for your deeds if ever they return to power. I cannot believe that this to-do will long continue, for where are the slaves to get their grain? And in their unbridled violence they have done such deeds as cause the crosses to doubt and to turn horn so as to restore order."

"You spoke of grain, Kaptah," I said. "Know that I have promised half our grain to Horemheb that he may wage war against the Hittites, and this you must immediately ship to Tanis. You shall have the other half milled and bake bread of the flour to be distributed to the starving people in all the cities and villages where our corn is stored. When your servants dispense this bread, they shall receive no payment but shall say, 'This is the bread of Aton; take ye and eat of it in his name, and give praise to Pharaoh and his god.'"

When Kaptah heard this, he tore his clothes, since they were but those of a slave, and cried out bitterly, "Lord, this beggars you, and where then shall I make my profit? You have caught Pharaoh's madness: you stand on your head and walk backward. Woe is me, poor wretch, that ever I should see this day! Not even the scarab will help us, and no one will bless you for the bread. Moreover, that damned Horemheb sends impudent answers to my demands, telling me to come myself and fetch the gold I have lent him in your name. He is worse than any robber, this friend of yours, for a robber takes what he takes, while Horemheb promises interest on what he borrows, thus tormenting his creditors with vain hopes so that in the end they burst their livers in exasperation. I see from your eyes that you are in earnest and that my lamentations are vain, and I must comply with your will although it will make you poor."

We left Kaptah to fawn on the slaves and to haggle over the sacred vessels and other valuables that the porters had stolen from the temples. All honest people had withdrawn into their houses and barred the doors; the streets were deserted, and some of the temples in which the priests had taken refuge had been set alight and were still burning. We entered the plundered temples to cut away the names of the gods and there met other adherents of Pharaoh engaged in the same task. We swung our axes and sledges so vigorously that the sparks flew. Every day our zeal increased, and we labored in order to avert our eyes from all that went on.

The people suffered hunger and want, and when the slaves and porters had rejoiced for a time in their freedom, they formed themselves into bands, which broke into rich men's houses to distribute their corn and oil and wealth among the poor. Kaptah hired men to grind corn and bake bread, but the people stole the bread from his servants, saying, "This bread has been filched from the poor, and it is but right that it should be shared among them." No one praised my name although I beggared myself in a single month.

Forty days and forty nights passed in this way, with the turmoil in Thebes growing steadily worse. Men who had once weighed gold stood begging in the streets while their wives sold their jewels to slaves so as to buy bread for their children. At the end of this period Kaptah came stealing to my house in the darkness and said, "My lord, it is time for you to fly. Aton's kingdom is soon to fall, and I believe no honest man will regret it. Law and order will be restored—but first the crocodiles must be fed, and more copiously than ever before, for the priests purpose to liberate Egypt from evil blood."

I asked him how he knew this and he answered innocently, "Have I not always been a faithful horn, and in secret worshiped Ammon? I have lent liberally to his priests, for they pay good interest and pawn his land for gold. Eie has made an agreement with the priests in order to preserve his own life, so the priests have the guards on their side. The leading men in Egypt have once more attached themselves to Ammon; the priests have summoned Negroes from the land of Kush, and the Shardanas, who have been plundering the country districts, are now in their pay. Indeed, Sinuhe, the mills will soon be turning again, but the bread which shall be baked of that flour will be Ammon's bread not Aton's. The gods are returning, the old order is coming back, and all will be as before, praise be to Ammon! For I am already weary of this confusion despite the riches it has brought me."

I was deeply agitated by his words, and said, "Pharaoh Akhnaton will never agree to this."

But Kaptah smiled slyly, rubbed his blind eye with his forefinger, and said, "He will not be asked! The city of Akhetaton is already doomed and all who stay there shall die the death. Once the rebels have the power in their own hands, they will block all the roads thither so that the inhabitants must starve. They demand that Pharaoh shall return to Thebes and prostrate himself before Ammon."

Then my thoughts cleared, and I saw before me the face of Pharaoh, and those eyes, which mirrored a disillusionment more bitter than death.

I said, "Kaptah, this iniquity must never be! We have walked many roads together, you and I. Let us walk this way together also, to the end. Poor though I now am, yet you are still rich. Buy arms; buy spears and arrows; buy all the clubs you can lay hands upon. With your gold buy the guards into your service. Distribute the weapons among the slaves and porters of the harbors. I do not know what will come of it, Kaptah, but the world has never yet seen such an opportunity as this to make all things new. When the land and the wealthy estates have been shared out, when the houses of the affluent are inhabited by the poor and their gardens are made playgrounds for the children of slaves, then assuredly the people will be pacified. Each shall then come by his own, each work as best pleases him, and all things shall be better than before."

But Kaptah trembled and said, "Lord, I have no intention of working with my hands in my old age. Already they have set eminent men to turning millstones, while their wives and daughters serve the slaves and porters in the pleasure houses. There is nothing good in any of this but only evil. My lord Sinuhe, do not require of me to tread this path. When I think of it, I think also of that dark house I once entered in your company. I vowed never to speak of that again, but now I speak because I must. Lord, you have once again resolved to enter a dark house, ignorant of what awaits you—and it may be that a rotting monster and a stinking death await you. If we are to judge by what we have seen, we may suppose that Pharaoh Akhnaton's god is as terrible as that of Crete, that he forces the best and most gifted men of Egypt to dance before bulls and leads them into a dark house whence there is no return. No, lord! I do not follow you a second time into the house of Minotauros."

And he neither wept nor protested as before but spoke to me solemnly, imploring me to turn from my purpose. At last he said, "If you will consider neither yourself nor me, think at least of Merit and of little Thoth, who love you. Take them away from here and hide them in a safe place. Once the mills of Ammon begin to turn, the life of no one here will be safe."

But my fervor had blinded me, and his warnings were to me foolishness. I said to him stiffly, "Who would persecute a woman and a little boy? In my house they dwell in safety. Aton conquers and must conquer, or life is not worth living. The people have sense, and they know that Pharaoh wishes them well. How could it be possible for them to return by their own desire to the tyranny of darkness and fear? Ammon's house is the dark house of which you speak, not Aton's. It will take more than a few bribed guards and scared nobles to overthrow him when he has the whole people behind him."

Kaptah rejoined, "I have said what I had to say and shall not repeat it. I burn to tell you a little secret, but as it is not mine I don't dare, and perhaps it would have no effect on you, obsessed as you now are. Don't blame me hereafter, lord, if later you gash your face and knees upon the stones in your despair. Don't blame me if the monster devours you. It is all one to me, being but a onetime slave with no children to bewail my death. Therefore, lord, I will follow you along this uttermost road, though I know it to be in vain. Let us enter the dark house together, lord, as before. If you will allow it, I will take a wine jar with me this time also."

On that same day Kaptah began to drink, and he drank from morning till night. Yet in his drunkenness he obeyed my commands and distributed arms in the harbor, and calling the officers of the guard

398

secretly to the Crocodile's Tail, he bribed them to take the part of the poor against the rich.

Hunger and riot prevailed in Thebes with this coming of Aton's kingdom on earth, and delirium seized the people's minds so that they were drunk without drinking. There was no longer any difference between those who bore the cross and those who did not, and the only things that counted were a weapon, a hard fist, and a loud voice. If anyone in the street saw a loaf in the hand of another he snatched it, saying, "Give me the loaf, for are we not all brothers in the sight of Aton?" And if he met another arrayed in fine linen, he said, "Give me your garment, for we are brothers in the name of Aton, and no man should be better dressed than his brother." If the horn was spied at a man's neck or on his clothes he was put to turning millstones or pulling down burned-out houses—that is, if he were not beaten to death and thrown to the crocodiles that lay in wait by the landing stages. Anarchy prevailed, and deeds of violence were daily multiplied.

Twice thirty days went by; no longer than this did Aton's kingdom on earth endure before it crumbled. For the black troops shipped from the land of Kush and the Shardanas hired by Eie encircled the city so that none might make his escape. The horn faction rallied in every quarter and were furnished by the priests with arms from the vaults of Ammon. Those who had no weapons hardened the ends of their sticks by fire, bound their pestles with copper and fashioned arrowheads from the ornaments of their women.

The horns rallied, and with them all who desired the good of Egypt. The quiet, patient, peaceful people also said, "We desire the return of the old order, for we have had more than our bellyful of the new, and Aton has plundered us enough."

4

But I, Sinuhe, said to the people, "It may be that wrong has trampled on right during these days and that many an innocent man has suffered for the guilty. Nevertheless, Ammon is still the god of darkness and terror and rules men through their foolishness. Aton is the only god, for he dwells within us and without, and there are no others. Fight for Aton, all you poor people and slaves, you bearers and servants, for you have no more to lose, and should Ammon win you would indeed taste slavery and death. Fight for Pharaoh Akhnaton's sake, for his like has never been seen on earth, and the god speaks through his mouth. Never has there been such an opportunity to renew the world; never will it be offered to you again!"

But the slaves and porters laughed aloud and said, "Do not prattle to us of Aton, Sinuhe, for all gods are alike and all Pharaohs are alike. But you are a good man, Sinuhe, although very simple, and you have bound our crushed arms and healed our broken knees without requiring gifts. Lay aside your club since in any case you lack the strength to swing it. You will never make a warrior, and the horns will slay you if they see the club in your hands. It matters little if we die, for we have soiled our hands with blood and lived well, sleeping beneath brilliant canopies and drinking from golden cups. Our feast is now at an end, and we mean to die with our weapons in our hands. Having tasted freedom and high living, we find slavery no longer to our liking."

Their talk made me ashamed. I threw aside my club and went to fetch the medicine chest from my house. For three days and three nights there was fighting in Thebes; many exchanged cross for horn and many more laid down their arms and hid in houses and wine cellars, in granaries and in empty baskets in the harbor. But the slaves and porters of the harbor fought on bravely. Three days and three nights they fought; they set fire to houses and at night fought by the light of the flames. Negroes and Shardanas set buildings alight also and robbed and knocked down all the folk they met, whether cross or horn. Their commander was that same Pepitaton who had allowed the slaughter in the Avenue of Rams, but now his name was Pepitamon again. He had been chosen by Eie because of his high rank and because he was the most learned of Pharaoh's officers.

I bound up the wounds of slaves and treated their broken heads at the Crocodile's Tail, while Merit tore up my clothes and Kaptah's and her own also to make bandages for them, and little Thoth carried wine to those whose pain must be soothed. On the last day the fighting was confined to the harbor and the poor quarter, where the war-skilled Negroes and Shardanas mowed down the people like standing crops, so that blood flowed along the narrow streets and over the quays into the river. Death never reaped so abundant a harvest in the land of Kem as it did on that day.

The leaders of the slaves came to the Crocodile's Tail while the conflict was raging, to refresh themselves with wine. They were drunk already with blood and the heat of battle. Smiting me on the shoulders with their hard fists, they said, "We have prepared for you a comfortable basket in the harbor where you can hide, Sinuhe, for doubtless

400

you have no desire to hang head downward beside us on the wall this evening? Is it not time for you to hide, Sinuhe? It is in vain you bind up wounds which are instantly open again."

But I told them, "I am a physician to the household, and none dare raise a hand against me."

At this they laughed, drank copiously, and returned to the fighting.

At length Kaptah came to me and said, "Your house is burning, Sinuhe, and the horns have stabbed Muti because she threatened them with her washing club. Now is the time for you to array yourself in the finest linen and assume all the emblems of your dignity. Leave these wounded slaves and robbers and follow me to an inner room, where we may prepare ourselves to receive the priests and officers."

Merit also put her arms about my neck and implored me, saying, "Save yourself, Sinuhe; if not for your own sake, then for mine and little Thoth's."

But grief, and lack of sleep, and death, and the din of battle had so befuddled me that I no longer knew my own heart, and said, "What care I for my house, for myself, or for you and Thoth! The blood that flows here is the blood of my brothers in the sight of Aton, and if Aton's kingdom fall, I have no desire to live."

But why I spoke thus wildly I do not know; it was another speaking, and not my vacillating heart.

Nor do I know whether I should have had time to fly, for shortly afterward the Shardanas and Negroes broke open the tavern door and forced their way in, led by a priest whose head was shaven and whose face gleamed with sacred oil. They began slaughtering the wounded. The priest put out their eyes with a sacred horn while the paint-striped Negroes jumped on them with joined feet so that the blood spurted from their wounds.

The priest cried, "This is the den of Aton; let us purify it with fire!" Before my very face they smashed in the head of little Thoth and slew Merit with a spear as she sought to protect him. I could not prevent it, for the priest struck me on the head with his horn, and my cry was stifled in my throat, after which I knew no more.

I came to myself in the alley outside the Crocodile's Tail, and at first I did not know where I was, fancying that I had been dreaming or that I was now dead. The priest had gone and the soldiers had laid aside their spears and were drinking the wine Kaptah set before them, while their officers urged them with their silver-braided whips to continue the struggle. The Crocodile's Tail was ablaze, for it was paneled with wood and burned like dry reeds on the shore. Then I remem-

401

bered everything and tried to stand, but my strength failed me. I began to crawl on hands and knees toward the burning door and into the fire, to find Merit and Thoth. My hair was singed off and my clothes caught fire, but Kaptah hastened to me crying out and lamenting. He dragged me from the flames and rolled me in the dust until the fire in my clothes was put out.

At this spectacle the soldiers laughed aloud, and Kaptah said to them, "Truly he is a little mad, for the priest hit him on the head with his horn and will no doubt receive punishment in due course. This is Pharaoh's physician, and it is not well for anyone to raise a hand against him. He is a priest of the first grade although he has been compelled to don shabby clothes and hide the symbols of his dignity so as to escape the fury of the people."

But I sat in the dust of the street, holding my head in my burned hands. The tears poured from my scorched eyes as I mourned and wept, "Merit, Merit! My Merit!"

But Kaptah nudged me wrathfully, saying, "Silence, you fool! Have you not brought enough misfortune on us by your idiocy?"

When I was quiet, he brought his face close to mine and said bitterly, "May this bring you to your senses, lord, for now indeed you have had full measure, and fuller than you know. I tell you, though it is now too late, that Thoth was your son, conceived when first you lay with Merit. I tell you this that you may gather your wits about you. She would not tell you because she was proud and lonely and because you put her aside for the sake of Pharaoh and Akhetaton. He was of your blood, that little Thoth, and had you not been raving mad you must have seen your eyes in his eyes and known again that line of lip. I would have given my life to save him, but I could not because of your madness, and Merit would not leave you. By reason of your madness they died. I hope that you will now come to your senses, lord."

I stared at him thunderstruck.

"Is this thing true?"

But I needed no reply. I sat on in the dust of the street, dry eyed, feeling no pain from my wound. All within me was cold and tight, and my heart closed up so that I was indifferent to all that went on about me.

The Crocodile's Tail stood in flames and with it burned Thoth's little body, and Merit's in its loveliness. Their bodies burned among those of butchered slaves so that I could not even preserve them to eternal life. Thoth was my son, and if what I believed was true, the holy blood of the Pharaohs had run in his veins as it ran in mine. If

I had known this, everything would have been different since a man may do for his son what he would not do for himself alone. But now it was too late. I sat in the dust of the street amid the smoke and flying sparks, and the flames from their bodies scorched my face.

Kaptah carried me to Eie and Pepitamon, for the fighting was over. The poor quarter was still in flames, but they sat in judgment on golden thrones on the stone quay, while soldiers and horns led forward prisoners for trial. Everyone caught with a weapon in his hand was hung head downward from the wall, and everyone caught with stolen goods on him was cast into the river to feed the crocodiles. Everyone found wearing the cross of Aton was flogged and sent to forced labor. The women were handed over for the pleasure of the soldiers, and the children were given to Ammon to be brought up in the temples. So death raged by the waterside in Thebes, and Eie showed no mercy for he desired to win the favor of the priests. He said, "I cleanse the evil blood from the land of Egypt!"

Pepitamon was exceedingly wroth because slaves had plundered his house and opened the doors of the cats' cages. They had taken the cats' milk and cream home to their children so that the beasts had starved and run wild. He also was merciless, and within two days the walls of the city were crammed with the bodies of men hung by the heels.

In jubilation the priests re-erected the image of Ammon in his temple and made very great sacrifice to him.

Eie appointed Pepitamon governor of Thebes and hastened to Akhetaton to compel Pharaoh Akhnaton to abdicate. He said to me, "Come with me, Sinuhe, for I may need the help of a physician to bow Pharaoh to my will."

And I answered, "Certainly I will come, Eie, for I desire my pleasure to be full."

But he did not understand what I meant.

5

Thus I sailed back to Akhetaton with Eie. Away in Tanis Horemheb had also heard of these events, and he made speed to man the warships and hasten up the river to Akhetaton. All was quiet in the cities and villages as he came; the temples were open once more, and the images of the gods had been restored to their places. He hastened to reach Akhetaton at the same time as Eie, to compete with him for power, so he pardoned all slaves who laid down their arms and punished no one who of his own free will exchanged the cross of Aton for Ammon's horn. The people praised him for his clemency, although it did not come from his heart but rather from his desire to save fit men for the fighting.

Akhetaton was a domain accursed; priests and horns guarded all the roads leading thither and slew every fugitive from it who refused to make sacrifice to Ammon. They had also barred the river with copper chains that none might make his escape that way. I did not recognize the city when I saw it again, for a deathly silence reigned in the streets, the flowers in the parks had withered, and the green grass had turned yellow now that no one watered the gardens. No birds sang in the sunshriveled trees, and all over the city hung the hideous odor of death. The families of high rank abandoned their houses, and their servants had been the first to flee, leaving all behind them, for no one dared to carry anything with him from the accursed city. The dogs had perished in their kennels, and the horses had starved in their stalls because the fugitive grooms had hamstrung them where they stood. Akhetaton the fair was already a dead city, breathing corruption, when I came.

But Pharaoh Akhnaton and his family lingered in the golden house. The most faithful among his servants had remained with him and also the elder members of the court, who could not conceive of a life elsewhere than with Pharaoh. They knew nothing of what had passed in Thebes because no courier had arrived in Akhetaton for a month. Provisions were running out, and by the will of Pharaoh their only food was the hard bread and the gruel of the poor. The more enterprising speared fish in the river or killed birds with their throwing sticks and ate this food in secret.

Eie the priest sent me first into the presence of Pharaoh, to tell him of all that had happened, because I was Pharaoh's trusted friend. So I went, but all within me was frozen. I felt neither joy nor sorrow, and even to Akhnaton my heart was closed. He raised his gray, haggard face with its dead eyes and said, 'Sinuhe, are you the only one to return? Where are all who were faithful to me? Where are those who loved me and whom I loved?"

I said to him, "The old gods rule again in Egypt, and in Thebes the priests make sacrifice to Ammon amid the rejoicing of the people. They have cursed you, Pharaoh Akhnaton, and they have cursed your city. They have cursed your name to all eternity and are already chipping it away from the inscriptions."

He moved his hand impatiently, and suffering was kindled again

404

in his face as he persisted, "I do not ask what has happened in Thebes. Where are my faithful ones and all whom I loved?"

I answered, "You still have your fair wife Nefertiti. Your children also are with you. Young Sekenre is spearing fish in the river, and Tut is playing at funerals with his dolls as usual. What do you care for any others?"

He answered, "Where is my friend Thothmes, who was your friend also and whom I loved? Where is he, the artist, by whose hand the very stones were imbued with eternal life?"

"He died for your sake, Pharaoh Akhnaton," I answered. "Negroes transfixed him with a spear and cast his body into the river to be devoured by crocodiles because he was faithful to you. Though he spat on your couch, do not think of that now that the jackal howls in his empty workshop."

Pharaoh Akhnaton raised his hand as if to brush a spider's web from his face; then he recited the names of those he had loved. Of some I said, "He died for your sake, Pharaoh Akhnaton." And at length, "The power of Aton has been crushed. The kingdom of Aton on earth is no more, and Ammon rules again."

He stared before him, and with an impatient movement of his bloodless hands he said, "Yes, yes. I know. My visions have told me of it all. The eternal kingdom cannot be contained within earthly boundaries. All shall be as before, and fear, hatred, and wrong shall rule the world. Better would it have been if I had died, and best of all if I had never been born to see all the evil that is done on earth."

His blindness so enraged me that I retorted heatedly, "You have not seen so much as the least part of the evil that has come about for your sake, Pharaoh Akhnaton! You have not seen your son's blood run over your hands, nor has your heart been frozen by the death cry of your beloved! Therefore your talk is empty, Pharaoh Akhnaton."

He said wearily, "Go from me then, Sinuhe, since I am evil. Go from me, and suffer no more upon my account. Go from me, for I am weary of your face—I am weary of all men's faces, for behind them all I see the faces of beasts."

But I sat on the floor before him and said, "Not so, Pharaoh; I will not go from you, for I will have my full measure. Eie the priest is coming, and at the northern boundary of your city the horns of Horemheb have sounded, and the copper chains that bar the river have been severed that he may sail to you."

He smiled slightly, threw out his hands, and said, "Eie and Horemheb, crime and violence: these then are my only followers now!"

405

Thereafter we said no more but listened to the gentle purring of the water clock until Eie the priest and Horemheb entered the presence of Pharaoh. They had disputed violently with one another, and their faces were dark with passion. They breathed heavily, and both talked at once without respect for Pharaoh.

Eie said, "Abdicate, Pharaoh Akhnaton, if you would preserve your life. Let Sekenre rule in your stead. Let him return to Thebes and make sacrifice to Ammon, and the priests will anoint him and set the red and white crown upon his head."

But Horemheb said, "My spear shall maintain the crown for you, Pharaoh Akhnaton, if you will return to Thebes and make sacrifice to Ammon. The priests may growl a little, but I will quiet them with my whip, and they will forget their grumbling when you declare a holy war to conquer Syria again for Egypt."

Pharaoh Akhnaton surveyed them both with a lifeless smile.

"I will live and die as Pharaoh," he said. "I will never submit myself to the false god, and I will never declare war and preserve my power by blood. Pharaoh has spoken."

With this he covered his face with a corner of his garment and went, leaving us three alone in the great room with the odor of death in our nostrils.

Eie spread out his arms helplessly and looked at Horemheb. Horemheb did the same and looked at Eie. I sat on the floor, for my knees had no more strength in them, and looked at both. Suddenly Eie smiled slyly and said, "Horemheb, you hold the spear and the throne is yours. Set on your head the two crowns you desire!"

But Horemheb laughed in derision and said, "I am not such a fool. Keep the dirty crowns if you want them. You know very well that we cannot go back to the old times again, for Egypt is threatened by war and famine. If I were to take the crown now the people would blame me for all the evil that must follow, and you would find it an easy matter to depose me when the time was ripe."

Eie said, "Sekenre, then, if he will agree to return to Thebes. If not he, then Tut; he will certainly comply. Their consorts are of the sacred blood. Let them bear the hatred of the people until the times improve."

"While you rule beneath their shadow!" said Horemheb.

But Eie replied, "You forget that you have the army and must meet the Hittites. If you can do this, there is no one more powerful in the land of Kem than yourself."

So they disputed until they perceived that they were bound to one another and could come to no solution save in alliance.

Eie said at last, "I freely admit that I have done my best to depose you, Horemheb. But now you have outgrown me, you Son of the Falcon, and I can no longer dispense with you. If the Hittites invade the country, I shall have no joy of my power, nor do I fancy that any Pepitamon could wage war against them, suitable though such may be as spillers of blood and executioners. Let this be the day of our alliance. Together we can rule the country, but divided we both fall. Without me your army is powerless, and without your army Egypt is lost. Let us swear by all the gods of Egypt that from this day forward we shall hold together. I am already an old man, Horemheb, and desire to taste the sweetness of power, but you are young and have your life before you."

"I do not desire the crowns but rather a good war for my ruffians," said Horemheb. "Yet I must have a pledge from you, Eie, or you will betray me at the first opportunity, so do not gainsay me. I know you!"

"What pledge would you have, Horemheb? Is not the army the only valid pledge?"

The face of Horemheb darkened as he glanced about the walls in hesitation and scraped his sandals on the stone floor as if he sought to wriggle his toes into the sand. He said at last, "I would have the Princess Baketaton to wife. Indeed, I mean to break the jar with her though heaven and earth should fall, and you cannot prevent me."

Eie cried, "Aha! Now I see what you are after; you are more astute than I thought and worthy of my respect. She has already changed her name back to Baketamon, and the priests have nothing against her. In her veins flows the sacred blood of the great Pharaoh. If you wed her, you win a legal right to the crown and a better right than the husbands of Akhnaton's daughters, for behind them is but the blood of the false Pharaoh. You have worked this out very cunningly, Horemheb, but I cannot approve—or at least not yet—for then I should be in your hands entirely and lack all authority over you."

But Horemheb cried, "Keep your dirty crowns, Eie! I desire her more than crowns, and I have desired her since the first time I beheld her beauty in the golden house. I seek to mingle my blood with that of the great Pharaoh, that future kings of Egypt may be the fruit of my loins. You desire only the crown, Eie. Take it when you consider the time ripe, and my spear shall support your throne. Give me the Princess, and I will not reign while you live—not though you should live long—for I have my life before me, as you say, and time to wait."

Eie rubbed his mouth with his hand, musing. As he mused his face brightened, for he perceived he had a bait by which he could lead

407

Horemheb in the ways that best pleased him. As I sat on the floor listening to their talk, I marveled at the human heart, which allowed these two to dispose of crowns while Pharaoh Akhnaton lived and breathed in the next room.

At length Eie said, "You have waited long for your princess, and may well wait a little longer, for you have first to wage a desperate war. It will take time to win the Princess's consent; she holds you in great contempt because you were born with dung between the toes. But I and I only have the means to incline her to you, and I swear to you, Horemheb, by all the gods of Egypt, that on the day when I set the red and white crown on my head I will with my own hand break the jar between you and the Princess. More I cannot do for you, and even thus I deliver myself into your hands."

Horemheb lacked patience to bargain further and said, "Be it so. Let us now bring this nonsense to a happy conclusion, and I do not think you will wriggle overmuch since you so earnestly desire these crowns—these playthings!"

In his excitement he had quite forgotten me, but when he caught sight of me again he said, disconcerted, "Sinuhe, are you still here? You have heard things not fit for unworthy ears, and I fear I must kill you, although unwillingly since you are my friend."

His words tickled me as I reflected how unworthy were these two men now dividing the crown between them, while I, sitting on the floor, was perhaps the worthiest man of any: the only male heir of the great Pharaoh whose sacred blood ran in my veins. Therefore I could not contain my laughter but pressed my hand over my mouth and tittered like an old woman.

Eie was greatly irritated and said, "It is unseemly in you to laugh, Sinuhe, for these are grave matters. We will not slay you, however, although you deserve it. It was well that you heard what passed. You are our witness. You can never speak of what you have heard here today, for we need you and will bind you to us. You too understand that it is high time for Pharaoh to die. As his physician you shall open his skull this very day and see to it that your knife goes deep enough for him to depart in the decent and traditional manner."

But Horemheb said, "I will not involve myself in this, for my hands are already dirty enough from having touched the hands of Eie. Yet what he says is true. Pharaoh Akhnaton must die if Egypt is to be saved; there is no other way."

I giggled again, then mastering myself I said, "As a physician I may not open his skull since there is insufficient reason and I am bound by the code of my profession. But be easy. As his friend I will mix him a good medicine. When he has drunk of it, he will sleep, never to waken again, and in this manner I bind myself to you so that from me you need never fear betrayal."

And I brought forth the fine glass vessel Hrihor had once given me and mixed its contents with wine in a golden cup; the smell of it was not unpleasant. I took the cup in my hand, and all three of us entered Pharaoh Akhnaton's room. He had removed the crowns; he had laid aside the whip and the crook and was resting on his couch with a gray face and bloodshot eyes.

Eie went up, took crowns and whip, and weighing these in his hands he said, "Pharaoh Akhnaton, your friend Sinuhe has mixed you a good potion. Drink it, be strengthened, and tomorrow we will talk again of sorrowful things."

Pharaoh sat up on his couch and took the cup in his hands, looking at each of us in turn, and his weary glance pierced me and sent a shiver through my spine. He said, "Men show mercy to a sick beast with a blow from a club. Have you mercy for me, Sinuhe? If so I thank you, for my disillusion is more bitter to my tongue than death, and death today is sweeter than the scent of myrrh."

"Drink, Pharaoh Akhnaton," I said. "Drink for Aton's sake."

And Horemheb said, "Drink, Akhnaton my friend. Drink that Egypt may be saved. With my shoulder cloth I will protect your weakness as once before, in the desert outside Thebes."

Pharaoh Akhnaton drank from the goblet, but his hand shook so that wine splashed down his chin. Then he gripped the cup in both hands and emptied it, and at last he sank back and laid his neck on the wooden rest. He said no word but stared with dim, bloodshot eyes into his visions. After a time he began to shiver as with cold. Horemheb slipped off his shoulder cloth and spread it over him, but Eie took the crowns in both hands and tried the feel of them upon his head.

So passed Pharaoh Akhnaton; I gave him death to drink, and he drank it from my hand. Yet why I did it I do not know, for a man does not know his own heart. I believe I did it less for Egypt's sake than for Merit's and for my son Thoth's. I did it less from love of Akhnaton than from bitterness, from hatred of all the evil he had brought about. But above all I did it because it was written in the stars that my measure should be full. When I saw him die, I believed that it was already full, but a man does not know his own heart, which is insatiable—more insatiable than a crocodile of the river.

When we had seen him die, we left the golden house, forbidding the servants to disturb him because he slept. Not until the following morning did they find his body and raise their voices in mourning. The golden house was filled with weeping, although I believe that the minds of many were easier for his death. But Queen Nefertiti stood tearless beside his bier, and the look on her face was such as none could interpret. She was touching Pharaoh Akhnaton's thin fingers with her beautiful hands and stroking his cheeks when I came, as my duty required, to attend his body to the House of Death. There I entrusted it to the corpse washers and embalmers, that they might preserve it for eternal life.

According to law and tradition, the young Sekenre was Pharaoh, but he was altogether beside himself with grief, and he stared about him unable to utter a sensible word, having been accustomed to take all his ideas from Pharaoh Akhnaton. Eie and Horemheb spoke to him and told him that he must now hasten to Thebes to make sacrifice to Ammon if he desired to keep the crown upon his head. But he did not believe them, being a childish boy and given to daydreaming.

He said, "I will make known the light of Aton to all people and build a temple to my father Akhnaton and worship him there as a god, for he was not like other men."

When Eie and Horemheb saw how stupid he was, they left him. On the following day when he went to spear fish in the river, it chanced that his reed boat overturned and his body was devoured by crocodiles. So the story went, but exactly how the matter fell out I do not know. I believe it was not Horemheb who had him slain but rather Eie, who was in haste to return to Thebes and keep his hold on the reins of government.

He and Horemheb next went to young Tut, who was playing on the floor in his room. He was playing at funerals, as his custom was, and his consort Akhsenaton played with him.

Horemheb said, "Come, Tut, it is time you rose from that dirty floor, for you are now Pharaoh."

Tut rose obediently and seating himself on the golden throne he said, "Am I Pharaoh? That does not surprise me, for I have ever felt superior to other people, and it is only right that I should be Pharaoh. With my whip I will punish all evildoers, and with my crook I will watch like a shepherd over all those who are pious and good."

Eie said, " Let us have no nonsense, Tut! You will do all I tell you without argument. First we will arrange a joyful procession into Thebes, and in Thebes you will bow down before Ammon in his great temple and make sacrifice to him. Then the priests will anoint you and set the red and white crown on your head. Do you understand?"

Tut reflected for a while, then said, "If I go to Thebes, will they build me a big tomb like the tombs of all the other Pharaohs? Will the priests fill it with playthings and golden chairs and fine beds? For the tombs of Akhetaton are narrow and dark, and I do not wish to have only paintings on the walls, but real toys, and my fine blue knife also, which the Hittites gave me."

"Assuredly the priests shall build you a fine tomb," said Eie. "You are a wise lad, Tut, to think first of your grave on becoming Pharaoh—wiser than you know. Tutankhaton is not a suitable name to bear before the priests of Ammon; from this day forward, therefore, let your name be Tutankhamon."

Tut made no objection to this but desired only to learn to write his new name since he did not know the characters by which the name of Ammon is represented. Thus for the first time the name of Ammon was written in Akhetaton. When Nefertiti learned that Tutankhamon was to be Pharaoh and that she herself had been quite overlooked, she arrayed herself in her loveliest dress, having anointed body and hair with rare ointments despite her widowhood, and went to Horemheb aboard his ship.

She said to him, "It is a preposterous thing for a boy yet in his non-age to become Pharaoh! Eie, my miscreant father, has taken him from my hands and rules Egypt in his name, although I am the queen consort and mother. Moreover men have looked on me with desire and called me a fair woman; I have even been called the fairest in all Egypt though that is exaggeration. Look on me, Horemheb, despite the sorrow that has dimmed my eyes and bowed my head. Yours is the spear, and together you and I might plan many things to the advantage of Egypt. I talk thus frankly to you because I think only of Egypt's good, and I know that my father, that accursed Eie, is a greedy and a stupid man who will do the land much harm."

Horemheb surveyed her, and Nefertiti let her robe fall open before him, saying that the cabin was very warm, and practiced every seduction. She knew nothing of Horemheb's secret pact with Eie, and even if—being a woman—she had guessed something of his desire for Baketamon, she fancied that she could easily supplant that inexperienced and haughty princess in his mind. But her beauty failed altogether to impress him.

Regarding her coldly he said, "I have been sufficiently dragged through the mire in this accursed city and am unwilling to defile myself still further with you, fair Nefertiti. I have letters to dictate concerning the war and lack the time to disport myself with you."

All this Horemheb related to me afterward, and although he must certainly have embroidered the facts, yet in the main the story was true. From that day forward Nefertiti hated Horemheb with a bitter hatred and did all she could to injure him and blacken his reputation. In Thebes she became the friend of Baketamon, whereby Horemheb suffered great injury as I shall later show. It would have been more prudent not to insult her but rather to keep her friendship and show kindness to her in her sorrow. But Horemheb was unwilling to spit on the couch of the dead Pharaoh. Strange though it may seem, Horemheb still loved Akhnaton, although he caused his name and image to be removed from all inscriptions and pulled down the temple of Aton in Thebes. As a proof of this I may tell how Horemheb ordered his followers to remove Akhnaton's body secretly from the tomb in Akhetaton to that of his mother in Thebes, that it might not fall into the hands of the priests. For the priests had desired to burn the body of Akhnaton and strew the ashes in the river. But these events took place much later.

6

As soon as Eie had Tutankhamon's consent he hastened to assemble many ships, and in these the whole court embarked. Akhetaton was abandoned by all save the embalmers in the House of Death, who were preparing the body of Akhnaton to live forever. The last of the inhabitants fled hastily and never looked behind them. In the golden house the eating and drinking vessels were left on the tables, while Tut's playthings lay abandoned about the floor in an eternal game of funerals.

Desert winds tore open the shutters; sand drifted over the floors where brilliant ducks flew through the ever green rushes and colored fish swam in salt water. The desert returned to the gardens of Akhetaton; fish pools dried up, irrigation ditches were blocked, and fruit trees withered. The mud of the house walls crumbled, roofs fell in, and the whole city decayed into ruins. Jackals howled through the empty halls, and on the soft, canopied couches they made their lairs. So perished the city of Akhetaton, as rapidly as Pharaoh Akhnaton had brought it to life.

The people of Thebes rejoiced greatly at the return of Ammon and the accession of the new Pharaoh. So foolish is the heart of man that he ever puts his hope in the future, learning nothing from his past errors and fancying that tomorrow must be better than today. The people lined the Avenue of Rams to greet their new Pharaoh with cries of joy and to strew flowers in his path.

But in the harbor and the poor quarter the ruins still smoldered; an acrid smoke arose from them and the river stank of carnage. Along the copings of the temple roofs, crows and vultures stretched their necks, too gorged to fly away. Here and there among the ruins and gutted houses, frightened women and children scrabbled after their household goods in the places where their dwellings had stood. I walked the quays, which still stank of stale blood, looking at the empty baskets and thinking of Merit and little Thoth, who had perished on Aton's account and through my madness.

My steps led me to the ruins of the Crocodile's Tail, and I thought of Merit, who had said to me, "Perhaps I am but the cushion to soften your loneliness when I am not your worn mat." I saw little Thoth; his cheeks and limbs were childishly soft, and he put his arm about my neck and laid his cheek to mine. With sharp smoke in my nostrils, I walked in the dust of the harbor, seeing before me the body of Merit transfixed and little Thoth's bloody nose and his hair matted and sticky with blood. I reflected that Pharaoh Akhnaton's death had been an easy one. I reflected also that nothing in the world is more terrible than the dreams of the Pharaohs, because the seed they sow is blood and death.

The jubilant shouts of the people reached my ears, as they greeted Pharaoh Tutankhamon in their delusion that this bewildered boy, whose thoughts ran only on a fine tomb, would root out injustice and restore peace and prosperity to the land of Kem.

I wandered thus wherever my feet led me, aware that I was alone and that my blood in Thoth had drained barrenly away. I cherished no hope of immortality; death was to me rather a rest and a sleep and the warmth of a brazier on a winter's night, Akhnaton's god had robbed me of my hope and my joy, and I knew that all gods dwelt in dark houses whence there is no return. Pharaoh Akhnaton had drunk death from my hands, but this held no consolation for me; with death he had drunk a most merciful oblivion. But I lived and could not forget. My heart was consumed with bitterness, and I nursed resentment against the people who were now bellowing before the temple like cattle, having learned nothing from the past.

My feet carried me to the ruins of the copperfounder's house; children hid themselves at my coming, and women digging amid the rubble for their pots and pitchers hid their faces when they saw me.

The mud walls of the house rose before me black with soot; the pool in the garden was dry and the boughs of the sycamore black and leafless. But a shelter, beneath which I saw a water jar, had been erected among the ruins. Muti came to meet me with earth in her graying hair, and limping because of her wound. She bowed before me on trembling knees and said in bitter mockery, "Blessed be the day that brings my lord home!"

More she could not utter. Her voice was strangled in acrimony. Squatting upon the ground, she hid her face in her hands. Her thin body had been wounded in many places by the horns of Ammon, but the wounds had cicatrized, and I could do nothing for them. I asked, "Where is Kaptah?"

"Kaptah is dead," she answered. "They say the slaves murdered him when they saw that he betrayed them and served wine to Pepitamon's men."

But I did not believe her, knowing that he could not die—knowing that whatever happened, Kaptah would live on.

Incensed by my skepticism, Muti cried, "It must be easy and pleasant for you to laugh now, Sinuhe—now that you have seen your Aton triumph! You men are all alike. Every evil in the world comes from men, for they never grow up. They remain boys; they throw stones at one another, strike one another—and their chief delight is to bring sorrow on those who love them and wish them well. Have I not always wished the best for you, Sinuhe? And how am I rewarded? With a lame leg, wounds in the body, and a handful of moldy corn! Yet I do not accuse you on my account, but on Merit's who was far too good for you and whom you knowingly and of set purpose sent to her death. I have wept my eyes dry for little Thoth, also, who was like my own son and for whom I baked honey cakes. But what do you care for all this! You come here smugly, with all your riches scattered, to rest beneath the roof I have raised here with such toil and difficulty, that I may feed you! I would wager much that before morning you will be whining for beer, and that in the morning you will beat me because I do not serve you as diligently as you would wish. You will set me to labor for you that you may lie idle. Such is the nature of men."

Thus she spoke, and her nagging was so homelike that I remembered Kipa and Merit, and my heart was flooded with such unspeakable sorrow that tears poured from my eyes.

At this she was much disconcerted and said, "You know very well,

Sinuhe, you hot-hearted man, that I mean no ill by what I say but speak only to instruct you. I still have a fistful of corn left, which I will grind and make into a good gruel. I will prepare a bed of dry rushes for you. Perhaps in a little while you will be able to follow your calling so that we may live. Do not concern yourself about this, for I have found washing to do in the houses of the rich, where there are quantities of bloodstained clothes, so that I can always earn something. Moreover, I fancy I can borrow a jar of beer from the pleasure houses where the soldiers have been billeted, to rejoice your heart."

Her words made me ashamed of my tears. I composed myself and said to her, "I did not come here to be a burden to you, Muti. I am soon going away and perhaps shall not return for a long time. For this reason I desired to see the house where I had been happy, to stroke the rough bark of the sycamore and touch the threshold that was worn by the feet of Merit and little Thoth. Give yourself no trouble for my sake, Muti. I shall send you a little silver if I can, that you may manage while I am gone. But I bless you for your words as if you were my own mother, for you are a good woman even though your tongue at times may sting like a wasp."

Muti sobbed and rubbed her nose with the back of her rough hand. She would not let me go but kindled a fire and prepared food for me from her meager store. I was compelled to eat lest I wound her, though every mouthful was near choking me.

Muti watched me, and with a shake of her head she snorted, "Eat, Sinuhe! Eat, you stiff-necked man, though the corn be moldy and the meal repugnant. I suppose you will now run your stupid head into all the nets and snares that come your way, but I can do nothing for you there. Eat, then, and gain strength, Sinuhe; come back again for I will faithfully await you. Have no concern for me, for old and lame though I be, yet I am exceedingly tough. I shall earn my bread well enough with washing and baking so long as there is any bread in Thebes if only you will come back again, lord."

So until darkness fell I sat among the ruins of my house, and Muti's fire shed a lonely glow into the sooty darkness. I reflected that it would be better if I never returned since I brought only sorrow and misfortune upon those who loved me—better to live and die alone, as I had come down the river on the night of my birth.

When the stars came out and the guards began to smite their shields with their spear shafts, to scare the people in the ruined alleys of the harbor, I said farewell to Muti and made my way once more to Pharaoh's golden house. As I walked along the streets toward the shore, the

415

night sky once more glowed red over Thebes and the lights of the great streets shone out; from the center of the city came the sound of music. For this was the night of Tutankhamon's enthronement, and Thebes was making festival.

7

But that same night the priests were laboring with great zeal in the temple of Sekhmet, clearing away the grass that had grown up between the flagstones, re-erecting the lionheaded image in its place, robing it in red linen, and adorning it with the emblems of war and devastation.

As soon as Eie had crowned Tutankhamon with the crowns of both kingdoms—the red crown and the white, papyrus and lily—he said to Horemheb, "Now is the hour, you Son of the Falcon! Let the horns sound and declare war! Let blood flow like a purifying wave over the land of Kem, that all may be as before and the people forget the memory of the false Pharaoh."

On the following day, when Tutankhamon in his golden house was playing at funerals with his dolls, in company with his royal consort —when the priests of Ammon, drunk with power, burned incense in the great temple and cursed the name of Pharaoh Akhnaton to all eternity—then Horemheb ordered the horns to be sounded at the corners of the streets. The copper gates of Sekhmet's temple were flung open, and at the head of picked troops Horemheb led the triumphal march along the Avenue of Rams, to make sacrifice to the goddess. Eie had his desire, for from the right hand of Pharaoh he ruled over the land of Kem. Now came Horemheb's turn, whose demand also was fulfilled, and I followed him to the temple of Sekhmet because he wished me to behold the greatness of his power.

Yet to his honor be it said that in the hour of his triumph he disdained all outward show and sought to impress the people by the simplicity of his demeanor. For this reason he drove to the temple in a heavy, workday chariot. No plumes waved above the heads of his horses; no gold gleamed on the wheel spokes. Instead, keen copper scythes slashed the air upon either side of the car. Behind him followed the ranks of the javelin throwers and bowmen. The thud of their bare feet on the stones of the Avenue of Rams was as deep and steady as the roar of the sea. The Negroes beat on drums fashioned of human skin.

Silent and awestruck the people beheld the stately figure erect in the

416

chariot, above the heads of all—beheld his troops who gleamed with health at a time when the whole country suffered want. They watched this progress in silence, as if suspecting that their sufferings were only now beginning. Horemheb halted before the temple of Sekhmet, stepped down from his chariot and entered, followed by his officers. The priests came to meet him with hands and robes splashed with fresh blood and led him before the image of Sekhmet. The goddess was arrayed in a red robe, moistened with the blood of the sacrifice so that it clung to her body, and the stone breasts rose proudly from the garment. In the twilight of the temple her savage lion's head seemed to move, and her jeweled eyes stared down as if alive on Horemheb as he crushed the warm hearts of the offerings in his hand and prayed for victory.

The priests leaped round about him, rejoicing, and gashing themselves with their knives, and they cried out with one voice, "Return as conqueror, Horemheb, Son of the Falcon! Return as conqueror, and the goddess will descend to you, living, and embrace you with her nakedness!"

But Horemheb did not allow the leaping and outcry of the priests to ruffle his composure; he performed the appointed rites with cool dignity and left the temple. Outside he raised his bloodstained hands and spoke to the waiting multitude.

"Harken to me, all people in the land of Kem! Harken to me, for I am Horemheb, the Son of the Falcon; in my hands I bear victory and deathless glory for all those who will follow me into the holy war. At this hour the chariots of the Hittites thunder over the Sinai desert; their vanguard lays waste the Lower Kingdom, and the land of Kem has never yet been threatened by so great a peril. The Hittites are coming, whose numbers are beyond reckoning and whose cruelty is an abomination to all men. They will lay waste your homes, put out your eyes, violate your wives, and carry off your children into slavery. Therefore the war I declare on them is a holy war; it is a war for your lives and for the gods of Kem. If all goes well, we will win back Syria when we have defeated the Hittites. Prosperity will return to us, and every man will receive full measure of corn and his full share in the spoils. Strangers have desecrated our country long enough; they have mocked at our weakness long enough and derided the impotence of our arms! The hour is now come for me to restore to Kem its military glory. Only by summoning our full strength can the day be won. Therefore, women of Egypt, twist your hair into bowstrings, and send out your husbands and your sons with rejoicing to the holy war! Egyptian men, forge your ornaments into arrowheads and follow me, and I will give you a war the like of which the whole circle of the world has never seen! The spirits of the great Pharaohs, and all the gods of Egypt—foremost among these Ammon, the exalted—fight at our side. Harken to me, all people! Horemheb, the Son of the Falcon, has spoken!"

He ceased, dropping his bloodstained hands to his sides and panting, for he had shouted with a tremendous voice. Then the horns sounded; the soldiers smote their shields with their spear shafts and stamped their feet. Here and there a shout rose from the multitude, the shout swelled to a storm of voices, and all the people cried exultantly together. Horemheb smiled and stepped up into his chariot, while warriors cleared a way for him through the roaring crowds.

He drove to the harbor and boarded his ship, for he was to sail directly to Memphis, having already tarried too long in Thebes. According to the latest reports the horses of the Hittites were even now grazing in Tanis. I too went on board, and none sought to hinder me when I went up to him and said, "Horemheb, Pharaoh Akhnaton is dead; therefore I am released from my post as his skull surgeon and am free to come and go as I please. I mean to go with you into battle, for to me all things are indifferent and I am nowhere happy. I would see what manner of blessing is to come of this war of which you have spoken throughout your life. I would learn whether your rule is better than that of Akhnaton, or whether the earth is governed by the spirits of the underworld."

Horemheb was overjoyed and said, "May this be a good omen—although I never should have supposed that you, Sinuhe, would be the first to volunteer for this war! No, this I could not have believed, knowing that you prefer comfort and soft couches to the strenuous exertions of the field. I fancied you might watch over my interests in the golden house—but perhaps it is better for you to come with me since you are a simple sort of man whom anyone may lead by the nose. In this way I have at least a clever doctor and may well find need for such. Truly, Sinuhe, my men were right to name you Son of the Wild Ass when we fought the Khabiri together, for you must certainly have the heart of that beast to feel no dread of the Hittites."

As he spoke, the oarsmen dipped their oars, and the vessel moved out into the current with floating pennants. The quays were white with throngs, whose shouting was like a gale of wind in our ears. Horemheb drew a deep breath and said smiling, "My oration made a deep impression on the people, as you see."

I followed him to his cabin, from which he drove his scribes. Then he washed his hands, smelled them, and said coolly, "By Set and all devils! I did not think that the priests of Sekhmet still performed human sacrifice. But the old fellows were no doubt excited, for the gates of Sekhmet's temple have not been opened for at least forty years. I wondered why they required Hittite and Syrian prisoners for the ceremonies, but I let them have their way."

So aghast was I at his words that my knees gave beneath me, but Horemheb went on indifferently, "Had I known, I would scarcely have permitted it. Believe me, Sinuhe, I was much startled to find a warm, bleeding human heart in my hand before the altar. But let us render to the priests what is theirs, and they will give us no trouble."

"Horemheb," said I, "is anything sacred to you?"

He pondered a little, and replied, "When I was young, I believed in friendship, and I believed also that I loved a certain woman, whose scorn drove me to madness. Now I know that no human being is an aim, but only a means. I am the center of all things; all things proceed from me and return to me. I am Egypt; I am the people. In making Egypt great and powerful I myself am made great and powerful. This is no more than fitting, as you may understand, Sinuhe."

His words made little impression on me, for I had known him as a boastful boy, and I had seen his parents, who smelled of cheese and cattle, although he had raised them to distinction. Therefore, I could not take him very seriously although it was plain that he sought to make himself divine in my sight. I concealed my thoughts from him and began to speak of Princess Baketamon, who was mortally offended because she had not been given a place of fitting dignity in Tutankhamon's procession. Horemheb listened to me greedily and offered me wine, that I might tell him more of Baketamon. So the time passed as we sailed down the river to Memphis, while the chariots of the Hittites laid waste the Lower Kingdom.

BOOK 14

The Holy War

I

WHILE Horemheb was in Memphis, collecting troops and equipment, he summoned the wealthy men of Egypt and addressed them.

"You are all affluent men and I but a shepherd boy born with dung between the toes. Nevertheless, Ammon has blessed me, and Pharaoh has entrusted me with the leadership of this campaign. The enemy that threatens our land is formidable and of hideous savagery as you well know. It has given me great satisfaction to hear you speak your minds boldly—to acknowledge that war demands sacrifices from everyone, for which reason you have curtailed the grain measure of your slaves and laborers and raised the price of goods all over Egypt. I perceive from your words and deeds that you also are prepared to make great sacrifices. In order to sustain the cost of war it will be needful for each one of you to lend me—and at once—one half of his estate, whether in gold, silver, or grain, in cattle, horses, or chariots. It is all one to me, so it be delivered promptly."

At this the rich men of Egypt broke out in loud expostulation; they tore their robes and said, "The false Pharaoh has beggared us already, and we are penniless men! What security do you offer us for the loan of half our estates, and what interest do you mean to pay?"

Horemheb surveyed them kindly.

"My security is the victory that with your help, my dear friends, I intend to win as soon as possible. If I do not win it, the Hittites will come and rob you of all you have; therefore, my security seems to me sufficient. As to the interest, I intend to make a separate agreement with each one, and I hope that my terms will prove acceptable to you all. But you protested too soon, for I had not yet finished what I had to say. I require at once one half of your estates as a loan—merely as a loan, my good sirs. At the end of four months you shall again lend me one half of the remainder; and after a year, one half of what you still have left. You yourselves are best able to compute the sum finally remaining in your possession, but I am well assured that it will prove more than adequate to supply your cooking pots for the rest of your lives and that I am in no way robbing you."

Then the rich men threw themselves down before him, weeping bitterly and hitting the floor with their foreheads until the blood came. But he consoled them.

"I summoned you because I know that you love Egypt and are willing to make liberal sacrifice on its behalf. You are wealthy, and each of you has made his fortune by his own efforts. I am sure that you will soon restore these fortunes; the rich man always grows richer even though superfluous juice be pressed from him now and again. You, most excellent men, are to me a precious orchard. Though I squeeze you as I might squeeze a pomegranate so that the seeds spurt out between my fingers, yet like a good gardener I would not harm the trees but only gather in the harvest from time to time. Remember also that I give you a great war—greater than you dream of—and in time of war the well-to-do man is bound to prosper. The longer the war, the greater his prosperity; no power in the world can prevent this—not even Pharaoh's taxation department. You should be grateful to me. I send you home now with my blessing. Go in peace, be diligent, swell up again like ticks, for there is none to hinder you."

With these words he dismissed them. They departed groaning and lamenting and rending their garments, yet as soon as they had passed the doors, they ceased their outcry. They began busily calculating their losses and planning means to repair them.

Horemheb said to me, "This war is a gift to them. From now on, when they rob the people, they may blame the Hittites for all calamities just as Pharaoh can blame them for the famine and misery the war brings on the land of Kem. In the end it is the people who pay; the wealthy will rob them of many times the sum they lend to me— I can then squeeze them again. This method suits me better than a war tax. If I levied such a tax on the people, they would curse my name. By robbing the rich to pay for the war, I win the blessing of the people and their favor as a just man."

At this time the delta country stood in flames. Roving Hittite bands set fire to the villages and grazed their horses on the sprouting corn. Fugitives came in hordes to Memphis, bringing such hideous tales of the Hittite frenzy for destruction that my heart quailed and I begged Horemheb to hasten.

But he smiled unconcernedly, saying, "The Egyptians must have a taste of the Hittites if they are to be persuaded that no grimmer fate can befall them than to be bound to the enemy in slavery. I would be

424

mad to set forth with raw troops and no chariots. Don't be uneasy, Sinuhe; Gaza is still ours—Gaza is the cornerstone on which this war is built. Until this city is in their hands, the Hittites dare not send their main force into the desert. They are not in undisputed control of the sea. I have sent patrols into the desert to harry the bandits and guerrilla fighters, and I am not so idle as you seem to think. Egypt is menaced by no exceptional danger until the Hittites are able to bring their foot soldiers across the desert to the Black Land."

Men were streaming into Memphis from every part of Egypt: hungry men, men who in Aton's name had lost homes and families and no longer valued their lives, and men who lusted for adventure and the spoils of war. Heedless of the priests, Horemheb pardoned all who had shared in the foundation of Aton's kingdom and freed the prisoners from the quarries so as to press them into his service. Memphis soon resembled a vast camp. Life here was turbulent. Fighting raged in the taverns and pleasure houses every night, and peaceful people locked themselves into their houses, to remain there in fear and trembling. From smithy and workshop came the ring of hammers. So great was the fear of the Hittites that even poor women gave up their copper ornaments to be forged into arrowheads.

Ships were continually putting in at Egyptian ports from the islands in the sea and from Crete. Horemheb commandeered them all and took officers and crews into his employ. He captured even Cretan warships and forced their crews to serve Egypt. Such vessels were now scattered about the sea and were cruising from port to port, unwilling to return home. It was said that insurrection had broken out among the slaves in Crete and that the city of the nobles upon the hill had been blazing like a torch for weeks past and could be seen far out to sea. Yet no one had any sure report of what was happening, and the Cretan seamen lied as was their custom. Some claimed that the Hittites had invaded the island, although how this could have happened when they were not a seafaring nation is hard to understand. Others maintained that a strange, fair-haired race from the North had sailed thither to lay waste the country and despoil it. But with one voice the Cretans declared that all calamities had come about because their god was dead. For this reason they were glad to take service with the Egyptians. Nevertheless others of their nation, who had sailed to Syria, allied themselves with Aziru and the Hittites.

All this was much to Horemheb's advantage, for exceedingly great confusion prevailed at sea, where it was all against all in the scramble for ships. Rebellion had broken out in Tyre against Aziru, and surviving rebels had made their escape to Egypt, where they enrolled under Horemheb. Thus Horemheb was able to muster a fleet and fit it out for battle with the help of experienced crews.

Gaza still stood. When the harvest was in and the river began to rise, Horemheb set forth from Memphis with his troops. He sent forward messengers by sea and land to penetrate the lines of the besiegers; a vessel that sailed into Gaza harbor under cover of night, laden with sacks of grain, carried the message: "Hold Gaza! Hold Gaza at any price!" While battering rams thundered at the gates and the roofs of the city blazed because no one had time to extinguish the fires, an arrow here and there came singing in with the message: "Horemheb commands you! Hold Gaza!" And when the Hittites hurled sealed jars over the walls containing venomous snakes, one of them would be found full of grain and among this Horemheb's message: "Hold Gaza!" In what manner Gaza was able to withstand the combined assault of Aziru's men and the Hittites is more than I can understand, but the irascible garrison commander, who had seen me hoisted up the walls in a basket, well deserved the renown he won by holding Gaza for Egypt.

Horemheb marched his forces rapidly to Tanis, where he surrounded and cut off a Hittite chariot squadron that had halted in the bight of the river. Under cover of darkness he set his men to digging out the dried-up irrigation canals so that the rising river filled them. In the morning the Hittites discovered that they were trapped on an island and began to slaughter their horses and destroy their chariots. At this Horemheb flew into a rage. His purpose had been to capture these unharmed. He sounded the horns and attacked. The raw Egyptian troops won an easy victory and cut down the enemy, who had alighted and fought on foot. In this way Horemheb captured a hundred chariots or more and above two hundred horses. The victory was more important than the capture, for after it the Egyptians no longer believed the enemy to be invincible.

Marshaling chariots and horses, Horemheb drove to Tanis at their head, leaving the slower foot soldiers and the supply wagons to follow. A wild fervor blazed in his face as he said to me, "If you strike, strike first and hard!"

So saying he thundered on his way to Tanis, heedless of the Hittite hordes that roved and ravaged through the Lower Kingdom. From Tanis he continued his advance straight into the desert, overpowered the Hittite detachments that had been posted to guard the water supplies, and captured store after store. The Hittites had stacked

426

hundreds of thousands of water jars at intervals across the desert for the use of their foot soldiers since, being no mariners, they dared not attempt the invasion of Egypt from the sea. Without sparing their horses, Horemheb and his men pressed onward. Many beasts fell exhausted during this wild advance, of which eye witnesses declared that the hundred careering chariots sent up a pillar of dust to the very skies and that their progress was like that of the whirlwind. Each night beacons were kindled on the ranges of the Sinai hills, bringing the free forces from their hiding places to destroy the Hittite guards and their supplies all over the desert. From this grew the legend that Horemheb tore across the wilderness of Sinai like a pillar of cloud by day and a pillar of fire by night. After this campaign his fame was so illustrious that the people told stories of him as they tell stories of the gods.

Horemheb took the enemy entirely by surprise. With their knowledge of Egypt's weakness they could not conceive how he dared to attack across the desert while their troops were harrying the Lower Kingdom. Their main forces were scattered among the cities and villages of Syria in the expectation of Gaza's surrender, because the regions thereabout could not support the colossal army the Hittites had assembled in Syria for the conquest of Egypt. They were exceedingly thorough in their warfare and never attacked until they had assured themselves of their superiority. Their commanders had noted on their clay tablets every grazing ground, every watering place, and every village in the area they intended to attack. Because of these preparations they had postponed their invasion and were thunderstruck at Horemheb's move, partly because never yet had anyone dared assail them first and partly because they had not believed that Egypt possessed chariots enough for so great an enterprise.

Horemheb's purpose had been at most to destroy the Hittite water store in the desert, to gain time for the ordered training and equipment of his men. But his amazing success intoxicated him; he whirled on like the wind to Gaza, fell on the besiegers in their rear and scattered them, destroyed their engines of war and set their camps on fire. Yet he could not go into the city. When the besiegers saw how few were his chariots, they rallied and counterattacked. He would have been lost had these troops had chariots also. As it was he was able to withdraw into the desert, having destroyed the water stores on the fringe of it before the infuriated Hittites could call up chariots enough to pursue him.

Horemheb rightly augured from this that his falcon was with him.

Remembering the burning tree he had once seen among the Sinai hills, he sent word to his javelin throwers and archers, ordering them to advance in forced marches across the desert along one of the roads constructed by the Hittites, where stood hundreds of thousands of earthenware jars containing water enough to supply a large body of foot soldiers. His purpose now was to fight in the desert, although the ground was better suited to chariot warfare. I think he had no choice, for after his flight from the Hittites his men and horses were so exhausted that they could hardly have reached the Lower Kingdom alive. Therefore he summoned his whole army into the desert, which was an act without precedent.

I got this account of Horemheb's first attack on the Hittites from him and from his men; I was not with him. If I had been, I should assuredly never have lived to write this. It fell to me to survey the traces of the struggle from my carrying chair as I followed the foot regiments on their forced marches through the scorching dust, beneath the glare of the pitiless sun.

When we had toiled across the wilderness for two weeks, which, despite the plentiful supplies of water, were exhausting enough, we saw one night a pillar of fire rising from a hill beyond the desert and knew that Horemheb awaited us there with his chariots. This night has stayed in my memory, because I could not sleep. Darkness brings chill to the desert after the burning day, and men who have marched barefoot through sand and prickly plants for weeks cry out in their sleep and groan as if tormented by demons. It is for this reason no doubt that men believe the desert to be full of such beings. At dawn the horns rang out, and the march continued, although ever more men sank down unable to rise. Horemheb's beacon called us, and from every quarter of the desert small groups of ragged, sun-blackened robbers and guerrilla fighters hurried toward the fiery signal.

If our troops hoped for time to rest when they arrived at Horemheb's camp, they were to be sorely disappointed. If they believed he might commend them for their rapid march and for having worn the skin from their feet in the sand, they were indeed deluded. He received us with rage in his face; his eyes were bloodshot with weariness.

Swinging the golden whip, which was flecked with blood and dust, he said to us, "Where have you been loitering, dung beetles? Where have you skulked, you devils' spawn? Truly I should rejoice to see your skulls whiten in the sand tomorrow; I am so filled with shame at the sight of you! You creep to me like tortoises; you smell of sweat

428

and filth so that I am compelled to hold my nose, while my best men bleed from countless wounds and my noble horses pant their last. Dig now, you men of Egypt, dig for your lives! This is work most fitting for you who have dug all your lives in the mud."

The raw warriors of Egypt were in no way resentful of his words but rejoiced at them and repeated them laughing to one another, having found protection from the terrifying wilderness in the mere presence of Horemheb. They forgot their flayed soles and parched tongues and began at his direction to dig deep trenches in the ground, to drive stakes between stones, to stretch rush ropes between these stakes, and to roll and drag huge stones down the slopes of the hills.

Horemheb's weary charioteers crept out from their crannies and tents and limped up to display their wounds and boast of their prowess. Of the two thousand five hundred who had set out there remained not five hundred fit men.

The greater part of the army arrived at Horemheb's encampment that day in an unbroken stream. Each man was sent immediately to dig trenches and build barricades, to keep the Hittites from the desert. He sent word to those exhausted troops that had not yet arrived that all must reach the fortified position in the course of that night. Any left in the desert at daybreak would die a fearful death at the hands of the enemy, should the chariots of these break through.

The courage of the Egyptians was notably strengthened at the sight of their own numbers in that empty wilderness, and they placed blind trust in Horemheb, confident that he would save them from the Hittites. But as they were building their barricades, stretching their ropes and rolling their rocks, they beheld the enemy approaching in a cloud of dust. With white faces and wavering glances they looked about them, in great dread of the chariots and their hideous scythes.

Night was drawing on, and the Hittites would not attack before they had surveyed the terrain or estimated the strength of their adversary. They pitched camp, tended their horses, and kindled fires. When darkness fell, the fringe of the desert was spangled with fires as far as the eye could see. All night long their scouts drove up to the barricades in light chariots, slaying guards and skirmishing along the whole front. But on either flank, where no barricades could be built, the ruffians of the free forces surprised the Hittites and captured their chariots and horses.

The night was loud with the thunder of wheels, the shrieks of the dying, the whine of arrows, and the clash of arms. The raw troops were sorely alarmed and dared not sleep. But Horemheb comforted them, saying, "Sleep, marsh rats, sleep! rest and smear you torn feet with oil, for I am watching over your slumbers, to guard you."

I did not sleep; I walked about the camp all night, dressing the wounds of Horemheb's charioteers, while he encouraged me, saying, "Heal them, Sinuhe, with all your arts. More valiant warriors the world has never seen; each of them is worth a hundred or even a thousand of those mud grubbers. Heal them, for I dearly love these scum of mine, and I have no trained men to put in their places."

I was out of humor from the toilsome journey across the desert, although I had performed it in a chair. My throat was dry with the acrid dust, and I was enraged to think that because of Horemheb's foolish obstinacy I must die at the hands of the Hittites, although death in itself held no terrors for me.

I said to him irritably, "I seek to heal these scum of yours purely for my own sake since to my mind they are the only men in the army capable of fighting. Those who came with me will fly as soon as they see the whites of enemy eyes. You would do well to pick out the swiftest horses and speed back with me to the Lower Kingdom, to muster a new and better army."

Horemheb rubbed his nose and said, "Your counsel does honor to your wisdom. But we have no choice save to defeat the Hittites here in the desert. Defeat them we must, having no alternative. I shall now take my rest and shall drink. After drinking I am ever exceedingly ill tempered and fight well."

He left me, and soon I heard the gurgling from his wine jar. He offered it to such men of his as passed, slapping them on the shoulder and hailing each by name.

So the night passed, and morning rose like a specter from the desert. Before the barricades lay dead horses and overturned chariots, and vultures were tearing out the eyes of Hittites who had died there. Horns sounded at Horemheb's order, and he paraded his men at the foot of the slopes.

While the Hittites were smothering their fires with sand, harnessing their horses, and whetting their blades, Horemheb addressed his troops. He bit at a chunk of hard bread and an onion as he did so.

"Look before you, and you shall see a great marvel. Ammon has delivered the Hittites into our hands, and we shall do great things this day. The enemy foot soldiers have not yet come up; they remain at the edge of the desert because they lack water. The chariots must break through our lines and capture the water stores in our rear if the army is to pursue its attack on Egypt. Already their horses are thirsty and lack forage, for I have burned up their stores and smashed their water jars all the way from here to Syria. They must therefore either break through or retire unless they pitch camp to await fresh supplies, in which event they will be unable to engage us in battle. But they are greedy men, and they have invested all the gold and silver in Syria in those water jars that lie strung out behind us, full, all the way to Egypt. They will not give them up without a struggle. Thus Ammon has delivered them into our hands. When they attack, their horses will stumble and entangle themselves in our barriers. They cannot hurl their full force against us, for the trenches you have so diligently dug and the rocks and the ropes will break the edge of their assault."

Horemheb spat out an onion skin and chewed the bread until the troops began stamping and shouting, like children eager for another story. Then Horemheb said, "My only fear is that in your feebleness you will let the Hittites slip through your fingers. Those rods you hold in your hands are spears whose points are designed to rip up the bellies of Hittites. To the bowmen I say: Were you true warriors and marksmen you would shoot out their eyes. But such counsels are vain. Aim at the horses, for these are bigger targets, and you could never hit the men who drive them. The nearer they come, the more certain will be your unskillful aim; I counsel you to let them come very near. I will flog with my own hands every man who wastes an arrow; we have not one to spare. And you, javelin throwers! When the horses approach, steady the butts of your spears against the ground with both hands and direct the points at the horses' bellies. In this way you incur no danger and can leap aside before the animal falls on you. Should you be flung to the ground, hamstring them, for only that way can you avoid being crushed by the wheels. This is your task, you rats of the Nile."

Raising a jar of water to his lips he swallowed a deep draught to clear his head, after which he continued, "Nevertheless, it is a waste of breath to talk to you. When you hear the war cry of the Hittites and the thunder of their chariots you will whimper and hide your heads in the sand, for lack of skirts to creep under. If the Hittites break through to the water supplies in our rear, each one of you is lost and will be lifeless before nightfall, because we shall be surrounded and all retreat cut off. As it is we have no retreat. If we abandon the defenses we have built, the enemy chariots will scatter us like chaff before the wind; I mention this in case any one of you should take it into his head to scuttle off into the desert. We are all

431

in the same boat and have no choice but to defeat the enemy. I will
be with you, fighting at your side. Should my whip lash out at you
rather than at the Hittites, that will be no fault of mine but yours
alone, my valiant rats."

The men listened to him spellbound. I confess I was growing
uneasy, for already the enemy chariots were approaching like distant
dust clouds. Yet I believe that Horemheb lingered designedly, to infect
the men with his own composure and to spare them the oppressive
time of waiting.

At length he glanced out across the desert from his high ledge,
raised his hands, and said, "Our friends the Hittites are on their way,
for which I give thanks to all the gods of Egypt. Go then, you Nile
rats, each man to his allotted station, and let none depart thence unless so ordered. And you others, you my old ruffians, pursue this
rabble—shoot over and round them—geld them if need be, should
they seek to fly. I might say to you: fight for the gods of Egypt, fight
for the Black Land, fight for your wives and children. Run now, boys,
run swiftly, or the chariots will have reached the barricades before you,
and the battle will be over before it has begun."

He dismissed them, and they set off at a trot toward the barricades,
shouting as they ran, whether from ardor or fear I cannot say. Horemheb followed them at a leisurely pace, but I remained sitting on the
slope to watch the battle from a safe distance. I was a physician, and
my life was valuable.

The enemy had driven their chariots across the plain to the foot of
the hills, where they formed into battle order. Their colorful standards, the gleam of the winged suns on the chariots, and the brilliant
woolen cloths that protected the horses from arrows presented a
magnificent and most formidable sight. The chariots worked in
groups of six, ten of these groups forming one squadron; in all I
believe there were sixty squadrons. But the heavy, three-horse chariots,
manned by three men, formed the center of their front. I could not
conceive how Horemheb's force were to withstand their assault, for
they moved slowly and ponderously, like ships, and demolished
everything in their path.

To the sound of horns the enemy captains raised their standards,
and the chariots moved off at gradually increasing speed. When they
had drawn near to the barricades I saw single horses tearing out between them, each with a rider clinging to its mane and drumming
with his heels on the sides of his mount to urge it to still greater
speed. I could not imagine why they should send their spare horses

in advance, unguarded, until I observed these riders leaning over and cutting away the ropes that had been stretched between the stakes. Other horses galloped straight through the breaches thus formed. Their riders rose up and hurled their spears in such a manner that they remained fixed upright in the ground, and from the butt end of each floated a bright pennant. This all occurred with the speed of lightning. I failed to catch their purpose, for the horsemen then wheeled about and tore back at full gallop to disappear behind the chariots, although some dropped from their mounts transfixed by arrows, while many horses fell and lay kicking and screaming hideously on the ground.

When the light chariots began their assault, I saw Horemheb rushing toward the barricades alone, where he tore up one of the spears and hurled it far from him so that it stood once more upright in the sand. He alone had instantly perceived that these spears and flags were placed to mark the weakest points in the defenses, where a breach might best be made. Other men who followed his example returned with the standards as trophies. I believe that only Horemheb's quick wits saved Egypt that day, for had the enemy hurled the concentrated weight of his first assault against those points the riders had marked, it is certain that the Egyptians could never have repelled it.

No sooner had Horemheb regained the cover of his troops than the light chariots of the Hittites were speeding against the barriers, driving in among them like wedges. This first clash was attended by so mighty a din and by such dense clouds of dust that from the hillside I could no longer follow the course of the battle. I saw only that our arrows brought down some horses in front of the barricades, but that succeeding drivers dextrously avoided the overturned vehicles and came on. Later it became clear that at one or two points the light chariots had penetrated the lines, despite severe losses. But instead of pursuing their course they halted in groups, while the spare men in each leaped out and began rolling away the stones and clearing a path for the heavier force, which had halted out of range to await its turn.

A seasoned soldier on beholding these enemy successes would have believed the day lost, but Horemheb's raw rats saw only the horses kicking in the death struggle before the barricades and in the pits. They saw that the enemy had sustained grave losses and fancied that their own valor had halted the onslaught. Howling with excitement and terror, they hurled themselves with all their might on the stationary chariots, to lunge with their spears at the drivers and pull

433

them down, or wriggled along the ground to hamstring the horses, while the bowmen let fly at the men who were dragging away the rocks. Horemheb allowed them to rampage as they would, and their numbers helped them. They captured many chariots, which they handed over, in a frenzy of excitement, to Horemheb's seasoned "scum." Horemheb did not tell them that all would be over when the heavy chariots came up but relied on his luck and on the vast pit he had had dug across the middle of the valley in the rear of the troops, which was concealed under bushes and brush. The light chariots had not come so far, believing that all obstacles were already behind them.

Having cleared a broad enough way for the heavy force, such Hittites as survived climbed again into their chariots and drove swiftly back, thus arousing great jubilation among Horemheb's men, who fancied that victory was already theirs. But Horemheb gave rapid orders for the sounding of horns, the replacing of rocks, and the planting of spears with points slanted toward the assailants. To avoid needless loss of men, he was compelled to station them on either side of the gaps. The scythes of the heavy chariots, turning with the wheels, would otherwise have mown down the troops like ripe grain.

This he did at the last moment. The dust cloud in the valley had not yet dispersed when the heavy chariots, the flower and pride of the Hittite army, thundered forward, crushing all obstacles in their way. They were drawn by powerful horses, a span higher than those of Egypt; their heads were protected by plates of metal and their sides by thick woolen pads. So massive were the wheels that they could overturn even large stones, and the horses with their mighty chests snapped the standing spears. Howls and blood-curdling shrieks rang out as the defenders were crushed beneath the wheeels or slashed in two by the scythes.

Soon the great vehicles burst through the dust cloud, and the horses, as they trotted forward in their colorful, quilted blankets with long bronze spikes jutting from their masks, looked like unknown, fantastic monsters. They clattered forward in column, and it seemed to me that no earthly power could halt them, nor any number of Egyptians block their way to the water jars in the desert. At Horemheb's order his men had withdrawn from the valley to the slopes of the flanking hills. The Hittites uttered a great shout and thundered on so that the dust rose in eddies behind them. I threw myself face downward on the ground and wept for Egypt's sake, for the sake of the defenseless Lower Kingdom, and for all those who must now die because of Horemheb's mad obstinacy.

434

The enemy were trotting briskly forward in a broad column when all at once the ground sank beneath them. Horses, chariots, and men tumbled higgledy-piggledy into the great pit the mud grubbers of the Nile had dug and camouflaged with bushes. This pit extended the whole width of the valley, from slope to slope. Scores of heavy chariots plunged into it before the remainder could be turned and driven along the edge. In this way the force was divided. When I heard the yell from our assailants, I raised my head from the ground, and until the rising dust veiled all beneath it, the spectacle I beheld was terrible indeed.

Had the Hittites been more circumspect, had they envisaged a possible reverse, they might yet have saved one half of their chariots and inflicted a heavy defeat on the Egyptians. They might have wheeled and returned through the breached barricades, but they could not understand that it was they who were defeated, being unaccustomed to that condition. They did not fly from our foot soldiers but drove their horses up the steep slopes to bring the chariots to a stand. Turning to inspect the field, they alighted from their vehicles to discover how best to cross the trench or to save their comrades who had fallen into it and to await the clearing of the dust that they might plan their next blow.

But Horemheb had no intention of allowing them to recover. With a flourish of horns he made known to his men that his magic had halted the enemy chariots, which were now impotent. He sent archers up the slopes to harass the Hittites, while other men were set to sweeping the ground with bushes and twigs to raise more dust, partly to confuse the enemy and partly to conceal from his own troops how great a number of Hittite chariots were still whole and fit for battle. At the same time he caused more rocks to be rolled down, to close the breaches in the barricades and thus, by holding the chariots in his power, complete his victory.

Meanwhile the light-chariot squadrons of the enemy had halted on the slopes to water their horses, mend their harness, and repair the broken spokes in their wheels. They saw the dust whirling among the hillocks. Hearing howls and the clash of arms, they fancied that the heavy force was routing the Egyptians and killing them off like rats.

Under the cover of dust, Horemheb sent his boldest javelin throwers to the pit, to prevent the Hittites from helping up their fallen comrades or filling in the hole. He sent the remaining troops against the chariots. They rolled great rocks before them with which to encircle the vehicles and deprive them of room to maneuver, and also if possible

435

to cut them off from one another. All along the slopes great stones were soon in motion. The Egyptians had always been well skilled in handling them, and among Horemheb's troops were only too many who had learned the art in the quarries.

The Hittites were greatly discomfited at the continued cloud of dust, which prevented them from seeing what was going forward, and many were picked off by the archers where they stood. At length their officers ordered the horns to be sounded to assemble the chariots and storm down again to the plain, there to reform their forces. But when they charged back along the way they had come, they did not recognize it. Their horses stumbled over ropes and traps, and their heavy cars overturned among the rocks. At last they were compelled to alight from them and fight on foot. Here they were at a disadvantage, having ever been accustomed to stand higher than their adversary and were at length overcome by Horemheb's men, although the struggle continued all day.

With the approach of evening a wind from the desert blew away the dust cloud, revealing the battlefield and the crushing defeat of the Hittites. They had lost the greater number of their heavy chariots, of which many with their horses and equipment had fallen unharmed into the hands of Horemheb. His men, wearied and fevered with the fury of battle, with their wounds, and with the reek of blood, were aghast at the spectacle of their own losses. The Egyptian dead in the valley far outnumbered those of the enemy.

The terror-stricken survivors said to one another, "This has been a day of horror, and it was well we saw nothing during the battle. Had we beheld the multitude of the Hittites and the numbers of our own dead, our hearts would certainly have leaped into our throats, and we should not have fought as we did, like lions."

The remainder of the Hittites, surrounded, raised their hands in the air. Horemheb caused them to be bound, while all the marsh rats of the Nile came up to marvel at them, to touch their wounds, and to pull from their helmets and clothes the images of double-headed axes and winged suns.

Horemheb distributed wine and beer among his men and allowed them to plunder the fallen, both Hittites and Egyptians, that they might feel they too had a share in the spoils. But the most precious gains were the heavy chariots and those horses that remained unharmed. That very night he sent word to the free forces on either flank, exhorting all brave men among them to take service with his chariots like his own "scum," for the desert folk were better skilled with horses than the Egyptians, who feared them. All horsemen answered his call gladly and rejoiced at the sturdy chariots and fine beasts.

I had my hands full with the wounded, stitching gashes, setting limbs, and opening skulls that had been crushed by the war clubs of the Hittites. Although I had many helpers, three days and three nights had passed before all were cared for, during which time many of the severely injured died.

Next day the Hittites launched a fresh attack with their light chariots, to recapture those they had lost. On the third day they still sought to break through the barricades, not daring to return to their commander-in-chief in Syria with news of their defeat.

But on this third day Horemheb was no longer content with defense. Having cleared a way through his own obstacles, he sent forward his "scum" in their captured chariots to chase the light vehicles of the Hittites and scatter them. We suffered great losses because the enemy were swifter and more accustomed to chariot warfare. Once more there was much work for me. Yet these losses, said Horemheb, were unavoidable, for only in battle could his ruffians learn to handle horses and chariots, and it was better to exercise when the enemy were defeated and discouraged than when, fully rested and equipped, they took the offensive.

"Without chariots with which to meet chariots we shall never conquer Syria," said Horemheb. "This fighting behind barricades is childish and profitless, despite the hindrance it has proved to the invasion of Egypt."

He hoped that the Hittites would send their foot soldiers into the desert also, for these, without sufficient water, would have been an easy prey. But the enemy were prudent, and apt learners. They held their troops in Syria in the hope that Horemheb, blinded by his victory, would send his men forward into that country, where they would have been rapidly annihilated by the fresh and seasoned forces of the adversary.

Nevertheless, this defeat caused profound consternation in Syria. Many cities rose in revolt against Aziru and closed their gates against him, weary of his ambition and of the rapacity of the Hittites. They hoped thus to win Egypt's favor and a share in speedy conquest. The cities of Syria have ever been at odds with one another, and Horemheb's spies fanned their discontent, spreading exaggerated and alarming reports of the great desert defeat.

While Horemheb rested his troops among those victorious hills,

437

while he conferred with his spies and laid fresh plans, he continued to send his message to the beleaguered city: "Hold Gaza!" He knew that it could not hold out much longer, yet to win back Syria he must have a base on the coast. He set rumors about among his men of that country's wealth and of the priestesses in the temple of Ishtar, who with consummate arts give pleasure to the valiant. I did not know why he lingered, until one night a starving, thirst-tormented man crept through the barricades, surrendered himself as a prisoner and begged to be brought before Horemheb. The soldiers mocked him for his impudence, but Horemheb received the man, who bowed low before him, stretching forth his hands at knee level, despite his Syrian dress. He then laid a hand over one of his eyes as if in pain.

Horemheb said, "Why surely no dung beetle has stung you in the eye?"

I chanced to be in his tent when this was said and regarded it as idle chatter since the dung beetle is a harmless insect and hurts no one.

But the thirsty man said, "Truly a dung beetle has stung me in the eye, for in Syria there are ten times ten of them, all exceedingly venomous."

Horemheb said, "I greet you, valiant man. Speak freely, for this physician here in my tent is simple and understands nothing."

At this the spy said, "My lord Horemheb, the hay has come!"

He uttered no more than this, but I took him for one of Horemheb's spies. Horemheb left the tent immediately and gave orders for a beacon to be lit upon the hilltop. Soon afterward a chain of answering fires winked across the hills as far as the Lower Kingdom. In this manner he sent word to Tanis for the fleet to put to sea and engage the Syrian vessels off Gaza, should conflict prove unavoidable.

Next morning the horns rang out, and the army marched away across the desert to Syria. The chariots drove on ahead as an advance guard, to clear the route of enemies and to choose camping places for the troops. Yet how Horemheb dared give battle to the Hittites in open country was more than I could understand. The men followed him gladly, however, dreaming of the wealth of Syria, which was theirs for the winning. I stepped into my carrying chair and followed them, and we left behind us the hills of victory, where the bones of Hittites and Egyptians lay peaceably together, to whiten in the sand of the barricaded valley.

438

3

I come now to the war in Syria, although I have little to say of it, being unskilled in military matters. All battles look alike to me—all burning cities and plundered houses, all wailing women and mutilated bodies, wherever I may encounter them. My report would be monotonous indeed were I to speak of all I saw. The war in Syria lasted three years, a cruel, merciless war in which great numbers perished. Villages were laid waste, gardens were ravished of their fruit trees, and cities deserted.

But I must speak first of the guile of Horemheb. He led his troops fearlessly into Syria, removing the boundary stones erected by Aziru and allowing his men to plunder the villages and enjoy the women as a foretaste of the fruits of conquest. He marched straight on Gaza, and no sooner had the Hittites grasped his purpose than they mustered their forces on the plain near the city to cut him off and destroy him, this ground being well-suited to chariot warfare. They were confident of success.

But winter was already so far advanced that they had now to feed their horses on forage bought of Syrian traders. Before ever this battle began, the horses fell sick and staggered in the traces; their droppings were green and watery, and many of the animals died. Thus Horemheb could engage the enemy upon an equal footing, and having once beaten off the chariots, he routed the demoralized foot soldiers with ease. Javelin throwers and bowmen swiftly completed the work begun by the chariots. The Hittites sustained a worse defeat than ever before and left as many dead upon that field as did the Egyptians. It was known thereafter as the Field of Bones. As soon as Horemheb entered their encampment he set fire to their stocks of forage until all was burned. This forage had mixed with it certain poisonous herbs that caused the Hittite horses to sicken, although I did not then know in what manner Horemheb had contrived this.

Thus Horemheb reached Gaza, while Hittites and Syrians in the whole of the south took refuge in fortified cities, and he scattered the besiegers. Meanwhile, the Egyptian fleet sailed into Gaza harbor, much battered and disabled; many vessels were still burning after an indecisive battle that had raged for two days offshore. They brought provisions and reinforcements for Gaza and carried home to Egypt our wounded and disabled men.

The day that saw the opening of the gates of Gaza the impregnable to admit Horemheb's troops is still celebrated throughout Egypt as a day of festival. This winter day is the Day of Sekhmet when small boys with wooden clubs and reed spears re-enact the siege of Gaza. No city was ever more valiantly defended, and its commander well deserved the praise and acclamation he received. I shall give his name despite the indignity he offered me in having me hoisted up the walls in a basket. His name was Roju.

He was called by his own men Bull-Neck, which well describes his appearance and his nature, for a more dogged and suspicious man I never met. After the victory the horns of Horemheb blew all day long in vain before Roju would believe that it was safe to open the gates. Even then he would admit Horemheb only, to satisfy himself that the man was what he appeared to be and not a Syrian disguised.

Aziru's siege had been but child's play compared with the Hittites' ruthless and persistent attack. Day and night these had hurled in burning brands, and when we arrived, there were but few survivors among the inhabitants. A few women and old men crept out to us from beneath the gutted houses, shadowlike in their horrible emaciation. All the children had perished and the men had toiled and worn themselves to death under Roju's whip, repairing the breaches in the walls. The survivors showed no joy at the sight of Egypt's army marching through the battered gateway. The women shook their bony fists, and the old men cursed us. Horemheb distributed grain and beer among them, and many died that night in agony. It was the first time for months that they had eaten their fill, and their starved stomachs were unequal to the meal.

If I could I would portray Gaza as I saw it on that day of victory. I would describe the dried human skins hanging from the walls and the blackened skulls pecked at by birds of prey. I would speak of the charred ruins and of the sooty bones of animals lying in rubble-blocked alleys. I would reproduce if I might the hideous stench of that beleaguered city—a stench of pestilence and death that made Horemheb's men hold their noses. All this would I describe, to give some notion of that great hour of victory and to make plain why it was that I could not heartily rejoice on this long-dreamed-of, long-awaited day.

On every surviving soldier of the Gaza garrison Horemheb bestowed a golden chain; it cost him little, for less than two hundred fit men were left. It was a marvel that they had held on. But to Roju Bull-Neck Horemheb gave a chain of green precious stones set in gold and enamel, also a golden whip, and he made his men cheer Roju so that the walls trembled at the sound. All cheered in deep and heartfelt admiration for the man who had held Gaza.

When the shout had died away, Roju fingered his chain suspiciously and said, "Do you take me for a horse, Horemheb, that you adorn me with golden harness? And is this whip braided with pure gold or with alloyed Syrian gold?"

He said also, "Take your men out of the city, for their numbers distract me. I cannot sleep in my tower at night for their noise, although I slept soundly enough when battering rams were thundering at the gates and fires crackled on every side. Take your men hence, for in Gaza I am Pharaoh, and I will order my men to attack yours and slay them unless they cease their din and let me sleep."

And indeed it proved that Roju Bull-Neck could get no sleep now that the siege was over. Not even drugs or wine could give it to him. He lay brooding on his bed, striving to recall in what manner the stores had been consumed.

One day he very humbly approached Horemheb and said to him, "You are my lord and greater than I. Punish me, therefore, for I am accountable to Pharaoh for all the things he entrusted me with—and what shall I do? All my papers were burned when the Hittites hurled their jars of fire into my room, and my memory is enfeebled through lack of sleep. I seem to remember all other things, but in the stores there should be four hundred leather cruppers for donkeys, and I can't find them anywhere. My store scribes can't find them either although I whip them every day. They can now neither sit nor walk but crawl about the floor on hands and knees. Horemheb, where are those four hundred cruppers, which were never needed because we long ago ate the donkeys? By Set and all devils! Have me flogged in the sight of all, for Pharaoh's wrath fills me with dread. I shall not dare to enter his presence as my rank requires if I do not find the cruppers."

Horemheb sought to calm him, saying that he would gladly give him four hundred of these, but the proposal threw Roju into yet greater agitation.

He said, "It is evident that you seek to lure me into deceit, for if I accept these, they will still not be those entrusted to me. You do this that you may degrade me and accuse me before Pharaoh, because you are envious and covet the post of garrison commander in Gaza! I will not consent to your deceitful proposal but I will find those four hundred cruppers if I have to tear down Gaza stone by stone to do it."

Unknown to Horemheb, Roju ordered the execution of the store clerk who had endured all the hardships of the siege by his side and set men to tearing up the floor of his tower with pickaxes to find the lost harness. When Horemheb saw this, he ordered him to be locked in his room and watched, and then he consulted me. I visited Roju, and with the help of many strong men I bound him to his bedstead and then administered a soothing draught. But his eyes blazed like those of a wild beast; he writhed on the bed, foaming at the mouth in fury.

He said to me, "Am I not commander in Gaza, you jackal of Horemheb? I remember now that there was in the fortress dungeon a Syrian spy whom I captured before your master came. By reason of my many duties I forgot to hang him from the wall. This spy is an exceedingly cunning fellow, and I now understand that it is he who has made off with those four hundred cruppers. Bring him before me that I may squeeze them out of him and sleep in peace once more."

He raved so long about his Syrian spy that I grew weary, and taking lighted torches I descended into the dungeon, where a number of rat-gnawed bodies sat chained to the walls. The guard was an old blind man whom I questioned as to a certain Syrian spy who had been imprisoned before the end of the siege. He vowed and declared that all the prisoners had perished long ago, having been first questioned on the rack and then left without food or water. I knew human nature, and the old man's demeanor aroused my suspicions.

I pressed him hard and threatened him until he prostrated himself before me, saying, "Spare my life, lord, for I have faithfully served Egypt all my days and in the name of Egypt have tortured prisoners and stolen their food. But this spy is no ordinary man. His tongue is strange and whistles like a nightingale, and he has promised me great wealth if I will feed him and keep him alive until the coming of Horemheb. He has also promised to restore my sight, having been blind himself until a great physician healed his one eye. He has promised to bring me to this great physician that my sight also may be restored and that I may live in the city among my fellows and enjoy my wealth. He already owes me more than two million deben of gold for the bread and water I have given him, and I have not told him that the siege is over and that Horemheb has come to Gaza, that he may incur yet heavier debt with every passing day. He swears that Horemheb will release him and give him chains of gold, and I must believe him for the twittering of his tongue is not to be resisted. Yet I do not intend to bring him before Horemheb until he owes me three million deben of gold. That is a round sum and easy to bear in mind."

My knees had begun to quake and my heart to melt in my breast, for I seemed to know of whom he spoke. But I controlled myself and said, "Old man, there is not so much gold in all Egypt and Syria put

442

together. From your words I know that this man is a great deceiver and merits punishment. Bring him before me instantly, and pray to all the gods that no evil may have befallen him, for you will answer for it with your blind old head."

Weeping bitterly and calling on Ammon to help him, the old man led me to a little cellar behind the others, the mouth of which was blocked up with stones that Roju's men might not find it. When I shone the light of my torch into this hole I saw chained to the wall a man whose Syrian dress was tattered, whose back was raw, and whose emaciated paunch hung in folds. One eye was blind, and in the torchlight he blinked the other and turned it toward me.

He said, "Is it you, my lord Sinuhe? Blessed be the day that brings you to me, but let the smiths make speed to free me from these fetters. Bring me a jar of wine that I may forget my sufferings, and let slaves wash me and anoint me with the finest ointments, for I am accustomed to comfort and a life of abundance, and these sharp stones have rubbed the skin from my backside. Nor have I anything against a soft couch and a few of Ishtar's virgins for company, seeing that my belly no longer hampers me in the delights of love. Yet—believe it or not—within a few days I have eaten more than two million deben worth of bread."

"Kaptah, Kaptah!" I cried, falling on my knees and throwing my arms about his rat-bitten shoulders. "You are incorrigible! They told me in Thebes that you were dead, but I would not believe it, for I think you can never die. My best proof of that is to find you here in the cellar of the dead, living and in good health among the corpses, notwithstanding that those who have perished in their chains all about you were more respectable men and more pleasing to their gods than you. It rejoices me indeed to find you alive."

Kaptah said, "You are still the same vain prattler, my lord Sinuhe. Talk not to me of gods, for in my distress I have called on all the gods I know—even those of Babylon and of the Hittites—and not one of them has helped me. I have eaten myself into beggary because of this rapacious guard. The scarab alone has helped by leading you to me, for the commander of this fortress is a madman and believes no sensible words. He allowed his men to plunder me and to rack me in a very terrible manner, so that I bellowed like a bull on their wheel. But the scarab I kept, to my good fortune, for when I saw what was to come I concealed it in a part of my body that it is an indignity for a god to inhabit but that may have been agreeable to the scarab since it led you to me. Only to that can such a remarkable meeting be attributed."

443

He showed me the scarab, which was still foul from its unpleasing hiding place. I ordered the smiths to release him from his chains and then led him up into my rooms in the fortress, for he was weak and his eye was unaccustomed to the light. At my order, slaves washed and anointed him and clothed him in the finest linen, and I lent him a gold chain and bracelets and other ornaments that he might make an appearance befitting his dignity. He was shaved also and his hair curled. Meanwhile he ate meat and drank wine and belched in contentment. But the prison guard wept and lamented behind the door, shouting that Kaptah owed him two million three hundred and sixty-five deben of gold for the preservation of his life and for his food in the dungeon. Nor would he abate one single deben from this sum, saying that he had risked his own life in preserving Kaptah's and in stealing food for him.

I wearied of the outcry and said to Kaptah, "Horemheb has been in Gaza for more than a week and the old man has cheated you. You owe him nothing. I will order soldiers to flog him, and if need be they can cut off his head, for he is a deceitful fellow and the cause of many deaths."

But Kaptah was shocked at my words, and said, "I am a man of honor! A merchant must hold to his engagements if he is to preserve his good name. Had I guessed that I should survive, I should of course have bargained with him. When I smelled the bread in his hand I promised him what he asked."

I stared at him in consternation.

"Can this be Kaptah? No, I can't believe it. Some curse lurks in the stones of this fortress so that all who remain within it go mad. You also are mad! Do you mean to pay him all you owe? And with what will you pay it? Since the kingdom of Aton fell, I fancy you are as poor as myself."

But Kaptah was now drunk, and he said, "I am a pious man. I honor the gods and keep my word. I intend to discharge my debt to the last deben, although of course he must allow me time. In his simplicity he would doubtless be content if I weighed out a couple of deben to him, for never in his life has he squeezed soft gold between his fingers. He would be beside himself with joy to receive only one deben, but this does not release me from my bond. I don't know where I can find so much, for I lost a very great deal in the Theban riots, having been compelled to fly thence in an ignominious manner, leaving everything behind me. The slaves were persuaded that I had betrayed them to Ammon and sought my life. After that I did great service to Horemheb in Memphis until the hatred of the slaves pursued me even there. I then did him even greater service in Syria, for I lived here as a merchant and sold grain and forage to the Hittites. I estimate therefore that Horemheb already owes me half a million deben of gold—and more, because I was forced to make my escape to Gaza in peril of my life on the sea in a very small boat. The Hittites, you understand, were enraged because their horses fell sick of the forage I had supplied. In Gaza I ran an even greater risk. The mad commander imprisoned me as a Syrian spy and tortured me on the wheel, and assuredly my hide would now be hanging from the wall had not this crazy old man hidden me and vowed that I had perished in the dungeon. Therefore, I must discharge my debt to him."

Then my eyes were opened, and I understood that it was Kaptah who had been Horemheb's best agent in Syria and his chief spy—had not the thirsty wretch who visited Horemheb's tent by night covered one eye as a sign that he had been sent by a one-eyed man? I perceived that no other could have performed such wonders, for in guile Kaptah had no peer.

I said to him, "What if Horemheb does owe you much gold? You know very well that he never pays his debts."

"That is so; he is a hardhearted and ungrateful man, more ungrateful even than this mad commander, to whom I conveyed grain in sealed jars. The Hittites fancied that the jars were full of venomous serpents, for in proof of this I broke one of the jars and the serpents bit three Hittite soldiers so that they died. After this the Hittites felt no desire to open further jars. Failing a recompense in gold, Horemheb shall appoint me receiver of harbor dues and of similar contributions in the captured cities. He shall turn the whole of the Syrian salt trade over to me, and much else, and by this means afford me satisfaction."

There was sense in what he said, and yet I marveled.

"Do you then intend to toil all your life to pay this old lunatic who is making such a to-do behind my door?"

Kaptah drank wine and smacked his lips, saying, "Truly it is worth languishing for a week or two in a dark hole, with hard stones beneath one and foul water to drink, to enjoy the full delight of soft seats, good light, and the taste of wine. No, Sinuhe, I am not as mad as you suppose. Nevertheless, my word is my bond, for which reason you must restore his sight according to my promise, that he may learn to dice with me. He was an eager gambler before his blindness came on him

—and if he should lose to me, what can I do? You understand, of course, that I mean to play for very high stakes."

I saw that this was indeed the only honorable way for Kaptah to discharge his huge debt, for Kaptah was a skillful player—with dice of his own choosing. I promised to devote all my arts to restoring the old man's sight, or at least so much of it as would enable him to distinguish the pips. In return, Kaptah undertook to send Muti enough silver to rebuild the copperfounder's house in Thebes and to maintain herself there in comfort during my absence. I called the old man in, and Kaptah assured him he would pay off the debt if given a little time. I examined his eyes and found that the blindness was not a result of living in the dark but of an old, neglected disease. On the following day I cured it by means of the needle, according to the method I had perfected in Mitanni. How long his sight would last I could not say, for eyes that have been so treated are apt to scar within a short space of time, and the resulting loss of sight can be neither prevented nor cured.

I brought Kaptah to Horemheb, who rejoiced to see him. He embraced him and called him a brave man, assuring him that all Egypt was thankful to him for his great achievements.

But Kaptah's face fell, and he began to weep, saying, "Behold my belly, which has shrunk to an empty bag from my exertions on your behalf. Cast your eye upon my lacerated rear and on my ears, which the dungeon rats of Gaza have nibbled into rags! You talk to me of gratitude, which puts not a grain of corn into my mouth nor so much as moistens my throat. Nowhere do I see the bags of gold you have promised me! No, Horemheb, I ask for no thanks. I ask you to pay what you owe me, like a man of honor, since I also have debts to discharge. Indeed I stand very deeply in debt—more deeply than you dream of."

Horemheb scowled, and smiting his leg impatiently with his whip he said, "Your talk is that of a fool, Kaptah. You know very well that I have no plunder to share with you and that I use all the gold I can lay hands on to prosecute the war against the Hittites. I myself am a poor man, and glory alone is my reward. This much I can do for you: I can imprison your creditors, accuse them of many crimes, and hang them from the walls, and so acquit you of your debts."

To this Kaptah would not agree. Horemheb laughed harshly and said, "Kaptah, how did you come to be bound to the wheel as a Syrian spy and cast into the dungeons? Mad though Roju is, yet he is a fine warrior and must have had some reason for his action."

446

Kaptah tore his fine garment in token of innocence, beat his breast, and cried, "Horemheb, Horemheb! Was it you who but now spoke to me of gratitude, only to insult me with false accusations? Didn't I poison the horses of the Hittites and smuggle corn into Gaza? When you lay encamped in the wilderness, didn't I hire bold men to bring you details of enemy dispositions? Didn't I hire slaves to slit the water skins in the chariots with which the Hittites attacked you? All this I did for you and for Egypt without thought of gain. It was but fair and right that I should perform certain harmless services for the Hittites and for Aziru. For this reason, when I fled to Gaza, I had about me a tablet of safe-conduct from Aziru. A wise man protects himself at every point and carries many arrows in his quiver. Neither to you nor to Egypt should I be of the smallest use were my carcass now hanging out to dry upon the wall. I carried the safe-conduct with me, for had you tarried too long, Gaza might have fallen. But Roju is a suspicious man, and it was in vain I covered my blind eye and spoke of venomous beetles as we had agreed. He believed in no passwords but stretched me out on the wheel until I bellowed like a bull and said that I was a spy of Aziru's."

Horemheb laughed and said, "What you have undergone shall be your reward, my good Kaptah. I know you, and you know me. Pester me no longer in this matter of gold, for such talk vexes me and puts me out of temper."

But Kaptah persisted until at last he had extracted from Horemheb the sole right to buy and sell all war plunder in Syria. He could purchase, gamble for, or barter for beer, wine, and women any spoils that had been shared out among the soldiers. He was also authorized to sell Pharaoh's share of the booty, or Horemheb's—or exchange it—for goods of which the army stood in need. This right alone would have made him a rich man; nevertheless, he demanded the same conditions for all Syrian plunder whatsoever that Horemheb's army might come by in the future. Horemheb agreed since it cost him nothing, and in return for this concession Kaptah promised him liberal gifts.

4

When Horemheb had repaired all his chariots, summoned auxiliary forces from Egypt, assembled in Gaza all the horses of southern Egypt, and exercised his troops, he issued a proclamation declaring that he came as liberator to Syria and in no way as conqueror. Under the kindly protection of Egypt, said he, all the Syrian cities had enjoyed freedom and unrestricted trade, each under its own king. By the villainous treachery of Aziru these cities had been forced to yield to his tyranny. Aziru had bereft the kings of their lineal crowns and oppressed the cities with burdensome taxation. In his greed he had sold Syria to the Hittites, of whose cruelty and evil practices the Syrians had daily proof. Therefore he, Horemheb the Invincible, Son of the Falcon, came to liberate Syria from the yoke of slavery, to encourage trade, and to reinstate the former kings so that under the protection of Egypt the land might flourish and prosper as before. He promised his help to every city that expelled the Hittites and closed its gates to Aziru. Those cities that continued to resist he would burn, plunder, and destroy, level their walls forever and carry away the citizens into slavery.

Finally Horemheb marched on Joppa and sent his fleet to close the harbor. With the help of his spies he noised abroad his proclamation, which aroused much uneasiness and indecision among the cities and disputes among his enemies, which was indeed its sole purpose. But Kaptah, like the cautious man he was, remained within the walls of Gaza in case Horemheb should suffer defeat, for both Aziru and the Hittites were gathering together a mighty force inland.

Roju Bull-Neck was reconciled with Kaptah, who cured him of his delusion by explaining that the soldiers, ravenous during the siege, had stolen the four hundred cruppers from the harness store and eaten them, for they were of soft leather and could be chewed to dull the edge of hunger. When Roju heard this, his frenzy subsided so that he could be loosed from his bonds, and he forgave his comrades the theft because of their great valor.

When Horemheb had departed with his men, Roju closed the gates of Gaza, vowing that never again would he admit any troops into the city. He drank wine and watched Kaptah's play with the guard. At the time of Horemheb's departure, Kaptah had won back from the old man only one and a half million deben of gold. They drank and threw dice from morning till night; they quarreled and hurled the dice in each others' faces; they spat in their palms and cast the dice from the cup so that they rolled on the floor. The old man was miserly and desired to play for small stakes only, and he mourned and bewailed his losses. When Horemheb laid siege to Joppa, Kaptah made the guard raise his stakes, and when a messenger brought news that Horemheb had breached the walls, Kaptah beggared his opponent so thoroughly in a few throws as to reverse the debt to the tune of some hundred thousand deben of gold. Kaptah was magnanimous, however, and forgave it. He bestowed new clothes on him and a handful or so of silver so that the old man wept for joy and blessed him as his benefactor.

I do not know whether or not Kaptah cheated and played with loaded dice. I know only that he played with great skill and unbelievable good fortune. The tale of this gamble for a stake of millions—a gamble that continued for many weeks—spread throughout Syria, and the old man, whose blindness soon returned to him, lived for the rest of his days in a little hut by the walls of Gaza. Travelers even from other cities would visit him, and he would tell them of the play. After the passage of years he could repeat the score at each throw, for the blind have good memories. But he was proudest when he spoke of the last throw of all by which he lost one hundred and fifty thousand deben of gold, for never had such high stakes been played for with dice. People brought him gifts to persuade him to tell his story, so that he suffered no want but lived in greater comfort than if Kaptah had pensioned him for life.

When Joppa fell, Kaptah went there in haste, and I with him. We saw for the first time that wealthy city in the hands of the conquerors. And though the boldest of its citizens had risen in revolt against Aziru and the Hittites when Horemheb stormed in, yet he would not spare it. For two weeks he allowed his men to plunder and despoil it. Kaptah amassed a huge fortune in this city, for the soldiers bartered priceless carpets and furniture and statues, and such things as they could not carry away, for silver and wine. A handsome, shapely Syrian woman could be had in Joppa for two copper rings.

It was here that I realized fully the brutality of man to fellow man. During this time of drunkenness, robbing, and burning, every kind of abomination was committed. The soldiers set fire to houses for their own amusement, so that at night they could see to loot, to rape, and to torture merchants and force them to disclose where their treasure lay hid. There were those who diverted themselves by standing at a street corner and, with club or spear, taking the life of every Syrian who came by, whether men or women, children or the aged. My heart was hardened at the sight of man's iniquity. All that had happened in Thebes on Aton's account was trivial beside what was done in Joppa because of Horemheb. He gave his soldiers a free hand, to bind them more closely to himself. To avoid sharing the fate of Joppa, many of the cities along the coast drove out the Hittites from their midst.

I will speak no more of those days, for in recalling them my heart

449

turns to stone in my breast and my hands grow cold. I say only that at the time of Horemheb's attack there were in the city, besides Aziru's garrison and the Hittite soldiery, nearly twenty thousand inhabitants. When he departed there were not three hundred left alive.

Thus did Horemheb wage war in Syria, and I went with him, dressing his men's wounds and witnessing all the evil that one human being can do another. The war continued for three years, during which Horemheb defeated the Hittites and Aziru's troops in many battles. Twice his own forces were surprised by Hittite chariot squadrons, which wrought great destruction and forced him to withdraw behind the walls of captured cities. He contrived to maintain sea communications with Egypt, and the Syrian fleet was never able to get the better of his own, which was now seasoned in war. He could always call up reinforcements from Egypt after his defeats, and gather strength for renewed thrusts. The cities of Syria were laid in ruins, and men hid themselves like wild beasts in the recesses of the hills. The whole region was laid waste, and ravaging hordes trampled the crops and broke down the fruit trees, that the enemy might not live off the land he claimed. Thus the wealth and man power of Egypt drained away, and Egypt was like a mother rending her garments and strewing ashes in her hair as she sees her children die. All along the river, from the Lower Kingdom to the Upper, there was no town, no village, no hovel that had not lost husbands and sons in Syria for the sake of Egypt's greatness.

During these three years I aged more rapidly than in all my earlier years. My hair fell out, my back grew bent, and my face became as wrinkled as a dried fruit. I snapped and spoke harshly to the sick as many physicians do when they grow old, despite their good will. In this respect I was no different from other doctors, although I saw more than most.

In the third year the plague came to Syria, for this follows ever in the wake of war, being engendered in any place where great numbers of rotting corpses are heaped together. The whole of Syria was but one huge, open grave. Whole races died out so that their speech and customs fell into oblivion. Pestilence slew those whom the fighting had spared. Within the armies of both Horemheb and the Hittites it claimed so many victims that warfare ceased and the troops fled into the mountains or the desert, where the scourge could not follow. This plague was no respecter of persons: high and low, rich and poor were its victims, nor was there any known remedy. Those who sickened lay down on their couches, drew a cloth over their heads, and most often died within three days. Such as survived bore terrible scars in armpit and groin, where the pestilent humors were forced out during recovery.

The disease was as capricious in sparing as in slaying. It was not always the strongest and healthiest who survived, but often the weak and starving, as if in these it had found too little to feed on. In tending patients, I came at last to let as much blood from them as I dared and to forbid them food so long as the sickness lasted. I cured many in this way, but a like number died under my hands, and I could not be sure that this treatment was correct. Yet I was compelled to do something for them, that they might retain their faith in my arts. A sick man who loses faith in his recovery and his physician's skill dies more easily than one who believes in them. My treatment was better than many others since it was at any rate cheap for the patient.

Ships carried the plague to Egypt, but fewer died there. It lost its virulence, and the number of those who survived exceeded that of the dead. It disappeared from the land that same year with the rising of the waters. In the winter it departed from Syria also, enabling Horemheb to muster his troops again and continue the war. The following spring he crossed the mountains into the plain before Megiddo and defeated the Hittites in a great battle. When Burnaburiash of Babylon saw the successes of Horemheb, he took fresh courage and remembered his alliance with Egypt. He sent his troops into what had been the land of Mitanni and drove the Hittites from their grazing grounds in Naharani. When the Hittites perceived that the devastated country of Syria was now beyond their grasp, they offered peace, being wise warriors and thrifty men, unwilling to hazard their chariots for empty glory when they needed them to quiet Babylon.

Horemheb rejoiced at this peace. His forces had dwindled, and the war had impoverished Egypt. He desired to build up Syria and its trade and so draw profit from the land. He agreed to make peace on condition that the Hittites yield Megiddo, which Aziru had made his capital and which he had fortified with impregnable walls and towers. Therefore, the Hittites took Aziru prisoner, and having confiscated the immense wealth he had amassed there from all over Syria, they handed him over with his wife and two sons in chains to Horemheb. They then plundered Megiddo and drove the flocks and herds of Amurru northward out of the country, which by the terms of peace was now under Egypt's control.

Horemheb did not quibble at this. Having brought the fighting to an end, he held a banquet for the Hittite princes and chiefs and drank wine with them all night, boasting of his prowess. On the following day he was to execute Aziru and his family before the assembled troops, in token of the eternal peace that should thereafter prevail between Egypt and the land of Hatti.

I would not partake of his banquet but made my way in the darkness to the tent where Aziru lay in chains. I went to Aziru because in the whole of Syria he now had no friend. A man who has lost all his possessions and is condemned to an ignominious death never has any friends. I knew that he dearly loved life, and I hoped to persuade him, by all that I had seen of it, that it was not worth living. I desired to assure him as a doctor that death is easy, easier than life's torments, sorrows, and sufferings. Life is a searing flame, death the dark waters of oblivion. I desired to say all this to him because he was to die the following morning and would be unable to sleep because he loved life so dearly. If he would not listen to me, I thought to sit silently beside him, that he might not lie alone. A man may live without friends, perhaps, but to die without one friend is hard indeed—hardest of all after a life of kingship.

He and his family had been brought in a shameful manner to Horemheb's camp, where the soldiers mocked him and cast mud and horse droppings on him. I avoided him then and covered my face with my garment. He was an exceedingly proud man and would not have wished me to see his degradation since I had once beheld him in the days of his majesty and power. I now went in darkness to his tent, and the guards said one to another, "Let us admit him, for he is Sinuhe the physician and his errand must be lawful. If we forbid him, he will revile us or by witchcraft deprive us of our manhood. He is malignant, and his tongue stings more fiercely than a scorpion."

In the darkness of the tent I said, "Aziru, King of Amurru, will you receive a friend on the eve of your death?"

Aziru sighed deeply, his chains rattled, and he replied, "I am a king no longer and have no friends—but is it indeed you, Sinuhe? I know your voice even in the dark."

"It is I."

"By Marduk and all the devils of the underworld! If you are Sinuhe, bring a light. I am weary of lying in the darkness; I shall have enough of that by and by. The accursed Hittites have torn my clothes and crushed my limbs in torture so that I am no pretty sight. Yet as a physician you must be accustomed to worse ones, and I am not ashamed, for in the face of death it is not worth while to blush for one's wretchedness. Bring a light that I may see your face and put

452

my hand in yours. My liver aches, and water runs from my eyes because of my wife and my boys. If also you can fetch some strong beer to moisten my throat, I will rehearse all your good deeds tomorrow in the kingdom of death. I cannot pay for even a mouthful, for the Hittites have robbed me of my last copper piece."

I bade the guards bring a suet lamp and light it, for the acrid smoke of torches stung my eyes. They also brought a jar of beer. Aziru rose up groaning to a sitting posture, and I helped him put the reed to his mouth, that he might suck up the Syrian beer, which is muddy with husks and malt. His hair was matted and gray, and his splendid beard had been torn when the Hittites tortured him, and great patches of skin had come away with it. His fingers were crushed, his nails black with blood, and his ribs broken so that he groaned as he breathed, and he spat blood.

When he had drunk and spat sufficiently, he gazed at the flame of the lamp and said, "How clear and gentle is that light to my weary eyes, now that I have lain so long in darkness. The flame flickers and will die—and so also does the life of man flicker and die. I thank you, Sinuhe, for the lamp and the beer, and I would willingly make you a gift in return. You know well enough that I have no more presents to give, for my Hittite friends in their rapacity have broken the very teeth you gilded."

It is easy to be wise after the event, and I would not remind him that I had warned him against the Hittites. I took his crushed hand in mine and held it, and he bowed his proud head and wept, so that the tears fell on my hands from his bruised and swollen eyes.

He said, "I rejoiced and laughed before you unashamed in the days of my glory; why then in sorrow should I be ashamed of my tears? Know, Sinuhe, that I do not weep for myself or for my riches and my crowns, although I have ever clung greedily to power and to this world's goods. I weep for my wife Keftiu—for my big, handsome son—and for my little, little son—because they also must die tomorrow."

I said to him, "Aziru, King of Amurru! Remember that all Syria is but one open, stinking grave because of your ambition. Numberless are those who have died for you sake, and it is only fitting that you should die tomorrow since you have lost. Perhaps it is right that your family should die with you. Know, however, that I begged Horemheb to spare the lives of your wife and sons. He would not consent, for he means to wipe out your seed and your name and your very memory in Syria. Therefore he will not even concede you a grave, Aziru, and wild beasts will snarl over your remains. He does not wish the men of Syria to gather at your tomb in times to come and swear iniquitous oaths in your name."

Aziru heard this with dismay and said, "For the sake of my god Baal, make sacrifice of meat and wine before the Baal of Amurru when I am dead, Sinuhe, or I shall be condemned to wander in perpetual hunger and thirst through the dark regions of death. Do this service also for Keftiu, whom you once loved, although because of your friendship you gave her to me—and also for my sons, that I may die with a quiet mind. I do not blame Horemheb for his decision, for no doubt I would have treated him and his family thus had he fallen into my hands. Truth to tell, Sinuhe, though I weep, yet I am glad that my family is to perish with me and that our blood shall mingle in its flow. In the land of death I should forever suffer torment at the thought of Keftiu in the arms of another. She has many admirers, and minstrels have tuned their strings in honor of her luxuriant beauty. Well is it also that my sons perish, for they were born kings and wore their crowns even in the cradle. I would not have them carried into slavery in Egypt."

He sucked again at the beer, and for all his misery he grew a little tipsy. He picked with broken fingers at the filth the soldiers had cast on him, and said, "Sinuhe, my friend, you accuse me falsely in saying that Syria is an open grave through my doing. I am to blame only for losing the war and allowing the Hittites to deceive me. If I had won, all the evil that has come about would have been laid at Egypt's door, and my name would be praised. Because I lost, the blame is cast on me, and my name is anathema throughout Syria."

The strong beer mounted to his head, and tearing his graying hair he cried aloud, saying, "O Syria, Syria! My torment, my hope, my love! I did all for your greatness, and for the sake of your freedom I rose in revolt—but now on the day of my death you cast me out. Fair Byblos, blossoming Smyrna, wily Sidon, Joppa the mighty! All you cities that gleamed like pearls in my crown, why did you forsake me? Yet I love you too dearly to hate you for your desertion. I love Syria because it is Syria: false, brutal, capricious, and ever ready to betray. Races die out; nations rise up only to fall; kingdoms dissolve; fame and glory flee like a shadow—nevertheless endure, endure, my proud cities! Let your white walls sparkle against the red hills of the coast—shine on from age to age—and my dust, borne by the desert winds, shall fly to caress you!"

My heart was filled with sadness to see him yet imprisoned in his

454

dreams, but I would not rebuke him since they brought him comfort on the eve of his death. I held his maimed hands, and he held mine moaning.

We talked throughout the night, recalling our meetings in the time when I dwelt in Smyrna and we were both in the pride of our youth and strength. At dawn my slaves brought us food that they had prepared, and the guards did not forbid them, for they also had their share. The slaves brought us hot fat mutton and rice cooked in fat, and into our cups they poured strong wine from Sidon, spiced with myrrh. I bade them wash Aziru clean of all the filth that had been cast on him and comb and dress his hair and hide his beard in a net fashioned of gold thread. I hid his tattered garments and his chains beneath a royal mantle, for his fetters could not be removed, being of copper and welded on him, so I could not array him in fresh clothes. My slaves did the same service for Keftiu and her two sons, but Horemheb would not allow Aziru to see his wife and children before they met at the place of execution.

When the hour came, and Horemheb, laughing loudly, stepped from his tent with the drunken Hittite princes, I went up to him and said, "Truly, Horemheb, I have done you many services, and it may be that I saved your life when in Tyre I drew the poisoned arrow from your thigh and dressed the wound. Do me this service: Let Aziru die without indignity, for he is the king of Syria and he fought bravely. Your own honor will be enhanced if you accord him this. Your Hittite friends have tortured him enough and crushed his limbs in forcing him to disclose where his wealth was hidden."

Horemheb looked very black at my words, for he had thought of many ingenious ways to prolong the death agony. All was prepared, and already at dawn the army had gathered at the foot of the hillock on which the executions were to take place. The men were fighting among themselves for the best places, that they might make the most of a diverting day. Horemheb had arranged this not because he took delight in torture but in order to amuse his men and spread terror throughout Syria, that after so terrible a death no one might dare even to dream of revolt. I must say this to Horemheb's honor, for he was not by nature cruel, as he was reputed to be. He was a warrior, and death to him was no more than a weapon in his hand. He allowed rumor to exaggerate his brutality, that it might strike terror into the hearts of his enemies and gain him the veneration of all. He believed that men had more respect for a cruel ruler than for a mild one and that they regarded gentleness as weakness.

455

He scowled, and taking his arm from about the neck of Prince Shubattu, he stood before me swaying and striking his leg with his golden whip.

He said to me, "You, Sinuhe, are a perpetual thorn in my side. Unlike any men of sense you are cross grained. You revile all who prosper and raise themselves to honor and affluence; you are tender and ready with consolation to those who fall and are vanquished. You well know with what toil and cost I have brought the most skillful executioners here from every corner of the land on Aziru's account; even to set up their many racks and cauldrons has cost a great quantity of silver. I cannot at the last moment deprive my marsh rats of their pleasure, for all have suffered hardships and have bled from many wounds on Aziru's account."

Shubattu, the Hittite prince, slapped him on the back and laughed, "You say rightly, Horemheb! You will not now deprive us of our pleasure. To save him for your enjoyment we tore no flesh from his bones but only very carefully pinched him with pincers and wooden screws."

In his vanity Horemheb resented these words, nor did it please him to be touched by the prince. He frowned and said, "You are drunk, Shubattu. As for Aziru, I have no other purpose than to show the whole world the fate that awaits any man who trusts the Hittites! Since in the course of this night we have become friends and have drunk many fraternal cups together, I will spare this ally of yours and for friendship's sake will give him an easy death."

Shubattu's face was distorted with rage, for the Hittites are tender of their honor, although as everyone knows they betray and sell their allies without a thought if profitable. Indeed all nations do so and all able rulers. The Hittites are more barefaced in their behavior than others and made no effort to find pretexts and excuses to disguise the matter and give it some veneer of justice. Yet Shubattu was wroth. His companions laid their hands over his mouth, and dragging him away from Horemheb, they held him fast until his impotent fury caused him to spew up the wine he had drunk, and he grew quieter.

Horemheb summoned Aziru from his tent and was greatly astonished to see him step out into the sight of all with the proud bearing of a king, wearing a royal mantle over his shoulders. For Aziru had eaten fat meat and drunk strong wine. He tossed his head and laughed aloud as he walked to the place of execution and shouted insults at the officers and guards. His hair was combed and curled, his face gleamed with oil, and he called to Horemheb over the heads of the

456

soldiers: "Horemheb, you filthy Egyptian! Fear me no longer, for I am defeated and you need not hide now behind the spears of your troops. Come hither that I may wipe the dirt from my feet on your cloak, for such a sty as this camp of yours I never saw in all my life. I would enter the presence of Baal with clean feet."

Horemheb was delighted at his words, and laughing loudly he shouted to Aziru, "I cannot approach you, because the Syrian stench of you turns my stomach, notwithstanding the mantle you have somehow stolen to hide your uncleanly carcass. Yet without doubt you are a valiant man, Aziru, to laugh at death. I give you an easy death, for the sake of my own honor."

He sent his bodyguard to escort Aziru and to prevent the soldiers from casting mud on him. The ruffians of Horemheb surrounded him and smote with their spear shafts at any who offered him abuse, for they no longer felt any hatred for Aziru because of the great sufferings he had brought on them; they admired his courage. They escorted Queen Keftiu also and Aziru's two boys to the place of execution. Keftiu had adorned herself and painted her face with red and white, and the boys stalked to the fateful spot with the bearing of princes, the elder leading the younger by the hand.

When Aziru saw them he weakened and said, "Keftiu, Keftiu, my white mare, my love and the apple of my eye! I am grieved indeed that you must follow me even into death, for life would still have been very sweet to you."

Keftiu answered, "Be not distressed for me, my king. I follow you willingly. You are my husband, and your strength is that of a bull. There is no other man who could content me after you had gone. During our life together I have sundered you from all other women and bound you to me. I will not permit you to go alone into the land of death, where all those fair women who have died before me are assuredly awaiting you. I would follow you there though my life were spared—I would strangle myself in my own hair, my king, for I was but a slave and you made me queen, and I bore you two fine boys."

Aziru was elated at her words and said to his sons, "My handsome boys! You were born into the world as the sons of a king. Die then like princes, that I need not blush for you. Believe me, death is no more painful than a drawn tooth. Be valiant, my sweet boys!"

With this he knelt upon the ground before the headsman. Turning to Keftiu he said, "I am weary of seeing these stinking Egyptians all about me, and their bloodstained spears. Bare your sweet bosom to

457

me, Keftiu, that I may behold your beauty as I go. I shall die as happily as I have lived with you."

Keftiu bared her opulent breasts, the headsman raised the great sword and at one stroke swept Aziru's head from his shoulders. It fell at Keftiu's feet, the rich blood spurted violently from the great body with the last beats of the pulse and splashed the boys so that they were stricken with horror, and the younger one shuddered. But Keftiu lifted Aziru's head from the ground, kissed the swollen lips, and stroked the torn cheeks. Pressing the face to her bosom she said to her sons, "Hasten, my valiant boys! Go to your father without fear, my little ones, for your mother is all impatience to follow him."

The two boys knelt down obediently, the elder one still holding the other by the hand, and the headsman smote their heads from their young necks with ease. Then, having thrust their bodies aside with his foot, he severed Keftiu's fat, white neck at a stroke. Thus all of them received an easy death. But by Horemheb's order their bodies were thrown into a pit to be devoured by wild beasts.

5

Thus my friend Aziru perished without seeking to bribe death, and Horemheb made peace with the Hittites. He knew as well as they that this peace was but an armistice since Sidon, Smyrna, Byblos, and Kadesh were still under their sway. The Hittites had made a strongly fortified base of Kadesh for the control of northern Syria. But now both the Hittites and Horemheb were weary of war, and Horemheb was glad to make peace, for he had interests in Thebes that required his supervision. He needed also to restore order in the land of Kush and among the Nubians, who in their freedom had run wild and refused to pay tribute to Egypt.

Tutankhamon reigned in Egypt during these years, though he was but a stripling and took interest in nothing but the building of his own tomb. The people blamed him for all the loss and misery resulting from the war. Their hatred for him was bitter, and they said, "What can we expect of a Pharaoh whose consort is of the blood of the false Pharaoh?"

Eie did not quell such talk but rather spread new stories among the people, of Tutankhamon's thoughtlessness and greed, and of his attempts to gather all the treasures of Egypt into his tomb.

Throughout this time I was never once in Thebes but traveled

458

everywhere with the army, which required my skill, and I shared its hardships and privations. Yet from the men of Thebes I learned that Pharaoh Tutankhamon was frail and sickly and that some secret illness consumed his body. It seemed that the war in Syria had used up his strength. Whenever news come of a victory for Horemheb, Pharaoh fell sick. After a defeat he recovered and rose from his bed. This, they said, had every appearance of sorcery, and anyone who kept his eyes open could see that Pharaoh's health was bound up with the Syrian war.

As time went on, Eie grew ever more impatient, and time after time he sent this message to Horemheb:

"Can you not cease this warfare and give peace to Egypt? I am already an old man and weary of waiting. Conquer, Horemheb, and bring us peace that I may have my agreed reward. I will see to it that you too have yours."

For this reason I was not at all surprised when, after the war was over and we were sailing up the river in warships decked with banners, we were met by the news that Pharaoh Tutankhamon had stepped into the golden boat of his father Ammon to sail to the Western Land. It was said that Tutankhamon had had a severe attack on the day that tidings reached Thebes of the fall of Megiddo and the conclusion of peace. The nature of the fatal disorder was the subject of dispute among the physicians of the House of Life. It was said that his stomach was blackened with poison, but no one had certain knowledge of the cause. The people would have it that he died of an access of his own malignance when the war ended, because his greatest delight had been to see Egypt suffer.

I know that in pressing his seal into the clay at the foot of the peace treaty, Horemheb killed Pharaoh as surely as if he had thrust a knife into his heart. Peace was all that Eie had been waiting for before sweeping Tutankhamon from his path and ascending the throne as the "Peace King."

We were compelled to soil our faces and to haul down the bright pennants of the ships, and Horemheb, in bitter resentment, loosed and threw into the river the bodies of Syrian and Hittite commanders, which, in the manner of the great Pharaohs, he had hung head downward from the bows of his ship. He had left his marsh rats in Syria to bring peace to the country and to stuff themselves on the fat of the land after all the hardships and tribulations of the war. His ruffians—his scum—he brought home with him, to celebrate the peace in

459

Thebes. These also were bitter and cursed Tutankhamon, who even in death destroyed their pleasure.

So I returned to Thebes and resolved never again to leave it. My eyes had seen enough of man's evil ways, and there was nothing new beneath the ancient sun. I resolved to remain and live out my days in poverty in the copperfounder's house. All the wealth I had acquired in Syria had been spent on sacrifices for Aziru, being riches I had no desire to keep. To me they smelled of blood, and I should have had no joy of them.

Even yet my measure was not full. A task was now allotted me that I did not desire and that filled me with dread. I could not evade it, and once more, after only a few days, I departed from Thebes. Eie and Horemheb believed that they had spun their webs and carried out their plans with great sagacity, so as to bring power fully into their hands. But this power slipped through their fingers before they knew it, and the destiny of Egypt hung on a woman's whim.

BOOK 15
Horemheb

IN ACCORDANCE with the bargain struck with Horemheb, Eie was to be crowned Pharaoh as soon as Tutankhamon's funeral obsequies were over. He therefore hastened the embalming and stopped further work on the tomb, which remained small and insignificant in comparison with those of the great Pharaohs. By the same agreement he had engaged to coerce Princess Baketamon into marriage with Horemheb, thus enabling Horemheb to prefer a lawful claim to the throne after Eie's death, despite his low birth. Eie had arranged with the priests that, after the period of mourning was over and Horemheb came to celebrate the festival of victory, Princess Baketamon should appear before Horemheb in the guise of Sekhmet, in Sekhmet's temple, and there give herself to him, that their union might be blessed by the gods and Horemheb himself become divine. Such was Eie's plan, but the Princess, with much care and forethought, had made her own, in which I know Queen Nefertiti encouraged her. Queen Nefertiti hated Horemheb, and she hoped also to become—next to Baketamon—the most powerful woman in Egypt.

So godless, so iniquitous was this plan that only the guile of a malignant woman could have conceived it. So incredible was it that it came near to succeeding. Only when this scheme became known could the magnanimity of the Hittites be accounted for, as shown in their offers of peace, their yielding of Megiddo and the land of Amurru, and in their other concessions.

Since the death of Nefertiti's husband and her enforced submission to Ammon, the Queen had been unable to endure the thought of being set aside from the throne and becoming of no more consequence than any other lady about the court. She was still beautiful, though her beauty now required meticulous care for its preservation. It won to her many of Egypt's nobles, who hung like drones about the court and its inconsiderable Pharaoh. By her intelligence and guile she also won the friendship of Princess Baketamon, whose innate haughtiness she fanned to a blaze until what had been pride became mania. The

Princess became so arrogant that she would not suffer the touch of any ordinary mortal nor even allow anyone to pass through her shadow. She had preserved her virginity in the belief that there was no man in Egypt worthy of her and was already past the normal age for marriage. Maidenhood had gone to her head, but I believe a good marriage might have cured her.

Nefertiti persuaded Baketamon that she was born to achieve great things and to liberate Egypt from the hands of low-born usurpers. She spoke to her of the great Queen Hatshepsut, who fastened a royal beard to her chin, girded herself with a lion's tail, and ruled Egypt from the throne of the Pharaohs. She declared that Baketamon's beauty resembled that of the great queen.

She also spoke much evil of Horemheb so that the Princess in her maidenly pride began to dread him as a man of low birth and as one who might possess her with a warrior's roughness and defile her sacred blood. Yet I believe she was secretly fascinated by his rough strength—she had looked on him overmuch and been inflamed by his glance, although she would never admit as much even to herself.

Nefertiti had no difficulty in exerting her influence over the Princess when, as the Syrian war drew to an end, Eie's and Horemheb's plans became ever more evident. I do not fancy that Eie attempted to conceal his purpose from his daughter Nefertiti. But she hated her father because, having made what use he could of her, he had thrust her aside and kept her hidden in the golden house because she was the widow of the accursed Pharaoh. Beauty and intelligence united in a woman whose heart the years have hardened are dangerous qualities— more dangerous than knives unsheathed, more destructive than the copper scythes of chariots. The best proof of this lies in the scheme Nefertiti contrived and in which she persuaded Princess Baketamon to join.

The plot came to light when Horemheb, having just arrived in Thebes, began in his impatience to loiter about the apartments of Princess Baketamon in order to see and speak with her, although she refused to receive him. Chancing to see there a Hittite envoy who sought an audience of the Princess, he wondered why she should receive such a man and give him so long an interview. Of his own accord, therefore, and without taking counsel of any, he arrested this Hittite, whose manner was haughty and who addressed him in terms only to be used by such as are sure of their authority.

Horemheb then reported this to Eie. At night they forced an entry into her rooms, slew the slaves who guarded her, and discovered certain correspondence she had hidden in the ashes of a brazier. Profoundly dismayed at the contents of these tablets, they imprisoned Baketamon in her rooms and set a guard both on her and on Nefertiti. That same night they came to the copperfounder's house, which Muti had had rebuilt with Kaptah's silver; they came in an ordinary carrying chair, concealing their faces. Muti admitted them, muttering angrily when they ordered her to wake me. I was not asleep; ever since witnessing the horrors in Syria, I had slept badly. I rose from my couch while she was yet grumbling, and having lit lamps, I received these strangers in the belief that they required my help as a physician.

When I saw who they were, I marveled, and when Muti at my order had brought in wine, I sent her back to bed. In his great fear Horemheb would have slain her because she had seen their faces and might hear their talk. Never had I seen Horemheb so frightened, and it gave me the greatest satisfaction.

I said, "I shall not permit you to slay Muti; you must be brain sick to talk so wildly. Muti is a deaf old hag who snores like a hippopotamus. If you will listen, you will soon hear her. Drink wine, therefore, and be assured that you need not tremble because of an old woman."

Horemheb said impatiently, "I have not come here to talk of snores, Sinuhe. What is a life more or less when all Egypt is in mortal danger? It is Egypt you must save."

Eie bore out his words, saying, "Truly Egypt is in mortal danger, Sinuhe—and I also! Never before has so great a peril menaced the land; in our distress we turn to you."

I laughed bitterly and threw out empty hands. Horemheb brought out King Shubbiluliuma's clay tablets for me to read and also copies of the letters Princess Baketamon had sent to him before the war ended. I read them and had no further desire to laugh, and the wine in my mouth lost its savor. Princess Baketamon wrote thus:

"I am Pharaoh's daughter, and in my veins flows the sacred blood. There is in all Egypt no man worthy of me. I have heard that you have many sons. Send a son to me that I may break the jar with him, and he shall rule over the land of Kem at my side."

So incredible was the tenor of this letter that the cautious Shubbiluliuma would not believe it and by the hand of a secret envoy returned a suspicious inquiry as to terms. In a further letter Baketamon repeated her offer, with the assurance that both the Egyptian nobles and the priests of Ammon were on her side. At this Shubbiluliuma

465

was persuaded of her sincerity and had hastened to make peace with Horemheb and was even now preparing to send his son Shubattu to Egypt. It was agreed that Shubattu should set forth from Kadesh on an auspicious day, with a great quantity of presents for Baketamon. According to the last clay tablet that had been received, he was already on his way to Egypt with his suite.

"By all the gods of Egypt!" I said in amazement. "How am I to help you? I am but a physician and cannot incline the heart of a mad woman to Horemheb."

Horemheb replied, "You helped us once before, and he who once takes up the oar must row whether he will or no. You must journey to meet Prince Shubattu and see that he never reaches Egypt. I do not know how you will contrive this and do not wish to know. I say only that we cannot openly murder him, for this would cause another war with the Hittites. I prefer to choose the time for that myself."

His words alarmed me, and my knees began to tremble. My heart turned to water, and my tongue stumbled as I said, "Though it be true that I once helped you, yet I did it as much for my own sake as for Egypt's. This prince has never wronged me, and I have seen him but once outside your tent on the day of Aziru's death. No, Horemheb, you shall not make an assassin of me. I would rather die, for there is no more shameful crime. In giving poison to Pharaoh Akhnaton I acted for his own good; he was sick, and I was his friend."

Horemheb scowled and smote his leg with his whip, and Eie said, "Sinuhe, you are a wise man and can see that we must not lose a whole kingdom beneath the couch of a capricious woman. Believe me, there is no other way. The prince must die on his way to Egypt—whether by accident or by illness is indifferent to me. You must journey to meet him in the desert of Sinai; you will go at the orders of Princess Baketamon, as a physician, to examine him and see whether he is competent to fulfill the duties of a husband. He will readily believe this and will receive you cordially, with many questions as to Baketamon. Even princes are human, and I fancy he is most curious to know by what manner of sorceress Egypt hopes to bind him. Sinuhe, your task will be easy, and you will not despise the gifts its fulfillment will bring you, for they will make you a rich man."

Horemheb said, "Choose quickly, Sinuhe, between life and death. Should you refuse, we cannot allow you to live now that you know so much, though you were a hundred times my friend. The name your mother gave you was an ill omen; already you have learned too many of the secrets of the Pharaohs. One word, and I slit your throat from

466

ear to ear—though unwillingly, for you are our best agent and we cannot entrust the task to any other. You are bound to us through a joint crime, and this crime we shall also share with you—if indeed you call that a crime which frees Egypt from the power of the Hittites and of a mad woman."

Thus I found myself caught in a net my own deeds had knotted, and of which I could break not one mesh. I had bound my destiny with those of Eie and Horemheb forever.

"You know very well that I do not fear death, Horemheb," I said, in a vain attempt to give myself courage.

I write for myself, without seeking to appear better than I am. To my shame I must confess that the thought of death filled me with fear that night, chiefly because it came on me so swiftly. I thought of the swallows' darting flight above the river and of the wine from the harbor; I thought of the goose Muti roasted in the Theban manner, and life was suddenly very sweet to me. I thought also of Egypt and reflected that Pharaoh Akhnaton had had to die that Egypt might live and that Horemheb might avert the Hittite attack by force of arms. Yet Akhnaton was my friend. This prince of a foreign land was quite unknown to me, and doubtless he had done such deeds in the course of the war as to merit a thousand deaths. Why should I hesitate to murder him to save Egypt once again since I had already slain Akhnaton?

I answered, "Lay aside your knife, Horemheb, for the sight of a blunt knife is irritating to me. Be it as you say. I will save Egypt from the power of the Hittites, though how I do not yet know. In all probability I shall lose my life in the doing of it, for the Hittites will certainly slay me if the prince dies. But I care little for my life, and I do not desire the Hittites to rule in Egypt. I undertake this for the sake neither of gifts nor of fair promises, but because the deed was written in the stars before my birth and may not be evaded. Receive the crowns from my hand, Horemheb and Eie; receive your crowns and bless my name, for I, an insignificant physician, have made Pharaohs of you!"

I felt a great desire to laugh as I said this. I reflected that the sacred blood ran most probably in my own veins and that I was the only rightful heir to the throne of the Pharaohs, while Eie was by origin no more than a minor priest of the sun and the parents of Horemheb smelled of cattle and cheese. At that moment I saw them both for what they were: robbers despoiling the dying body of Egypt, children play-

467

ing with crowns and emblems of power, so chained and fettered by their desires that happiness could never be theirs.

I said to Horemheb, "Horemheb, my friend, the crown is heavy. You will learn this some hot day when toward evening the cattle come down to the water's edge to drink and the voices about you fall silent."

But Horemheb said, "Make haste now and go. A ship awaits you, and you must meet Shubattu in the Sinai desert before he reaches Tanis with his suite."

Thus I departed once more from Thebes, suddenly and by night. I went aboard Horemheb's swiftest ship, taking my medicine chest, some wine, and the remains of the roast goose that Muti had served me for dinner.

2

Once more I was alone, in a loneliness exceeding that of other men, for there was no one to whom I could lay bare my innermost thoughts and reveal the secret that, if it were made known, would have occasioned the death of thousands. I had therefore to be wilier than a serpent, and I was goaded on by the knowledge that if caught I should suffer a hideous death at the hands of the Hittites.

I was sorely tempted to abandon the task and seek refuge in some remote place, like my namesake Sinuhe of the legend, and let destiny roll forward over Egypt. Had I acted so, the course of events might well have altered and the world today been otherwise. Yet now in my old age I perceive that all rulers are in essence alike and all nations also. It signifies little who rules or which nation oppresses another since ultimately it is the poor who suffer.

But I did not flee, being weak. When a mortal is weak, he lets himself be led even to the commission of a fearful deed sooner than choose his own way.

Therefore, Prince Shubattu must die. Sitting beneath the golden awning with a jar of wine beside me, I strove to hit on some way of killing that would remain undiscovered, so neither I nor Egypt might be held answerable. The task was no easy one, for the prince would certainly travel in a style befitting his rank. The Hittites, being suspicious by nature, no doubt kept a sharp watch upon his safety. Even if I met him alone in the desert, I could not have slain him with such means as offered, for spear and arrow leave traces, and the crime would have been manifest. I considered whether I might lure him to seek me with the basilisk of the desert, whose eyes are green stones, and hurl him into a crevasse so that I could report that his foot had slipped and that he had broken his neck. But this plan was childish, for I was certain never to be left alone with him. As for poison, the Hittites were ever attended by cupbearers who tasted both food and drink beforehand so that this also was impracticable.

I then remembered stories of the secret poisons of the priests and of the golden house. I had heard that there were ways of introducing poison into fruit still growing green upon the tree so that whoever plucked and ate the fruit when ripe met his death. There were also certain scrolls that brought slow death to him who opened them, and flowers whose scent, when priests had handled them, was fatal. But these were secrets of the priesthood, and I fancy that many of these tales were tales only. Even had they been true and I conversant with them, I could not well have cultivated fruit trees in the desert. No Hittite prince would open a scroll; he would hand it to his scribe. Nor were the Hittites in the habit of smelling flowers but rather slashed at their stems with whips and trod them underfoot.

I wished I had Kaptah's cunning to help me, but I could not involve him in this affair. Besides, he was still in Syria collecting his dues. I summoned up my powers of invention and all my medical science, for a doctor is familiar with death, and with the materials at his command he may bring death as readily as life to his patients. If Prince Shubattu had been ill and I appointed to tend him, I could have tended him to death at my ease, according to all the laws of medicine, nor could any self-respecting physician have condemned my treatment since throughout all ages the medical faculty have helped one another to bury their dead. But Shubattu was not ill, and if he were to sicken he would summon a Hittite rather than an Egyptian physician.

I have set forth my musings in detail, to show how exacting was the task Horemheb had laid on me, but now I will speak only of what I did. In the House of Life at Memphis I replenished my stock of drugs, and no one marveled at the prescriptions I wrote, for what to a layman is deadly poison may in the hands of a physician be a sound remedy. Then without further delay I continued my journey to Tanis, where I hired a chair and was furnished by the garrison with an escort of chariots to attend me along the great military road through the desert.

Horemheb's information proved correct. I met Shubattu and his suite three days out from Tanis, encamped by a well. Shubattu also traveled in a chair to save his strength, and he brought with him many pack asses laden with gifts for Princess Baketamon. Heavy chariots ensured safety on his journey, and light chariots reconnoitered the road ahead, for King Shubbiluliuma had commanded him to be prepared for all surprise attacks, being well aware that the expedition was far from agreeable to Horemheb.

But the Hittites displayed great cordiality and courtesy to me and the officers of my modest escort, as is their way when they receive as a present what they cannot attain by force of arms. They received us in the camp they had pitched for the night, and having helped the Egyptian officers to set up our tents, they surrounded us with many guards, saying that they desired to defend us against robbers and against the lions of the desert, that we might sleep in peace. When Prince Shubattu heard that I had been sent by Princess Baketamon, his curiosity got the better of him, and he summoned me into his presence.

He was a splendid-looking young man whose eyes—now that he was not drunk as when I had last seen him—were large and limpid. Happiness and interest brought color into his dark face. His nose was as noble as the beak of a bird of prey, his teeth gleamed like the teeth of a wild beast, and he laughed with pleasure at the sight of me. I handed him a letter from Princess Baketamon, forged by Eie, and stretched forth my hands at knee level before him with every mark of veneration, as though he were already my sovereign. I was greatly diverted to note that before receiving me he had arrayed himself in the Egyptian manner and now found himself embarrassed by these garments, to which he was unaccustomed.

He said to me, "Since my future consort has confided in you and you are physician to the household, I will conceal nothing from you. When a prince marries, he is bound to his partner. My consort's country shall be my country, Egypt's customs my customs. I have striven as far as may be to adopt them already, that I may not come as a stranger to Thebes. I am impatient to see the wonders of Egypt of which so much has been told me and to become acquainted with its mighty gods, which henceforth shall be my gods also. But most eager am I to see my royal consort, for by her will I found a new ruling race in Egypt. Tell me about her, therefore. Tell me of her size and her figure and of the breadth of her loins as if I were already an Egyptian. Do no conceal any flaw in her from me, but trust me like a brother, as I trust you."

His trust was shown in a group of officers who stood behind him with drawn swords and in the soldiers who guarded the tent door with spears directed at my back. But I feigned to notice nothing of this.

470

Bowing to the ground before him, I said, "My royal lady, Princess Baketamon, is one of the fairest women in Egypt. Because of her sacred blood she has preserved her virginity although she is some years older than yourself. Her beauty is timeless, her face is like the moon, and her eyes like lotus flowers. As a physician I can assure you that her loins are fit for childbearing although narrow, like those of all Egyptian women. She has sent me to meet you, to satisfy herself that your royal blood is worthy of hers and that you can fulfill the bodily requirements of a husband without causing her any disappointment. She awaits you with impatience, having never in her life been possessed by a man."

Prince Shubattu threw out his chest and raised his elbows to shoulder level to display the muscles of his arms, and he said, "My arms can draw the strongest bow, and with the grip of my knees I can squeeze the breath from an ass. There is no fault to be found with my face, as you may see, and I cannot remember when I was last ill."

I said to him, "You are indeed an inexperienced youth and ignorant of the customs of Egypt if you think that an Egyptian princess is a bow to be drawn or a donkey to be gripped between the knees. This is far from being the case, and it is clear that I must give you a few lectures in the Egyptian arts of love, that you may not cover yourself with ignominy in the eyes of the Princess. She was indeed well advised to send me hither so that as a physician I may initiate you into the customs of Egypt."

My words sorely wounded Prince Shubattu, for he was a high-mettled boy and like all Hittites was proud of his virility. His officers burst out laughing, and this still further incensed him. He whitened in fury and ground his teeth. But to me he sought to maintain the suave Egyptian manner, and he said as composedly as he could, "I am no such inexperienced boy as you seem to think, and my spear has pierced many a fair skin! I do not think that your Princess will be ill content with the arts of the land of Hatti."

I answered, "I readily believe in your strength, my ruler, but you must have been mistaken when you said you could not remember when last you were ill. I am a physician and can see by your eyes and your cheeks that you are sick now and are troubled by a flux."

There is no human being who does not end by believing he is sick when assured long and constantly that he is so. At heart everyone feels the desire to be pampered and tended. Doctors in every age have been aware of this, and the knowledge has made them rich. I had the fur-

471

ther advantage of knowing that the desert springs contained lye which loosens the bowels of those who are not seasoned to it.

Prince Shubattu was astonished at my words and cried, "You are certainly mistaken, Sinuhe the Egyptian. I feel in no way ill, although I must admit that I have a flux and have had continually to squat by the roadside in the course of my journey. But how you know this I cannot think. You must certainly be more skilled than my own physician, who has taken no note whatever of my disorder."

He listened to himself, and feeling his eyes and brow he said, "In truth I do feel a burning in my eyes after staring all day at the red sand of the desert. My forehead also is hot, and I am not as well as I could wish."

I said to him, "It would be well for your physician to give you a medicine to ease your stomach and give you a good sleep. The stomach disorders of the desert are severe, and I know that a number of Egyptians died of them on their march to Syria. No one knows the origin of these complaints. Some say that they are born of the poisonous desert winds; some blame the water, and others the locusts. I do not doubt that tomorrow you will be well again and able to continue your journey if your physician will mix you a good draught this evening."

He began to ponder at this. His eyes narrowed, and glancing at his chiefs, he said to me, smiling like a mischievous boy, "Do *you* mix me such a potion, Sinuhe. Without doubt you are more familiar with these strange desert diseases than my own attendant."

But I was no such fool. I raised my hands in protest and said, "Far be it from me! I dare not prepare any such remedy for you. Should you become worse, you would blame me and say that as an Egyptian I wished you ill. Your own physician will tend you as well as I, and better. He is familiar with your constitution and your former disorders. He need do no more than give you a simple binding medicine."

He smiled and said, "Perhaps your counsel is good. I mean to eat and drink with you, that you may tell me of my royal consort and of Egyptian customs, and I do not desire to be forever running out and squatting behind the tent during your account."

He summoned his own physician, who was an irritable and suspicious Hittite, and we took professional counsel together. When he found that I had no desire to compete with him, he conceived a liking for me and did as I advised. He prepared a binding medicine of exceptional strength, which I had my own reason for prescribing. When it was ready, he drank from the cup before handing it to the Prince.

472

I knew that the Prince was not sick, but I desired his suite to believe that he was. I desired also to bind his stomach, that the draught I proposed to administer might not pass through him overrapidly. Before the meal he had ordered in my honor I went to my tent and drank my stomach full of oil—despite the nausea it caused me—so as to preserve my own life. I then took a small jar of wine with which I had mixed the poison. This jar, which I had resealed, held enough for two cups only. I returned to the prince's tent with it, sat on his mat, and ate the dishes his slaves set before me, and drank the wine his stewards poured into our cups. Despite severe nausea I related lurid stories of Egyptian customs to divert the Prince and his followers.

Prince Shubattu laughed with flashing teeth; he slapped me on the back and said, "You are an entertaining fellow, Sinuhe, Egyptian though you be, and when I have settled in Egypt I will make you my physician. Truly I choke with laughter and forget my disorder when you tell of Egyptian marriage practices, although I fancy the Egyptians have adopted them only to avoid the begetting of children. I mean to teach Egypt many Hittite practices, and I will make my officers regional governors—which I think will be most beneficial to Egypt—so soon as I have given the Princess her due."

He smote his knees, and being by now somewhat exalted with the wine, he laughed and said, "In truth I could wish the Princess already lay on my mat, for your tales have greatly inflamed me, Sinuhe, and I know I shall cause her to groan in her ecstasy. By the holy heavens and the Earth Mother! When the land of Hatti and Egypt are united, no kingdom on earth will be able to withstand our power, and we shall gather under our sway the four corners of the world. But Egypt must first be imbued with iron and fire until every man there believes that death is better than life. All this shall come about, and soon!"

He raised his goblet and drank, and he poured libations to the Earth Mother and to the heavens until his cup was empty. By now all the Hittites were somewhat fuddled, and my merry tales had melted their misgivings.

I profited by the occasion and said, "I would not insult you or your wine, Shubattu, but it is plain that you have never tasted the wine of Egypt. Had you tasted it, all other wine would seem to you as insipid as water. Forgive me, therefore, if I drink of my own wine, for that alone can make me drunk, which is the reason I always take it with me to the banquets of strangers."

I shook my wine jar and broke the seal before his eyes, and in feigned drunkenness I poured the wine into my cup so that it slopped on the ground. I drank and exclaimed, "Ah, this is the wine of Memphis—pyramid wine paid for in gold—strong, sweet, and heady—unparalleled in all the world!"

The wine was indeed strong and good, and I had mixed myrrh with it so that the whole tent was perfumed when I opened the jar. Even through wine and myrrh I tasted the tang of death. I spilled much of it down my chin as I drank, but the Hittites attributed this to my fuddled condition.

Prince Shubattu was curious, and holding out his cup to me, he said, "I am no stranger to you. Tomorrow I shall be your lord and Pharaoh. Let me taste your wine, or I shall not believe it is as excellent as you say."

But I pressed the wine jar to my breast and refused him earnestly, saying, "This wine does not suffice for two, and I have no more with me, and I desire to get drunk this evening because this is a day of great rejoicing for all Egypt and the land of Hatti—hee-haw, hee-haw!"

I brayed like a donkey and pressed the wine jar closer. The Hittites doubled up with laughing and smote their knees, but Shubattu was accustomed to having every wish granted. He begged and besought me to let him taste of my wine until at last I wept and filled his cup until my little jar was empty. Nor was it hard for me to weep, so great was my terror at this moment.

When Shubattu had been given the wine, he looked about him as if warned by some misgiving. Then in the Hittite manner he held out the cup to me saying, "Hallow my cup, as you are my friend, and I will do you a like favor."

He said this because he did not wish to seem suspicious and let his cupbearer taste the wine. I took a deep draught from his cup, whereupon he emptied it, tasted the wine, and seemed to be listening to his body with his head on one side as he said, "Truly your wine is strong, Sinuhe! It mounts to the head like smoke and burns the stomach like fire, but it leaves a bitter taste in the mouth, which I will rinse away with wine from the mountains."

He refilled his cup with his own wine, thus swilling it out. I knew the poison would not take effect until the morning because his bowels were bound and he had eaten copiously.

I swallowed as much wine as I could and pretended to be very drunk. I waited yet half a water measure's time before I bade them lead me to my tent, lest I should arouse suspicion in the minds of the Hittites. I clung tightly to my empty wine jar that it might not be left behind to be examined by them. When the Hittites, with many coarse jests, had put me to bed and left me to myself, I rose hastily. Thrusting my finger down my throat, I vomited the poison and the protecting oil. So acute was my fear that the sweat poured off me and my knees trembled, and perhaps the poison had to some extent affected me. Therefore, I rinsed my stomach many times; I drank cleansing draughts and vomited repeatedly until at last I threw up from pure fright without the help of emetics.

Not until I was as limp as a wet rag did I rinse out the wine jar, smash it, and bury the pieces in the sand. After this I lay sleepless, trembling with fear and with the effects of the poison. All night long Shubattu's great eyes gazed at me; I saw his face before me in the darkness and could not forget his proud, careless laugh and his dazzling teeth.

3

Hittite pride came to my aid. Next morning when Prince Shubattu felt indisposed, he would not confess to it or put off the journey because of the pains in his stomach. He stepped into his chair denying that he suffered, although this required great self-mastery. The journey continued all day, therefore, and when I passed his chair, he waved to me and strove to smile. His physician twice administered binding and pain-killing medicines, thus aggravating his condition by allowing the poison to exert its full effect. A powerful purge might even then have saved his life.

In the afternoon he fell into a deep coma. His eyes turned in his head, and his drawn face assumed a yellow pallor, striking terror to the heart of his physician, who summoned me to his aid. When I saw his desperate plight, I had no need to feign terror, for it was real enough and chilled me despite the day's heat. I felt ill already from the poison. I said that I knew the symptoms to be those of the desert sickness, of which I had warned Shubattu the evening before and of which I had read the signs in his face, although he would not heed me.

The caravan halted, and we tended him where he lay in his chair, giving him stimulants and cleansing draughts and laying hot stones to his stomach. I saw to it that the Hittite physician alone mixed the drugs and administered them, forcing them between the Prince's clenched teeth. I knew that he would die and desired by my counsel to render his death as painless and easy as might be since I could not do more.

When evening came we bore him to his tent. The Hittites gathered outside to mourn aloud, to rend their clothes, strew ashes in their hair, and gash themselves with knives. They were in mortal fear, knowing that King Shubbiluliuma would have no mercy on them if the Prince died in their charge. I watched with the Hittite physician at the bedside of the Prince and saw this fair youth, who but the day before had been robust and happy, wasting away in pallor and ugliness before my eyes.

The Hittite physician, filled with suspicion and despair, made continual examination of his condition, but the symptoms were no different from those of a severe stomach disorder. No one thought of poison since I had drunk the same wine from his cup. I had carried out my task with noteworthy skill and with great profit to Egypt; yet I felt no pride as I watched Prince Shubattu die.

On the following day he regained consciousness. As death approached, he called softly for his mother, like a sick child. In a low, pitiful voice he moaned, "Mother, Mother! My lovely Mother!" But when the pains loosed their grip of him, his face lit up in a boyish smile and he remembered that he was of royal blood.

He summoned his officers and said, "Let no one bear the blame for my death, for it has come on me in the form of the desert sickness, and I have been tended by the best physician of the land of Hatti and the most eminent physician of Egypt. Their arts have not availed to cure me, because it is the will of the heavens and of the Earth Mother that I should die—and assuredly the desert is ruled not by the Earth Mother but by the gods of Egypt, and it exists to protect Egypt. The Hittites must not seek to cross the desert, for my death is a sign of this, even as the defeat of our chariots in the desert was a sign although we would not heed it. Give the physicians a present worthy of me when I am dead. And you, Sinuhe, greet Princess Baketamon and say that I release her from her promise and feel great sorrow because I may not carry her to her marriage bed for my own joy and hers. Bring her this greeting, for as I die I see her floating in my dreams like a story princess, and I die with her timeless beauty before my eyes though I have never seen her."

He went with a smile on his lips, for death comes at times like bliss after great agony, and his eyes before they faded saw strange visions. I surveyed him trembling, forgetful of his race, his speech, and the color of his skin; I remembered only that he, my fellow man, died by my hand and my wickedness. Hardened though I was by all the deaths

476

I had witnessed during my lifetime, yet my heart quaked at the passing of Prince Shubattu, and the tears poured down my cheeks.

The Hittites laid his body in strong wine and honey that they might bear it to the royal tombs, where eagles and wolves watched over the eternal sleep of kings. They were touched by my emotion, and at my desire they willingly certified on a clay tablet that I was in no way to blame for Prince Shubattu's death but had exerted every art to save him. They attested this with their seals and with the seal of Prince Shubattu, that no shadow might fall on me in Egypt because of their lord's death. For they judged Egypt by themselves and believed that when I told Princess Baketamon of Prince Shubattu's fate she would have me put to death.

Thus I saved Egypt from the power of the Hittites, and I ought to have rejoiced. I did not, being oppressed with the sense that death followed ever at my heels. I had become a physician that I might heal and give life, but my father and mother died because of my wickedness, Minea died because of my weakness, Merit and little Thoth because of my blindness, and Pharaoh Akhnaton because of my hatred and my friendship and for the sake of Egypt. All whom I loved died a violent death—Prince Shubattu also, whom I had grown to love during his death agony. Everywhere, a curse went with me.

I returned to Tanis, to Memphis, and at last to Thebes. I gave orders for my ship to be made fast at the quay of the golden house, and having entered the presence of Eie and Horemheb, I said to them, "Your will has been done. Prince Shubattu has perished in the Sinai desert, and no shadow falls on Egypt because of his death."

They rejoiced greatly at my words. Eie took the golden chain of the scepter bearer from his neck and hung it about my own, and Horemheb said, "Relate this also to Princess Baketamon; she will not believe us if we tell her of it, but will fancy that I have had him assassinated out of jealousy."

Princess Baketamon received me. She had painted her cheeks and mouth brick red, but in her dark, oval eyes lurked death.

I said to her, "Your chosen, Prince Shubattu, released you from your promise before he died. He died in the desert of Sinai, of the desert sickness. No arts of mine availed to save him nor yet those of the Hittite physician."

She took the golden bangles from her wrists, and setting them on mine, she said, "Your news is good, Sinuhe, and I thank you for it. I have already been initiated as a priestess of Sekhmet, and my crimson robe is in readiness for the festival. Nevertheless, this desert sickness is only too familiar, and I know that my brother Akhnaton, whom I loved with a sister's love, died of the same. Accursed be you, therefore, Sinuhe—accursed to all eternity! May your grave also be accursed and your name fall into perpetual oblivion. You have made the throne of the Pharaohs a playground for robbers, and in my blood you have desecrated the blood of the Pharaohs."

Bowing deeply before her, I stretched forth my hands and said, "Be it as you say."

I left her, and she bade her slaves sweep the floor after me all the way to the threshold of the golden house.

4

During this time the body of Tutankhamon had been prepared to withstand death, and Eie had the priests bear him swiftly westward to his eternal resting place, which had been hewn in the rock in the Valley of the Tombs of the Kings. He had with him many presents, although Eie kept for himself a great portion of the treasure that Tutankhamon had intended for burial. As soon as the entrance to the tomb had been sealed, Eie pronounced the period of mourning at an end, and Horemheb sent his chariots to occupy the streets of Thebes.

None rebelled when Eie was crowned Pharaoh, for the people were weary, as a beast that is goaded with spears along an endless path is weary. No one questioned his right to the crown.

Thus Eie was crowned Pharaoh. The priests, whom he had bribed with countless gifts, anointed him with holy oil in the great temple, and the people shouted his praise for he distributed bread and beer among them, and so poor had Egypt become that these were now munificent gifts. But many were aware that henceforth the true ruler of Egypt was Horemheb, and they wondered silently why he did not himself take the power into his own hands instead of allowing the aged and detested Eie to ascend the throne of the Pharaohs.

But Horemheb knew well what he was doing, for the people's cup of suffering was not yet drained to the dregs. Bad news from the land of Kush summoned him to war against the Negroes, and after that he still had to renew the conflict against the Hittites for the conquest of Syria. For this reason he wanted the people to blame Eie for their sufferings and want, that later they might praise the name of Horemheb as victor and restorer of peace.

Eie never considered this, being dazzled by power and by the glitter of the crowns, and he willingly fulfilled his part of the bargain he had struck with Horemheb on the day of Akhnaton's death. The priests brought Princess Baketamon in ceremonial procession to the temple of Sekhmet, where they arrayed her in the crimson robe and raised her on Sekhmet's altar. Horemheb arrived at the temple with his men, in celebration of his victory over the Hittites. All Thebes shouted his praise. Having distributed golden chains and tokens of honor among his men, he let them go. Then he stepped into the temple, and the priests closed its copper doors behind him. Sekhmet appeared to him in the shape of Princess Baketamon, and he took her. He was a warrior and had waited long.

That night all Thebes celebrated the festival of Sekhmet, and the sky glowed red with the light of lamps and torches. Horemheb's scum drank all the taverns dry and smashed in the doors of the pleasure houses. At dawn the soldiers once more assembled before the temple of Sekhmet to see Horemheb come forth. When the copper gates were opened and he stepped out, they cried aloud and swore in many tongues, for Sekhmet had been faithful to her lion's head. Horemheb's face and arms and shoulders were scratched and bleeding as if a lion had torn him with its claws. This diverted his men greatly, and they loved him for it. But Princess Baketamon was borne away by the priests to the golden house, without showing herself to the people.

Such was the bridal night of my friend Horemheb, and I know not what pleasure he had of it. Shortly afterward he mustered his troops and went to mobilize his army at the First Cataract in the south, in order to march on the land of Kush.

Eie exulted blindly in his power, and he said to me, "In the whole land of Kem no one stands higher than myself, and it matters not whether I live or die: Pharaoh dies not—he lives forever! I shall step aboard the golden boat of my father Ammon and sail across the heavens into the west. I am already an old man, and my deeds glare out at me from the darkness of night. I am glad that I need no longer fear death."

But I mocked him, saying, "You are an old man and I believed you wise. You cannot suppose that the stinking oil of the priests has rendered you immortal in the twinkling of an eye? Royal headdress or none, you are the same man still. Death will soon overtake you, and life depart."

His mouth began to quiver, and fear glinted in his eyes as he said plaintively, "Have I then committed all these crimes in vain? Was it in vain that I sowed death about me all my days? No, no—assuredly you are wrong, Sinuhe. The priests will save me from the abyss of death and will preserve my body to all eternity. My body must be immortal since I am Pharaoh, and for the same reason I cannot be held guilty for my deeds."

Thus did his reason begin to fade, and he had no joy of his power. In the horror of death he coddled himself and dared not even drink wine. His diet was dry bread and boiled milk. As time went on, he was filled with ever increasing dread of assassins, and whole days passed during which he dared not taste food for fear of poison. His old age found him entangled in the net of his own actions, and he became so suspicious and cruel that all shunned him.

A seed quickened for Baketamon, and in her rage at this she harmed herself in attempting to destroy the child while it was yet in her womb. The life in her was stronger than death, and when her time came, she bore a son to Horemheb, and in painful labor, for her loins were narrow. The physicians and slaves were compelled to hide the child from her lest she do it harm. Many tales were afterward told of this child, such as that he had been born with the head of a lion or with a helmet. I can bear witness that there was nothing abnormal about the boy, who was healthy and robust. Horemheb gave him the name of Rameses.

Horemheb was still fighting in the land of Kush, and his chariots wrought great destruction among the Negroes. He burned their straw-built villages and sent women and children into slavery in Egypt, but he enrolled the men in his army, where they proved good warriors, no longer having any families to distract them. Thus Horemheb built up a new army with which to meet the Hittites, for these men were strong, and when once they had worked themselves to a frenzy with the sound of their sacred drums, they felt no fear of death.

From the land of Kush Horemheb also sent great herds of cattle to Egypt so that grain grew luxuriantly once more in the land of Kem, the children had no lack of milk, and the priests were well supplied with beasts for the sacrifice. Whole tribes fled from their homes in Kush into the jungles—into the regions of the elephants and giraffes—beyond the boundary stones of Egypt. For years the land of Kush was deserted.

After two years of war Horemheb returned to Thebes, bringing with him much booty. He distributed gifts and held victory celebrations for ten days and ten nights. All work stopped, and drunken soldiers crawled about the streets bleating like goats, and the women of Thebes were delivered in due time of dark-skinned children.

Horemheb held his son in his arms and taught him to walk, and he

480

said to me proudly, "See, Sinuhe! A new race of kings has sprung from my loins, and in the veins of my son runs the sacred blood although I was born with dung between the toes."

He also went to Eie, but Eie in his fear shut and barricaded the door against him and cried in his shrill old voice, "Begone from me, Horemheb! I am Pharaoh, and I know that you have come to slay me and to set the crowns on your head."

But Horemheb laughed heartily, kicked open his door, and shook him, saying, "I do not mean to kill you, old fox! You old bawd, I shall not take your life, for you are more to me than a mere father-in-law and your life is precious. It is true that your lungs whistle, and your mouth slobbers, and your knees are feeble—but you must hold out, Eie! You must survive another war, that Egypt may have a Pharaoh over whom to pour out its wrath while I am away."

To his consort Baketamon, Horemheb brought great gifts: gold dust in plaited baskets, heads of lions he had killed, ostrich feathers, and live monkeys.

She would not even look at them and said to him, "In the sight of men I am your wife, and I have borne you a son. Be content with that, and know that if ever you lay hand on me again I shall spit on your couch and deceive you as no wife has yet deceived her husband. To bring shame on you I will take pleasure with slaves and porters and will lie with donkey drivers in the public places of Thebes. Your hands and body smell of blood, and they sicken me."

Her opposition inflamed Horemheb's desire for her; he came to me complaining bitterly and said, "Sinuhe, mix me a draught which I may give her to make her sleep so that at least I may go to her then and have my way with her."

I refused, but he sought out other physicians who gave him dangerous drugs. He administered these to her secretly. When he rose from her embrace, she hated him more bitterly than before and said, "Remember what I told you—remember my warning!"

Soon Horemheb departed for Syria to prepare his campaign against the Hittites, for as he said, "The great Pharaohs set up their boundary stones in Kadesh, and not until my chariots have entered Kadesh once more will I be content."

When Princess Baketamon perceived that once more a seed quickened within her, she shut herself into her room in the desire to be alone with her degradation. Servants were obliged to leave food for her outside her door, and when her time drew near, the physicians had her secretly watched. They feared lest she bring forth the child alone and send him down the river in a reed boat, as those mothers did who incurred shame by giving birth. She did not do this: when her time came she summoned her physicians. The pains of her labor brought a smile to her lips, and she brought forth a son to whom, without consulting Horemheb, she gave the name of Setos. So bitterly did she hate this child that she called him He who was born of Set.

When she recovered from her lying in, she bade her slaves anoint her and array her in royal linen. Having been ferried over to the other shore, she went alone to the fish market in Thebes. There she spoke with donkey men and water carriers and gutters of fish.

She said to them, "I am Princess Baketamon, the consort of Egypt's great general, Horemheb. Two sons have I borne him, but he is a dull and slothful man and smells of blood. I have no pleasure in him. Come and take pleasure with me that I may enjoy you, for your scarred hands and your wholesome smell of dung please me, and I also like the smell of fish."

The men of the fish market marveled at her words. They were frightened and sought to evade her, but she followed them with persistence, and baring her beauty to them she said, "Am I not fair? Why do you hesitate? Know that even should you consider me old and ugly, yet I desire from each of you no other gift than a stone—and let the stone correspond in size to the pleasure I give you."

Such a thing had never before happened to the men of the fish market. Their eyes brightened at her beauty. The royal linen of her dress lured them, and the perfume of her salves mounted to their heads.

They said one to another, "Truly she must be a goddess who reveals herself to us because we have found favor with her. We should do wrong to oppose her will, and the pleasure she offers us must be divine."

Others said, "At least our pleasure will cost us little, for even Negro women demand at least one copper piece. No doubt she is a priestess who is collecting stones with which to build a new temple to Bast, and we shall perform a deed acceptable to the gods if we do as she bids us."

They followed her to the reed swamps by the riverbank, where she led them to be out of the sight of men. And there all day Baketamon gave pleasure to the men from the fish market, cheating them of none of their delight but greatly favoring them. Many brought her large stones such as are bought of quarrymen at a high price, so highly did they rate the pleasure she gave them.

They said one to another, "Truly we have never met such a woman.

Her mouth is melted honey and her breasts ripe apples, and her embrace is as hot as the charcoal bed on which fish are grilled."

They begged her to return soon to the fish market and promised to gather many large stones for her. She smiled at them modestly, thanking them for their kindness and for the great joy they had given her. When in the evening she returned to the golden house, she was obliged to hire a sturdier craft to ferry across all the stones she had collected in the course of the day.

Next morning, she took a heavier boat, and when the slave women had rowed her over to Thebes, she left them to await her on the quay and made her way to the vegetable market. There she spoke to the farmers who came into the city at dawn with the oxen and asses, men whose hands were hardened by the soil, whose skin was rough and weather-beaten. She also spoke to the street sweepers, the emptiers of latrines, and the Negro guards, luring them and baring her beauty to them so that they abandoned their loads of farm produce, their oxen and their donkeys. They left the streets unswept and followed her to the reed swamps, saying, "Such a delicacy does not come the way of the poor every day. Her skin is not like that of our wives, and the scent of her is like the scent of the nobles. We should be mad not to take the pleasure she offers us."

They took pleasure with her and brought her stones. The farmers brought doorsteps from the taverns, and the guards pilfered stones from Pharaoh's buildings. In the evening Princess Baketamon offered modest thanks to all the men from the vegetable market for their kindness to her and for the joy they had given her. They helped her to load the boat with stones until it was so deeply laden that it was near sinking, and the slave women had much ado to row it across the river to the quay by the golden house.

That same evening it was known to all Thebes that the catheaded goddess had revealed herself to the people and taken pleasure with them. The strangest rumors ran rife about the city, for those who no longer believed in the gods found other explanations.

The following day, Princess Baketamon went among the men of the charcoal market, and that evening the reed swamps by the river were sooty and trampled. The priests in many small temples complained bitterly, for the charcoal sellers were godless men who thought nothing of tearing stones from the temple walls with which to pay for their pleasure. They licked their lips and boasted among themselves, saying, "Truly we have tasted paradise. Her lips melted in our mouths, her breasts were like glowing brands in our hands, and we did not know that such delights existed in the world."

When it became known in Thebes that the goddess had appeared to the people for the third time, the city was filled with a great unrest. Even respectable men left their wives and went to the taverns, and at night they took stones from Pharaoh's buildings so that next morning every man in Thebes went from market to market with a stone under his arm, impatiently awaiting the appearance of the catheaded one. The priests were perturbed and sent forth their guards to arrest the woman who was the source of this outrage and scandal.

That day Princess Baketamon lay in the golden house, resting after her exertions. She smiled at all who addressed her and behaved in a notably agreeable manner. The court were much astonished at her demeanor, and no one dreamed as yet that she was the mysterious woman who had appeared to the people of Thebes and taken pleasure with charcoal burners and cleaners of fish.

Princess Baketamon, having surveyed the stones of varying size and color that she had collected, summoned into her garden the builder of the royal cattlesheds and said to him, "I have gathered these stones by the riverbank, and they are sacred to me. Each one is linked with a joyous memory; the bigger the stone, the more joyous the memory. Build me a pavilion with these stones that I may have a roof over my head, for my consort neglects me, as you have doubtless heard. Let this pavilion be spacious and its walls high, and I will collect more stones as you need them."

The master builder was a simple man and he said humbly, "High Princess Baketamon, I fear that my arts may not suffice to build a pavilion worthy of your rank. These stones are of different sizes and colors so that the fitting of them together will be a matter of great difficulty. Lay this task rather on some temple builder or artist, for I fear that my lack of skill may spoil the beauty of your thought."

But Princess Baketamon touched his bony shoulder shyly and said, "I am but a poor woman whose husband is neglectful, and I cannot afford to call eminent master builders to my service. Nor can I offer you a worthy present for the work, as I should wish to do. When the pavilion is completed, I will inspect it with you, and if I find it well done, I will take pleasure with you there; this I promise! I have nothing to give you but a little joy."

The master builder was greatly inflamed by her words, and surveying her beauty, he remembered the tales in which princesses fell in love with humble men and took pleasure with them. His fear of

484

Horemheb was great, but his desire greater, and the words of Bake tamon flattered him exceedingly. Swiftly, he began to build the pavilion, exercising all his arts in the work and dreaming as he built. He built his dreams into the walls of the pavilion. Desire and love made of him a great artist, for he saw Princess Baketamon every day. His heart glowed and he toiled like a madman, growing ever paler with labor and with longing. From the stones of different colors and sizes he built a pavilion such as had never before been seen.

The stones Baketamon had amassed were soon exhausted, and she went once more to Thebes where she collected stones in all the markets, in the Avenue of Rams, and in the temple gardens. At last there was no part of Thebes where she had not gathered stones.

By this time her doings were known of all, and the members of the court gathered in the garden to steal a glimpse of the pavilion. When the women of the court saw the height of the walls and the number of stones in them, great and small, they clapped their hands to their mouths and cried out in amazement. But no one dared say a word to the Princess, and Eie, who with the authority of Pharaoh might have been able to curb her, was crazily jubilant at her behavior, believing that it would cause Horemheb exceedingly great vexation.

Horemheb waged war in Syria; he captured Sidon, Smyrna, and Byblos from the Hittites, and sent many slaves and much plunder to Egypt, and to his wife he gave many magnificent presents. Everyone in Thebes knew what was going on in the golden house, but there was no man bold enough to tell Horemheb of his consort's behavior. His own men, to whom he had assigned high positions, shut their eyes to it, saying among themselves, "This is a family matter, and it is wiser to put one's hand between the upper and nether millstones than to interfere between husband and wife."

For this reason Horemheb heard nothing of the matter, and I believe that this was best for Egypt, for the knowledge would most certainly have distracted his thoughts from the campaign.

5

I have spoken much of what happened to others during Eie's reign, but little of myself. There is little to relate. The river of my life raced no longer, but ran smooth and slow again over a shallow bed. Year after year I lived under Muti's care. My feet were weary of trudging dusty roads, my eyes were weary of beholding the restlessness of the world, and my heart was weary of the world's vanity. I shut myself in my house and received no patients, save for a neighbor now and again and the very poor who had no presents to give the regular physicians. I had another pool dug in the courtyard and filled it with colored fish, and I sat all day beside it under my sycamore. Donkeys brayed in the street before my house, children played in the dust, and I gazed at the fish that swam lazily about in the cool water. The sooty sycamore put forth leaves again, and Muti tended me well, preparing good food for me and letting me drink wine in moderation when I so desired. She saw to it that I slept enough and did not overtax my strength.

But food had lost its savor, and wine gave me no joy. When the chill of the evening came, the wine brought before me all my evil deeds—Pharaoh Akhnaton's dying face and the young face of Prince Shubattu. The desire to heal men had left me, for my hands, which I had hoped might be good hands, were accursed and engendered death. So I watched the fish in my pool and envied them. Their blood was cold, and their delights were cool, and they lived out their lives without having to breathe the hot air of the earth.

As I sat there in my garden, I spoke with my heart and said, "Be still, foolish heart; the fault is not yours. All is madness; good and evil have no meaning; greed alone, with hatred and desire, rule the world. The fault is not yours, Sinuhe, for man is man and will never change. In vain you may try him with war and want, with pestilence and burning, with gods and with spears. By such trials he is but hardened to a greater savagery than the crocodile's, and the only good man is the man who is dead."

But my heart gainsaid me, "You may sit there and watch your fish, Sinuhe, but I will give you no peace. Thousands and again thousands have died because of you, Sinuhe. They have died from famine, pestilence, and wounds. They have died beneath the wheels of chariots and have perished on desert marches. Because of you children have died in their mothers' wombs; because of you bent backs have come under the lash; because of you injustice tramples upon justice; because of you greed triumphs over good; because of you robbers rule the world. Truly, countless numbers have died because of you, Sinuhe. All who have died, and all who are yet dying are your brothers and die because of you. For this reason you hear their weeping in your dreams, Sinuhe, and their weeping takes the savor from your food and lays waste all your happiness."

But I hardened my spirit and said, "The fishes are my brothers because they cannot utter vain speech. The wolves of the desert are my brothers and the lions of the wilderness, but man is not my brother because he knows what he does."

My heart mocked me and said, "Does man then know what he does? *You* know; you have learning, and therefore I shall make you suffer until the day of your death, but the others do not know. You alone are guilty, Sinuhe."

Then I cried aloud and tore my clothes, saying, "Cursed be my knowledge, cursed be my hands, cursed be my eyes! But most cursed be my mad heart, which gives me no peace but besieges me with false accusations. Bring me the scales of Osiris, that my lying heart may be weighed!"

Muti came hurrying from the kitchen, and wetting a cloth in the pool she bathed my head. With severe reproaches she put me to bed and gave me many bitter draughts until I grew quiet. For a long time I lay sick and raved to Muti of the scales of Osiris, of Merit, and of little Thoth. She tended me faithfully, and I fancy she was overjoyed to be able to keep me in bed and feed me. She forbade me to sit in the garden in the heat of the day, because my hair had all come out, and my bald head could not bear the poisonous rays of the sun. Yet I had not sat in the sun but in the cool shade of the sycamore, watching the fish, which were my brothers.

After my recovery I was more peaceable and became reconciled even with my heart so that it no longer tormented me. And I spoke no more of Merit and of little Thoth but kept them in my heart, knowing that their deaths were necessary if my measure were to be full and I to be alone. Had they dwelt with me, I should have been happy and at peace, and my heart would have been silent. But I must always be alone, according to the measure meted to me, in token of which I had drifted alone down the river on the very night of my birth.

One day I dressed myself secretly in the coarse garment of the poor, kicked the sandals from my feet, and left the house. I went to the quays and bore heavy burdens among the porters until my back hurt and my shoulders were crooked. I went to the vegetable market and gathered its trampled refuse for my food. I went to the charcoal market and worked the heavy bellows for the smiths.

I did the work of slaves and porters; I ate their bread and drank their beer and said to them, "There is no difference between one man and another, for all are born naked into the world. A man cannot be measured by the color of his skin, or by his speech, or by his clothes and jewels, but only by his heart. A good man is better than a bad man, and justice is better than injustice—and that is all I know."

Thus I spoke to them before their mud huts in the evenings, as their wives lit fires in the street and the air was filled with the smell of fried fish.

They laughed at me and said, "You are mad, Sinuhe, to do the work of slaves when you can read and write. No doubt you are involved in some crime and would hide yourself among us. In your talk there is a hint of Aton, whose name we may not utter. We shall not betray you to the guards but shall keep you among us to divert us with your prattle. But do not compare us with dirty Syrians and miserable Negroes, for though we be but slaves and porters we are at least Egyptians, proud of our color and our speech, our past and our future."

I said to them, "That is senseless talk. So long as a man is proud of himself and believes himself better than other men, so long will mankind be persecuted by fetters and flogging, by spears and by birds of prey. A man should be judged by his heart alone."

But they laughed aloud and smote their knees, saying, "Truly you are a madman and must have grown up in a sack! A man cannot live unless he believes himself better than others, and there is no one so wretched but feels in some way above his neighbor. We are content to be wiser than you and craftier, although we are but poor men and slaves while you can read and write."

I said to them, "A good man is better than a bad one and justice better than injustice."

But they answered bitterly, "What is good and what is evil? If we slay a bad master who flogs us and cheats us of our food and lets our wives and children die, our deed is a good deed, but the guards bring us before Pharaoh's judges and cut off our ears and noses and hang us head downward from the wall."

They gave me fish to eat, which their wives had cooked, and I drank their thin beer and said, "Murder is the lowest crime of which a man can be guilty, and it is as wicked to slay in a good cause as in a bad. No man should be slain but rather healed of his evil ways."

They laid their hands over their mouths, looked about them, and said, "We do not desire to slay anyone, but if you would heal men of their wickedness and set justice in the place of wrong, go first among the nobles and the wealthy, and among Pharaoh's judges. You will find more wickedness and injustice there than among us. Do not blame us if because of your words they cut off your ears and send

488

you to the mines or hang you head downward from the walls, for the words you utter are dangerous. Horemheb, our great commander, would without doubt have you killed were he to hear you speak thus to the people, for to slay in war is man's glory."

I listened to their counsel and left them. Barefoot and clad in the gray garment of the poor I wandered about the streets of Thebes. I talked to the merchants who mixed sand with their flour, to the mill owners who gagged their slaves with sticks that they might not eat of the corn they ground, and I spoke to the judges who stole the inheritance of the fatherless and gave wrong judgment in return for gifts. I spoke to them all and accused them because of their evil-doing, and they listened to me in great astonishment.

They said one to another, "Who is this Sinuhe who speaks thus boldly, despite his slave's garment? Let us be careful, for he must be a spy of Pharaoh's, or he would never venture to speak so to us."

They listened to what I said, and inviting me into their rooms, they offered me presents and gave me wine to drink. The judges sought my counsel and gave judgment in favor of the poor against the rich so that there was great discontent in Thebes. Men said, "In these days not even Pharaoh's judges can be trusted. They are more dishonest than the thieves they try."

When I went to the nobles, they reviled me and set their dogs on me and had me driven off with whips so that my humiliation was very bitter and I ran through the streets of Thebes with a torn robe and with blood dripping from my legs.

The merchants and judges saw my degradation and listened to my words no longer. They drove me away, saying, "Should you come to us again with false accusations, we will have you condemned as a slanderer and agitator."

I returned then to my house, perceiving that all my labor was in vain; my death would have done no one any service. I sat once more beneath the sycamore in my garden and watched the silent fish in the pool and so found peace, while the donkeys brayed in the street and children played at war and cast dung on one another.

Kaptah came to visit me, for at last he had ventured to return to Thebes. He arrived with pomp in a finely decorated chair carried by eighteen black slaves. He sat there on soft cushions, and costly salves trickled from his forehead to spare him the evil smells of the poor quarter. He had gotten considerably fatter, and a Syrian goldsmith had made him a new eye of gold and precious stones, of which he was exceedingly proud although it chafed the socket so badly that he took it out as soon as he had sat down beside me under the sycamore.

First he embraced me and wept for joy at this meeting. His weight was mountainous as he laid his broad hands on my shoulders, and the seat Muti brought out broke to pieces under him. Having turned up the skirts of his garment, he sat on the ground. He told me the war in Syria was nearing its end and that Horemheb was just then besieging Kadesh. He boasted of the great business he himself had done in Syria and told me that he had bought an old palace in the wealthy quarter and hired hundreds of laborers to rebuild it, that it might be worthy of his affluence.

He said to me, "I have heard evil of you in Thebes, my lord Sinuhe, where it is said that you have been stirring up the people against Horemheb and that judges and other eminent men are incensed against you because you have accused them of many injustices. I counsel you to be careful. Perhaps they will not dare to condemn you, because you are in favor with Horemheb, but they may come one dark night to kill you and burn your house if you continue with your talk and stir up the poor against the rich. Tell me what is the matter with you and what has set these ants running in your brain, that I may help you as a good servant should help his master."

I bowed my head and told him all that I had thought and done. He listened to me and shook his head until his fat cheeks wobbled.

When I finished, he said, "I know that you are a mad, lonely man, my lord Sinuhe, but I thought your madness might have improved with the years. It seems to have grown worse, although with your own eyes you saw what happened in the name of Aton. I believe these whims attack you because of your idleness. It would be better if you would ply your trade again, for by healing one sick man you do more good than with all your talk, which only does harm to yourself and to all whom you lead astray. If you have no wish to continue in your profession, you can always pass your time in some useful occupation, like other wealthy men. You could collect jewelry and other objects fashioned during the period of the pyramids. In truth, Sinuhe, there are many ways of passing the time and so keeping these vain fancies from your mind. Women and wine are in no way the worst means to this end. For Ammon's sake dice; waste your gold on women; drink yourself insensible; do anything! But do not hurl yourself to destruction with vain talk—for I love you dearly, my lord Sinuhe, and I desire no harm to come to you."

He said also, "Nothing in the world is perfect. The crust of every

490

loaf is burned, every fruit has its worm, and when a man has drunk wine, he must suffer next morning. For this reason there is no perfect justice; even good deeds have evil consequences, and the best motives may lead to death and defeat, as Akhnaton's example should have taught you. Look at me, my lord Sinuhe! I am content with my mean lot and grow fat in harmony with gods and men. Pharaoh's judges bow before me and the people praise my name, while the very dogs defile your garments. Take life quietly; it is not your fault that the world is as it is—that has ever been so and ever will!"

I contemplated his corpulence and his wealth and greatly envied him his peace of mind, but I said to him, "Be it as you say, Kaptah. I will ply my trade once more. Tell me, is the name of Aton still remembered and still cursed? For you spoke his name although it is forbidden."

Kaptah said, "Truly, Aton's name was as quickly forgotten as the pillars of Akhnaton were effaced. Yet I have seen artists draw in the manner of Aton, and there are storytellers who tell dangerous tales; one may see now and again the cross of Aton drawn in the sand and upon the walls of latrines, so it may be that Aton is not yet quite dead."

"Be it as you say. I will ply my trade, and as a recreation I will also start some collection as you have counseled me. As I have no desire to mimic others, I will collect all those who yet remember Aton."

But Kaptah fancied that I spoke in jest, for he knew as well as I how much evil Aton had brought on Egypt and on myself. After this we talked agreeably of many things. Muti brought wine, and we drank together until slaves came and helped him to rise. Because of his great weight, he found difficulty in getting to his feet. He left me, but on the following day he sent me munificent presents, which secured for me such comfort and plenty that nothing would have been wanting to my happiness, if I could have been happy.

6

So I set up the physician's sign above my door and took up my work again, requiring gifts according to the means of my patients. But I required nothing of the poor, and sick people squatted in my courtyard from morning until night. I asked them very cautiously about Aton, being unwilling to frighten them or to give rise to evil report since my reputation in Thebes was already sufficiently black. But I found that Aton had been forgotten and that no one any longer understood him. Only agitators and those who had suffered injustice remembered him, and the cross of Aton was used as an evil symbol to do men harm.

When the waters fell, Eie the priest died. It was said that he had starved to death because his dread of poison would not allow him to eat. Then Horemheb brought the war in Syria to an end and allowed the Hittites to keep Kadesh since he could not win it back. He returned in triumph up the river to Thebes, where he celebrated all his victories. He observed no period of mourning after Eie's death but declared publicly that Eie had been a false Pharaoh who through his ceaseless warfare and extortionate taxation had brought only suffering to Egypt. Having put an end to the war and closed the gates of Sekhmet's temple, he persuaded the people that he had never desired war but had been forced to obey the false Pharaoh. Therefore, the people greatly rejoiced at his return.

But as soon as Horemheb had arrived in Thebes, he sent for me and said, "Sinuhe, my friend, I am older than when we parted, and my spirit has been sorely oppressed by your words, with which you accused me of being a bloodthirsty man who brought only harm to Egypt. I now have my desire and have re-established the might of Egypt so that no danger threatens the land: I have snapped the points of the Hittite spears and shall leave the conquest of Kadesh to my son Rameses. I have had my fill of war and mean to build a powerful kingdom for him. Egypt is as filthy as a poor man's stable, but soon you will see me heave out the dung, replace wrong by right, and give to every man his full measure. Truly, my friend Sinuhe, with my coming the old times return, and all shall be as it was. For this reason I intend to efface from the line of kings the miserable names of Eie and Tutankhamon—since Akhnaton's has already been removed— that it may seem as if their times had never been. I shall reckon my own reign from the night of great Pharaoh's death when I came to Thebes spear in hand with my falcon flying ahead."

He leaned his head moodily in his hand. The war had carved lines in his face and there was no joy in his eyes as he said, "The world is indeed different from what it was when we were boys, when the poor had their full measure and when even in the mud huts there was no lack of oil and fat. But Egypt shall be fruitful and wealthy again. I will send ships to Punt; I will set work going once more in the quarries and deserted mines that I may build bigger temples and gather gold, silver, and copper for Pharaoh's treasury. In ten years

492

you will not recognize Egypt, Sinuhe, for you shall then see no more beggars or cripples in the land. The weak shall give place to the strong, and I will wash away the sickly blood from Egypt and make of it a sturdy nation, which my sons shall lead into battle for the conquest of the world!"

I did not rejoice at his words. My belly sank to my knees, and my heart was seized with a deadly chill. I did not smile but stood before him dumb.

This angered him, and scowling as of old, he said, "You are as sour as ever, Sinuhe. You are like a barren thornbush in my sight, and I do not know why I expected to feel such joy in meeting you again. I called you to me before ever I had lifted my sons in my arms or embraced my consort Baketamon, for war and power have made me lonely. There was not one single man in Syria with whom I could share my sorrow and joy, and when I spoke I had always to weigh my words. From you, Sinuhe, I desire only friendship. Yet it appears as if your friendship has burned out and as if you felt no joy in my return."

I bowed low before him and my lonely soul cried out to him. I said, "Horemheb, of all the friends of our youth you are the only one now living. I shall always love you. Now the power is yours, and soon you will set upon your head the crowns of both kingdoms, and no one will be able to curb your power. I beg you, Horemheb: raise up Aton once more! For the sake of our friend Akhnaton, raise up Aton! For the sake of our most terrible crime raise up Aton, that all men may be our brothers and that there may be no more war!"

When Horemheb heard this he shook his head in pity and said, "You are as mad as before, Sinuhe. Don't you see that Akhnaton threw a stone into the water with a great splash, but now I smooth the surface as if he had never been? Don't you see that my falcon brought me to the golden house on the night of the great Pharaoh's death so that Egypt might not fall? I bring back the old ways, for men are never satisfied with the present: in their eyes only the past is good, and the future. I will unite past and future. I will milk the wealthy of their abundance; I will milk the gods who have grown too fat. In my kingdom the rich will not be too rich nor the poor too poor, and neither god nor man will compete with me for power. Yet I talk to you in vain since you cannot comprehend my thought. Your own thoughts are those of a feeble man, and the weak have no right to live in the world but are made to be trampled underfoot by the strong. So is it also with nations; so it has ever been and ever will be."

493

Thus we parted, Horemheb and I, and our friendship was diminished. When I left him, he went to his sons and lifted them in his strong arms.

From his sons he went to Princess Baketamon's room and said to her, "My royal consort, you have shone in my thought like the moon during these past years, and my longing has been very great. Now my work is done, and you shall soon sit by my side as your sacred blood entitles you to do. I have shed much blood for your sake, Baketamon, and for your sake cities have burned. Have I not earned my reward?"

Baketamon sweetly smiled at him, and stroking his shoulder shyly, she said, "Truly you have earned your reward, my consort Horemheb, great warrior of Egypt! I have built in my garden a pavilion the like of which has never been seen, to receive you as you deserve. Every stone in its walls I have collected myself in my great longing for you. Let us go to this pavilion, that you may have your reward in my arms and that I may give you joy."

Horemheb exulted at her words, and Baketamon led him into the garden. The members of the court hid and held their breath at what would follow. Slaves and stableboys fled also. Thus Baketamon led Horemheb to the pavilion. When in his impatience he would have seized her, she defended herself gently and said, "Bridle your manhood for a while, Horemheb, that I may tell you with what great toil I have built this pavilion. I hope you remember what I said when last you took me by force. Look carefully at these stones. Each one of them —and they are not few—is a memorial of my pleasure in another man's embrace. I have built this pavilion with my own pleasure, and in your honor, Horemheb. This great white stone was brought to me by a gutter of fish who was enchanted with me; this green one was given me by an emptier of latrines in the charcoal market; and these eight brown stones set together were brought by a vegetable seller who was quite insatiable and who warmly praised my accomplishments. Have patience, Horemheb, and I will tell you the history of every stone. We have plenty of time. Many years lie before us, but I believe the story of these stones will last me until my old age, if continued each time you seek my embrace."

At first Horemheb would not believe her words but took them for some grotesque joke, and Baketamon's modest demeanor deceived him. When he looked into her oval eyes, he saw there a hatred more terrible than death, and he believed what she told him. Mad with rage

494

he seized his Hittite knife to slay the woman who had so hideously dishonored him.

She bared her breast to him and said mockingly, "Strike, Horemheb! Strike the crowns from your head! For I am a priestess of Sekhmet—I am of the sacred blood—and if you kill me you will have no right to the throne of the Pharaohs!"

Her words brought Horemheb to his senses. She held him bound, and her revenge was complete. He dared not tear down her pavilion, which confronted him whenever he looked out from his rooms. After reflection he saw no other course than to appear ignorant of Baketamon's behavior. To tear the building down would have been to betray to everyone his knowledge that Baketamon had let all Thebes spit upon his couch, and he preferred laughter behind his back to open shame. From then on he laid no hand on Baketamon but lived alone. To Baketamon's credit be it said that she embarked on no more building works.

Such was Horemheb's return, and I fancy he had little joy of his majesty when the priests anointed him and set the red crown and the white on his head. He grew suspicious and trusted no one, believing that all derided him behind his back because of Baketamon. Thus he always had a thorn in his flesh, and his heart knew no peace. He numbed his grief with work and began to clear the dung from Egypt, to restore the old ways and to put right in the place of wrong.

7

In justice I must speak also of Horemheb's virtues, for the people praised his name and held him to be a good ruler. After only a few years of reign he was numbered among the great Pharaohs of Egypt. He milked the rich and eminent, that none might compete with him for power, and this greatly pleased the people. He punished unjust judges and gave the poor their rights; he revised the taxes and paid the tax gatherers regularly from the royal treasury so that they could no longer enrich themselves by extortion from the people.

He traveled incessantly from province to province, from village to village, seeking out abuses. His journeys could be traced by the cropped ears and bleeding noses of corrupt tax gatherers. The cracking of whips and cries of lamentation were heard far and wide from the places where he set up his courts. Even the poorest could approach him, and he dealt out incorruptible justice. He sent ships again to

Punt. Once more the wives and children of seamen wept on the quays and gashed their faces with stones as custom required, and Egypt prospered exceedingly. Of every ten ships that sailed, three returned every year laden with treasure. He built new temples also and rendered the gods their due, favoring no one god save Horus and no one temple save that in Hetnetsut, where his own image was worshiped as a god, to whom the people made sacrifice of oxen. For all these things the people praised his name and told fabulous tales of him.

Kaptah also prospered mightily until no other man in Egypt could vie with him in wealth. Having neither wife nor children, he had named Horemheb his heir, that he might live in peace for the remainder of his life and gather ever greater riches. For this reason Horemheb extorted less from him than from other wealthy men.

Kaptah invited me often to his house, which with its gardens formed a whole district in itself so that he had no neighbors to disturb his peace. He ate from golden dishes, and in his rooms water ran from silver taps in the Cretan manner. His bath was of silver and the seat of his privy was of ebony, and the walls of this were inlaid with rare stones fitted together to form diverting pictures. He offered me strange foods, and wine from the pyramids. During his meals he was entertained by singers and players, while the fairest and most highly skilled dancing girls in Thebes performed marvels in their art for his enjoyment.

He said to me, "My lord Sinuhe, when a man attains a certain wealth, he cannot become poor but grows even richer without lifting a finger to help himself, so strangely is the world ordered. My wealth originated with you, Sinuhe, so I shall ever acknowledge you as my lord, and you shall lack nothing all the days of your life. For your own sake it is well that you are not rich, for you would never use your means to the best advantage but would sow unrest and bring about great calamities."

He also favored artists; sculptors hewed his image in stone, giving him a noble and distinguished appearance. They made his limbs slender, his hands and feet small, and his cheekbones high. In these sculptures both his eyes had their sight, and he sat plunged in thought with a scroll on his knee and a pen in his hand although he had never even tried to learn to read and write. His scribes alone read and wrote and totted up huge sums on his behalf. These statues greatly amused Kaptah, and the priests of Ammon—to whom he had given vast presents that he might live in amity with the gods—set up his image in the great temple, and he bore the cost of this himself.

I was glad for Kaptah's sake that he was rich and happy. Indeed, I was glad of everyone's contentment and no longer sought to deprive men of their illusions if they were made happy thereby. Truth is often bitter, and it may sometimes be kinder to kill a man than to take his dreams from him.

But no dreams cooled my own forehead, and my work brought me no peace although at this time I tended many sick people. Of the patients whose skulls I opened only three died so that my reputation as a skull surgeon stood high. But I lived in continual discontent and found fault with everyone. I nagged at Kaptah for his gluttony, at the poor for their sloth, at the rich for their selfishness, and at the judges for their indifference, and I was satisfied with none. Sick people and children I never chided but healed my patients without giving them needless pain and let Muti share out her honey cakes among the small boys in the street whose eyes reminded me of Thoth's.

Men said of me, "This Sinuhe is a wearisome, bitter man. His liver is swollen, and gall bubbles out of him in his speech so that he can find no delight in life. His evil deeds pursue him so that at night he finds no rest. Let us pay no heed to what he says, for his tongue stings himself more viciously than it stings others."

It was true. Whenever I had poured forth my bitterness, I suffered for it and wept.

I spoke malignantly of Horemheb also, and all his deeds were evil in my eyes. Most of all I spoke ill of his "scum," whom he maintained out of Pharaoh's stores and who led an idle life in taverns and pleasure houses, boasting of their prowess and violating the daughters of the poor so that no woman could walk safely in the streets of Thebes. Horemheb forgave his ruffians all they did. When the poor turned to him with complaints about their daughters' plight, he told them that they should be proud because his men were begetting so sturdy a race.

Horemheb was growing ever more suspicious by nature, and there came a day when his guards visited my house, drove away the sick from my courtyard, and brought me into his presence. Spring had come again, the river had fallen, and swallows were darting above the sluggish, muddy waters. Horemheb had aged. His head was bowed, and the muscles stood out like cords on his long, thin body.

He looked me in the eye and said, "Sinuhe, I have warned you many times but you do not heed my warnings. You continue to tell the people that the warrior's profession is the most degraded and contemptible of all. You say that it would be better for children to die in their mothers' wombs than to be born warriors. You say that two or three children are enough for any woman and that it is better for her to be happy with three children than unhappy and poor with nine or ten. You have said also that the god of the false Pharaoh was greater than all other gods. You have said that no man should buy or sell another as a slave and that the people who plow and sow ought to possess the land they cultivate, though it be Pharaoh's or a god's. You have declared that my rule differs little from that of the Hittites. And you have said much that was even more outrageous. Any other man would have been sent to the quarries long ago. I have been patient with you, Sinuhe, because you were once my friend. As long as Eie the priest was alive, I had need of you because you were my only witness against him. Now I need you no longer; you may rather harm me through your knowledge. Had you been wise, you would have held your tongue, lived a quiet life, and been content with your lot— for truly you have lacked nothing. Instead, you bespatter me with slander, and that I will no longer endure."

His wrath increased as he spoke; he slashed his thin legs with his whip, scowled, and went on, "You have been a sand flea between my toes and a horse fly on my shoulder. I allow no barren trees that bear only poisonous thorns in my garden. I must banish you from Egypt, Sinuhe, and never again shall you see the land of Kem. If I allowed you to remain, the day would come when I should have to put you to death, and that I do not wish to do because you were once my friend. Your extravagant words might be the spark to kindle the dry reeds. When once dry reeds have caught, they blaze away to ashes. I will not allow the land of Kem to be gutted again—no, neither for gods nor for men. I banish you, Sinuhe, for you can be no true Egyptian, but some strange abortion of mixed blood. Sick notions throng your head."

It may be that he was right and that my heart's torment arose from the mixture in my veins of Pharaoh's sacred blood and the pale, dying blood of Mitanni. Yet I could not but smile at his words, though I was half stunned by them, for Thebes was my city. I was born and brought up there and desired to live in no other place.

My laughter enraged Horemheb. He had expected me to fall prostrate before him and implore his mercy. He cracked Pharaoh's whip and shouted, "Be it so! I banish you from Egypt forever. When you die, your body shall not be brought home for burial, though I may permit it to be preserved according to custom. It shall be buried by the shore of the Eastern Sea, from which ships put forth for the land of Punt, for that is to be your place of exile. I cannot send you to Syria, for Syria's embers are yet glowing and need no bellows. Nor can I send you to the land of Kush since you affirm that the color of a man's skin has no significance and that Egyptians and Negroes are of equal worth. You might instill foolish ideas into the black men's heads.

"But the land by the seashore is deserted. You are welcome to make your speeches to the black wind of the desert, and from those hills you may preach at your pleasure to jackals and crows and serpents. Guards shall measure out your domain, and if you stray outside these bounds, they shall slay you with their spears. Save for this you shall lack nothing. Your couch shall be soft and your food abundant, and any reasonable request shall be complied with. Truly loneliness is punishment enough, and because you were once my friend, I have no desire to oppress you further."

I did not dread the loneliness since all my life I had been alone and was born to be so. My heart melted in sadness to think that never more should I behold Thebes or feel the soft soil of the Black Land beneath my feet or drink the water of the Nile.

I said to Horemheb, "I have few friends, for men shun me because of my bitterness and my sharp tongue, but you will surely allow me to take leave of them. I would gladly take my leave of Thebes also and walk once more along the Avenue of Rams, to breathe the perfume of sacrificial smoke among the bright pillars of the great temple and to smell the fried fish at nightfall in the poor quarter of the city."

Horemheb would assuredly have granted my request if I had wept and prostrated myself at his feet, for he was a very vain man. But weakling though I was, I would not humble myself before him, for learning should not bow to power. I put my hand before my mouth and hid my fear in yawns, for I had ever been overcome by drowsiness when most afraid. In this I believe I differ from other men.

Then Horemheb said, "I shall permit no needless farewells since I am a warrior and dislike weakness. I will make your journey easy and send you immediately on your way without arousing public excitement or demonstrations. You are known in Thebes—better known than perhaps you are aware. You shall leave in a closed chair, but if anyone desires to accompany you to your place of banishment, I will permit it. Nevertheless, he must stay there all his days, even should you die first. He too must die there. Dangerous thoughts are a pestilence readily transmitted from one to another, and I do not desire your sickness to return to Egypt with any other man. If by your friends you mean a certain mill slave whose fingers have grown together and a drunken artist who portrays a god squatting by the road-

499

side, and a couple of Negroes who have frequented your house—then you need not seek to take farewell of them; they have gone on a long journey and will never return."

In that hour I hated Horemheb, but I hated myself more. Once again my hands had sown death, and my friends had suffered through me. I said nothing but stretched forth my hands at knee level and left him, and the guards took me away. Twice he opened his mouth to speak to me before I went, and he took a step forward. Then he stopped and said, "Pharaoh has spoken."

The guards shut me into a chair and carried me away from Thebes, past the three hills and eastward into the desert along a stone-paved road that had been built at Horemheb's command. We journeyed for twenty days until we came to the harbor where ships took aboard cargoes for the land of Punt. There were people living here, and so the guards carried me a three days' journey from there, along the coast to a deserted village where fishermen had once dwelt. Here they measured out an area for my walking and built me a house in which I have lived all these years. I have lacked nothing. I have lived the life of a rich man. Here are writing materials and paper of the finest, caskets of black wood in which I keep the books I have written, and all the requirements of a physician. But the book I now write is the last, and I have no more to say for I am old and tired, and my eyes are so dim that I can scarcely distinguish the characters on the papyrus.

I do not think I could have survived had I not recorded—and thus relived—my life. I have written to make clear to myself the reason for my existence; yet now that I bring my last book to an end I am more ignorant of it than when I began to write. Nevertheless, writing during these years has greatly comforted me. Every day the sea has been before my eyes. I have seen it red; I have seen it black. I have seen it green in the daytime and in the darkness white. On days of searing heat I have seen it bluer than blue stones. It is enough, for the sea is vast and terrible for a man to have before his eyes forever.

I have also beheld the red hills about me. I have examined sand fleas; scorpions and serpents have been my confidants, and they no longer shun me but listen when I speak. Yet I believe they are bad friends to man, and I have had as great a surfeit of them as of the endless, rolling billows of the sea.

I should mention that in the course of my first year in this village of whitened bones and tumbledown huts, when ships were sailing once more to Punt, Muti came to me from Thebes with one of Pharaoh's caravans. She greeted me and wept bitterly at the sight of my wretchedness, for my cheeks had fallen in, my belly had shrunk, and my mind was steeped in indifference.

She soon recovered and began to scold me, saying, "Have I not warned you a thousand times, Sinuhe, not to run your head into snares in your foolish man's way? Men are deafer than stones—they are little brats of boys who must always be cracking their heads against the wall. Truly you have run your head against the wall often enough, my lord Sinuhe, and it is time you settled down and led the life of a wise man."

But I rebuked her, saying that she ought never to have left Thebes, for she had now no hope of return. By her coming she had bound her life to the life of a banished man.

In reply she railed at great length. "On the contrary: What has happened to you is the best thing that has ever happened, and I believe that Horemheb has shown himself your true friend in bringing you to so peaceful a place in your old age. I too have had enough of the bustle of Thebes, and of those whining neighbors, who borrow cooking pots without returning them and empty their garbage into my court. When I come to think of it, the copperfounder's house was never the same after the fire. The roasting pit burned the meat, and the oil turned rancid in the jars. There were drafts along the floors and the shutters rattled unceasingly. Now we may make a fresh start and build everything to our liking. I have already chosen an excellent place for the garden. I shall cultivate herbs and watercress, which you greatly enjoy, my lord. I shall give work enough to these lazy drones whom Pharaoh has set to protect you from robbers and evil-doers. They shall hunt fresh game for you every day—they shall catch fish and gather mussels and crabs on the shore, although I suspect that sea fish are not so good as those we had from the river. Moreover, I think of selecting a suitable burial place, if you will permit me, my lord. Having come so far, I never mean to leave here again. I have had enough of wandering from place to place in search of you, and journeys frighten me since never until now have I set foot outside Thebes."

Thus did Muti comfort me and cheer me with her grumbling. I believe that it was thanks to her that I stretched forth my hand to life again and began to write. She goaded me to it although she could not read and secretly regarded my writing as nonsense. Yet she was glad for me to have some occupation, and she saw to it that I rested between times and enjoyed all the good dishes she prepared for me. She fulfilled her promise and set Pharaoh's guards to work, making their lives a burden to them so that they cursed her with great feeling behind her back and called her a witch and a crocodile. But they dared not oppose her, for then she reviled them volubly, and her tongue was sharper than an ox goad.

I fancy that Muti's influence was most wholesome. She kept the men in continual activity so that their time passed quickly. She rewarded them by baking good bread for them and brewing strong beer in great jars. They had fresh greenstuff from her herb garden, and she taught them how to vary their diet. Every year when the ships sailed to Punt, Kaptah sent us many donkey loads of goods from Thebes. He commissioned his scribes to write to us of all that went on in the city so that I did not live altogether in a sack. All this was of benefit to my guards. They learned new skill from Muti and grew rich from the presents I made them so that they did not long too sorely for Thebes.

Now I am weary with writing, and my eyes ache. Muti's cats jump on my knee and rub their heads against my hand. My heart is weary of all I have written, and my limbs long for their eternal rest. Though I may not be happy, yet am I not unhappy in my loneliness.

I bless my paper and my pen, for thanks to them I could become a little boy again in the house of my father Senmut. I have walked the roads of Babylon with Minea, and Merit's lovely arms have been about my neck. I have wept with those who mourned and shared out my grain among the poor. But I will not remember my evil deeds or the bitterness of my loss.

All this have I, Sinuhe the Egyptian, written, and for my own sake. Neither for gods nor for men, nor to immortalize my name, but only to bring peace to my own poor heart, whose measure is now full. I know that the guards will destroy all that I have written as soon as I am dead, and by the command of Horemheb they will pull down the walls of my house. Yet I do not know whether I greatly care.

Nevertheless, I am carefully preserving these books I have written, and Muti has plaited a strong cover of palm fiber for each of them. I keep these covered books in a silver box, and the silver box lies within a casket of hard wood, and that again within a copper one, just as the divine books of Thoth were once enclosed, to be sunk to the bed of the river. Whether my books will thus escape the guards, and whether Muti will hide them in my grave, I do not know, nor am I much concerned.

For I, Sinuhe, am a human being. I have lived in everyone who existed before me and shall live in all who come after me. I shall live in human tears and laughter, in human sorrow and fear, in human goodness and wickedness, in justice and injustice, in weakness and strength. As a human being I shall live eternally in mankind. I desire no offerings at my tomb and no immortality for my name. This was written by Sinuhe, the Egyptian, who lived alone all the days of his life.

CRETE

KNOSSOS

THE OCEAN
(MEDITERRANEAN SEA)

THE WORLD OF
SINUHE
THE EGYPTIAN

BLACK LANDS

RED LANDS